TAKEN

A Truth or Lies World Collection I

ELLA MILES

TRUTH OR LIES WORLD COLLECTION SERIES ORDER

ENZO & KAI'S STORY

Taken (Collection I)
Stolen (Collection II)

ZEKE & SIREN'S STORY

Sinful (Collection III)
Broken (Collection IV)

LANGSTON & LIESEL'S STORY

Vicious (Collection V)
Endless (Collection VI)

TAKEN BY LIES

CHAPTER 1
ENZO

Alcohol.

It can lower your inhibitions.

Transform you into somebody society accepts.

Make you relax enough to ask the hot girl at the end of the bar out on a date.

Alcohol has so much power.

The power to tempt me.

To take me away.

To make me forget.

It should be only an act of rebellion. An underage misdemeanor, done as much for attention as to feel the effects. That's all alcohol should represent. I'm only seventeen. Still a long ways from twenty-one, but alcohol has never been a healthy pastime.

As soon as I tasted the liquid, I knew it was a habit I would never give up.

Not because I'm an alcoholic. That's one thing I could never be, even when I drink in large quantities. Even when I need alcohol as much as I need to breathe.

I need it to forget.

I finish the last drop of the amber liquid in my glass. One drink isn't nearly enough for me to forget. If there were another way to erase my demons and slip me into amnesia, I would take it. But I've never found another option. This is my only option.

"Another round," I say to Zeke and Langston who are sitting in the corner booth with me. It's not a question, but a statement.

I need more, and they will both stay with me, drinking until my past is erased for another hour.

Slinking out from beneath the corner booth hidden in the shadows, I stand and cross the width of the room before climbing onto a stool at the bar. We have a waiter, but I don't have the patience to wait for her to realize we need more drinks.

I eye Blake behind the bar. He knows when he sees me to drop his other patrons and serve me immediately. His tip, along with his job, requires it. This is just another bar my family owns. It's nothing in the grand scheme of things — just a place for me to retreat to when necessary. And lately, I've found coming here on a daily basis is very necessary.

Blake spots me out of the corner of his eye. He politely ends his conversation with the flirty woman at the end of the bar and walks my way, before pouring me another glass of the finest bourbon we have. I reach for the glass he sat in front of me and wait while he continues to make drinks for my friends.

I lift the glass to my lips taking comfort in the fact that soon my nightmare will be over. My memory will be obliterated, at least until I have to meet with my father later today.

The door flies open, and a girl falls through. She stumbles once as she drops to her knees. But her cheeks don't flame with embarrassment. Instead, fear threatens her eyes as she scans behind her. As if, any second, the evil she is running from will find her.

She stands quickly and brushes herself off out of habit, not because she's dirty. Her skin is a light olive color, but it's impossible to know what ethnicity she is just from the coloring. We live in Miami; everyone is tan. But her skin hints at more than just spending too much time in the sun. Hers promises a past and culture far more intriguing.

Her legs are too skinny I realize as I soak up her body and ingrain it in my memory like I do with everything. My memory is flawless, and even if it wasn't, there is no way I would forget such a spark of beauty like her.

Her clothes are too big for her. Her blue jean shorts engulf too much of her legs. Her tank top hangs like a tent instead of showing the curves beneath it. Dark black hair hangs down her neck in thick waves hiding her face.

But then she flips her head back and blows the rest of her locks from her face. Gone is the fear. Gone is the clumsy girl. Gone is the awkward girl uncomfortable in her own skin. I even forget her clothes are two sizes too big.

She's transformed from meek girl to powerful woman with one toss of her hair. Her steps are bold and robust as she struts toward the bar, only taking her three steps to reach the edge.

She smiles at the bartender, and Blake floats over to her, as under her spell as I am. I don't know what she says as she whispers to Blake, but I know he will retrieve whatever drink she ordered without verifying her age. And I'm right. Blake slides a beer to her without glancing at her ID. An ID that would either be fake or show she isn't any older than I am.

Her age doesn't matter though. The way she looks at him with piercing greenish blue eyes and unending poise is enough to persuade him to risk his job for her.

Blake may be used to serving underage clients, but that's only because of me. I've never seen him serve anyone unassociated with me who's so clearly a minor.

The girl lifts the glass to her lips, and the foam sits on her upper lip as she drinks down the golden liquid like it is the only thing keeping her alive.

That I can understand.

I shouldn't approach her. I shouldn't think about her. I shouldn't invite more evil into her world when it's clear she running from enough herself. But I can't fight the pull. I'm not strong enough.

I leave the drinks Blake placed in front of me for Langston and Zeke. I only take my drink as I slide into the stool next to her.

Her gaze never leaves her drink as I move next to her. She doesn't realize the danger that has approached.

"What's an innocent creature like you doing in a bar like this?" I ask.

Her eyes roll gently in her head, but it's the only sign she heard me. Otherwise, I don't exist to her.

But I'm a patient man. I know she heard me, and I know she is uncomfortable with me sitting so close. She'll answer. If for no other reason than she's curious as to why I converged on her in the first place. She may not show any fear right now, but she's running from something. And the tension in her neck is enough for me to know she's terrified of me outing her and returning her to whatever she's trying to evade.

She doesn't know I would never stop her from escaping. It's a feeling I understand too well. I would never stop someone from feeling free, if only for a moment.

"I needed something to eat. There isn't anything but bars on this road for miles."

I frown. *Food? That's her excuse?*

She downs her drink, and before the last drop crosses her lips, Blake brings another bottle to replace the empty beer still in her hands.

I smirk. "It seems you need alcohol a lot more than you need food."

She shrugs. "Alcohol helps too."

"This bar doesn't serve any food. You are out of luck."

She nods. "I know." She still doesn't look at me as she speaks. It's like she's talking to a ghost. Like I don't exist to her.

"I could turn you in for underage drinking. My family is close to the cops in this town. I could have you arrested. A permanent mark on your record. But maybe that would help you. Get you somewhere safe and away from whoever you are running from."

My words finally get her attention. Her bright eyes, looking more green now than blue, finally fall on my dark orbs. Her pink lips purse, and I think she's going to yell at me or plead for me to do anything but call the cops. I expect her to beg or to dash out the door again running in fear.

"You won't turn me in, and even if you do, I don't fear the police."

My finger traces the rim of my drink instead of tracing the outline of her soft lips like I want.

"I'm not a nice man. My conscience will have no problem turning you in. I'll sleep just fine knowing I put you in jail for a night."

She licks her plump lips, and my patience teeters on the edge of a cliff. *Why the hell do I want to taste her lips?* She's just a girl. Just like all the rest of the girls I went to high school with.

I groan silently. She's not like other girls. I don't know much about her, but I know she is *nothing* like other girls.

Her bright eyes narrow into slits about to tear out my throat, and I think I finally unnerved her.

"You're not a man. You're just a boy. Just like I'm a girl, not a woman. You're not twenty-one any more than I am."

She inches closer until her face is a breath away from mine. Her lips so close I could easily take them into my mouth before she could react and stop me.

She nibbles on her bottom lip as if she knows that's exactly what I want to do.

"You may control the police, but right now, I control *you*. You won't dare call the police on me."

I exhale, my eyes squinting as I study this fascinating girl in front of me. I've never met someone who spoke so many truths and so many lies in one sentence. I lurk forward, and she stills, exhaling harsh breaths but refusing to back down.

I lick my own lip, and I watch as her bottom one trembles. Our gazes lock in a fierce battle. Neither of us will back down. I could take what I wanted without a fight from her because she refuses to show weakness. I would guess she's always this strong.

Her life is as much a struggle as mine. We would make quite a pair. But I'm afraid our lives aren't meant to do anything but intersect for a brief moment. She's here to give me a tiny sliver of entertainment. She's a distraction from my own hauntings.

Blake places a plate of burger and fries in front of the girl.

My eyes widen for less than a second, but it's long enough for her to take it as a win. She smiles as she leans back in her chair before turning to her plate of food.

"I guess you don't know everything about this bar, *boy*," she says before shoveling a fry into her mouth.

I can't help but grin at her. The way she says boy, it doesn't feel like an insult, even though that's how she meant it. It feels freeing to seem like a boy in her eyes instead of a man who has too many responsibilities. I'm not the only one she has under her spell. This bar doesn't serve food, but it didn't stop Blake from ordering food from the nearest diner for her.

"I'm Enzo. I'm rarely proven wrong, but I'm happy to be proven wrong by..." I pause waiting for her to tell me her name.

Her eyes cut to me. "I don't give anything away for free."

"I don't either." My unblinking gaze holds hers. I gave her my name; now I expect her to give hers just as freely.

She finishes her second beer. "Buy me another drink, and maybe I'll tell you."

I finish my drink and slam it down on the bar. She jumps at the sound the glass makes as it hits the rough wood.

She startles easily.

I don't say a word, but I know Blake got my silent order loud and clear. Get me another drink and bring one for the girl.

Two minutes later, half of her burger is gone, and Blake brings another bourbon for me and another beer for her.

"Name," I command, my voice low and rumbling. I won't wait for her to follow an order. I need her to follow my demand as much as I need to drink this glass of bourbon.

She smirks. "Impatient?"

I grab her wrist as it loosely holds a fry inches from her mouth.

Her eyes widen for a millisecond before she regains her control. She's afraid of me. Or at least she doesn't like strange men gripping her wrist.

I lean forward, and my teeth snap a bite of the french fry she's still grasping.

She frowns and her body radiates anger as if me taking a bite of her fry is the greatest sin I've committed so far.

"Jocelyn."

"What?"

"You heard me."

"Jocelyn what?"

She shakes her head. "Enzo what?"

I growl, but it's so low I'm not sure it was audible.

"Jocelyn," I say again. It's a pretty name. A strong name, but for some reason, it doesn't fit the girl in front of me. I'm sure she goes by a nickname. Maybe Josie, or Jose, or Lynn. But I haven't earned her nickname. The one that only her family and friends call her. And she hasn't earned more than a first name from me.

"So Jocelyn, what are you really doing in my bar?"

Her eyebrows shoot up. "Your bar, huh?"

"Yes, *my* bar. Everything I enter becomes *mine*."

Jocelyn coughs at my words—choking slightly on the piece of burger stuck in her now dry throat.

She winces as she finally swallows the piece down, but doesn't immediately grab for her beer to relieve her throat. This girl is used to dealing with pain. It barely fazes her. And apparently speaking words to me is more important than dealing with her discomfort.

"Yours?" She drags her teeth across her bottom lip, and my dick, along with the rest of my body hardens to stone.

"You may own everything you enter, but I control everything I touch." Her hand moves to my glass sitting on the edge of the bar. Her finger lazily traces around the rim of the thick glass just as I had done before. And then her finger dips into the center, pulling up a drop of whiskey before she brings her finger to her mouth and sucks her finger dry.

I groan.

She purrs in response as if drawing me closer to her. She's playing with fire.

I grab another fry off her plate and bite off the end with my mouth, needing to regain my composure and at least the illusion of control. This twig of girl can't control me. She has no power over me. Even my father, the ruthless man he is, can't tame me.

But somehow, this girl did. If only for a moment, she claimed me as hers and made me want to do whatever I could to please her. But just as quickly the spell she cast over me broke.

She growls and snatches the remainder of her precious fry out of my hand before shoveling it into her mouth, along with the rest of the food on her plate until not even a crumb remains.

My breathing slows. *How did I not notice before?*

The spaghetti strap shirt she wears lowers, and I see the thin frame of her collarbone protruding more than what is healthy. I glance at her wrist I held only moments before. Now it seems so frail I could snap it with the twist of my hand. And I swear I can see her hip bone sticking out through the thin fabric of her shorts.

She's too skinny. Too frail. Too hungry.

I've known women like her. Some were drug addicts.

But from the lack of needle marks on her skin, I know that is not that case. And even though she's drunk a lot of beer, I don't get the feeling that she is an alcoholic. Her body doesn't tremble at the sight of alcohol.

Others I've met were whores.

But from the innocent way she keeps biting her lip, I can't imagine her selling her body to survive.

And others...others were sold.

"Who did you escape from?" I need to know if she escaped from an enemy or from one of my own. If she escaped from my enemies, then I will have great pleasure in keeping her from them, but if she fled from one of my own...

She cocks her head to the side, studying me, trying to understand the hidden meaning behind my words.

"Answer me." I grab her wrist again firmly, showing her I won't let her go without an answer.

Her breathing speeds, and I feel her pulse skipping rapidly through her icy veins. I was right. She was sold. I just need to know who her master was. Then I can decide what to do with her.

I don't agree with men kidnapping and selling women like cattle. But right now, staring at this endearing creature, I get the appeal.

She closes her eyes, and I imagine she's picturing her master's eyes, his commanding voice, even his cock as it drives inside her.

I study her body. She's thin, but not bruised. She hasn't been broken yet. He may have not even fucked her yet. She's just hungry and hasn't been taken for long, which makes me want to break her myself.

I'm sick.

Jocelyn isn't mine. And I won't take her and be her master. I just need to know who I should return her to.

"I belong to myself. I've never been sold. And I will never be taken."

Her eyes puncture mine with sharp ice, and I realize she's speaking the truth. I've always been good at judging people. I know when someone is telling the truth or a lie.

"Then why are you starving?"

She trembles and her eyes are downcast as if that was the question that hurt her. Not the one before, assuming she was a slave.

I feel the tsunami of emotions behind her olive eyelids, before she opens them and erases any remnants of pain.

"I'm not starving. Not anymore. I'm surviving."

Jocelyn looks to where I'm still gripping her wrist, as if her eyes have any control of my hand. But somehow I can't resist what her eyes demand. I release her.

She stands. She's done with our conversation. I'm almost done too, but it doesn't stop me from getting the last word in. I stand, and our bodies collide in the thin space between our bar stools.

Her movement is fast. So fast I shouldn't even notice it. No normal person with an ordinary upbringing would notice her action. My buddies sitting in the booth deep in the corner of the bar wouldn't. And no one sitting the length of the bar would.

But I do.

It's the oldest trick in the book.

She turns to leave, acting as if nothing just happened between us.

"Jocelyn," my voice is harsh as I say her name, and as I expected, she halts. A skill I have perfected. I can control people as easily with my voice as I can with my fists.

I slowly walk to her, and I can feel the anxiety dripping off of her in thin droplets. Her body doesn't show any outward hint of worry, but I can smell the panic as it festers inside her.

I stand in front of her, and she continues to hold her head high. She won't show weakness. She won't show fear.

I shouldn't do this. I should just let her have what she took. I should be kind. It could be the difference between her eating another good meal and withering away into nothing. But I'm not kind; I'm heartless. And I don't tolerate thievery.

I hold out my hand and look down at her with displeasure. I don't have to say a word. She knows what she did.

She reaches into her back pocket and places the thick leather wallet into my hand.

I grin. "Good girl."

Her eyes meet mine, and for a second I think I see something more. Something like winning in her gaze. But she didn't win, *I did*.

"Thank you for lunch," she says. And then she's gone before I can respond or stop her from running out without paying her bill.

I smirk at my thick wallet and glance at the bar. She didn't steal from me or the bar by not paying for her food and drinks. She thought she won by stealing three beers, a burger, and fries from me. But I won't be paying her bill.

I never pay my own. That's why Zeke and Langston are here. Not that I can't afford to pay for something so inexpensive. But why should I pay? I own everything in this town. I shouldn't have to pay myself for something I take.

I walk back to the booth in the corner and take my seat.

"You let some pussy almost steal from you?" Langston says, smirking.

I glare, and the smile leaves his face. He hides behind his drink that Lana, our waiter, must have brought him while I was entertained by the girl.

"No one steals from me."

They both nod. They know the consequences if someone stole from me.

"She your whore now? Or can I have a taste of her?" Zeke asks.

I lean back in the booth and drape my arm over the back. I don't want either of them going after Jocelyn. She's mine, even if I never get to touch her.

"I think you have too much work to do to be chasing pussy," I say.

Zeke huffs but doesn't push the subject. Lana drops off the bill that I know covers our drinks in addition to Jocelyn's tab. Langston places his credit card on the bill without looking. He knows better than to balk at paying. It's why I pay him so well. Even though my family owns the bar and I don't have to pay, it's a way for my friends to show loyalty to me by covering our drinks.

"What time are you meeting your father?"

"Three."

I glance at my watch and freeze.

Instead of the shiny silver face of my Rolex staring back at me, I see the faint tan line of where the watch used to sit.

I smirk.

I may be the devil, but Jocelyn is a thief. She left this bar knowing she had won. She never had any intention to steal my wallet. She wouldn't have gotten much from my wallet anyway. There is nothing more than a couple hundred dollar bills tucked in its depths along with credit cards I would have been canceled before she could use them and would only leave a trail for me to find her.

Instead, she stole the one thing of real value on my body. The watch is worth over ten grand.

Round one goes to the thief, but the devil only ever gets deceived once. Jocelyn has no idea who she stole from. But soon, I'll make sure she never forgets.

CHAPTER 2
KAI

I stole.

I swore I would never do it again. But I didn't have a choice.

It wasn't about my survival. If it were only me, then I wouldn't have stolen. Even from someone like Enzo, who has more money than he could possibly spend in a lifetime, based on the expensive clothes he was wearing. But I didn't steal for me. I stole to save my father.

And now I owe another debt that will take me years to repay.

I hold the silver watch in my hand, running my fingers across its smooth face. The watch is warm despite it being made of metal. I make a mental note to repay Enzo when I can, but the reminder won't be necessary. I'm afraid I will remember Enzo forever.

His hair was darker than night. His chiseled jaw covered with the dark shadow of his stubble will haunt me for not feeling how the rough edges would feel when I kissed him. And his deep eyes spoke of pain and heartache that no boy our age should have ever experienced.

I glance back down the street to where the bar sits. I could still return it. Enzo doesn't deserve to feel any more pain. This watch is expensive, and although I don't know anything about Enzo, he appears not to be hurting for money. *But what if the watch was given to him by his father? Or his mother? What if it was passed down for generations? What if the love of his life gave it to him? What if it is irreplaceable?*

I study the timepiece further. It's new and barely worn, without a single scratch on it. Almost like today was the first day he wore it. *It can't mean much to him if he's never worn it, can it?*

A man walks down the sidewalk toward me. I keep my gaze down, trying not to draw attention to the fact that I notice him.

He's not here for me, I repeat to myself.

He's just a stranger walking down the sidewalk. But it doesn't stop the chill running down my spine.

I will repay Enzo someday. I will make things right. Even if I hate him.

No, hate is too strong of a word. I don't hate him. Although I've never been so tempted to kiss someone in my life. Never wanted to forget about myself more than I did when I was near him. And also never wanted to be swept off my feet by a prince charming who would take me far away from here. Someone who would protect me and ensure I never had to worry about where my next meal came from.

But Enzo isn't my prince charming, and even if he were, it's not what I want. I will find my own way out of this mess I'm in.

I may not hate Enzo, but he reminded me temptation is real. And I can't lose focus. I can't let myself fall for a boy like Enzo. I don't know anything about him except the look on his face when he taunts me.

I don't remember Enzo from school, but I know he can't be more than a year or two older than me. Seventeen or eighteen I would guess. Not that I attended much school. It's a waste of time when you need every hour to make enough money to eat.

I continue walking down the sidewalk, past the row of bars. It's mid-afternoon, so the streets near the bars have yet to grow busy, but in a few hours, they will be filled with people washing their worries away with a drink and loud music.

My feet carry me automatically, knowing these streets like the back of my hand. My fingers find the door of the pawn shop on the corner, three blocks over. I slip inside without any guilt.

I always repay my debts. Always. No matter the cost.

The door chimes loudly, announcing my presence, not that I need to be announced. Jim is standing behind the counter like he expected me. I haven't been here in a while, but I have no doubt he heard of the debt my father owes. This is the only way I know how to make enough money to pay off his debt quickly, and Jim knows it.

I don't hesitate. I walk to the counter, ignoring the smell of sweat and desperation that seems to always hang in the air here. People come here not because they are greedy, but because they have no other choice but to sell some prized possession or stolen item to survive. The same reason I'm here.

I pull the stolen watch from my pocket and lay it on the counter. Jim picks it up without a word, already knowing what I want from him.

He studies the watch carefully, running this thumb across the face's surface just as I did earlier. He looks for scratches or signs of damage. He taps the metal; I assume to test for authenticity.

I don't know how to determine if a watch is counterfeit or not. If I found this watch on the street, I would have a fifty-fifty shot at guessing its value. But after meeting Enzo, I know he would only wear the real deal. He's not fake. He has money. He's grown up in an entirely different world from me. And while it still pains me to take it from him, not knowing entirely what it cost him, I will not let the value of the watch go to waste.

"Five thousand," Jim says, meeting my gaze as he lets the watch lie flat on the counter while we haggle.

I've done a few deals with Jim before. Never for anything of this much value. I know he's a fair man, but I also know I have to be willing to lose the sale to get the full worth out of it.

I can't lose.

I don't have time to find another pawn shop to sell to. The next pawn shop owner might not be so kind. I may have to show my ID or proof of ownership. This is my only shot.

I stare at the watch, reminding me too much of the owner I only just met.

I know the exact amount I need. I also know how much I need to feed myself and my father for a month. The amount to give us some breathing room. To pay for our rent.

But this watch is only about one thing—getting one more day of freedom from my father's debts.

I won't be selfish. I won't take more than I deserve.

"Eight thousand," I counter.

Jim smiles. "That's an awfully high price for a watch, Miss Miller."

I glare back at him. "I know its worth, Mr. Wilson. I know it is easily worth more than ten thousand, and it is in pristine condition. I know you will easily sell it for more than ten grand because you are a good salesman. You could sell a fake for that much easily. You'll sell the real deal for more."

He chuckles. "I am a good salesman, but that doesn't mean I'll pay you eight grand."

I reach out like I'm going to take the watch back. "No, you would give me ten if I pushed the subject because it's a good investment for you that you can easily make a couple grand off of and because you know if you treat me well, I will bring you more quality items to sell in the future."

I grab the watch. It feels good to have it in my hand even though I know the cost of keeping the watch for myself. But I can't stop myself from wanting the watch. From wanting *him*. I slide the watch across the counter toward me before Jim grabs my wrist stopping me.

"Seven-five, final offer."

I smile. I need seven thousand three hundred to pay off the debt. Two hundred extra. But I won't spend it on food, clothes, or shelter. It will be the first step to paying off my new debt.

"Deal."

Jim nods and then looks down at my hand still gripping the watch while he still holds my wrist. He releases me and waits for me to turn the watch over.

Instead of letting it go, I hold the watch tighter. I'm not ready to let it go. I'm not ready to let Enzo go. Not that either was ever mine in the first place. But there was something about Enzo that taunted me with a future I have always wanted. Money, protection, and adventure.

Something my current life lacks. My life is destined to become the same over and over. I have no future—nothing beyond working my ass off to repay debts. No man would ever want to take me on, not when they realize the money they would owe just to ensure we would be free.

"Miss Miller?"

I cling to the watch for a single second, reminding me of the promise in Enzo's eyes. He wanted me. Somehow I know a single night with Enzo would have been more adventure than I ever dreamed my boring life could have.

"Miss Miller?"

I turn and meet Jim's gaze.

He holds out his hand, and I raise mine over his. The watch doesn't fall out of my hand willingly. It glides reluctantly through my grasp like I'm letting my future slip away—a future I can never have.

Jim takes the watch, and my eyes burn with regret as I watch him place the watch in a small black box. Its gleam disappears beneath the lid as he closes it away from me. He then turns to the cash register.

"Cash or check?"

I swallow hard as my mind returns to my reality of what I need to do.

"Cash."

He nods, already knowing what my answer will be. He pulls out the cash and counts it into my hand.

"Stay safe, Miss Miller. I wouldn't want anything to happen to one of my best customers."

The wad of cash is large, too bulky to conceal in anything but a purse or bag I don't have. And I won't spend a dime on any of the purses lining the rack at the front of the pawn shop, even if I should to ensure I make it back home with all of the bills. I tuck a handful into each of my two pockets and then shove the remaining into my bra, not caring that Jim eyes my cleavage as I do.

"I always do."

His eyes seek mine, and I swear I see a hint of concern etched in the wrinkles that form around his eyes. "See that you do."

He knows where the watch came from. I don't know how. I didn't notice any etchings or name written across the band. But Jim knows, and he's warning me. I'm not going to get anything else out of him though—no other help or words to explain why he's worrying. I'm not afraid of anyone, including the boy I stole the watch from.

I turn without another word and leave the pawn shop, leaving only the ringing chimes of the door as I exit.

The sun blazes hotter as I step outside, causing instant blisters to form on my bare shoulders. I wish I had a car, a bike, any form of transportation to get me home faster. I would even settle on a hat to shade my head from the burning rays causing sweat to bead down from my forehead to my back. Even my ass is sweating.

The heat doesn't stop me from running. I have two miles to run to make it back to the trailer and not a minute to spare. So I run, despite my flip-flops, despite the intense heat, and knowing what awaits me when I get home.

My flip-flops slow me down, so I take them off and run, risking piercing my foot on broken glass that tends to clutter the sidewalks from drunk tourists. Risking tetanus with each step doesn't stop my feet from running.

Running should make me feel free. My feet are moving so fast, my body flying. But I only run out of fear. Only one thing makes me feel free. Only one thing brings me a moment to forget. I close my eyes as sea salt sprays my face. The ocean is the only place I truly feel free.

My body collides with that of another. The body isn't strong enough to knock me down, just enough to make me stop.

"Mason," I gasp and fling my arms around my only friend in the world.

He holds me tightly in his scrawny arms as I bury my face in his chest, breathing in his cheap cologne so different from the rich, musky scent that oozed from Enzo. I may have called Enzo a boy, but he carries himself like a man. Mason, on the other hand, is a boy through and through. Mason is skinny, not from lack of food, but because he hit a growth spurt recently and his body has yet to catch up with his new found height. His muscles are there, but thin against his frame in long bands, not thick with years of working out. His hair hangs in long waves around his tanned face, made for the beach. But no one would ever call him anything but a boy.

I pull away and see the hauntingly worried look in Mason's face. I can't call him anything but a friend, even though I felt him sniff my hair as he held me. Even though I felt his body go rigid, his cock stirring against my flat body.

His feelings have only recently developed. A few months ago he thought of me as nothing more than a friend. More like an annoying younger sister than as a girl he craves. But things changed. I don't know how or when exactly. But they did. Mason stopped seeing me as a girl and started thinking about me as a woman. But he's wrong. I'm nothing but a naive girl and Mason is my friend. That's all.

"What are you doing here?" I ask as I pull away, out of his clutches. Mason is standing at the entrance to our trailer. He rarely comes here. When we hang out, it's at school or his home. An actual house. Not here. Not where we are both reminded of how I come from nothing, and he has everything.

"You haven't been at school in weeks. I was worried about you." He strokes my face, and I see the fret all over his.

I nod. "I've been busy working. I should have called and told you I was fine."

"You don't seem fine. You wouldn't have run into my arms that way if you were fine."

I smile making sure the edge of my mouth reaches my eyes, so it seems genuine. "I missed you, Mason. And I wasn't expecting to see you again until I go back to school."

"Don't lie to me, Kai. You're not planning on returning to school, not now that you are sixteen and not legally required to go. You've been slipping away more and more to work on that boat. To pay back debts that aren't yours to be burdened with." His fingers twist the ends of my hair between his fingers. "Stay with me, Kai. Finish school. You could live in Colton's room, now that he is away at college. My parents wouldn't mind. And then after you and I could—"

"I can't." I won't let Mason finish his thought. I don't think I can ever think of Mason as more than my friend. I don't think I can think of any man in that way. Not if I want to survive.

"You can."

I shake my head. "My father needs me."

"Your father is a grown man. He can take care of himself. Come with me."

I hear the footsteps behind me, the rough sand shifting beneath their feet and their voices echoing throughout the trailer park. This is a world Mason doesn't belong in, and I won't let him become a part of it.

"You should go. My shift starts soon."

Mason nods. "I can give you a ride."

"Dad is giving me a ride on his way into town."

Mason studies me a moment, trying to determine if I'm lying or not.

"I need to change. I'll see you at school next week. I promise." I pat his shoulder and smile. He seems to accept my words as truth. He doesn't realize his friend would ever lie to him. He doesn't understand what it's like to do anything to survive.

"I'll see you next week, Kai." He smiles back at me brightly, thinking our world will go back to normal.

He walks away with a small skip to his step. My smile drops watching him. I hate lying, but I won't let myself bring him down with me.

The voices grow closer, and I turn in their direction.

"Where's your father, *girl?*" The man who speaks can't be much older than I am. Maybe early twenties if I had to guess. His voice is harsh and demanding. He's used to getting what he wants with his threatening voice and stony stare. I see the glint of a gun at his side beneath a jacket that is too warm to be wearing here.

"My father's not here."

The man growls as he approaches and grabs my arm, pushing me hard against the side of the trailer.

I wince but quickly bring my face back to neutral. *Never show weakness.*

"I've been chasing you all day, girl. And I have no time for games. Where is your father? If you don't find him, I'll make sure *you* repay his debt."

I hold my breath to keep my body from trembling in fear. To keep him from noticing the speed of my heartbeat. I saw him earlier today. Hunting my father and me down like animals.

That's why I ducked into the bar.

That's why I stole from Enzo.

Not to keep this man from hurting me. I already know I will lose my virginity by a man like him. Repaying a debt neither my father nor I could pay.

I've accepted it.

I don't need to be a fortune teller to know my future. It's the same as any of the other girls living in the trailer park.

But I stopped it happening for one more day. I stopped my father from being beaten, tortured, and killed for one more day.

One more day.

That's all I can ever buy. That's all I can ever steal.

"I have what you came for."

The man's hand moves to my throat.

I gasp.

I can't help it. It's natural to fight for breath when he touches me like this. I can't resist my natural instinct to survive. To find air where there is none.

I recoil into my body, trying to keep my fear inside.

His eyes travel up and down my body, assessing me, deciding if my body is enough to forgive my father's debt.

He chuckles in anger. "You are far too skinny for my liking.

You're not even a woman yet. You haven't filled out with curves that I can sink my teeth into."

I growl as he speaks about my body and then spit in his face.

His laughter deepens as he studies my mouth. "Although, pushing my cock into your throat so you can't speak or breathe might please me. It will not be enough to repay the debt your father owes, but it will entertain me until he returns."

He pushes me toward the trailer. I stumble into the door.

Asshole.

I feel him walking toward me, but I won't let him touch me again. I turn with a fierceness surging through my veins.

"I have the money to pay you back."

He eyes me up and down again. "I won't take a check from you, girl. I know anything you write will bounce."

"Good, because I intend to pay you in cash."

I dig into my bra and pull out the first wad of cash. His eyes grow big as he stares at the thick bundle.

"How did you get the money? Did you already whore yourself out to protect dear old daddy?"

My eyes tighten into slits. My body tenses, and I dig my heels into the hard sand to keep myself from attacking this man. "Do you want the money or not?"

He nods.

I pull the rest of the money from my pockets, careful to keep the last two hundred in my pockets away from his eyes. If he saw I had more money, he would take that too, as interest.

I shove the wad of money into his hands.

"How do I know this is everything?"

"Because unlike you I'm not a filthy liar. I keep my promises and pay back everything I owe. Now leave." I turn and march into the unlocked trailer before he says another word. I slam the door shut and stick the broom through the door handle to lock the door. It does no good when we leave the house, but there isn't anything inside worth stealing. All it does is provide some level of protection to keep men like him out.

I shake against the door, my breathing fast and heavy. Even so, I don't get enough oxygen into my lungs. Goosebumps cover my thin arms and my gut wrenches at the thought of being violated.

I close my eyes and try to forget about him grabbing my neck. About threatening to rape me or stick his cock down my throat. I try to forget it all, but I never can. It's not the first, nor the last time I'll be threatened.

A knock pounds at the door making me jump. *He got his money. What could he possibly want?*

My mind races with what to do, how to save myself. I run to the drawer in the kitchenette. I yank it open and rummage through the drawer looking for a knife. All I find is a butter knife.

The knock rattles the entire trailer this time, and I grip the dull knife in my hand aiming it toward the door. Maybe I'll be able to jab it in his eye, and he will leave realizing I'm not worth the struggle.

"Kai, it's me." My dad's voice travels through the door, weak and worried. He must have seen the man he owes a debt to. He doesn't know I paid it. That I'm still alive with my virginity still intact.

I race to the door, pull the broom handle out, and open the door still gripping the knife.

Father lets out a breath when he sees me. "Are you...?" He can't finish.

I drop the knife. "I'm fine."

It's the truth. I'm fine. I'm always fine, but never more.

Never safe.

Never happy.

Just fine.

"Good." He nods. "I can't stay. Mr. Bramble is—"

"I took care of it." I step back to let father into the trailer. He doesn't offer me a hug, although I can tell he was concerned about him. And even if he did, I wouldn't relish the embrace the way I did Mason's. Father may care about me, and I may risk my life to take care of him, but it doesn't stop the anger or pain we both feel toward each other. We just haven't been able to find our way after we lost my mother.

He studies me a moment and then nods. He doesn't thank me.

He doesn't ask how I came up with the money. He doesn't tell me he's sorry for the life he's forced me in to. Nothing, but a nod.

He walks to the recliner in what most would call a living room and sinks into it, putting his feet up in the chair. He'll be asleep within minutes. The trailer has only one bedroom that is big enough for one tiny twin bed. I sleep there; he sleeps here.

We shouldn't hate each other, but we do. We shouldn't resent each other. It's neither of our faults, not really. My father does his best captaining various vessels, mostly yachts for the rich. They pay him well, but we will never get out of the debt my mother caused us.

Cancer.

She died of cancer when I was little, so young I can't even remember her. She fought a long time, over five years. But the entire time she was nothing but a vegetable. But that didn't stop my father from trying to save her. Through chemo, treatment, the nurses and doctors costing more than we could ever afford to repay.

Most men in the trailer park have addictions that have cost their families everything. Gambling, drinking, drugs.

Not my family.

My family will forever be haunted by the ghost of my mother. If only her body had given up when her spirit did, then we would just have thousands of dollars in debt to repay instead of millions.

Then my father wouldn't have to take on more loans from nefarious people to pay the medical bills that never end.

Then I would be able to attend school instead of working all day long.

Then maybe father and I would have a relationship beyond two people merely surviving in the same trailer.

That's not life.

That's a fairytale.

I watch as my father closes his eyes. Sometimes I think he'd rather stay on the fancy yachts, away from here, where even his debts can't find him. Instead of coming home to this dump. I haven't seen him for three weeks, but it makes no difference to me. He's the only family I have and just as he works to protect me, I work to protect him.

I don't wake him as I head out the door, even though I should, to ensure he pushes the broom handle back through the door, so he's safe. I just slip out of the trailer and start my long walk to the docks. Because even though I stole over seven grand today, it's not enough.

It's never enough.

I ensured our survival for one more day. But we don't have enough for food for tomorrow. And now, I have my own debt to repay.

CHAPTER 3
ENZO

I step into Surrender and my eyes automatically darken. The club's name is simple and is a little on the nose. There are no windows and very few lights. It's like stepping into darkness, forcing you to relinquish your sight, body, and soul when you enter.

My spine straightens, my lips thin, and every muscle in my body tightens as I morph into the cruel vulture I was taught to be. Gone is the boy I only occasionally let out when I think no one is looking. Everyone's eyes fall on me as soon as I step foot into the club. I'm underage, far too young to be in a place like this. But I've been coming here since I was seven. This club is what twisted my soul and made sure when I die I won't be going anywhere but hell.

My eyes don't acknowledge the stares as I walk. I know better than to give any of the drunks sitting near the entrance the time of day. They only come here to gawk at the dancing women, get drunk, and forget.

I envy them. They live a simple life, one where drinking actually makes them forget, because the worst they have to ignore is their cheating wives or inability to pay rent from their pathetic jobs.

It's the men that sit further into the club I have to worry about. They are the ones who have real money. They have power.

I walk deeper into the club, keeping my head up. I won't make eye contact with any of them, but I feel their eyes on me.

I'm the youngest man in this club and despite being younger, smaller, weaker; I'm their prince. This is all mine to collect.

Mine to rule.

Mine to control.

And because I'm the prince, every man here wants me dead.

I haven't earned the right to rule them, but I will. I don't have a choice if I want to live.

But for now, I get to continue breathing. I've made the mistake before, of staring at one of the men. It was a mistake I won't repeat. Fights don't break out in the club often; it's not allowed unless it's part of the entertainment. But each man in here feels they have to protect their pride, and when that pride is challenged, they fight. No rule is going to stop them.

I can fight. I've won plenty, lost more. Sometimes I come here seeking them out, wanting to feel the pain and adrenaline, the high that only comes when my fist connects with a jaw as blood spurts in my face. But today isn't that day.

And I've gained enough respect after my last fight that most here wouldn't dare to threaten me. At least not personally. They would send some of their minions to fight against me. Most likely sending several men to a fight that wouldn't be fair.

My lips curl up into a smirk as I think back to my last fight where I broke a glass and used the shards to draw blood against my weaponless opponent. *Not that I fight fair either.*

Deeper and deeper I descend into the abyss, into the cave of the club that will one day be mine. My heart grows darker along with the light surrounding me. There are no windows this deep into the club. The light from the lamps only illuminates how black the room is.

I don't need the light to guide me; I know how many steps it takes to get to my father's room. I know where to avoid stepping to keep my feet silent, instead of making the hardwood floor creak. I know where to walk to stay in the shadows instead of shimmering in the light.

It's not necessary to creep through the club silently, trying to be invisible. It's not possible anyway. Not with the security cameras and men everywhere. Not when every man here knows exactly who I am. But it's a habit I can't break. I'm only visible, only heard when I want to be.

The thick door is shut to my father's room, but I don't knock. I turn the knob and step inside, letting the door fall closed behind me.

My lip twitches as I see my father sitting in his favorite chair toward the back of the room. Three women, more naked than clothed, dance around and on him. Two other men sit in chairs next to them. All have two fingers of the finest scotch in the glass in their hands.

This room serves as many things for my father.

His lair.

His office.

His sanctuary.

He's fucked countless women in here and punished every man who has dared to cross him.

I don't think he'd ever leave this room if he didn't need to prowl the rest of the club and city to maintain his power.

"Gentleman and ladies, I need to speak with my father."

The women look to my father for their cue what to do. My father's gaze penetrates through me as he waves them off. They start walking toward the door in the back that leads out to another hallway. One of the women turns back winking at me as she runs her hand down her neck and across her pointed nipple—indicating she'd gladly fuck me later and wouldn't care if I paid her like my father.

I understand why. The woman is in her early twenties. Most men in this club are in their thirties or forties. Some in their fifties. She would love to go a round with a man closer to her age. I may be seventeen, but my life experience has hardened me and makes me seem older.

Maybe I'll find her later. I could use a fuck to get out some of my pent up energy. Especially after meeting Jocelyn. Gorgeous, intriguing, and a thief. Her deep sea-colored eyes will haunt me the rest of my life. Because as much as I'd like to find her and make her pay for stealing from me, I won't. My reputation is still intact. No one knows she stole. And if I found her, I would punish her.

Cruel.

Mercilessly.

Until I possessed her.

Jocelyn deserves to be punished, but I've never disciplined a woman before. Not because I'm too good, kind, or chivalrous.

One day I will. Whether by choice or necessity. And then my fall into darkness will be complete.

But I'm still young. I still have a drop of light left in my veins, and I'm not ready to relinquish it yet. Because if I touched her, I would ruin her.

Break her.

Own her.

The two gentlemen remain in their seats. I've known both men my whole life. They are two of my father's best men. Highest in rank, and trusted with his very life. But I know what this meeting is about, and they won't be privy to it.

"Alone," I growl.

I may be half their age. I may be heir to this kingdom. But I've earned my right to get to speak to the king alone. Being his son has nothing to do with it.

The threat of what I'd do if the men stayed is evident in my voice. I don't care if they are my father's men. I would kill them.

Both men start to turn to my father to ask what to do, but my unyielding glare along with the low rumble of my throat make them rethink their plans. They stand immediately, and head for the door the women exited through.

My father smirks as they leave.

"Good to know you are finally learning something from your old man," he says.

I ignore him as I take a seat in the chair his number two emptied. I help myself to the glass of scotch Baldwin left as he scurried out like a worried rat.

"You summoned me." I sip the scotch, letting the warm liquid seep through me, making my already hot skin race with the fire of the liquid. I'm always hot, ready to attack—a blaze of sweltering fire that can't be stopped.

"I did, and you came, like a good little son."

It's an insult. All of his words toward me are. He says them to get a reaction out of me, but I've long learned to pretend his insults and threats don't exist.

"Did you have a point in bringing me here? Because I have a full schedule for today, including ensuring you make millions and the men are in line."

"Impatient fuck as always." He shakes his head. "I would have thought any son of mine would have learned to respect his elder, his leader."

My eyes darken as my lids fall, only allowing the tiniest slit of my eye to remain open. I know how to close off from this man. I know how to keep my composure. I'm seventeen. Practically an adult. No longer a boy. But around this man, who calls himself my father, I struggle to be anything but a ten-year-old boy who disobeyed. I won't be that scared little boy anymore. Not around him.

Instead, I sip on my drink like I want to be here, and I wait. I have more patience than my father ever will. I could sit here all day and all night without flinching. I know how to go deep within myself and ignore everything else. Food, drink, feelings, *everything*. I know how to shut out the world. If he wants me to be patient, I will be. And he'll lose.

He sighs. "I have a target for you."

I raise an eyebrow but don't speak. I know he has more to say.

I've killed men before, nine to be exact, so this isn't an unusual request. What is strange is that he brought me here, to the place he holds holy to give his order, instead of sending one of his men. So what's different about this one?

"How?" I know it's the right question. Does he want me to make this man suffer or kill him quickly? What kind of man am I dealing with? Am I taking out a monster or enemy? Dispatching the leader of a gang or disposing of one of our own who dared not to follow orders?

My father's body stills as he considers his next words.

"You decide."

My eyes widen, and I almost choke on my scotch. I never get to make a decision. I may rule a group of men who will follow every order I give, but it's not the same as having free will to decide when and who we strike. I'm only following my father's orders when I give my own.

His mouth curls down at my reaction. Disappointment, I've seen it before.

I stiffen again into stone, ensuring I won't show a moment of weakness again.

"Who's the target?"

My father remains silent as he sips his drink. His pupils widen as he imagines the target in his head. Whatever this man did to deserve my father's wrath is bad. And now I decipher his meaning. I know what the real test is, why my father won't tell me how to dispose of him. Because once I know what this man did, it's up to me to prove my worth to my father, by correctly dispatching of him. By giving him the correct punishment for his crimes, and seeing that justice, at least in the eyes of my father, is done.

"What did he do?"

He turns toward me, his lips finally curling into the evil grin I'm used to seeing.

"Nothing."

Fuck.

I've killed in self-defense before. Injured many men, fighting battles to defend my family's power.

I've killed men who hurt my family or this club. Killed those who were planning to take us down. But I've never killed someone who was innocent.

It doesn't mean my father is telling me the truth either. This man could be innocent or my father's greatest foe. It makes no difference. I'll kill him all the same.

Because that's what I am—a killing machine. My father trained me my entire life to be an assassin so I could prove my worth to him. My first kill was when I was thirteen, and it has been my life ever since.

My father sees the change in my body despite the wall I put up. He knows I'll follow his every command without hesitation.

"Good." He nods at me.

My stomach drops feeling like my transformation into the devil is complete. Except the devil is still sitting three feet away from me. *How can I be the devil when he's still alive?*

"One more thing. You do this kill, *the right way,* then you will get power."

If it's possible my body stills even more. Except for my bloody heart. It thumps loudly in my chest. This is what I've been waiting for, for seventeen years—this chance.

"Kill, and you will no longer take orders from anyone. Kill, and your debt will be paid. Kill, and you'll owe me nothing. Kill, and you'll be free."

Free.

It's all I've ever wanted. Freedom.

My father is offering me what I've sought all these years.

But I doubt doing this will indeed set me free. If anything it will bring me deeper into the darkness with him. And he knows that.

It doesn't matter. This is what my whole life has been leading me toward—this final kill.

Who am I kidding? This won't be my final kill, but maybe it will be the last one I do for my father.

I growl. My father doesn't tell the truth often, at least not to his men. He doesn't have to explain himself to anyone, but he's never lied to me. So I have no reason to believe he is lying now. If I do this, then I'll be free. At least of him, but never this club. *Never this life.*

I nod, agreeing to his terms, cementing my place in hell.

He pulls out a pen from his pocket and takes the napkin on the table where his drink sat. He scribbles on it, then hands it to me.

I unfold the napkin and stare at the name before downing the rest of my scotch.

Kai Miller, you're a dead man.

CHAPTER 4
KAI

I feel him before I see him.

I shouldn't know how he feels when he's around me. I've only met him once. I've barely had time to study the curves of his face. Barely had time to notice the richness of his voice. The small wave of his hair. The light scruff on his face. The way he walks, tall and strong. I shouldn't have noticed any of it, but I did. And now I could sense Enzo out of a crowd of a million. I would zero in on him immediately.

I sense him approaching easily; he sucks all the oxygen out of any room he is in, casting a dark shadow as he moves like a predator. Even though I'm standing on the front deck of a large yacht and there is air all around me, I can't breathe.

Enzo's steps are quiet, I shouldn't be able to hear his feet hitting the dock, but I do. He moves silently, a skill I'm sure he uses to his advantage to do whatever nefarious things he spends his days doing.

I try to ignore him and continue mopping the wooden floor of the yacht, but it's hard for me to pretend I don't notice him.

His feet still on the pier next to the yacht and my arms slow their movement as I stare down at his dark black boots.

Boots? Why the hell is he wearing boots?

It's summertime in Miami. Most people here wear flip-flops, boat shoes, or go barefoot. The only people who wear boots around here are those that work. Those that clean or catch fish for money to bring back to their families. People like my father or me. Not the kind that was handed daddy's money. Enzo doesn't understand anything about hard work. He's a spoiled rich kid.

I can't help but curl an eyebrow up as my eyes travel further up his body. Gone is the dark pants and buttoned-down shirt, replaced with jeans and a tight black shirt. He looks like he could disappear into the night, even though it's the middle of the afternoon.

Enzo folds his arms across his chest, and he looks at me sternly. A look I've seen plenty of times from my father when he's about to give me a whooping. The look is meant to intimidate me into doing whatever he wants, but it takes a lot more than a look to cause me to worry.

I suck in a breath and then get back to work. I've almost finished cleaning the yacht. It wasn't as disgusting as the one I did last week. That one had puke, piss, and blood all over it. I'm hoping the second one I'm supposed to clean is as easy as this one.

"Thief," Enzo says.

Shit.

But of course Enzo noticed I stole his watch. He realized immediately that I took his wallet, even though that was the plan all along. To get him to catch me stealing his wallet, so it would be easier to steal his watch. I just didn't think he would care enough about his watch to track me down.

There is no point denying what I did. I can't pretend he lost his watch or he was the victim of a desperate pick-pocketer. We both know what I did.

I stand up straighter and stop mopping. I wipe the sweat from my brow. He's changed in the hours since I saw him, but other than tying a bandana around my hair to keep it off my face, I haven't. I look the same, except sweat beads down my skin and more dirt clings to my flesh than before.

I nod. "I stole your watch."

His eyes lighten. "You did."

Shit, he's not going to make this easy. But I'm not going to collapse and beg for forgiveness on my knees. I did what I had to, to survive.

"I'm sorry I stole your watch."

He jumps onto the yacht despite the high gap between the deck and the pier. It's a large jump most people wouldn't dare take, but he does it with ease, like he's made the leap thousands of times and never once thought of plummeting into the water if he were to miscalculate his movement.

I take a step back before I can help myself.

He grins like I just showed a weakness.

"Are you now? Because you don't look sorry to me."

"I'm sorry, I would have never stolen it if I had a choice."

He laughs. "You had a choice. You chose to steal from me. Do you have any idea what I do to thieves?"

I stare down at his clenched fists. "I'm sure I have an idea."

He cocks his head as he takes another step closer. This time, I don't step back. I let him inch closer, but I squeeze the mop handle harder. I will use it as a weapon if I have to.

"But it doesn't scare you. I don't scare you?"

"No."

He shakes his head. "Stupid girl."

I narrow my eyes into deep slits. "I'm not stupid."

He sighs. "Then why did you steal from *me*? There were countless other men in the bar you could have stolen from."

I feel the color returning to my face. This question is easy. "Because you needed the watch the least. You have more money than anyone in that bar—more money than most people in this city. You could call someone and have the watch replaced in five minutes, and you wouldn't even notice the downward tick in your bank account. You were the least likely to be hurt by my actions."

My words surprise him. It's clear in the way his body hardens, his eyebrow inches up, and his jaw twitches.

"Unless..." I start. "Unless, the watch was a family heirloom or gift. Did your father or girlfriend give you the watch? Is it irreplaceable?"

I don't know why I ask. I wouldn't rat out Jim. I can't track down the watch and get it back for him, but at least I will know how much I truly have to repay Enzo.

He laughs. Long, hard, and his voice sounds like he's gone maniacal. I don't know what's so funny, but I watch him slowly stop.

"I don't do the girlfriend thing."

Those words make me sad, because the tiniest part of me wanted him to take a chance and make me his girlfriend. But that's stupid because I don't do the boyfriend thing either. I don't have time for it, and I won't let some man take care of me.

"And my father has never given me a damn thing."

His eyes are serious as he says them and I see a pit of his pain. I see how broken he is in his dark orbs where he tries to hide his shattered pieces from the world. But he can't hide it from me, I see it as clearly as I see the sun shining in the sky.

He shakes his head again. "Why did you steal it? Planning on buying more burgers and beer with it?"

My lips curl up a little at his teasing. "It was for my father."

"Aww, I see. You're a daddy's girl. So tell me, daddy's girl, how does dear old daddy treat his daughter? Is he a drug addict? Alcoholic? Does he gamble away the money he's supposed to use to pay rent and feed you?"

"Stop."

His lips do curl up, happy he finally hit a nerve in me.

"I used the money to repay a debt my father owes, but my father isn't a bad man. He works hard and does his best to take care of me. He's not a drug addict, alcoholic, or gambler. He's just my dad."

His entire body exhales as if he disagrees with me, but knows there is no point in arguing with me.

I dig into my pocket and find the two hundred dollars extra I received from selling the watch. I hold it out to him.

He stares at the money like it's a snake about to bite him.

"What's that?"

"This is me repaying you for the watch."

"If all you got was two hundred dollars for the watch, then you made a bad deal. That watch cost me twelve grand."

I shrug. I should have gotten more than the seven and a half I got. I didn't make the best deal, but I was desperate. Just like I was when I stole the watch in the first place.

"I know. I got more than that, but that's all I have left after I paid off the debt." I square my shoulders to him and hold out my hand. "I will repay you. All of it, plus interest. No matter what it takes or how long. You have my word."

He takes my hand in a dominating grip. "I don't need the money, daddy's girl."

"Don't call me that."

"Would you prefer I call you, stupid girl?"

"No, I'd prefer you call me by my name."

"Jocelyn," the way he says the name sends shivers down my spine. "But that's not really your name is it?"

I freeze. *How did he realize I'd given him a fake name?*

"You don't go by Jocelyn. You go by Josie, or Jos, or Lynn, but never Jocelyn."

I don't move. He thinks he's so smart, but he can't even figure out a sixteen-year-old girl's real name.

Enzo studies me, his thick eyelashes shading his eyes as he does. "I don't need the money Jocelyn, and as for the watch, I have dozens more at home."

I still. "Then what do you want?"

"I'm looking for someone. I was told he works down here by the docks, and seeing as you do too, you might be able to help me find him while being more inconspicuous. Help me find him tonight. And I'll forgive your debt."

It's a good deal. It will take me most of my life at my current rate to pay back the debt I owe him. "What do you want with this man?"

He shrugs nonchalantly, but nothing he does is ever casual. Every movement is planned out. His actions are orchestrated to make me as uncomfortable as possible. Make me hate him, while wanting to plant my lips on his at the same time.

"Does it matter?"

No, it doesn't. I'm heartless, but he doesn't need to know that. I don't care what happens to this man. I don't care if he beats him, extracts a debt from him, or kills him. It won't be on my conscience.

I squeeze his hand and shake. "Deal."

He smirks.

"You can tell me what you know about this man while I finish mopping. I have one more yacht to clean tonight."

"You aren't cleaning another yacht tonight until you help me."

I roll my eyes at his bossiness. "I might, if I think this man will be on it. The other yacht is on the other side of the harbor. If I think we will have better luck finding him there, then it will be more inconspicuous to be cleaning then going in guns blazing like I'm sure you plan on doing."

"You think I'll just take out my gun and starting shooting to get people to talk?"

"I don't think, *I know*." I eye the back of his shirt where I know a gun is hidden. I also do not doubt he has more weapons on him. He has a knife stashed in his boot or another gun hidden in his pant's leg.

"What world were you brought up in, Jocelyn, where you can tell if a man is carrying a gun or not?"

"The kind where I have to know if a man is carrying a gun or not for my own survival."

A calmness passes between us. An understanding of each other. He may be rich, and I may be poor, but we aren't so different, the two of us. We are more alike than we are different.

I continue mopping while Enzo scrutinizes me, studying me like I'm an alien from another planet he's just now recognizing as one of his own. When I finish, I dump the water overboard and stow the mop and bucket in the cleaning closet. Enzo follows as we both hop off the expensive yacht and onto the pier.

I can feel him smiling at how effortlessly I made the same jump he did, instead of using the ramp.

"So, who are we looking for?" I ask.

Enzo pulls out a napkin and hands it to me.

I take it hesitantly. I feel a sense of doom come over me, and I swear a dark cloud descends overhead just to cover the spot where I stand.

I unfold the napkin and read the name written on it. My name. *Kai Miller.*

Shit. Fuck. Shit.

I should have pressed harder about what Enzo wanted with the man he thinks he's hunting for. I try not to react at the name, but I feel Enzo studying my reaction. *Is he testing me? Did he know this was me all along? What does he want with me anyway, other than to give him back the watch?*

"Jocelyn? Do you know this man?"

"Yes," I breathe.

"Who is he? Where can I find him?"

I close my eyes trying to find a way out, but I don't have a way out.

I don't know for sure that what Enzo wants to do with me is bad. *Liar, yes I do.* This man oozes evil. *Is he here because my father owes his family a lot of money? What else could it be?*

Shit.

Enzo's going to kidnap me and force my father to repay the debt. Enzo likes me. He won't really hurt me. I might even be able to make a deal on my father's behalf. Promise to steal something for Enzo that he wants more than the money my father borrowed from him. He's seen how good of a thief I am.

"Jocelyn? Where is he?"

I grin. If I'm going to do this, I'm going to do it with my pride intact. "This man you are looking for. He did something to you, didn't he? Stole from you, hurt you, outsmarted you maybe?"

Enzo sighs, getting annoyed with my games. "Yes."

"So he's smarter than you?"

"I didn't say that."

"No, but you can't find him on your own, so he must be."

"Sure, but when I do find him, and I will, with or without your help, I will have outsmarted him. And if I do it without your help, you will still owe me your debt."

I nod, *men and their pride.* But I'm no different. I want my pride too.

"Where is he?" he repeats.

"He is standing right in front of you." I fold my arms across my chest and grin, my eyes daring him to doubt me.

Enzo's eyes narrow as he looks around for a man to jump out from behind me. It takes him a second to process that I'm not Jocelyn, I'm Kai Miller. Katherine is my actual name, but I haven't gone by that since I was three and declared my name was Kai. I've always been Kai.

His lips curl into a grin. "I knew you were a thief; I didn't realize you were a liar too, *Kai*."

I smile back, tauntingly. "A liar who could have slipped through your cracks and been on the run for a lot longer than you were prepared to search for me. But I didn't run. I owe you a debt, and now that debt has been repaid."

He nods. "Your debt is forgiven. But it was a stupid trade, my beautiful, Kai." He grabs my arm. "Let's go for a ride on the waves, Kai. I have something I want to show you."

CHAPTER 5
ENZO

This can't be right.

This girl can't be Kai Miller.

It has to be a mistake.

Even if she is Kai Miller, my father must have written down the wrong name.

Or there must be a different Kai Miller.

She doesn't belong in my world.

She doesn't deserve to die.

Even though she stole your watch without any way to pay you back?

Shut up, I tell the voice in my head.

There is a difference between being punished and dying. She deserves to be punished for her crime, that's all.

"Show me your ID," I say.

Jocelyn, or Kai or whatever her name is, bites her lip in the adorable, seductive way she does when she's thinking hard.

I groan inwardly, but don't let her see how such a simple movement affects me. I want to kiss her, not kill her.

"I don't have an ID."

"What? Did you leave it at home?" I ask, not sure why she would. I don't know where she lives, but surely she drove to the pier. I know she doesn't live in any of the large seaside houses that cost millions and are the only homes nearby.

"No, I don't have an ID."

I grip her wrist, not believing a word out of her mouth. "You're older than sixteen, which means you have a driver's license."

She shakes her head.

"You're not at least sixteen?" *Shit, how young is she?*

"I'm sixteen; I turn seventeen next week." She hesitates as if she's ashamed to say the rest. "But I never got my driver's license."

I narrow my eyes into slits, demanding her to tell me the truth.

"Why would I need a driver's license? I don't own a car, and even if I did, I don't know how to drive."

My heart throbs. I learned to drive when I was thirteen. No one taught me, just like no one taught me how to throw a punch or fire a gun. I learned because it was necessary to survive. But since I was sixteen, I've been driving a Lamborghini. I can't imagine never driving. It's one of the world's greatest escapes. I feel powerful and unrelenting when I drive. And suddenly, I have the urge to teach her how to drive and watch as she takes control.

"I'm Kai Miller," her words are calm and steady.

"How do I know that? How do I know you aren't lying to me so I'll forgive your debt?"

Anger flares on her face, as steam flows from her ears. She's pissed. It's cute, but not enough to make me believe her.

She huffs. "Do I look like a Jocelyn to you?"

"No."

"My name is Kai. My father calls me Katherine because he thinks Kai is too masculine sounding. But I chose the name Kai when I was little and thought Katherine was too long. It means—"

"Sea."

She nods slowly.

Kai looks like the sea. Her eyes match the greenish blue color of the ocean, and her skin thrives under the sun making her tanner instead of burning. I would guess she's grown up her whole life near the water, but instead of learning about the ocean, she's been cleaning expensive yachts...for my father, I realize. This is one of his yachts.

Fuck. She really is Kai. Whether the name on her birth certificate is Katherine or Kai, it doesn't matter. This is who my father meant when he wrote the name on the napkin. And she knows something, or my father thinks she does, which is why I have to kill her.

But I need to learn more. *So much more.* I have so many questions Kai needs to answer. I need to take her somewhere private, not here on the pier. Somewhere I can figure out what to do.

I look down at her lean body. I could grab her arm and force her to go with me. She might struggle or even scream, but it won't be enough to draw much attention to us. The sailors know who I am, and they wouldn't dare cross me or my family. Even if the police are called, it would be too late. I would already have her.

But she might answer more of my questions if I lure her, instead of taking her.

It's not in my nature to persuade someone with the carrot rather than the stick. But with Kai, I think it's the only way.

Her eyes widen as she realizes I believe her, and I want something from her.

I hold out my hand.

"I'm not going with you. Not until you tell me why you were searching for me."

I let my shoulders drop, attempting to seem relaxed. I feign a smile, and let my eyes grow soft, so I stop looking like such a demon.

"Have you ever been on a yacht before?"

She chuckles incredulously. "Are you serious? You just saw me on a yacht."

I smile more genuine now at seeing her brighten. "I meant, have you been on a yacht like this out in the ocean? Not when you were working, but when you could truly enjoy its grace and extravagance?"

"No," she exhales in sadness.

I extend my hand to her, making it easier for her to accept. "Let me take you out on one. It could be fun. Just the two of us." I wink.

Kai stares at my hand, and I know she's debating with herself.

She wants to take it. She wants to have fun, have an adventure. Pretend that cleaning away nonstop isn't her life.

But she knows the danger. I don't know much about her, but this much I know. She was wary of me in the bar, and she continues to be now. She should be. I don't know what made her different than most kids our age, but I know she doesn't get to spend her days going to school, doing homework, and flirting with boys her age. Her life has hardened her to the truths of the world. She knows danger when she sees it, and I'm danger.

"Do you know how to drive a yacht?"

I smirk; I've got her. "I guess you're just going to have to trust me if you want to go out the ocean."

She ignores my hand but walks closer to me. "Let's go then."

I let my hand drop despite my urge to touch her. I need her hand, waist, or entire body in my clutches. I need to ensure she can't escape. But it's more than that. I'm desperate to feel what I know will be deliciously warm flesh against mine.

"This way then," I say as I start walking down the pier toward a yacht I know isn't being used tonight. I let her feel like she has power and is making this choice. I don't force her to follow me. But if she ran, I would chase.

I hear her hesitant steps clanking down the pier in her flip-flops. My head shakes the tiniest bit. She definitely doesn't belong in my world; she doesn't even know how to walk without being heard.

I reach the black beast of a yacht at the far end of the pier. It's not the biggest yacht in our collection, but it still looms over us, taunting us with its majesty.

Kai stops next to me, her breathing heavy as she stares up at the boat.

"It's tiny," she says, trying to lighten the mood with her joke.

A wave of her black hair has fallen on her neck, and I brush it back, feeling the iciness oozing, prickling my hot skin as I whisper in her ear, "Trust me, it's not small."

She blushes and bites her damn lip again, like she's trying to contain her excitement.

Shit, it's infectious.

Some stairs lead up to the main deck of the boat, but what fun are stairs? I jump up to the main deck and turn to tell Kai about the stairs or to help her across.

Thud.

I turn and see Kai smiling next to me. She landed on the deck, although not quite as gracefully as I did.

God, this creature intrigues me. She's made for this life on the ocean, full of thrill and risk-taking. Unfortunately, this might be the last risk she ever takes.

"This way, sweetheart." I wink at her and start walking toward the bow.

"Ugh, really? Sweetheart?" She chases after me.

I shrug. I haven't found a nickname that suits her yet.

Why am I trying to come up with a nickname for her? I shouldn't be getting attached.

I enter the wheelhouse and find the first mate.

"Out," I shout to the man I barely recognize. He's been to the club before and works for my father, but I couldn't tell you his name.

"Yes, sir." He doesn't hesitate as he exits the room. He knows the consequences.

"And ensure no crew or cleaning staff remain on the yacht. I will be taking it for a spin, *alone.*"

Kai's eyebrows raise as the man scurries off.

I walk behind the wheel and start-up the yacht.

"We're really doing this?" Kai asks, her voice hitched.

"Yes," I hiss, although I don't know what *this* is. *Does she think I'm going to take her to some private island and fuck her?* She's probably a virgin for goodness sakes. And she's young. *Sixteen.* Almost seventeen. She feels far too young for my seventeen, almost eighteen years, or maybe it's the difference in life experience that makes us so far apart.

We are both too young for any of this. She may not have seen death or taken it as I have, but she's experienced pain and fear. We are teenagers who shouldn't be thinking about fucking, yet that's where both our minds are.

I don't know what I'm going to do when I get her out on the ocean, but I do know I won't be fucking her.

"Do you know how to untie us and remove the buoy?" I ask.

She gives me a wicked smile. "Of course."

"Good, do it then."

Kai tucks her hair behind her ear that has fallen from the bandana and then runs off.

I shake my head as I watch her leave, giving her another chance to get free of me.

No, giving her another chance to trust me before I ruin her.

A minute later the anchor is up, and we are pulling away from the pier. Kai's eyes are big as she watches me steer out of the marina.

With her eyes on me, I feel unsettled.

"You should go to the front and feel the breeze in your hair before we pick up speed. There is nothing like it," I say.

"What about you?" she asks, innocently.

My eyes darken. "Somebody has to steer the boat."

She sighs in disappointment.

"Don't worry; I'll have us stopped somewhere before the sun sets."

Kai smiles weakly and then does as I say. She moves to the front of the boat, where I can unfortunately still see her as I drive us out into the ocean. Her body becomes part of the wind. She throws her arms back, her eyes close, and her hair flies.

Beautiful.

I steer us out into the ocean, finding a quiet place where we won't be disturbed. And then I enable the GPS autopilot to keep us stopped at this exact location, since the ocean is too deep here to use the anchor.

"Beautiful," I whisper as I approach Kai.

"It is, isn't it?" She looks out at the ocean where the sun is beginning to set while I look at her.

"How long have you been cleaning yachts?"

She shrugs, her eyes cutting to mine and her smile faltering. "A long time."

"That's not an answer."

"Maybe you haven't earned an answer."

I grab her arm that is gripping the railing and turn her toward me. She stares at my touch. She's so cold to my fiery fingers. We both gasp before she pulls her arm away.

"I haven't earned an answer? I forgave your debt after you stole from me. I'm spending my time and money on gas to take you on a fancy joy ride. How have I not earned some answers to my questions?"

Her hand grips the railing again as she turns from me.

"What does your father do for a living?" I ask.

Nothing.

"How about your mother?"

Silence.

"How long have you been cleaning yachts?"

It doesn't matter what question I ask. She won't answer.

Does she know who my father is? Does she know who I am? Did she witness something at the club? Did she witness a murder? What?

I grab her arm and shove her back. She catches herself on the railing, her back now to it, instead of her front.

I cage her in with my arms. I've been nice, trying to butter her up to answer me, but it didn't work. Now, I need answers.

Time is ticking, and I need to decide what to do with her.

She blinks rapidly, and then her eyes grow defiant as I box her in.

"You don't scare me."

"I should."

She huffs. "You don't think I haven't been dealing with men like you my entire life. Well, I have. And you are by far the least scary. You're nothing but a *boy*. Whatever you want from me, you won't get unless I want you to."

I growl and push myself against her until her breathing stops, proving just how far I'll go to get the answers that I need.

We both stare at each other, neither of us backing down—neither of us giving in.

Her mind is whirling. I can see it going a million miles an hour trying to figure a way out of this. And she may be able to with whatever low-level men come to collect her father's debts, but she won't be able to figure a way out with me. She will answer me if she wants to live. And even if she responds, there is no guarantee of living. That was her mistake when she told me who she was, when she willingly got on this yacht with me.

"Fine, I'll answer."

I back away only an inch.

"If you win at a game of truth or lies," she continues.

I narrow my eyes, pressing my body hard against hers again. "No, you will tell me everything I want to know."

She shakes her head slowly. "I will answer any question you ask, if you win. It's clear you have questions you need to ask. That's why we are here. My father probably did something stupid, and you need information about him. But I will only answer if you win."

"No."

She smirks. "You don't have a choice, pretty boy. Otherwise, I'll refuse to talk, and you'll have to report back to your boss that you didn't get the information you need."

"And if you win?"

"Then you answer my questions."

I frown. I don't like this at all, but if I win, she will answer without me having to hurt her. And if I lose, then I guess I will torture her until she tells me.

"What are the rules?"

"We each tell two truths and lie." She thinks for a moment. "Although, since neither one of us want to reveal much about ourselves, we will play it in reverse. We each will tell two lies and one truth."

"How do you win?"

"When you correctly guess the truth."

"And if we both guess the truth?"

"Then we will both be answering a lot of questions."

I look over her shoulder and watch the sun hover over the horizon. In thirty minutes or less it will be set, and I'll be out of time. I want to determine if she deserves to die, tonight.

I look at her. Kai's street smart. She knows how to survive. She stole from me without me noticing. She's sly. But now that I know that about her, I know what to watch for. I've spent my entire life reading people; I'll know if she's telling the truth or not.

"Deal."

Her grin reaches her eyes, and then she looks down at where I'm pressed against her body. My cock has hardened against her stomach; her nipples are sharp points beneath her tank top. If I kissed her right now, I don't think she'd stop me, but then she'd never answer me.

I take a step back, and she exhales sharply.

I walk to the sliding front door of the cabin, throwing it open, disappearing inside. When I step back out, I have two glasses and a fifth of whiskey.

"Sit," I say at the table near the front of the ship.

She takes a seat hesitantly, as I pour us both half a glass of whiskey, fearing we are both going to need a lot to get through this night.

She takes the glass without a word and sips on the drink. She doesn't turn up her nose in disgust like most girls her age when they drink anything straight. She doesn't wince at the burn; she welcomes it.

I breathe in the drink before I taste it and return to the state of numbness I feel when I drink it. But somehow I don't think there is enough alcohol on this boat to make me numb when I'm around her. Every electrode in my body is firing.

"You go first," I say.

She nods.

"My first truth or lie is I've never given a blow job."

My eyes darken at her words. This is how she wants to play this. *Dirty.*

"I've never come."

Damn her, and her dirty distractions.

"I've never been kissed," she breathes.

Somehow her last one feels as dirty as the previous two. *Something so innocent, yet so delicious.*

She leans back after she finishes and puts her feet up on the table, relaxing. She said each sentence with equal weight; she's used to lying to protect herself.

"Your turn."

But I'm good at lying too...

"I've never shot a man.

"I've never raped a woman.

"I've never killed a man."

My truths and lies are darker, instead of dirty like hers. But it does the job I was hoping.

Shock.

Even if my body betrayed me on some level when I told the truth instead of the lies, she wouldn't notice, she was too busy being frazzled by my words—hating herself for getting on a boat with such a vicious man.

"Now what?"

"Now we make our choice. We only get to pick once. One chance to pick the truth."

"And if neither of us chose correctly?" I ask, even though I doubt it will happen. One of us will choose correctly and one of us won't. I have no doubt I'll be the victor.

"Then I guess we don't get any answers."

I nod, agreeing.

I think back to the three choices:

I've never given a blow job.

I've never come.

I've never been kissed.

I eye her suspiciously as I think them over and how she said each sentence. The first sentence was easy falling from her lips, meant to shock me as I had her. The second was breathy, like she was thinking about coming when she said it and how good it would feel. The third she said almost playfully, like she was daring me to kiss her.

I smile.

"Have you decided?" she asks.

"I can eliminate one easily."

"And which one is that?"

"I've never come is easily a lie. I felt how you pressed back against my body when I was touching you. You know your body well. You know how it feels to make yourself come. You know that exquisite feeling when you touch your clit and explode."

Her cheeks blush just a little, but otherwise, she doesn't show any confirmation that I chose one of the lies correctly.

"And what do you think? Do you think you know any of mine you can eliminate?"

She cocks her head to the side as if she's hiding something. "You've never shot a man. That one's easily a lie. I saw your gun. I can only assume you've used it."

I swallow hard, and she knows she guessed the lie correctly.

"Now comes the hard part though."

I nod.

We both eye each other, waiting for either to give away our secrets with a look, a breath, a word. Neither of us does.

I watch her weigh her two options in her head. Either I've never raped or never murdered. Neither makes me a saint, both make me a sinner. She knows nothing about me, but I know the hope she has will make her choose I've never killed a man, because she views that as the worse crime. She will choose the lesser of the two evils. *Wrongly*.

I think between my two options.

If I believe she was telling the truth when she says she's never been kissed, then that means she's given a man a blow job without having been kissed first. I stare up at the woman in front of me. She's not that kind of woman. She may be desperate, but she knows her own worth. She wouldn't sell herself, so she wouldn't give a blow job for money. And if a boyfriend asked, he would have had to have been chivalrous. Taken her out on date after date to gain her kiss, let alone to earn her to blow him.

"Ready?" she asks.

I nod.

She lifts her drink, and I raise mine. We both down our drinks until the glasses are empty, our eyes never leaving each other.

"Your truth is you've never given a blow job," I say as I gently set the glass on the table, happy to declare my victory. I don't care if she guesses correctly. I will get my questions answered.

Her lips slowly curl. "Wrong."

What? She's given a blow job but never been kissed?

She leans forward on the table. "And your truth is you've never raped a woman."

My eyes glare back at her as she smirks. I don't have to open my mouth for her to know my truth. She already knows she won.

CHAPTER 6
KAI

I won.

I know without Enzo confirming it. I guessed correctly, although it never felt like speculation. I've always been good at telling the difference between a lie and the truth. Enzo is harder to read than most, but even he has his tells.

He's never raped a woman.

It warms me a little to know he never did anything that horrible.

But he has.

He's shot someone. *Killed someone.*

I don't know the circumstances around either. It could have been self-defense. I have no doubt, if I could afford a gun, I would have shot someone by now and killed if my aim was good.

Somehow, I don't think Enzo has done either only in self-defense.

Enzo glares at me, frustrated I won and he lost. I expect him to argue with me about my truth and lies. I expect him to call me out and claim that surely a sixteen-year-old like me has been kissed, especially if, as I claim, I've given a man a blow job. I expect him to whip his dick out and force me to suck it, to prove I've given head before.

Instead, he's a statue, giving me nothing of what is going on inside his body.

"You're not going to question my truth?"

His head cocks to the side as if he's trying to figure out what game I'm playing. "No."

"You sure?"

He nods his head. "Yes, I know you wouldn't deceive me during the game. I know you've masturbated before. And I know you've sucked off some man's dick like a whore."

I wince at his harsh words.

His eyes meet mine, filled with want. "And I know you've never been kissed."

I bite my now sore lip, that aches to be kissed, but I'm sure is red and swollen from the number of times I've chewed it today to keep myself from kissing this boy. This very dangerous, off-limits boy who I shouldn't be on this yacht with.

Enzo stands up and walks back to the railing, where the sun is now well below the horizon. The sky has opened up, allowing the darkness to begin to overtake the heavens. Soon there will be nothing left but the stars and the moon to shine down upon us.

I consider pouring myself another drink before I approach him, but I've had enough alcohol. I need my wits about me around him. He won't express it, but I can feel the anger radiating off him as I approach. He has considerable control though to not let it show on any of his features.

I stop next to him, ensuring I don't touch him.

"Ask me."

His voice is low and rumbling. It's deepened since he was talking to me earlier. This voice is the one he uses to scare people. It should frighten me. Instead, I want to hear it again.

I know how he expects me to use my newfound power. To ask questions about the game. To ask who he's shot or killed and why he's never raped a woman before if he's done the other two.

"How did you learn to drive a yacht?"

His head turns to me, and I can see his thick, dark eyebrow raise. "I grew up around the water in this business. You were taught to take care of the yachts, while I learned everything else about them. How to drive them, maintain them, sell them. There is nothing I don't know about how a ship like this works."

I inhale and then exhale, trying to remind myself to keep breathing. *What is he doing to me?* They are just words. I shouldn't be so hot and bothered when he merely speaks. And I've let it affect my judgment. I know better than to get on a boat in the middle of fucking nowhere with a strange man. A man who has already admitted to killing someone. But his words are intoxicating, pulling me deeper until I have no brain cells left and will do whatever he wants.

"Who do you work for?"

"Black."

I stop breathing. *Black.* His name is synonymous with evil. He's a myth and a legend. I'm not even sure he's a real person, but I have no doubt Enzo works for the most dangerous man in the city.

I need to gain back some power, because even though I won, it doesn't feel like I have any control.

"Have you ever been kissed?" I ask, wiggling my eyebrows trying to break the serious mood.

"Yes, Kai. I've been kissed. I'm not wide-eyed and bushy-tailed like you." He pauses. "And before you ask, yes I've had women kneel in front of me, pleading with me for the pleasure to suck my cock."

My eyes drop to his dark jeans, and I swear I saw his cock grow against the zipper.

No, it must be my imagination. He can't be turned on.

Enzo faces me now and takes my hand in his. I watch in horror and excitement as he lifts my hand to his lips and kisses my palm tenderly. It should be innocent enough, but I feel a warm tingle cascade through my body.

"Do you have any other questions, Kai?"

I close my eyes, trying to still my racing heart. "Why did you bring me here?" My words are a whisper, but I know he hears me, despite my eyes being closed.

I feel his hand at my neck, and I gasp, opening my eyes. His body is so close to mine I can feel the electricity in his body. He's so warm; he burns me when he grazes my skin. But other than his hand at my neck, he doesn't stroke me, just thumbs my neck, melting a layer of skin from my hard shell. He's so full of restraint.

I lick my lip, because I can't stand not to feel something pressed against my lips.

"Kai," he says, his voice threatening, but I don't understand why.

"Enzo," I say his name like a curse.

His eyes tell me what he's going to do before he does it—giving me one second to stop him.

I don't stop him.

His lips crash with mine.

I always thought my first kiss would be sweet, gentle. I thought it would be the first step on the way to falling in love. I thought it might be clumsy or awkward, but the second kiss would more than make up for it.

That's not what this is.

This kiss in an explosion, setting off a desire neither of us is allowed to feel.

A second after our lips crash, his tongue sweeps into my mouth. My arms wrap around his neck like I've done it a thousand times, while his hands grip my waist, almost suffocating me with their grip.

My tongue fights with his. Both of us needing control over the kiss. He demanded my first kiss from me, and I gave it willingly. But now, we need more.

I purr into his mouth as his tongue massages mine and his body presses into me, smoldering me in the process. And I'm cursing the fabric between us, wishing we were in swimsuits or better yet, nothing at all.

We could fuck.

Here. Now.

Enzo might not be who I dreamed of being my first. But he's better than the alternative. He's better then selling my first time or having it taken from me, which is what will happen if I stay at the trailer park.

He might not cuddle with me in bed afterward or even talk to me about what happened. He wouldn't be gentle or concerned with making sure I was adequately prepared before he would take my virginity. But he would take it, and I would give it as willingly as I gave this kiss.

I shouldn't be thinking about sex. I'm too young, not even seventeen yet, but in my world, I don't have the luxury of waiting, of remaining innocent.

He bites my lip.

I feel the tingle of the blood in my mouth.

What do you want with me, Enzo?

It should piss me off, but it only turns me on more.

Dammit! What am I doing?

This is precisely what he wants, me thrown off guard. Me, letting down my guard so he can attack. It's the reason he brought me here. To get something from me.

I might let him fuck me, but I won't let him take advantage of me.

The kiss will end soon. I can feel it. So I do the only thing I can to gain more information.

I slip my hand into his back pocket and fish out his phone. I know he didn't notice. I'm an expert at picking pockets when I want to be. I let him catch me with the wallet so I could more easily retrieve the more expensive watch.

The kiss ends.

I don't know who stops it. It just happens.

Enzo's eyes stare intently at my swollen lip. His thumb brushes across the sore. I see the blood before his thumb moves to mouth, and he sucks it off.

Neither of us speaks about what just happened. We just stare and pretend that kiss didn't change everything.

I slip his phone into my back pocket before he realizes it's missing.

"Bathroom..." I say suddenly needing a moment alone.

I don't wait for him to nod or tell me where one is. I dash away, through the sliding door where Enzo retrieved our drinks. I don't care where the bathroom is; I don't need it. I need to stop letting Enzo affect my body and use my head. I need to realize the danger I put myself in.

I open the nearest door and step inside before shutting it and locking it. I slip the phone out of my pocket and stare at it.

It's password protected.

Of course, it is.

Shit, what was I thinking?

It buzzes.

I jump, staring at it like it's just come alive.

The phone may be locked, but the message still shows up on the home screen.

The message is from Black, his boss.

BLACK: IS KAI DEAD YET?

I BLINK. OVER AND OVER.

I'm not reading that right.

But every time I reread it, it says the same thing.

Eventually, the screen goes dark, and when I hit the home button again the message is gone, only an alert left that he has an unread message.

Dead.

That's what Enzo is doing here. He was sent to kill me.

The door opens, but I don't have to turn to know Enzo has a gun pointed at my head.

"Do you have any more questions, thief?"

His words cut through me like glass. I may be a thief, but he's an assassin.

I turn to him with defiance in my eyes. I always knew something horrible awaited my future. He may think I'll die quick and swiftly, or I'll beg for my life.

I'll do neither because I've been prepared for this day. And I won't go down without a fight.

"Just one.

"Why?"

CHAPTER 7
ENZO

Why?

I promised to reply to any of her questions if I lost, but this is the one question I can't answer.

"Why?" Kai asks again, her voice steady, though I can see the quiver in her lip as she speaks. A lip still swollen and stained red from the drop of blood I drew when I kissed her.

Kai won't let this go.

I hold the gun loosely in my hand, still pointed in her general direction, but not aimed directly at her. I should pull the trigger and end this. Put a stop to the questions I can't answer.

"Why?" her voice is stronger now, more determined. "You are going to kill me anyway. It won't hurt to tell me why if you are just going to shoot me. I won't be able to tell anyone."

I don't react, not even with my eyes. She's right of course, but that doesn't mean I'm going to answer her.

Her eyes grow dark and angry. "We made a bet. You played the game. You lost. Now answer me! *Why?*"

My eyes close for a second longer than they should be closed. I expect her to take her chance and escape. She's smart, observant, and will do anything to survive, but she doesn't take her opportunity when I show the tiniest weakness. Her need to know the answer is greater than her need to live in this moment.

I want to answer her.

I want to know why myself.

But I won't lie to her, and I don't know the answer.

Her legs tremble, and she falls, the bed behind her catching her into a seated position. Her hand shakes against her chest, and if I were to feel her pulse I know it would be flying through her body, her fight or flight response kicked into gear.

"You don't know, do you?" Her words are sharp and determined.

"No, I don't know why."

"Did you even ask why when you were given this assignment?"

"Yes."

She nods slowly. "I understand. You're not high up enough in Black's crime organization to get to know why. You blindly follow orders. I knew you were a criminal. I knew you did bad things when I met you. I knew you were dangerous, but I didn't realize you were heartless and cruel. I didn't know you were a fucking coward, a nobody, a lowlife who only cared about earning cash when you took a life!"

Her breathing is hurried, but she doesn't stop. "I thought if you were to kill me, you would at least give me the courtesy of deciding I deserved to die yourself, not because some king in a castle told you to. I thought you were your own person, but now I realize who you really are. A fucking pussy with no control and no future."

"Are you finished?"

She huffs. "You're the one with a gun. You tell me."

I lower it just a little; she exhales realizing I'm not going to shoot her, not yet.

"You're right. I'm a fucking coward who won't stand up for myself. I follow orders. But you're wrong about my ability to control my future. I may not be able to control what I do on this boat, but I will after."

"How?"

"Because this is my final assignment. After this, I'm free."

She sucks in a breath, and for the first time, I see real terror in her eyes. She realizes there is nothing she can do to stop me from killing her. That my desire to be free is greater than my desire to save her.

Kai takes a second to compose herself, and then she stands. She walks to me, ignoring the gun in my hand pointed toward her leg.

Her lips pout, and her body sways as she walks toward me.

My pulse races, my jaw twitches, and my cock hardens.

I want her.

There's no denying it. It's been a while since I've felt a kiss like the one she just gave me. *No, I've never had a kiss like that one.*

It was passionate, mysterious, sweet, and full of promise. Her first kiss was everything a kiss should be. *Too bad it will also be her last kiss.*

I want Kai.

More than I want to breathe.

More than I want my freedom.

I could have both. Spend the day kissing her, fucking her, using her. Then get the freedom I'm desperate for.

As Kai moves closer, I know that is what she is offering me too. Her body on a platter. She thinks it is the only possibility she has at keeping herself alive. If I develop any feelings for her, then I won't kill her. But that's not going to save her. Nothing will.

She reaches out hesitantly, touching my face.

My eyes stay glued to hers as I watch her tongue caress her bottom lip. And then I remember how good it felt to have her lips pressed against mine. But I've had years of training in self-control. No matter how much Kai tempts me, I won't give in.

She presses her lips to mine, softly.

"You can try to seduce me all you want; it won't save you."

"I beg to differ," she purrs back before her lips crash hard against mine.

After putting my gun back in my waistband, I close my eyes as my hands grip her body, jerking her to me. Her body is cold, soft, and so breakable in my arms—everything I've always wanted but never been able to taste. The mix of hot and cold together creating a tsunami in both of us.

The only women I've been with were whores or worked for my

father. They were all skilled in how to kiss, how to fuck. It was business to them. Not Kai. She's a breath of fresh air, untamed and wild with her movements.

Her tongue pushes deeper, exploring my mouth without the finesse I'm used to. And damn, that turns me on.

"Fuck," I growl as she knees me in the balls.

I knew it was coming. Despite knowing she would try something like this, it didn't stop me from taking the brief moment of pleasure. Something I almost always deny myself, because it makes me weak.

Kai runs, but I take my time chasing after her. The ship is big, but not so large I won't be able to find her. And even if it were too large, I would still be able to find her. I'm too drawn to her not to notice her heart beating, begging me to stay away and yet still hoping I will find her and claim her.

After adjusting myself in my jeans, I feel the pain ease, and I start walking. The gun has returned to my hand as I walk.

I should be pissed and angry about what she did. I should find her and shoot her on the spot without giving her another second to breathe. But I know I won't, because she intrigues me.

I hear the engines roar.

I shake my head, knowing exactly where she is.

I walk slowly to the engine room. I try the door, but I already know it's locked.

The engines burn louder, but we won't move because the GPS autopilot is engaged and she doesn't know how to turn it off.

I kick the door in easily.

Kai stands frozen as I enter, but I don't raise my gun.

"What's your plan now?" I ask because I know she has a plan B and a plan C, etc. She won't stop until I've decided I've had enough.

She faces me stoically, with no fear. She won't die terrified.

"To cause as much pain as possible to you before I go."

I nod. "I don't think that's your real plan."

"It is."

"Liar. You haven't given up yet. You'll only change to trying to hurt me to extract revenge when you've given up trying to survive."

She frowns, hating I know her so well.

"You don't have to do this. You don't have to kill me."

I raise an eyebrow and wait. Apparently plan B is persuading me not to kill her, although I'm guessing there's more to her plan. With Kai, there always is.

"I'm not a snitch. I won't tell anybody this ever happened."

I nod, believing if I let her go free, she would never mention this to anyone.

"I haven't witnessed anything else. I know nothing about the organization you work for. I don't know the name. I don't know who your boss is. Or what crimes anyone has committed. I've never seen anyone steal, or rape, or shoot, or murder. And even if I did, I would know well enough to keep my mouth shut to survive."

My eyes harden. I believe her. My father wants her dead, and I have no idea why. It may not even be about Kai. It might be that he is just testing me to kill someone innocent to ensure I would do anything for him.

"I will pay my debt to you. And I will pay any debts my father owes if that is what this is about. No matter how high of a price, I will find a way to pay it back. My stealing your watch and using it to pay my father's last debt should prove that to you."

I smirk. "I have no doubt you would. You're a thief. You know how cruel the world can be. But you are also a survivor. I would guess one of the reasons you've never been kissed is because the men in your life have only caused you more pain. None of them were worthy of taking something so innocent from you. You protected something so simple that most people give without thinking. You only gave when you were desperate for it. But I have no doubt you would sell your body, even your soul to survive. To protect your father. You would give everything."

She nods, her throat tight, and the vein in her neck pulsing hard. She's already relented to the fact she would eventually sell her body to survive. Like so many women from her part of town do.

I raise the gun again as anger pulses through me. I can't stand the thought of her selling herself to another man. She's mine. "You won't be selling yourself, thief."

She swallows and licks her lips.

"Don't kill me…"

I hesitate.

"…not with your gun. If you're going to kill me, then do it with your bare hands."

I smirk, both liking and hating her plan C because the only way I could truly kill her is by touching her. But her touch will end me too.

CHAPTER 8
KAI

Itry to look past the black metal aimed at me, to the man behind it. The gun might lead to my death, but Enzo will be the one squeezing the trigger.

I don't know why I ask him to kill me without using the gun. It will make no difference. I will be dead no matter how he does it. A gun might even make my death swifter.

I don't want to die from a bullet to the head.

If Enzo is going to kill me, I want him to do it with his bare hands. I want him to feel the life he's taking, and how desperate, determined I am to live. And a tiny part of me hopes he won't be able to kill me if he's forced to endure my heart stopping, my breathing slowing, and my essence leaving my body.

I swallow hard, trying to remain calm.

No, it won't make a difference. He will kill me either way, unless I find a way to escape. But at least this way, I will have some amount of control over when and how I die.

Enzo doesn't lower the gun.

I'm going to die.

Right here and now.

Instinctively, I close my eyes, like somehow not seeing the bullet coming will make dying easier.

I should be thinking about my mother, whom I miss. Or how my father will be lost, unable to survive without me. I should be thinking about the friends I will never get to see again. About the future I will be deprived of.

I will never fall in love...

Get married...

Or have kids...

Not that I ever thought those things were really in my future anyway.

But my brain doesn't go to any of those things. All I can think about is that damn kiss. The first one, the second one...I want *more*.

I let my lips curl up in a smile. At least if I'm going to die, I'm going to die with something happy in my head. Even if it is twisted that I'm thinking of Enzo when he's the one who's going to destroy me.

One second.

Two...

Three...

Nothing.

My eyes flutter open. Enzo's eyes darken as he looks at me. He lowers the gun, empties the ammo, and tosses the gun to the side while the bullets fall to the ground next to him.

"Why?" I ask, my bottom lip trembling.

"You ask that question a lot, thief."

"That's not an answer, killer."

"Because you asked me to. You didn't beg, you asked with dignity. And after not being able to answer the one question you want answers to the most, I owe you."

"Thank you."

"My debt has now been repaid. We owe each other nothing."

I nod. "Nothing."

Enzo steps toward me, and I reciprocate.

I should be running. I should be searching for a weapon to fight back. To kill him before he kills me.

The pull to him is too strong. I want him more than I want to live.

What's wrong with me? Am I that desperate for a small taste of what love could feel like?

Yes.

Because I know without a doubt if the circumstances were different, I could love the boy standing in front of me. He's handsome, my attraction to him overwhelms me. But it's more than his looks. He has an old soul, like me. Dangerous, yet truthful. Controlling, demanding, and merciless. He's honest, yet holds the secrets of the world. He's complicated and simple. He craves freedom, like me.

I could love a monster like him.

We both take another step closer. Neither of us knows what the other is going to do when we meet.

I hold my head high as I edge closer. My lips are parted, and my breathing is slow. Time creeps. I should be thankful. I could live a lifetime in this moment with Enzo; maybe then I could live forever.

Closer, closer, closer.

One more step...

We collide. Our bodies attach like magnets. My arms go around his waist, and his hands go to my throat.

The electricity between us is unfathomable. It dances between us like tiny fairies trying to bind us together.

We are together. Now, what the fuck do you want?

"Why?" his voice grumbles.

I cock my head, not understanding his question.

"Why do you trust me, when I've threatened to kill you?"

"You're an honest man. You may hide truths, but you don't lie. I trust you will keep your promise and kill me."

He strokes my cheek. It's not meant to be comforting; he just needs to touch me.

"I don't want to die, though. Dying would be the easy way out."

"Why?" he asks, again.

Enzo doesn't know why he's supposed to kill me, and I don't know why I keep getting close to him even though every nerve in my body is screaming for me to run away. He didn't answer me; I won't answer him.

"Kiss me," I demand.

He isn't used to being bossed around by anyone other than the man he works for. I doubt a woman has ever commanded him to do anything. But for some reason, he does as I demand without question.

Lips crash down on mine, hungrier than the last two times we kissed combined.

The kiss is reckless, for both of us. But soon all thoughts are lost, fading away as quickly as they started.

I nip on his bottom lip before he has a chance to torture mine again.

He gasps from the way I take over the kiss. And then I bite hard, drawing blood the same way he did me.

He jerks away, and I see the small pebble of blood on his bottom lip. His tongue licks over his tiny wound and the lust in his eyes deepens.

The fire grows between us. No kiss will be able to extinguish it. It will burn, long after either of us are gone. That will be my legacy—an intense fire that will reign hell down on those who hurt me.

My mouth waters, needing him again.

He gives me a predatory glare. I smirk back, tempting him to devour me again the way I want.

He does.

His lips suck on mine as his tongue invades my mouth, demanding for me to give in to his power. *Not going to happen.*

I fight right back, my tongue dipping deeper into his mouth. Our tongues continue dancing with each other for dominance. Our groans grow heavier with each lap of our tongues, and our lips are swollen from the vicious kisses.

We would make a fiery match. Both of us unrelenting and stubborn. We both have pasts that have made us ruthless and savage. We would be one of those couples with an inextinguishable passion that would turn to fighting any time we left the bedroom. The arguing would be worth it though to be kissed like this.

My hand slides under his shirt, my nails dig into his back as I push his shirt up, before tearing it off his body.

I gasp.

Enzo's hard body terrifies and intrigues me. He's not fit in the same way the football players at my high school are. His muscles aren't even or crafted in a weight room. I doubt he's ever worked out in the traditional sense, but his body is hard as steel. It's rough and sharp along the edges of his muscles that have been built with years of hard work in the streets instead of in the gym.

He's seventeen, barely a man, still a boy by most people's tabulation. Young enough to still be in high school, although I doubt he attends, he has no need for an education a typical school can provide. He's smart and sly despite little formal education. That's all the skill he needs.

I stop our kisses as my hands move over his rippled abs and up to his chest. Scars darken his once flawless skin. He doesn't have any tattoos I can see, which surprises me. Only scars. Too many for someone so young to have.

I have almost as many. Though none of mine come from being shot like his. But the knife scars I recognize. I've had the unfortunate experience of getting a knife jabbed into my arm before.

"Rape me," I say.

His velvety eyes widen as he tucks my hair behind my ear gently. How can he be so tender right now? "It wouldn't be rape," his voice threatens.

My body burns with an ache I've never felt before. He's right. It wouldn't be rape, even though that should be the only way his cock gets inside me—by force.

I want him to fuck me, to tear away my virginity, to be my first.

"It wouldn't be," I agree, my eyelids growing heavy as I trace over a scar in his shoulder that appears to be a bullet wound. My body pulsates with blistering need.

My heavy eyes meet his and the whole world stills. The ocean waves calm, the motor stops, the seagulls stop squawking. Even the wind is silent.

"Fuck me; I don't want to die a virgin."

I wait for him to tell me that fucking me won't save me. He won't fall in love with my pussy and keep me so he can fuck me again. This man has fucked plenty of women in his short life, I'm sure.

He doesn't say any of those things though.

Instead, he kisses me softer than he ever has before—a goodbye kiss.

Like hell it is! He doesn't get a goodbye kiss.

I press my body to his naked front and feel his erection thrust into my stomach. He wants me, so much. Maybe more than I want him.

I don't let him kiss me softly; I pull him back into our rough dance.

This time, it's rougher than the first.

I kiss him hard.

He slams my body against the wall.

I nibble harder on his lip.

He grabs my neck, threatening to kill me with his hands around my throat, his lips against mine, and his cock hard against my stomach. If I die, will he fuck my lifeless body?

The glare and determination in his eyes say no. He wants me very much alive.

Pain starts in my neck as he narrows his grip.

I can't breathe.

I try sucking in.

Nothing.

I gasp, which makes it worse as all my oxygen leaves my body.

My head feels dizzy, cloudy.

This is it.

His mouth pushes to me again, his grip loosens, and he breathes into my body.

He's not ready, yet. But soon, very soon...

"We could leave. Run away together. If we are both trapped, maybe leaving together would set us free," I say. It's a lie. I won't leave my father even if Enzo allows me to live. And the look in Enzo's eyes says he knows I'm lying too.

I push back, knowing my frail body can't compete against his hard one, but he lets me shove him.

I relish the space between us and hate it at the same time.

I push again, and he stumbles through the open doorway.

I storm after him.

I push him against the railing, and my hands go around his throat the same way his did mine. I tighten, knowing he can stop me at any second, and I'm not even sure I'm strong enough to strangle him, even if I wanted to.

He lets me. I kiss him and squeeze his neck at the same time, cutting off his oxygen the same way he did to me.

I don't see panic in his eyes, but I didn't reveal my terror when he did the same to me earlier. Not because I didn't think he would kill me, but because I'm stupid enough to trust I'm supposed to leave this world at his hands. I trust him to kill me in the way I deserve.

When his face starts to turn purple, I release.

And he inhales before releasing a tiny cough.

His eyes threaten mine. "Yea, we could run away and escape all of this. Or we could stay. I could protect you, make you my queen. Make you untouchable by any of my men."

More lies.

Whatever hold Black has is more than Enzo will ever hope to gain. Enzo won't give up his freedom for me.

His hand comes over my hair, removing the bandana, and letting my dark black hair fall to my shoulders.

He grabs my waist and pushes up the thin material of the spaghetti strapped shirt I'm wearing.

Yes, I moan inwardly. Take me, make me yours. I'd rather die belonging to someone than alone.

But then, we've changed positions. My body is arched over the railing as he clenches my bruised neck again.

"Why do you follow orders?" I whisper.

"Because I'm just as trapped in my life as you are in yours. I'm wealthy, I have more money than you could ever imagine, but that doesn't mean I'm free to spend it on the life I want. I do horrible things that are asked of me because I'm a monster. And even if I'm set free, the devil within will never let me go."

Tighter his hands move, just enough that the oxygen I pull through my throat to my lungs thins to a whispered breath.

"You don't seem trapped," I say—*another lie.* I may not understand it, but he's as confined as I am. If he weren't, he would have fucked me like any other boy our age would when given the chance.

He squeezes tighter, and his eyes close.

Dammit! Look at me! But my throat is closed. I can't scream at him.

He's going to kill me without even looking at me.

My hands flail, fighting against his hand taking my life. But he has more strength in his hand than I do my entire body.

I try to kick his groin, as I did before, but he has my legs pinned to the railing.

I can't move.

I can't breathe.

And I can't speak to get him to change his mind.

He's shut out the world, gone to whatever dark place allows him to kill the innocent and condemn his soul to hell.

I close my eyes as the pain overwhelms me again.

I'm alone.

I stop fighting.

I let the darkness come.

But just before it reaches me, something happens.

I can't explain it.

Maybe I'm already dead. I thought I would go to hell for the life I've lived. The stealing, the hurt I've caused my father, my disobedience. Maybe an angel saved me, and I'm going to heaven instead.

For a second, I'm floating. I must be out of my body.

And then just as quickly, I'm falling.

Down.

Down.

Down.

Until my body crashes into the cold water.

CHAPTER 9
ENZO

The water burns my skin as I plunge into the ocean.

My skin is always hot, like fire. The water is frigid in comparison and slices through my flaming skin like ice.

I have a love-hate relationship with the sea. I love the freedom it offers, and yet it can just as easily cause death. The ocean, for all its beauty, has to be experienced cautiously. For it can take life as easily as it gives it.

I kick hard and break the surface of the water. I suck in a deep breath, filling my lungs with oxygen.

I forget what caused me to tumble into the water. I forget everything as I breathe in the salty air. Right now, I love the ocean. I love how it makes me forget by stealing my brain cells and using my body to keep me afloat.

A gasp next to me brings me back to reality quickly.

My eyes bulge as I realize Kai is next to me, gulping for air. She's not getting enough oxygen. And then she begins floating down, under the water.

Before I think, I'm next to her. Pulling her body up, above the waves. She keeps opening her mouth, trying to catch her breath, but it's not enough.

Kai's body is colder than usual, her throat has a bruise where my hand once squeezed too hard around her precious neck, and her body is limp in my hands.

Shit.

She's going to die.

But that's what I want.

She's supposed to die.

I open her mouth and place mine over hers, giving her a breath. It's not enough.

I squeeze hard around her stomach just under her chest. Over and over I press until finally, the water expels from her lungs.

She coughs and then shivers. Her body is trying to survive in the cold water that threatens to take her life as I did.

"Shh, Kai. I've got you." I hold her against my heated body, trying to offset her temperature.

She lets me hold her. She shouldn't. She should never trust me, but she does. Or she realizes she doesn't have a choice but to accept my help for the moment, until her body regains its strength.

Her head rests against my shoulder, and her body shakes viciously trying to get warm. I continue treading water, keeping us alive.

I shouldn't be doing this.

I should let her die.

But I don't think about my responsibilities.

I don't think about what I'm going to do after I keep her alive.

But holding her in the cool water makes my heart speed up. I don't know what my heart is doing. It's never beat so swiftly before. Never pounded in my chest before her.

My body never reacts to its surroundings. I'm hot as fire, but I don't change. I let the burning build inside me, but never let it out. I don't feel pain nor happiness. I feel nothing.

Until her.

I can't make sense of what I'm feeling. *Happiness maybe? Hope? Lust?*

Something like emotion is there, stirring in my beating heart. But I can't put a word to it.

Slowly we rock in the waves, drifting further away from the yacht in the middle of the night.

Kai's eyes flicker open wide. She smiles at me.

Stupid girl.

And then the fear returns.

She begins thrashing in my arms.

"You...you tried to kill me," her voice trembles.

"I did."

"Help!" she cries out.

The ocean waves beat harder against us, giving her a silent answer. *No one will save her.*

"I killed you, but I also brought you back to life."

She pants heavily just out of reach. Her strength has returned, and her blood pumps with adrenaline.

Even in the dark of the night, I can see her emerald eyes shine with resolution.

"Why would you do that? So you can have the pleasure of watching me die again?"

Her eyes scorch mine as she waits for me to answer.

I take a deep breath. "I don't know why."

She shakes her head, and laughs gently.

Her laugh, even though it is meant to be unnerving, is beautiful and light—like her.

The waves calm as do her arms, and she begins floating more than wading, letting the sea hold her up. She belongs here, in the water.

I can't kill such a beauty.

Not because I love her or even care for her. I just can't. Something has been holding me back from the moment I met her.

My father lied to me. There is a reason he wants her dead. She's not an innocent, naive girl. She has a secret, one I haven't discovered yet.

I can't kill her.

And that makes me weak, a coward, a fool.

Killing Kai doesn't make sense. I won't kill her, screw the consequences.

"I think you've earned the power to choose your own fate."

"Why?"

"You're asking the wrong question. I don't know why, only that I think you deserve more than to be killed at my hand." I brush against the bruises I caused on her neck.

She straightens with a stoic expression.

"How do I get to choose my fate?"

"Because I have a choice other than death. I can kill you here and now. I could drown you easily in the ocean you love dearly. It would take but a minute or two. Or, you can live, but not in Miami. You will leave and never return."

"You'll let me live?"

"Yes," I breathe.

"My father. I can't leave—"

"Yes, you can." I sigh. She continues to think of that bastard she calls a father over herself. She doesn't understand she's a million times more deserving of life than he is.

"I can't just—"

"The choice is yours, but don't worry about your father. He has a good job, and I'll ensure his debt is taken care of." I don't know her father, but I suspect he works for my father, just as I know she does. She just doesn't realize it.

Kai doesn't speak, for a long time. The moon shines down upon us, lighting up the sky and the sea.

"Choose Kai, will you run away and live, or stay and die?"

"Live; I want to live."

"Good," I nod.

I soak her up one last time as she floats effortlessly in the water with a willpower I don't understand. I hope to remember this image of her, forever. To remember what weakness feels like and what strength looks like.

I turn and swim hard to the yacht without looking back. I'm sure she is swimming after me, but it will make no difference.

I reach the yacht first and climb up the ladder in the back. I disengage the autopilot before Kai has a chance to make it to the yacht. When I walk back to the side and look down, I see Kai has stopped swimming and is floating a couple feet from the boat.

"I'll die if you leave me in the ocean," she whispers angrily.

She looks up at me. "You weren't giving me a choice. I was going to die either way. You are just too much of a coward to kill me yourself! You'll let the ocean take me instead."

My heart does a weird fluttering in my heart again, trying to convince me to jump back in and warm her. But I can't. This is the only way. My gut-wrenches as I force myself to stay on the boat.

"You won't freeze or drown if you truly want to live."

"I'm not strong enough."

"Kai may not be your given name, but it is who you are."

"How do you know my real name isn't Kai?"

I shake my head. "I don't; you just confirmed my suspicion."

"I'll die."

I lean against the railing, getting as close as I can to her, even though we are a deck away as I stand up on the main deck, and she floats in the depths of the water.

"Kai means sea in Hawaiian. You were raised by the ocean, just like me. You know how to tame it as easily as I do. If you want to survive, you will."

Her lips part and her eyes deepen as she begins slowly drifting away from the yacht.

I could have Kai so easily. Steal her and make her mine, but as evil as I am, I won't risk my own death to take her. Only to save her.

I shake my head as I watch her float further away. She knows enough about currents to make it back to shore. I'm not the one who's saving her; she's saving herself.

"Leave Miami, if you are strong enough to survive," I say roughly into the night with a threat in my voice of what will happen if she stays.

CHAPTER 10

KAI

My neck aches as if a thousand-ton elephant sat on it.

My throat burns with the salt of the ocean water sticking to my lips and hair.

And my core aches for a boy who left me here to die.

I'm alive, but for how long?

I shiver again in the cold water, wishing Enzo was here to keep me warm. If it were daylight, the sun would heat me, but at night there is nothing except my trembling muscles to regulate my temperature. And every second my body spends energy shivering is one less second I will have to survive. I can't afford to waste any energy on anything but swimming to shore.

The yacht speeds away, further and further until it melts into the horizon and the sound of its engines no longer vibrate through me.

Dead.

That's what I should be. He all but killed me with his hands before we plummeted overboard.

I don't remember much after I fell into the ocean. I must have gone unconscious. And Enzo must have brought me back to life, only to wipe his hands of me.

I can't survive.

Enzo knew I would be dead before my body washed up on the shore.

I know how to float in the water, but I won't be able to with my body shivering like it is.

I'm miles away from shore, much too far to swim.

And it's too dark for other boats to find me except by pure luck. I'm more likely to get run over than found.

No, I'll drown or freeze by morning. I'm too skinny to survive in this cool of water.

If I'm lucky, a shark will find me and give me a quick death. But that's unlikely.

Fuck you, Enzo.

Fuck your evil grin.

Fuck your delicious mouth.

Fuck your masculine cologne.

Fuck your dirty, filthy mind.

Fuck your ability to make me trust you and want you, even though I knew I should never believe the devil.

I feel a cool plastic bump into me from behind.

I turn around slowly, not sure what has touched me.

A lifesaver floats amply behind me.

I eye it suspiciously for a second before throwing my body on it and clinging to it.

Life.

I choose life.

"Fuck you, Enzo!" I shout into the night, even though I know he was the one who left this lifesaver.

He wanted me to live, and he gave me all the help me could without risking his own life.

The waves pick up as does the wind, and I move a good ten feet as one wave pushes me further out to the ocean.

No.

I will not let the ocean take me, not after surviving Enzo. The sea is my friend.

I cling to the lifesaver as I kick hard, trying to move out of the current taking me further away from shore.

Kick.

Kick.

Kick.

I am strong. I can do this.

It takes everything I have, but I finally evade the pull of the current.

I pant heavily as I lay my head on the edge of the lifesaver.

Live.

Keep living.

But then what?

Can I really leave the only home I've ever known? The only connection I have to my mother? Can I leave my father, who can barely take care of himself? What explanation would I give him or my only friend Mason for leaving?

If I want to live, I will leave.

I will start over, maybe even convince my father to come with me. We need a fresh start. Perhaps someday we will find a way to return to Miami.

Right now, I just have to survive.

I need rest.

My eyes close. I'll nap for a minute; then I'll find the strength to find a current that will help guide me back to shore.

The sun starts coming up, waking me up. I slept most of the night.

Shit.

I cling to the lifesaver as I glance around. Shore is a couple of miles away.

I smile for the first time since I discovered Enzo planned to kill me. *I'm going to live.*

I consider my options. I could keep floating and hope I drift in the right direction, to shore. I could stay and wait, hoping a boat will pass by and spot me soon. Or I could swim to shore.

My first two options are the safest, but I could be out here for hours longer.

There is only one option I accept. I abandon my lifesaver and start swimming.

I've been swimming my entire life, since I was a baby. It comes easily and naturally to me, but it's still difficult in my current state. I'm weak and exhausted from spending all night at sea.

Why?

The question floats around in my head encouraging me to swim harder.

Why was Enzo supposed to kill me?

Why did Enzo spare my life?

Why?

It doesn't make sense. I've done nothing wrong. I've seen nothing. I've stolen nothing from the man Enzo works for.

There is something I'm missing. Some secret I have yet to discover.

But it makes no difference now. My fate has been decided. I will leave my home, never to return.

I feel the sand beneath my fingers before I realize where I am.

Shore.

I made it.

I cough, my lungs panting for oxygen that isn't tainted with salty ocean water.

My arms and legs ache and my stomach wretches, needing food.

I smile.

I'm alive.

I lay on the shore on the edge of the water, the waves still hitting me with each push of the tide, covered in sand and saltwater.

The sun bakes me, warming my freezing core. I want to stay here lying on the beach, but I don't want Enzo or the people he works for to find me alive.

I force myself up onto my legs. Then, I walk.

If I thought the swim was lengthy, the walk is even longer.

I wish nothing more than to call my father or Mason to come to get me and drive me home. But I don't have a phone or any money. The little money I had must have been swept away with the waves.

I walk...

And walk.

And walk.

Each step is hurting more than the last.

When my trailer finally comes into view, I stumble. Falling to my knees as tears pour from my eyes down my sand covered cheeks.

I'm alive but for how much longer?

I have no money to leave with, and right now, I don't even have the strength to ride in a car, let alone walk or ride a bike out of town. I don't even have the money for a bus fare. And if I don't put food in my belly soon, I'll end up sick.

Just a little further.

I'll sleep in the trailer, hide away from all of this. I think there are some ramen noodles still in the pantry I can cook. And then tomorrow, I will find a way to leave.

I just can't find the strength to stand up.

I feel cold hands wrap around my arms, dragging me to my feet.

"Who are you?" I try to say, but the words never leave my throat.

For a second, I can see the man's face.

"Enzo?" I ask.

The man doesn't answer.

And then I feel the coldness of his hand, the wretchedness in his eyes, and the rough, unbathed smell he oozes.

This man isn't Enzo. Neither is the man to my left. They are both too cold to be Enzo.

I can't walk, but it doesn't seem to matter to them.

They drag me to a van.

I have nothing left in me to fight as they toss my broken body into the back. No strength to prevent them from tying my arms and legs with rope. And then blackness covers my eyes.

I don't understand why they are kidnapping me, and I know better than to ask, Enzo reminded me of that.

Enzo.

Is he behind this?

Or is Black, the man he works for, responsible?

It doesn't matter.

All I know now is that I'm being taken, and I no longer have any strength left in me to survive.

CHAPTER 11
KAI

Broken.

For one thousand and ninety-five days I've done every-thing to keep myself from breaking.

Shut off my mind off during the beatings.

Escaped the depths of the darkness in the night.

Locked down my body during the rapes.

Imagined a new life when I was tortured.

Gritted my teeth through the violations.

Tried every tactic I needed to survive.

Closing myself away.

Envisioning a better life.

Plotting my revenge.

None of the strategies worked long term.

I hate Enzo for what he did to me, but my need to extract revenge was never enough to keep me alive.

I would try blocking my reality out by pretending my stomach didn't constantly ache, and my body wasn't bruised, my bones shattered.

That would keep me alive for a few weeks.

But then came the loneliness.

Being alone was worse than the pain. Not having a friend, a family, or anyone who loved me, that was what made me give up hope more than anything.

It's been over three years since I was taken.

When those strong arms grabbed me, and the hood went over my head, I didn't know what my future held.

Nothing.

I am nothing.

I am nobody.

I am a ghost.

A commodity to be bought and traded.

I was sold for one million—that was my worth.

I look down at my naked, bruised body. There isn't a patch of skin that hasn't been colored. I doubt I'm worth as much now as I was when I was originally sold.

Who would want a pile of bones like me?

The boat rocks, and I heave. There is nothing in my stomach to come up, though. Sometimes I think it would be easier if I would just starve to death, but no matter how much I've tried, my body won't give into the sweet release. My body has adapted and learned to survive on far less food and water than what it should be capable of.

I've tried finding weapons to end my life, but there are none to be found on this yacht.

I've searched, no man carries a gun—not even a knife.

I don't understand the men who keep me.

Nothing about it makes sense. I don't even know who is in charge. *Who is my master?* They all share in the torture. They all revel in the pleasure of watching me slowly disintegrate.

No.

I won't break.

That's the only thing keeping me sane for the last one thousand and ninety-five days.

The thrill at watching the men in frustration as I continue to hold on to who I am and what I'm capable of.

Their primary goal is breaking me.

I overheard them placing bets on how long it would take and who would deliver the final blow.

Three months...

Six months...

One year...

When I made it one year, they stopped betting. I think most of them thought I would never break at that point.

I won't.

I can't.

Staying strong doesn't mean I'm safe; it means I'm foolish. Giving in to them would be easier.

They wouldn't torture me as often.

They could give me a command, and I would obey.

I would resolve that this is my life, and the last drop of hope I've been holding onto would leave.

They could keep the door unlocked. Maybe even stop at a port and get off this godforsaken boat.

But I can't break.

I'm not sure it's possible.

I don't know why.

At first, I was stubborn, defiant even.

I wouldn't give these men the pleasure.

But then, my strength left. And now, I have no idea why I won't crack.

Three years is a long time. I should feel changed, different.

When I was taken I was just a girl; now I'm a woman. I've spent many of my formative years held captive on a boat full of dangerous, cruel men. Rapists, savages, devils.

I close my eyes as another wave hits the side of the yacht. If my body had any muscles left, I would be shivering from the cold and fever that has continuously taken over my body. I would be vomiting everything in my stomach. But all my body can do is cringe, I can't even brace myself to keep from sliding on the slick floor as the boat tosses me about.

I hate boats.

I hate the water.

I hate the men.

I hate Enzo.

Right now, I hate the water most of all as we rock viciously side to side. I don't know where we are except that it has to be deep in the middle of fucking nowhere. That's the only way the waves get this big, unless a hurricane or tsunami is chasing us. With my luck, I have no doubt a storm is afoot.

I should have hated the water from that first day when Enzo left me to drown in it. But I didn't hate it; I'm not even sure I hated Enzo then. He was just following orders from his boss, Black, when he tried to kill me. He was surviving as much as I was, and then he gave me a chance at freedom. Swim to shore and leave Miami, and then he wouldn't kill me. That was the arrangement.

It sounded like a fair deal at the time. And the night I spent out in the ocean didn't make me hate the water, I grew to appreciate it more. Its power, strength, and freedom I envied and respected.

It was when I made it to shore, and Enzo's men kidnapped me, breaking our arrangement that I could live as long as I left, that I learned what hate was.

I know more about hate than I do love.

I don't think I'm capable of love anymore.

You hear that? I can't love. You broke me! You win!

Another wave crashes, sending me against a wall.

Maybe if I told them I was broken this would stop?

No, this never stops. This never ends.

The boat rocks again, proving my point that this is now my life. Stuck on a boat with the worst of humanity.

I could end it, that tiny voice in my heart whispers again.

I can't with a weapon. I can't with food, but I could let the sea take me. With the storm pursuing us, I would be gone in seconds.

The pain would be gone.

At first, I couldn't imagine taking my life. I was too proud. Too full of hope. Filled with a determination not to let them win. That vanished the first year.

The second year, I couldn't because of my father. He is the only family I have, and even though we don't always have the best relationship, he loves me. He would find me. I couldn't give up for him.

The third year was the hardest. I had no one to live for, not even myself. I'd given up at ever having a normal, healthy life again, even if I was to escape this torturous boat ride. My father had surely given up on me, or at least, I had given up on him. The only thing keeping me alive was *Enzo*.

I can't even explain it.

It wasn't revenge; I'd long given up on getting revenge or even needing it.

I only had one question I needed Enzo to answer... *Why?*

Why me?

Why when he took me out on his yacht three years ago did he choose torture over killing me? Was it the only way he could keep me alive? Because if given the choice, I wish he would have just killed me that day.

Why?

The question will haunt me forever. It might be the only thing keeping me alive.

Until now...

The yacht seesaws and lugs causing my body to slip from the wall I was leaning against and slam into the door to my bedroom.

Bedroom, ha.

This isn't a bedroom.

It's not even a gilded cage.

The room has four walls and a floor. No bed. No dressers. No bathroom. Nothing that would bring me comfort. When I first arrived, I was given a blanket and pillow, but that was soon taken away from me.

Now I have nothing, not even clothes. And in some way, having nothing is freeing.

Another quake of the boat, this time bigger than the last. I instinctively grab the door handle to keep from sliding back against the far wall. Not because it will hurt—it will—but pain means nothing to me anymore. Because despite the three years at sea, I still want to control my own fate, no matter how hard these men and the sea try to take it from me.

My pathetic grip on the door handle is barely enough to keep me against the door as the yacht is thrown again in the waves and wind of the sea.

Fuck.

We are going to die.

We've never experienced a storm quite like this. *This is the end.*

Dammit.

This is not how I want to go. When I die, it will be when and how I decide.

"You hear me! I decide when I die!" I shout out.

Yelling like that used to get me a beating from one of the men. They tried to get me to give up my voice along with my body and soul.

I never ceased. Eventually, they stopped responding, learning being alone was harder for me than dealing with their brutal violence. But today, even if they wanted to hear me, they couldn't. The wind's cry is too sharp to hear anything except its wicked howl.

Another creak and bang of the boat sound as the yacht violently slaps against the water.

My door flies open, the door handle ramming into my stomach knocking all the air out of me.

I gasp for breath as I fall to the floor in agony.

Even the sea wants me to break.

"Never!" I cry when I finally catch my breath.

I get to control how this ends.

Another sway and my body slides into the opening of the door. I inch out into the darkness of the hallway. I'm used to darkness, my hole of a room has no light, no electricity, and no windows to the outside. My eyes have adjusted to the pitch black of night, but the hallway almost always has light. The storm must have taken out our power.

I smirk, taking comfort in the fact that the men who held me captive for years won't survive past tonight either.

They don't deserve a quick death. Tonight I hope the storm traps them in this vessel as they slowly suffocate or starve. However, it's unlikely that they will suffer a slow death. The odds are far greater that they will be knocked out by a massive chunk of the ship or the water will drown them quickly, but I can hope.

I move one hand in front of the other as I begin to walk.

I feel my shattered bones crunch into more and more despair with each movement. My bruises burn into my body with each brush against the floor begging me to stop.

I won't stop. Not until I take my last breath.

The yacht lurches forward sending me the length of the hallway to the stairwell.

Shit, stairs.

I have to make it up a flight of stairs.

I haven't climbed in months. *Can I really ascend stairs?*

I bite my lip, more determined than ever to choose how I'll die.

I stare down at my broken toe I earned after I shared my food with one of the other women the men kept on board. I haven't seen or heard another woman on board in weeks. If I did, I would have to free them as well, so they too could choose their own fate and how they will die.

I grab the railing and pull myself up. I wince as I again put pressure on my broken foot that hurts like a motherfucker.

Broken bones are the worst. Nothing but time will heal them. And I have nothing to set the bones correctly. The fingers in my left hand won't bend fully because they healed crooked. The broken ribs are worst of all, because the shattered splinters slice into my lungs making every breath painful.

Stop wallowing in self-pity and do something to end this.

One step, then another, then another.

It's painstakingly slow, especially since I have to stop each time the yacht veers to the side, and I use all of my energy just holding the ground I made up the stairs.

The door is the last obstacle before I'm on the main deck. But one simple turn of the knob and the door bursts open in my face. It hits me hard, but I smile.

Almost there.

I'm thrown onto the main deck as the boat jerks forward again and then stops suddenly, like we're traveling in a car that has just thrown on its brakes to narrowly avoid hitting a child playing in the street.

But we don't have any way to control how the yacht moves, not in this storm. Mother nature decides when the boat moves forward or stops. Or even if it stays afloat at all.

The rain pelts down on me as I lay on the main deck. I tilt my head upward feeling the cold droplets cascade over my face in one heavy stream.

Kai means sea in Hawaiian. You were raised by the ocean, just like me. You know how to tame it as easily as I do. If you want to survive, you will. Enzo's words come back to me. I knew before he told me what the name I called myself when I was three means. I was born Katherine but never felt like it fit. Kai is more fitting.

I shake my head.

Kai means sea. I was born by the sea. I will die at sea, I say in my head, already knowing my fate and how wrong Enzo's words were. How wrong the name I chose for myself was.

Unlike three years ago when Enzo tossed me overboard and I eventually saved myself, this time I won't be coming back up. I won't have a buoy to hold onto through the night. I won't have the strength to swim for shore. We are in the middle of the fucking ocean—no one can save me.

And that brings me peace.

I let the rock of the boat push me to the railing on one side of the boat. *Thank you, gravity.*

The railing is the hard part. I won't let the waves push me over; I want to do this myself.

With the rain pouring down, it's hard to feel like I'm not already letting the ocean take me. I grip the slippery railing cautiously, one wrong step and I'll be gone.

Slowly I climb up on the railing with my feet on the bottom rung, my hands gripping the top.

I suck in a breath, but it's mostly water entering my throat at this point. It burns down my lungs, making me cough and gasp for a clean breath.

I don't have much time if I'm going to be the one to decide.

Carefully, I hike one leg over the top of the railing and then the other until there is nothing between me and the ocean but letting go.

A wave splashes hard onto my body, knocking me back against the railing. I don't know how the surge didn't take me then. I shouldn't be strong enough to hold on and fight the wind, rain, and waves.

I close my eyes, trying to feel one moment of freedom. One moment that's mine. One where I can forgive the sea for the pain it's caused me and let it take me in mercy. In one swift pull, I'll be gone.

I have no one to say goodbye to. Nothing left to think or worry about.

I don't think of heaven or hell.

I've been living in hell, and I can't imagine such a place as heaven after what I went through.

No, I long for darkness to take me and never give me back. I ache for a long sleep where I never wake up.

Peace.

I feel it for a moment. The sea seems to calm as if accepting me and preparing me to take the plunge.

"Take me," I say. I let go.

I fall for only a half a second, before a hand grabs my wrist. My feet didn't even leave the bottom rung.

"What the hell?"

I turn back and see Jarod holding my wrist. When I first arrived, I thought he might have the most empathy. He was the one I tried to break and persuade to show me compassion, but it only made him try harder to break me—more determined than all the rest. And if I had to say who the leader is, it's him.

He's the captain of the boat, the leader of the crew. *But only here.* Enzo is the leader back home.

No, Enzo isn't a leader either. He follows orders from Black. Black is the one I should hate the most.

"Let me go," I cry, knowing one slip of his hand and I'll be free.

But Jarod is strong. One sharp pull and I'm back on the other side of the railing, but not to safety. I've learned there is no such thing. But I'm no longer on the edge of death like I was before.

"You crazy bitch," he curses.

Another wave crashes and knocks us against something sharp. My head pounds, and now along with the water flowing down my face, I feel the ooze of blood.

My eyes grow heavy, and the world turns foggy.

"Shit," Jarod curses.

He tosses me over his shoulder as he carries me inside. To my surprise, he doesn't take me to my room. It's the only room I've been in for months. No, instead he brings me to another room—to one with a bed.

A bed?

Why would I need a bed?

Are they going to rape me in a bed instead of on the floor?

I should fight, but I have nothing left.

I've given up.

I have no hope.

I have no fear.

I am nothing.

I don't shiver.

I don't react.

I'm not even sure I'm breathing.

Jarod tosses me on the bed, and I don't move, not even to cover my naked body or gain warmth.

My eyes are open, but I don't see the men standing over me. I see nothing except darkness. *Am I dead or dying?*

They say you see a white light before you die, that your entire life flashes before your eyes. That isn't my experience. I see nothing but gloom and death.

"Is she dead?" a voice asks.

"No," Jarod answers.

I'm not dead. I almost feel like crying at that, but I don't. I'm still alive, and as much as I wish I were nothing, I still have hopes and dreams. My dreams are no longer shiny and pleasant. I hope to be dead.

"She's broken," Jarod says.

What? Broken? I'm not broken. Am I?

"Broken." The word travels through the men like a ghost of a whisper. Each mutters it, not sure that it is true until he gets a chance to speak the word himself.

Broken.

I'm not broken. I feel no different from before. My wounds might be worse, and I might die if I don't recover, but I'm not broken.

Never.

But one by one they test the word themselves.

Broken.

Broken.

Broken.

Each time they say the word, I begin to believe it myself more and more.

I'm broken.

They finally broke me.

This is what it feels like.

"Does that mean...?" one of the men asks tentatively.

"Yes, we can go home now. Our job is done," Jarod answers.

What?

Their job was to keep me until they broke me. *That makes no sense.*

What are they going to do with me now? Are they finally going to kill me?

No.

They won't. Otherwise, Jarod wouldn't risk his life to keep me from killing myself.

Men start filing out of the room, and for once the heavy rock of the boat begins to return to a gentle sway as mother nature agrees that she has broken me, and there is no reason left to keep tormenting us with her wrath.

I feel a blanket go over my skin.

I want to fight it. I don't like it touching me. I've yearned to be touched, to be comforted, to feel a soft, warm blanket for years. But now that I feel it, I hate it. I want it gone.

But I don't have the strength to say anything or even remove the blanket from my body. I'm a frozen corpse.

Jarod looks down at me grimly. "You're broken," he says almost like he's trying to convince me I am.

I'm not, comes the tiniest of voice. *I'm not broken.*

I know Jarod sees the defiance in my eyes. It's the only thing I can give him to show how wrong he is. Any other time it would be enough for him to fight me and try again to break me. He knows he didn't truly break me, so why is he saying it.

So they can go home.

The men had one job: to break me. For years they failed in their task. None of them thought the task would last this long. The storm shook up more than just me. They all thought they were going to die. They want to go home. I just don't know what they are going to do with me.

Jarod leans down and whispers in my ear, "You're broken, now you're free."

CHAPTER 12

KAI

Home.

I never thought I'd be returning home.

I thought I would die at sea.

But here I am, lying on a park bench in baggy shorts and a T-shirt.

I look homeless.

That's because I am.

Miami isn't my home anymore.

It hasn't been my home for over three years.

I'm not sure it was ever really my home, even when I was living in Miami. The trailer I inhabited with my father barely ensured I had a bed to sleep in and a roof to protect me from the rain. Most of the clothes I owned had holes in them. And my belly was never fully fed. Although, I would go back to that time in a heartbeat.

Back then I wasn't really starving. Back then I'd never experienced pain or understood loneliness. Back then I wasn't completely alone. Sure I only had my father and Mason, my best and only friend. I felt lonely, but I wasn't really. I didn't understand the word until recently.

Loneliness isn't about being alone. It's about realizing you have no one. No one who loves you. No one who misses you. No one who even cares to talk to you.

It's what leads you to be so desperate as to talk to the spider in the corner of your room like they are your best friend. Then you talk to your shadow. Then you start talking to yourself like the little voice inside you is another person and not yourself.

It's when you realize no one will ever talk back; no one will bury or mourn you if you die. That's when you understand what true loneliness feels like.

I slowly sit up, as the sun burns my now pale skin. I haven't seen the sun in years. I used to wear a tan year round, but after spending three years locked in a dark cave, the hint of sunlight scares me. I will blister immediately if I don't find shelter.

I don't remember coming back. My last memory is falling asleep on the lumpy bed on the yacht. It should have felt like a luxury; instead, it felt too soft to fall asleep on. But the pull of exhaustion made me sleep, despite the lack of comfort I felt lying in the five hundred count sheets.

I don't remember getting dressed.

I don't remember leaving the yacht.

I don't remember the swaying stopping.

As I sit up, I realize the swaying truly hasn't stopped. *Maybe I'm still on a boat after all? This is all some dream.* I used to dream about Miami a lot that first year. I tried to remember what the sun felt like even when I was cursing it for causing me to sweat so much. This is a dream.

I stand up, and the ground shakes.

Shit.

I grab the back of the bench to steady myself.

The ground seems real enough. Grass tickles the bottoms of my feet.

I stare down at my bare toes. I may have gotten dressed, but I'm not wearing any shoes—*not that I want shoes*. I can't remember why people would ever want to wear such things.

I take a step, and the texture of the grass is intense. It tickles and itches the bottom of my foot.

So their feet don't have to feel this, that's why people wear shoes.

One more step, and I let go of the park bench. The ground still shifts back and forth, and I'm sure I look drunk as I walk, but I don't care.

It's early in the morning, and other than a few early morning joggers and homeless people, there isn't anyone around to judge me.

I keep walking, slowly at first, and then my steps become more regular as I get used to the wobbling. I know the way without thinking. My past has been buried for years, but now it blasts back into my consciousness as if I was here yesterday.

I don't take in my surroundings as I walk; the sounds and noises would overwhelm me if I did. Instead, I let the sounds of the cars honking and whizzing by drift into the background. I don't focus on the grass, or sand, or sidewalk changing under my feet, making it more difficult to walk with each change in the terrain. I keep my eyes down, so I don't have to register the bright sun or the vibrant colors all around.

All I want to do is make it to the trailer and lock myself up in my room for days.

Finally, the trailer appears in front of me in the same place it's been parked for almost twenty years. It never occurred to me, as I walked over here, that father could have moved or sold it.

The ratchety old door creaks open, and I realize the door still doesn't latch properly. My father never fixed it.

And then, as if my thought of him called him to existence, my dad stands at the top of the three steps that lead up to the door. Enzo kept one of his promises to ensure my father stayed alive.

We both eye each other, standing tall and stiff. Neither of us breathes. We just look. I don't have to speak to tell him what I've been through the last three plus years. He can see every mark and hand that was ever laid on me. If he thought I ran away from home, that doubt has now been pushed away.

I've changed completely; he looks the same.

If there were ever a time where we would react differently than our usual, unaffectionate selves, now would be that time. But that isn't who we are. We don't do hugs. We don't do warmth. We may love each other, but we don't stoop to such weakness. It's not who we are. I doubt my father even hugged me when my mother died.

I can't remember ever hugging this man.

I don't know how long we stand just looking at each other. It could be seconds or hours. My ability to comprehend time was taken from me, along with my body and sense of worth.

Finally, my father moves. He takes the three steps down the stairs and stops in front of me.

"You shouldn't have come back," his voice cracks.

I agree, I shouldn't have.

I don't speak though. I don't nod. I just let his words fill me.

Is there a tear in the corner of his eye?

No, that can't be. My father doesn't show emotion, ever. He doesn't cry.

But yet, I think that's precisely what he's doing.

And then he's gone, walking away from me. Our reunion is over.

"Kai? Is that you?"

Mason.

I turn and look at the boy I grew up with. Even he hasn't changed much. His body is a little thicker, his hair a little longer, his voice deeper. There are a few thin lines around his eyes I don't remember before, but otherwise, he looks exactly the same. He's the same boy I've been friends with since I was five.

I should speak, reassure him, because he looks like he's seen a ghost. And after he realizes it's really me, he will see the bruises, the scars, the broken bones. He will see how frail I am and then he will lose it.

He'll rush me to the police or the hospital. I'll have to answer questions I never want to explain.

I'm not ready to speak. I've talked plenty of times, mainly to myself, but talking right now feels like opening myself up to let someone in again. And as much as that person should be Mason, I can't.

He hasn't changed, but I have.

And a part of me hates him. For not finding me. For not preventing me from being taken. For not saving me.

Mason and my father were the only people who would have missed me. My father could barely feed himself. I don't blame him, but Mason has money, resources, connections. He loved me. He wanted more from me. He could have found me.

"Jesus, it is you." Mason runs toward me with open arms threatening to engulf me.

His fingertips barely touch me, and I wince, taking a step back. The light touch feels like fire against my ice cold skin.

"Christ," Mason curses as he runs his hand through his long blonde surfer locks.

My eyes turn downcast. I can't watch him realize what happened to me. I can't take his empathy, his concern, his anger. *He has no right to feel any of those things!*

"What happened?" he asks.

No answer.

"Kai? You can talk to me. I won't hurt you." His hand brushes against me, and I jump out of my skin.

I can't. You can't touch me, I shout inside.

My eyes meet his, telling him to stop with a sharp glare as a dog would warn a stranger thinking of coming onto its property.

"Okay, no touching. Can I drive you to a hospital or police station?"

I freeze. *No.*

"Kai? A doctor should see you. You could have broken bones. I will pay for everything."

I do have broken bones, you idiot.

Slowly, I shake my head no.

He sighs.

"Okay, I won't push you. Let's go inside though. Maybe after a bath and food, you might reconsider going. I could even have a doctor come to you if you prefer."

Mason puts his hand out, offering it to me like a crutch to walk with.

He thinks I'm weak, *maybe I am?* But I don't want his or anyone else's help.

I ignore his hand and walk to the stairs and then enter the dilapidated trailer.

I take a deep breath, and everything returns—the smell of bacon and coffee, my father's usual breakfast. The stench of cigarette smoke, alcohol, and bad decisions hangs in the air.

I don't hear Mason behind me, but I'm sure he's followed me into the trailer. He's never come inside, not once in all the years I've known him. I was always embarrassed of my home. I didn't want him near it; now it doesn't matter.

Mason may think we have a future together if he doesn't already have a girlfriend. I glance behind me, spotting his left hand. No ring. He's not married, but he could be dating.

It doesn't matter.

I don't have a future. And anything I do from here on out won't involve him.

Mason slowly moves by me to the single bathroom at the back and then returns a moment later.

"I started the water for a shower. I wish there was a tub to soak in, but a shower will have to do for now," he says.

Shower.

How long has it been?

I reek, I'm sure, but I can't tell anymore. This is how I smell, like rotting flesh and death.

"Do you want help?" his voice shakes a little as he asks.

I shake my head. I'm not even sure I want a shower, but I want to be alone. I spent years yearning for someone to talk to, and now that I have someone, I want nothing more than to hide away by myself.

"I'll make you something to eat."

I don't answer. I should eat, but my stomach no longer cries for food. It's used to surviving on nothing. It doesn't matter if I eat or not.

I walk past Mason and head into the tiny bathroom. I pull the door closed and strip the dirty clothes off my body. The shorts were so baggy. I'm not even sure how they were staying on my body.

The steam begins to fill the small room, and it draws me to the water.

Water—*my enemy, my friend, my everything.*

It reminds me of the ocean and angers me that I never got the end I wanted. I'm alive when I shouldn't be.

I step into the small corner shower. I don't bother to pull the curtain closed as the water drips down on me in thin streams. There was a time when I thought the water pressure wasn't enough, certainly not enough to wash the shampoo out of my hair. But now, it's too much. It feels like it is dumping on my head, the same as it was the night of the storm on the yacht.

The warm droplets are too hot for my icy skin, and I immediately want to retreat. But that means facing Mason again—something I'm not ready for. So I force myself to stand under the heavy stream.

I don't use shampoo or soap. I don't try to remove the caked on dirt, sweat, or filth. I just let the water do the work.

Time passes, again, I don't know how long. But eventually, I turn the faucet off. I let the water drip from my hair down my skinny frame. I've always been thin, but now I can see every bone in my body. I should have curves; instead, I have protruding bones.

There is a towel lying by the sink, and I use it to dry off before stepping out of the bathroom and then walk to my bedroom.

Sleep; I need sleep.

I fall onto the bed in a heap still wet, but it doesn't matter. The bed feels too soft. I'm not going to be able to sleep on it, I realize instantly.

"I made you soup." Mason steps into the small room. "Oh my god! I'm sorry, I should have knocked first."

He stops and shields his eyes.

I look around the room, confused by what he is shocked and sorry about.

It takes me too long to realize I'm naked. The towel that was wrapped around me has fallen open. My nakedness doesn't bother me, but it does Mason.

So I reluctantly wrap the towel around myself.

Mason peaks from behind his fingers and then straightens to bring me the bowl of soup he prepared and a cup of tea.

"I wasn't sure if you could handle more than soup, but if you can keep this down, I can get you whatever you want to eat."

I look at him with big wide eyes. *Food.* He would get me anything, anything I craved. *Doesn't he realize I don't crave anything anymore?*

Mason sits on the edge of the bed next to me and holds out a spoonful of the soup to my lips. I look down at the cup of tea he sat on the small end table. I take that instead, lift it to my lips, and drink slowly.

He sighs in exacerbation and sets the bowl next to me.

"I will do anything to help you, Kai. I don't know what you've been through. I don't know who took you or what evil you've experienced. But I..." He takes a deep breath. "I love you, Kai. I have since we were five. I've just never had the courage to tell you. Not having you all these years, thinking you ran away and never called was hard. Realizing the truth is harder. I love you. I will never stop loving you."

His words should comfort me. Make me stop feeling so alone. They don't. I don't feel anything anymore. All I feel is numbness.

So I don't speak. There are no words to say back. And if I speak, he might ask questions I don't want to answer. I don't want to talk about what happened. I don't want to see a doctor or a therapist.

His eyes travel over my body again. They slowly meet my eyes.
Broken.
He thinks I'm broken.

He sees my frail, ruined body. He thinks my spirit has been crushed; my heart ripped out of my chest. My soul trampled on.

I'm not broken, I say inwardly. *I can't be broken.* I swore they would never break me.

He doesn't hear or see that though. All he sees is a broken doll he thinks he can fix.

I don't need fixing. I need answers.

This is who I am now. I need acceptance.

I finish my tea and then eat some of the broth soup before I pull the covers up and close my eyes, pretending to sleep.

Mason eventually leaves me alone in the room and shuts the door.

Finally, alone.

I stand out of the bed, letting the towel drop, and curl up on the carpet floor. Even that feels too soft.

I want cold.

I want ice.

I don't want comfortable and warm.

But the floor is better than the bed. And my body is too tired to find a better, harder bed.

So I sleep.

The next morning, everything happens again.

Mason is still here. He must have slept on the recliner. He feeds me. He encourages me to talk. He talks. He tries to get me to shower. To eat. To go to a doctor.

The only thing I do that makes him happy is eat.

Otherwise, he looks at me with pity in his eyes. He winces when my bones creak. He swears when he sees new bruises. He tries to take care of me, but it's not what I want.

Mason is a good man; I should have dated him before. He would have made a good boyfriend. Maybe if we were together when I was taken he would have tried harder to find me?

Now, I'll never know.

Now, we can never be.

Time passes, and our routine stays the same.

I sleep.

I eat.

He asks questions and pushes.

I don't know how much time passes, except eventually I don't feel like sleeping so much. My bruises and pains are still there, and I haven't gained much if any weight, so I doubt much time has passed. But some did.

Enzo.

His name floats back into my head again.

Why?

That becomes my new focus. Not on avoiding Mason, but on thinking about Enzo.

Not the good. Not the adrenaline at stealing Enzo's watch when we first met.

Not when he took me on my first yacht ride, the last one I will ever enjoy.

Not when we played our two lies and one truth game, and I won.

Not when he gave me my first kiss.

The only thing I think about when it comes to Enzo is why?

Why me?

Why didn't he kill me, when he was ordered to?

Why did he have me kidnapped and sold, instead?

Why did Jarod let me go when I was his favorite plaything?

I need answers, to so many questions.

But it is all really one question. *Why?*

I don't know how to find Enzo. I don't even know his last name or if he still lives in Miami. I don't know if he's even alive anymore. He worked in a ruthless business. He could be dead.

No.

I feel it.

He's alive.

He's why I'm still alive.

He's why I'm here.

I need answers.

Not necessarily revenge, although I'll take that too.

I can't think past what I'll do when I figure out my answers.

I listen carefully and hear Mason sleeping in the other room. The faint sound of the old television blares and skips. I'm surprised the television still works.

I need to get out of here to get my answers.

But where?

First clothes, then where.

I go to the rod in the corner of the room that holds my old clothes. I stare at them. I don't want to put them on, but I need to if I don't want to get arrested or sent to a psych ward.

And I need them to cover my body. My scars and bruises need to be covered.

I pull on a pair of jeans and a long-sleeved sweater. It's summer, but it's the only thing that will hide my body.

I run a brush through my midnight black hair and leave it

down, even though it descends far down my back almost to my butt. It needs to be cut; the ends are uneven and frayed. It would look better up, but I need my hair down to cover my neck and cheeks. Now people will only notice the bruises on my face if I look up.

I take a step, and the jeans fall off my hips.

Shit.

I rummage through my drawers until I find a belt.

The clothes itch and burn against my skin, but I don't take them off.

Shoes.

I need shoes.

I try on tennis shoes, closed-toe shoes, flip-flops, even heels; but I can't. It's too much for my feet. They all feel like a vice grip.

People go barefoot in Miami all the time; this is a beach town after all. Hopefully, no one will notice my feet.

I open my door and listen carefully. Mason is still asleep.

I tiptoe through the small trailer, ensuring my feet don't make a sound.

I should feel bad for leaving Mason without talking and without a note. A reasonable person would, but I don't have feelings anymore. *Those were taken.*

I get to the door, knowing this is the most dangerous part. I could wake him up, and then how would I leave without him following?

I touch the handle and pry it open inch by inch.

The creak softens, and I stare intently at Mason. He's out. Exhausted from trying to take care of me and break through my walls—walls no one will ever knock down.

When I'm outside, I breathe again.

I'm free, at least of Mason.

Now, where?

I rack my brain, thinking hard for the first time in forever. My mind is foggy, and it hurts to use, but the thought finally comes to me. Where the most dangerous people in town go...

Surrender.

The name of the darkest underground club in town floats in my hazy brain.

It's for the wealthy, the secretive, the criminals.

It's shady, but it's where all the elites and those that cater to them go.

My clothes won't get me into the club. Even if I were dressed up, I wouldn't get in. It's invitation only.

But somehow, I know that's where Enzo is. If he's there, he'll let me in. And if he's not, then I'll find a way in. I'll find someone who knows him.

Because Enzo is the only way I'll get my answers. The club is where all the darkest creatures that crawl the earth lurk. If Enzo is still alive, he'll be there.

I shouldn't go. I should stay far away from the man who sold me, but I can't. I need answers more than I need to live. I'll be breaking our deal by coming back to Miami, by not staying away, but Enzo broke our deal first when he had me taken.

CHAPTER 13
KAI

The door to Surrender looms across the street from where I stand. I can't make my legs move toward the door, but I can't walk away either.

There is no sign above the frame—no advertisement as to what sins men partake in behind the door.

There is nothing to indicate that anything happens here or that this is even a club.

It's simply an unmarked door. I shouldn't know it exists, but when I was fifteen, I was desperate for money. To eat. To survive. And to pay off my father's debts. Debts he accrued when my mother fought a long battle against cancer.

I found a boy at school who sold drugs and offered to help him to make some quick cash. So I sold weed; I couldn't bring myself to sell anything harder. But this is where he wanted to meet me, outside this club. This is where most of his clients were, and that's how I knew this place existed.

It's exclusive and private.

No one knows about the club or gets in without an invite.

There is no way I'll get in.

But I have to get in.

I try not to seem too interested as I stare at the door. I'm sure a hundred security cameras are looking at me right now, cameras that extend well beyond the door of the club. A place like this needs to know who is approaching. They need to know if the person is dangerous or one of their members before they even decide if they are letting them in or not.

I scan the top of the brick building but don't see any cameras. No guard stands outside the door, but I have no doubt there is one inside. I may make it through the door, but that may be as far as they will let me go. They could kill me for just knowing about the club when I shouldn't. And even if I make it to Enzo, even if I get my answers, he will kill me.

This is a suicide mission.

But at least I'll have my answers.

I stop stalling, and I walk slowly toward the door, like Enzo might jump out and aim a gun at me at any moment.

Nothing happens.

I hesitate at the door. I have to be the old Kai. The one who could walk and talk her way into anything. I didn't have curves, or a body men would die for, but I knew how to exude strength and confidence.

I close my eyes. *I am her.*

I open my eyes as I open the door and push myself inside the den of the most evil men in the world—men who kill, torture, and sell women.

I expect arms to grip me. A man to tackle me. Some movement to try to throw me out. So when I feel nothing but the warm air of the club against my cold skin, I exhale sharply. I'm emitting steam and ice in a place built of fire.

I force myself to keep my head high and meet the customers' eyes as I walk into the large room holding men seated at tables with drinks and half-naked women dancing around them.

I don't belong here, but maybe they will think I'm one of the dancers who hasn't changed into her stripping attire yet.

If they looked at me at all, they would know that isn't the truth. They would realize I'm just a broken bag of bones and flesh.

Surrender is precisely what anyone would expect a club to look like. You would never know these men are more dangerous than the average. Other than the furniture being more luxurious and talent of the dancers being better than most, I've stepped into numerous clubs like this along the Miami coastline.

This isn't where I'll find Enzo. This isn't the deepest, darkest place of the club. This is for appearances, so if anyone like me stumbles inside, they won't realize what they found.

I don't think Enzo is these men's leader, but even if he were, he's proud enough not to bother mingling with the men at the bottom. At least he was three years ago.

The covered clothes I'm wearing feels like a mistake. The sweater and jeans are suffocating me and make it impossible to pretend to be a dancer or a waiter, which are the only role a woman has in a club like this.

But I keep walking, and no one stops me. No one asks me a question. No one even raises an eyebrow.

It's eerie how the men continue on. I feel like a ghost. *Maybe I am? Maybe I did die at sea, and I've come back to haunt Enzo's ass?*

I make it out of the main room and find myself in a hidden hallway darker than the main rooms. The blackness should scare me; the amount of light here only makes the wickedness harsher. It does nothing to brighten my way.

But I prefer the dark, the night. The black trapped me for years, but it taught me how to see even without the moonlight.

I walk easily, somehow feeling more at ease as I walk down hallway after hallway.

I should be stopped. I know I'm on camera, but no one stops me.

It's like Enzo wants me to find him.

I see more light pour through at the end of a hallway, and I hear music again for the first time since I left the main room at the entrance.

This, this is where I'll get my answers.

I stand in the shadow of the door, wishing I could see what is going on in the room without being seen myself.

I wish I could steal my answers from Enzo as easily as I stole his watch the first time I met him.

Instead of recoiling, I step forward out of the shadows and into the doorway.

Enzo.

He's seated in a large, red chair at one corner of the room. It looks like it was made for royalty, not his traitorous ass.

His eyes meet mine the instant my body appears in the doorway, as if he knew I was walking down the hallway toward him. No one else notices me. Just him.

Rage, like I've never felt before, explodes like shockwaves through my body. This is the man responsible for my years of torment, pain, and suffering. This man chose to sell me to Jarod and his men. This man ensured I hated the sea forever. This man took my life and twisted it into something I'll never be able to claim as my own. He took my freedom and exchanged it for retching pain.

This man.

This fucking gorgeous, evil man.

Last time I saw Enzo, he was a boy. Tall, his muscles strong, but young. He looked older than his age of seventeen, but now he's all man. He's grown into bulk muscle, hardened into a monster of beautiful veins and cords twisting through his body. A shadow of his dark hair covers his rigid chin, sharp lines form his cheeks, and slits for eyes that resemble a snake. His hair is a little longer than before, twisting into black threads weaving his victims under his spell, making it appear he's innocent when he's the epitome of evil.

My air is gone as he stares at me. I've imagined this moment for years, replaying this moment in my head and all the ways it could play out. With me slapping him, yelling at him, giving him some of his own medicine when I tortured him. I imagined so many variations of what I would do when I first saw Enzo again.

I never expected to freeze like a pussy. I'm strong and fearless. There is nothing left to fear when everything has been taken from you. But standing in front of the man responsible for my breaking is too much for my brain to process.

Enzo stands, brushing off a well-manicured hand that was tracing over the lapel of his suit jacket. A suit that melds over his sculptured muscles like a second layer of skin. I thought he looked good in his clothes before, but now he radiates confidence as he moves like nothing and no one will stop him from getting what he wants.

My eyes widen, their attention drifting from Enzo to the women lounging and dancing around him. Five women, all in various states of dress. Skin tight clothing revealing their breasts and asses, to lingerie, to completely naked. Then I see the men. Two of them wear suits like Enzo's although they don't fit as well. And three wear jeans and hoodies. None of the men acknowledge the women, treating them like they are inanimate furniture and decorations instead of real people. It should disgust me, but these women are treated like queens compared to the women on the yacht I've spent too much of my life on.

Everyone's focus is on Enzo as he stands, still gawking at me like he doesn't believe I'm really here. I doubt he even recognizes me. It's been years, and I was nothing to him but a paycheck he collected when I was sold to ensure I kept our deal and stayed away. He's probably just amazed that one of his slaves made it through his security to his door without being thrown out.

Enzo walks toward me, and the room falls silent as their eyes shift to me. I should be terrified of being in a room full of so many predatory men. Men who probably knew about my fate or have helped Enzo do similar things to other women. I don't feel anything about the other men, only Enzo.

"Out," Enzo says without tearing his gaze from me. He's not speaking to me though, he's speaking to everyone else in the room. His throat growls as he says the word in his deep, authoritative voice. His voice was always strong and powerful. It sounds much the same as I remember, but somehow deeper than before.

The women scatter, but their eyes give me a curious glance before leaving. I watch them from the corner of my eye. They are all beautiful and unbroken, unscarred, untouched.

The men in the hoodies and T-shirts leave next through doors in the back of the room.

The two men in suits linger. One opens his mouth as if he wants to question Enzo's authority, but he resists the urge. They leave slowly after the rest.

Enzo worked for one of the most powerful men in all of Miami, maybe the world—definitely one of the most dangerous. It seems in the time I've been gone, he's gained more power in the organization. He told me once if he killed me, he'd be free.

He didn't kill me. So I guess he never got free.

What did selling me get him? *Power*, women who dance for him, men who shoot without asking questions.

Now that we are alone, my heart speeds. The last time he touched me, he almost killed me with his bare hands on one of his yachts. Then he saved me from drowning when he threw us overboard. I'm not ready for him to touch me again.

But I can't back up and show my fear.

I take a deep, painful breath as my ribs expand and the broken bones dig deeper inside. I push my chest out, standing as tall as I can in my loose jeans and pale colored sweater.

"You should have killed me," I say, my first words in days.

Enzo stops a foot in front of me. He doesn't react to my words, but his eyes read recognition. He knows exactly who I am. The girl he should have killed, turned woman. Because now that I survived, I will get my answers. And I will ensure his life is hell.

I don't know why Jarod set me free. Maybe Enzo gave him instructions when he sold me to him that I could only go free if I was broken enough to never want to return to Miami. Jarod grew bored of me and set me free, thinking I was broken. But I wasn't. I'm not. That was his mistake.

"That can be arranged," his voice is harsh.

I grit my teeth as my legs begin to tremble beneath me. I don't even have the strength to keep standing. *Why would I think showing up here and demanding answers was a good idea?* He'll sell me again or dispose of me with a click of a gun. I'm nothing to him.

No, I'm something. He was supposed to kill me, not sell me. Whether he thought selling me was a better fate than death I have no idea.

And I'll ensure he kills me before another man touches me. I'm not afraid of death. And I'm not afraid of Enzo.

"Then what are you waiting for—kill me," I say. He won't. I can see he has as many questions behind his eyes as I do. He wants to know what happened to me. *How I escaped my master? Why I'm here?*

He tilts his chin as if that will give him a better angle to view my thin-as-a-toothpick body. That's all he can see though: how skinny I am. The broken bones, the bruises, and the scars are mostly hidden. Unless he examines my toes or fingers, he won't see any broken bones. My nose has been shattered several times, but my left eye has a deep bruise that would be impossible to hide even from makeup.

"I could kill you," he nods as if considering it. "Or we could play a game."

My heart stills. I know exactly what game he is talking about—truth or lies. The same game I taught him last time. The game I won. Winning the game didn't matter though. I ended up an empty shell of the woman I once was.

"I think I'd rather be dead."

His eyes narrow and his jaw tenses. "Why?"

"Because in death I might finally be free."

He walks toward me again, and I still, silently begging him not to touch me. My body screams on the inside to stay away, but I'm afraid if I speak, he will stroke me intentionally. My skin crawls at that thought.

He doesn't touch me as he circles me like a hawk determining how to snatch its prey. After circling he stops in front of me.

"Death won't free you." He steps back, giving me space to breathe.

"Yes, it will. I'm broken, can't you see? I am nothing. When you sold me to those men, you ensured my death. I should have died three years ago when you had your men take me before selling me, even after our arrangement. You didn't give me the chance to leave Miami. You lied. You did this to me..." my voice cracks in a high pitched squeal, and I know tears are threatening. *Do not cry.* Not in front of this man.

I think back to when I was first kidnapped. I was exhausted after swimming to shore all night, and then the hands came around me. At first, I thought it couldn't have been Enzo. I thought it was one of my father's debt collectors.

After Enzo spared my life, I thought he had compassion. There was no way he would have done this. And then I overheard the men talking about Enzo, about his boss Black. When I was brought to a room full of wealthy men, plodded out on stage like cattle, and sold to the highest bidder, it was Enzo's name who was given as the seller. He may not have been there, but it was by his order that I was sold.

Enzo must have realized I would have never stayed away from Miami and my father. But he couldn't kill me, so he sold me.

I swallow the tears back down. "You ensured I was broken, by selling me to the worst men. It's my turn to give an ultimatum: kill me or answer my questions, because I will not live another day in this hell without understanding why you didn't kill me that day. Why you were tasked with killing me in the first place."

I spit my words out, but he doesn't flinch. Each word is like a punch to his gut. But he's invincible; he can't be fractured. He has a natural armor I would die to possess.

"You're right. I sold you, not to the highest bidder, but to the cruelest man to ensure you a life of pain. One who didn't even want you, but loved knowing he would ruin you for any other man. Now that you are broken he has no use for you, so he dumped you on the nearest shore."

I should sob at his words. Or feel validated for confirming my suspicions. Enzo is responsible for my pain, and I have a chance to hurt him for hurting me.

"You are wrong about one thing," he says.

"I doubt it."

He smirks. "The men failed. I've seen shattered women. I've tortured enough men to understand when that last bit of desire to live leaves, when the whites vanish from their eyes, and they relinquish their souls to me. I know what it takes to drive a person to the edge of existence and ensure they never want to hold on. Your body may be in agonizing pain, your mind clouded with fear, but you, Kai Miller, are not broken."

I gasp.

I'm not broken.

I've known it the whole time, yet I needed confirmation from someone else to believe it. My father didn't say it. Mason couldn't even imagine it. But Enzo said it without me even asking or pleading with my eyes. It's what I needed to hear to survive.

"I know I'm not broken, despite what everyone keeps telling me."

He nods slowly with a tiny twinkle in his eye.

"Now that we've settled that, you don't truly want me to kill you. It's time to play a game."

"No, no more games. Even if I win, you'll find some twisted way to deceive me."

"And you never deceived me?" he asks.

"No, not during the game."

He nods. "I never lied to you during the game either. You won the game. I answered all the questions I could."

"All but the one that truly mattered." *Why? Why did he come to kill me?* The one question he never answered and I need to be answered more than anything.

"I was a boy with little power then. Now, I'm a king." He gestures to the grand room that looks more like a lair than a room.

"You will answer any question I ask if I win the new round?"

"Yes, if you win, I will answer any question."

This is why I came. To get answers to my questions. To understand why, of all the millions of women in the world, the devil found me. I can't trust Enzo, but this might be my only chance to get answers.

Why was Enzo assigned to kill me?

Why didn't he kill me?

Why did he take me?

Why did he have his men sell me?

Why was I tortured to the edge of breaking?

Why?

"You'll tell me why?" I ask, not including all the questions, knowing his answer would encompass all the questions.

"Yes, I'll tell you why."

Enzo may be evil, but he'll tell me the truth if I win. He wants answers too. He's itching to ask me endless questions. To tie me down, beat me, and force me to answer. I don't know why he doesn't go with that method. It wouldn't work; I know how to endure the worst torture imaginable. Maybe Enzo senses that. I have nothing to hide. Losing and having to answer his questions isn't really a loss.

"And if I lose, I'll answer your questions," I say.

"No."

I wait with bated breath for him to speak his next words. His wolfish eyes and growl of his throat already giving way to what he wants. *Me.*

"No, if you lose, I win you," he says.

CHAPTER 14
ENZO

I thought Kai was a ghost.

I thought I was dreaming, imagining her standing in the doorway to my lair.

But then she spoke, and I knew Kai was real.

She's been gone so long. I made sure she would never appear in Miami, in Surrender, in my life. Yet, here she is...

Skinny.

Beaten.

On the edge of death.

Kai shouldn't be alive. I don't even understand how she's standing.

I remember how tiny she was before, but this is on a different level. The years that have passed since the last time I saw her have turned me into a hard machine of muscle. No one would ever mistake me for a boy. Kai should have filled out the curves of her body; instead, she's thinned into almost nothing. A strong breeze could blow her over. I could snap her frail neck between my thumb and fingertips.

Her clothes hang baggy; her bones poke out beneath long sleeves and pants that I'm sure hide the unconceivable—bruises, scars, pain.

Her midnight dark hair has grown in length but is uneven and frazzled. The swelling around her eye is what has me entranced the most. Black and blue coloring around her now pale skin, lightened from lack of sunlight and nourishment.

For years, I've done my best to forget what happened. Forget her beautiful pouty lips, her gorgeous wavy black hair, her silky skin. I tried to erase her snark and tenacity from my head. I pretended that night was all a dream. That I never put my hands on her and threatened to kill her. That I didn't force her out of Miami and into a world of pain.

As much as I tried to forget, it was impossible. Not because she was the only girl I've ever wanted and couldn't have. A girl who intrigued me and sparked a stirring inside me I didn't know could exist. But because getting rid of Kai gained me power.

I'm no longer a prisoner to my father, but a ruthless, free man.

I decide my destiny now. And I have men who will fight to the death to ensure I get my way. And I've never forgotten what it cost me to gain that authority—Kai.

She was the sacrifice for my freedom. She was never supposed to return. I was never supposed to deal with the consequences of my sin. But here she is.

Kai was stupid to come back. She was free. She could have gone anywhere, and saved herself. Rebuilt her life. It would have taken time, but she had that choice. She chose to come back here, to me.

It's clear from the look in her defiant eyes she wants to destroy me, but she wants more than that. She wants answers.

I sigh.

I understand her need for truth, to make sense of what happened to her, but it's a stupid reason to give up her life. When the answer is simple—I sacrificed her to save myself.

But I'm not going to enlighten her. Not unless she wins.

"Sit," I say, indicating to the chair Langston, my right-hand man, was occupying before.

Kai's eyes cast down to the chair, but she doesn't move. If she doesn't sit down soon, she will collapse from exhaustion.

"Sit," I practically shout, my voice bellowing throughout the room. I'm not used to my orders not being followed immediately and completely.

Kai doesn't shutter at the loudness of my voice, but my command finally registers. I expect her to fight and argue with me at every step. Instead, she steps toward the chair. Her legs wobble and shake, barely keeping her upright with each step. But she doesn't seem to notice her flawed body shutting down.

She stumbles, and I reach out my arm to catch her, but she pivots at the last second, catching herself instead of tumbling into my grasp.

I sigh and move my hand to the back of my neck, rubbing hard, trying to get the frustration out on my tense muscles.

I shouldn't want to help or even touch her, but I can't help the pull this woman has over me.

I need a drink. Kai needs food. I don't know when the last time she ate was.

Fuck.

How could I let this happen? I'm a cruel, sadistic bastard, but I never meant for this betrayal to take over her life. I hate how hollowed-cheeked she is. I hate how much pain she's in. But most of all, I hate that any man ever touched her.

She's *mine*.

Then why'd you let her go?

Because I didn't have a choice.

I leave Kai in the room as I walk to the kitchen to get some food. I should be worried about what Kai will do in the minutes I'm gone. What secrets she will find in my private room. I'm more concerned that her weak heartbeat will stop or her lungs will give out and she'll be dead before I return.

I don't know what food is nourishing for a person who has been to hell and emerged on the other side. So I just throw the first things I find onto a plate: strawberries, old pizza, crackers, and olives.

I jog back to the room, my feet silent as I move.

When I enter my lair again, Kai is still sitting in the chair, her fingers brushing against the hem of her shirt.

She startles when I enter.

I should apologize. I should make her feel better, but I don't. I want her to eat, but I also want her on edge. I want to win our game of truth or lies. I want to take her and secure her as mine.

I don't know why I suggested the game, when I could just as easily take her by force. She's too weak to fight. I could toss her over my shoulder and take her to my home. Lock her away forever.

But it doesn't seem fair. I like giving her a fighting chance, even if the result is the same in the end.

I set the plate of food on the end table next to Kai and then pour us each a glass of water. I'd offer her alcohol, but I'm afraid it would burn what little lining is left in her stomach after years of eating itself in order to survive.

"Eat."

She stares at the food, like it's a pile of worms and bugs I'm asking her to eat.

"Kai, eat," my voice warns.

Her eyes flutter up to me as her breathing slows. "I didn't come here to eat; I came to get answers. Are we playing the game or not?"

I sigh. She's the most frustrating woman. "When we play, and I win, you will eat. You will do everything I say, because I own you."

She releases a breath. "You forget that I won last time. And now I'm more determined than ever to win again."

"You may have won before, but by the end of tonight, you will be mine."

"I will belong to no one, but myself," she snarks.

I grin. "There is the fighting girl I remember."

She huffs. "She's gone. Kai Miller drowned in the ocean."

"So you're Katherine now, then?" I ask, remembering the name she said her parents called her before she declared her name was Kai.

"No, I'm nobody. I don't even exist."

We breathe in unison, both needing air, but I'm not sure the room has enough for both of us. And what's left of the air is pushing us together. We both try to resist, but somehow I'm leaning toward her, reaching my hand up to brush a strand of hair that has fallen into her face.

Kai brushes it away glaring at me before I can touch her. She hates me, of course, she doesn't want me to touch her.

"The rules?" she asks.

"Same as before. We each get one guess to identify the truth from the lies correctly."

She nods. "I win; I get my answers."

"I win; I get you." I expect her to ask questions. *How long would I take her if she were to lose? What would she be expected to do if I take her?*

She doesn't ask. Being taken no longer scares or concerns her. She's lost her life before, because of me. This is no different to her.

And I need to win for so many reasons. There is the attraction, the pull that begs me to take her, make her mine, fuck her and show her pleasure she's never experienced before, while ruining her more than she already is. But I need to take her for more than just my own sexual desires. The power and life I've gained require her to stay hidden. I can only do that one of two ways. The same two choices I had before: kill her or take her.

"You can start."

I sit back in my chair, sipping on my water like it's scotch. I should have poured myself a drink, but I want to be acutely aware of her. Ready to tell when she's lying or telling the truth before she even speaks. Last time we played, I was naive. I thought I had experience, and that she didn't. Time has changed us both. Me into brawn, her into vengeance. We both have the skills needed to win the game, but hopefully, her brain is too clouded to think clearly.

Kai clears her throat as her head drops to her hands. She's covering her face as she thinks about the lies and truths she will reveal, hoping that by hiding her face, I'll be less attuned to her.

My lips curl—*as if not feeling her was possible.* I feel her more than I see her. Her icy breath pierces my burning heart with each exhale. And my blood pumps slower through my veins matching her slow, irregular beat. Even thousands of miles apart, I would occasionally feel a chill down my back or a sharpness in my side and think of her. We are connected, and right now I feel her pain, along with her determination.

Slowly, Kai reveals her face to me again; she reaches for the water takes a sip and then stares straight at me.

"I hate my father.

"I hate the ocean.

"I hate you."

I smile loving the theme she chose this time. The last time we played she chose lust, temptation. She tricked me by making me believe she was more innocent than she was. This time, she's chosen her strongest emotion—hate. It's easiest for her to fuel into every sentence equally, making me believe every word out of her mouth.

She wants to play with the strongest emotions to win. Then I will too.

"I love my family.

"I love the ocean.

"I love money."

"I didn't think you were capable of love," she snarls.

I shrug. "Everyone is capable of loving something."

Her face darkens. She doesn't think she's capable of loving, not anymore.

I stare down on the deep purple colored bruise on the inside of her wrist, exposed as the sleeve pushes up her arm. Then to her bare feet where several of her toes bend the wrong way.

I doubt anyone who has been through what she's been through is capable of loving anything anymore.

"Which is my truth?" Kai asks, impatiently.

"So eager to lose."

"I want my answers."

"Which do you hate the most, Kai?" I pick up my glass and swirl the water around as I contemplate my choices.

"The easiest and most obvious choice would be that you hate me. I tried to kill you. I left you in the ocean. I told you if you survived, to leave Miami. And then I caused torment worse than death."

I pause, waiting for her to argue or yell at me for any of those points. She doesn't.

"But the most obvious choice doesn't mean it's your truth. Although, I have a hard time thinking you could hate anyone as much as you hate me." But maybe she uses a different word in her head for what she thinks of me. After all, hate and love are two sides of the same emotion. And if she hates me, then it means she has the capacity to love me. She could never love me; therefore she could never hate me.

"Your father would also be easy to hate. He was supposed to protect you. Or at the very least rescue you. He didn't." But she's too much of a daddy's girl to truly hate him. Not for his incompetencies, even though she should.

"The ocean is worthy of your hate too. I left you in it to drown. Who knows what hardships you experienced on the sea?"

Her eyes dilate a millimeter.

"Have you made your choice?" she asks.

"Yes, have you?"

"I still don't think you are capable of love. But between loving your family, the ocean, or money the choice is easy."

I smirk. *Bingo, I have her.*

And I know her truth.

"You go first," she says.

"You don't hate your father. And as much pain as I've caused you, you don't hate me. You hate the sea." It's plain as day. She hates the sea. Sea equals Kai. She hates herself. She hates what she's become. She hates being broken and weak. She could never hate her father, and she sees me as nothing but a soldier following orders. Who ultimately kept her alive, even though she was tortured because of it. She hates the sea.

"And you love the ocean," Kai says.

Neither of us blinks. Or breathes. Or moves. Neither reveals who the winner is. The thread of connection between us looms revealing our winner. One of us chose correctly, and the other wrongly.

"The ocean represents freedom for me," I say.

Her eyes widen, realizing her mistake. "But you don't long to be free anymore; you are free," she whispers.

I nod.

"And you don't love money," she says.

I nod.

"You love your family."

I nod. "I love my family. Those men, Langston and Zeke, are my family. Maybe not my blood, but they are my family in every other sense of the word."

She nods. She doesn't call it cheating. We both chose our words carefully. Family means whatever it truly means to me, not the technical definition of the word. Family means Zeke and Langston.

"The ocean represents everything I lost," she says.

I nod.

"I could never hate my father for not being strong enough to rescue me."

I nod.

"I don't even hate you..." her voice cracks. "Hatred requires me to feel anything toward you, and I don't believe you are human enough for me to hate. You're a beast who broke every promise and then sold me to a bigger monster."

Her bottom lip trembles. "I hate the ocean because it took everything from me, and instead of letting me die and be free, it sent me back here to you."

I should be kinder. I should feel empathy and let her go. I won't, but I should.

"I lost," she whispers while she holds her head high. Her lips purse and her icy cheeks pale.

"And now, you're mine."

CHAPTER 15
KAI

I lost.

I won't get my answers.

This was a one time deal; no way will Enzo give me this chance again to get the answers I seek. And now, because I was blinded by the need to understand why I endured punishment and pain for years, I'm his.

I traded one unknown master for this man.

I should be scared, terrified.

He could take me and sell me again. He could beat me, rape me, kill me. He could do whatever unthinkable things he wants with me, and I couldn't stop him. Enzo could have taken those things anyway, whether I won the game or not. But he didn't have to resort to that. I offered myself up willingly, all so I could win a bet. And now I've lost everything.

No, I didn't have anything left to lose. That's why I could offer up everything.

Enzo devours me with his hungry glare. My stomach aches, but not from the lack of food, but because of the lust that stirs inside me every time I'm around Enzo. It shouldn't be there. I should hate him with every fiber of my being. Instead, my body longs to feel something, anything, even an ache for a monster.

Maybe it's because he spared my life that I don't feel the hatred I should feel towards him? Maybe deep down, despite how devastatingly difficult life was on that yacht, some part of me preferred to live rather than die. I just need to find that piece of myself again.

"Come," Enzo says.

I consider fighting him, but as he stands and inches toward me, I know if I don't follow his directions, he will grab me and force me to obey his orders. Something I'm used to. But not something I will allow anymore.

I stand up.

Enzo raises an eyebrow in surprise and then starts walking toward the back of the room. I follow slowly, wincing as my broken toes swell with each step. He pushes on the back wall, and a hidden door opens.

He steps through the door.

Then I do. And then we are back in the darkness.

Enzo knows his way as we weave down unlit hallways, much the same as when I made my way to his room. He doesn't stumble or bring up a light on his phone to see the way. It appears he can see in the shadows as easily as I can.

He turns his head back toward me once, but not to see if I'm still following, we both can sense each other more than we'd like. There is an attraction, a pull. Like magnets that pull as much as they push. His fire and my ice begging to be brought together, while knowing the second we touch we will explode. Cold and heat aren't meant to mix, just exist close to each other.

And then the light is burning my retinas as we step into the light. He was warning me with his gaze, I realize, now that the sun is burning down on me.

Enzo studies my every movement as I recoil into my sweater. I hate the fucking sun. Ridiculous thought, after spending so many years begging to feel its warmth. Now it's too hot, too bright, too much.

"Get in," Enzo says.

That's when I notice the car. The very fancy, blacked out car. It's a two-seater, shiny, and very fast looking.

And suddenly I don't want to get in the car. I can't remember the last time I rode in a car. A car looks claustrophobic. It looks dangerous. It looks—

"Kai, get in the car."

Fuck.

I will not let Enzo see my fear. It's just a car. I've ridden in them countless times before. I can handle it—even a tiny, suffocating car like this one.

I walk to the passenger side, open the door, and slide in. My foot instantly relieved to no longer be standing on it.

I close my eyes and try to take a few deep breaths.

"Afraid of the car or my driving?" Enzo asks.

My eyes pop open as I snarl at him.

He chuckles. "It's not my driving you should be worried about."

I still. I know exactly what I should be worried about. This isn't my first rodeo. He isn't my first capture. But Enzo isn't like the other men who took me. We have a connection that saved me last time; I'm not sure that link will save me a second time.

I'm jerked backward, slamming against my seat as Enzo speeds off.

"Seatbelt, Kai. We wouldn't want anything else to happen to damage your pretty face."

"Really? You're making jokes now?"

He shrugs as he zips around another corner.

I grab the seatbelt and clasp it across my body despite hating how trapped I feel.

"I wouldn't call them jokes. I enjoy watching you squirm. And the faster you learn you are no longer in control, the easier your life will be."

I will never confess I've given him control, just like I never admitted I was broken. My life may have never been my own, but it doesn't mean I don't have some control.

"So stubborn," he says, turning sharply.

"Motherfucking bastard. Fucking slow down. I'm weak, I feel trapped in this car, and I'm about to hurl all over the upholstery."

He smiles and then slows. It seems that is all he wanted: for me to show weakness.

I close my eyes again as my stomach churns from the turns and being in such a small space. I can barely breathe. Bile rises in my throat; I'm going to vomit.

"Open your eyes, Kai."

I don't want to open them. *Why does he want me to open them anyway?* So he can see the terror on my face he's causing. He's sick.

His voice softens, "Open your eyes."

I open them.

"Look at the road ahead. It will help."

I watch the road and notice our speed has slowed tremendously. Cars are now passing us, speeding down the highway. I watch the road in front of us and the pressure building in my stomach subsides a little.

"Good, just like that. Now breath in through your nose and purse your lips as you breathe out."

I do what he says, my breathing calm. He's so nice, so kind.

"And if you need to puke, tell me. If you thought those men tortured you before, you haven't felt wrath until I punish you for destroying my car."

I frown—*from cruel to nice in the flip of a switch.*

He notices my reaction. "I was joking."

"It wasn't funny."

He sighs and then turns back to driving, ignoring me for the most part. I do occasionally see his eyes cut to mine when my breathing grows erratic again, whether for the safety of his car or for me.

I expect us to drive to some underground society. Or to a condo high above the city. I assume Enzo might live in a mansion high up on a cliff. Or worst yet, a yacht. What I don't expect is the house we stop in front of before Enzo cuts the engine in the driveway.

"This is your home?" I ask, as I stare at the modest house on the beach.

"Yes. Were you expecting something grandeur?"

I look at the modern, sleek looking house that can't be more than two to three thousand square feet. I'm sure the home is expensive, it sits on a large private piece of beach property, gated and secluded, but it still seems modest compared to what I figured he could own based on his fancy suit and expensive car. But somehow this fits Enzo—no magnificence is needed to show his power and attraction.

"No, this was exactly what I was expecting."

"Welcome to your new home, Kai."

Home.

This will never be my home. I don't have a home.

Enzo steps out of the car and doesn't wait for me to follow. He jogs to the door and opens it, smiling as he steps inside.

I look around as I sit in the car. He never gave me an order. I could continue sitting in the car for the rest of the day, and he couldn't get angry at me for disobeying. I don't know why he trusts that I will stay. I lost the bet, but that doesn't mean I'll make it easy for him. I never promised not to run away.

I get out of the car, my eyes scanning, trying to find my best method of escape. A habit I've developed after years of being captive. But one step on my injured foot and I realize why Enzo isn't worried about me running and escaping. I can barely walk, let alone run. I would have no chance against him.

So, reluctantly, I follow through the door where Enzo went.

"Mr. Black, welcome home. It's been a while since we've seen you," a man in a suit who appears to be a couple decades older than us says to Enzo.

Black.

I frown as I try to make sense of what the man said. Enzo said that Black was who he worked for. But he never told me his last name.

Enzo turns to me and reads the confusion on my face. But he doesn't answer my question.

"This is Mr. Westcott. He works for me and takes care of this house while I'm away. If you need anything and I'm not here, he can assist you," Enzo says.

"It's very nice to meet you, Kai," Mr. Westcott says.

"How do you know my name?" I feel out of the loop, like everyone else knows the answer to a secret, but I'm not even aware of what the secret is.

Mr. Westcott smiles. "Mr. Black texted me that he would have a guest by the name of Katherine Kai Miller, but that you preferred the name Kai."

I glance between the two men. The story checks out.

"I'll leave you two to tour the house. Mr. Black, please let me know which rooms you would like prepared. The fridge is fully stocked, but if you need anything else, I'll be in my office." Mr. Westcott says before walking away.

"Mr. Black?" I ask, staring at Enzo with my hands folded across my chest.

He narrows his eyes. "You need to eat, Kai."

"I want my question answered, *Mr. Black.*"

"Eat first; then you can ask questions."

I frown. I don't like this tit for tat game, or him expecting me to win a round of truth or lies to get a question answered.

Enzo turns down a hallway and like before, he doesn't ask me to follow him. He walks, and I'm expected to follow like a trained dog. Reluctantly, I do.

He stops in the kitchen and has his head buried in the fridge, pulling out all manner of food. He frowns after pulling a platter full of fruit and raw vegetables out. "I don't have any meat, which might help you heal faster, but eat this for now, and then I'll get you something more substantial to eat."

I stare at the mound of food as I stand next to the island. "I can't eat all of that."

He laughs. "Eat some of it while I talk."

"Okay."

He smiles and slides the food on the island in front of where I stand leaning against the counter.

I pick up a grape and gnaw at it. "Talk."

"There isn't much to say really. My last name is Black. I'm Enzo Black."

"How?" I mumble, my mouth still working on the first bite of grape.

"My father's name is Black. He owned the empire. The bars, the yachts, the men."

"Owned?" I ask, realizing he used the word in the past tense.

He nods. "Yes."

"And now? Who rules the empire now?"

"Me." I can see it in his eyes. How he got the power he now wields. *Me.* I don't understand how disposing of me gained him control over his father's empire, but I know I had a lot to do with it. And he won't tell me anything further than what he just told me.

I swallow, the sour taste of the grape lingering on my tongue. I stare down at the platter, trying to pick a fruit that has the least flavor, but I can barely remember the taste of any of the fruits. I haven't had anything this fresh in years. Instead, I opt for a snow pea stalk. I take a bite off the end.

And then anger fumes inside me. "He was the king, and you were the prince. You had more power back then than you let on. You could have decided I didn't have to die or be sold. You could have convinced your father."

He shakes his head. "No, I would have ended up dead. I traded your life to save mine. I did all I could to save you. I'm sorry you aren't grateful for that."

"Grateful! You expect me to be grateful! Do you have any idea what I've been through?"

He looks at me sheepishly, his face fallen and hurt. It wounds him, what has happened to me. Yet another thing that doesn't make sense about this man. He can't care for me. Not if he sold me to cruel men. That's not caring; it's the opposite of caring. It's savage.

He's silent though, not giving me any more insight into his thoughts or reasoning.

"But you're the king now?"

"Yes."

"So you have the power to decide my fate? You could let me go."

"Yes."

"But you won't?"

"No, you controlled your own fate when you offered up your life to me. Now you're mine."

"To what? To beat? To rape?"

He shrugs. "If I like."

My eyes flitter, looking deep into his. He might decide one day to rape me, but that isn't the purpose of him taking me. At least I don't think it is.

"Or will you sell me when you get bored of me?"

His eyes dilate, and his nostrils flare at my words.

"You. Are. *Mine*. I won't sell or share you with anyone."

That warms my insides. I'd rather be with the monster I know than one I don't.

"Besides, I wouldn't get my money's worth now that you've already been touched and broken."

I shudder. He's right, but I hate his words. *Why isn't that enough for me to hate him? Why do I still feel like there is more to the story I'm missing— like why me?*

I stop eating and turn toward the large window behind me that overlooks the ocean, trying to process what's happening. Enzo is callous yet considerate. Merciful yet punishing. I have no idea why he took me or what he intends to do with me.

"It scares you, doesn't it?"

"What?" I ask.

"Being so close to the ocean."

I nod. There is no point denying it. I'm in one of the most gorgeous, secluded places on a private beach, and I won't go near the ocean for however long I'm here.

"What happened to you, Kai? What made you so afraid? Of the water above everything?"

I freeze.

"You were afraid of the car. Wounded by the sunlight. But both of those you were willing to face. With time you will stop fearing them. But the ocean you look at like it's the enemy. You look at it with a hatred you don't even give me."

"Jarod, the man you sold me to, you had no contact with him after you sold me? He never told you what happened?"

Enzo looks at me wide-eyed. "No, I had no contact with the man who owned you."

I nod. Then he won't be getting the truth from me. He doesn't deserve to know what happened to me. He doesn't get to understand my fears. There is nothing that can fix me anyway. And I have a sinking suspicion that the only reason Enzo would try to heal me would be so he could ruin me again himself.

"Kai..." His hand reaches out and touches my wrist. I don't know why or what purpose, but everything else falls away but his touch.

It burns.

The heat overwhelms my body, and it feels like fire is flaming my skin. I stare down at the spot wide-eyed, expecting red blobs of fire to be flying from his fingertips to my wrist.

It's too much.

His touch.

My body.

It's too damn much.

I step backward, trying to get out of his grasp. *Don't touch me. Let me go*, I plead in my brain, but I can't form the words.

Everything goes dizzy.

Cloudy.

Then black.

I feel myself falling.

Like before.

I'm falling.

Down.

Down.

Down.

Maybe this time, if the ocean catches me, it will keep me, drown me until I'm gone.

Watching Kai collapse to the ground shouldn't affect me. It shouldn't bother me in the slightest. *But then why do I have this gut-wrenching, heaving, gnawing feeling in my stomach as I watch her ailing body fall and then bounce against my hardwood floor?*

I should have moved faster; then maybe I would have caught her and prevented the forceful impact of her body. But I was too focused on the bruise on her wrist. The blues and purples drew me into her pale skin, but I couldn't tell if it was fractured, sprained, or just a bruise. The desire to hunt down Jarod, the man who dared to hurt her flooded through me, while simultaneously wanting to tie her down and fuck her, giving her more wounds and scars from the ropes I would use to tie her up.

Fuck, there is something wrong with me.

"Kai?" I bend down to offer my help for her to stand, even though I know she won't take it. She all but hates me. She thinks I'm going to torture her and rape her like the last man who owned her. She should think that way. I'm not safe. Although it's not my style to force a woman against her will, women line up to be fucked by me. I pay the most beautiful women in the world to work in my club, and they have no problem extending their services to me when their shifts are over.

Kai's different; she wears the battle she's endured on every piece of her flesh. And all the scars do is make me wonder what she sounds like when she screams with tears running down her cheeks. Because I'm a sick, fucking monster.

I don't know how she ended up on the floor. I reached out wanting to touch her bruise and wanting to see if the cold still pulses through her veins. And then she was on the floor.

I don't know how...

Did exhaustion finally catch up with her?

Lack of food?

Or was it panic I saw in her eyes at the thought of me caressing her?

"Kai," I say louder, keeping my hands by my side instead of touching her, in case my almost brush against her was what caused the panic attack.

She doesn't stir.

Shit.

"Kai," I scream.

Westcott runs into the room, "Enzo? What happened? I heard a scream." His face is full of shock as he stares down at Kai's lifeless body.

"She just collapsed," I answer.

"I'll call 911," Westcott says.

"No," I hiss.

Westcott frowns, and I know he will disobey me if I don't do something soon. He's worked for my family for a long time. He's one of my most loyal employees, but he doesn't put up with my shit. He doesn't have to worry about me firing him; I won't. And even if I did, I pay him well enough that he could retire now even though he's only fifty.

Westcott pulls out his phone, threatening me. He's the only person in the world allowed to bully me and not get reprimanded or killed for his trouble. In some ways, he was the father I always wanted but never had.

What do I do?

"Kai, wake up!" I scream as I roll her over onto her back.

Ice. Her body shoots off frosty sparks through my warm body. She's as bone-chilling as I remember, possibly colder. I shudder for a second as her cool combines with my fire causing the hair on my arm to stand as goosebumps form.

I survey her, looking for any sign of the injury that would have caused her to collapse and not wake up. But other than the bruise that was already covering her eye, I don't see any visible head injury.

And then I watch her chest rising and falling. She must have knocked herself unconscious when she fell. I know I shouldn't move her, but I can't keep her lying on the bare floor. She needs a bed; she needs sleep and food. She needs medical support and therapists to heal, but I'm not sure I'm willing to let anyone else see or touch her even to help her. *She's mine.*

Gently, I cradle her head and scoop up her legs. Having her in my arms does something primal to my body. It arouses an urge I haven't felt since the last time I kissed her. I feel alive even though her skin prickles mine—a steady, calmness pulses from her thin veins to my thicker cords. I feel more settled and more urgent at the same time. An awakening builds inside as my stomach clenches at what I let happen to this beautiful woman in my arms; she still seems like a girl to me in so many ways.

"What are you doing to me, Kai?" I whisper into her ear.

Her breathing is still slow and constant in my arms.

"Sir?" Westcott asks with concern in his eyes.

"She's breathing. I think she just collapsed from exhaustion. Is the master bedroom ready?"

He nods.

"I'll call an ambulance."

"No," my voice cuts through the room. I won't have anyone take her away from me. *Not now.*

I rush past him to the bedroom I usually occupy when I'm staying here. This is my favorite house out of all the ones I own. If I can't be on the sea, then I'll take this beach house as a close second. But I just got back last night and slept at the club before coming here. None of my stuff is here or unpacked.

Kai can have the master; I'll take one of the spares, I decide as I climb the stairs to the second floor. She doesn't stir the entire time I hold her.

I kick open the door to the spacious master bedroom. An oversized white canopy bed sits against the far wall with white linen sheets giving off a beach vibe as it gets the perfect view of the ocean out the floor to ceiling windows—one of the windows pushes out as a concealed door leading out to the private balcony. There isn't much else in this bedroom. I like to keep everything simple and elegant. Only a door impedes the bare walls and leads to the deluxe bathroom suite where the walk-in closet is.

This room will serve as the perfect gilded cage for Kai. I haven't figured out what I'm going to do with her yet. Killing her would be the easiest, but as I've already determined from our last encounter, I can't kill this girl. Locking her away is the next best thing to ensure I keep my power. This room isn't exactly a prison, but to her, it will feel like one.

I carefully lay her down on top of the covers on the bed. A quiet moan escapes her lips, but otherwise, she doesn't stir.

I walk quickly to my closet that is always filled with the basics for when I stay here and pull out one of my shirts for her to sleep in before I return to her side.

She's still breathing, still knocked out when I return.

So I begin the slow, torturous work of removing her sweater and jeans. Her feet are already bare, filthy from spending days walking barefoot, swollen, and covered in deep lesions. The only parts of her body I can see are her hands, feet, and face—and if they are any indication of what lies beneath her clothes, I'm not sure I can bear it.

I pull her sweater up her smooth stomach attentively as I'm not sure what I will reveal.

I'm not a squeamish man, but when I see the cuts, bruises, and scars marking her skin, I want to hurl. I force myself to stay put and continue removing the sweater from her frozen, defeated body. I finally get the sweater over her head, and I lose my mind.

What the fuck did Jarod do to you?

What did I do?

I thought death was the worst thing that could have happened to Kai, my pretty girl, but I was wrong. This—this is the worst thing anyone could ever experience.

Every inch of her skin is covered in her anguish and pain.

Scars.

Bruises.

Cuts.

All of her is broken.

Misaligned.

Torn.

Injured.

Jarod didn't spare one inch of her precious body. Every part is marked.

He fucking claimed her. He made her *his*. He ruined every part of her body, and there is no telling what he messed up inside her, both internally and in her mind. I don't know how anyone recovers from this.

I understand now why Kai thinks she was broken. She is broken, but somehow, an essential part of her spirit remains. Despite what her body has gone through, the fight persisted. She wouldn't have come to find me if she didn't want to battle—to take back her life.

I have no doubt when her body is strong enough; she will once again fight for her freedom. She might even win.

I can't let that happen. We are both two parts to a whole. We both can't survive in this world. If she escapes, I'll cease to exist. The only way we can both live is if the world thinks she's dead—at least my world does.

I try to purge the fuming rage that has built up inside me and is now exploding out of me with passion from my body. I want to call on all of my men to hunt the bastard down who did this and make him wish he only had to experience the pain Kai did after what I plan on doing to him.

But if I send my men to find them, it would be admitting Kai is alive.

So I push the feeling down, something I'm an expert in.

I take the T-shirt in my hand and pull it down covering her

stomach and the tops of her thighs. Only then do I undo the jeans and gently pull them off her body. I want so badly to lift the T-shirt up and catch a glimpse of her gorgeous cunt I've dreamed about for so long. But I'm not a sick fuck who dreams of corpses, which is basically what she is in this state. And if I see that her pussy is as broken as the rest of her body, I'll throw all my rational thoughts out the window, and I'll do something that will get me killed in the end.

So I quell my dark desires, locking them deep inside the cage where I keep everything else.

I tuck Kai under the covers as her breath continues to rise and fall.

What am I going to do with you?

I reach into my back pocket, and I call Westcott.

"Sir?"

"Call a private doctor to the house for Kai. The best, one who specializes in her condition."

"Absolutely, sir. I'll have a doctor here right away."

I end the call. Kai won't want a doctor to see her. She won't want the help, but she doesn't always get a choice in her life. She'll die if not.

I don't know what to do, but stand over her and ensure she continues breathing until the doctor arrives.

"Enzo?" her voice croaks.

"Yes, I'm here," I moan back in agony at seeing her in pain.

Her eyes don't open, and I'm not even sure she's conscious.

"I'm so cold," she whispers.

I nod. I love her arctic skin against mine. I love how it centers me and makes me crave her.

"Hold me, Enzo. Make me warm."

Fuck.

I stare at her a minute, not sure she wants me to touch her. But then she shivers despite being under the pile of blankets.

I kick off my shoes, remove my suit jacket, and loosen my tie before climbing into bed next to her. I don't dare take off any more clothes. My self-control is already hanging on a thread as it is. I can't feel her skin to skin.

But as I wrap my hot skin against her cool ice, I feel every part of her connect with me.

Body.

Heart.

Soul.

What are you doing to me, pretty girl? And why do you have this hold over me?

I pull her tighter to my body, our skin regulating each other's temperature and bodies as we doze while we wait for the doctor to arrive. My cock hardens, pressing against her ass.

Not going to happen, I try to convince my cock, but to no avail.

And I know that as I hold her, I can never touch her again. I'm the devil, but I'm done being a monster to her. I will stay far away. She will be safe as long as she never leaves these four walls. And I will continue to be the monster with power over the world, and control everything, except her.

CHAPTER 17
KAI

The chill returns to my body. My eyes fly open.

Where am I?

What happened?

I'm in the most magnificent room I've ever seen in either real life or a magazine.

The bed I'm lying on is enormous. Much bigger than a traditional king. It's a white canopy bed with white linen sheets softer than a pile of feathers. Floor to ceiling windows line the wall, giving me a view of a balcony most people would pay a fortune to sit on, because it has the most unobscured, private view of turquoise blue water I've ever seen. You can't even see any sailboats on the horizon, that's how reclusive it feels. Like you are on your own tranquil piece of paradise.

But I want to sprint over to the curtains and pull them shut, blocking out the fucking sun and the divine view that makes my stomach want to hurl.

I chuckle to myself when I notice the see-through curtains. There is nothing in this room that will block out the sun's rays.

I stare down at the stark white sheets and comforter covering my body. They may be made of the softest fabrics known to earth, but they irritate my skin—making me feel like I need to scratch my reddened flesh like I have the chicken pox.

I can't decide if I'd rather bury myself under the covers to block out the sun or throw the scratchy covers from my body.

I try to remember where I am and how I got here.

Enzo.

I remember the club. I remember losing the game. I remember collapsing.

Shit.

I collapsed. Passed out. That's the one thing I never wanted to let happen. Because when I'm unconscious, I can't control what happens to me. I can't fight. I can't prevent the torture.

My body stills. But I don't feel the usual pain that comes after being abused. I don't think I was touched...

But I remember being warm.

How is that possible? I never feel warm. Even with the light shining in and the mountain of covers on top of me, I'm not warm.

Now, I'm cold. It must have been a dream of feeling snug.

I actually feel colder than usual.

That's when I take in more of my body and feel the stick of the needle in my hand, pouring the biting liquid into my body.

My eyes widen, and my body trembles. I want it out. *Now.*

I look around the room, searching for someone to explain what the fuck happened and why I have an IV. I don't need an IV. I don't need a doctor. I don't need anyone.

"It's good to see you awake, Miss Miller," a man sitting in an armchair on the other side of the bed says.

I shake at the unexpected sound.

"I didn't mean to startle you; I'm Dr. Gould."

Fuck.

I recoil further up on the bed, inching to the farthest corner away from this stranger, covering myself with the evil covers.

The doctor's smile drops when he sees my reaction.

"Mr. Black brought me here to help you, Miss Miller. I won't hurt you. You can trust me."

Liar.

I can't trust anyone.

The doctor purses his lips when he sees my reaction.

"You've been passed out for three days. I inserted an IV to give you proper nutrition. And I only did the bare minimum of examination to ensure you didn't need any further treatment while you were unconscious. I didn't think you would appreciate anything more while you were out."

He's right; no one should touch me while I'm passed out.

"Where am I?" I ask, even though I already know the answer. I want confirmation.

He eyes me carefully, trying to study my reaction. "Mr. Black's beach residence."

He doesn't say more, but I know I'm in Enzo's room. I can smell and feel him everywhere. His musky cologne and ocean salt scent covers the room.

Why the fuck does Enzo live in a box of light?

He should be living in a dark cave in a hillside—*not this.*

I need the dark, not the light.

The doctor rounds the bed to the side I'm hiding under. I want to move to the other side, but he moves faster than I can crawl away.

His sad eyes stare down at me as he stands tall overhead.

"Miss Miller, can you tell me what you remember?"

I frown and huff steam from my nose.

He nods.

"Can you nod and tell me you remember, though? I'm worried you might have brain damage."

I nod. *I remember.*

"That's good. I know you've been through a lot these last few years. I need to give you a more thorough exam. I believe you have several broken bones and some have started healing while not aligned. After I examine you, we can talk about getting some x-rays and prioritize your injuries. I promise you will recover from this. I've helped countless women heal from similar situations. You will get through this."

I raise my eyebrows as a chill runs through me. Enzo didn't just get any doctor to look after me; he hired one who knows exactly how to treat women like me.

I can see in the doctor's eyes he wants to touch me, comfort me in some way. He tells me with his body first, then his words.

"Let's start with something simple. I'm just going to check your pulse. Is that okay?"

I don't answer. I can't. I'm frozen.

He hesitantly reaches his hand out, and his fingers press against the inside of my wrist.

I jump.

I can't fucking stand the touch. No matter how comforting he intended it. It feels like he's trying to stab my body. To ruin and torture me.

My body springs up like a scared cat, my body on alert, my claws out, and a hiss from my mouth.

"Miss Miller, I'm sorry. Come back to—"

I can't hear the doctor's words. I can't be here a second longer.

I spring from the bed, feeling the tug of the IV trying to keep me in.

Fuck that.

The pain of the needle barely registers as it pulls from my hand. But I feel free as I leave the bed. The covers no longer trapping me, and my body safe from being touched.

I don't know where I'm going. Enzo started the tour of the house yesterday, but he never finished it. Instead, I collapsed like a pussy. Enzo will think he can take whatever he wants from me—that I won't fight back. I won't be surprised if he comes to my room tonight and takes whatever he wants from me.

I can't think about that. I'll figure out how to protect myself soon enough.

I run to the stairs.

Fucking stairs.

I'm so tired, but the adrenaline from needing to get away from the doctor is stronger than the weakness and dizziness I feel.

Down the stairs I go, half running, half falling.

When I stumble down the main floor, I keep moving my legs,

still not sure where I'm headed or why. My fight or flight has kicked in, and I can't stop until someone slows me down.

I keep going, sweat soaking my body, chills shooting up and down my spine, panic weighing down my legs.

Keep running, flee, escape.

Those thoughts play on repeat through my head.

I can't stop.

I can't get a reprieve from the exhaustion I'm feeling. Nothing will stop me.

"Stop," a deep, authoritative voice echoes in the walls.

What? Stop? I can't.

"Stop."

I feel my legs slowing, although I don't understand why.

"Stop, Kai."

My legs come to a halt as if I hit a brick wall.

I didn't, but I came close.

Enzo is standing less than a foot in front of me.

I pant heavily, knowing I can't catch my breath. I've pushed my body too hard. I'm about to faint again.

"Breathe," comes the same steady voice. I hang on to that voice, letting it fill my lungs as if it were oxygen.

The fog covering my eyes lifts, and I see Enzo, really see him for the first time.

He's so close to me, yet I don't get the urge to run away from him. He's not attempting to reach out or touch me in any way. His eyes are locked with mine, and it's almost like he can see inside my head. Our stupid connection, I don't understand. One we've had for far too long and needs to be severed, immediately.

Enzo nods, encouraging me to continue to slow my body down until I'm calm again, or at least my version of composed.

Once he sees that I've returned to my less erratic state, his eyes darken, his lips twitch, and the vein in his head pops out.

"Why aren't you dressed?" Enzo hisses at me.

My fists clench at his harshness, but I don't step back. Neither does he.

I stare down at my body for the first time. I was wearing an oversized shirt when I left the bedroom. Now I'm wearing nothing. I don't remember removing the shirt, but I must have on my way down the stairs, needing the itchy clothing off me as much as I needed the sheets to stop constricting my body.

I huff. "Does it matter? I've seen the way you look at me. It doesn't matter that my body is broken. That other men have touched me. You're just as sick as them."

He growls and then steps closer to me.

I don't retreat, even though I feel the blood frosting my body as it pumps faster. *Don't let him intimidate or threaten you.*

"You will wear clothes anytime you leave your bedroom," he fires into my ear.

I grow rigid. "Don't you mean, *your* bedroom?"

He shrugs. "It doesn't matter what it *was*, only what it *is*. You can pretend it's your sanctuary, your cage, my bedroom, or whatever fantasy you create in your head to make sense of what is happening to you. But while you are here, it is *your* bedroom."

He takes three giant steps back, and I can breathe again. Then he does something I don't understand. He removes the T-shirt he's wearing.

My eyes hone in on the rippling muscles over his stomach, so defined and tight, then jump up to his hard pecs. He would be a perfect specimen if it weren't for the healed scars that cover his body—like mine. His make him look stronger though, more rugged—nothing like mine.

He tosses the shirt to the floor a foot in front of me.

I cock my head.

"Put the shirt on, Kai."

My eyes narrow, not understanding why he cares if I'm dressed. He's seen my naked body before. He must have, how else would I have gotten out of my clothes? I doubt the good doctor would have undressed me. *That means Enzo has touched me.*

Fear rakes through my body at that thought. He just touched me; he didn't violate me.

I finally take the room in. It appears to be a large office, but it is not just occupied by Enzo. Two other men stand behind him. All three men are wearing jeans and dark shirts, and I can see sweat on all of their brows. They've been working.

I recognize the two men standing by Enzo; they were the same men at Surrender with him. One of the men tries hard to avoid eye contact with me or gazing at me at all, as if he thinks looking at me will burn his retinas. The other man only looks at my eyes, ensuring his eyes never drop lower to my naked body.

A tiny smile crosses my lips. Enzo is mad because he doesn't like these men staring at my naked body—whether because he wants me to himself or because he's embarrassed by the state of my body and them knowing he wasn't the one to break me in. I don't care. I kind of like that he wants me to himself instead of sharing me with others. Unlike my last master, I won't be shared around like a whore.

Enzo's body hardens as he notices my carelessness about my body. I've had disgusting men stare at my body and violate me. I don't care that I'm making him uncomfortable now.

But my eyes return to the two men. They seem to be Enzo's right-hand men. They might have the answers I seek. They might be able to tell me why Enzo's father ordered him to kill me.

The only way I'm going to get a chance to ask is by putting clothes on so they can all stop acting like they are innocent men who have never seen a naked woman before.

I step forward and pick up the shirt, and quickly pull it over my head. It's warm like Enzo, smells like salt and sweat, and covers most of my body. I don't hate it against my skin, but I don't love it either.

"Who are you?" I ask the two men.

"I'm Langston."

"And I'm Zeke."

Enzo motions with his head, and both men disappear without a command.

Damn him. I forgot he can practically read my thoughts.

A knock on the door startles me.

Enzo's nostrils flare as he looks behind me. I turn as Dr. Gould enters.

"Miss Miller, you really should return to bed. I won't examine you now if you need time, but I would recommend an exam sooner than later if you want to ensure you heal a hundred percent back to your previous state."

Enzo rushes past me, and hurries the doctor out of the office—leaving me behind. I fold my arms across my chest as the cold nip returns. I'm used to being cool, I thrive in it, but the shakes are different. It reminds me of how weak I am.

I try to distract myself by inspecting the office. But there isn't much to look at. A large desk with multiple chairs all made of modern materials. White walls and gray floors. And of course a stellar view of the ocean from behind the desk.

I suspect every room in this house was built around the spectacular views. Views I long to erase from my head.

And then I hear their voices.

"I did what I thought was best to care for the girl. She needs immediate medical attention. It can't wait!"

"I hired you because you were the best. That you wouldn't hurt her, but it's clear you couldn't even do that right."

Muffled voices continue.

"You're fired."

My mouth falls open as Enzo returns to the office.

"You fired him?" I stutter out.

He nods.

"Why?"

"Because he wasn't very effective in his job. He's supposed to do no harm, but he hurt you."

I swallow hard. "Will you hire another doctor?"

He doesn't answer, and it's clear he hasn't decided.

"You need to put a bandaid on your hand," Enzo says, holding one out to me.

I glance down at my hand where the IV was and see blood slowly oozing out. I take the bandaid from Enzo, careful not to brush our fingertips together, and then I apply the bandaid.

"Thank you."

He smirks. "Don't thank me, Kai—for anything."

"What do you want with me?" I ask, my voice shaky, afraid of his answer. Because I can see the heat in his eyes. I already know the answer.

He shakes his head. "I want you to go upstairs to your room, keep your clothes on, and eat the food I provide you. And the next time I hire the best doctor in the world to examine you, you take the help."

He moves out of the doorway for me to leave.

"Why are you keeping your distance? Avoiding touching me?"

His body darkens as he steps closer. "Because I will *never* touch you. Never. Why would I want to claim what has already been tainted? Why would I want you?"

I feel the tears behind my eyes. I should be happy to hear he won't touch me, even if his words are harsh and cruel. He can't hurt me if he doesn't touch me. But then that means I'm nothing to him.

"Why keep me? Why keep me alive?"

"You didn't win the game. You didn't earn your answers. You are mine for as long as I want to keep you. Now go to your room and don't come down until I can no longer see every fucking bone in your body."

"So I'm a prisoner to my room?"

"Until you learn to obey the rules, yes."

I feel the sickness take hold of my body. I don't want to give in, but I don't have a choice. If I stay defiant, I will blackout.

"Go, before I'm forced to carry your body to bed again, myself."

I storm past him and then reach the stairs.

Shit.

Now I wish Enzo would really carry me upstairs, because I will have nothing left in my tank by the time I reach the top. But I'm too stubborn to return and ask for his or anyone else's help.

So I climb. It's ruthless, unforgiving, and I feel new bruises forming as I knock myself against the stairs as I move upward. But I make it.

I walk down the hallway to the bedroom he calls mine, and I stare at the bed. I won't get in that cloud of heaven.

Instead, I stumble to the farthest corner of the room from the windows, I remove the shirt, and lie down on the smooth hardwood floor. At least his home is floored with hardwood instead of carpet. I curl up on the ground, tucking my knees to my chest, and close my eyes.

Sleep will easily overcome me. But Enzo will haunt my dreams. He was the boy who saved me, only to sell me. He was my first kiss. My first taste of what falling in love could feel like. He was freedom to me. And now he's my master, who's so disgusted by me he doesn't even want me.

I thought I knew loneliness, but loneliness is only now coming for me. Because even Enzo can't hate me. I am nothing. I am no one. I should be dead, but no one will kill me. Instead, I'm trapped in this cage of gleaming light until I find a way for it all to end.

ENZO

I watched as Kai climbed the stairs with bated breath.

It took her twenty minutes to reach the top, something that should have taken her thirty-seconds to do. It took everything in my body to restrain myself, to keep my feet planted at the bottom of the stairs hidden in the shadows, instead of tossing her over my shoulder and carrying her to bed. But I can't touch her, for both our sakes. *Never again.*

If I touch her, I would fuck her, rape her, hurt her. That's a line I won't cross, no matter how my twisted brain wants me to. I won't harm her.

That's a lie. I'm hurting her by keeping her captive—by not telling her the truth.

She reaches the top, and I wait for as long as I can stomach before heading up the stairs. For one, I need a new shirt, my clothes haven't arrived yet, and the only ones I have are hanging in the closet off the room she now occupies. And two, I need to know she isn't passed out again.

I run up the stairs and creep at the doorway to the room. Kai didn't bother shutting the door, so it's easy for me to loom in the dark. She's not in the bed.

Fuck.

I walk inside, expecting to see the worst. Instead, I hear her snores.

I shake my head as I see her curled up in my shirt on the floor. I don't know what she's been through to prefer the hard floor to a comfortable bed. To prefer walking naked than be clothed. To prefer to be left alone than touched.

I want to grab a blanket from the bed and cover her. I want to support her head with a pillow. But both would wake her up, and she needs sleep above everything else.

She slept for three days straight after she first passed out. I spent most of the night holding her in her sleep, keeping her warm, as she requested when she was unconscious. I close my eyes remembering how good it felt to not be burning hot all the time. To let the rage inside me cool. To feel comforted even though she wasn't awake to hold me back.

Never again.

I leave her and head to the closet. I grab another black T-shirt and pull it over my head. And then I walk back over to Kai. She's still asleep on the floor. I need to call another doctor to monitor her. To provide an IV if she starts sleeping for days again, one who will be more cautious when she tries to persuade Kai to do anything.

I need to touch her. To feel her. She's like a drug pulling me to her. Too bad I can't have her. Too bad she's going to be trapped here for the rest of her days. Because she could be the one person who could save me.

My fingers graze her hollow cheeks, and I suck in a breath at the power that pulses through me at the connection.

Fuck, I could live off this feeling.

I can't keep doing this. If I keep touching her when she's unconscious, I won't be able to resist caressing her when she's awake. And the faster I can get her to trust that I won't touch her, or hurt her beyond keeping her here, the faster she will heal and settle into her new life. Then I can leave her in Westcott's trust. Then I can be free of her, forever.

I take the stairs two at a time as I try to put my thoughts of Kai behind me. Not an easy task.

Langston leans against the doorframe leading to the living room. His arms are crossed across his chest, his muscles bulging and revealing tattoos wrapped in black ink around his bicep. His lips wear a knowing look.

"What?" I grumble.

"Nothing." Langston smiles.

I roll my eyes. I don't have time for whatever games he wants to play.

"Who's the girl?" he asks.

I glare at him. "You don't get to ask about my life."

I storm past him and head to the kitchen to get a bottle of water to calm me down. I feel like I'm about to boil over and no one is safe when I let my temper loose. I can't control what happens. I'm worse than a hurricane running through town. I destroy everything in my path; I don't leave anyone behind.

"Actually, I think we've earned the right to know everything about your personal life, boss," Zeke says entering the kitchen.

Great, they are ganging up on me.

I down a bottle of water, crush the plastic, and toss it on the ground, my anger palatable in the air.

"Are you running a hospital or something now? Taking in the sick? Or is she something more?" Langston asks.

Both men stand on either side of the island in the center of the kitchen. I stand between them. *Trapped.*

Kai is more. She's everything. Everything I ever wanted. Everything I ever dreamed about: her strength, her influence over me, her resilience.

She's also everything I hate. She revealed my own weaknesses. She's the only one who could take away the power I've gained. And I won't go back to being the powerless boy I was when I met her.

My eyes cut back and forth between the two men. They are my best men. And my best friends. Not always a good mix. Since they are my friends, they think they can pull shit like this. Try to force me to talk to them.

I've known them since we were kids. Zeke was always the brute force in our little group. He could kick anyone's ass with his size alone. Langston was never as gifted with muscle as Zeke, although he's worked hard and gained plenty of muscle, he was more of the brains. He preferred security and doing surveillance. And I was the leader of the group. The decision maker even before I had any power in my father's organization.

I blow hot steam from my nose as I glare between the two men.

Langston laughs, throwing his head back like it's the funniest thing in the world.

"What's happening?" Zeke asks confused.

"Black here, has it bad," Langston force out between laughs.

"Has what bad?" Zeke asks.

I groan. "Langston thinks I have the hots for the broken girl currently occupying my bedroom. I don't. And even if I did, it doesn't matter. I don't fuck another man's goods."

Langston cocks his head. "There is so much more to this story. And I'm dying to know. But right now, we have a decision to make. Reko has been breaking the rules. He's been smuggling drugs without your consent. He needs to be dealt with."

I nod, my blood cooling as I think about work and let the taunting about Kai go.

"Who is his lead man?" I ask.

"Warwick," Langston answers.

"Good, I know the man. He's a regular at Surrender. He will be easy to snatch."

"And what are we going to do when we snatch him?" Zeke asks, I can hear the itch in his voice to do some damage.

"Torture him until he either gives up his boss or he's dead. Either way, it will send a message."

"How long?" Langston asks.

I smile. "Two weeks." I need out of this fucking house. Westcott will be able to handle Kai for two weeks, especially in her weakened state. And I need to get to the ocean. We always do our business on the sea. It's easier to clean up and dispose of the bodies. We throw a lavish yacht party while doing business. It gives us a good alibi, and we can continue to learn about what goes on in the city and on the sea, my jurisdictions.

I don't love the party part, but it's the easiest way to get information out of people. Surrender is good, but the yachts are better. At Surrender, people aren't really trapped. On the yachts, they have no place to go until I say. Not unless they want to take a dip in the water.

But there is another purpose to wanting to be gone. I decide against my better judgment to pay Jarod a visit. Repay him for how he took care of Kai.

Langston and Zeke both smile. They love the water as much as I do.

"Maybe after a day or two of being apart from the girl, we'll be able to get more information out of mister romantic here," Langston teases.

I growl, threatening him.

But Langston runs off, like he knows exactly what he's doing to me. He knows me too well. I've never brought a woman here. This is our place. It's as much Zeke's and Langston's as it is mine. We have all crashed here at various times. But we have one rule, it's just us. No girls. I broke that rule, and they know it was for a very real purpose.

I've broken too many rules for Kai so far. By my rules, she should have died a long time ago. I won't break any more rules for Kai. From now on, I do everything by the book.

♡

"What did this Jarod guy do?" Langston asks suspiciously.

He destroyed what was mine—Kai. He brutalized her, burned her flesh, stabbed her, broke her bones, raped her. He did so many unthinkable things no man should ever do to a woman. But I don't want Langston or Zeke to know the real purpose for tracking Jarod down for the past two weeks.

"He destroyed some property of mine to the north," I say

keeping my words vague so I'm not technically lying to my best friend. I hate lying if I can avoid it.

My words seem to be enough for Langston. Neither he nor Zeke need much to follow my orders. They trust me with their lives. They will do anything I ask with zero questions.

"So what's the plan?" Zeke asks as we crouch down near the railing of my own yacht staring across the black sea to Jarod's yacht.

"We sneak onto the boat silently, then take out every man until we find Jarod," I answer.

"And when we have Jarod?" Zeke asks.

"I send a message that no one touches what is mine," I say.

Zeke and Langston's exchange knowing glances. They are more than capable of getting their hands dirty without me being involved. My father would have let his men carry out his orders, but I prefer to be more hands on. It sends a better message. And this is personal.

Langston stares across to the boat. A light flickers off. It's time. This is as unguarded as the yacht will ever get. There are only three of us and who knows how many men on Jarod's yacht, but we will win. I could have sent Langston or Zeke by themselves on this mission, and they would have slaughtered everyone on board with ease. The three of us doing this job together is overkill.

"Let's go," I say as I silently jump into the water with the tiniest of splashes.

They both follow as quietly into the ocean. And then we begin swimming, careful with our movements to hide in the waves and avoid making a wake, but quick and efficient.

I reach the ladder leading up the back of the boat first. I ascend, my blood boiling with need for revenge. I should have brought Kai with me. Let her take out the man who hurt her so viciously, but that might lead her to believe I am a good person. I'm not. I'm not doing this for her. I'm doing this for me, so I can sleep better at night. I should have never let Jarod touch her in the first place.

I hit the deck of the yacht, and pull my silenced gun out from my waistband. I don't find a guard right away. Amateurs.

I don't wait for Langston or Zeke to come up the ladder. I start moving like a ninja in the night. My body blends with the shadows and creaks of the boat as it rocks gently in the sea.

My first target doesn't appear until I walk inside. A man asleep at the helm. I shake my head as I shoot him in the head. He almost deserves to die solely for being so poor at his job, not just for having a part in hurting Kai.

I hear a couple quick fires in the distance. Zeke and Langston have boarded the ship and taken out their first men.

I smile.

I always come alive in moments like this. When I'm hunting deserving men. Giving them their justice. I don't always kill evil men. Sometimes the men I kill are just mixed up in the wrong business, but the cruelest are my favorite to end.

I creep deeper into the yacht and open the first bedroom door. A man asleep in the bed. I sigh as I pull the trigger. This is almost too easy. I really should have come alone.

Another door, this man is up, having heard the sounds of the men dropping and our guns firing softly. He draws his gun, but he's too slow as I shoot him in the chest. He falls with a thud.

I open door after door and find no one. I open one door that sends chills down my spine. The room is empty—not even a bed. I should leave, not step inside, but I do. It pulls me in.

It's then I see the scratches on the door, walls, floor. I see the marks where a body hit the wall. Blood stains the floor. I trace my fingers over the scratches on the door.

Fingernails.

Rage fills me. This is the room Kai stayed in. The room Jarod kept her in. Tortured her in. No wonder she hates my bed. She's been used to the floor.

I storm out. A hurricane force beats inside me, yearning to do damage to the man who hurt Kai. How the fuck could I let this happen? How could I have been the reason for this cruelty?

Because I was a stupid, fucking coward.

"Zeke has him tied in the room on the end," Langston says when I enter the hallway.

"Good, stand guard on deck," I say.

I throw the door open and see Jarod tied to a chair. His eyes burn in confusion when he sees me. Sweat covers his forehead and fear rakes his body.

Good, he should fear me.

"Black," his voice trembles as if he's seeing the devil himself.

"Good, you know who I am. I didn't think you would."

I give a look to Zeke, and he departs us immediately.

"Black, I'm sorry. I didn't—"

I punch him hard in the jaw. I don't want to hear his apologies. His body careens as he falls sideways to the floor.

He spits out blood. "I didn't do anything wrong. I was just following orders. I don't deserve to die for doing what was commanded."

He's right. He doesn't deserve to die for following orders. "Too bad I don't believe in being fair. You touched the girl, that alone means you deserve to die."

His pupils dilate in terror.

I grin.

I love this part.

I spot the tape Zeke used to tie Jarod to the chair. I tear off a piece and cover his mouth with it. I don't want to hear him speak anymore. His muffled screams will be enough to excite me.

"You deserve to feel everything you did to Kai. Too bad I don't have years to spend torturing you. A few hours will have to do."

I kick him hard in the stomach. He gasps and wretches. Possibly even vomiting in his mouth.

"I'm sure you kicked Kai when she was down. I've seen the bruises and broken ribs."

I kick three more times for good measure as his body slams against the wall, breaking him free of the chair, but his hands are still trapped behind his back. He stumbles to his feet.

Good, I'll enjoy the fight more now that he's standing.

I slam my fist into his jaw over and over in quick succession. His face coloring and swelling before my eyes as blood swells from the cuts.

"Did you punch her like this? Bruising her body repeatedly? Did you enjoy it like I am?"

He twists away, but he has nowhere to escape.

"What about stabbing?"

His eyebrows raise as I pull a knife from my pocket and extend it. He tries to retreat back, but I grab his arm and thrust the sharp blade into his shoulder and twist.

He cries out, but it's muffled.

"How many times did you stab her? Three, four, five times?" I ask, pulling the knife out before jabbing it back into his other shoulder, extracting more vengeance.

Tears start down his eyes. Stirring more energy in me to continue as I know how many tears he pulled from Kai. Zero. She would never cry in front of this monster. She kept them all buried inside. One day she will explode, and I will curse myself when those tears fall.

"You burned her too?"

I find a lighter on his nightstand and hold the flame to his neck. He screams as the flame sears his skin—music to my ears.

For hours I continue the torture well into the night until I've lost track of time. I let the devil live inside me all in the name of getting revenge for the pain Kai lived, but I don't do it for her. I do it for me. Because the evil inside me needs a life to defeat.

Jarod lays broken on the floor. A mess of blood, tears, and piss.

I lean down close to his ear, knowing he is seconds away from begging for a conclusion. For me to kill him.

"I think we've covered everything you did to her, except one. Rape."

He sobs and closes his eyes in fear.

"Don't worry; I'm not a sick fuck like you. I won't rape you."

I pull the gun from my waistband. "But I am done with you."

I fire—killing him. And closing the biggest mistake of my life. I let this man hurt Kai, and now I've rectified the situation. It won't matter to Kai. She'll still think I'm a monster for what I did, and rightfully so. But at least now I took back what was mine.

CHAPTER 19
KAI

Enzo's gone.

He has been. For almost three weeks.

He vanished. It's like he wasn't even here. I imagined him.

No.

He was real. He is very, very real. Otherwise, I wouldn't be trapped in this fucking, gorgeous beach house. I shouldn't complain. I'm being treated better than I have ever been treated in my entire life. And that includes before I was kidnapped.

My father had nothing. And my mother died when I was little, leaving behind a legacy of hospital bills for us to spend our entire life paying off.

And for the first time in a long time, I don't know what my future holds. When I was living with my father in his trailer, I knew what my life would entail. I would live in the trailer with him, and clean yachts for a living. Until one day the debt collectors would come and demand more from me. And then I would sell my body to pay the bills. I knew my destiny, and it didn't look bright. It wouldn't include school or a career or a husband and kids. My life outlook was bleak, so I never dreamed.

And then I was kidnapped, and my future changed. I no longer worked to put food on the table. I was lucky to get a scrap of bread on that yacht. I knew what my future was. Death.

But now that I'm trapped in a house on the beach, I have no idea what my future holds. I can guess...rape, beatings, death. Maybe a little bit of everything I thought my future held before. But if my future here does include those things, it will be behind the glow of the modern walls of this beach house. It's too pretty for anyone to think anything heinous happens here.

And Enzo... I have no clue what to think about that man. He's dark, dangerous, and powerful. I should be scared of him. He's worse than any master who could ever own me. Killed more men than an army. But he hasn't hurt me. He specifically said he would never touch me. *Never.*

But then why am I trapped here?

Why keep me?

Isn't that the question? One I'm afraid I will never get an answer to.

A light tapping rattles on the door. It's Dr. Miranda. She's been overseeing my progress these last few weeks. And when I say overseeing, I mean overseeing. She's never touched me, not even to place an IV. She did convince me to use one for the first week to increase my strength and nutrition without overwhelming my stomach. But instead of inserting it herself, she taught me how.

"Come in," I say, knowing she will stand outside my door all day and never enter until I give her permission.

The door creaks open as Dr. Miranda pokes her head inside.

She smiles at me sweetly when she sees me sitting in my usual corner of the room on the floor. She doesn't berate me or tell me my bones would heal easier in the bed. She also never asks how I'm doing—realizing that even if I'm doing better, I'm still in a dangerous place and that isn't an encouraging question to ask.

Instead, she sits cross-legged on the floor in front of me.

"How many hours did you sleep last night?"

"Three or four."

She nods, showing no reaction to my answer. She never does.

"Still getting nightmares?"

"Yes, I woke up three times from them and after the last one, I just decided to stay awake." I went from sleeping twenty-four hours a day from exhaustion to only sleeping three. My body doesn't know how to react. So I go from one polar extreme to the next.

"Have you been able to keep food down?"

"Yes."

She never asks how much I've been eating. I eat enough, but not as much as she'd like, I'm sure.

"How is walking?"

"Still difficult, but the swelling in my foot has gone down."

"Would you like to show me?"

I bring my foot out from beneath me and show her. She nods at the progress.

"How is your pain overall?"

"Manageable."

Miranda looks to my bottle of painkillers that have been sitting on the nightstand. I haven't taken a single one. Not because I enjoy the pain, but because I'm afraid they will knock my frail body out. It's one of the reasons I don't sleep well either.

"Would you like me to prescribe you something to help you sleep?"

"No."

She purses her lips, obviously wanting to tell me something, but not sure she should say it. She doesn't like pushing me. I don't know if it's because Enzo threatened her, or if she just realizes if she pushes she might lose any progress we have made.

"What?" I ask.

"I was thinking about your sleep. Sleep is the most important part of your healing process. Of course, I would like you to eat more. I would like you to take more medication and get some x-rays done. But if I had to choose one thing to focus on for you, it would be sleep."

I sigh. "I can't control when my nightmares come or how much sleep I get. And I won't take anything. It doesn't make me feel safe."

She nods. "I'm not asking you to take anything."

"Then what are you asking?"

"I'm asking if there is anything that would make sleeping safer for you?"

I look at her wide-eyed. I'm pretty sure there is something, although I would never ask for him. I'm not even sure if it was a dream or reality. But the first few nights I was here and slept for hours uninterrupted, Enzo slept with me. He held my body all night, keeping me warm without overpowering me. I've never slept so peacefully, but maybe it was just because I was so exhausted and it had nothing to do with him.

"Maybe a stronger lock on the door would help you? Blackout curtains? Sleep during the daylight and staying awake at night, if that is more what you are used to. Take a relaxing bath before you sleep. All I ask is that you try to get more sleep. It's the most important thing for your body to heal."

"I will try."

"Good, thank you."

Miranda studies me a second longer. "For what it's worth, Kai, you are healing. Your cheeks are filling back out into light shades of pink, your eyes aren't empty holes anymore, and you have fat and muscle returning to your body. I know the healing process can be frustratingly slow, but be patient with yourself. You will get better. And you will heal in ways you didn't even realize you needed healing —just be patient."

I nod.

She stands. "If you need anything at all, give me a call. Mr. Westcott has my number. Otherwise, I'll come back in a couple of days."

Miranda doesn't wait for a goodbye or acknowledgment from me at all. She leaves without expectation of a hug or a handshake or a verbal goodbye. I like her as much as I can like a person, which isn't much, but I'm thankful to have someone watching over me and ensuring that I'm healing. Albeit slowly and on my own terms.

I lean my head back against the wall. I know what comes next, and I'm not sure I can handle it. I wish everyone were as gentle and understanding as the doctor.

A loud tapping rattles the door.

I don't have to welcome him in, he just enters.

"Good morning, Miss Miller," Westcott says with a large tray of food.

"It's Kai," I say for the millionth time.

He ignores me and sets the tray on the nightstand.

"I brought you pancakes, eggs, bacon, sausage, and toast. There is also a side of fruit. A smoothie, yogurt, and orange juice. And then I brought you both coffee and tea since I wasn't sure which you preferred and you still haven't told me." He looks resentful.

I haven't told him because I don't even know which one I prefer. Not anymore.

"Would you like to eat out on the balcony today? It's a beautiful day. It would be a shame to waste the sunshine. Vitamin D is essential for healing you know."

I frown. If it were so important, then the doctor would have recommended it.

He sighs when I don't answer and lifts the tray to set it down on the spot on the floor next to me, knowing this is the only way he'll get any food in me, if it's within my reach.

I take a piece of the bacon off the plate and start nibbling on it. Its probably not the best for my stomach, but it tastes good.

"Is there anything else I can get or arrange for you today?" he asks.

"My freedom."

He ignores me as he always does.

"Actually..." I sit up straighter. "You can do something for me."

His eyes grow big and an automatic smile forms.

"Can you arrange for blackout curtains to be installed in the room? And several locks on the door that can only be locked from the inside."

He frowns.

"Westcott? Can that be arranged?"

"Yes, of course. Mr. Black wanted you to have anything you requested."

"Except my freedom. I'm to stay locked in this room?"

"The door is never locked. You are not a prisoner in this room as much as you think you are. You are welcome downstairs or on the balcony or to visit the beach if you so wish."

I smirk. I can go anywhere on the grounds where they can keep an eye on me.

"When is Enzo coming home?"

Westcott doesn't answer me. But I think it's because he doesn't know, not that he was told not to tell me.

"Anything else, ma'am?"

I shake my head.

Westcott leaves me to try to muster down some of the food and drink. I decide to test the coffee and tea today. I should know which one I prefer. I taste both, and my stomach feels like hurling, the bitter taste they both leave in my mouth is too much for my bland tastebuds.

Gross, how do people drink either? I know some people want an IV of coffee hooked up to them, but I don't understand why.

I sigh. I don't like coffee or tea. I'm not sure I can like anything anymore.

I nibble more on the bacon. I guess I like the bacon.

I continue my best to eat, and within an hour there are men in the room installing curtains and more locks on the door. I try not to hide and shrink away when they enter the room, but I can't help it.

They won't hurt me, I repeat to myself. *They won't hurt me.*

As soon as the men leave, I run to the door and close all the locks. Each one is different and uses a different mechanism to close along a different part of the door. Some high, some low, some in the middle. It would take a lot to get through the door.

Then I move to the curtains and close them tight. The room descends into blackness.

I smile.

Finally.

I might be able to sleep.

I go back to my corner of the room where it's now dark enough to try to sleep even though it's the middle of the day. And that's what I do. I sleep.

♡

My body is shivering uncontrollably in the tiny room the men left me in. It's so fucking cold. I'm used to the cold. My body always runs cold, and our trailer doesn't have heat. Not that we need it much in Miami, but we can't afford jackets or blankets either.

I'm somewhere much colder than Miami.

I was unconscious when they brought me into the room.

The room heaves.

What the hell?

We keep rocking, and it takes me a minute to realize I'm on a boat. The water—my favorite thing in the world, and also my enemy.

I hear men's voices outside of my room, and I remember.

I was kidnapped.

I was sold.

And now a man owns me.

I don't have to be told why a man would buy a woman. I know the purpose they have for me.

The door opens, with a loud thud as it slams against the wall. A toothy man steps inside. He doesn't look particularly strong. He doesn't have defined muscles, but he's a heavy-set man, that could throw his weight around and hurt me.

"It's time to break in the new whore."

No.

My shivering changes to uncontrollable trembles. My body is not prepared to be raped. I can't. I don't want to become a shell of a woman who can't function after this, if I ever get free.

The man comes into the room, and I inch backward, looking for a weapon, for anything I can use to hurt him. I find nothing.

He smirks, like he knows what I'm doing.

I can't hurt him, but I can run.

That's what I do as he moves forward. I'm faster than him, so I run around his body. I dart out of the room, not sure what my next step is. I just won't let them take me easily. I won't let them hurt or violate me.

I make it to the hallway, and I see another man with arms crossed smiling at me. "I win the bet. I told you she would try to run."

"Fine, fine," the man from the room says as he closes in from behind me.

My heart races, and my body continues to shake violently like that is going to help. I'm more scared than I realized.

No, don't let them have my fear. *I will fight, and they might still claim my body, but that's it. I will keep everything else. I will not be a broken, scared girl when I leave here.*

I force my body to still, which only makes the toothy man smile brighter.

"You're a fighter. Good, it's been a while since we had a fighter. It will be more fun when you finally break. I give you a month."

"Nah, I give her three. She's more determined than you think," the man behind me says.

Each man walks closer, and I don't know what to do. Which man is weaker? Which do I attack and hope I can break free of?

I don't get to make a decision. Both of them grab an arm at the same time.

I fight—viciously. My legs start kicking, my arms flail, my nails dig into their skin, and I try to bite their skin with my teeth.

I can do this all day.

Until the fist makes contact with my jaw.

Black dots surround my vision as a pain in my head overwhelms me. I've never felt anything like this before. And I know I can't keep fighting. Not when the fight is so unfair.

They can do whatever they want to me. I'm weak. I have no strength.

They start pulling me to a different room—one filled with men. The shakes return, and my eyes widen. I thought only one man would take my virginity. I thought only one man would rip me apart, violate, and ruin me. But there are six men in the room.

I don't know what they plan, but I'm outnumbered. I turned seventeen yesterday. Still too young for anything like this to happen. But being too young won't stop it.

I don't know what I expect. But I don't expect this. I feel a kick in my side, then a slap to the face, followed by being thrown into a wall.

When they said 'break' they literally meant break.

And my body starts the slow process of turning into a shattered pile of bones.

Another hit.

Another kick.

A yank of my wrist.
I try not to cry out, to keep my voice and pain to myself, but I can't.
I scream.

MY EYES FLY OPEN. *IT'S A DREAM. IT WAS JUST A DREAM.*

I pant heavily as cold sweat covers my body.

My body burns as it did that night. I don't know if that night was the roughest they were on me, but it was the hardest night for me. It was the beginning. The not knowing what to expect. The unfamiliarity of the agony with each hit, putting fresh wounds onto my body for the first time. That was what destroyed me.

I scream at the pain. Even though I'm awake, I can still feel it, still hear their grunts, still see their smug smiles brighten at the enjoyment they got from hurting me.

"Kai." A loud pounding comes at the door.

I still.

"Kai, open the door."

Enzo.

He's back.

And I don't know how to feel.

He came back. That should make me shrink in terror, but I like that he came back. It means I'm not alone anymore.

I should go open the door and let him in, but I'm pissed. At him for keeping me captive. For leaving me alone. For letting me endure my nightmares when he could easily stop them by sleeping here with me.

So I don't open the door.

Enzo doesn't get to see my pain, my tears. He doesn't get to see what leaving me did to me. Because as much as I want to be free, this is the only place I have a chance of healing.

I pull my knees tight to my chest as I rock myself in the corner, trying to calm myself. I can't. My icy veins are pulsing so hard I'm afraid my heart is going to give out from the speed.

I close my eyes even though the room is already dark from the blackout curtains. The darkness often saves me, but it can't save me from this.

I hear the door handle rattle as Enzo tries to get inside.

I don't know why he wants into my room so badly. *Is he pissed I had men install locks on the door? Did his business dealing go badly and now he wants to blow off steam on me?*

He can't get inside. There are six locks on the door, none which have keyholes on the other side. They are all various chains and bolts keeping anyone and everyone out.

I'm safe in here.

My eyes focus in on the locks. *I'm safe, but then why do I feel anything but secure?*

Sweat continues to ooze from my pores like my body is trying to expel the nightmares through my skin. My mind tries to shut off, but it can't block out the men. And I can't get rid of the shakes that ricochet through my body.

The door handle stops rattling. I exhale. Enzo realized he couldn't get in.

I'm alone.

And I don't know how to feel.

I'm alone to face the demons in the dark. Alone to heal myself. *What if I can't heal myself? What if I just stop eating and drinking until my body finally gives out?*

Dr. Miranda wouldn't allow me to do that. Neither would Westcott or even Enzo. Enzo would hire someone to break through the locks and force feed me before he let me wither away into nothing. I still have my suspicions that the only reason I'm here is so he can heal me and then get more money when he sells me.

But for now, I get one more day alone.

I hear a loud crack.

I jump.

The door.

Another pound against the door, followed by another crack.

Shit.

I grip my knees tighter as my teeth begin to chatter.

Pound.

Pound.

Pound.

Then crack.

The door splits along the edge. Enzo pushes the door open wide enough for him to step through.

He's dressed in a black suit; his tie has loosened around his neck like he just came home from a normal day at the office. But that's where the normalcy stops. His dark hair is ruffled and longer than the last time I saw him; he could use a haircut. The shadow of hair on his sharp jawline has thickened. Sweat trickles down his forehead.

Blood.

Tiny droplets of blood rest on the collar of his shirt, tie, and cufflinks.

What have you been doing Enzo? And do you plan on doing the same thing to me?

I had so many questions of why he wanted to break down the door before. Most ended in something horrible happening when he made it through the door. But now seeing his face, those worries vanish.

Enzo is shattered.

His eyes are dark with fear, his brow wrinkled with worry, and his lips tight with anxiety.

He's concerned about me—about what he would find when he opened the door.

My lips open to comfort him, to tell him no one was torturing me, it was just a nightmare, but I can't, because I'm not fine.

His eyes travel over every inch of my body, inspecting, trying to figure out where I'm hurt and where I've healed.

We both continue to stare at each other, like whoever stops first loses.

Neither of us knows what to say.

I don't offer up any information about what I'm going through, and he doesn't tell me whose blood stains his clothes.

But despite the connection of our gazes, I long for more. To understand this man, who for one second shows he cares only to show later how monstrous he can be.

His body wants me. I can see his cock lengthen and harden in his pants at the sight of me this way. Sweaty, scared, and broken.

That's how he likes his women.

Yet, he denies himself the one thing he seems to want—*me*.

Finally, he swallows, and our connection is lost. He glances around the room at the curtains and then to the locks that were preventing his entry.

"I see you did some redecorating while I was gone."

I snarl.

He ignores my response and cocks his head to the side.

"You are supposed to be dressed."

"No, I'm supposed to be dressed when I leave this room," I snap back.

He smiles a little at my firey response.

"There was no need to barricade yourself in this room."

"Why not? I was told not to leave this room until I had fully healed. Might as well ensure no one gets in. Although, I see my plan backfired."

He winces at my words, and I explode.

"You're a fucking asshole! You've kept me locked in this fucking room, this house, for weeks!" I stand feeling my anger from him leaving me, and the nightmare overtakes any other thoughts.

He doesn't blink as I yell. He just lets me berate him.

"You don't tell me fucking anything! You just give me mixed signal after mixed signal. You were supposed to kill me but didn't. You should have sold me or raped me by now, but you haven't. You want me to heal, yet you spend your time yelling or ignoring me. You're a fucking coward! Nothing has changed since you were a boy."

"Are. You. Done?" I feel his temper rising with each word, but he doesn't let it free. This man is practiced in self-control.

"No, I'm not fucking done!"

I realize I've taken several steps toward him as my anger took control of me. I'm dangerously close. Close enough he could touch me. Last time he did, I passed out for days. I won't let that happen again. I know how much his touch burns.

But I won't retreat either.

The shiny piece of metal captures my attention. He has a gun.

None of my previous captors had a gun. At least they never wore their guns around me, as if they sensed I would steal it if the opportunity presented itself.

Here's my chance.

I'm risking everything by doing this.

I'm out of practice with pickpocketing.

My movements are slower than usual.

He could touch me in the process.

Or realize what I'm reaching for and shoot me before I have the chance to shoot him, if he no longer thinks I'm worth keeping alive.

But I have to try.

"You're a cruel, evil monster. Don't think I didn't notice the blood of your victim on your clothes."

"Who said the man I killed was a victim?"

I inch closer, keeping my gaze on his instead of the gun. "Because no one deserves to die by your hand. You aren't God."

He smirks. "To most women, I am. Any woman who's had the pleasure of spending a night in my bed has called me God over and over."

I hesitate. I have no doubt Enzo is good in bed with a willing partner. My mouth waters at the thought of how he might be in bed. Powerful, strong, and merciless. He would ensure his partner came, while also taking everything he wanted from her. Fucking her harder than she's ever been fucked, spreading her wider, pushing her beyond her limits. There would be spanking, a rough taking, and rope to tie her up like they were in some Fifty Shades of Grey novel.

A willing partner is the key. *I wouldn't be willing? Would I?*

I snatch the gun before I answer my silent question. I take a step back at the same time as I aim the gun at Enzo.

He doesn't move. He doesn't offer his surrender or try to take the gun from me, even though I'm sure he could easily.

"Do it, pull the trigger. Put me out of my misery," he says.

His misery?

He doesn't know what misery feels like. He can't with a body like his, a mind that has been through schooling, and a company, albeit an illegal organization, he runs that makes him millions.

"Don't tempt me. I should. You are not my master."

He shakes his head. "I'm not your master. No one could control such a creature like you. You are like the sea; you can never truly be owned by any man." His words seem to sadden him, like he's just now coming to this realization.

I can't kill him.

Just as he couldn't kill me.

But I can kill myself.

I change the direction of the gun. I point it toward my heart.

One squeeze and I'll be gone. Even if I miss my heart, my body couldn't take the blood loss.

I see Enzo's body tighten. He doesn't tell me to stop, but every muscle in his body is pulling, forcing him to stay when he wants to snatch the gun from my hands.

I sigh.

I can't fucking kill myself. Not after everything I've survived.

I drop the gun.

He doesn't go to pick it up. Instead, he walks to the bathroom. When he returns, he has a wet washcloth and a glass of water.

He holds them both out to me.

I take them carefully before taking a seat back in my corner of the room. I use the washcloth to wipe the sweat from my body, and then I drink the water.

He watches me carefully until I'm lying on the floor again, and then he exhales sharply.

"Can you at least put a shirt on around me?"

"Huh?"

"Just...fuck. I know for whatever ridiculous reason, you feel more comfortable naked than wearing clothes, but I just can't—I can't."

"You can't look at how disgusting I am?" I spout my anger.

He rubs his neck. "I can't look at how attracted I am to your brokenness."

My eyes widen at his admission. I knew he was attracted to my pain, but now I've confirmed it.

"I'm twisted, Kai. I'm not your savior, and I'm not your monster. I may have been the boy who saved you only to turn into the savage who destroyed your life. But now, all I want is for you to disappear again like before."

Shit.

"I'm not going to sell you. Though sometimes we don't get what we wish for."

His eyes bury into mine, and I can feel everything. His lust at wanting me, his fight at holding back. And his desire to go hunt and kill the man who hurt me. Enzo Black may be a monster, but he may be the kind that protects me instead of hurts me—at least this new version of him. I can see the regret in his eyes at selling me, but I can't forgive him. I can never forgive him.

Never.

He seems to regret that too.

But I can't make his life easier. I won't wear a shirt, because it will make sleep harder, even if I'm tempting his self-control. Even if I'm risking him fucking me by exposing my body to him.

I lay down in the corner, naked.

He sighs.

"What am I going to do with you, Kai?" he says to himself.

I'm broken, you don't have a choice of what to do with me. Just let me go. Stop hurting me.

I expect him to leave—find a different room to sleep in.

Instead, he starts removing his clothes.

Shoes, then tie.

Then the slow unbuttoning of his shirt, until his rippled body appears. And then his pants slide down his thick legs.

I expect him to stop.

He doesn't.

He removes his boxer briefs.

My eyes burst, and my heart pumps wildly at the sight of his thick, long cock. It's only partially erect, but it's the most glorious thing I've ever seen.

"What are you doing?" my body freezes. He's told me many times he won't fuck me. Or even touch me. He's disgusted and turned on at the same time. *But then why is he naked in my room?*

"I'm going to sleep. I prefer to sleep naked too. If you get to sleep naked, then so do I."

I frown.

"This isn't your room."

He rolls his eyes. "Are you going to be able to sleep without me here?"

I flame. "What?! You are one cocky ass if you think I can only sleep with you here."

He raises an eyebrow at my explosion. "The last time I stayed with you, you slept for three days straight. How much sleep have you gotten since I was gone?"

I don't answer him.

"That's what I thought."

I watch in horror as he pulls the pillows and blankets from the bed and starts making himself a cot on the floor next to my spot.

"You really don't need to be here," I say.

"I do. I need you healed."

"So you can fuck me?"

"No," his eyes sear.

"So you can sell me?"

He groans. "I'm not going through this with you again." He fluffs his pillow and then lies down on the pile of covers and blankets. But doesn't cover himself. His perfect round ass sticks straight up in the air.

"I'll have a new door and locks installed for you in the morning."

"You're not mad I had them installed?"

"No."

"Why?"

He shrugs. "This is your room now; you can do whatever you want with it."

"Because I'm never leaving this room?"

He doesn't answer, which means his answer is yes.

I sigh and decide not to continue our circle of usual conversation any longer.

"Sleep, Kai."

I curl up on the floor watching him as he closes his eyes. He looks so peaceful lying on top of the covers like that. I don't ask why he doesn't cover up. I know how hot he runs. He doesn't need covers to be warm.

I'm the one who needs covers, but I can't tolerate them.

I need to be warmed.

Enzo could warm you. But I won't ever ask or risk the burn I felt before.

I'm alone.

Always alone.

I close my eyes and try to sleep, but I already know what I'll dream about, and in some way it will be a worse nightmare. One of the only things that kept me sane all those years was Enzo. I'd dream of him, his kiss, his body. I'd imagine his cock as I rode him. I'd imagine the look he would give me, the want. I would fantasize about him saving me, fucking me when the other men were touching me.

Enzo saved me more than once in these last few years, and now that I've seen his real cock, I've seen the glaze of his eyes as he imagines fucking me, I won't be able to stop fantasizing about him. Even though I can never have him. Even though he's the worst kind of man, he still saved me numerous times in my dreams—once for real. As much as he's a monster, he will always be my savior.

I can pretend I can never forgive him for selling me, but he did it to save my life. To give me a chance to stay alive. He was hiding me from someone more dangerous than him. And someday soon, I will get my answers.

CHAPTER 20
ENZO

Kai's screams will forever live in my head.

I always thought the next time I'd hear her scream was with me thrusting in her tight cunt. But that will only ever happen in my dreams. I won't hurt her.

Instead, the scream I heard hit me to my core. I thought someone had broken into the house and was torturing, raping Kai.

My feet have never flown so fast up the stairs, determined to kill the intruder for touching what was mine. But I was met with a door that wouldn't open. I couldn't protect her.

I chewed Westcott out big time for allowing Kai to install such locks on the door, even though I knew why he did it, and it was the right move. Then again, I couldn't stand to not be able to save and protect her from whatever devil was on the other side of the door.

Breaking down the door was easy when I had that much adrenaline and willpower running through my veins.

And then I saw Kai. Alone. No torture was happening, at least not in the present. It was a nightmare.

A nightmare I couldn't save her from.

Fuck, fuck, fuck.

How did I let this happen? How did I let her get hurt? And why have I grown so soft as to care for her when I've only ever cared about my own survival? This girl threatens my survival more than anything.

I will never forget the agony on her face, and her naked body still bearing every mark the bastard laid on her. It makes me want to return Jarod from the depths of the ocean only to kill him again for hurting her.

Then she found my gun. I wish she would have pulled the trigger and ended my life, but when she turned it on herself, I realized how much more she mattered to me than I was aware. *Why do I think her life is worth more than mine?*

It made me admit how much I want her, even though I'm fucked up. I'm the worst possible man in the entire world to want her. I thought telling her one bit of the truth would warn her to stay away and hide her body from me. Of course, Kai did no such thing.

And then I did the stupidest thing I've done in a while. I decided to sleep on the floor next to her. It's the middle of the day, but it doesn't matter. The sun no longer shines in due to the blackout curtains. And my sleep schedule is fucked up. I work more nights than days. I'm used to sleeping in the daylight.

I slept on the ground next to her; it was purgatory. Not just because the hardwood floor is the most uncomfortable place to sleep, even with my pile of blankets, but because I was so near to Kai and couldn't touch her.

The last time I slept next to her, I got to touch her. I got to feel her cool skin, and it slowed my unsteady heart, cooled my veins, and relaxed me. Being so close, but not being able to press against her was excruciating, even if it was for both our benefits. It's not some-thing I want to repeat.

But even that wasn't the worst part. The worst part was worrying she might have another nightmare—one I couldn't save her from.

It's obvious from spending time with her she doesn't want to be touched. And I'm happy to oblige. *But what if she's in the middle of a nightmare and it's the only way to pull her out? Then what would I do?*

Thankfully, I don't have to answer that question, because Kai sleeps undisturbed—whether from my presence or sheer exhaustion.

I watch her sleep. It's been almost eight hours since I've laid down next to her. She's been asleep the whole time. While I've struggled to keep my eyes closed for more than an hour at a time. I don't need much sleep, I've adapted to survive. You don't get to sleep much when dangerous men with guns are hunting you down. And I'd rather watch her sleep than rest my own eyes.

Kai coils her body tightly into a coil; I'm sure that's the only thing keeping her remotely warm. I'm desperate to cover her with a blanket to warm her if she doesn't let me touch her. But I resist.

I try to look past the bruises and scars, but I want to feel every one. I deserve to feel the pain for what I did.

I deserved that pain, not her.

I was the coward.

I chose my life over hers.

If only I could change the outcome.

"Enzo," she whispers.

My attention draws back to her. I expect her to wake, but she doesn't. She's still asleep, dreaming about me.

"Yes, Enzo, like that."

Wait? Is she having—

"Fuck yes, Enzo. Fuck me harder."

A sex dream.

I smile. *God, please don't let this be the last time I hear her curse my name like this in anticipation of coming.* It probably will be the last time, so I revel in it. I let it fill me for all the times I will never get to experience her beauty, her passion, her rage.

I want to feel everything Kai has to give. She would have the passion in bed most women lack. Most women I've been with only go through the motions. They think it's all about how big their boobs are or how they sway their ass or the sweet coos that leave their too plump lips as I fuck them. I don't give a shit about any of that. I've always wanted a woman who could equal me—who would fight me in bed—a woman I'd have to tame in order to touch. Worship to be worthy. Love to be her king.

Kai Miller is the only woman who ever seemed like she could fit the bill.

Maybe because she was always off the table, it was just a fantasy I could never confirm or deny. Never realize if Kai is just like all the rest of the women or not.

Hearing her beg for me in her dreams is enough confirmation to know exactly what I'm giving up by not consuming her. She is the woman I've pined for all these years. All it would take is for me to turn into the monster she already thinks I am.

Kai's eyes open, and she smiles at me sweetly.

I smirk. *You wouldn't be smiling at me so sweetly if you knew what I just overheard.*

I lay on my side, and her eyes widen as she notices my rock hard cock. Her mouth waters as she stares openly, not hiding her shame at gawking at me.

"Don't be getting any ideas. My cock is off-limits."

Her smile vanishes, and she scowls at me. "I wasn't thinking about wanting your cock. Trust me; I could live the rest of my life without fantasizing about another cock."

"Hmm, somehow I don't think that's true."

I stare between her legs, even though I know I'm playing with fire.

She doesn't cover herself up.

"So if I asked you to put a finger between your thighs, you wouldn't be wet right now?"

"No."

"Prove it."

"Why? What do I get if I win?"

I shrug, overly confident. "Whatever you want."

She smiles. "And if you win?"

"The pleasure at being right."

"Deal."

She places two fingers between her legs. Her face immediately drops. She's soaked.

I smirk. "Told ya."

I continue to smile as I walk into the bathroom where the cold tile hit my feet. My cock is hard as a rock thinking of her desperate moans.

Fuck.

I pride myself on my self-control, but this is impossible. *How am I going to keep resisting her when I have to be so close to her? How can I resist her naked body?*

Avoidance.

I turn the shower to cold and step inside. Not even allowing myself to jack off to her—that would be giving in and showing weakness. I am not weak. I will not let her or anyone else control me.

The cold droplets should help. Instead, they just remind me of her.

Jesus Christ, I curse as I squeeze my eyes shut. I can't even get relief from a shower. I need to get the fuck out of here. So that's what I do.

DAY AFTER DAY PASSES, AND OUR ROUTINE ONLY FORTIFIES INTO the same.

During the day I sleep on a cot on the floor next to a naked Kai. And at night I get work done. I'm ruthless in my endeavors. I work harder than I've ever worked, turning my money into more money and ruling the underground, sparking more fear at the sound of the Black name.

I should be thrilled Kai is fueling such dedication to my work, but I'm not happy. I can't keep going on like this. I try my best to be a machine. I turn off my feelings and work, but it's impossible to keep Kai from my mind when I get a new image of her naked body every night.

She's started healing. Her body has begun to fill out now that she's eating and sleeping properly. If she wore clothes, it would be easy to think of her as normal, albeit a little skinny. But she never clothes herself unless I demand it—which I haven't. It's like she wants to taunt me with the scars I allowed to happen on her body. I have my own scars, so there is no need for an imagination for me to understand the pain she endured in getting hers. It makes my skin crawl thinking about Jarod hurting her. *Thank fuck he's dead.*

I've spent the night turned away from Kai, but I can still hear her heavy breathing. It almost sounds like panting.

I squeeze my eyes tighter, wishing I could do the same to my ears. I'm a wreck. I'm sweating; my cock is hard, my balls blue from not allowing myself to jerk off to her.

It's been weeks now.

Weeks.

I've gone this long without sinking my dick into a woman before, but it's different when I'm so desperate for such easy prey right next to me.

My alarm goes off, and I don't care that its blaring wakes her up. She's gotten enough sleep.

"Morning," Kai says. "Or should I say good evening."

I frown, ignoring her pleasantries. I need to get out of here faster than usual today. I need to find a new solution because I can't keep sleeping next to her on the floor. For one, my back can't handle it anymore.

I stomp to the bathroom, preparing myself for another cold shower. But at the last minute, I change the water to steaming hot. I've tried cold too many times. It only reminds me of Kai's icy skin. I need hot.

And then I step under the steaming water.

"Hey!" I hear Kai's voice.

I close my eyes, *ignore her.*

"Hey, asshole! You aren't even going to talk to me anymore now?"

I count to three.

One.

Two.

Three.

It usually helps me gather my rage before I speak. I am in control —just not around her.

"No, I'm not going to fucking talk to you, Kai!"

My rage overwhelms me. I know Kai has questions, and she's just lonely. Well, she wouldn't be so alone if she would ever leave this fucking room, but she hasn't since that first day.

I have questions too.

Like why the hell does she sleep on the floor instead of the bed?

Why won't she let anyone touch her?

How did she get every bruise?

And most of all, what happened to her that made her forget the truth of what happened to her?

I turn the water off and step out.

Kai stands with her arms crossed as she glares at me.

I grab a towel and start drying off, not caring to hide my body from her. We are both too comfortable with each other's bodies now. There is nothing left to hide.

"What do you want, Kai?"

"You know what I want," she breathes.

I roll my eyes. "You don't always get what you want or even what you need. You of all people should have learned that by now."

I walk to the closet and begin getting dressed in a dark gray suit. She follows.

"Why do you sleep on the floor?"

Her eyes widen, and her head whips back. "What?"

"You heard me. Why?"

She doesn't answer me, she just blinks.

I huff. "You want your questions answered, well I have questions of my own."

Her breath rises and falls in her chest, pushing her hard nipples toward me.

I close my eyes again, trying to think of anything but her tempting body. In my angered state, I can't help but want her. And I know my self-control is growing dangerously close to losing.

When I open my eyes, she's somehow made her body even more appetizing. Her lips are parted, I can see her taunting tongue between her teeth begging to be in my mouth. Her nipples are pointing at me, and her legs are squeezed together as if hiding a secret.

I stride toward her with a look meant to scare her. She doesn't back down.

She stands taller, stronger.

I growl.

She huffs back.

This is never going to end. I'm never going to be free of her until I understand what she went through—seeing that bastard and the yacht she was tortured on isn't enough. Only once I hear her story in her own words can I heal her. Only then can I leave and never look back. My favorite house will become hers; I will sail away on my yacht and leave Miami in Langston's control. I prefer the sea anyway.

I need this to end.

I need to get away from her, stop thinking about her. Then I can go back to fucking any woman and return to my normal life of self-control.

What would end this?

I smirk as the answer finally comes to me.

"How about a game of truth or lies?" I ask.

A slow grin forms on her face. "Stakes?"

"Winner gets to ask the other three questions. *Any* three questions."

Her face lights up. I don't care if she wins. Her winning might actually let me leave faster. But even if I lose, I will still end up with more answers, because in the game, she always reveals more about herself. And I need to know everything about Kai to free us both.

CHAPTER 21
KAI

Enzo wants to play.

It seems the only way either of us will share information is through the game. And I'm ready for redemption after the last time we played and I lost.

I'll do anything to get answers. And I've already lost everything, my freedom included, and got nothing in return.

Enzo continues to dry his dripping body off with a towel, feeling free to show me every inch of him.

I don't like being touched, but it doesn't stop my body from aching to be stroked by him. I want to sink my claws into his sculpted abs. I want to outline the mysterious wounds marring his body. Run my tongue over his thick jawline until I taste his salty lips.

"I'll meet you in the bedroom when you're finished getting dressed," I say, turning to leave. If I'm not gaping at him, I won't be as tempted. He doesn't thirst for me anyway. And I don't want him to crave me. If he did, he would have already forced himself on me. And neither my body nor soul could handle it.

"No."

I pause, snapping my head toward him. "Change your mind?" *Please tell me you didn't.* I need more information. Even if I lose, I'll learn more about this strange man. And I'm tired of being alone. Our nights together are our only interaction. And we barely speak one sentence to each other.

The only real conversations I have are with Dr. Miranda and Westcott. Although neither talk about anything other than whether I'm healing or not. I'm tired of being alone. Even if it just means playing a game where we both try to hide the truth.

"We aren't playing in the bedroom," he says.

I gape.

"You will need to leave the bedroom," he continues.

He wants me to get dressed. To wear clothes, so I don't distract him.

"I'm not wearing any clothes," I say defiantly.

He smirks and drops the towel. "Neither am I."

Shit. Why did I think this was a good idea again?

Because now as much as he's going to be tempted by my body, I'm going to be distracted by his. And I can't let it show. I can't let him see my weakness.

Enzo winks at me like he knows the dirty thoughts plaguing my head. And then he strides past with his glorious, godlike body.

I follow, chills running through my body as I walk. My body feels sore and stiff. I haven't left the bedroom in weeks, or has it been months? I've forgotten how long I've been here, unlike when I was taken before and counted every single day.

Being held captive by Enzo isn't that bad, but the loneliness is the same. I still feel like property. I'm still owned. Enzo just doesn't act on his dark desires as my previous master did.

We step into the hallway single-file. The lights are off, and only the moonlight shines through the window overhead.

We continue in silence down the stairs that are no longer my adversary. The swelling in my ankle has reduced and other than an ache of stiffness, I'm able to keep up with Enzo's quick steps.

My eyes dart around on the first floor, looking for Westcott. I don't know what he does except bring me regular food.

"Westcott's room is separate. He lives in a small cottage on the grounds. He isn't here."

I exhale. I don't know why I care if Westcott is here. He's seen me naked almost every time he's brought me food. It's not about that. It's that this feels different. This game we are playing is ours—our secret. I don't want anyone else to know.

I don't know where we are headed. I have yet to tour the entire house. So when Enzo makes a sharp turn, I suck in my breath as I stand in the double door entrance to a grand room.

He steps inside, but I gawk. Not at his tight bare ass I want to lick, but the room. The room stretches two levels and has floor to ceiling windows that seem to float out over the ocean. Large bookcases line both walls, the kind where you need a ladder to reach the top shelves. The room is dark, and Enzo doesn't turn the light on. The only light illuminating the room is the moonlight, which is more than enough for both of us to see. I've learned that Enzo prefers the night almost as much as I do. Probably because it's easier to attack people in the dark than the light.

"You like books?" I ask, stepping inside.

"No, I hate them," he says stone-faced.

"That would be a lie. I win round one," I say smiling.

He grins as he pulls two chairs up, right next to the window overlooking the sea.

"We should sit back here. That way you're supposed hatred for the books will keep you distracted," I say barely stepping into the room.

He shakes his head. "The ocean can't hurt you."

I cringe, hating that I told him my secret about hating the ocean.

That's the problem with the game. No matter if you win or lose, you always reveal more about yourself.

He takes a seat and waits.

I edge closer, like I'm waiting for a lion to jump out and eat me. I stare at the surf knocking about in an endless calm of rolling waves. We are high above the water. There are panes of glass and several yards between me and the sea.

The water won't hurt me.

I sink into the other chair. I swallow hard, pushing the ache in my throat down.

"This isn't fair you know. You have the advantage."

He raises an eyebrow. "No, it's a fair game."

"How?"

"You are afraid of the ocean. And I'm afraid of you."

I huff. "Afraid of me?"

"Of what I would do if I lost my self-control."

"You mean you would torture me?"

He's silent—*which means yes.*

I look away from him and back to the ocean.

"How you can be more frightened of the ocean than of me, I don't understand."

I glare back. "Because all you've ever done is threaten. You threatened to kill me, you sold me, you held me captive, yet you've never once physically hurt me yourself. And although I don't know why, I do know for some reason, you can't hurt me."

He growls and jumps out of his chair, stopping only millimeters from burning my skin.

"Be lucky all you've ever experienced is a threat from me. Trust me; you may be the only human on the planet I've threatened without following through. You think you've experienced pain, but I'm the king of pain."

"You won't hurt me," I spit back.

His eyes trail all over my body. "Not today; I can't promise I won't tomorrow."

He sinks back in his chair.

I tremble a little from the booming voice that just fell silent.

"Let's just play," I say.

He nods.

"Ladies first."

I let my mind still as I think of my lies. I should try to appear sexy, use my body to try and distract him, although he only seems attracted to my injuries because he thinks about how much enjoyment he'd get from breaking me again.

I clear my throat and focus. I want to win. I want my answers. And he won't give me much truth in what he reveals about himself.

"I never want to be touched.

"I enjoy sleeping on the floor.

"I want to fuck you."

His throat growls when I say the last one. His body monitoring mine as if searching for some hint of truth to any of my words, relaxing after seemingly finding what he was looking for.

"My turn," he says.

I nod.

"I'm never letting you go.

"I hate that I let another man hurt you.

"You were taken for six years, not three."

I gasp.

He looks pained—like every word he spoke was fire from his mouth.

Suddenly, my truths and lies no longer matter. Because all I can focus on are Enzo's. *I was taken for six years, not three. How is that possible? It can't be true, can it? It has to be a lie, but then why would it hurt Enzo so much to say it?*

I'm never letting you go is obviously true. He's told me as much before.

And he's also implied that he hates the scars on my body. That he wasn't the one to cause them, because he's a fucking sadist as well as a cruel bastard.

Six years...

I lost three years more than I thought.

Three whole years.

Fuck.

What else was I wrong about?

I ticked off the time in my head so clearly, but I remembered wrong. *Did I block it out? What else don't I remember? What did I get wrong?*

I can't speak, but thankfully Enzo can.

"The third one is your truth, the rest are lies."

He doesn't call me out. He doesn't prolong the inevitable. He doesn't say why he believes that to be true. Or even brag that even though he's my captor, I still want to fuck him.

Just because I want to doesn't mean I will ever act on it. It's just lust after a hot man. Because two-seconds after I want him, I remember all he's done, and I go back to hating him.

"Your turn, Kai."

I could win. Actually, we would tie if we both guessed correctly. I know the truth. They are all truths. I just refuse to say it. Because if I say it, then it makes it true. And it can't be true. None of it can be.

"All of yours are lies," I say unable to meet his eyes, which leaves me looking at his bare feet.

"Kai," he commands.

One word and my head raises.

"Are you sure? That's your choice?"

I nod.

He sighs, knowing I just threw the game.

I narrow my gaze. *Did he want me to win? Well, I can't! I can never win! Because I'll never be free.*

"You win," I whisper. *I lose. I always lose, even when I win.*

CHAPTER 22
ENZO

Kai let me win.

Because she can't face the truth. She wishes every word out of my mouth was a lie.

She hates that I care that another man hurt her.

She hates that I've claimed her forever.

And she hates, most of all, that I know something she doesn't. That six years have passed instead of three. That the reason time seemed to move so slowly over the years was because it was standing still for her.

My choice was easy, even if she hadn't thrown the game. I know her well enough to know even though she needs to sleep on the floor, she yearns to find comfort in the soft cloud of fabric covering the bed. Even though she's afraid of my touch, her body begs to feel that exquisite warmth she remembers from our first encounter all those years ago.

Six years ago.

And I saw the way her body heated when she said she wanted to fuck me, I've heard her cries for me to fuck her in her sleep. Those were the hardest words I've heard leave her mouth. It pushed my restraint to the limit. Because I'm desperate—for anything. A touch.

A caress. A brush. *Anything.* I need that spark that occurs when cold and heat mix.

I need more.

I need her lips pressed against mine as I suck on her swollen lip. I need her body aligned with mine, writhing beneath me. I need to watch her gasp and moan as I flick her harden nipples between my fingers. And most of all, I want to watch the tears well in her eyes as I spread her wide with my cock. And I want to watch the tears change as her eyes roll back in her head and the pain changes to ecstasy.

Yet I don't get to touch her. She's just desperate for a chance to feel any pleasure after being denied joy for so many years.

I need a drink.

Kai shouldn't drink when she's this weak, but the only way I'll get to drink without her protests is to offer her some too.

So I walk over to the bar cart in the corner. I grab two glasses and pour some scotch into both before I bring the drinks back. I hand one to Kai.

She takes it with shaky hands. She doesn't even focus intently to ensure our hands don't brush as she snatches the glass from my hand. I should have brushed my fingers against hers since she wasn't on guard. That might have been my only opportunity to touch her.

I sigh as I sit and sip mine.

Kai's hands continue to tremble violently as she brings it to her lips. I know she tastes the liquid, but her eyes have glazed over into a blank expression.

I take the glass from her hands and set it down on the floor beside her. Her body is too focused and unsteady for the alcohol at the moment.

"Six years," she whispers.

I want to speak to explain. I want to take away the last six years for her, but I can't. *I want to take it away for myself.*

Finally, her head whips toward mine. "It's been six years since we fell into the ocean off the side of your yacht?"

"Yes."

She closes her eyes harshly, as she sucks in a breath. Her knees come up to her chest, trying to reassure herself.

I could comfort her so easily with a hug. I'm sure a hug would help. But it's not something I'm used to giving, nor have I experienced in recent years.

And then I see why her eyes are closed so tightly. Tears. Tiny droplets are escaping out the side of her eyelids.

I gasp.

Out of everything she's endured, I never imagined she cried. Kai's too proud and strong to let any man see her pain—including me. The only reason I get to see them is because this revelation took her by surprise. She spent her time in captivity trying to remain in control, I'm sure, but now she realizes she was never really in control.

She brushes the tears from her cheeks as they roll down, but no audible sob escapes her lips.

I shake my head, admiring her strength.

I wish I were as strong.

Her eyes open after several minutes pass. The redness in her eyes the only sign remaining that she cried.

"I was taken at sixteen. Just two weeks shy of my seventeenth birthday. I thought I had only lost three years, but I lost six. So instead of twenty, I'm twenty-three years old."

There is nothing to say, so I say nothing.

"I'm twenty-three." She laughs at herself as if that is the only logical thing to do. Then she looks at me with wildness in her eyes. "Age is nothing but a number. Twenty isn't that different from twenty-three. That's not what makes it hard. It's realizing how long I was gone. How much I endured. How much control I lost."

I disagree. Twenty is very different from twenty-three, at least the three years made a huge difference in my own twenty-four years on this earth, but I won't tell Kai that. She needs to deal with the realization on her own.

She slumps back in her chair, her legs falling back to the floor. Then she turns her attention back to me. "You won. Ask your questions."

And then I realize why she let me win. This answer, finding out she lost more years, was enough for tonight. She can't endure any more truths.

What do I want to know? I get three questions. I start with what I assume will be an easy answer.

"Why do you sleep on the floor instead of the bed?" I assume it has to do with the six years she was taken, but I need confirmation.

Her eyes go blank again. "Because for three—I mean six years—I was never given a bed, pillow or blanket. The floor I slept on was hardwood. Over time I guess my body adapted. Anything else is too soft for me."

I nod. I appreciate the truth, but I need more. And the only way to get more is to push her out of her comfort zone.

"Why don't you like being touched?"

She bites her lip. "Get touched against your will for six years and then tell me how you like other people's touch."

My eyes darken. "There's more to it than that."

She shakes her head. "No, that's it."

"No, that's not it."

"How do you know? You've never been through the torture I have."

"Yes, I have!"

Her eyes widen, our bodies halt, but my voice carries, bouncing off the walls, echoing through the room. We wait for the reverberations to stop.

Her tears threaten again. This is what I need an answer to. *This.* I've finally hit a lie I need the truth of. It's the key to healing her.

"Why don't you like being touched?" I slow my voice.

She looks down, ignoring me.

"Why don't you like being touched, Kai? I've experienced torment before, but it doesn't make you stop hating other people's touch. If anything, it makes you seek it out more. It makes you desperate for pleasure, comfort, love, anything that can erase the pain."

Nothing.

"What happened, Kai?!"

I grab her forearm before I realize what I'm doing.

Kai screams, but I'm not sure if it's from surprise at being grabbed, pain, or pleasure. Her scream carries, as the electricity pulses back and forth between us. Pushing us to the edge of joy before ripping us down with the sharp ache as the heat and cold fight with each other.

I only touch her for a second, before I correct my mistake, but it's enough to know she is definitely hiding the truth from me. Because her reaction is beyond anything normal.

Instead of pushing her again, I change my tactic. "Why come back to the barbarian who sold you?"

She holds her forearm carefully in her other hand, as she stares at the spot where I touched her. A single tear rolls down her cheek.

"Because I am nothing. I can't be healed. They broke me, permanently.

"I used to think someone would save me. My father or best friend would come and rescue me. I even fantasized you might come and take me away. But when I broke, they said I was free.

"When I came back to Miami, I knew I wasn't. I was alone, surrounded by people who didn't care enough to come for me. I didn't want to go back to them. The only thing that seemed to matter was my need for answers. I risked everything to learn the truth. I risked my life because I already knew no one would save me. I couldn't even save myself. The truth became my everything, but now that I know one truth, I realize the truth isn't worth my life."

More tears fall down her rosy cheeks.

"If you could take our previous game back, where you lost your life to me, you would?"

"Yes."

CHAPTER 23
KAI

"**Y**ou saved yourself, that's how you got free," Enzo says encouraging me despite me never having asked a question, trying to pretend like my life isn't the mess that it is— trying to give me some sense of encouragement.

My eyes glisten with the tears. I didn't cry for six years—hardly a single tear fell. And now, I feel like I can't shut them off for the stupidest of reasons.

"No, I didn't save myself."

"Then, how did you get free?"

I've already told him, but he wasn't listening, or he needs confirmation that the words I spoke were true, and I wasn't exaggerating.

"I was deemed broken. It was a game to them. Jarod wanted to break me, and then the men had no use for me anymore. Jarod said I could be free if I broke, so I broke. And then they dumped me on a park bench."

Enzo curses under his breath. It's beautiful how he feels all of my agony. It makes me more attracted to him than solely his physical allure. It's a stupid thought to think he could be more than a beast.

"Where did they keep you?"

"In a room with no furniture."

"Where?" he asks again.

My eyes flutter down as I think of the yacht and why I hate the water so much. I glance out at the ocean in front of me.

"Okay, no more questions," Enzo sighs.

He stands, and I think I should follow him, but he motions for me to stay seated. So I do.

I hug my knees to my chest again as I try to self-soothe. I wish I could let someone embrace me. I would love to feel comforted again. I look out as the moon rises higher over the sky. I don't know what time it is. Usually, Enzo leaves by this time of night and heads to Surrender or to kill whoever dared to cross him.

I don't know what he's still doing here with me.

A few minutes later, Enzo returns. I gaze at him as a pair of sweatpants now cling to his legs a tray of food in his hands.

Neither of us has worn clothes around each other in weeks. It was a silent protest, a game we both wanted to win when one of us backed down. It seems I at least won one game.

"Come outside with me, Kai."

My eyes widen. My body stiffens at the thought. "No."

"The sun won't warm you as it's not out. And I promise not to toss you into the ocean like before," he smirks trying to lighten the mood. It doesn't exactly work.

I bite my bottom lip. I can't go outside. I'm a prisoner. And I'm afraid. *Can't you see that, Enzo?*

"Do I have to win another round of truth or lies to get you to go outside?"

"No, I hate that game."

He nods.

"Come eat some food and drink some wine on the deck with me," Enzo says.

I can't.

"You can ask me questions while we eat."

It's tempting, but I know what he's not saying. I can ask questions, just not the question I need an answer to.

"Kai," his voice warns. I don't know why he's so insistent on me going outside with him. But I know if I don't go willingly, I will be forced to go. And on some level, I want him to force me. I want to see him as the devil again. Not the man who seems concerned about what happens to me.

And also because I want to feel him touch me again. The last time he did, sparks flew. I wasn't sure if I was experiencing pleasure or complete agony. It was a mix of both. But I could see the potential in the touch. With time, I could crave his touch.

"I'm not going to hurt you, Kai."

"Why?"

He shrugs. "Because I can't. You should be dead. And when you returned, I should have tortured you for information about your master. I should have ensured you weren't a spy. I should have used you and disposed of you a long time ago, but I can't."

"Why?" I whisper again.

"Because you are the only one who could save me."

He doesn't elaborate. He just carries the tray out through the glass window that turns into a swinging door, when he pushes against the pane.

I could run back to my room and lock him out. But I'm tired of being afraid. I won't live in fear. I'm safe, even if I'm only safe because I'm in a new prison with a guard who won't touch me.

My feet touch the rough wood of the deck, and I want to recoil back inside. *Push through; you can do this.*

I take another step. Then another, then another. And then I feel the cool ocean breeze hit me.

I freeze.

The salt is rough against my skin; it tangles in my hair and makes me want to run.

I don't run, but it doesn't mean I can move.

"Sit, Kai. The ocean can't hurt you."

I know his words make sense, but I can't. I can't move.

"Kai, you can do this. Sit."

My legs collapse, and I fall onto the couch outside next to Enzo. Tears stream down my face again.

Dammit!

This isn't what I want. I want to be strong. I want to face my fears with courage, not weakness.

"I'm such a coward."

Enzo growls, forcing my head to look at him.

"You are the strongest fucking person I know. I still don't know the whole story, but I know enough. Don't let anyone, yourself included, ever tell you you are anything but strong."

"All I ever did was survive."

"That's more than anyone else in your position would have been able to do."

I shiver as the cold spritz from the water hits me again. It's windier than I would have expected from inside; the weather looked so clam. Or maybe it's because I haven't felt fresh air in so long that everything feels more intense.

"Do you want a blanket?" Enzo asks, with hope in his voice.

I don't.

"It will protect you from the wind and salt in the air."

"Okay."

He dashes inside and returns with a lightweight blanket before I change my mind. He hands it to me, and I take it. I wrap it around me instinctively and close my eyes as I feel trapped beneath its material.

"Here, I made you a sandwich."

I open my eyes and see what appears to be a grilled cheese sandwich on a paper plate that he removes from the tray on the coffee table in front of us.

I smile. "A grilled cheese sandwich? Are you a chef or something?" I tease.

He smiles back. "Nope, I just decided to fix the worst thing for us. It's all grease, processed bread, and gooey cheese. It is the worst thing for our stomachs, but hopefully, it will put some more weight on your bones."

I frown. "It bothers you how skinny I am, doesn't it?"

"Yes," he hisses.

I take a bite of the grilled cheese; the cheese immediately melts in my mouth before sliding down my throat.

"How does it taste?"

"Better than most of the stuff Westcott has been trying to get me to eat. Except the bacon. I like bacon."

Enzo smiles. "Everyone likes bacon. I'll tell Westcott to add grilled cheese to his menu for you."

I nod and continue to scarf down the sandwich. Maybe if I eat quickly, we can go back inside.

When he's satisfied that I ate my entire sandwich, he pours me a glass of red wine.

I take it and smell it first. I've never had a good glass of wine, but I expect this is more expensive than what most people drink. I've seen enough people smell it first before taking a sip to know that's what you are supposed to do.

I sip. It tastes bitter and dry, but soothing at the same time.

The sadness overcomes me immediately.

"What's wrong? Do you not like the wine? I can get another."

"No, the wine is fine. I just…"

I look up at Enzo. "This is the first time I'm drinking, legally."

He holds out his glass. "To drinking legally as an adult. May we drink smarter than our previous, reckless selves."

He waits, but I don't know what he's waiting for. "You are supposed to clink your glass with mine."

"Oh." My cheeks burn as I clink my glass with his.

Enzo Black, what are you doing to me? My eyes travel up and down his bare chest again, and I give a silent plea for him to find a way through my walls. To make it so he can touch me again. So one day, he can fuck me. And I can find the pleasure I've been missing all these years.

We both sip our glasses, while our bodies yearn to touch. Like a magnet, I feel my body reaching out and trying to join with his. But I'm not brave enough to even brush my hand against him.

"How has work been this week?"

"Huh?" Enzo asks.

"You never talk about work. I don't even really know what being the all-powerful ruler you are means."

"It means I make the rules and all the men follow. It means I make millions of dollars a day. It means I own the underground, the darkest places in Miami and the ocean surrounding. No one takes a foot in this town without me knowing about it."

I nod. "I know that, but what do you do every day? Where do you go?"

"Surrender mostly. That's where I can get information and gather my team to ensure everyone is doing their jobs, which mainly means running the clubs and yachts and protecting those that have paid us for protection. I spend my day looking as menacing as possible, so no one dares defy my rule, and if someone does, I make an example of them."

I sip more wine.

"And women, you can't forget the women who dance all over you and let them fuck you at night," I force a smile to my face as I say the words that hurt more than they should.

Enzo isn't yours. He can fuck whoever he wants. And even if he were yours, he shouldn't be. You can't forgive him for selling you.

"Yes, the women make the job more enjoyable," his jaw hardens as he speaks.

"Ever had a serious girlfriend or someone you considered making Mrs. Dangerous?"

"No."

"Why not?"

"Because there will never be a Mrs."

"It seems a King needs his Queen."

"Not this King."

I take a long swallow and finish the wine in my glass. I hold it out, and Enzo pours more into my glass.

"You should come with me," he says suddenly.

"Go with you?"

"To Surrender. It would be good for you. It would help you heal faster."

"How would watching naked women dance on the most disgusting vile men help me?"

"Because you need to face your fears to heal."

"I'm not afraid of Surrender."

"No, you're not. But you are afraid of clothes and light and going outside. I'm sure being around strange men isn't exactly your idea of a great day either. You need to push yourself to heal."

"You trust me enough to go and not run away?"

"No, I don't trust you. Try running and see what happens."

"That sounds like a threat you will never follow through on."

He smirks. "Maybe I won't, but Langston will."

"Fine. As long as I don't have to strip, I'll come with you."

He laughs. "You walk around naked all the time in front of me and anyone else who enters my house. Why would stripping be so bad?"

I laugh. "I guess it wouldn't. My strip show would end quickly though since I'm already naked."

We both laugh at the ridiculousness. And then Enzo's gaze turns serious.

"Stop looking at me like that," he says.

"Like what?"

"Like you want me to take you to bed and pound you until you come screaming."

"I'm not looking at you like that."

"Liar."

"I'm not."

He sighs. "I will never fuck you, Kai. I will do my best to never touch you. I can't have you, Kai. I will ruin you."

"I'm already ruined."

He reaches his hand out.

I freeze.

He stops short of stroking my black hair like I want.

"No, you're not ruined. You're just hurt. You're just in pain. Someday soon you will break free of the walls you put up to protect yourself. And when you do, you'll realize just how amazing you are."

I try to cling to his words, but I can't. My eyes are growing heavy. I just slept almost eight hours. I shouldn't be so tired, but I am. So, so tired. My body starts loosening like jello, and I fall into a heavy pile on the couch.

CHAPTER 24

ENZO

I *tighten the rope around Kai's wrist. She moans as the sharp pain digs into her flesh.*

My eyes glaze at the sight, knowing she'll wear a bright red scar tomorrow because of me.

I stand back and admire my work. Kai is spread eagle on my bed. Her arms and legs are tied by a crude rope to the bedposts. My tie is around her mouth so she can't speak.

She doesn't move, but her eyes beg me—don't hurt me.

I'll do my best princess. The pleasure will be worth any pain.

She swallows hard, her neck muscles flexing as her saliva slides down her throat.

My eyes can't stop soaking her in. Her hardened nipples are begging to be licked. Her stomach has flattened, preparing for my kisses. And her pussy is dripping with anticipation.

And then I see the scars...

On her neck, her breasts, her stomach, her legs. They are everywhere. Reminding me of what I gave up. I let another man touch her.

Wild hunger stirs deep inside me. I don't know why I've waited all these weeks to touch her. I'm hungry and desperate for her, and her body is more than ready for me.

I climb up on the bed and settle between her legs, careful not to touch her. I want our bodies to connect in one swift movement as I slide inside her. I want an explosion.

I warn her with my eyes, and she braces herself on the bed but doesn't tell me to stop. She wants this.

I grab her hips and slam my cock into her body in one long stroke.

Damn, she's tight. So fucking tight.

"Jesus, Kai. I've never felt anything this tiny, this chilling to my bone, this comforting." Her pussy molds to my cock in cool perfection. Christ, even her pussy is cold compared to my skin. *But it's the perfect balance for me.*

She sucks in a rough breath through her nose; her whole body is tense. I've hurt her.

I've hurt her.

I need to stop. Give her time to adjust.

Stop, I can stop. I'm self-control. I'm not a monster.

I stop, but then her pussy tightens, a soft cry escapes her throat, and a tear trickles down her precious face. Any normal man would stop seeing her react like that, but I'm not normal. I was raised by the devil and revel in the darkness. So instead, I lose myself.

I pump hard, my full-length inside her.

Her gentle tears turn to streams. She's fighting inside, trying to get me off her, trying to make me stop.

But now that I've started, I can't stop. I won't stop. Not until I've destroyed her.

In.

Out.

Harder.

Faster.

Her tears are spilling from her eyes, but I need more. I love to see her in pain, knowing I'm the one to give her that experience. I'm the only one who gets her tears.

"Cry for me, baby. Beg for me."

"Stop."

"Yes, just like that."

"Stop, Enzo. Please."

I freeze, staring at her mouth still tied up. She can't talk. It's not possible. But I know I heard her speak.

"Please."

I OPEN MY EYES.

"Enzo," Kai whispers in her sleep on the floor in her usual spot in the corner of my bedroom.

It was a dream.

My body is pressed against her as I hump her leg like a sixteen-year-old horny boy.

Shit.

I scurry away, shocked that I haven't woken her up. I'm a sick, disgusting prick. My dream alone is reason why I can never touch her, or permit myself to fuck her even once. I'm not a good man.

I remember last night. How many secrets were revealed, and how many more are left to say.

She passed out so easily. At least this time I don't think it was from exhaustion. She's just a lightweight after not drinking alcohol for years and having lost so much weight.

But it gave me another excuse to carry her to bed. Well, the floor since she won't sleep in a bed.

But I can't even carry her anymore if this is the result—me humping her while dreaming of torturing her.

I'm sick.

I need to find a way to get her out of my life quickly before I do more damage than I've already done. She doesn't deserve any more pain.

I stare down at her still sleeping body. She reaches out like she's trying to grab something, but I'm no longer there for her to grab onto.

It's for the better, Kai. You don't want me. Maybe before, if we had fucked on that yacht before she was taken. *No, she was too young then.* She wasn't ready to be fucked.

If she hadn't been taken by a man as sadistic as I am, then maybe

I would have a chance. She could learn to enjoy how twisted I am in bed. Many women before her have enjoyed my sick fantasies. But Kai never will. She's been through too much. She will always see me as the same monsters as them.

Kai was a virgin. She'd never been with a man. Never even been kissed before I hurt her.

It makes me nauseous knowing her first time was with a man set on breaking her. And I was the catalyst to that happening. I'm the reason she isn't still cleaning boats and stealing to make enough money to eat.

Either way her life would have sucked, but not as bad as now. I took her innocence and gave it to a man who didn't deserve her.

And now she's lost.

Destined to break beyond repair if I don't get her away from me.

"Are we going to Surrender today?" she asks with big eyes.

I don't know how long she's been awake, but I don't know what to say. I don't want her to come to the club with me. I can't be around her. But I told her to come. She needs to heal; that's my best plan for being able to leave her—by continuing to lie.

"Yes."

She fidgets with her fingers.

"We will leave in twenty minutes. You need to get dressed."

I walk into the bathroom, grab one of my suits, and then head to one of the other bathrooms to get ready. I can't be near her. I can't help her put clothes on. I doubt she will wear anything suitable to go out in public in any way. I'll just tell her she has to stay, and I'll deal with her a different day.

I glance at my watch after twenty minutes exactly have passed.

"I'm leaving. You ready?" I shout up the stairs. I continue fidgeting with the watch, remembering the one Kai stole when I hear her footsteps stomping down the stairs. Even as light as she is, she has no idea how to be quiet on her feet.

I look up when her feet still in front of me.

"Fuck," I curse.

"That bad?" she asks.

I don't know what to say. I thought at most she'd wear a loose T-shirt. Maybe she'd find an oversized dress I had Westcott pick out to fill her closet. But I didn't expect this.

Kai is dressed in tight dark jeans, a flowy black halter top that pushes her boobs up, and strappy heels. She's not wearing any makeup, but she's combed her hair into shiny tendrils framing her face in dark lines.

"I couldn't find any makeup, and my hair could use a trim, but I thought I looked alr—"

"You look beautiful, Kai. You don't need makeup or anything at all, but I'll make sure Westcott buys you some before your next outing."

She smiles with a nervous lip.

"You going to be able to walk in those shoes?"

"I didn't figure I'd be walking far."

"You never know when you'll need to run away from danger at Surrender." *Or me.*

If she would find a way to disappear, then I could let her go. I'm just not sure she's strong enough to leave alone.

She follows me to the garage and hops in my Porsche without waiting for me to tell her to. It's like something has changed in her overnight. She's tired of living scared. It's like knowing that more of her life was taken than she realized made her want to start living her life now instead of waiting.

I'm in my own head on the drive over, trying to decide why I want her at the club.

Because Surrender is where the truth will eventually come out—whether that's today or a year from now. Eventually, she will learn the truth here.

I pull up outside the back entrance to the club. No one knows of this entrance but me, and now Kai. Everyone else enters through the single entrance at the front.

"Ready for this?" I ask.

"I don't know. I'm guessing I will pass out in fear and you'll have to carry me home again."

"Please don't do that."

"Why?"

"Just don't. I won't push you. If you need a break, just tell me or Langston or Zeke, and we will find a private room for you by yourself."

"No, push me. I need to be pushed to heal."

I lead her inside. Through the dark hallways that only she and I can see in. It's nice not to have to touch her to lead her or turn on a light. I prefer the black.

We walk to one of the main public rooms, and I find Langston prowling.

Kai stalks in behind me, holding her head up and proud.

"Katherine, would you like a drink?" I ask using her true name instead of the one people might recognize here as the dead coming back to life.

"Sure," she says.

She doesn't tell me what she wants to drink, but I decide something light like champagne that she hopefully won't drink too quickly. It's more for her to have something to hold and be more comfortable. I give Langston a look to watch her before I retrieve our drinks.

I grab her champagne and me a whiskey. When I turn back around to give her her drink, I see Langston reaching his hand out to touch her.

I drop the glasses and run to her. Her body is frozen in fear at the looming touch.

I don't know how I reach them just in time. I don't know how to stop Langston except to tackle him to the ground, so that's what I do.

"What the hell?" Langston wrestles me, trying to push me off him.

All eyes in the club are on us.

"Sorry," I say, before I throw a punch at his face. I need to send a clear signal no one touches Katherine. And even though I stopped Langston, I need everyone else in the club to keep their distance. So the punch was necessary.

"No one hits on my girl. You hear me—Katherine is mine," I yell, making it clear why I hit him, even though he's my best friend, and what will happen if anyone else touches her.

I stand up and wipe the sweat from my knuckles. I give Kai a look and walk out of the room. Turns out it wasn't Kai who would need to go cool off in another room; I needed it.

I leave her with Langston without explanation. She's free to wander. But she won't run or escape. As much as she wants freedom, I saw the look on her face when I punched Langston—thanks and relief. She's come a long way, but she's still terrified of the world. She won't leave, because she feels safe with me, the monster she knows. That's a mistake.

CHAPTER 25
KAI

I hate Enzo.

I can say that with certainty now.

Hate.

I hate the contradictory feelings he stirs inside me.

I hate that he is the only person who I can truly talk to.

I hate how he makes me lust after his muscular body.

I hate that he tries to heal me, never allowing me to stay broken.

I hate that he protected me from a single touch by acting like a jealous lover.

But most of all, I hate that no matter what he does, it will never be enough for me to forgive.

My heart has blackened because of him. My soul tormented, and my body changed. I'm thankful that he spared my life, although the consequences he faced for that seem inconsequential. But I can never forgive him for selling me.

It doesn't seem Enzo does any of these things because he expects my forgiveness. More like it's a meticulous plan that will somehow end in me out of his life again.

Despite how I hate Enzo, my heart softens every time he does something to save or protect me. And he just saved a night or possibly weeks of pain by preventing Langston from touching me. And my stupid heart likes Enzo more than it should for protecting me from that pain.

Enzo stormed off without a word to Langston or me. All eyes in the club are on us. It's a strange feeling, after being alone for so many years. I'm not used to so many people in one room, especially when all the attention is on me. But I refuse to show weakness. Or hide the scars or marks on my body.

I want to chase after Enzo and find out why he prevented Langston from touching me. And why he stormed off afterward. He brought me here to push me, to heal me faster. He thought that would happen sooner if he made me face my fears.

"Are you okay?" I bend down to ask Langston, who is still lying on the floor in shock.

Langston nods slowly, as he stares at me with large eyes. He stands up quickly, and I give him a wide berth, so he doesn't touch me. Langston gives one look to the crowd, and the stares stop, the voices begin again, and the dancers continue as if the last few moments didn't happen.

"I'll get you some ice for your face," I say.

"No, I can't show weakness."

I study his eye; it doesn't look too bad right now. But it will swell up and blacken my morning.

"I'm sorry," I say.

"Why are you sorry? You weren't the one who hit me. I just didn't realize you and Enzo had gotten so serious so fast. Enzo isn't exactly the dating type."

I snort. "We aren't together."

Langston frowns as his eyes dart around the room at men who are most likely listening to our conversation. "Follow me."

He walks down a hallway to a locked door, buried in the depths of the club, but not as far as Enzo's office. Langston unlocks the door and then steps inside. I follow while keeping my distance. I shut the door behind me.

The room is small compared to Enzo's office, but Langston's office appears more for regular work than Enzo's. Langston's has a desk, laptop, papers, and a small seating area. But Langston doesn't sit down. Instead, he walks over to a mini-fridge in the corner where there is a bar setup. He opens the freezer and pulls out a bag of peas, placing it over his eye.

I try to hide my smile, but I can't. "You a big fan of peas or does this happen often?"

He walks over to the rolling chair behind his desk and slumps down, as he continues to hold the frozen peas to his face.

"In my line of work, this happens often—although Enzo isn't usually the one throwing the punches at me." Langston pauses, studying me as if trying to understand who I am and what I'm doing in here.

"Should I call you Katherine or Kai?"

I shrug. "Ask Enzo."

My feet are aching from standing, and the only seats in the room are the small couches in the corner, not close enough to talk to Langston. He notices my stares and gets up from behind his desk; he collapses down on one of the couches in a lump of pain. His head is obviously throbbing. He wouldn't crumble in such exhaustion from a simple punch if it didn't have force behind it. I know the difference between a weak punch and one with the full weight of a body behind it.

I walk to the other couch, but I'm not used to my heels and my feet are already twinging. I step, and the heel moves out from under me, causing me to stumble.

Langston reaches his arm out to catch me. I see it the split second before I would crash into his hand. But I can't let him touch me. I contort my body and fall away from his hand to the floor.

We both stare openly at my reaction to his almost touch.

"What is going on? Why don't you like to be touched?"

My eyes drift down to the now visible marks on my arms and chest, my clothes not hiding them this time. This time when I entered this club, I didn't want to hide behind my clothes.

"You know why. You saw me that day naked. You saw how broken my body was and how it continues to be. It shouldn't come as a surprise that I don't like to be touched."

"No, I guess not. It still doesn't explain who you are or what you are doing in Enzo's life."

I settle myself on the floor and lean against the couch rather than sitting on it. The floor is more comfortable for me anyway.

"If you figure out what I'm doing here, let me know."

Langston continues to study me with his one good eye. "Enzo and I have been friends a long time. We've both taken bullets for each other. Committed the worst sins together. Trust me; I will learn why you are here. So you might as well tell me now and save me the trouble."

I cross my arms as anger floods my eyes. "You want to know what I'm doing here! It started six years ago. Enzo was looking for someone by the name of Kai Miller. *Me*. He was sent by his father to kill me. Except when it came down to it, he couldn't do it. He didn't kill me. Instead, he had me kidnapped and sold. A few weeks ago, I was returned to Miami. I was pissed and went in search of Enzo. I wanted to know why. We played a game of truth or lies. I lost. Now I'm forced to live my life as his prisoner. That's why I'm here, because I lost a stupid game. And I will never understand why."

Langston freezes as I tell my tale. I hope he has the answers. He will be able to tell me why, if he knows Enzo as well as he claims. Langston should know why Enzo's father ordered him to kill me.

Langston's mouth eventually drops as he realizes the truth. He knows my answers.

"Why? Why was I ordered to be killed?"

A knock followed by a head poking through the door halts our conversation.

"Langston, there has been a security breach," a man says while entering Langston's office. I don't recognize him. I haven't met him before.

Langston stands, dropping the bag of peas on the coffee table as he starts walking to handle the issue.

"Langston? Answer me?"

He stops at the door and turns and faces me.

"Please," I beg.

His lips thin as he stares like he's seeing a ghost. "It's not my truth to tell. I'm sorry."

And then he's gone.

I slump, my shoulders rounding over my chest.

Now what?

Enzo won't tell me. Langston won't answer me. But someone in this club knows my answers. I just have to find the man willing to answer me. I'm not going to wait here for the men to return. I'm going to get my answers.

I force myself up onto wobbly legs. I really shouldn't have worn these heels, but I knew after the last time I came here that I wanted to look my best. I wanted to fit in, instead of standing out.

I make it to the hallway, but I have no idea where to wander. I know where Enzo will be. I remember the string of corridors that lead to his lair, but do I want to find him?

I start walking, being drawn this way or that way, not thinking as I walk, just feeling and letting my body wander through the hallways. The hallways are mostly dark, and occasionally I'll walk by a room that is lit up and noisy. I walk by the entrances quickly, not ready to be in the throws of large groups of people again. If I'm going to get my answers, I'm going to need to do it one on one.

Slowly, I realize I am indeed headed toward Enzo's office. I stop just outside the solid door to his office that is now closed. I consider knocking, but that doesn't feel right.

I grab the handle, just as I hear sounds behind the door.

I pause my hand on the door as I listen, hoping to catch the end of a conversation Enzo is having. Hopefully, a discussion that will give me answers.

But I don't hear words.

Moans escape through the cracks in the door. Then panting.

Sounds I would only recognize in my dreams.

I squeeze my eyes shut, trying to keep the tears in my eyes. I manage to keep them on the edge of my eyelashes.

I shouldn't be upset that Enzo is inside fucking a whore. He has every right. He's not mine, and I don't want him to be.

I just don't like that he gets to experience any amusement after what he did to me.

My hand tightens again on the door handle. I should leave and find a man who might talk. I'm sure there are plenty of drunks around here that would be willing to spill Enzo's secrets with the right persuasion. But I can't. I'm too focused on what's happening behind the door.

I turn the handle slowly and crack the door open. My eyes focus in on the dark room and the shadows moving on the lavish couch. Enzo and his whore don't notice me.

Maybe Enzo does, but he doesn't care that I'm watching.

I don't have to step inside to see, I can see just fine through the dark slit in the door.

I see Enzo flip the woman over, spreading her legs wide, her ass in the air. He pushes his pants down and then sinks his cock inside her. He gathers her hair into a ponytail at the back of her head and pulls hard as he fucks her.

He's brutal with his thrusts, just as I would expect. He doesn't kiss her or caress her in any way. He takes what he wants without considering how it makes her feel—like a whore.

They both pant and moan as their naked, writhing bodies collide. I can hear their skin slapping together. His ass tightens as he pushes himself deeper inside.

"Sweet Jesus," she moans.

I don't know how his movements feel good to her. He's pounding into her so hard; he must be bruising her insides. But her soft cries of delight tell a different tale.

My mouth parts as his tongue licks over her ear, whispering dirty words as he fills her cunt.

I remember his tongue, how commanding and deep it went into my mouth, how he could make me drip between my legs from just his tongue on my lips.

He grabs her hips harder as her body jerks backward against his. And I remember how his hand felt against my stomach as our bodies hardened against each other, both resisting and begging to be connected together.

And then he grabs her neck—just like he did me. He squeezes, although not to snuff out her life as he tried with me all those years ago. More to heighten her senses, to demonstrate his power, and relinquish her control to him. Because that is what he needs above all else. Power and control.

Why would I ever dream about a man like Enzo? She may be enjoying herself, but it's not from what he's doing. He's taking what he wants without giving back. He's just like the men who took me.

I can't keep watching, but I can't tear myself away. Instead, a single tear falls at the loss of something I can never have.

"I never took you for a voyeur," Enzo's voice booms behind me.

I jump. Enzo isn't fucking the woman on the couch. He's standing behind me, and the fact that it brings me any relief at all burns me to my core.

CHAPTER 26
ENZO

I lost control.

I never fucking lose control. And now I've done it twice in a span of twenty minutes.

I punched Langston, something I haven't done since we were kids and wrestling around testing our strength. It needed to be done. And it helps my image at the club; the men respect brute force. But I haven't had to use my muscles like that in the club in a while.

What I did after though was a complete loss of myself. I walked off in a whirlwind of rage, thinking after a stiff drink and time alone, I would be better. Composed, back to my usual controlled self.

Instead, I spiraled.

I drank four glasses of whiskey. I haven't drunk that quickly since I was a teenager. I needed to take the edge off of the restless feeling stirring in my chest. But the drinks did nothing to calm the wild storm brewing inside me.

Instead, I went to my private bedroom. I laid on my bed, took my cock out, and jacked off to the thought of Kai.

There are dozens of women, scantily clad throughout this club. Any one of them would love the pleasure of being mine tonight. And they would do more than be mine, if I paid them well for their time

"

with me. Most nights if I needed a woman, I'd have Zeke select one for me. She would be paid well for her time with me, although no woman ever complained about how I treated them in bed. Every woman I've been with would have let me fuck them for nothing. No money was needed, but the money bought me a sense of protection from the expectation of more. It also let me have my way with them because I was paying for the night.

But I saw the way the women I fucked looked at me. With eyes of lust when they saw my sharp muscles and rugged body. They are used to entertaining men, most of the men in the club are older, ragged with life experiences. They are wealthy, dangerous men, but the women never fear, because they know I protect them. I protect all of them. If a single woman were ever hurt in one of my clubs, the bastards that touched them would die for their mistake.

The women see me as their salvation. A way to make money they never could otherwise. I'm their defender and savior. And if they get selected to spend a night with me, they see it as winning a prize. I pay them more for a night than they earn here in a year. And I pay them well for a year's worth of work.

They think I'm a saint compared to the other men. They're wrong. I'm worse because I'm the only one with the power to save them, but I don't.

I fuck them. Give them the best night of their life. One filled with passion, pushing their limits as they take my large cock in every orifice.

And then I leave, treating them like whores. Not because I think of them that way, but because I will never date. Never marry. Never have anything more than one night.

Ever.

But I haven't had any of the women in the club in weeks. Not since Kai stumbled back into my life.

I don't understand the pull she has over me. Maybe it's because she is the only one who threatens everything I've worked to obtain. She could destroy me. And being with someone who has that kind of power over me is thrilling. It terrifies and excites me. Pushes me, and that is something I rarely experience.

So I slid my thick, rock hard cock into my hand and pretended it was Kai's lips wrapped around it instead. I came hard on my bare stomach. But it wasn't enough. I immediately fisted myself again, imagining it was her pussy I was sinking into, which wasn't hard to visualize since I've seen her naked more than I've seen her clothed. Her thin legs wrapped around my waist, and though frail, digging into me with all her might. Her fingers clawing as her legs squeezed me tight. I would drown in her body, our heavy breathing outpacing our flowing blood. I would fuck her until I simultaneously pulled a tear-filled cry and a rippling orgasm from her body. Only then would I slam my cum deep into her and adorn her with her first moment of pleasure during sex.

I came again, imaging her battered body surrendering to mine for the first time. Her eyes glittered with overcoming joy and terror at letting me be the one to show her the beauty of fucking.

When I was finished, I cleaned myself off and went in search of Langston to chew him out. He's the reason I lost control. Seeing him with her brought me to my weakest point.

Instead of finding Langston, I found her.

Kai was standing in the darkness at the door to my office. The door was cracked, and her body was stiff as she stared inside.

I heard the familiar sound of panting and heaving as two bodies fucked. It's a regular sound in a place like this—expected even.

But I could understand what it might trigger in a woman like Kai, one who only associates sex with suffering.

And I know exactly who is behind the door she's listening to. *Zeke.*

Fucking bastard.

I really need to get him a bigger office with a couch or bed. That way he'll stop bringing women into my room.

"I never took you for a voyeur," I say.

Kai exhales, as if she'd been holding the world inside as she watched. Like hearing my voice shook her to her core.

I narrow my eyes, as I study her features in the dark. Luckily, I can see so well in the night because I see the glistening on her cheek

—wetness from crying. But it's like all her tears were sucked back up when she heard my voice.

My voice saved her.

I stare back at my friend and his hookup for tonight.

She's not upset because she is watching a man fuck a woman. She's not imagining that it's her or he's fucking her against her will.

She's upset because she thinks the man was me.

"I was looking for you," she says, finding her voice. It's gruff and laced with desire.

"I see that."

We are both quiet, listening to the muffled sounds of sex.

"Jealous?"

"Of what?" she asks.

"The woman," I nod in the direction. "Do you miss getting fucked daily?"

She slaps me.

And I deserve it. My words were harsh and cruel. But I need her to hate me, to be afraid of me, and keep her distance. Because I'm losing my battle at keeping her away from me, and cruelty is the only thing she will respond to. I've been too kind these last few weeks; I've begun to let her into my world. And it has to stop.

Her touch continues to sends sparks. It was a brief interaction of our skin, but I'm dizzy with the aftershocks, the tingling her flesh offers. It was the first time she touched me willingly. And I almost want to make a snide comment again just to feel her hand against my face, no matter how sharp the sting on my face.

"Rape isn't fucking," she says.

When I gaze at her again, my eyes are heavy with tension.

"I was only pointing out you must have needs. Wants. Desires. You need to heal. And at this club, you can find whatever man you want to fulfill you. You're not ready yet, but if you want to heal, you need to find that man."

"I'm not going to find a man to fuck in your sex club."

"This isn't a sex club."

She rolls her eyes. "Yes, it is."

I resist the urge to move in on her and box her in with my body and capture her wrists. "No, one of the purposes of this club is sex, but more importantly this is a place where business and pleasure mix. Men come here for a good time, yes, but more importantly they come to meet other men who can assist them in their endeavors. They try to befriend me, so I might be in debt to them and owe them a favor."

"And the women? What do they get other than being whored out?"

"Protection. Safety. Money. Everything they desire."

"As long as they sell themselves."

I shake my head. "The women don't see it that way. They might be desperate when they come to work for me, but they live like queens. Worshiped and wanted. They are never forced to fuck or even touch a man. They don't even have to dance. They can simply serve liquor and get paid a six-figure salary to work for me."

She gasps.

I close the door to my office. I'll deal with Zeke fucking in my office later.

"You can't hide your secret lust from me. I see it as plain as I can see your tits in my mind. I've seen the look too many times not to notice."

She glares.

"There is no shame in feeling lust. Just because your innocence was taken doesn't mean you stop wanting to find the joy in a good lay. It's not sick or twisted. I'm the sick one, not you," I say.

"I agree; you're sick."

"I am, so stop looking at me like I could save you. I can't. Not with protection. Not with my body. Not at all."

"I know you can't save me from the demons that haunt me; nobody can. And even if I get better, I'm still a prisoner in your home with no hope to work off my debt."

My eyes darken. I can think of plenty of ways she could work off her debt to me.

"Langston will drive you home. The club was too much for you. From now on, you can stay a prisoner in my house," I say, my jaw clenching as I say the word *prisoner*. But that's what she is, until I release her. Or someone else figures out the truth.

"Why not you?"

"Because I have work to do. And Langston owes me."

"Thank you for stopping Langston," her words explode out of her in a whisper.

I huff. "You obviously haven't learned anything if you are thanking me. I'm not your protector, Kai. You should know by now that I could set you free; I just never will."

And then I walk away, despite my urges to stay. To drag her into a spare room and make her realize what it's like to be fucked and enjoy it.

I feel her staring as I round the corner. *I can't save you, but you can save us both.*

CHAPTER 27
KAI

Enzo said I need to have sex in order to heal. I need a man to pleasure me. That's the only way to truly get over my fears.

I'm sure he's right, but I can barely tolerate clothes, I can't sleep in a bed, I hate the sunlight. I'm not ready for sex. I don't think I'll ever be.

I stand frozen in my spot after Enzo leaves me at the closed door to his office. I can't believe I thought the man in the room was Enzo. I can't believe I cared, but I do. I'm not even sure I'm jealous because I want Enzo to be the one fucking me. I'm clearly not ready for sex. I just don't want him fucking anyone.

If I'm his possession, then I want him to be mine. But it doesn't work that way. Only one of us gets to be the object, the other a person with a life.

"Katherine," Langston says cautiously from behind me.

I turn, and it's clear from his stoic expression he's been given orders from Enzo. I'm now Katherine instead of Kai. *Why am I Katherine here? What does my name mean? If I spoke my name aloud to the men in this club, what would happen?*

"Are you ready to go home?" he asks.

Home.

Enzo's place is anything but home. I don't have a home. Even if Enzo would let me go, I don't know what I'd do. I don't have a high school diploma. I have no money, no experience, and I can't even tolerate being touched. I don't know how I'd get food if I were truly free. I should be thankful Enzo keeps me, even if I don't understand the purpose.

I nod.

Langston leads me out the front, but not through the crowded rooms at the entrance. Through the door and outside into the night, he doesn't walk slowly or wait for me at all as we stride down the street. My feet ache in the shoes. I feel the flicker of early light, as the sun slowly begins to rise. *How is it already almost morning?*

I'm exhausted. The night was long, even though the time spent away from the house was relatively short.

Langston stops in front of a Maserati and opens the door. I slide into the passenger side before he hops into his side.

My heart races fast, my palms sweat, and my pupils dilate as Langston eases onto the road. Driving here was easier with Enzo at the wheel, but I don't know Langston, I don't trust him. But Enzo didn't offer to drive me home. Because I'm nothing to him. I need to remember that even when he offers me a brief moment of kindness.

I close my eyes to try to block out the car ride. My plan works, because we arrive at Enzo's house before dawn breaks.

Langston hesitates as the car idles, he's looking at me. And as much as I want to run out of this car and into the safety of the house, to my room, I don't. I can tell from Langston's hurried breath he wants to say something to me, but he's not sure how to say it. I wait, hoping it will give me some insight into Enzo, the man they all call Black.

"Be careful."

I narrow my gaze. "Careful?"

"Yes, careful. This is a dangerous world you are now a part of. Black may be a king. He may rule all, but Enzo is different than the man he portrays at Surrender. He's frailer than you realize. Don't hurt him."

"Don't hurt him! Are you serious? Shouldn't you be telling him not to hurt me?"

Langston looks me over. "It doesn't appear you have been hurt in weeks. Enzo is helping you, not hurting you."

"I wouldn't say keeping me as a prisoner is helping."

He leans across me, and I freeze trying to keep my chest from bumping against his arm. He's careful not to touch me as well. He opens my door.

"Then leave. Go. Be free. I won't stop you. Enzo won't stop you."

He smiles smugly when I don't move. "That's what I thought. You need him to survive. So stop thinking of yourself as a prisoner. You're as much a prisoner as Enzo is."

I frown, and then I realize Langston thinks of Enzo as a prisoner as well. *To what, I don't know? His father? His job? What?*

Slowly, I step out and walk inside. Langston waits until I close the door before he speeds off.

Westcott welcomes me with a smile. "Can I get you a coffee or tea? Some breakfast maybe?"

Does the man sleep? Why is he up so early? And hasn't he realized it's not morning for me? The sun is up, which means it's time for bed.

Except, I don't know when or if Enzo is coming home. He seemed pissed off the last time I saw him. He may leave again for weeks just to avoid me. And I haven't slept alone on the floor in weeks.

I scrunch up my nose at the thought of tea or coffee. "No, I'll just be in my room."

I practically run to the stairs before I kick out of my heels, leaving them on the floor as I dash up the stairs. I get to the bedroom and slam the door shut. I lock the six locks Enzo had installed again. And then I begin to strip the constricting clothes off. When I'm free of them, I sigh.

No.

I need to continue to make progress. I lost six years. I need to make up for it. Get my life back.

But I'm tired of wearing tight jeans. So I walk to the closet and let my hand stride over the fabric. Half of the closet is filled with

Enzo's suits, jeans, hoodies, and sweatpants. The other half is filled with clothes I'll never wear. Dresses, jeans, skirts. I tolerated the jeans, pushing myself. I need to settle now on wearing clothes, any clothes. Something I can sleep in.

I pull the largest T-shirt on my side of the closet I can find, and I slip it on. It hangs down to my knees.

It's a start.

I walk back to the bedroom and stare at the bed. It still looks like the most uninviting thing.

One step at a time. Today I wear clothes. I went out in public. Soon I can try the bed again.

I stare at the blackout curtains blocking the sunlight. *Maybe just one more step?*

I walk to the curtain, grip the edge, pull it open and let the light in. I lean against the window forcing myself to feel the warmth, forgetting some windows in the house turn into a door when the appropriate pressure is applied. The window falls open, and my body trips out onto the balcony.

I wince as the brightness of the sun burns my eyes. It's so fucking sunny. But it's warm and relaxing at the same time.

Just five minutes. I'm already out here. *Five minutes.* Tomorrow it will be six, then seven, then eight. *I will get my life back; I'm not a prisoner.*

There is a couch with a small table and chairs on the balcony. I want to sit on the hard chair, but I choose the soft couch. I curl my legs up, compelling myself to try and get comfortable.

Four minutes. Just four more minutes.

I am strong.

I am not broken.

I can heal myself.

I don't need Enzo.

I don't need anyone.

I close my eyes, trying to block out some of the sun's rays.

But my body shakes at the heat. I shift in my seat trying to get comfortable. I grab the hem of the shirt I want to rip from my body. It itches and scratches, driving me mad.

I try to adapt to my old ways. Shutting everything out. Squeezing my fists to the point of pain to distract myself. Counting. Blocking. Guarding. None of it works.

Enzo.

I know it's the one that will work, because it's what saved me time after time. There is nothing wrong with it. Fantasizing about him doesn't make me sick. It's just because he's the only man in my life. The only man who hasn't physically hurt me.

That's not true—Mason didn't hurt me either. But I'm not attracted to Mason like I am Enzo. He doesn't have that rugged, beckoning, mysterious look Enzo has. Enzo is the only boy I've ever kissed. He's the only one whom I can imagine.

♡

Kiss me.

His lips brush against mine, stopping just shy of giving me what I fully want.

Kiss me, *I say in my head again.*

This time, he doesn't resist. His lips devour me; his tongue slips deep inside, threatening a groan to escape my throat. I hold the sound in, not ready to show him how much pleasure a simple kiss gives me.

More.

He tangles my hair in his fist as our bodies rub against each other. I shift my weight, pressing my body closer.

Want me, fuck me.

He pushes me back, and I fall against the soft fabric of the couch. His dangerous eyes leaving me dazed as he exposes me, pushing up my shirt.

"Touch yourself," he says.

I nod.

I want this. *The fire between my legs is begging to be touched, stroked until I explode.* I need this.

I slide my hands down between my legs.

"Like this?"

"Yes baby, just like that."

I begin rubbing slowly over my swollen nub. Small circles and then bigger,

I move my fingers, stroking faster. And then I reach inside, pulling some of my liquid out, and drag it over my clit, intensifying the feeling.

Yes, God, yes. This is what I've been missing—an orgasm to pull me from my shell.

"Faster," Enzo commands.

I do as he says. I can feel myself growing with need and tingles ripple through my body heating me and bringing me closer to the edge I seek.

I look up at Enzo with heavy eyes, I'm close, but I need his help to get me to the brink.

"Your turn," I say.

He frowns, looking at me with disgust.

I stop. "What's wrong?"

"Why would I want to fuck a whore like you? You're disgusting. You have no curves. Your skin is battered, permanently. You have no fight left. No man will ever want to touch such a revolting whore like you."

I pant heavily. No, I'm good enough. Touch me!

"No."

♡

I JOLT, MY EYES WAKING FROM THE FANTASY I WAS PLAYING IN MY head. I breathe recklessly in and out, knowing I can't get enough oxygen to calm my body any time in this century.

I stare down at my body wide-eyed, which doesn't help my anxiety. My hand had slipped between my legs, trying to act out the fantasy. Of all the times I've imagined Enzo in my head, I've never attempted to act it out. That's what went wrong.

I can't tolerate touch—not even by myself. That's how fucked up I am. That's what those men did to me.

I wipe my moist hand on the edge of the T-shirt I'm wearing and pull it down as I sit up, my body still spinning a million miles an hour. I need to go back inside and try to sleep. Forget this day even happened, but I'm not sure it's possible.

A loud popping sound startles me. I curl into the farthest corner of the couch, as I hesitantly look over the edge of the railing to see what is happening below.

I don't see anything.

"Fucking ladder," Enzo curses.

A metal ladder thumbs against the railing again, this time staying against it.

I bite my lip, and try to remain calm as I watch Enzo climb up the ladder to the balcony. I'm not sure he knows I'm up here. So I stay silent.

But he came back. I smile.

He reaches the top, swings a leg over the top, and then jumps out of his skin when he sees me. He starts falling backward, and I reach my hand out, trying to grab him to keep him from tumbling over.

He rights himself before I reach him.

We both stare at my hand outreached to help him. I would have never offered to touch him in order to help him before. *This is a step.*

"Progress," he says, smiling.

"What are you doing?"

"You locked the door."

I nod. "Yes, I locked the door to keep you out."

He shrugs. "That's not how this works. You lock the door to keep yourself safe. You've already decided I won't hurt you."

He stares at me wearing a white T-shirt sitting on the couch. "The better question is, what are you doing?"

I tremble. "Pushing myself."

"I see." His tense eyes travel over me. "I think you've had enough."

I nod.

He walks to the door and holds it open for me as I step inside. I immediately run to my corner and fall to the ground, my body shaking violently.

Enzo rubs his neck, looking frustrated. I don't know if the look is for himself or me.

There is a knock on the door, and I freeze. *What the hell?* Westcott never comes up here and disturbs us if Enzo is here. Enzo always calls him if he wants him.

Enzo looks at me with a silent sorry on his lips.

I hug my legs, bite my lip, and let my hair fall to my face. I'm done with people today. I've pushed myself far enough, and now I'm about to shut down.

Enzo slowly undoes each of the locks, his eyes cutting to mine at the sound of each mechanism unlocking, making it easier for them to get to me. *The monsters.*

I close my eyes.

I'm safe.

I'm fine.

Slowly, the door opens, and Enzo slips out through the crack. I'm alone.

I consider racing to the door to slam it shut and lock out Enzo again, but as much as I want to declare my independence from him, as much as I want to run away, I can't. I'm not strong enough to survive on my own, not yet.

And I need Enzo to sleep next to me in order to rest myself. Especially tonight after getting myself so worked up. I need the edges of his muscles to focus on, his rippled chest, his gruff face covered in dark shadows. I need to hear his soft snores rocking me to sleep. I need him.

The bastard. Maybe this was his plan all along. To get me to rely on him. So I could never leave. He wouldn't need a cage or guard to keep me trapped. I would do it myself.

I need to form a plan to stop relying on him, but right now I just want to sleep.

The door creaks open, and Enzo returns. He considers for a second and then walks over to me. He kneels down in front of me like I'm a child.

He bites his lip before he speaks. "Can you do me a favor?"

"No."

He smirks. "Then do yourself a favor. Let's go to the bathroom."

I raise an eyebrow. "Got a new fetish? Like watching me pee or something?"

He laughs. "No, just trust me. I need to change before we try to sleep."

"And you need me for that?'

"Yes," he sighs.

I stare at the door. He's hiding something from me behind it. But whatever it is, I don't want to be in here alone when it arrives.

So I stand and walk awkwardly to the bathroom.

Enzo shuts the door and locks it, something he never does. I stand silently as Enzo begins removing his jacket and tie.

"How was the car ride with Langston? Did he drive as cautiously as I told him to?"

Why is he asking about Langston? We seldom talk about normal things.

"It was fine. Yes, he drove like a grandma." Even though it didn't help me trust him or feel safe.

"Good. Has his eye started turning black and blue yet from my punch?"

"No, it was just swollen and red."

"Damn, I didn't hit him hard enough then," he smirks, a hint of a dimple on his cheek showing.

I open my mouth to thank him again for preventing his touch, but then I remember he told me to stop thanking him, so I don't.

Enzo kicks out of his shoes, leaving them a mess on the floor. It isn't like Enzo. He's organized and controlled. He usually hangs or folds his clothes when he's done with them. Even the dirty ones are folded in a pile for Westcott to collect.

"What's going on?" I ask.

He frowns. "I'm talking to you like a normal person while I get undressed."

"Except we don't do normal."

He shrugs.

The bedroom door slams. I flinch.

He sighs. "We can go back to the bedroom now." He hasn't finished getting undressed for bed. He's still wearing his shirt and slacks, but since it was just a distraction anyway, it doesn't matter.

I unlock the door and open it, terrified of what I will find. The way I'm acting, you would think there would be a wild animal on the other side ready to attack me.

I open the door but don't notice anything different about the room. The room is empty; no animal or person jumps out at me. I hesitantly enter the room, and that's when I notice the bed.

It has a different mattress on it than before. The covers have been removed and replaced with silk, thin and light. There is no comforter or blanket on the bed. And the pillows look like rocks.

"What's this?" I ask.

Enzo steps behind me, staring at the new bed.

"I'm fucking tired of sleeping on the floor. So I found the hardest, most uncomfortable bed I could find for us to try."

Us.

That word is dangerous. There is no us. *No we.*

There is Enzo, the man whose last name fits him—Black, like his heart. My new master who will soon snap and stop treating me like his damaged queen.

And then there is me—the woman filled with secrets and shame.

There is no us.

Us would mean we have a future together. Us means he thinks of me as more than his property. Us means I forgive him. And I can never do that. No matter how kind he's being, I can't forget about the cruelty inside.

CHAPTER 28

ENZO

The bed was a mistake.

Kai's not ready to be pushed any further. She's been pushing too hard already. She's going to crack if she keeps going at this rate.

Six years she was hurt and beaten. It's going to take more than a few weeks to bring her back to life after that cruelty.

It's all my fault Kai is pushing beyond her limits.

I put her up to this when I brought her to Surrender. And now she's going to lose any progress she's made by going too far.

The bed sounded like a good idea in my head, when I was driving back. I called and ordered the firmest bed on the market to be delivered upon my arrival back home. Normally, the mattress company doesn't deliver so quickly, but when you have money as I do, the impossible easily becomes possible. I only wish my problems with Kai were as easily fixable.

Langston and Zeke are out meeting with a new gentleman in town who wants to acquire a yacht. I would usually meet with a new client, as this man is willing to pay big bucks for what he wants. I intended to meet with them after delivering the mattress for Kai to try. But seeing her now, I know I can't leave her.

Even though I should.

I feel unsettled no matter what I do, stay or leave.

Fuck.

I don't know what to do. Not when it comes to Kai. I want to help her, but it's as much about helping her as helping myself get rid of her.

I try to stare at the bed, instead of her. I can't believe she's wearing clothes now; even if it's just a T-shirt, it's more than I've seen her in since she arrived.

I should let the issue of the bed go, and continue to sleep on the cot I've made on the floor. But my back is killing me, and I'm more irritable than usual after our outing at the club. I doubt I'll be able to sleep, but if Kai sleeps, it will be worth it. She needs as much sleep as possible to continue to heal.

I walk closer to her, careful not to get too close and accidentally brush against her. I inhale her scent, knowing this is the best I will get tonight, or ever. But her scent will stay with me in my dreams.

Kai usually smells of the wildflower shampoo she uses. But tonight she smells different. She smells of lust, desire, and sex.

My eyes widen, and my heart races. *Did someone touch her? Rape her? No, I would have known.*

"Show me your hands, Kai."

She turns with concern on her face. "What? Why?"

"Just do it." I give her a warning look.

She hesitantly holds up her hands.

I lean down, lowering my head to her hands stopping just above them. I inhale deeply. Her fingers are laced with the same scent that hung in the air before.

I straighten, studying her face. She blushes and bites her lip nervously.

I cock my head, realizing what happened. She pushed herself even further than I realized. She pleasured herself, but from the anxious look on her face, it didn't appear to go successfully.

I suck in a breath. I could fix her problem so easily. Make her come with a few strokes of my fingers. Give her undo pleasure. But that would require her to be touched. Tolerate a bed.

"Didn't go successful, did it?" I ask, raising an eyebrow at her hands.

Her blush deepens. "No."

I'm surprised by her honesty. We both know what I'm talking about.

I stare at the bed and then back to her. I don't know what's gotten into me. My own sexual frustration has heightened. And I'm afraid what I'm about to do will make it worse.

But I know how healing it could be for her, how freeing to let go of one tiny bit of her own frustration.

"Get on the bed, Kai."

She blinks and swallows slowly. "What if I can't?"

"I'm not asking you to sleep. Just lie down on the bed."

"I'm not sure—"

"You can. It's not an option; it's an order. Get on the bed."

Kai slowly walks over. She takes her time climbing up, her legs moving awkwardly. And then she lies down flat on her back. Her breathing speeds as I walk over, her body trembling slightly.

I have an uphill battle if I'm going to have any success with my plan. I don't even know if it can be done, but if anyone can do it, I can.

I smirk, *I'm a cocky son of a bitch.*

Kai must see something on my face. Something that makes her say, "I trust you."

Those words crush me. Because I haven't earned her trust. *Not ever.*

"Good, because I'm going to give you back something that never should have been taken."

CHAPTER 29
KAI

I trust you.

I don't know why I said those words.

Trust.

I don't trust Enzo.

But it seemed those were the words he needed to hear to carry out his plan. And it seemed I would be rewarded if I let him get his way.

So despite every bone in my body begging me to run, I stay. I lay on the cool bedsheets face up. I expected to hate and curse the bed the second I laid down on it—but I don't hate it.

The bed is firm. The sheets feel brisk, my skin adapting to the temperature easily. And the pillow is supportive under my head and neck, not soft and mushy.

I'm not sure what Enzo has planned as I lay face up on the bed, but I'm tired of living in fear. Today, I will claim something back. Something bigger than wearing clothes or stepping out into the sunlight. *But what?*

"Turn off that brain of yours," Enzo says.

"I can't."

He sighs. "What was the last good memory you have?"

That's too invasive of a question. My last good memory should be the time Mason and I played hooky from school and spent the whole day at the beach getting sunburned and drinking vodka. That day should have been the day I got my first kiss.

Or maybe it should have been a memory with my father. Sharing a simple meal I cooked, and not worrying about bills and payments, before watching Jeopardy together on the TV.

Neither were my best memories.

"Kai? It doesn't matter what it is; I just need you to think of a positive memory. Something that will help you relax."

My one good memory bubbles up; it's the one I've played in my head every day for years. The memory that saved me from death. The one I could use to escape when my body couldn't.

"You kissing me."

He shakes his head. "Not your happiest memory with *me*. Your happiest memory *ever*."

I swallow, hating myself for the words I'm going to say, because I'll be giving him a lot. But I say the words anyway. "You kissing me *was* my best memory."

He gasps. His eyes latch onto mine, and I swear I see moisture in his eyes. It's sad that my only good memory is my first kiss with a man who moments later tried to kill me—who succeeded in selling me. But there it is. My life is too tragic to be true.

He nods. "Okay, that's good. It will make this easier."

This. What's this? What are you doing, Black?

"We are back on the water."

I tense—*fucking ocean.*

He notices and changes the narrative. "We are here, in bed. In the only place you feel safe. The door is locked. No one can get in."

"The ladder?"

"It's gone. No one can use it to get to you."

I nod.

"Close your eyes."

I do.

He pulls the curtains tight, blocking out the last strips of light poking through. I feel the darkness descend around me before he walks back to the edge of the bed, standing over me, but not touching.

I open my eyes when he nears.

"Tell me what you remember of our kiss," he says, his voice thick with desire.

"I remember how unexpectedly good it was. How powerful I felt even though you were in control. I could push back against you. I remember the collision of our lips. How good it felt to enjoy the scolding hot for once. How your lips made me surrender to you, no matter how much disdain I felt for you. In that moment, I wanted you. I would have given you everything. Trusted you with my body. Let you take my innocence."

"I should have," his voice is pained. "I should have taken your innocence. Then, Jarod wouldn't have. You would have at least had that."

My lip trembles. *Would it have been better? Would I be as broken as I am now if Enzo would have taken my virginity?*

Yes, it would have been better. Even if he sold me afterward, it would have been better.

"Take off your shirt," Enzo says.

I hesitate but give in. I don't care that he can ogle my body. He's done it a million times before. But for some reason after telling him one of my most intimate of memories, it's harder to strip naked in front of him.

I pull the T-shirt over my head and hand it to him; he sniffs the shirt slowly then tosses it on the floor.

Enzo starts undressing—pants, buttoned-down shirt, and underwear.

I should be freaking the hell out. Alarm bells should be going off, warning me of what a naked man with a predatory gaze wants with me. *To fuck.*

Something I imagined a million times, but can't let happen. I can't touch myself; he would ruin me if he tried to fuck me.

He smirks, noticing my reaction. "It's a good thing I can't touch you. Otherwise, I'd have you tied up, and bent over this bed, while I sink my cock into you with no apologies at how tight the fit would be in your petite body."

I nibble on my bottom lip. "If you aren't going to touch me, what are you going to do?"

His eyes brighten, a wicked grin spreads across his scruffy face, and I know without him saying what he plans.

"Make you come, of course."

"But how? If you can't touch me? I'm not ready."

"Because the only way you won't be truly terrified of life anymore is to experience some pleasure."

"Giving me my freedom would make me happy."

"No, it wouldn't. Stop lying to yourself."

I glare. "How would coming make me happy?"

He freezes. "You don't remember, do you? I know your last few memories have destroyed you, but you don't remember before?"

I suck in a breath giving him a silent answer.

"Don't you remember when you'd lie in your bed at night with a boy you thought you could love in your head? One who would smile at you in the hallways at school, hold your hand innocently. One whose crotch you'd stare at enough times to get the general sense of how big he was beneath his jeans. With that image in your head, you'd let your hand trace circles all over your body, priming yourself for what comes next. You'd let your breathing get heavy, and your head floats away in the clouds, imagining that one special boy was the one gently and carefully removing the clothes from your body like he was unwrapping the most precious gift.

"Then as your hand slipped between your panties, you'd pretend it was him. His fingers finding your clit and knowing how to rub to make your juices spill from between your lips. Maybe you'd imagine he'd go down on you, putting his head between your legs, his tongue taking the place of his fingers. You'd writhe beneath your fingers as you circled that beautiful pink clit of yours faster and faster. Building yourself up to images of him. You'd take your time because you wanted to drag out the feeling. You wanted the dream to be real, and yet you didn't because you were afraid reality with a boy wouldn't be as good as you could experience on your own. You'd be right; boys your age wouldn't be able to find your clit, let alone know what to do with it. And then you'd come. That tiny explosion would start at your core and then grow as it trickled outward to the tips of your fingertips and toes. Don't you remember, Kai?"

My breath is caught in my throat. "No, I don't remember." I want to, desperately. I want to own my body again. I want to be able to touch or have control over my emotions and feelings. *But I can't.*

His face drops. "Then let me help you."

Enzo rounds the bed; my eyes follow him as he climbs up on the bed next to me and lies down. I stare at his naked body with muscles so defined he looks like he competes in wrestling matches. His body isn't flawless. It's marked with scars, but no tattoos that I can see. I don't let my eyes drift down to his cock. I keep my eyes up, like if I don't stare at his cock, I'll be saved. From what I don't know.

Maybe if I had met Enzo earlier, I would have dreamed about him in high school. He would have been the dangerous boy that everyone knew they should stay far away from, but secretly pined for at the same time. He would have been every girl's crush and every boy's nightmare.

Enzo's eyes aren't as forgiving as mine. He doesn't shy away from staring at my body. And the way he slowly licks his lips lets me know he likes what he sees.

"Moisten your lips, beautiful."

Beautiful. I focus on the word. Hold onto it. I haven't heard a compliment like that in forever. But I'm not beautiful. The healing has made me more human but not attractive.

He scowls. "If this is going to work you have to trust me. You promised you would. You have to believe every word I say is true. I won't lie to you. Not now. You're beautiful, Kai."

I moisten my lips, but I'm not sure I believe him.

"Good. Part your lips, run your tongue over your bottom lip slowly. Take your time."

I hang onto his words, my body responding before I have time to process them. I let my tongue explore my own mouth, running my tongue over my bottom lip slowly, like it's the most delicious popsicle I want to taste.

"Good girl. You're so fucking sexy when you do that. I remember how you taste. I've never forgotten."

I raise an eyebrow. *Not possible.*

"I haven't. You tasted like the sea. Like salt and cool, refreshing water. You were the most invigorating woman I've ever kissed. So eager and yet so in control of your own body."

Control, I want that back.

"Now, take a deep breath and exhale slowly with me." He sucks in a breath, and I do the same. We hold our breath for what seems like forever before he steadily lets us exhale. In and out we repeat, until I'm breathing slowly on my own.

"You are so beautiful, so fucking strong and in control."

Beautiful and in control, I repeat his words in my head.

"Now let your hand fall against your body wherever it wants. Don't force it anywhere."

My hand rests against my chest, feeling my speeding heart beneath it.

"Perfect, Kai. Let your fingers dance across your flesh. Let it feel the tingles as you trace the scars, but more importantly, the untouched skin that will heat your body."

My fingers barely move at first, focusing too much on a scar over my chest on the left side. A knife wound. I thought it would kill me, that I'd bleed out.

"Move your fingers, Kai."

I do, letting them move to skin that feels good instead of evil. My fingers trip over the point of my nipple.

Enzo sucks in a sharp breath, and his eyes deepen with his own lust. "See that hard nipple? It's hard because it knows what it wants. It wants to be flicked, stroked, touched. It's peaked in anticipation of what you will do to your own body."

I pause over my pointed nipple. *How did it get hard?*

"Squeeze it between your fingers."

My thumb and fingers squeeze.

"Ah," I cry at the unfamiliar sensation.

Enzo grins seductively. "Good girl, see how your body reacts. Your other nipple has hardened. Ready for its turn. Lick your finger this time before you touch it."

I slowly lick my finger, letting my saliva soak it before dripping it over my nipple. It feels better than the first, as I move my finger in slow circles.

My body arches into my hand as my nipple tenses beneath my touch.

"You're so beautiful taking control of your body like this, Kai. You're making me use all of my self-control to not touch you. Because goddammit, I've never wanted a woman more than you."

His words are like my own special chorus singing to me. I want him to want me, even if I never want him to touch me.

"Now what do you want, Kai? What are your fingers eager to touch next? Let them go."

Down. My fingers slip down.

"Part your legs."

I let my legs fall to the side, as my fingers slide down my marred stomach.

"Wider."

I spread my legs as open as I can and realize I'm opening not for my fingers, but for Enzo's dirty gaze. His tongue licks his lips, and I feel the sensation in my core.

"Fuck," I jerk at the unexpected sensation even though he didn't touch me.

He bites his lip in an evil grin.

"Touch yourself, Kai. Show me how you like it."

"What if I don't remember?"

He shakes his head. "Trust your body. You do. And if you don't, I know what you like. How you like to be touched."

My fingers are between my legs, and I let them move as one, caressing my cunt, taking all of my lower lips in.

"You're wet," he says, and I confirm with my touch.

"Yes."

"Move your hands in big slow circles."

I do, as I exhale the intensity of the touch and his devouring stare is too much.

I can't.

I stop and start moving my hand away to give myself a break.

"Don't you dare. Keep your hands on your pussy. You don't get to stop until you've come all over your delicious fingers."

I clench my teeth together at the overwhelming sensations I can barely handle.

"You're ready."

"For what?"

"To sink your fingers inside. To feel the walls of your pussy."

I nod. *That sounds incredible.*

"Start with one finger at your entrance."

Yes, one finger.

"Now slide it in through your slickness."

In my finger slides as he growls deeply, and my skin burns. His growl urging me on as if knowing this step was going to be hard for both of us.

My finger stills. It's just one finger. I can barely even feel it inside me, but its enough to send me into a frenzy of anxiety.

"You got this, beautiful; hold onto my voice."

But I can't. A tear burns my eyes. *Why is this so difficult? Why can't I touch myself?*

I start panicking. Sweat drenches my body, and I start pulling my finger out.

"Look at me, gorgeous."

I blink back my tears as I turn my head to Enzo. *I failed. I can't.*

"Look at my cock."

I do, and I gasp.

His hand has his cock firmly in his grasp, and I've never seen him so hard. "This is what you do to me. You make my cock hard and thick. You make it ache to thrust inside of you. You make me into a fucking desperate son of a bitch who only bursts for you."

He strokes himself. *God, he's so big.* Bigger than any man I've seen.

His cock is long, thick, and veiny. It grows the more he strokes it, as he devours me with his wolfish eyes.

"I haven't had another woman since you arrived. I used to get laid weekly, daily if I wanted it. But not one single woman since you."

"Why?" I breathe.

"Because of you. All I think about is you. Your naked body. Your fight. You drive. Your tears. I want it all, Kai. Every buried emotion, I want it. To claim and own myself.

"Don't let me take it. Your emotions and experiences are yours—not mine. No matter how much I want you, only you can give yourself to me. And I don't deserve you. Take back your body. Take back yourself."

He continues to stroke himself, and I realize my finger starts sliding in and out of myself the same as his rhythm stroking his cock.

"Add another finger. Stretch that pretty cunt."

Another finger slides in and out, but I don't stop at two. I add three.

His heavy growl at my addition drenches my fingers.

My other hand drops lower and begins to circle my clit finding the swollen nub easily now that I'm so turned on.

"Yes, Kai. Touch yourself. Feel how incredible your body feels beneath your fingers."

"God," I moan as another surge makes my toes curl. The sensations start coming back, and I remember how it feels. I remember what to do.

My back arches into my hand as my fingers work. My lips part and my legs spread wider as my fingers sink deeper.

"Beautiful, are you close? I'm so fucking close because of you." He's stroking himself so hard I don't know if he's pleasuring or punishing his cock for wanting me.

"Take it back, Kai. Take back what is yours."

I feel my body clenching around my fingers, my body tensing, arching for more. So close, but even though I'm the edge, can I really fall over the cliff? Can I let myself feel the intense joy and feel the peace afterward?

"Let go with me, Kai. Let go. Come on those dirty, filthy fingers. Come because you control your body. No one else, just you."

I hear his words. And they help. But I also feel myself stirring inside—a voice of my own stepping out of the dark shadows of my heart.

I'm here.

I'm strong.

I'm in control.

I scream as I finally push myself into an orgasm. My muscles squeeze my fingers rhythmically as I come. My body clenches and then releases my orgasm as it bubbles then bursts in tiny explosions throughout my body, releasing all of the darkness of my past and giving me back my body—giving *me* back.

I gasp as I try to regain my normal breathing, and then I watch Enzo jerk his own beautiful orgasm from his body. His eyes roll back, no longer focused on me, as his cock hardens before the thick, white liquid spills onto the tight muscles of his stomach.

God, what would it feel like for his cock to spill his seed inside me?

I'm not sure I've seen anything so breathtakingly attractive as a man coming on himself when he wanted to fuck me instead. He could have. He could have taken me and destroyed me. Fucked me into oblivion. But he didn't.

He didn't touch me.

And it's never made me want a man more. I just came, just experienced that sensation again for the first time in years, but I think I'm already crazier with need than before. I'm horny and lusting after the handsome man lying next to me.

I can never forgive him, but this...giving me back a piece of myself is as close as I will ever get to absolving him.

But right now, I can't think. The heavy pull of sleep is too much. And I let it consume me.

♡

I WAKE UP TO AN EMPTY BED.

Enzo is gone.

But I slept in a bed; albeit a hard, cool one.

And I made myself come.

I'm healing, faster than I thought I would heal in a lifetime, and it makes me want to think about a future. *What does my future look like?*

Will I ever be free? Finish school? Hold a job?

Or will I end up a whore? A slave again?

I climb out of bed, before I realize my legs are woozy from last night.

I smile. I have a new favorite memory. The only way it could have been better would have been to combine the two memories. Kissing while coming would have made it better.

I don't know what time it is. I fell asleep in the early morning. I pick up my discarded shirt from last night and put it on before I walk over to the curtains and pull them open. The sun is low in the sky. It's almost sunset. I slept all day, no wonder Enzo left the bed. He's probably at work.

I don't hesitate, I push the glass open and step outside. I take a deep breath of salty air, feeling like a new woman as I walk over to the edge of the balcony and lean against the railing. Today is a new start. I don't need answers to heal anymore. All I need is me.

I can decide my own future. And Enzo will just have to deal with it. He won't stop me. I'm his kryptonite. I can have anything I want, and he'd give it to me. I just need to figure out what I want.

Him.

Shit, I think.

"You're entering a brave new world," Enzo says from behind me in his suit.

I smile. "Thanks to you."

He frowns. "No, I had nothing to do with it."

That's not true. He gave me back myself after being the one who took it in the first place. I feel settled for the first time in years.

"Here," he says holding out a tall drink with a straw to me.

"What's this?"

"Try it."

I take it from him and sip. It's crisp and sweet and delicious.

He grins, his dimple showing as my eyes light up. "It's iced coffee with cream and sugar. I know Westcott has been trying to get you to drink coffee or tea when you wake up. But I knew you would enjoy something cold more than hot at the moment."

"Thank you."

He sighs. "Stop thanking me."

"I can't. You helped me. Why do you keep being so nice to me?"

"Trust me; I'm not nice. If you knew what was going on in my head, you wouldn't be thinking that way. I have my own devious reasons for helping you. And in the end, you will hate me again. So don't let yourself like me for a second. Because I will just use it to destroy you."

I don't believe him. I misjudged him. He's my savior.

I step toward him.

Closer.

Closer.

Closer.

My hand outstretched as I hesitantly lay my hand against his chest.

Spark.

Fire.

Fuck.

The sensation of only our touch is more than the explosion I felt last night when I came. His heart squeezes at my touch—his dark, dangerous heart. The one that can be cruel or kind.

"I'm glad you didn't take my innocence that night. The kiss was enough to survive on."

He looks pained as I continue to touch his heart.

"Sex with a worthy man was something to look forward to. A goal to get back to."

He grabs my wrist forcefully. The most forceful touch I've felt since I was released.

"Stop looking at me like you see me bringing you chocolates and flowers. I'm not your knight in shining armor. I'm not your savior. I made a mistake all those years ago. One I plan to rectify very soon. I just need you healed before I carry out my plan. Because I'm not so ruthless to destroy a broken girl."

He releases me and steps back. "You aren't broken anymore. Now I can ruin you."

He walks away.

I want to be fucked by a worthy man. Enzo Black isn't that man. He never will be.

ENZO

Kai is no longer afraid.

She can walk in the light.

She dons clothes instead of going bare.

She slept in my bed.

And her body is hers again.

She's healed. There are still fragile parts, pieces that will take longer to fit back into her body. Pieces that still appear broken and can't be fixed in a single night. But she doesn't need me anymore. She's healing on her own.

There is no denying she isn't broken. The shattered pieces of her icy cage are being put back up, but this time, she let me in first.

It was the one thing she shouldn't have done—trust me.

Healing her broke me in ways I wasn't expecting. She's no longer shattered, but I am. Because as much as I want to pretend it's better that she's healed, it's not. I know what darkness comes next, even if I don't want to face it.

The door to my lair at Surrender opens, and Langston walks in, followed by Zeke, Westcott, and Archard, my lawyer.

I motion for all the men to take a seat at the long conference like table I have brought in for meetings like this.

"You all know why I gathered you here for this meeting," I start.

"The girl," Langston answers.

I nod.

"She's the one? Kai? The one you killed six years ago?" Langston continues.

"Yes, one and the same."

"But how is she alive, if you killed her?" Zeke asks.

All of the men stare at me with bated breath as they wait for my answer.

"Because I didn't kill her."

"Why not?" Zeke asks.

"Because Black's in love with her," Langston slumps back in his chair. "I told you that pussy would be what destroyed us. Everything we've spent our entire lives working for. All the shit your father put us through will be lost because you want to fucking get laid."

I slam my fist down on the table. "No, I don't love the girl." *Truth*. "And I sure as hell don't want to fuck her." *Lies*.

"Then what, Mr. Black? Why didn't you kill her?" Westcott asks this time.

"Because it's not who I am. It's not who any of us are. I didn't want to start my reign by killing someone who didn't even know what could be hers. It didn't seem fair."

The men nod.

"I was a boy. I was stupid. I won't make the same mistake again."

"So you're going to kill her now?" Zeke asks.

"No, I'm going to follow the rules and earn my kingdom the way the contract was written. I'm tired of feeling like a fraud."

"Kai's not ready for that. She's weak. It would be kinder just to kill her," Langston says. He's the only one who truly got any insight into who Kai really is. Westcott may have spent time with her, but he doesn't know her. She never opened up to him.

"She is now," I say.

"What changed?" Langston asks.

"Everything," I answer.

I turn my attention to Archard, my lawyer. The real reason I brought all of my most trusted men together. To understand what my next steps are now that I know the last few years have all been a lie.

"So tell me what happens now," I say to Archard.

He thumbs the papers. "Well, the contract you signed three years ago is void now that we know the conditions haven't been met."

I nod, I knew they would be. But everyone else in the room gasps, realizing what it means.

"What are my choices now? What are the conditions for me to regain everything I just lost?" I ask.

Archard looks concerned as he pulls the paper and slides it over to me. The paper I haven't seen in over twenty years. One I only faintly recognize. I skim quickly, already realizing what I have to do.

It's the same choice as before. *Save her or save myself. Never both.*

I'm used to surviving. I don't know how not to survive. I don't know how to lose.

Kai is stronger now; it could be a fair fight.

Liar. It would never be a fair fight. I should have just killed her all those years ago. I should have snuffed out her life like you put a wounded dog to sleep, because it's kinder than letting them suffer.

I could choose her this time. I could save her, and find a way to lose.

But it's no longer just about me. I look at the four pairs of eyes focused on me. Their lives rely on me too, as well as the hundreds of other men who work for me. The entire city's survival depends on having a strong Black at the helm—protecting them from the evil. And as much as I'd like to think you need good to drive out the bad, it isn't true. Only the cruelest, darkest of men can do what is needed to drive out the darkness.

I'm the worst kind of man. Because I brought Kai Miller back to life, only to destroy her. She thought she was broken before, but when I'm done with her, she will never recover. This time she will remain broken.

CHAPTER 31
KAI

"Meet me in the library," Enzo says, poking his head out on the balcony where I drink another iced coffee as dawn ascends. I don't know why I've resisted sitting out here for so long. *Why have I resisted everything?*

"Okay. Why?" I ask, not tearing my eyes from the still haunting ocean.

"For once, can you just do what I fucking say without asking any questions?" Enzo snarls before leaving.

I frown. *What the hell is up with him?* The last time we were in the library we played truth or lies. *Is that what he wants again?* We still haven't talked about what happened the last time we slept when he made me come. He vanished afterward.

I hate following orders, but right now it seems necessary to get my answers.

I run my hand through my long black hair that now reaches almost to my butt. I could really use a haircut. *But why does it matter what I look like?* I'm a prisoner. He wants me locked away, even if I won't stay hidden much longer.

I'm wearing jean shorts and a spaghetti strapped shirt. The same type of outfit I was wearing the first time I saw him. I thought my life was devastatingly horrible then, but I didn't realize how tragic my life was destined to be.

I carry my iced coffee to the library doors, which are closed surprisingly enough. I raise my hand to knock but stop myself. This is my home—at least for now. And Enzo invited me to the library. He's expecting me.

I push the heavy door open and step into the dream-like room. I've never been a big book lover. I've never had time to read books; it was hard to find the time when I was focused on finding enough food to fill my belly. And I never had money to spend on lavish things like books. But being in this room makes me want to get lost in the spines. I want to go on an adventure and never return. Books might be the only way for me to do that.

Enzo is the only silhouette I see in the moonlit room, but with every second that passes, light continues to pour in as the sun rises in the sky. We will only be veiled in darkness for a few more minutes.

I walk and notice the chairs we sat in before are gone. Instead, there is a small table with two chairs at either end. This is business. Whatever he brought me here for, it's not casual.

Neither is he. He's dressed in a suit. Usually, when he arrives home, he loosens the tie or kicks off his shoes. He doesn't today. His tie is still done up to his neck. His jacket still buttoned. The only hint that he's already put in a day of work is the scruff of shadow on his chiseled jaw.

Enzo notices me. His eyes take every drop of me in from head to toe. He notices the clothes and the way they still hang loose on my body. He notices that I tried to brush my hair and that my skin has slightly more color after spending a few hours sitting out in the sun. But he doesn't speak. Words are reserved for the meeting.

Instead, he sits in one of the chairs. I mirror his movements and sit in the other. I expect now that I'm seated he will start explaining why I'm here. He doesn't.

The door opens, and Westcott enters. I cock my head. He never enters when it's just the two of us.

He carries in a large tray with what looks like orange juice in tall skinny glasses, a tray of fruit, and cheese and crackers. He hands each of us a glass and puts the food on the table before leaving. I watch intently as he goes.

Enzo holds out his glass, and I clink mine to his before sipping. It's bubbly as it goes down. There isn't just orange juice in the glass; there is also champagne. It tastes nice going down.

"Since it's morning, I figured mimosas would be more appropriate than wine or liquor. Even though we will both be going to sleep in a couple of hours."

Mimosas, that's right. That's what these things are called.

"Stop stalling. What am I doing here?"

His lips thin as he cautiously sets his drink on the table. "Isn't that the question you've been dying to know the answer to?"

I bite my lip. *Is he finally ready to talk? Will he tell me why I'm here? Why he was sent to kill me in the first place?*

"Want to play a game?" he asks.

My lips part in anticipation. *Do I? More than anything.*

I clear my throat. "Stakes?"

"The usual, winner asks all the questions. *All of them*, until they are satisfied."

I nod. I feel like this is a setup. Like he's going to lose on purpose in order to tell me his truth. *But do I want him to win?* Because after he made me come, I realized I want to tell my own secret.

I want to spill all of my secrets. I want to tell Enzo what truly happened, every painful memory. I want to tell him why I don't like being touched. Why as much as I've healed, I will always be broken too. My secret could change everything. How Enzo feels about me. How he treats me. How he looks at me. And I'm not sure I'm ready for that. But I'm not sure I'm ready to hear his truth either.

Because I care about Enzo, I've learned to hate him less, and knowing the truth will probably cement his place in my send to hell list.

So I'll play the game as always. I'll do my best to deceive and figure out his truth. This time, I just don't know if I want to win or lose.

"I've never been sold.

"I've never been raped.

"I've never been tortured," I say.

He gasps as each word is spoken. Obviously not understanding any of my words or how a single one could be true. But we've bent the rules before. Last time we played, all of his were truths. So he knows that all of mine could be lies. Or all truths. And he doesn't get to protest the results.

That's how we play the game now. The truth is always well hidden, even from the game itself.

"Your turn," I say, raising an eyebrow.

"I will never fuck you.

"I don't regret letting you go.

"My real name is Rinaldi."

I don't react. I knew whatever he chose to tell me was going to be shocking. But after our last game, learning I've been gone six years instead of three, nothing he says will surprise me now. *Nothing.*

But his words still hurt. And all of them hold an air of truth.

He's said plenty of times that he won't fuck me. I'm damaged to him. *Why would he want a woman another man's touched and abused?* He has plenty of playthings back at his club.

And of course, he doesn't regret letting me go. Nothing touches him. Even the complication of me returning.

The last one makes the least sense. His real name is Rinaldi. *Is Enzo his middle name or nickname or something?* It seems completely out of left field if it isn't true.

They could all be truths. They could all be lies. But I've made my decision.

From Enzo's hungry stare, it's apparent he has as well.

"They are all lies," he says.

I take a deep breath in and out. Deciding how to answer so he will believe me. Because one of them is the truth, the rest are lies. I shake my head slowly, waiting for the confusion and acceptance to clear his face.

One second passes, then another as we both stare. He tries to read my face. Tries to understand which of the three is the truth—which pain I never suffered. Or how I could make one of them fit my truth in my messed up head, even though it truly happened.

Finally, he slumps in his chair and says, "You were never tortured. At least you don't feel you were because it would make you weak. It is the narrative you can control. They beat you, but torture requires the other person to submit to it. If you blocked them out, they never got in."

I don't confirm or deny his statement. I just choose my answer, preparing for the answers I've been waiting years for.

"Your name is Rinaldi."

"Good answer. Yes, my name is Rinaldi."

I narrow my eyes, not understanding. And it's clear he feels he needs to give me more confirmation. But I believe him. My true name is Katherine after all, even though I've always been Kai.

He clears his throat loudly, and the doors open again. Langston, Zeke, and Westcott all walk in.

I cock my head. *Have they all been outside listening this entire time?*

"What is my name?" Enzo looks to the men.

"Your name is Enzo Rinaldi," Langston says.

Zeke and Westcott, both nod, confirming the statement.

"Thank you; that will be all for now."

The men file out of the room.

"What was that about? If you say your name is Rinaldi, then I believe you. No need to drag out men that would lie for you to prove your point."

"My name has everything to do with it."

"Okay?" I say slowly. "Then explain. Why do you go by Black if your name is Rinaldi? Did your father change your last name or something because he thought it sounded more menacing?"

He shakes his head.

"Black wasn't my father's true name either. We were both born Rinaldi. There is only one way you get to become a Black. You earn it. Black is a legend, a myth. The name alone sparks fear in anybody who understands the true origin of the name in this city. Black has been around for hundreds of years—passed on from leader to leader. It's the name assumed when a new leader is born to Surrender. To the sea. To Miami. *The world.* It has to be earned."

Black. Living in Miami, of course, I'd heard the name. I knew

Black was the most dangerous man in the city; myth said the world. He offered no mercy. No prisoners. No survivors. But I never thought the myths were true. Always over exaggerated to get people to do his bidding. I thought he was Enzo's father and that Enzo now became Black because his father either died or got too old to do the job properly. If Black doesn't truly exist, it's only a name assumed by a family of men when they take power; it makes more sense why all the rumors exist around the name.

But one sentence he spoke concerns me more than the rest. *The position has to be earned.* My eyes flutter up, my jaw clenches, and my hands fist.

"What did you do to earn the title?"

"I took out my opposition."

I exhale. That doesn't seem so bad. And it doesn't seem to have anything to do with me or my predicament.

"Who was your opposition?"

His jaw tightens. "Only one of two people can take over the title —from two families with an arrangement. The most powerful offspring of each fight, in each new generation, for control."

I nod, understanding more about him. How he felt trapped in this world from birth. He was. Destined to fight for a crown he may not have even wanted. But only the strong survive. So he had to be ruthless to gain his freedom. But he's free now as their leader. Free to make any decision he wants.

"Ask," he says.

"Who are the families?"

Maybe I know the other family, and that's why this pains him. He killed someone he thinks I cared about.

I silently laugh.

He doesn't realize there is no one I care about anymore—no friend worth saving. He could have killed Mason, and it wouldn't have hurt me much after Mason failed in rescuing me. It may be heartless, but I lost my heart six years ago.

"The Rinaldis," he says indicating his own family.

I nod, of course.

"And the Millers."

I gasp.

"What? Miller as in..."

He nods. "Your family."

"No," I shake my head viciously as I laugh out loud this time. "You're joking. My family isn't strong. My family has nothing and is nothing. We have no money, no power, no control. We wouldn't know the first thing about running an evil empire. This is ridiculous."

"Your family was strong the generation before your father. They had money, power. Your grandfather was Black. He ruled the empire, but then your father lost to my father, and that started the Miller's downward spiral."

What?

"Usually, the loser helps the next generation out, getting ready to fight for the next battle by preparing them. Ensuring whoever becomes Black is the strongest of all the men."

"But my father never told me. He never spoke of this to me. I had no idea that..." I can't even say the words.

"That you are heir to a criminal empire."

I nod.

"You are."

"No, I can't be. And you said *man*. I'm not male."

"Usually, it's a boy chosen as the one to fight. But since you are an only child and have no cousins..."

"I'm the only choice." I drink down the mimosa with shaky hands not understanding any of this but needing something to soothe my nerves.

He sighs and then clears his throat again.

The door once again opens. A different man enters carrying a stack of papers. He brings them to me.

"I'm Archard, Enzo's lawyer. These are papers going back generations explaining how control of the Black name and empire works. Here's your father's signature. And—"

"Mine," I say looking at the ridiculous signature. It might as well be in crayon as big and half written as it is. But there it is—*Kai M*. I couldn't write Miller yet, it doesn't look like I'm much older than five from the way my name is written.

"We've met before?"

"Only once when we were kids. Our fathers were the ones to set out the rules for the next generation. That's how it is done."

I nod, my new world sinking in as Archard leaves.

Why didn't you tell me the truth, dad? Why didn't you prepare me for this? For the evil in the world? Why didn't you protect me at least?

"This doesn't matter anymore," I lift the papers. "You won. You're Black. You defeated me when you sold me. And even if you didn't, the Millers aren't strong enough to run an empire. We would have lost."

"The Miller family has been weak for a long time, but it's strong again." His eyes stare at me. He means *me*; I'm the strong Miller he's talking about. "But you don't belong in this world."

"I'm in it whether I want to be or not. But I don't know why you are telling me this. You're Black. You won."

"No, I claimed the name wrongly. If I had killed you, I would have won. I would have a rightful claim to the name. The contract would have been finished, safe for another generation."

"But there wouldn't have been another generation of Millers."

He nods. "The Rinaldi's would have claimed the name forever. The old ways would have been over."

"Why didn't you kill me?" I whisper.

"I don't remember signing those papers any more than you do. But I've known since I was a kid what my destiny was. My father trained me hard, assuming that when the battle came, I would win no matter my opponent. The families are usually tight-lipped on the number of children each has. Keeping secret who will fight in each generation. But in this generation, only a single child was born to each."

I nod. He's a machine, I don't even know what the battle would entail, but I assume it's dark and dangerous. It would involve using a weapon, having other men attack. It would involve killing and blood —not things I could ever do.

"Of course you would win. But why didn't you kill me? That would have ensured you the name and title—your freedom."

"When I was given the assignment to kill you, I didn't know who you were. I didn't know you were the one to be my opponent. But when I met you, I sensed something. Something wasn't right. I wanted the truth, but it was clear you didn't know your own truth."

He sighs.

"All I had to do was kill you, and the empire was mine. I couldn't. It didn't seem fair. You obviously didn't understand what you had a claim to."

Enzo could have killed me. He could have won without making it messy. Defeated me and taken the name. But he didn't. He showed me mercy, something I'm sure his father punished him for. But when he sold me, he was given the title. I used to think death would have been better than what I went through. But I'm not sure anymore.

"Thank you for sparing my life. I can't forgive you for what occurred afterward, but I understand now the position you were in. And I thank you for doing the only thing you could to keep me alive while winning your own life back. But now that you have won the right to call yourself Black, to be the leader of savages, you can let me go. You don't have to worry about me sticking around. I have nothing to stick around for. I'll leave Miami forever."

"I figured you would say that, but there is one important part you don't understand."

I stare at the papers in the middle of the table I have yet to read thoroughly. *What's the catch? Do I actually have to be dead for him to retain the Black name? Is he really going to kill me this time?*

"I'm no longer Black. The second you were confirmed to be alive, I lost my title, my empire. I'm just Enzo Rinaldi again. I have no more power than you do."

"I don't understand."

"You're alive. The rules of the contract have not been met."

"Then I surrender. You win; just let me go."

He frowns. "It doesn't work that way. I can't. Too many people know you are alive."

"Then what do I have to do?"

"You choose. You have three choices."

I don't like where this is going.

He pulls out his gun and lays it on the table.

"One, I kill you now, and claim what I've spent my entire life earning."

Not going to happen. If he couldn't kill me before, he can't now.

"Two, we fake your death, and you stay locked away in my room forever. The men will think you are dead, and I will keep my power. But you will wish you were dead. I've been kind and merciful for the past few weeks. That time has passed. You've healed, and I will claim that tight little pussy as mine as many times as I want. And as you said before, you will surrender to me. I will take it, and you will beg for more."

His lips twitch, and I know that's the most appealing option to him. The fucking part is appealing to me too, even though he's the devil. A night or two in his bed doesn't sound so bad. But I would be trapped. I would be taken. I would be a prisoner.

"Or three, you play the new game and lose. In the end, your surrender will be taken. I will rightfully and legally claim my empire. And you will go free."

I sigh, three is obviously the only choice I have if I want to be free. This isn't about me choosing. It is about Enzo getting his way—as always.

"But know, this new game isn't like our truth or lies game. This game is dangerous. Your life will be on the line every single day. If you play, and aren't strong enough, you'll die. And there is nothing I can do to prevent that. More truths and lies will be revealed. And they will hurt worse than anything I've told you so far."

I smirk, I've experienced pain. I can handle any truth.

"If I chose three, where will I live? Will you let me free?"

He growls as his eyes bare down on me, and I know his answer.

"No, you're *mine*. You already lost one game. You don't get to back out now. And I'm done playing a nice host. Any choice other than death will leave you tied up in my bed."

"I only get to go free when the game is over?"

He nods, but it pains him. He doesn't want me to go free *ever*. But I assume it's one of the fine prints of the contract I should be reading before I agree to anything. But I don't. Because as I thought before, this isn't a choice. I've never had a choice. Never been able to dream or fantasize about my life. My life has been predestined from the start.

"And what if I win the game?" I ask. I don't know what this new game entails. But if it involves truth or lies, we both know I'm just as capable of deceit as he is. If it involves pain, then I can survive agony and torture. I've lived it longer than him. Enzo only wins when it comes to weapons and killing.

When he brought me here, I wouldn't have had a chance. If he brought out this contract then and forced me to play, I would have lost before the game started. But that's not what Enzo wanted. He wanted a fair fight. That's why he was so determined to heal me.

He's not a kind man; he just wants to sit on his throne, knowing he earned it like every generation before him.

He smirks. "You won't," his cocky ass mouth says. But there is a hint of a smile and glimmer in his eyes. He's more than ready for a fight—a battle—both in and out of his bed. His dark desires read all over his face.

But he won't win both battles. I'm strong enough to win one—whether it's saving my body or claiming an empire I don't even want. I just don't know which fight I will win. Because as much as he can only win one battle, I can only surrender to one. Will it be my body or my life I surrender to him? And which will I claim?

"Let the games begin," I say with a smug smile. I'm going to enjoy kicking his ass.

BETRAYED BY TRUTHS

PROLOGUE
ENZO

My eyes open before dawn. Not because I'm an early riser or enjoy watching the sunrise. But out of necessity —survival.

My feet hit the ground before my body is fully awake. My senses put out feelers in every direction, trying to determine any threat before it ends me. I pull the gun from under my pillow and aim it around the room. I no longer sleep without it. Not after my father's last "test" left me fighting off a dozen men with nothing but my thirteen-year-old body's scrawny muscles to defend myself.

I still my breathing and heartbeat as I focus. But I know immediately there is no one in my bedroom but me. The room is silent and dark.

I put my gun in the back of my jeans. *Yes, I sleep in jeans.* I've gotten too many early wake-up calls needing me to be ready to fight. And I'd rather fight with pants on than in my boxers. My junk feels better protected with another layer of clothes on, even if in the end it makes no difference.

I grab the black T-shirt that lies on the chair in the corner of my room and pull it over my head before stepping into my work boots. Then I slink to the window, thumb the drapes open just enough to see out through the thin slit in the fabric to the early morning sky. The sun is hovering on the horizon bringing with it the light.

I let the drapes fall closed, and then move with silent feet through the house—through corridors and down staircases. Through the house I will inherit someday when I become the king of evil incarnate and take over from my father.

Demolishing the house will be the first thing I do when I take over. I hate this fucking house. I hate its thick brick walls. The cold, drafty hallways that weren't built to accommodate air conditioning. The gargoyle statues that seem from another time, not meant to stare out over the seas of Miami. It's like my father lifted this house from medieval France and plopped it on a hillside in Florida. It's completely out of place here among the rows of beach houses.

And to me, it feels like a prison I have no hope of ever escaping.

I stumble to an abrupt stop when I reach the kitchen. My father's eyes sear into mine, and I know my fate from the way his nostrils flare at the sight of me.

"What are you fucking doing? You think you deserve to eat breakfast before even putting in an hour's work?" he asks, lifting a cup of coffee to his lips.

Yes, I fucking need to eat breakfast! I don't know how he expects me to pack on muscle if I never get to eat.

I don't say that. It might make me feel better for a second, but in the end, it would earn me a beating.

"Just awaiting your orders, sir."

That pisses him off more. *Dammit, what did I say?*

Father stands from the stool he's been sitting on while, waiting for me to make a mistake. His grip on the mug tightens until it shatters and hot coffee spills from the broken mug. The liquid must burn my father's skin, but he doesn't notice nor care.

I eye the broken shards, knowing my father could use it as a weapon against me at any second. I count the pieces preparing for an attack.

But I should know better than to think my father would be predictable.

Instead, he marches to me with all his furry behind him. Oozing from his pores as steam shoots from his nose. His face darkens to a shade of red that can only be used to describe the devil. All he's missing are horns and pitchfork.

"Awaiting orders?" He reaches for my neck, a move he's done countless times. I escape with ease, darting around to the other side of the kitchen island.

"Awaiting fucking orders?! Really, Enzo? Have you learned nothing from all our years of training! No son of mine awaits fucking orders. You give them! You rule them! You never take them!"

My father launches himself at me before I can escape. I may be quick, but he has years of experience, thick muscles, and more rage than I ever thought one man could contain behind him—while I live in fear.

He pins me against the cabinet with his forearm shoved against my neck, and his leg shoving hard into my stomach. He grabs my gun and quickly disarms me, tossing it to the floor behind him.

I'm powerless. He could kill me right now, and there is nothing I could do about it.

He won't. He needs me.

That's what I keep reminding myself every day.

I can't die. He can't kill me.

But sometimes, in the gloomy pain that encompasses my every day, I wish he would. Eternal sleep has to be easier than the torture I go through every day just to survive.

I don't flinch as his fist pounds into the side of my head. I jolt into the cabinet ensuring a dent in the wood as my head makes contact. The familiar taste of blood coats my mouth, but I don't think he knocked any teeth out this time.

Who needs coffee when you have dear old father to jolt you awake with a good morning jab to the face?

"Look at me, son."

I whip my head back to face him with nothing but disdain.

Dad sighs, exhaling his frustration, coffee, and whiskey. He may have just been drinking coffee, but I know his day is wrapping to a close, not starting. He was out late last night, chasing down a yacht from one of our enemies who threatened his control of the seas.

From the anger waving off of him, the chase didn't go well. But my father returned, and the only way that would have happened would be if he eliminated the bastard for daring to kill a single crew member from our ranks.

He shakes his head as he peers into my broken eyes. "Do you want to become Black?"

I nod my head, knowing any other answer will land me another blow to the head. Although, I'm not sure I want to become Black. Black is synonymous with my father. And he's the last person I want to become.

"Then you have to put in the work. The Millers will be preparing their heir to take over. To defeat you. He will be stronger than any foe you've ever faced. You can't lose."

I squint my eyes. My father would never allow me to come home if I lost. Good thing he'll be dead when it's finally time for me to do battle. That's what triggers the next Black to take his place. And I can't imagine a world where my father will ever die. So I don't expect to face my opponent until I'm ninety.

"You will be Black. The legend, the myth, the ruler. You will take my place someday. And when that day comes, you'll be more dangerous and ruthless than I ever was. You have a better teacher than I did. You will be more prepared to take over than any heir before you."

If this is what I have to do to prepare, then I don't want to be Black. I don't want any part of it. I'd rather lose and live my life on the sea, learning how to sail, and working hard than go through another day of my father's training course.

"And when you become king, like me, you will be free."

Free.

He said the magic word.

The one thing I crave more than anything—*freedom*.

My father grins, his eyes deepening as if he unlocked the key to the greatest treasure, instead of just finding the key to getting me to take his training seriously.

"Good," he says releasing me.

I ball my hands into fists, instead of reaching for my pounding head like I want. *Never show weakness.* I learned that lesson when I was seven and cried when I skinned my knee on the sidewalk after riding my bike too fast. Father whipped me for every tear I shed, which only made me cry harder and earn more lashings. When my tears had finally dried up, I had changed. I've never cried since that day. I'll never cry again.

Never flinch.

Never wince.

Never cry.

I am invincible. At least that is what the world thinks of me. I'm unstoppable.

His lips curl up higher as the evil wheels in his brain turn with an idea.

Fuck me.

I'm screwed.

Last time he had an idea, I was forced to run barefoot through the forest behind the house. I ran for three days straight with him hunting me on horseback with the promise that if he caught me, he'd shoot me.

My stomach lurches thinking of what happened when he finally caught up to me. My feet were bleeding; my body was frail from not eating; I was delirious with dehydration. He should have been proud that I lasted for three days. I hadn't slept or eaten. I never stopped moving. It took him three whole days to track me down and find me. He had the advantage of horses, scent dogs, and a weapon.

But father wasn't proud. I don't know how long he expected me to last or if shooting me was the plan the entire time no matter what I did. But my shoulder will never be the same.

He shot me without a word—only a dark stare of disappointment.

I was in shock, so I didn't realize what had happened until he motioned for me to follow.

I took one step and collapsed from the pain. When I awoke, I expected to be in a hospital or at least in my bed at home. Instead, I found myself covered in dirt, my shoulder still bleeding from the wound my father caused.

I could have died!

The bastard.

But I can't die. So I pulled myself up and walked home. Father wasn't there when I arrived, but I knew better at that point than to call a doctor. So I called Langston, one of my best friends. His father is a doctor, so I thought he could help. But all he could do was pull out the bullet, wash it clean with vodka, and then force the vile liquid down my throat until I passed out again to avoid the pain.

My shoulder still throbs six months later. That's when I started keeping a gun under my pillow. That's when any spare moment I have I'm practicing shooting or deflecting. I will not let any man shoot me again. Not without fighting back.

"Come," my father says like I'm a dog as he walks away from me.

I take the moment to inspect my head, but I don't find any contusion, bump, or blood. Probably just another concussion to add to the endless list of pain my father has caused me.

He picks up my gun before I have the chance.

Fuck.

I straighten my spine. *I will not let him shoot me again.*

Although, that's what I feel like I'm walking into. A shooting range where I'll be the target.

We descend down more stairs, and the prickling on the back of my neck tells me exactly where we are going—*the dungeon.*

My father doesn't hold very many men prisoner. And the ones he does he doesn't keep for very long. But there are a few rooms on the premise for this very purpose. To hold dangerous men, torture them, and then kill them when he gets the information he requires.

I swallow down the fear that begins to rise with each step.

We pass door after door of cages meant to loosen tongues into speaking, and then we stop at the last door. My father takes a key from his pocket and opens the door to the darkness. I already know what awaits me.

Nothing.

Blackness.

Loneliness.

This won't be a test of physical pain; it will be mental as all of his most ruthless tests are.

I don't wait for him to tell me what to do. I don't take orders. *Ha.* He forces me to take orders every single day.

But one day, I won't.

I'm already starting to get big enough that I can imagine a day when I'll have enough muscles and skills that I won't have to follow my father's orders. Except he has the power of the entire Surrender crew behind him. Most men in Miami would follow his every order just to stay alive or earn a favor from the notorious Black.

I walk into the cold, damp room. When I turn I see my father's smirk on his face. He doesn't want me to follow any orders, except his. He wants me to be his puppet he can control, even from the grave.

He tosses my gun into the room. I watch as it lands on the dirty floor at my feet.

Maybe I was wrong? Why the hell do I need a gun if he's just going to lock me in the room for a few days?

"This is a test of patience and self-control," he says.

I bend down and pick up the gun, not taking my eyes off of my father and my senses going on high alert.

"Why the gun?" I ask as he closes the door.

He grins, with a wicked glare. "Because before I open this door, you'll want to kill yourself rather than survive through one more minute of the pain. And you need to learn self-control, self-preservation. You need to prefer pain to death."

The door latches with a loud thud. Locking me in for longer than I ever want to imagine.

This should be an easy test for me. I have more patience than my father. I thrive on being alone. I can sleep for days uninterrupted and dream of a better world where I don't have to handle endless nights of pain just to show I'm worthy.

Easy.

But my days and nights are anything but.

I don't get food—not even scraps.

And my only choice for water is the occasional trickle that seeps through the walls when it rains that I'm forced to lick from the dirty bricks. I resort to drinking my own pee in hopes of getting the tiniest drops of liquid. But I haven't peed in days.

I've lost track of time. *How many days have passed and how many left to endure?*

My body won't survive much longer. It aches to move, to think, to breathe.

So I don't do anything.

I've even learned to shut off my mind.

I just exist.

And then I see the flicker of the gun that rests in the corner. I could end this.

Yes, that's what I'll do. End this.

I just have to make it to the gun.

Move body, move!

Now that I've made my decision, I want it to end—now.

But I can barely think, let alone move.

Every thought becomes a struggle.

I reach one arm out, then the other. Now pull my body forward as my legs push. I gain an inch. Then another. And another.

Until my fingers brush against the gun.

I smile for the first time in weeks.

This is going to end. I'm going to end it. I'll piss off father, leave him without an heir. That thought alone sparks my happiness. My final act won't be to kill my father, but myself. That will enrage him more than anything else ever could.

I grasp the gun and put it to my head.

My hands are shaky, but it doesn't matter if I miss the center of my head as long as I hit some part of my body. I'm too weak to handle a gunshot. I'll die from blood loss within minutes. It will just prolong my agony.

I keep my eyes open staring into the dark abyss, and then I pull the trigger.

CLICK.

Shit.

I remove the gun from my head and pull again.

Nothing.

The bastard removed the fucking bullets.

I fling the gun towards the wall, but my arms are too weak for it to even reach it. The metal falls to the dirt with a soft thud.

That's when the door flies open, and my father's chuckles fill the room.

"You failed. You're weak. I think it's time I teach you a lesson."

I should speak. Tell him how strong I am for surviving as long as I did, but my voice doesn't even work. Nothing does.

I know he's kicking my stomach because my body jars, but I don't feel it. I've shut out the world—the darkness. Even though I'm not dead, I feel dead. I'm gone.

More kicks, punches, and whips. I feel blood oozing, my body moving, but I don't fight back. I have nothing left.

"You're a fucking piece of worthless shit. I didn't raise a coward, a fucking pussy. Get up! Fight back!"

I can't.

You try to fight when you've been starved for weeks.

And then I see it—*my salvation.*

I see the glimmer from his knife sticking from beneath his pant leg. But he's stopped kicking me, instead preferring punches.

So I turn to him and spit my frustration.

His face turns to steely rage. And I brace as his foot makes contact. I ignore the force and grab his leg holding on for long enough to grab the knife, and then I stab hard into his foot.

I know the jab isn't deep, given the tough leather of his boot, but it's enough to make contact. *Enough to end this.*

My father doesn't make a sound at the pain he's in. His impervious armor is up all around him as always.

But he stops the torture.

"Pick yourself up," he says.

I summon everything inside me to get myself to stand.

He smirks in approval.

"Maybe you'll earn the right to call yourself Black after all." And then he's gone.

I smirk. I won. My first win against this monster. It feels good. And if I can win once, I can win again and again. Until I'm free.

CHAPTER 1
KAI

What the hell did I just agree to?

I stare across at Enzo, who is more my enemy than I ever realized. *How could I not know that I had a claim to an empire?*

This house, the money Enzo's acquired, the resources, the men—they could have all been mine as easily as they are his.

I didn't have to grow up thinking I had no choices, no chances at ever becoming something more. I could have had everything—all the money I could ever spend. I still can.

But only if I beat Enzo—at a game I don't even understand.

A game where only the strongest win. I don't even know if I will survive the tests, I'm so weak.

But I want to play. It may be my only chance to truly be free.

Archard, Enzo's lawyer, reenters as if he has been listening to our entire conversation and knows now is the time to arrange things.

Westcott appears too, carrying a chair for Archard, because apparently, this conversation is going to last longer than the previous time he was here and stood watching us.

Archard sits in the chair Westcott provides. Westcott looks to Enzo who simply nods, and Westcott leaves us.

"So it appears the two of you have agreed to the terms of the contract," Archard says.

Enzo doesn't respond; he just glares into my soul waiting for me to back out or change my mind. So I answer, "Yes, although I'd like to know a little more about the contract."

"Of course, Miss Miller. We have lots to discuss."

Archard retrieves the large pile of papers from the center of the table. And then pulls two more stacks from his briefcase. "These are copies of the contract between your two families for you to keep," he says, passing a stack to each me and Enzo.

Enzo nods but barely glances at the papers. It's clear he's seen them before, while I grasp onto them like they are my lifeline to a past and future I don't understand.

"This contract was written to ensure Surrender, and all of its entities, go to the proper heir. *The true heir.* The one capable of running the organization properly," Archard says.

"Surrender? You mean the club? The winner only gets the club?" I ask.

"No, Surrender is one of many clubs and entities the winner, or heir apparent, will control. I'm sure Mr. Rinaldi will give you a tour of everything you could inherit. Surrender is also the name of the umbrella company that encompasses everything," Archard pauses.

Enzo, or Mr. Rinaldi as Archard called him, tightens his lip and gives the slightest of nods.

"But according to the records here," Archard flips a page before continuing to read. "The winner will receive ownership of sixty-five bars and clubs, ten superyachts, and seven estates. The winner will also be given control of the entire organization including the over a thousand employees that work for Surrender and encompassing companies that include bars, clubs, yachts, and security."

My eyes widen with every word.

"The winner will be given the power to a ten billion dollar organization that runs Miami and most of the sea between here and the Bahamas," Enzo says with a threatening tone in his deep baritone voice. He steeples his hand on the table as if this is an ordinary day, a regular meeting—not one deciding our destiny, the fates of over a thousand employees, and the status of the underground of Miami.

But it's clear from Enzo's expression he doesn't think I can do this. Even if I were to win, I couldn't run the empire properly.

"So if I win, I get everything?" I ask.

Archard nods. "Yes, you would have the keys to the world. You would never want again. You would have more money than you could ever spend—more power than most kings. But you also need to understand how serious the power you would gain controls. You would take the lives of thousands of people into your hands. You would be responsible for ensuring Surrender, the name of the organization, not just the club, continues to grow and thrive. You would be responsible for ensuring the company continued to be profitable. And the clients that hire Surrender for protection are ruthless. If you fucked up, they would come for your head. Becoming Mr. or Miss Black is a dangerous job. One you shouldn't take lightly."

I let it sink in. All that I stand to gain if I win. I would obtain money, power, control. But I would also inherit danger, darkness, cruelty. I would acquire everything I hate.

Maybe I could change it?

Somehow I don't think you can change a criminal organization overnight.

"And what does the loser get?" I ask, because I have to know. I'm much more likely to lose. I wasn't prepared for a life of power.

"Nothing," Archard says with thinned lips.

Nothing.

I won't be any better off than I am now. I have nothing to gain by playing, except maybe my freedom from this house.

"Shall I continue?" Archard asks again looking to Enzo for permission.

My rage rises, although it shouldn't. Archard is Enzo's lawyer. He works for him, of course he would ask him the questions. But I want to be looked at like I have a chance to win this too.

"If Miss Miller is ready to continue," Enzo bounces the attention back to me.

I try my best to smile to rid myself of the negative feelings. "Yes, let's continue."

Archard flips the page, and I do the same with the papers in front of me.

"Let's discuss the rules."

Rules.

I glance to Enzo expecting him to be studying the paper in front of him, but instead, he's studying me.

I shift nervously in my seat, wishing on some level I could be having this meeting alone with Archard, instead of getting unnerved by Enzo's constant gaze. But on the other hand, I welcome the heat pouring off Enzo. It both calms and excites me.

"The first term is that only one person from the new generation can compete. The oldest direct heir gets the right to decide if they compete or if someone else from the same generation is better suited for the task and job at hand. Now is the only time to swap out for someone different. If there is a different sibling, cousin, etc. from this generation you would rather have compete from your family for the name of Black and all that comes with it, let it be known now," Archard says.

"I don't have any siblings or cousins. It's just me," I say.

Archard turns to Enzo, although I would guess he already knows his answer. This is just a formality.

Does Enzo have any siblings or cousins he fought first to earn this right?

"I will be the one competing," Enzo says blankly.

"Good, now let's discuss how a winner will be determined," Archard says.

I stare down at the next page where Archard begins reading.

"There will be five rounds to determine who can claim the name Black. The first person to win three rounds will become the winner."

Five rounds. That doesn't seem so bad.

"The first and third round rules were determined by Miss Miller's father."

I raise my eyebrows. *Dad? He determined two of the games?*

My heart aches. *Why didn't you tell me about this Dad?* You could have prepared me to fight. To win. Instead, you left me in the dark.

Did you even choose a game I could win or did you expect me to lose as quickly as possible?

"The second and fourth games were determined by Mr. Rinaldi's father."

I gulp as I look across to the darkest man I know. If his father won the games before, then I expect him to be even crueler than the man in front of me. Which means whatever games he chose, I'm fucked.

"And the final game, if needed, was determined by both fathers."

They had to agree? What game would they agree to? I doubt our families would agree on anything if they've been doing battle for generations—where the winner gets to live like a king, and the loser barely survives in a trailer park. No wonder we struggled so much.

What else did you hide from me dear old Dad?

I need to find my father. He has some serious explaining to do.

"The winner of each round should be easy to determine. There is no subjection to the games. There is a clear winner or loser as determined by the rules of each game. But if a winner needs to be decided, or a rule determined to be won or broken, I'm the one to make such decision."

"*You?* Wouldn't that give Enzo an unfair advantage since you work for him?" I ask.

"No, Miss Miller, my loyalty lies with the Surrender organization and the man or woman who claims the title of Black. As Mr. Rinaldi no longer holds that title, I have no loyalty to him," Archard says.

I frown. I don't like this one bit. It feels rigged.

Enzo smirks as my reaction. "Don't worry, Miss Miller."

I hate when he calls me by my last name.

"You'll soon learn this game is the epitome of fair," Enzo continues.

I snark. He means these games will be anything but fair. But that's the point. Surrender isn't run fairly. This life, this world isn't. I of all people understand that.

Archard ignores our exchange. "The games begin upon the demise of the previous Mr. Black. As he died three years ago, that means the games should start immediately."

I suspected Enzo's father was dead, but this confirms it.

Enzo doesn't react to Archard's words. He doesn't get emotional at the thought of his father being dead. I don't know what that means, but I suspect he didn't have any better relationship with his father than I did with mine. At least his father was honest about him about this world.

I wonder how his father died, but neither Enzo nor Archard explain. I don't know how old his father was or what his health condition was like, but if what Archard said was true, even the winner is at risk of dying young. Black may have all the riches of the world, but also the enemies. It's a dangerous job.

Do I even want to become the next Black? I would have to do the job. Be ruthless. Order people dead to protect my own. *Could I do such a thing?*

I stare at Enzo across from me. Tall, dark, handsome. But also merciless, powerful, God-like. He's muscle, steel, and strength.

He was bred for this.

Trained for this.

He's been doing the job for the last three years. He was brought up by a father who won and knew what it would take to continue to win.

While I grew up in a trailer park with nothing.

No mother. Barely a father.

No money.

No food.

No energy to form muscles needed to fight.

No guns to wield as weapons to learn how to fire. And after being broken by the worst of men, I'm even weaker than before. I have no chance of winning. *None.*

This battle is worse than the odds of David and Goliath. David did win, but that was fictional. This is real—and I won't bet on me winning.

"When do we find out what the games are? When will they take place?" I ask.

"You will be given at least twenty-four-hours notice of when and where each game will take place along with any items you need to complete the task. Your fathers determined the rules of each game and when the rules of the game will be revealed. The first game rules, as determined by your father Miss Miller, will not be revealed until the game starts," Archard says.

Fucking father. He couldn't even give me a warning to allow me a day or two to prepare for his stupid game. Unless the game is surviving the longest without food, I have no chance of winning.

I might as well surrender now. The sooner I lose, the sooner Enzo might let me leave. The sooner I will be free.

"When does the first game start? Is this our twenty-four-hour warning to the first game?" I ask.

"First, I need you both to sign, agreeing you are the heirs who will be playing, and then I will set everything in motion. It will take a day or two at least to get things sorted, and then I will notify you both twenty-four-hours before the first round. This isn't that warning."

Archard slides the papers to me. I sign below my name I wrote practically in crayon when I was five and agreed one person from my generation would fight.

Except I'm the only one from my generation. I'm the only chance the Millers have of winning.

I slide the paper across to Enzo. He signs and then glances to the door behind him.

Langston and Zeke enter.

I frown. I'm sure they were listening to everything as well. *Why does he get henchmen to help him while I get nothing?*

"Sir, there is a situation at Surrender," Zeke says.

Enzo nods. "I'll be right there."

"No," Archard answers.

We all freeze.

Archard turns to Enzo. "You are no longer Black. You should have never claimed the title to begin with. You no longer get to make any decisions or wield any power."

"But the organization can't run for days or weeks or months or however long this fucking farce lasts. I will be the winner anyway.

Isn't there some clause in there about who runs the organization while the heir is decided?" Enzo snarls.

"Yes, you are required to run it together," Archard says.

Together.

I silently laugh. *Good luck with getting us to agree on anything.*

But the way Enzo is staring at me, I think he wants to do a lot more than run an empire together. He wants to slam our bodies together, and he wouldn't be giving me any control in the matter. I would have to surrender my body to him.

"Come on then, we have an empire to run," Enzo snarls.

The contract is signed.

I never thought this day would come—the end.

I thought I'd be forever trapped in a lie I could never escape. I thought pretending Kai was dead would save me. I thought not having a Miller line to fight for their right to the throne would have satisfied me.

Instead, it made me restless.

I didn't earn my position.

I was given it.

But now, I can claim it rightfully.

You hear that, Dad?! In a few weeks, this will all be over, and I'll be the winner. I'm the rightful heir. I will be Black.

I exhale deeply, trying to let go of every drop of discomfort my father caused me over the years—the pushing, torture, ruthlessness. I should let every painful feeling go.

I can't.

Not until I've won.

Then I can pretend all the suffering I went through was worth it. Then I can prove my father wrong.

Kai Miller may be strong. In fact, she's the most relentless person

I've ever met. But unless all five rounds are who can withstand suffering the longest, she has no chance of winning. Even if I hadn't trained my entire life for this job.

Her chances are hopeless.

I could have prepared hard for a year and still beat her. Not because she's a woman, but because of the last six years. Her body is badly beaten and still recovering. She barely has enough fat covering her bones, let alone real muscle. And despite being capable of doing whatever it takes to survive, she's still too kind to do this job.

Kai would only ever kill in self-defense, not because it was necessary for the greater good of the organization.

She would never take from those less than her.

Never yell or demonstrate her power to show her strength.

Kai has a heart, even if she keeps it locked away behind a metal cage.

I'm heartless.

My father made sure of that years ago. I'm the only one merciless enough to do the job.

But what will happen to Kai when she loses?

She'll go back to the trailer park with her father. Possibly even ask me for a job to keep her afloat until the next generation attempts to take my power.

Blood boils in my veins at another generation having to face what Kai and I have been through, all to play a stupid game where the winner wins everything and the loser is lucky enough to be left alive.

I stare at the gorgeous woman across from me. Jean shorts hang off her hip bones engulfing her thin legs that I can only imagine will strengthen and tone with time. The spaghetti strapped shirt drapes loosely over her breasts that have started to fill out again. The weight she has gained has begun going to all of my favorite places on her body—her breasts and ass. Her jet black hair reaches far too long down her back in uneven tendrils.

But her physical looks aren't what make her beautiful. I'm sure with more self-care, a beautician, and hair cut, Kai would be a knockout. Her thin frame makes her every supermodel's dream body. But

I've had models before; actresses, strippers, every kind of attractive woman.

Kai is gorgeous because of her piercing green-blue eyes. The color sucks me in every time she looks at me. And behind the eyes that trap me is her spirit. The part of her that signed the papers without surrendering, even though she knows her chances of winning are less than one percent.

Her fight to not only survive, but find something better for herself. Something she deserves. I do not doubt that whatever the outcome, she will find what she's looking for one day.

And that will be the worst part of winning—losing her.

I could offer her a job to keep her around, but she wouldn't take it.

Give her money and one of my many houses to keep her close to me, but she won't be bought. No matter how poor she is.

Kai Miller is the most independent, self-sufficient, kick-ass woman I've ever met. Even if she doesn't realize it herself yet.

For now, she's mine.

Trapped under my roof.

For now, that's enough.

My cock hardens in my pants, reminding just how much it's not enough. And how I need a new solution. I want her to be mine forever. Not because I love her and want to make her my wife. But because when I want something, it's mine.

I'm not a monster. I won't take her body by force. She will give it to me willingly, or I won't have her at all.

I cringe thinking about what she's been through. I should set her free of living in my house at least.

But she wouldn't be safe.

Not until I figure out the truth. Because I have an inkling that someone is hunting her after I killed her previous master. Jarod may have been the one who got his hands dirty, but he wasn't the one who owned her.

I head toward the bedroom I've shared with Kai since I stole her for myself. Kai walks silently behind me.

We should be headed to sleep; instead, we are headed out to work in the daylight.

I'm used to going with no sleep—Kai is too. But I don't like her missing any amount of sleep. She needs all the healing powers it can offer her to continue to grow stronger.

I walk to the closet, deciding I'd rather wear jeans and a dark shirt in case whatever emergency we are dealing with is messy. I don't like getting blood on my designer suits.

"What should I wear?" Kai asks.

I freeze and turn to her. "Whatever clothes you can handle."

She frowns crossing her arms. "I can handle wearing clothes."

I smirk. "Since when?"

She huffs. "Since I realized you're a complete asshole and I can't rely on anyone but myself."

My head snaps around looking in her direction as she stomps to her side of the closet and begins pulling her shirt off over her head until her torso is naked like she prefers.

"You think you're tough now? Huh? You think you're done healing?" I ask.

"Yes."

My grin turns evil as I let my dick decide my actions instead of my brain.

I move like a force of wind blowing through the closet. The only thing saving her from my grasp is that I'm so used to not touching her—not having her.

Instead of touching her, the intimidation of my movements pushes her back against the wall, until I box her in with my hands.

I was expecting fear under her pretty eyelashes. Or at least shock.

Instead, she bites her plump lip. Stealing all of my control with one suck.

Fuck.

Her large eyes stare up at me as if waiting to see what I'll do next.

"I'm not afraid of you," she whispers.

"You should be."

"I'm not. I may hate you, but I'm not scared."

Hate.

What does she know about hating me? Because I sold her? That's why she hates me. But I'm keeping her here for her safety. Or at least that's what I keep telling myself.

I could change the hate-filled lust I see in her eyes with one truth. One truth would change her whole perspective on me.

Her hatred for me would vanish with one sentence.

But do I want her hatred gone?

No, it's better if she hates me.

I lean in close, so close the stubble on my face lightly prickles against her cheek. "You're not scared. And you might hate me, but your hatred doesn't prevent you from wanting me. I gave you the best orgasm of your life, and now you want more. Your eyelids are getting heavy at the thought of my cock filling you."

"You will never fuck me," she spits back.

"Not without your permission, no. I'm the devil, but that doesn't make me like *him*," I say, referencing Jarod.

She sucks in a breath.

"You won't fuck me," she says again, to assure herself and me.

I lick my lips and growl low and breathy against her ear, careful not to touch her with any part of me but my breath.

"We'll see," I say as my eyes travel down to her pointed nipples.

Her cheeks pink, but she doesn't hide her breasts from me. She's not embarrassed by her body. And this image of her will sit in my head, stealing my thoughts, the rest of the day.

Damn her.

I won't be able to focus the rest of the day.

She stares down at my cock pressing against my pants.

"We will see," she grins.

I huff.

"Get dressed, Miss Miller, if you would like to accompany me today. We leave in five minutes."

She snarks. "We will leave when I'm ready. As Archard said, you don't get to go anywhere without me."

Fuck the contract. And fuck Archard.

He doesn't control me.

No one does.

Except the fiery woman standing in front of me half-naked. The woman who I could disarm with a brush of my hand because the touch alone would be too much for her. The woman who is the only person who has truly ever stood up to me. Only she is capable of taking me by the balls and leading me wherever she wants.

Luckily for me, she doesn't realize the full depth of her control of me—at least not yet.

"Five minutes, Miss Miller. I'm leaving in five minutes. I extended to you the invitation to ride with me, but if you aren't ready by then, then you are welcome to figure out how to drive yourself in any car you own. Or pay for an Uber with your own money. But if you want a ride from me, I leave in five."

I don't give her a chance to respond.

I leave.

Down the stairs to wait for her.

Sharing a room was a mistake.

Bringing her here was worse.

Letting her sign the contract will be my undoing.

I pace at the bottom of the stairs while I wait for her and try to figure out what I'm going to do with her.

I should have had a dungeon built as my father did; that way I could just lock her up when she pissed me off.

I shake my head.

I won't be a monster.

I will never be that cruel. Even though it's in my blood.

Six minutes later Kai descends the stairs as if to tempt me with leaving. Trying out her newfound power over me as if this is all a game.

It is.

But not one she should be playing. Because she will lose, and the consequences will devastate her.

Kai is wearing dark black pants and a shimmering top that hugs to her skin tighter than anything I've seen on her. Her hair is up in a bun, no longer hiding her face. She must have decided to dress up a little to match me since I never changed out of my suit.

"Is this acceptable to wear, Your Highness?" she asks snakily, knowing she looks hot as hell in this outfit. Men would do what she wants just for a chance to fuck her.

I growl my disapproval in her wearing anything so revealing.

She smiles.

"I think I'll take that as a yes," she says.

"Only if you keep calling me Your Highness. It has a nice ring to it. Maybe I'll have other people start calling me that when I win."

She glares at me. "Don't count me out yet."

I won't.

I would never count Kai Miller out.

"Besides, I did the best I could with limited clothing and no makeup."

I don't want her wearing nice clothes. Or makeup. Or a stylish haircut. It will only make her more attractive to other men. But it's not fair to her. And I'm also a selfish bastard, who wants to see what she would look like dolled up when she dresses to the nines.

"Westcott," I snap, knowing he is waiting down the hallway for any orders I have to give him.

"Yes, Mr. Bla—" he starts and then catches himself as I glare at him.

Kai giggles.

I turn my glare to her, but it doesn't stop her snickering.

"What do you need me to do, sir?" Westcott says instead.

"I need you to talk to Kai and ensure she has everything she needs. Clothing, makeup, a hair stylist. The best of everything on my credit card. Understood?"

"Yes, sir."

Kai's mouth falls open.

"I'll have a stylist stop by later so Kai can choose herself," Westcott says.

I turn to Kai, waiting for her to give her approval, but she's frozen as a statue.

"Kai? Will that work for you? Or would you rather go to a store?" I ask.

She nods instead of answering my questions.

"That will be all, Westcott."

He leaves silently, knowing better than to ask any other questions.

"Let's go. Langston and Zeke already headed to Surrender. There is no telling what mess awaits us." I start toward the driveway where I know Westcott had my car brought out from the garage.

"Um..." she starts.

"What?" I snap. I don't have time for this.

"I have a proposition for you."

I roll my eyes. "I can fuck you later. We need to go, now."

Her eyes darken in defiance. "Do you want to go to Surrender by yourself?"

I stop.

Of course, I do. I don't want to have to babysit her or convince her why we need to do tasks my way.

"What are you proposing?" I ask.

"You go handle the crisis at Surrender."

"And?"

"I go see my father."

My jaw twitches. I want to go to Surrender by myself. But I don't want Kai to go see her father.

It makes sense why she wants to. To find out why he never told her about the deal between the families. And see if she can get him to give her any hints of the tasks he chose.

I understand why. I would want the same myself if I were in her situation.

But I know my answer.

I won't trade or back down.

I don't know why I don't want her going to see her father exactly. I don't trust they will play by the rules, but honestly, I'd prefer it if she knew the first task. It might keep her safe if she was able to practice her skills for a couple of days first and have some sort of plan.

But I don't like sending her to a man who could barely provide her with food. A man who didn't keep her safe. A man I don't trust.

And more importantly, Kai is mine. She lost our truth or lies game. She relinquished herself to me, even if she hasn't let me have her body yet. But I won't share any of the time I have with her. Even with her father. Even if it saves her.

I'm sure I can do my own task efficiently while ensuring she is also safe. That she isn't walking into a trap where another man would hurt her.

"No deal."

"What?" she exclaims.

I start walking to the door, and she scurries after me as we file outside.

"Why not? You don't want me to come. I just want to talk to him. You can send one of your bodyguards to ensure I come back. I just want to know why my father never told me the truth for years."

"No."

Anger flares on her face and despise pulses through her veins. "You don't get to control me anymore. You're not Black. You don't have power over me. I can do what I want."

I snap toward her, reaching my hand out to grab her, unable to resist her skin against mine. I grab her wrist loosely in my hand. The gesture is kind and caring, not like she's my enemy. But the movement is anything but kind. Because she's not prepared for my touch.

I've touched her before, but she's still sensitive to it if she hasn't prepared herself. If I'm being affectionate and lust is flowing through her making her clit throb for me, then she can ignore the panic inside.

Right now she hates me. So she can't escape me.

The touch sends her spiraling to a place she thought she had left. The darkness covers her.

It's cruel.

One of the cruelest things I've ever done to her.

But I can't let her have power.

I can't let her think she has control.

Because if she does, she might think she is free. She might run.

And she has no idea the danger she is in now that she's signed the contract. Word will soon spread that she's the girl who was supposed to be dead come back to life. And all of our enemies will descend thinking of her as a weakness instead of a strength.

I will do my best to keep her hidden. To keep the truth hidden from our enemies. No one needs to know I'm no longer in control and I have to compete against Kai to keep what's mine. But I can't promise our enemies won't find out the truth.

And after what I made her endure before, I won't let her get hurt again. I will protect her the only way I know how.

By fear.

By pain.

By control.

Kai jerks her hand out of my grasp, realizing I'm trying to control her with my touch. "You bastard."

She holds her hand against her chest, away from my reach.

"You're not in control, Kai. You never will be; I know you too well. And I won't let you win—you're mine. Accept it, and I will make your life so much easier."

"And if I don't?"

I pause, letting the wind rustle through us. When it calms, I speak.

"Then you will continue to hate everyone, including yourself."

I beep the car fob and climb into the car, waiting for her to make up her mind. Go back inside or come with me. Because going to see her father isn't an option.

I have more security here than she could ever imagine. Westcott has more skills than she realizes for a fifty-year-old man; he's more security guard than butler.

She will never escape. Not until I determine it's safe.

I owe her that.

She climbs into the passenger side.

"You don't scare me," she repeats her words from earlier.

"I know."

"You won't fuck me."

"I know."

"Then what do you want with me?" she asks.

I press my foot down on the gas, not being gentle as we speed off.

Everything. I want fucking everything.

I stride into Surrender like I own the place.

And I guess technically I do—at least I own it as much as Enzo does. And he walks in like everything and everyone should bow to him as soon as he enters. So I mimic his behavior.

I am strong.

I am fearless.

I am losing my fucking balance in these heels.

Why is it heels are what women are supposed to wear to feel powerful and in control? Why didn't society pick something like tennis shoes, or better yet, furry slippers for women to wear?

But no, society decided women only look hot when balancing on six-inch spikes.

Instead of following Enzo, I walk next to him. Trying my best to look like an equal, instead of his pawn. I don't know where we are going, but I assume Enzo's office.

I was right.

We enter his office and almost immediately there is a knock on the door. We don't even have a chance to speak to each other privately about what our game plan is in dealing with whatever the crisis is.

"Dallas Fell is here to talk about his security. He claims he lost five million dollars because our security entail didn't protect him. He's threatening to kill you and everyone you sent to protect his assets," Langston says poking his head in.

Langston glances from Enzo to me, and it's clear he's worried. This man must be dangerous and pissed at Enzo for failing him.

Enzo just nods like he deals with this every day. He probably does.

"I'm sure he does. Five million is a lot of money to a man like him," Enzo continues.

"Should I send him in?" Langston asks.

"No, we need a few minutes to discuss our game plan first," Enzo says.

"Really? He's irate and causing havoc—flipping tables and shit. I don't think leaving him alone is a good idea," Langston says.

Enzo ignores him as he stares at me. His wheels are obviously turning in a different direction.

"Take him to your office and offer him our best liquor while he waits. Assure Dallas he will have ten million added to his account, and that's what I'm handling while he waits. Then bring him to my office in fifteen minutes," Enzo says, his voice calm and collected.

Ten million! He's going to give this man ten million dollars because he fucked up.

Langston rolls his eyes, and I suspect Enzo acts like this all the time, while Langston is less calm and collected.

"You'll owe me for any damage the asshole does to my office," Langston says.

Enzo smiles tightly. "I always do. Bring Zeke with you. He can rough him up if he gets too out of control."

Langston nods and then leaves.

"Ten million dollars? Don't you think if you are just going to throw that kind of money at someone to fix a problem you should run it by me? That's a fuck ton of money," I say.

"No, it's not a lot of money. Not to *Black*."

I scowl. "It's a lot of money to *me*."

He shakes his head. "Not anymore.

I sigh—he's right. If I win, ten million dollars will be nothing. And if I lose, the money won't be mine anyway.

"Fine."

He grins. "I knew you'd see it my way."

"I do, but from now on run it by me first. I don't want to have to tattle on you to Archard," I smirk.

"You won't tattle on me."

I step closer taking a deep breath as his eyes heat. "I will," I tease.

His eyes drop from my face to my cleavage peeking out from beneath my shirt.

He wants me.

I want him.

And after he brought me to orgasm without so much as touching me, I've been dying to know what it would be like for him to fuck me —but I'm too fucked up for sex.

And I can't get past him selling me.

If I shared my truth would things be different?

Maybe he'd truly want me.

Maybe I'd let myself have him.

Maybe we could fuck like two normal adults who are attracted to each other.

There is no chance of anything but fucking—not after the lies and deception. Not after our families made us enemies from the day we were born.

But toe-curling orgasms might make everything more worthwhile. Because Enzo is definitely the kind of man who would ruin me for any man after.

Right now, despite the lust in Enzo's eyes, he won't touch me. His hands are in his pockets as if he's trying to hold himself back with the thin fabric. And the only time he's touched me was to prove a point.

I could want Enzo if I let myself.

If I let go of the pain.

If I let him heal me.

If I forgot all of his wickedness.

If I told him the truth.

But I'm not ready to share what really happened to me yet. If he keeps staring at me though like he's undressing me, then I'll be spilling my guts and stripping my clothes, begging for him to take me.

I'm not ready for that.

But I want to be.

I clear my throat. "So what are we doing about Dallas? We were in charge of his security?" I ask, hoping to put a stop to the sparks flying around the room. We both know nothing is going to happen between us—at least not today. So it's better if we squash all the heat in the room.

Enzo takes his time answering as he pours us both a glass of whiskey. He hands it to me, and I take it but don't plan on drinking much. Last time I drank, I passed out. I'm stronger, but not sure my body is healthy enough to handle any alcohol yet.

He eyes my drink. "Yes, we handle Dallas' security. Most of our clients hire us for security, and we provide it. We also design, build, and sell yachts, but again only to those who want the most secure vessels. And as for what we are going to do about the situation, you should drink some of that first."

"Why?"

"Trust me."

I laugh. "Trust you?"

"Yes."

"Why would I trust you?"

"Because despite what you may think, I do want to do right by you."

I freeze at his words.

"And I want to do what is best for Surrender. You may hate this organization. You may hate the cruelty that happens here, but trust me, we do a lot more protecting the innocent than evil schemes. It just so happens that protecting the innocent involves killing the immoral."

I nod and take a small sip, preparing myself for whatever he's going to say.

"Marry me."

The color drains from my face. "What?"

"Marry me."

He's right; I need more alcohol if we are going to discuss marriage. It's probably buried in that stupid contract somewhere. Or he's going to pull his gun and force me to marry him—although he's never forced me before.

I down my drink. "You must be joking."

"I'm not. We don't have to get married legally. Just go through the motions."

"Why? What would that solve? Are you saying you don't want to go through with the competition? That we will just share the name and power together?"

"No."

"Oh." That would have been nice, ruling with Enzo—working together. It would have led to endless fights, but the sexual tension would only increase until...

No, don't go there! It's not right.

I turn back to Enzo, his head is cocked, and I can see the vein throbbing on his neck.

Dammit, why do I want him so much?

"We would take pictures of our elopement and pretend to be married. You would go by the name of Black, same as me here. I would say I gave you fifty percent ownership of the company. That way the men would accept your power. And I wouldn't have to explain that I gave up the name of Black and look weak. The company would continue to thrive until we determined the true Black."

"Married," I say the word slowly, trying to absorb it.

"Pretend we are married—that's it."

I sigh. *Be married without any of the perks?*

Except for the power—the money.

Why do they feel like nothing when I wouldn't have Enzo?

Why do I want Enzo?

Fuck.

"And you could do that? Pretend to love me?"

"Easily."

He raises an eyebrow as if asking if I could pretend to love him. *Do lust filled eyes count?* Because I'm afraid that's what I look like right now.

"Wouldn't that make the men think you were a pussy for letting a woman like me have that much power?"

"No, not after they see how strong you are."

Jesus. Why does he have to keep complimenting me? It makes me forget all the shit he did before.

I nod.

"And we won't be legally married?"

"No, no one will ask. And if they do, I'll say we got married over-seas and be able to provide a marriage license that appears real enough. Actually getting married would fuck up the contract between the families, and I don't want that."

"What about Langston and Zeke and—"

"Those close to us will know the truth. But they won't share it with anyone here. Langston, Zeke, Archard, and Westcott will play along because it preserves the empire. We will tell no one else about the contract and fight between us for control of Black."

"What about when the game is over? What then?" I ask.

"Then we get fake divorced and whoever the winner is, stays as Black."

I nod. "You have it all figured out."

"I do."

I don't actually have to go through with a marriage. I just get to use the name Black, same as him and pretend to be his wife while at the club. *Easy enough.* It's the best, for both of us.

"Fine. Let's get fake married."

"Good." Enzo walks over to a painting of a deer on the wall. He slides it open revealing a safe behind it.

I chuckle.

"What?" he asks.

"I just feel like I'm in some sort of spy movie. I didn't realize anyone really kept safes behind paintings."

He shrugs. "This isn't my safe. It belonged to my father, and I haven't opened it since he died."

"Why are you opening it now?"

He enters a code, and it pops open before he reaches inside.

My breathing stops as I wait to see what he's retrieving, but somehow I already know.

A small box appears in his hand. He walks over to me and holds out the box.

I set my glass down on one of the end tables next to several luxury chairs before I carefully take the box from his hands without touching him.

I open the box.

A simple diamond ring sits in the center. I couldn't tell you if it was a princess cut or emerald cut or what. I couldn't tell you if the diamond were real or fake. All I know is it is the most beautiful, elegant ring I've ever seen.

Whoever wore this before wore it with love. I can feel the love oozing from the metal ring.

"It was my mother's," Enzo says.

"It's beautiful."

"If you don't like it, we can get you any ring you want. And when we are done, you can sell it for money. The ring is worth millions. You could live off the money for the rest of your life if you lose."

My gaze slowly drifts up to his—this sad boy's eyes. And in this moment, I forgive him a little more.

For almost killing me.

For forcing me to survive a night in the sea.

For selling me.

For betting against my life and claiming me.

For the lies.

I'm as close as possible to forgiving him for all of it.

Because in his eyes I can see how much this ring means to him. The only treasured possession from a forgotten mother. Something we have in common. A mother who left us and was the only one who ever truly loved us.

Enzo is willing to give it up to provide me with security if I lose.

"You would do that for me?" I ask.

"I don't hate you, Kai. And I abhor what I put you through. Now I just want to protect you. Give you back your life."

I bite my lip as I stare at the ring.

"And I know you don't believe me, but I want to win as much to protect you from this life as to win myself," he says.

I believe him.

I should let him win.

It's what's for the best. But I won't. I want to win. I want to destroy him for the pain he caused me.

"Thank you, but I can only accept the ring for as long as we are fake married. It means too much to you."

"No, you'll keep it."

"I could never sell it."

His eyes darken. "Then I'll sell it for you. This is the only way I can protect you. Take it."

I won't promise him I'll sell it because I won't. Not because I'm not above handouts. Enzo owes me a lot. But I won't use his mother to hurt him.

We are as even as possible—this gesture for his world to see me as his equal and of giving me security afterward.

"Are you going to make me put the ring on myself?" I ask.

His eyes widen at my offer to let him touch me.

He takes the box and removes the ring.

"My heart belongs to the devil," he says reading the inscription on the inside of the ring.

It seems fitting if his mother loved his father.

"You will never get my heart. Nothing more than my captivity I lost in a game, which I will soon win back."

Enzo swallows, and I watch his throat bob. He doesn't agree nor disagree with me.

I hold out my hand, waiting.

I push down the anxiety, and then I feel his touch on my hand. My cold interior instantly warms. I feel calm, secure, safe.

Not loved. That's not what this is. We are both too broken to ever experience such a thing.

But it's different—a sense of trust between us, even though we've both lied and will continue to lie to each other.

The lies are to protect each other.

To help each other.

To keep each other safe.

Enzo pushes his mother's ring onto my finger.

And somehow, I think this is the closest I will ever get to being married.

CHAPTER 4
ENZO

arried.
It's not real.
It's fake in every way that matters.
But Kai still said yes.
She let me put my mother's ring on her finger.

This is the only "marriage" I will ever have. I will never let a woman into my life; it's too fucking dangerous.

And kids, forget it.

The Black line will end with me.

And if I know Kai, she wouldn't dare bring kids into this world either.

This will end with us.

I stare at the sparkly ring on Kai's finger that fits perfectly, as if it were made for her. I still hold her hand in mine. My thumb lazily playing with the ring on her finger. Waiting for the reaction of fear to surge through her.

It doesn't come.

My heart belongs to the devil. The inscription my mother had inscribed after my father gave her the ring. Good thing Kai's heart is too strong to fall for such a monster like me.

Her big, bold eyes look up at me, as if she can feel my pain through where our hands touch. And I can feel hers.

Too bad this can never be more. I might eventually persuade her into my bed, but that's as far as this will go. When one of us is declared the winner, we will go our separate ways. Then this will be only a terrible memory that we both spend our whole lives trying to forget.

A knock brings us back to reality.

We both take a deep breath in unison. The corner of my mouth twitches with the need to protect her. That's what I do, protect the innocent. And Kai is an innocent. I've failed her before; I won't again.

She smiles softly back trying to reassure me. But this is her first test. This is the first peek at what her life will be like if she wins. And as much as I'd love for her to find a way to win—she's more worthy than I will ever be—the job isn't a kind one, it turns you into the devil. Hardens you until there is nothing left of who you truly are.

It's my burden to bear.

Kai picks up the drink I poured her while I walk over and take a seat in my chair that looks as much like a throne as a chair. I used to hate how my father sat in it, acting like an actual king. But after I've become Black, I understand. The throne has power. And you need every drop of it to control these bastards.

Kai hesitates for a second and then wisely chooses to sit next to me. You don't show that you rise for any man. You sit and let the weasels come to you. You don't show them respect. They are nothing but low life worms that you need to control in order to keep people safe.

Another impatient knock.

"Enter," I say, my voice deep and commanding.

I feel Kai's eyes burn into me. I rarely use my voice like this in front of her. I know with a single syllable I sound threatening and demeaning—like I could squash everyone in this club with a word. *I could.* That's how powerful my voice is.

The door opens, and Dallas Fell enters.

"You kept me waiting long enough, Black," Dallas spits as he storms in our direction. "I'm tired of your watchdogs holding me back. You fucked up! Now it's time to pay the price!"

I feel Kai shuddering next to me.

You don't belong in this world, this life. Go as soon as you have a chance, I plead. Knowing that even if she heard me, she wouldn't leave. She's too stubborn, bull-headed, and determined. She thinks she can change things, make the world a better place if she were to win. She doesn't understand that I am making the world a better, safer place by handling the criminals myself. No one else can do this job.

"Sit down, Dallas, if you want me to pay for my mistakes," my voice booms, bouncing off the walls in an echo of fierceness.

Dallas scowls but pulls up a chair and sits across from us. His anger is still there, but he seems to accept that I will fix his problems as he eases into the chair.

Until his attention moves to Kai. He must not have seen her when he first entered, but now she's all he can look at.

"Fetch me a drink, whore. And then strip, I want to feast on your body while Black and I do dealings," Dallas says.

Every bead of blood in my body seethes with a furry I haven't felt in years. I feel a tornado of anger and rage swirling, and if Dallas doesn't get out of Surrender, Miami, and the country within the next five minutes, I'll kill him.

Kai just laughs like it was the funniest thing she's heard, and then she leans forward, playful determination on her face like she's about to tell the sweetest secret.

"Fetch your own fucking drink, jackass. I am not your slave. I won't be doing a damn thing for you. And I sure as hell will never be stripping for anyone but *my husband.*" She flashes the diamond I just put on her finger for Dallas to see. Then she places her hand seductively on my inner thigh.

Fuck.

I feel the sweet relief as I always do whenever we touch. The flames flying calm at her touch then start swarming again, but this time in her direction instead of his. *God, I want her so much.*

"Wait? Are you telling me you two—" he starts.

"We eloped last week," I answer.

"Holy shit," Dallas leans back staring between the two of us—accepting her as my wife so easily. I thought I would have to show him our marriage license. Or at least show more affection—kiss her to get him to believe us. Something I'm not sure Kai could handle.

"I suggest you treat my wife with more respect, before I hang you upside down by your balls and leave you writhing in pain for the whole world to see," I say.

"I apologize, Mrs. Black. Please, let us start over. I never meant to treat you with such disrespect. You must be a truly special woman to get a man like Black to settle down and risk everything for you," he says.

She narrows her gaze. "Mr. Black isn't risking anything for me. He loves me, and he knows I am more than capable of living in this dangerous world. I can handle men like you just fine. I accept your apology, for now, but if you say a word against me, the Blacks will no longer work with you in any capacity. You will become our enemy, and it will be you whose life will be threatened."

I grin. *Kickass.*

I couldn't say it better myself.

Dallas smiles as well.

"You have found a fiery match, Mr. Black. I assume you sleep with one eye open to ensure she doesn't cut off your balls in your sleep," he says.

I wink at Kai. "She's everything I ever wanted in a woman. You can see now why I made her my wife to ensure she never became an enemy."

He nods. "Please introduce us properly so we can part as friends."

"Dallas Fell, please let me introduce you to Katherine Black, my wife. Katherine, please meet Dallas, the weasel of the underworld who makes enemies, not just because of how he runs his mouth without thinking, but because he is truly a slimeball who steals from those he claims are his friends. And then expects not to be hunted down like the rat he is," I say.

Dallas chuckles. "That was a good description of me. Thank goodness I have the loyalty of the Blacks to protect me. Pleasure to meet you, my dear," he holds out his hand to Kai.

And for the first time, I see the fear return. The anxiety is apparent in her eyes. She can tolerate touching me and having me touch her for brief moments, but not others. If she shakes his hand, she won't be able to control her fear, and then he'll see her weakness. *He can't see her weakness.* He'd exploit it himself, or sell her weakness to the highest bidder to try and use it against me later.

I can't let them shake hands.

I grab my drink that is filled and thrust it into his outstretched hand. "We don't have time for any more pleasantries." I stand and walk over to the bar cart to pour myself a drink before sitting again.

Dallas seems perturbed but sits back and doesn't question why my wife doesn't shake his hand.

"What are your qualms, Dallas? You know the rules. We protect you, but only if you follow our rules. You broke them; we can't protect you if you don't listen," I say.

He chuckles. "So I'm guessing what your lap dog said about there being ten million dollars in my account to replace the lost money is a lie."

My eyes turn devilish. Ten million is nothing to me, but I don't give out money to the undeserving. Of course, it was a lie. I said it to keep him calm while giving Kai and me time to get our stories straight.

"I want to get what I pay for," Dallas says, his eyes heating as he turns to stare at Kai's cleavage.

I growl—low, menacing, and audible.

Dallas doesn't stop. He's testing me. Trying to see if Kai is my weakness. He's that kind of a son of a bitch.

"Beautiful, will you excuse us for a moment? It seems that Dallas needs to be shown some manners," I say. I expect a fight. I expect her to say that she has as much right to be here as I do.

Instead, Kai shoots daggers to Dallas as if he wasn't only looking at her but touching her. Her hate will be what allows her to put away her pride and leave.

This isn't your world, Kai.

This is a world of sick, disgusting men. No woman belongs here.

I'm all for equal rights, but there is a reason woman are better than men. They would never let such impure thoughts into their heads.

She stands, peering down at him with disgust. "Hurt my husband, and I'll hurt you. Understand?"

Dallas chuckles in his disgusting way that makes his oversized belly laugh.

"I would never hurt your husband."

She glares. "You did when you took his business and then didn't follow his rules. You put his reputation and mine at risk by letting a breach happen. I may not know everything about this organization or world yet, but I'm a fast learner. I'm not his weakness; I'm his partner. And by being here, I was able to expose your feebleness. That you are a slimy man, who will hit on women giving them no respect. You're lucky I'm letting my husband deal with you instead of dealing with you myself. I'm not as merciful as my husband. And he cares more about money than I do. Because if I dealt with you, you would be wishing you were dead."

Kai storms out swaying her hips and standing taller than I've ever seen her.

This woman.

She says she's not my weakness, but she is. She's my kryptonite. And as soon as she figures it out for herself, I'm a goner.

As soon as the door shuts behind her, I turn back to Dallas.

"Such a firecracker," he says.

"Don't speak about my wife."

He smiles. "Fix your mistake."

"It wasn't my mistake. It was *yours*. And I won't be paying you back. You'll be lucky if I let you leave intact."

He rolls his eyes. "You will because I have leverage now. Your wife is your weak spot."

My heart rumbles in my chest. "Katherine is anything but a weakness." I struggle to call her Katherine instead of Kai, but it's necessary. No one gets to know she's Kai Miller. It would be too dangerous. I don't know who among us is a snake and who is an ally. Who would take destiny into their own hands and kill her to ensure I win and keep my loyalty.

"We will see."

"No, we won't see. Because you've just sealed your fate. If you think I will let you walk out of here unharmed after threatening my wife, you're deranged."

Color drains from his face.

"I'm sorry, Mr. Black. I didn't mean any disrespect. I've been a long-standing client of your father's and I mistook my place. Your wife is safe. I would never harm her or tell anyone else to harm her. I just meant I can see why you like her so. And I thought it would allow me to get more from our arrangement if I played on your weaknesses. I was wrong. Please show me mercy."

"Why should I?"

"Because I will double your fee. I will pay you more to protect my assets, and I will play by your rules. I value our friendship."

"Ha, we don't have a friendship."

"I value our relationship, and I would never want to become your enemy."

"Fine. You pay double, and I'll let you leave here alive. But if I hear one whisper against my wife, I will hold you personally responsible for the rumors."

He sucks in a breath. "Thank you for your mercy, Mr. Black."

We both stand—our dealings done. I don't keep him alive out of mercy. I keep him alive because he's a weasel that may lead me to who is hunting Kai. I can track him and find out who he's working with easier if he's alive instead of dead.

"Now, help a man out and tell me where you found a woman like Katherine. Who did you buy her from? It's clear from the markings on her body that she was a whore you bought and then marked as your own."

I lose it.

My full furry comes down on him as I punch him in the face. Then riddle him with more punches to every part of his body.

Maybe I was wrong. Maybe he's worth more dead than alive. At least my conscience will survive another day. At least I can protect Kai from one more monster. Because this bastard deserves to die.

CHAPTER 5
KAI

I shudder as I storm down the hallway, not able to get away from Dallas fast enough. He's a vile, disgusting man. And as much as I wanted to show my strength, that I'm Enzo's equal, I was happy to have Enzo deal with the wretched man by himself.

Enzo—my fake husband.

I thought we were done with the lies, but at least this time, I'm in on the lie. Everyone else is left seeking the truth.

The ring feels heavy on my finger. The metal frosting against my cold skin as if molding to the temperature of my body.

The ring could ensure my future, even if I lose.

But I won't accept it. I don't need money to survive. To flourish. Not even to live.

I may forever hold hatred and pain for Enzo, but I won't cause Enzo the same pain. I might hurt him, but not by taking the only thing left that reminds him of his mother.

Why would I want any part of this life?

Even if it could provide me with security.

I would lose myself, go mad, if I had to deal with disgusting men like Dallas every day. No wonder Enzo has darkened until there is nothing left but his fiery exterior that is ready to burst every second with a temper that can't be calmed.

I envy the fire in him. It keeps him warm and ensures he never backs down. Never loses himself. Never gives up.

I need to leave.

I need to run.

I need to be free.

I usually wouldn't go back on my word. But after feeling trapped in a room with a man that makes Enzo look like a saint, I have to get to air.

I don't think.

I just go.

My legs moving quickly through the hallways in the shadows. When I pass a group of men, I walk boldly, like I'm their queen.

"Katherine, would you like me to pull the car around for you?" Zeke asks.

I pause realizing he is one of the men in the group. I clench my teeth trying to figure out how to avoid a confrontation.

"Who is the broad?" one of the men asks Zeke.

My eyes tighten into dark holes where only demons can exist as I stare at the group of men. "My name is Katherine Black."

A collective gasp shakes the hallway as every man realizes what it means. One by one they turn their gaze to my hand, searching for the ring I wear.

I purse my lips and stand as proud as possible when they take in my scars trying to determine what they mean.

"I've lived with the devil before I defeated him. And I'll do the same to any man who crosses me or my husband," I say, knowing I can't show fear or weakness in front of these men. Even though I'm only one woman and they are many. They could hurt me before Enzo ever came to protect me. I have to show my own strength.

I turn to Zeke. "No, Zeke. I won't be needing my car. See that these men return to work."

Zeke eyes me curiously, knowing my claim of Black is a farce. But as Enzo said, Zeke will play along here. Enzo trusts him, so I have no choice but to do the same.

I walk, leaving the men behind to no doubt stare at my ass.

I reach the door that Enzo and I entered the club through. I open the door and let the brightness blind me. I usually seek the dark, but for now, I need the light—something to burn the ickiness from my meeting with Dallas.

"You shouldn't be out here."

The voice sends blood boiling shivers through my body.

"Dad?"

I turn and see my father smoking a cigarette while leaning against the brick wall.

"What are you doing here?" I ask.

He drops the cigarette, putting it out.

"I should ask you the same question."

"You don't get to ask me anything. Not after you've hidden everything from me for my entire life!"

His eyes turn cool. It's where I get my own iciness from—my father.

And suddenly I want to be nothing like him. Because I can't imagine lying to any child of mine for their entire life.

"You don't understand anything, Katherine."

"Then explain to me!"

He shakes his head. "You aren't ready for the truth. You never will be."

"Fucking coward!"

He doesn't flinch as he walks to the door leading into Surrender.

"Wait, you work at Surrender?"

My father doesn't answer, but it's clear from his non-answer that he does.

"You work here. Your whole life is here, yet you never prepared me once for the life I was fated to live in. Enzo's father prepared him his entire life for this life. He prepared him to win. I have no chance. I have nothing because of you!"

My anger overtakes me, and I charge.

"You were supposed to protect me, and you didn't!" I scream as I throw my arm back to punch him.

His hand grabs my fist, stopping me from making contact.

Shooting pain rips through my palm, down my forearm, and into my chest.

My father, a man I should love. The man who raised me. Fed me. Clothed me. Now with his touch wreaks havoc in my body. My body responds like he's the enemy instead of my protector.

Tears water in my eyes, but my father still grips my fist.

"Leave Katherine."

I close my eyes.

Fear, hatred, rage. All of the emotions fill me as my father controls me with his touch. I can't break free.

How can I ever win against Enzo when I can't even tolerate my own father's touch?

I can't.

At least not now—and I don't know how long I have until the first task, but I will find a way to at least tolerate touch.

I will not be held captive by another man's grasp ever again.

"Let her go," Enzo's voice booms.

My father turns in Enzo's direction, but his grip doesn't loosen.

"I said. Let. Her. Go."

My father lets go, and I can breathe again.

Enzo walks toward us. Each step breathing more life into me with his calm fierceness.

Enzo's eyes run up and down me, looking for any sign that I'm hurt. I'm sure from the expression of terror on my face he thinks my father hurt me.

He did, but not in the way Enzo is imagining. My father hurt me by never protecting me. He was never a real father. True fathers don't lie to their children.

When Enzo is satisfied I'm not truly hurt, he turns back to my father. "Clean up the mess in my office, Miller."

I should cringe at the cruel way Enzo treats my father. But I don't. My father deserves it. And if I can't dish it out, then I'll let Enzo.

My father looks at me one last time. And I see blankness in his eyes. No emotion. No caring. I'm not sure if he ever truly cared about me. Or if I was just the stupid girl who thought her father was different than all the rest.

And as much as I want to feel nothing back, I do. I still feel hope. Hope that the reason my father never told me of this world was for my protection. That he tried to hide me from this world to keep me safe and now that I'm here in it, it hurts him so much that he turned off his emotions.

"Yes, Mr. Rinaldi," my father says, using Enzo's real name.

Enzo frowns, his lips tighten into slits ready to order my father around.

"We aren't done," I say as my father begins to walk inside. My voice has more hope than I wanted to convey. Hope that my father does really love me; he just doesn't know how to protect me now that I'm no longer a child.

My father nods in agreement before disappearing inside to clean up the mess Enzo ordered him to clean up.

Wait...mess?

"What mess is my father cleaning up?"

I stare at Enzo, and that's when I see the cuts on his knuckles. The blood splatter on his jacket.

He killed Dallas.

There is no doubt in my mind.

I can't handle this. Not now.

I turn and start walking away. Where to, I don't know. Just away.

"Wait," Enzo says his hand brushing against the same wrist my father gripped before Enzo realizes what he's doing and begins to pull away.

I place my hand over his, stopping him from letting me go because unlike the pain I felt with my father touched me, I feel something different with Enzo. A feeling I've only ever felt with Enzo. A feeling I can't even describe. I feel weightless, floating through the air above my body. I'm no longer weighed down with grief and anger. I'm flying. I'm free of my past when Enzo touches me.

Every time he does I feel more alive than before. Even when he purposely hurt me with his touch, it wasn't the same as when my father touched me. Enzo's touch calmed me even if it was too much at the same time.

His eyes widen as he looks at us touching.

"I'm sorry. I didn't mean to touch you. You just can't run off. Our enemies could be lurking nearby. It's not safe to leave without protection," he says.

I barely register his words. All I feel is our bodies connecting in a way that is bigger than the flesh contacting. It's more than emotion or feelings. It's like his presence is bringing me back to life.

I lick my lips.

Why does Enzo's touch save me, when even my own father's hurts me?

CHAPTER 6
ENZO

I touch Kai and my world stills.

All of my focus, energy, everything becomes hers.

I've claimed her as mine, but I am just as easily hers. I'm captivated and engrossed in her body. And I would worship at her feet for a chance to be with her.

Despite my desire that grows more restless in my body with each passing second, my lust isn't my focus. My body may be hard and growing harder having her in my clutches. But the calmness on her face covering the pain that was there a moment ago is what has me fascinated.

I shouldn't be able to calm her.

She should tremble every time I touch her. But it seems after I gave her my mother's ring, giving her security for the rest of her life, she no longer feels panic at my touch. By protecting her, I gave up my greatest strength against her. I can no longer control her with a simple caress.

"Does everyone lie to me?" she asks, her hand still holding mine to her wrist in the same place her father was grabbing her when I came out.

Zeke warned me he was concerned Kai would run. He saw the look in her eyes as she wandered through the hallways.

I knew she needed air after our meeting with Dallas. But I never expected what I saw when I chased after her. I expected her to run as soon as she tasted fresh air. I expected to chase her through the city. Instead, she stood terrified by the grip of her father.

I'd known that he had worked for my father and then me when I took over. As he's a ship captain, I've rarely seen him. He's almost always at sea. But I pay him well as I do all of my men. He shouldn't be living in a trailer. His daughter shouldn't have had to steal to survive. Even if he did owe a debt for his wife's medical bills. He shouldn't have been living with nothing.

And Kai should have had plenty.

Instead, they lived in destitute. Her father lying to her every day about the money he has, who he works for, and even her own destiny.

Seeing him grab her, and the pain it caused her, took every drop of self-control in my body not to attack him. The only thing keeping me from doing so was knowing that he is still Kai's father. That she still loves him despite the pain. And I don't understand his intentions.

My father was the devil. That was clear from the moment I was born. There was no question who he was or what he wanted.

But Kai's father is a mess of contradictions. *Does he love her? Is he trying to protect her by lying? Keep her out of this world? Or is he hiding his demons inside?*

I don't know the answer, but I will find out.

Because if her father is her ally, then I need to keep him away to ensure he doesn't help her win.

And if he is her enemy, then I need to keep him away to protect her.

Either way, Kai needs to stay away from her father.

"Men lie, Kai."

"Why didn't you tell me my father worked for you?"

"The same reason I didn't say that you also worked for me."

"What?"

"When you were cleaning yachts as a teenager you worked for Black."

She pulls her hand from my grasp breaking whatever connection we shared.

"Is the loser required to work for the winner?" she asks.

"No."

Her eyes drop. "Why didn't he tell me the truth? Why didn't he prepare me for this? Why didn't he protect me?"

A tear rolls down her pinked cheek.

I test my newfound theory that my touch can no longer rise panic within her. I stroke her cheek removing the wetness from her face. And the look I get is far more reward than I deserve for such an action.

She bites her lip.

"I don't know why. Only he can answer that."

Her face tightens as she frowns. "And you won't let me speak to him again?"

"No."

"Why?"

"Because I don't trust him."

"Him or me?"

"Him."

She shakes her head. "I don't think you can tell me who I can and can't speak to."

"You're right. I can't, but I'll ensure you never see him so you'll have no chance to speak."

She growls, and her fists fly up and pound into my chest. "You can't keep him from me. He's my father! If I want to talk to him, I will."

I pull her to me, wrapping my arms around her body to keep her from fighting me. But it doesn't stop the wildness in her eyes or the flailing of her body trying to get free in my arms.

"It's for your own good," I say.

"You don't get to determine what's best for me!"

"Yes, I do!"

"No! You sold me! You don't get a say in my life."

"And it's because of my fuck up that I must do everything I can to protect you!"

I let her go.

She takes a step back.

"Keeping me from my father and the truth isn't protecting me."

"It is, and you know it."

She breathes, and I see the fight leave. She knows I'm right. She can't trust her father any more than she can trust me. Her father is trying to protect her by keeping her innocent and weak so she has no chance of winning and becoming part of this life. Or he's a monster who doesn't love his daughter. Maybe there was another sibling that was born. A son he kept hidden trying to raise to take Kai's place, but something happened to that boy, and now it's too late.

My father ordered me to kill Kai when he realized she was my competition. If he knew of a son, he would have done anything to kill the child to ensure I won. My father never thought I was strong enough.

"What if I don't want your protection?"

I take her left hand in mine, my thumb tracing over the diamond sitting on her thin finger. "This ring may not be a vow of marriage. It's not a pledge of my loyalty for all of eternity. It's a vow to protect you, forever. I fucked up once, but now I realize my mistake. I owe you a lifetime of making it up to you, and that means protection, whether you want it or not. I'll protect you with my life."

Another tear falls.

I wipe it away, relishing the chills her skin sends through my body.

"My words aren't meant to make you cry."

She smiles lightly. "To most women, they might sound like heaven, but to me, I realize the truth. Your protection is just another way to control me. I don't want your protection, Enzo."

I sigh as she pulls once again out of my grasp.

"I'm sorry, Kai, but you don't have a choice."

She shakes her head. "I always have a choice. I'd rather die than be controlled."

"I'd rather you be alive."

"Why?"

I shrug. "Maybe saving you from death will absolve me of some of my other sins."

"It won't."

"We'll see."

Kai stares at the door, and I know what she's thinking. Of running inside and finding her father before I banish him. But I'm not the one keeping him from her, he is. He's had every opportunity to speak to her, and yet he's never tried. And I'm going to find out why.

"Come," I say.

It's a command, and I'm not sure she will follow it. As much as I wish she were truly mine, she's not. She's free willed and does what she wants, even if I know what's best for her.

I smile when I hear her heels on the sidewalk behind me. She catches up with me easily, but then stops in her tracks when she sees where we are headed.

"Go for a ride with me?" I ask as I stare at the gorgeous yacht looming in the distance. If she wants to get over her fear and no longer need my protection; then this is the way to do it—by facing it.

She takes a step back. "No."

How can she survive in this life if she can't face the water?

She can't.

"Then you'll have to accept my offer of protection."

Kai nods silently accepting my words as truth. She doesn't have a choice. If she can't protect herself, then I am all she has.

CHAPTER 7
KAI

Enzo wants to protect me.

But it's as much about control as it is protection.

And I'm tired of being a prisoner.

Enzo stops the car outside of his home. *His home*, a place that will never be *mine*. This house will never be anything but my cage. And only I can set myself free.

I throw the car door open and run.

I know it's useless—that Enzo, my captor, will chase. But it feels good to run, to fight, instead, of letting my body fall for the handsome man who offers protection.

That protection can feel good, comforting, safe. But then it also traps me as Enzo can just as easily turn into an insufferable ass who thinks he's God and can control my every movement.

Enzo catches me faster than I expected. We fall to the ground in a lump of arms and legs. I fight. My fists flying into his chest and he lets me.

Pound.

Pound.

Pound.

My fists make contact over and over as I sob into his shoulder.

This is the most contact I've had with him—this exercise in getting out all of my grief.

At first, I continue to take out my pain on him. My frustration and hurt for what he did to cause my current situation overtakes me, allowing me to let it out with my fists in a way I haven't been able to until now. Because now that I can touch him, I'm free of him.

Enzo rolls to his back, and I continue my assault on him. Moving from his chest to his face as I take out my furry. He does nothing but holds my hips as I rest on his.

I punch him until I have nothing left.

And then I collapse on his chest.

I exhale everything inside me, hating him with every breath in my body. Until I hear the thump of his heart, it speeds so fast like he's been running for his life instead of just suffering at the fate of my fists.

Fists that are too weak even to draw blood. He might have a couple of bruises in the morning, but that is the worst that will happen to him. A man like Enzo has faced fists much worse than mine. My assault hardly fazed him, more of a nuisance than real discomfort.

I lift my head, studying him.

"Why is your heart beating so fast?" I ask.

His shifts beneath me, and I feel his hard length between my legs.

"Because you are in my arms."

I gasp.

I've known I turned him on, but I've never felt him. Never felt his desire so plainly displayed for me.

I thought my reaction to realizing the depths of his lust would be fear. I thought I'd run in terror. Instead, I want to feel more.

I rock, ever so slightly, feeling his erection beneath my body.

"Careful, Kai," Enzo's voice warns as he grits his teeth together as if in pain.

I still. My eyes wide and unyielding.

"Let me go," I say, changing the subject even though our bodies don't agree. I throb, wanting more of him but determined not to give in to the stupid wants of my broken body.

"I can't," he says.

I glare. And I know he will never let me go. Not because his cock is begging for me, but because he thinks of me as his property. He can pretend to be self-righteous all he wants. I know the monster within him.

I get up in a huff, but it feels more like I'm ripping my body from his. Each step I take toward the house is difficult. I want to go back.

What is wrong with me?

I storm into the house.

"Miss Miller, can I get you anything?" Westcott asks as soon as I enter.

"Is Archard here?"

He narrows his gaze. "Yes."

I frown. *Is Archard here to tell me it's time to start the games?*

"Where is he?"

Westcott hesitates. "Mr. Black's office."

I frown at the way he says Enzo's last name, but I won't argue about it now. I stomp to the office.

"I need a word with you, Archard," I say.

He's relaxing on the couch in the office.

"Mr. Rinaldi said you would."

"What? Enzo said I would want to talk to you?"

He nods.

Fuck Enzo.

"And what did he say I wanted to talk to you about?"

"You wanted to speak to Archard about me letting you go," Enzo says from behind me.

I ignore Enzo. "Enzo can't hold me captive. He's no longer Black. He has no power. If this is to be a fair fight, I should be free to leave."

Archard looks over my shoulder to Enzo.

"Don't look at him! Look at me. If you are not loyal to Enzo, then ensure this game is fought fair. I can't properly prepare if I'm a prisoner."

Archard sighs. "You're right. Enzo is no longer Black."

I smile, turning to Enzo to demand he let me go free.

"But there is nothing in the contract between the families that says this game is fought fairly. You are welcome to do whatever acts you please in regards to each other. You can try to undermine, hurt, steal, deter, even kill one another in preparation for the games. The games don't pause just because it's not one of the five tasks."

I gasp.

"Enzo can't use the power of Black to hold you here. But he can use whatever means he desires. Force, wit, lust." Archard stands. "If you want to go free, then you have to figure out how to do it yourself. I can't be involved."

I breathe deeply in and out; my anger is furying inside me.

Archard stops at the door. "I came to let you know preparations have begun for the first game. It won't be too long now."

And then he's gone.

I glare at Enzo. "I will leave."

He shakes his head. "Not until you are safe. You lost fair and square. You're mine until I say you can go."

"There is nothing fair about this."

"No, but that was a lesson you learned long before me."

His eyes glaze over, and I see his cock still straining against his pants.

"You need to shower and change. Your last sin still clings to you," I say talking about the blood on his shirt.

"It wasn't a sin if I was protecting an innocent."

He means me. He thinks he protected my honor or something by killing Dallas.

My eyes focus in on his crotch. I try to imagine what his cock would feel like inside me. *Would it burn my insides as he took me? Or would my body welcome him in, feeling whole for the first time?*

"Don't act like you don't want me," Enzo says, his voice dripping with lust.

"Why haven't you fucked me?" I ask.

"When you ask, I will."

I frown. "What does that mean? It's clear you want me; what's stopping you?"

"I don't hurt women."

"Ha! You don't hurt them yourself; you just sell them and have other men do it for you."

Enzo doesn't argue. And I'm tired of fighting. I need to save all my strength to find a plan to escape and then the rest to pull the truth from my father.

A knock interrupts us.

"Miss Miller, the stylist has arrived," Westcott says.

I exhale, trying to let go of my frustration because I need to get a haircut and new clothes if I want a chance of being taken seriously.

"Thank you, Westcott."

I follow Westcott upstairs to the bedroom I share with Enzo. That will stop. I won't share anything with him—not anymore.

"Claire Holland, this is Mrs. Black," Westcott says, introducing me as Enzo's husband.

I eye Westcott, waiting for him to leave as the perky blond woman approaches me with a broad smile on her face. Westcott leaves us.

"It's a pleasure to meet you, Claire," I say.

She smiles brightly holding her hands out to take mine in hers.

I can't let her touch me.

"I'm so excited to see what clothes you brought." I move past her toward the racks of clothes now hanging throughout the room.

She squeals in delight instead of trying to take my hand again. "I'm so excited to dress you! You have an incredible body, Katherine. So thin! You have to tell me your diet and exercise secrets."

I give her a tight smile. *Get kidnapped and live on a yacht that makes you sick for six years.* "Sure," I say, instead of the truth.

"Westcott said you needed a whole new wardrobe, that you were newly wed and wanted to refresh your clothes?"

"Yes."

"Yay! I'm so excited; we better get started." She moves to the closest rack and starts talking about dresses, when the door opens and Enzo enters.

I glare at him.

"Sorry ladies, I don't mean to intrude. I just need to shower. I won't be in your way. Continue," Enzo says as he strides toward the bathroom.

The bubbly Claire falls silent as she stares wide-eyed at Enzo. Her mouth parts as she drools after my fake husband.

If Enzo notices her gawking, he doesn't give any sign. Instead, he winks at me before disappearing into the bathroom.

I never thought I'd be jealous of any woman staring so openly at Enzo, but I am.

"We should get started," I say, practically hissing between my teeth.

♡

I NOW HAVE ENOUGH TO FILL A LARGE CLOSET WITH DESIGNER clothes. I have a huge pile of makeup and beauty products fit for a queen. Now all that is left is a haircut.

Claire brought with her a large mirror, table, and chair for her to cut my hair. She loves fashion and clothes, but it turns out she started as a hairstylist.

I sit in the chair staring at myself in the mirror as I let my long hair out.

Claire has already been shocked by the scars marking my body. I told her I was in a car accident when I was younger that hurt my body, but I can't hide the long uncut hair. There is no reason for my hair to look like this.

Her mouth falls open as I undo the bun on top of my head and let my ragged, dark hair fall.

"Um...how long has it been since you had a haircut, Katherine?"

"Several years. I got busy and usually wore my hair up, so it didn't matter how uneven it was. But I'd like to get something more modern now."

"Of course," Claire says, smiling. "Let's wash it first, and it will be easier to cut wet."

Enzo still hasn't left the bathroom, even though I heard the shower turn off at least twenty minutes ago.

I walk to the door and slowly open it, peaking my head inside to see Enzo in the closet buttoning up a new dress shirt.

"More business?" I ask as I enter the bathroom.

He shrugs. "You never know when business will arise."

But I realize he isn't dressing in a suit. He's wearing a tux. I remember him saying he wanted to take some photos of us at our fake wedding so we would have some proof if the need arose. He must want to have it happen sooner than later.

Which means once that's done and word spreads that I'm Mrs. Black, it will be even harder to leave the cage I'm in. When Enzo first said he wanted to pretend to be married so we could be seen as equals, I thought he was doing it to help me. Now I think he's doing it to keep me trapped.

"Can I come in?" Claire's high voice rings through the bathroom.

"Yes," I say, not taking my eyes off Enzo's hard chest.

Claire comes in, and I know her eyes are on Enzo the same way mine are.

"Where do you want me?" I ask turning to Claire.

She sighs, and I know the image of Enzo won't soon leave her head.

"Leaning over the tub. That way I can wash your hair and get a feel for your hair's texture," Claire says.

I turn the water on the tub and then kneel before it.

I can do this.

I can do this.

I can do this.

I force my body still as I prepare for Claire to touch me. I close my eyes as I tilt my head forward over the tub, my elbows resting on the tub's edge. My heart races, and my breathing speeds so fast I'm afraid I could have a stroke.

Tears threaten.

Panic rises.

Anxiety overtakes.

I jerk.

And then I feel the touch.

My eyes fly at the warmth. It's too warm to be Claire's hands touching my shoulder. Too warm to be anyone's but Enzo's.

"What are you doing?" I ask as he kneels next to me.

"Washing your hair, and then cutting it," he says.

My eyes search, but I don't see her. "Where is Claire?"

"She's gone."

"Why?"

"Because you had a panic attack. And I won't let you suffer anymore."

I crinkle my nose. I don't remember anything. I don't remember if she touched me or not. I don't remember hearing them talk, but they must have if Claire's gone.

"She laid but a single finger on you before you panicked. You completely locked yourself away into a dark place in your mind. So I sent her away. When I touched you, you came to," Enzo explains.

I frown. I really need a haircut, and I'm frustrated that I can't tolerate anyone touching me for the few minutes it would take to get the job done.

"If she left her scissors, I'll try cutting my hair."

"No, I will."

"Do you know how to cut hair?"

"She gave me a few lessons before she left."

"The water is warm," he says as he tests the water.

He removes the half-buttoned down shirt and then kneels once again next to me. He waits patiently for me to lean forward. And when I do he gently uses a cup to pour water over my hair.

I close my eyes to keep the water from splashing into my eyes.

"Shampoo," he says, warning me before his hands run through my hair.

I moan at his delicate touch.

His fingers stop, my head tilts, and my eyes open to meet his.

"Sorry," I say, at my unexpected outburst of pleasure.

"Don't be."

He starts scrubbing, his fingers digging into my scalp in the most luxurious, pleasurable way.

I try to keep my moaning inside, but every once in a while, a small whimper escapes through my parted lips.

He stops and rinses my hair before applying conditioner, then rinsing again. His touch on my head warms and sparks every nerve in my body. He could ask anything of me, and I would give it to him, if only he kept scrubbing my head.

"I'm finished," he says almost reluctantly, like he too was enjoying touching my head.

I sit up, and he holds my long strands in his hands before wrapping them in a towel. Then he leads me to a chair he set up in the bathroom in front of the mirror. He removes the towel and watches my wet hair fall.

He picks up scissors lying on the counter.

"Um.." He clears his ruff throat. "How short do you want it?"

I motion to just above my breasts indicating where I want him to cut.

He nods and swallows, his Adam's apple bobs as he does.

He pulls my hair back gently.

"You trust me?" he asks with a grin.

I nod silently. Because I do trust him—*too much*.

It gives him too much power over me.

I watch his breath rise and fall in his chest slowly as he takes my strands in his hands and begins to work. I feel my head getting lighter with each snip. I enjoy watching the focused look of his brow as he works. His concentration stays on my hair and not me—giving me a chance to study him. The scars on his chest. The muscles that seem to grow bigger with each passing day.

My mouth waters thinking of what it would feel like to kiss his abs. Slip my tongue between the hard ripples. Feel his muscular body between my legs. I feel my body heat and not just from Enzo's warm touch. For a desire to have him.

"Finished. What do you think?"

I flick my hair in front and watch the even strands fall to the length I asked Enzo to cut it.

"I'm impressed. When you lose your empire to me, you should take up hair styling," I tease.

He smiles. "If it means I get to cut your hair, then I'll do it."

I give him a weak smile. *How can he be so kind to me?*

He's a monster. He hurt me. This is just an act.

But it's what makes me fall for him. It's what tricks my mind and allows my body to take over which is desperate to feel him—to fuck him.

Enzo is attracted to me too, but not enough to act on it. And I will never show weakness by asking for the man who sold me to fuck me. No matter how much I want his body. No matter if it would heal me to feel that of a man who I actually desire inside me. I will not give him the satisfaction of knowing I want him.

And Enzo isn't attracted enough to me to actually woo me—no man is.

So I'm destined to live out the rest of my years alone.

Enzo steps back. "There is a white dress I picked for you to wear hanging in the closet. Put it on, and then Westcott will take some pictures he can send to the newspapers."

And just like that Enzo is back to ordering me around. He leaves before I go in search of the dress that will serve as my fake wedding dress. I open the closet door and see the most beautiful lace dress.

Can a monster really pick out something so beautiful? Can the devil protect an angel?

Not without clipping her wings.

CHAPTER 8

ENZO

I prepare for Kai to yell at me for my plan. She's not going to like the location of our fake wedding.

I stand at the base of the stairs in my tuxedo. I considered wearing something more casual, but I need this to look as convincing as possible.

Kai's feet clink loudly on the stairs as she descends. And I try to keep my eyes down. I know my body will betray me when I look at her and show how desperately I want her. I can't imagine her looking like anything except a beautiful angel in her dress. A dress I'll want to rip from her flesh as I drive my cock inside her. And I need as much self-control as possible to keep my hands off her after getting the pleasure of feeling her silky hair in my hands.

But after two steps, I can't help but look.

Gorgeous doesn't do her justice. The lace dress clings to her body, giving her curves I didn't realize she had. She's curled her hair, and it hangs elegantly to just above her chest. She's painted her face with a light layer of makeup that highlights more than overpowers her features. But her dress is anything but angelic. It's sexy as fuck. There is a slit up to her thigh I didn't realize existed when I picked the dress from Claire's cart of clothes and the V at the top dips down to between her breasts. The dress is as fit for a red carpet as it is for a wedding, but it will do perfectly for the pictures.

I just have to persuade my cock to behave.

"How do I look?" she asks when she hits the last step.

I smirk. "You already know from the heat in my eyes."

She smiles. "You don't get to touch me," she warns.

"I get to touch you plenty. We are supposed to act like we are married."

Her cheeks flush.

I hold out my hand, and to my surprise she takes it. Maybe this will be less of a fight than I thought.

"Are we back on good terms? Or are you going to try to run again?"

"You cut my hair. I guess I owe you."

I lead her to the back door. "Good, because it's going to take all of your strength to repay me."

I can see from her amused expression she thinks I'm asking for sex, until I nod in the direction I'm leading her where an arch of flowers hangs in front of the ocean.

"You're kidding. I can't go there."

"Where else do you suggest our fake wedding take place?"

She sighs. "Fine, but I'm only giving you five minutes. And my face will be wrinkled with anxiety the whole time. I'm not exactly sure those will be the pictures that will convince the world we are married."

I grin. "Trust me." Because I already know this is more than just about getting some wedding pictures. This is about getting Kai one step closer to being free.

I lead her out of the house onto the back deck. She goes easily; the harder part will be when we reach the sand.

"Ready?" I ask.

Her eyes grow large. "Don't let me go," she whispers, gripping my hand tighter.

I don't plan to. *Ever.*

In unison, we step down from the last step onto the corse sand.

Kai isn't wearing any shoes, and she wrinkles her nose as the warmth tickles the bottom of her foot.

I don't take my eyes off her face. She doesn't react in anxiety. But then it's not the sand that she fears. It's the water. The sea. The danger.

I hear Westcott move to the deck behind us, ready to take pictures of us as we walk hand in hand to our fake wedding.

"You got this," I say as we take another step.

"I don't need a pep talk."

I smile, Kai's sassy as always.

Another step, and then another, inches us closer. With each step, I wait for the panic and anxiety to rise in her. Instead, I feel her squeeze my hand tighter.

"Who's that?" she asks.

I look in the direction her eyes travel to the man walking to the arch.

"Our fake priest."

She smiles. "This is crazy."

"Don't worry; soon we will be getting fake divorced."

This earns me a tiny laugh. Something I rarely see and want more of. But doubt I will see it again. I don't deserve it. And our future together will be riddled with more pain.

The arch of flowers sits several feet from the edge of the ocean. And we make it all the way without a panic attack.

"Maybe you've been cured," I say.

She shakes her head. "No, this is just far enough away that the water doesn't scare me."

I take her other hand, and we face each other standing in front of our fake priest. Maybe it's my touch and presence that calms her.

I reach up and pluck a red flower from the arch, before tucking it behind her ear.

Her cheeks blush, and her eyes brighten in a thank you.

"What are we supposed to do now? I've never been to a wedding," she says.

"Me neither."

Justin leans in. "Just stand here and promise each other the world even though you will likely cheat and lie within the first month of marriage resulting in one or both of you having your heart ripped out."

We both raise an eyebrow at our fake minister.

"Sorry, I didn't mean to interrupt. I'm Justin."

"Kai—"

"Katherine, this is my wife, Katherine. And I'm Enzo."

Kai stares at me, at my correction of her name. I hired him under the guise that we wanted to relive our marriage in photos since we eloped and didn't hire a photographer the first time.

"I'm sure you two will beat the odds and live a long and happy life together."

Kai laughs. "I'm sure we will."

Justin smiles. "Would you two like a private moment to relive the vows you said to each other before?"

"No, we remember our vows just fine."

He smiles.

Kai's eyes cut to Westcott who has been firing off photos of us from the deck. He's not a professional photographer, but I figure the fewer people we could involve in this the better. Especially since I haven't decided if I want to announce our marriage or not. Not after how Dallas reacted. I don't know if it will help to pretend we are married. It doesn't hurt to have options though.

A wave crashes next to us, spitting drops of water onto our skin.

Kai tenses and tries to pull away, but I hold her hands firmer in mine.

"You two make a cute couple," Justin says.

"Thanks. I think we got all the pictures we need. You are welcome to go."

Justin frowns shaking his head. "I think you are forgetting one important picture."

Kai and I both turn to him with a raised eyebrow.

"What?" Kai asks.

"You got a picture of you walking together, holding each other, pretending to say your vows. I'm sure you'll get pictures of the ring you gave her. But none of that matters without the kiss."

Kiss.

"I don't think that's necessary," I say. "We remember our first kiss without a picture to remind us." These pictures are just to prove that we were married. Something I can show to people, display in my office, put online as proof.

Kai turns back to me trembling slightly. "Kiss me."

"What?"

"Kiss me, my husband."

I don't care that Justin is still watching us, I let the shock read all over my face.

Why does she want me to kiss her?

We have had an attraction to each other since the moment I met her in the bar. And it came back as quickly when she came back to me in Surrender, after spending years apart.

But she hates me—I want her to hate me. Because as much as I want her, I don't deserve her.

It's just a kiss. I've kissed her before. It's innocent enough. It's her motives I don't understand. *Why does she want me to kiss her?*

"Enzo."

I freeze.

I can't.

She can see it on my face—which for some reason makes her light up more.

"Thank you, Justin," she says.

He nods to us both. "Best of luck."

He heads back up the beach.

"Ready to head back?" I ask.

She laughs. "No."

I cock my head.

And then she jerks my hands toward her as our bodies collide and our lips crash together.

This kiss isn't clumsy or innocent. Not like the kisses I stole from her when we were teenagers. This kiss clutches at my heart begging me to finally feel something for this woman beyond regret, pain, and anger.

Her tongue parts my lips, and I know I won't be able to stop, not now that I've had her.

I grab her hips forcefully with a promise never to let her go. Her arms wrap around my neck as I take over the kiss, strengthening it with my own fire. My tongue pushes deep inside her mouth begging her to open wider for me. To let me in. To take this further.

She moans against my lips. Welcoming me in through her shields of ice. I've never felt such a strong desire for a woman before.

"Jesus, Kai."

She runs her tongue over her bottom lip before I pull it back into my mouth. Sucking, tasting, enjoying. I explore every inch of her mouth as my self-control evaporates.

My hands need to be everywhere. And I let them roam her body without thinking.

Down her back in the backless dress.

Over the lace fabric covering her glorious ass.

Up her sharp hips, to her tiny waist—to her cleavage.

I don't think.

I squeeze her breasts. *God, I've wanted to feel her body again for weeks now.* And hearing the tiny whimpers in her throat as I massage her breasts drive me wild.

I sweep her long hair off her neck and kiss her exposed skin that's like ice to my lips. I love how our differences in temperature only heighten the experience. I forgot how incredible it feels. Like tiny explosions firing every time I touch her.

I grab the hem of her dress hiking it up her body as I feel every part of her thigh. The rough scars ripple under my fingers where smooth skin should be.

Fuck.

What am I doing?

I have to stop.

But I don't.

It's like she's possessing me. It would take a nuclear explosion to stop me, and even then, I'm not sure I would stop until I was dead.

This is what makes Kai dangerous to me. This control she has. I've always prided myself on my self-control, but with Kai, it's different. She's different than all of the rest of the girls I've been with. She could consume me whole if I let her.

Stop.

My hand slides higher to her ass. *Jesus, she's not wearing any underwear.*

Stop.

I open my eyes, hoping a pained expression on her face will persuade me to release her before things go too far and I make the hatred she feels for me permanent. Not that that would necessarily be a bad thing. Her hating me might make protecting her easier.

When I open my eyes though, I don't see pain on her face. Nor terror, anxiety, or fear.

Kai's lost in the moment, sucking it all up, and begging for more with her lips as her body presses deeper into me.

Beautiful.

There is no reason to stop—she wants this.

I press into her, my cock pushing against her stomach when I really want it pressing much lower and deeper into her. So that's what I do.

I lift her up, and her legs wrap around me. My cock driving against her pussy as her legs tighten around me, trying to suffocate me like a boa constricting its prey.

Stop.

I kiss down her neck, to the curve of her upper breast. *More, I need more.*

I nudge the fabric of her dress off her breast, exposing it to the world. Good thing this is a private beach because I would gorge out anyone's eyes who saw her glorious breasts.

She gasps as my mouth envelopes her nipple pointed at me, begging for me to tease and taunt.

More, more, more.

Stop.

The voices continue taunting me—wanting one thing and knowing I should do the other. Like the devil and angel on my shoulder. But the devil will always win, because I was born from the devil.

There is too much of my father in me. He still has a hold over me, even in death.

I'm not strong enough to stop this—not until some force of power greater than me ends this.

The water.

I just have to force my legs to the water.

Kai grabs my neck, sinking her nails into my nape as she plants a passionate kiss on my lips.

Fuck, she isn't going to make this easy.

I get lost in the kiss, forgetting my mission until a wave splashes against my feet. The tide is rising, getting closer, meeting me halfway.

I hold onto Kai tightly and begin walking. I expect her to panic as soon as she realizes where I'm headed.

She doesn't.

She's too consumed with our kiss. Too lost. Too desperate.

She begins undoing my tie, loosening it while her legs grip me tighter.

My legs move automatically toward the water allowing me to deepen our kisses, while pulling at her dress, practically ripping pieces from her body.

Kai is everything.

If only this were possible.

I feel the water on my feet covering to my ankles, and I want to run in the other direction because I know how this will end. Instead, I take another step until the water is to my knees.

Kai still doesn't recognize what's happening. Her eyes are closed, and her body so lost in mine that fireworks could go off and I don't think she'd notice beyond the sparks flying between us.

End this.

Run.

I don't have the strength to stop this. All I have left is to fall.

The water engulfs us, and our bodies fly apart as if the waves forced us apart.

When I break the surface, Kai is flailing in the water.

"You fucking asshole!" she screams as she makes it to her feet, pulling her soaked dress up to cover her body.

The spell I was under breaks instantly at the loss of our connection.

I can't touch her—nothing beyond the most chaste of touches ever again. Our connection is too much for my self-control.

I'm just like my father.

Worse.

Because I pretend I only hurt the wicked, when in fact I am just as capable of hurting the beautiful—just like my father did.

Kai runs out of the water. And I chase after.

"Kai, stop!"

She does finally stop on the edge of the deck, whipping around with a cross look on her face.

"Why should I? You are a fucking bastard! You know how much I'm afraid of the water. Why would you do that?"

I stiffen. "Because I want to ruin you," I lie. *Because it's the only way to save you from me.*

She gives me a sly smile. "Don't worry; I'll ruin you first."

She stomps toward the house, and I follow. She throws open the sliding door and steps inside, walking through my house not caring that she's getting water all over my hardwood floor.

I follow.

We both head upstairs to the bathroom.

Kai begins stripping out of her dress when she stops, noticing that I followed her.

"You've got to be kidding? Do you really think I'm going to let you watch me strip after what you did?" she says.

"I'm dripping wet. I'm going to shower and change."

"You're not going to do that here."

"This is my house and my bathroom," I growl.

She smirks. "Not anymore. Get out!"

I roll my eyes but decide not to fight her on this. I walk into the closet to grab a pair of jeans and a T-shirt and storm out to go shower in the guest bathroom. Too bad cold showers don't work on me anymore because of Kai. I'm going to need something to convince my aching balls nothing is ever going to happen with her.

Twenty-minutes later I'm still steaming, but a knock on the door changes things.

"Come to apologize for kicking me out?" I ask as I open the door.

"We need to head out right now. The Savage sent out a mayday," Zeke.

"Shit."

I throw my shirt on as I race after Zeke. The Savage is the head of our fleet. It's the yacht I'm most often on. My favorite. Anders captains the ship for me. He's the best captain in my crew. If he sent out a mayday, then they were attacked by the best.

"Do we know what happened yet?"

"No, they've been radio silent ever since."

"Shit." Which means we were definitely attacked.

"Where's Kai?" Zeke asks.

"Probably still showering."

Zeke stops abruptly. "You need to get her."

"Why?"

"Because now that you are no longer Black, she has to come with us. Archard is downstairs. He heard the mayday call. You can't make this decision by yourself."

"Kai get your ass downstairs in the next five-seconds! Archard has something he needs to say," I holler, pretending Archard is here to tell us the game starts tomorrow. Instead of the truth.

The bedroom door flies open, and Kai emerges in tiny shorts and an oversized shirt of mine.

"Is the game starting?" she asks with a hint of trepidation in her eyes.

I ignore her and head downstairs.

She follows.

"Archard, is the game starting?" Kai asks.

Archard shakes his head. "No, I'm just here to ensure the rules are followed."

Kai looks to me then Zeke.

"We need to go," I say.

"Go where?" she asks.

"The docks. We need to get on a yacht right away. The Savage, one of our main vessels, sent out a mayday. We think we've been attacked," I say.

"Why are we going to the docks? How will that help?" Kai asks.

"We need to get on a boat and hunt down the bastards who attacked us."

"We?"

"Yes, *we*. We will lead a crew of men. I don't leave my men to take care of things themselves, not when it's this important."

"I can't get on a boat."

I narrow my gaze. "You're going to have to."

"No, I don't." Kai crosses her arms and stares at Archard, knowing she has his reassurance to back up her words.

I run my hand through my hair in frustration.

"We have to go! We don't have a choice. I don't leave my men when they need me."

"You no longer get to make the decision yourself."

"Goddammit, woman! You are the most infuriating person on the planet!"

"And you are the most selfish, demeaning asshole!"

"What the fuck do we do, Archard?"

"You don't both have to go, you just both have to agree how to handle the situation as a leader, or you don't get to be involved at all," he answers.

"Fine, I'll go. You stay." I like that plan better anyway. I have a feeling this is Alastar's men who attacked us. This sounds like his doing. He is my biggest rival. He's wanted my money and power for a long time. And I don't know if Alastar was the leader Jarod reported to. If his men are hunting us and want Kai back, I don't want her anywhere near them. *She's mine.*

"Like hell I'm letting you go! You'll get to make whatever fucking decisions you want by yourself if you go. The men will continue to see you as the leader instead of seeing me as an equal. You can't go."

"Jesus Christ! All I'll do is ensure my men are safe."

"Our men." Blood boils raging back and forth between us.

"I'm going."

"No, you're not."

I narrow my eyes as my cheeks redden, and my teeth grit to hold back my anger. I walk to her so I can hiss in her ear. "You are just doing this to get back at me."

Her eyes cut to mine. "You hurt me; I hurt you."

"You have no idea what you are doing."

"I'm ensuring you have the same power as me. I'm punishing you for hurting me because you can't stand not to have all the control."

"I won't leave my men to die."

"We will send Zeke and Langston," she says.

Zeke looks at me. We've already wasted too much time as it is. "Go." Hopefully, I'll be able to coerce Kai into letting me follow suit.

"And keep us informed of what is happening," Kai says.

I chuckle. She has no idea what we are facing. Zeke won't be able to give us a play by play. We won't know what happens until he returns.

"Stay safe," I say.

"Always do," Zeke answers and then disappears.

"Fuck!" I scream before pounding my fist into the wall leaving a large hole in its wake. I've never stayed behind when something this bad happened before. I hate not being there for my men.

"It's going to be fine. Not everyone needs an ass like you weighing them down."

"Oh sweetie, you have no idea the danger you've just put our entire team in, and yourself, by not letting me go after them. My men are fearless, but they need a leader. Zeke and Langston aren't those men. We always fight together—the three of us. If anything happens to any of them, it's on you. And when the danger isn't put out, you'll be who they come for next."

"Where are you going?" she asks as I storm toward the office.

"To work and hope I can find some way to help them from here." But I already know there is nothing to be done. Kai may try to seek further revenge, but I can't imagine anything worse than this. Whatever Kai plans after this will be nothing. At least I no longer have to worry about any physical connection between us, she just severed it.

CHAPTER 9
KAI

Fuck, that kiss.

That kiss was everything.

Passionate.

Gut-turning.

Toe-curling.

Explosions firing.

I never wanted the kiss to end. I was completely lost in the moment. I forgot about everything.

The pain.

The heartache.

The game.

Everything.

I forgot it all.

Nothing has ever consumed me as much as kissing Enzo did—until he dumped us in the water.

And then the hatred returned, more powerful than ever. Like I was baptized in the water and came up new. The lust vanished, replaced fully with the hate—and the need to destroy this man that has been the cause of every bad thing in my life.

Enzo is a monster. Not just to men who deserve it. He's the devil through and through. I never met his father, but Enzo is just like him if his father is as bad as everyone says.

And the best way to destroy a monster is to show them their reflection. Once Enzo sees his reflection as the devil he truly is, he will destroy himself. He won't be able to live with the self-loathing when I'm through revealing his truths.

I pound on the door Enzo threw shut to his office.

"Let me in!"

"No."

"You don't have a choice! I get to be involved in the business."

"What? You going to run to Archard if I don't let you in?"

"If I have to."

Archard left shortly after Zeke did, but not before warning us both that not following the rules would lead to penalties during the game.

I hear the lock of the door clink, and then the door opens. Enzo stands tall, towering over me. The look alone would bring most men to their knees, but I know Enzo's weakness—*me*.

"I'm sorry," I say.

He huffs. "No, you're not."

Enzo collapses into the office chair, while I take a seat on the couch.

"Fine, I'm not. But I didn't make the decision to get back at you from before."

"Then why did you?"

I hesitate. "Because I couldn't go with you, and I don't trust you." *And I would be petrified, worrying they might hurt you. I want to be the one who hurts you.* My feelings are so messed up.

He cracks his neck.

"What are we going to do now?" I ask.

"Nothing. There is nothing to do but wait. Zeke will call when he has the situation under control."

"Who attacked us?'

"I think Alastar. He's been trying to coordinate his allies to make a move against us for a long time. I've been distracted lately. They must have known and made a move."

"How dangerous is he?"

"A step below me."

"So basically an adorable, whiny kitten."

"This isn't a joke, Kai."

"Sorry, just trying to lighten the mood."

A knock rattles. "Excuse me, sir. I have the pictures on my camera here. You wanted one selected to send to the newspaper for the announcement. Would you like to choose?"

"Leave the camera on my desk," Enzo says.

Westcott places the camera on his desk and then leaves.

We both stare at it, silently stewing until I can't take it anymore.

I retrieve the camera, and kick my legs up on the couch, while I click through the pictures.

There are hundreds of pictures. Of us holding hands as we walk through the sand. Then staring at each other. Some of us smiling and laughing. Others more solemn.

I smile looking at us. We look like a bride and groom on our wedding day.

And then I get to the picture of us kissing. How locked in the moment we are. How right we look together—like we belong in each other's arms.

It was so easy to kiss him. To let him hold me, like we regularly make out while holding each other.

"Why the hell do I let you touch me like this when I can't even shake anyone else's hands?" I say.

"Because we have a physical connection neither of us can shake," Enzo says standing over me as he stares down at the picture of us making out. "And it's going to cause the death of both of us if we aren't careful."

He lifts my legs and then sits on the couch before placing my feet in his lap.

This feels so normal, how any regular couple might sit on this couch. Except one of us didn't try to kill the other. One of us didn't sell the other. One of us is cruel. And the other is about to get her revenge by ruining him and then winning this fucking game.

I reach out and touch his hand, trying to unnerve him, but instead, I do it to myself. I feel everything he's feeling when I touch him: the worry, fear, and concern for his friends.

Shit, what did I do?

I'm not a monster. I shouldn't stoop to his level. And I sure as hell shouldn't bring other people's lives into this.

"I'm sorry—truly."

I continue tracing circles on his palms, each circle I trace I feel more of his emotions. More pain. More hurt. More anger.

But also lust, desire, want.

He grabs my wrist and lifts my fingers from his palm. "Stop."

"Why?"

"Because if you don't, I won't be able to."

And what if I don't want you to stop? Enzo is the only one who has been able to drive out my demons so far. If we fuck, maybe they will be gone for good.

Enzo sighs. "Try to sleep, Kai. It's going to be a long night." He leans his head back and closes his eyes.

I swear I hear him snoring a few minutes later. Apparently, sleeping is how he shuts the world out when he wants to.

I close my eyes, but I know I won't be able to sleep. Not on this tiny couch with my legs on Enzo. Not with the tension between us. Not when I want him more than I want any sort of revenge.

Christ, what's wrong with me? How can I lust after a man who hurt me so much?

Because there are two sides to Enzo. The monster and the protector. Turns out I like it when he protects me. Because him staying home instead of going to the fight feels like protection. If he truly wanted to go, he would have fought harder.

I try to push Enzo out while I wait for news, but hours pass, and he's still the only thing on my mind. And I'm more conflicted than I've ever been about what I want and what I plan on doing next.

"Enzo!" Langston yells down the hallway.

Enzo's eyes pop open, and we both run at toward Langston's distant voice.

The front door is open, and Langston stands inside, holding a limp and bleeding Zeke in his arms.

Fuck. I fucked up.

CHAPTER 10
ENZO

If Zeke dies, I'll kill her.

I don't care that I've done everything I can to keep Kai alive. I don't care if she's too naive to realize the danger she put us all in. I don't care if she genuinely thought she was doing the right thing.

She's no longer innocent.

She fucked up.

She betrayed me. She betrayed Zeke. She betrayed all of my men.

I run to Langston. "What happened?"

"We were ambushed. It was all a setup, a trap. They used the attack on The Savage as bait. They wanted you, Enzo."

"How many did we lose?"

Langston's eyes drop. "We were the only ones to get out. And it wasn't because I was skilled. They let us go. They wanted us to go—to warn you."

Fuck. My enemies already think I'm weak. I need to squash them immediately—set an example.

"There are rumors you no longer are king. That you've abandoned your thrown—for pussy." Langston looks to Kai.

I don't have time to deal with it now. Now I need to ensure Zeke lives.

"Put him on the couch," I yell to Langston.

He does. There is so much blood. I've seen bad before, but I'm not sure I've seen a man continue to breathe with this much blood loss.

I stare at Kai who blinks rapidly as she takes in the scene. I toss her my cell phone from my pocket. "Call the emergency doctor listed in my contacts. Now!"

She starts fumbling with the phone.

I don't have time to ensure she does it. I need to take care of Zeke.

"Hang on, buddy. You're going to be fine. I got you," I say, but Zeke doesn't stir. He doesn't even open his eyes or moan.

I rip his shirt open, trying to identify his wounds to stop the bleeding.

Three holes cover his chest.

Fuck.

Langston and I exchange a quick, worried glance. He has less than a five percent chance of surviving and that's being generous.

"The first aid kit!" I yell to Langston who is already moving to where I keep it in the cabinet on the wall for emergencies just like this.

He opens the box and starts pulling out all the gauze he can find. I find the first bullet wound on his stomach spurting the most blood and pack the gauze tightly over the wound.

Langston does the same for the two wounds on his upper chest.

"Just hang on, Zeke," I repeat.

I scan more of his body trying to find other sources of the bleeding.

His jeans are soaked in red blood.

And then I see the slice on his upper thigh less than an inch from his groin.

Jesus, these men are savages. They tried to castrate my most loyal man. They won't get away with this.

"I need more gauze," I shout to Langston.

Langston's eyes grow big. "There's none left."

"Fuck!"

I stare down at what we have, but if I remove any of the already soaked gauze from his current wounds, he'll die. But if I don't stop the bleeding in his thigh, he'll die. Whatever I do, he'll die.

"Here," Kai says, pulling her shirt from her body and tossing it on his leg.

I cover the wound with the shirt, pressing hard and deep.

"Let me," she says, kneeling next to me.

I want to push her away and say she has no right to touch him, not when she is the reason he will die. If I had been there, this would have never happened. I have instincts my father taught me that Langston and Zeke don't. I would have realized the trap that was set.

"Push down hard on the wound with everything you have. Use your entire body," I say.

She nods, her fingers brushing against mine as she takes over applying pressure on his leg. When our fingers touch, I no longer feel the spark of connection. Instead, I feel anger and hatred. I've never wanted to punish someone so much in my life.

Never.

Kai has no idea what Zeke means to me, what Langston means. They are truly my family. Two of only a handful of people who actually care if I live or die—and she put a member of my family at risk.

Unacceptable.

She's not cut out for this life. And the sooner she realizes it, the sooner I can take over as Black again, on my own.

Langston goes white staring at Zeke.

"Is he breathing?" I ask.

"No."

"Don't you dare die on me!" I yell, my voice cracking as I scream. I don't get emotional often. I haven't cried since I was a kid, but I feel the water clouding my eyes. My heart aches and pounds in my chest. "Trade with me," I say to Langston.

He nods and moves, too shaken up to think straight.

I put my lips over Zeke's, breathing life into him, while applying pressure to his chest wounds. Langton struggles to contain the blood spurting from Zeke's stomach.

His chest rises and falls, confirming that oxygen is getting in, but I know his heart isn't beating hard enough to push what little blood is left in his body through his veins.

I start pumping over his heart, demanding it beat faster.

"You don't get to die, Zeke! Not today! Do you hear me?! You don't get to fucking die," I scream, as I continue to pump my hands over his heart, while Langston and Kai do their best to keep the blood inside his body.

I hear footsteps down the hallway. Westcott opens the front door to let the doctor in.

Finally.

I look to Langston and Kai who have yet to notice that help is on the way. The sound is too faint for either of them to hear or notice. But the doctor is coming.

I can't save Zeke, I'm not strong enough, but I have enough money and resources to pay for the best team. If anyone can save him, they can.

Footsteps grow louder as they run down the hallway to where we lay.

The door crashes open and a team of six doctors and nurses race inside, the lead doctor, Lester Patten, is in the front.

Thank fuck I pay him well enough to drop everything and come, no questions asked.

This isn't the first time he's had to come to save one of my men or me, but this is the worst he's ever had to deal with.

Patten's face falls ashen for a second when he makes a quick visual assessment of the situation. And my fears are confirmed—this is bad.

"Get him on the gurney. Now. We need to perform a surgery," Patten says.

The team descends, taking all of our places as they cover the wounds and move Zeke to a gurney.

"He's not breathing," I say, my voice suddenly calmer now that

I've accepted that Zeke will most likely die and there is nothing left for me to do here.

Patten looks to one of his men, who immediately starts performing CPR, while the rest pack in his wounds with more gauze to try and stop the bleeding.

"You should find everything you need to perform surgery in the room down the hall," I say, even though the doctor and his team already know which room to head to. I have one room that is always set up for this exact situation. You can never be too careful. We don't have time to get to the hospital. And even if we made it, Zeke wouldn't be safe there. Alastar's men would try to kill one of us there.

"I know," Patten says.

And then they are gone—whizzing Zeke down the hallway to do what I paid for—everything fucking possible to save his life.

Langston looks at me a second, trying to be loyal to me, but needing to go watch over Zeke. His eyes are red with worry, his cheeks stained with tears that must have fallen at some point, his face still white from shock, and his body tense with fear.

"Go," I say.

He doesn't wait for a second order. He leaves.

"I'm so sorry, Enzo," Kai says.

I close my eyes trying to conjure all the self-control I can muster. But Zeke's blood still clings to my fingers and clothes. I can't let what happened go.

"Do you have any idea what you just did?!" I scream at Kai.

Her lip trembles as my voice beams through the room, ricocheting off walls and pouring into her as if I just used my fists instead of my voice.

"I didn't realize—"

"Exactly. You don't fucking belong in this world. You have no idea what it takes to be Black. If you were to win, all you would do is get yourself and my entire organization killed. Your first decision as Black got Zeke killed!"

"He's not dead—"

"He might as well be."

"The doctor can save him."

My eyes protrude with all of my furry. My fists ball, my nostrils flare, and my heart pounds so loud I'm sure she can hear it.

"If he lives, he will carry scars with him forever. You of all people should know that."

A slow tear rolls down her cheek.

"You don't get to cry. You don't get to feel sorry for what you did. You may not have killed anyone before, but you just did—you killed Zeke."

More tears fall down her cheek, but I harden more. *I will destroy her.* I don't know why part of me felt any amount of sorrow for her before, but it's gone. I want Archard to walk in the door now and say the game starts tomorrow, because I need to take out my frustration on her, now. And killing her wouldn't be enough.

I need to find a way to fix this. Since I won't kill Kai, and I want her alive and healthy when I do my damage to her, I have to take my rage out in a different way. By ensuring everyone fucking knows I'm Black, and I don't show mercy. Alastar's men will die a torturous death for what they did to Zeke.

And then everyone will know why Kai is married to me. They will know I won her. And marrying her was just a way to claim her as mine. I'll make her nothing.

I start toward the door. "I'm leaving."

"What? Where are you going?" Kai asks.

"To get revenge for Zeke."

"But Zeke needs you here, if he wakes up—"

"Langston will be here if he wakes up." *Which is a big if.* "And when he wakes up, I want to be able to tell him I killed the man who hurt him. We can't show weakness, not fucking now."

"But—" Kai puts her hand on me.

I jerk back, like her touch burns me—I hate her.

I see the pain from my reaction on her face. "Don't you dare try to stop me! You stopped me from going before, and Zeke paid the price. If you try to stop me now, I'll kill you."

She doesn't terror at my threat. She stands tall, strong, fearless. *Fuck her.*

"And I would deserve it."

I narrow my eyes. Not believing she said that. But nothing she says will fix anything—*nothing*.

"Go."

"I don't need your fucking permission."

"And I'm not giving it."

I shudder as my anger fills me, needing a fucking escape hatch through my body. And then I disappear.

Without Kai's permission.

Without Archard holding me back.

I go because it's the only thing I can do for Zeke. A man who saved me too many times to count. My brother in every way that matters.

I failed him. I won't fail him again. I will kill the man who hurt him. And then when I return, I'll deal with Kai. Because my father had it right the first time when he ordered me to kill her when we were teenagers. She has no business being in this life. And the only way to prevent her from winning is by killing her.

CHAPTER 11
KAI

Enzo hates me.

And with good reason. I may have caused one of his only friends to die.

Enzo had said he considers Zeke and Langston to be family. But I didn't believe him until Langston carried Zeke inside lifeless in his arms. That's when I realized just how much Enzo cared for them.

I thought Enzo was heartless—I was wrong. He just doesn't care about me.

But he loves Zeke. He loves Langston. He loves his family.

And now Enzo's gone. To get revenge for hurting Zeke.

I never thought I'd be jealous of a dying man, but I am. Because Zeke was loved. And Enzo is going to make amends for what happened to Zeke.

When I was tortured, I got nothing. No revenge. No closure. *Nothing.*

I walk down the hallway cautiously searching for where the doctors brought Zeke. He looked so horrible when the doctors brought him in. Every inch of his clothes was caked in blood, and his gaping wounds were still bleeding, pouring more of his lifeline from his body until I'm not sure he had anything left.

If they save Zeke, it will be a miracle. Literally a miracle.

I knew it.

Langston knew it.

Enzo knew it.

The doctor saw it without even examining him.

Zeke is most likely already dead, and it's my fault.

I never thought I'd be ashamed of killing a man. Not after my trust in men was taken. But if Zeke dies, it will haunt me.

Why didn't I let Enzo go with them?

I'm not sure it would have made a difference other than Enzo might be lying side by side with Zeke, on death's doorstep. But it wouldn't be on my conscience. His death wouldn't be my fault.

Because I wanted to hurt Enzo.

I did hurt him—more than I ever bargained for.

I got my revenge on Enzo.

But I don't feel any better. Because as much as I'm pissed at Enzo for selling me, for being the catalyst that started this—Jarod was the one who hurt me every day. He's the one I hold responsible. Only when he's dead will I get my revenge.

I see Langston pacing outside of a closed door.

I don't know what to say, but I need to know, so I ask. "How is Zeke?"

Langston's head snaps so hard in my direction there was an audible sound to his hatred. With one look, Langston cuts to my core, ripping me open till I'm raw with emotion and pain.

I thought I knew torture and pain. It was nothing.

Knowing I hurt these men I thought were heartless and invincible kills me.

"He's dying. How do you think he is?" Langston barks.

"I'm sor—"

"I don't want to hear a pathetic apology from a bitch like you."

Langston had always been kind to me, but not now. Now he will hate me till the end of my days.

"Has the doctor said anything?" I ask, because I need to know.

He shakes his head. "He's in surgery."

"That's good. That means he's still alive."

"No, Enzo pays the doctor's so well they will fight for his life well beyond the length a normal doctor would give up and declare him dead. He could already be dead, and they will continue to work hours longer."

"There could be a miracle."

He glares at me. "A miracle would be if you dropped dead."

I suck in a breath at the invisible kick to the stomach.

"You're the reason he's in there! Do you understand that?"

I nod.

"I don't think you do! You prevented Enzo from going."

"I know, and I'm sorry, but Zeke would probably still be in there right now. Enzo would just be right in there with him."

"No." Langston hovers over me in an instant, and I wonder if he's going to slap me, grab me, or hit me. I deserve it, but I flinch, and he stops as if remembering what happened when he touched me the last time. How Enzo hurt him and threatened him never to do it again.

"Enzo wouldn't be in there. And Zeke wouldn't either. You've never seen Enzo in action, so you don't understand. He's unstoppable. He can hear things, see things, sense things we can't. His intuition is unmatchable. He knows where and what our enemy is doing before they do.

"Zeke and I's connection to Enzo is strong. Once Enzo figures out a plan, it's almost instantaneous that he conveys it to Zeke and me. And with Zeke's strength, my quickness, and Enzo's power we are indomitable. We've been hurt, but never like this. We've never been so caught off guard. Never been this close to death before."

"He could still survive," I whisper, feeling Langston's pain with each word.

"You still don't understand. Zeke wasn't the only man who was hurt. He might be the closest to Enzo, but he isn't the only one. They killed over twenty men, injured more, and captured the rest. Those deaths are your fault."

The color drains from my face, and I collapse to the floor. I let men die.

"You should have let Enzo go. You aren't cut out for this world. You aren't even cut out to fight to become Black."

"I let Enzo go now," I say, finally looking up at Langston again.

"What do you mean?"

"He said there was nothing he could do for Zeke here. But he's going to get revenge. I let him go, but..." I can't finish. *Did I just send Enzo to his death?* Because the man that hurt Zeke like that will mutilate the man in charge.

And if Enzo is dead, that means I become Black by default.

Langston's right, I can't lead. I don't belong in this world. If I were to lead, the men would be dead within the month.

Enzo might be cruel, but I doubt every man who works for him deserves to die because of my incompetence. Men like my father work for Enzo, and as upset as I am at my father right now, I don't think he deserves to die.

"Good, Enzo will get revenge for Zeke." The way he says it makes it seem there is no way Enzo will die getting revenge. He says it like it's his word. Like it's already done.

Tears fall again as I shiver in my cold skin against the wall.

I did this.

Please come back Enzo. I don't want the empire. I don't want revenge. I don't want anyone else to die.

Langston paces while I shiver for several minutes before I gather my strength and stand. I'm no good quivering on the floor.

I fucked up; now I need to do everything I can to fix this.

Zeker is still in surgery, so there is nothing I can do for him.

Enzo is gone.

But Langston...he's in anguish.

He's beyond torn up, practically driving his feet so hard into the ground with each step I'm surprised he hasn't gone through the floorboards.

I can't help Zeke or Enzo, but I can help Langston.

I get up off the floor realizing for the first time I'm shirtless, only a bra covers my indecency. I gave up my top to help Zeke. My hands are covered in blood the same way Langston's are. The same Enzo's were.

I walk upstairs to the bathroom off the bedroom I share with Enzo and then wash my hands under the water, watching in horror as the water turns red from the blood of a man I can't save. Wiping the blood away in part feels like I'm washing him away.

Why do I care? Zeke was a monster. He killed men on a daily basis, but he didn't deserve to die.

When I'm finished washing, I mindlessly walk over to the closet, pull out a shirt and jeans, and put them on. Then I grab one of Enzo's shirts and jeans. They will be too big on Langston. Enzo is at least two inches taller, his muscles are more defined, but Langston needs a change of clothes. He can't keep walking around carrying his friend's blood on him all day.

I head downstairs and into the kitchen, trying to find a way to help Langston. I doubt he would take food. My stomach is in knots; his is probably worse.

He might drink booze, and it might help him numb his feelings, but I'm not sure if that's a good or bad thing.

Coffee.

It will warm him up and keep him awake while he waits for his friend.

"Miss Miller, can I help you with anything?" Westcott says.

"No, I got it."

"If you need any food or drink I would be happy to make it for you."

Westcott and I haven't always gotten along. He always seemed too cold and loyal to Enzo for my liking.

"Thank you, but I need to do this myself."

He gives me an understanding look, his eyes filled with sadness. "The coffee is in the cabinet on your right."

My mouth drops. *How did he know I was looking for coffee?* I think I've underestimated Westcott.

I turn to the cabinet and pull out the coffee. Of course, Enzo has a fancy coffee maker that takes me ten minutes to figure out how to use. But I do it. Then I pour the coffee into a mug and head back to Langston.

He's still pacing outside the door. It's started to get late into the middle of the night. But he's so awake I don't think he could sleep if he were forced to.

"Drink this," I say.

He ignores me.

"Langston, drink this," I try again, holding out the coffee.

"I'm not doing anything that brings me comfort, not while Zeke might be dying."

I huff. *Stubborn man.* They all are. "Drink this," I shove it into his hands. "You need it to stay awake and alert for Zeke."

I said the magic words, because he takes the mug from me without a thanks. He just stares a penetratingly dark gaze with his otherwise blue eyes.

"You need to change too," I say, holding out the clothes. If I hesitate, he might slap me for showing weakness.

"No."

I take a deep breath, trying to figure out how to approach it. "When Zeke awakes, you'll scare the shit out of him if he sees you coated in blood. He won't know if it's yours or his. Either way, it might put him into a shock. Change."

"Fine," he relents. He removes his shirt tossing it in my direction.

I try not to wince, but I can't help it.

He smiles smugly at my reaction.

He starts undressing his pants, and I don't react. I know what he's trying to do—goad me into to telling him he shouldn't undress in front of me. But I don't care. I just want him to feel better.

He kicks his jeans off, then does his best to wipe the blood from his hand on the jeans before throwing them at me.

Langston is ripped. He has thick thighs, a slender waist, and muscular arms. His body is marked with scars, similar to Enzo. Similar to my own marks. He just has fewer than me.

He smirks. "Like what you see, baby? Does my body turn you on, while my friend is dying? You know a good fuck might be the only thing that could cheer me up."

It's clear he doesn't want to fuck me, he's just trying to find any way to hurt me. So I ignore his disgusting comment.

"I'm sorry," I say.

He huffs.

I nod toward his scars. "This life has hurt us both, remember?" I glance down at my own scars covering my arms from the cuts and gunshots. "You've just been given a chance to have control; I haven't. I promise to you; I won't mess up again. I may not be able to bring Zeke or any of the other men back. But I promise to you I will live my life carrying that pain as I do these scars. And I will do everything in my power to right my wrong. If that means throwing the games on purpose to let Enzo win, I will. I promise."

Langston's eyes harden, and I think he's going to attack me. But then he exhales as if my words brought him some level of comfort.

I want to hug him, but I can't handle touch. And he's practically naked.

But I can see the pain. He needs comfort even if he won't accept it. Even if he will throw me across the room for my effort.

I hesitantly start toward him, not initially letting my actions known. Then when I get close, I wrap my arms around him quickly.

It feels like fire in my lungs at the touch. Uncontrollable pain surges through me as I hug him, but I don't let go.

Langston tries to fight me off, but I hold him tighter despite my own agony.

"I'm sorry. I don't want or expect you to ever forgive me. But I promise I will spend my life making up for any death I caused."

He tries again to free himself from my grip, and he could if he truly wanted to. Instead, I tighten, and he relents. He needs this hug.

I feel the heated tears on my shoulder. I feel his warm breath on my neck. Both should feel like comfort. Instead, they feel like tiny knives stabbing me over and over. But I don't let go.

He cries hard into my shoulder, his arms finally wrapping around me as he breaks for his friend—grieving for what he might lose.

Forever passes. Or at least that's how it feels to me. Like hell has engulfed me before Langston finally lets go.

His eyes are puffy and red, but he no longer looks at me like he wants to kill me—*that's a start.*

I pick up the clothes and hand them to him. He slowly takes them and starts dressing silently. When he finishes, he says, "You really can't stand being touched, can you?"

I open my eyes, realizing I haven't been able to look at him since

I hugged him. My body shakes, icy sweat has soaked my body, and I'm frozen from the cold chill that has formed a layer over my skin trying to protect me from the evil.

"I can't."

"Then why did you do that?"

"Because you needed it."

His eyes soften, and I know he can't forgive me if his friend dies, but he respects me for what I just did. For putting him above my own needs.

"Those men really hurt you, didn't they?"

I can't answer. "I'll go get you more coffee," I say, needing a minute to myself after what happened.

I return a few minutes later with more coffee for both of us. Even though I prefer iced, I drink the warm liquid trying to calm myself as I sit on the floor. Langston finally sits as well. Staring at me as often as he stares at the door that still hasn't opened.

"You should get a blanket. Warm yourself up. You were like ice to my touch."

I shake my head feeling the panic take hold of me. "I can't."

He frowns. "Are you too cold to move?"

"No, the blanket just won't help. It's a survival mechanism my body learned when I was taken. To shut down so I can't feel as much. My skin turns cold, my heart barely beats, so my organs need less oxygen to survive."

"I'll get you a blanket."

"No, the blanket won't help. The panic attack is too great. I won't be able to tolerate the touch right now."

"But you let Enzo touch you?"

I feel the water in my eyes. "Yes."

"Why?"

I chuckle gently. "I have no idea. I should hate him as much as he hates me."

Langston nods.

And then we are silent. We wait for the door to open. But it never does. With each minute that passes, I know the outcome—*Zeke's dead.*

Finally, the door opens and the doctor stands in the doorway, covered in more blood than I knew was in a human body.

He's dead.

There is no way he survived this.

And with his death, I know I sealed my fate. Enzo will kill me for killing his friend. I've seen what he does to men who cross him. He will never forgive me for this.

Langston shoots up, but I remain seated. The fall will hurt less when I collapse from the pain if I'm already sitting.

"Did he?" Langston asks.

"Zeke's alive—for now."

He's alive.

CHAPTER 12
ENZO

He's alive.

That's the text message I received from Langston.

Zeke is alive.

I don't know for how long. I don't know if he will survive for another hour, another day, another week. Or if he's out of the worst of it.

But he's alive.

I grin, which means I can bring Zeke vengeance while he is still breathing. He will know I killed the man who did this to him before he breathes his last breath. Or he'll know when he finally opens his eyes and decides to rejoin the living.

Either way, it's what I've been needing to hear.

My heart aches a little less knowing Zeke is still alive. The tightness in my chest has loosened, which will make it easier to do the job I'm about to do. But my anger hasn't, which won't bode well for Billy, Alastar's right-hand man and the man who tried to maim Zeke. After doing some digging into Alastar's crew, I learned Billy was the most likely culprit of Zeke's wounds. They use our security equipment, so I was able to hack the system and get security footage. Billy was the fucker who hurt Zeke.

387

I climb up the ladder of the yacht Billy calls his home. My veins pumped with excitement when I realized he's at sea. I prefer to do my work here on the sea rather than back on land. I feel more alive on the water.

I didn't bring any of my men with me. I would never ask them to seek my revenge. Never put them in danger when I can handle the threat myself.

That's one of the reasons the name Black has become even more of a legend since I took over. My father was evil, killing men who didn't deserve to die. I, on the other hand, am fair, but when someone crosses one of my men, clients, or me, they pay with their life.

Killing Billy won't be enough. I need to make an example of him so no other man will ever cross me. And the world will know Black is still alive and well. That marrying Kai didn't make me weak, if anything, it made me stronger.

I thought pretending Kai was my wife would make me appear stronger, but it hasn't. I'm about to remedy the situation—by telling the world the truth. She's mine by force, not willingly. The only person to ever be told differently was Dallas, and he's dead now. The rest of the world has heard rumors I've married, which is why I was attacked. They will know the truth. She's my slave, nothing more.

Kai thinks I've mistreated her in the past. She has no idea what I'm truly capable of. She will be my slave in every sense. She deserves to feel the pain of hurting someone I love.

But for now, I need to focus on my current task.

My feet hit the top deck silently. The security on the ship is of the highest caliber. Alastar is wealthy and will ensure his men take no precautions. They have too many enemies to not be secure at all times.

But he forgets I invented most of the security he uses. The cameras are mine. The alarms are mine. Even the men who work for him were trained in my ways, the man I'm hunting included.

So getting around the security team is easy enough.

But I don't want to get around the security system. I don't want to go unhidden. I want to slaughter any man who dared to cross me.

So instead of sneaking through the ship to the main panel to shut off the cameras, I make my presence known immediately.

I remove my dark jacket, letting the white of my shirt underneath light up on the cameras.

"You want me! I'm here!" I say into the night, knowing every man on this yacht has been notified of my existence and is making plans to take me out.

They should. They should shoot me in the head on the spot instead of trying to torture me into telling them what they want to know.

But they are too stupid and cocky. They think a dozen men can easily hold me back while they torture me.

I silently laugh. They have no idea. No idea the training my father put me through. No idea what I'm capable of given the right motivation.

The men descend as I expect them to, with weapons drawn all aimed at me.

"Drop your weapons!" one man yells in my direction.

I don't even have a weapon out, but they already see me as a threat.

I slowly reach into my pants and produce my gun. I hold it up to them, then drop it on the floor, my heart racing fast not from the fear but in anticipation of what I know is coming.

"Put your hands up."

So predictable.

I do.

And then two men grab my arms, forcing them behind my back as they start walking me brutally forward.

They don't even bother tying my wrists together. They think two large men holding me with dozens of guns aimed at me is enough—they have no idea.

I'm walked down into the depths of the yacht—to their leader, Billy.

It's exactly what I want. I will kill these men for who they work for. But Billy is who I want. He's the one who tortured Zeke. He's the one who ordered Zeke to die because I wasn't there to torture instead.

Billy isn't the leader, but he is the leader of this ship. Similar in rank to Zeke. It's only fair that I repay him with the same scars he caused Zeke—the same pain. But unlike Zeke, he won't be surviving the night.

The door opens, and I'm shoved inside with the two men still twisting my arms behind my back roughly, like that is going to force me to do what they say. I can still feel the metal of their guns pointed on me from behind, but I don't give a shit about any of them.

I care about the man standing in front of me—Billy.

"I didn't think you'd be stupid enough to set foot on my ship, Black. Not after what I did to your man," Billy says not bothering to rise from his seat.

I smile smugly. *This will be too easy.*

"I just thought I'd repay you for your hospitality the last time you hosted one of my men."

His eyes darken. "It will be I who shows you the same hospitality I showed your man."

I growl roughly. "I'm giving you one chance, Billy. Save your men. Surrender to me now, and I'll let them live. I'll even give them a chance to change their loyalty and work for me. If not, they will all die."

"It will be you who dies after you tell us what we want to know."

"And what is that?"

"We want what everyone wants. We want the power of Black. We want to be granted the title. We know the title is earned, not born into. When we kill you, we will earn it."

I laugh. "You want to know if killing me is enough to grant you the title? You don't know the ways of my organization. There is only one way you become Black, and that isn't it. You can kill me, but it won't solve your problem. Black will just be reborn again, with a leader just as ruthless as I am." If I die, Kai becomes the leader. And that scares the shit out of me.

"Then we want to know how to destroy you. We want the codes

to your bank accounts. We want a list of your allies. We want the blueprints to your security systems."

"You can't destroy Black. Even if you were to torture and kill me, you would be no better off than you are now. In fact, you'd be worse off if you killed me, because the new Black would be pissed. He'd take over, and his first task would be to hunt you down and kill you, slowly. You're lucky I'm here."

"Why's that?"

"Because I intend to kill you quickly. Zeke's alive, and I want to go back and tell him the good news that I've killed you."

That's when I make my move. I jerk my arms, not caring if they pull my arms out of their sockets. The sudden twist of my arms brings the men on either side of me to my knees because they refuse to let me go. Refusing to let me go will be their deaths.

I dive behind one, as the bullets start raining, killing the first man. Then I grab the other and slit his throat with the knife they never took from my pocket.

Like I would board a hostile enemy's yacht with only one weapon—idiots.

I take his gun and start shooting. The men start retreating down the hallway. I slam the door I know is bulletproof and invincible to attack. I built this yacht after all. I know the security. I know Billy would keep the most secure room for himself.

And now he's trapped. His men can't get in, but they will hear his screams and know they are next. Some might even go overboard and swim for shore rather than let me kill them.

Billy's eyes go wide in fear. He may be the leader. He may be used to torturing and killing people, but he doesn't usually get involved in a fight until the enemy has been weakened.

He's used to hurting men who are already injured and weak. Men who are tied up, making them easy to torture.

I wipe the blood from my knife on my jeans. I want a fresh knife when I cut and dice him like he did Zeke.

"What do you want?" he already asks, his voice wavering with fear.

I smirk. "Already trying to bargain for your life, Billy? We haven't even gotten started yet."

"I have money; you can have it all."

Jesus, this man is pathetic. He'll be pissing his pants before I'm done with him.

"Don't do the crime if you can't do the time, Billy."

"I didn't. I didn't touch your friend."

I shake my head in disgust of this man.

"Lying, that's not going to save you."

I take a step forward, holding the knife loosely in my hand.

His eyes dart around the room, in search of an escape.

I wait for him to draw his weapon, but then I realize what he is looking for—a weapon.

I chuckle. "You are the worst. You don't even have a weapon on you at all times, do you?"

I toss him the gun I'm holding. "You get one shot, so you better make it good."

He barely catches the metal, bobbling it before gripping it like his life depends on it.

It does.

His hand trembles, and he fires in my direction without steadying it.

I don't even have to dive out of the way to avoid the path of the bullet, that's how far he missed.

"You missed." My lips curl into a devilish grin. "My turn."

I disarm him with ease. Then my knife presses hard into his chest, mimicking the first wound he caused Zeke.

Billy cries out from the plunge of my knife into his lungs.

"It hurts, doesn't it? Soon you'll have trouble getting oxygen into those lungs because of the gaping hole."

I pull on the knife then stab into the other side of his chest. His hand reaches up to try to stop me, but I bat it down like it's a fly.

"Oh, don't cry. We are just getting started. I haven't even got to the good part yet."

I stab him hard into his stomach, twisting to create as much damage as possible.

"I'm being kinder than you were, Billy. You used a gun to create most of the wounds on Zeke. A bullet that exploded into his body.

My knife goes in and out cleanly. It's more personal this way." The blood from his body oozes everywhere, and if I weren't holding him up, he'd have collapsed to the floor already.

His body jerks forward, trying to collapse from weakness.

"Not yet, you don't get to die yet."

He moans and cries.

"Please."

"Please what?"

"Just let me die."

I crack my neck. This is the best part—when you've finally broken them. They no longer wish for life, just death. Because not existing is better than living.

"Do you remember the last thing you did, Billy?"

"No," he moans.

"Then let me remind you. After you shot him multiple times, you beat him. But I don't have time for that, and you are too weak to survive. You tied his hands behind his back so he couldn't fight back. You had men holding him so he couldn't fight instead of facing him one on one like a man. Then you tried to castrate him."

He shakes in my grasp. "Please."

"You missed; I won't."

I stab him in the groin as he cries like the biggest pussy alive. I release him and let him crumple to the floor, but his screams don't stop. Every man aboard the ship hears his cries. And if they weren't terrified before, they are now.

The blood spills out of Billy quickly as I stand over him. He got off easy if you ask me. Because within a few seconds, he's dead.

I pick up the gun and head to the door to kill the rest of his men. Once I'm done, word will spread of what happened here. The Black name will be restored.

Then all I have left to do is deal with Kai for risking Zeke's life in the first place. I've never been so happy about punishing someone before. It will cement her hatred for me, but it's necessary.

No one goes unpunished—least of all Kai. I've been thinking of her as a weakling who I needed to treat with careful movements because of the pain she's been through.

But the second she signed the papers, wanting to become Black, the game started. And I can no longer treat her like a princess. She wants to be in this world; then she gets to live with the consequences of her decisions. And I don't regret that I'm going to enjoy punishing her.

CHAPTER 13
KAI

I've lost the right to see how Zeke is, so I don't enter the room when the doctor talks to Langston about Zeke's condition. Langston may respect me, but he hasn't forgiven me. I might have a chance at forgiveness now that Zeke has survived, but that won't come for a long time.

The doctor tells Langston that if Zeke survives the night, he will have an excellent chance at living.

I listen as Langston goes to his friend and cries gently at the possibility that his friend could die.

The doctors and nurses that treated Zeke file out of the room. The lead doctor stops when he sees me. "I'll make sure a nurse is always awake monitoring Zeke through the worse of it. I'll send most of my team home, but I'd like to stay in case something happens I can take him back into surgery quickly. Is there a place I can freshen up and get some rest?"

He talks to me like I own this house—like I could make such a decision. I will never make a decision again after what happened to Zeke.

The doctor sees the pain in my eyes. "I don't make assurances I can't keep. But Zeke is a fighter. I've stopped the bleeding and gave him a blood transfusion. I mended the broken bones. He has a real shot at surviving."

I shake my head. "It's not that..."

He sighs. "I never ask questions or get involved in my high profile client's lives. But I can tell you, this isn't your fault."

"It is," I say sternly. I will feel this pain for the rest of my life because I almost caused him to die. "Westcott will see you to a room," I say, hoping the man is behind me as usual.

"Follow me this way, Dr. Patten," Westcott says.

I sit on the floor outside of Zeke's room, knowing I can't enter, but also that I can't leave. I need to know Zeke is okay. I need to apologize to him, but I won't as long as Langston is there.

I listen to Langston talk to Zeke even though he's still out. "I'm so sorry. It should have been me. I wish I could trade places with you." He really does love him like a brother.

I smile. I wish someone loved me like that. But I don't have anyone. My father lied to me my whole life. I have no siblings. Mason likes me, but we didn't have this kind of connection. Not one where we'd give our lives to save the other.

I have no one.

I hug my knees, feeling alone. I hate being alone.

"Miss Miller, you should get some sleep. Mr. Black wouldn't like to know you aren't taking care of yourself," Westcott says.

"Mr. Rinaldi wants me dead for what I did. I don't think he cares if I sleep or not," I say, never letting Westcott forget Enzo hasn't earned the Black title yet.

Westcott sighs. "Mr. Rinaldi is a complicated man. I think you should sleep."

"I can't." The tears fall as I look at the closed door that leads to Zeke. "I won't be able to sleep until Zeke is up and walking on his own."

"That could take weeks."

"Then, that's how long I'll wait."

Westcott must realize arguing with me right now will lead nowhere. So he leaves me to sit quietly outside Zeke's door, alone.

Hours pass, and eventually, Langston stops talking.

A new nurse arrives, and I stand, peaking my head inside as the nurses change shifts. I see Langston passed out in the chair next to Zeke's bed.

I enter cautiously, like Langston might wake and drive me away.

He doesn't. He snores loudly, utterly exhausted as he sleeps in the oversized chair.

The room is set up like a hospital room in one half; the other half a makeshift surgery room.

"Do you know if there are any extra pillows or blankets in here?" I ask the nurse.

She smiles and walks to the closet retrieving one of both for me.

"Thanks," I say.

She studies the machines around where Zeke lays, while I cover Langston with the blanket and slip the pillow behind his head so his neck won't be sore when he wakes.

"I'll give you some privacy," the nurse says.

"No, you don't need to do that."

"Don't worry." She holds up her computer. "All the machines are hooked up so I can monitor him from my laptop. And if you need anything, just press the button over his bed and it will alert me."

I nod as she leaves.

I pull a chair up next to Zeke's bed and study him. He looks so lifeless it's hard to believe he is truly alive. Except for the rise and fall of his chest, he looks like a corpse. His face is white, his body still, and tubes jet into his broken arms and legs. Bandages cover what I can see of his head and arms, and I can only imagine what his chest and legs look like beneath the covers.

I reach out and touch his hand, shocked at the initial pain of the touch, but I push through it to comfort him. He doesn't stir. "I'm sorry. I'm so sorry," I say as tears fall.

"I never meant for anyone to get hurt. I was just trying to hurt Enzo for selling me. You were never supposed to get hurt—I'm sorry."

Zeke doesn't react to my words. He just lays lifeless.

And I don't want him to forgive me for what I did anyway. So I just hold his hand hoping he knows how sorry I am.

Zeke's body starts writhing beneath the blankets.

"Zeke," I say hesitantly, seeing him stir.

"Zeke, it's okay. No one can hurt you."

His eyes fly open as his body jolts. And then I realize what's happening—pain.

He must be in incredible pain.

"Squeeze my hand as hard as you need." I reach up and press the button for the nurse. "The nurse will bring you more pain medication."

Langston wakes up from the noise. When he sees me, he stills, "What are you doing? What did you do to him?"

"He's waking up. I called the nurse. I'm just trying to keep him calm until he gets more pain medication."

Zeke moans, and Langston forgets about me. He grabs his friend's hand. "It's okay. I'm here. You're going to be fine."

The nurse rushes in.

"He woke up, and he's in a lot of pain," I say.

"I'll get him more pain medication," she says, racing toward the cart with the meds.

"No," Zeke says.

We all turn to him as he says his first words. Both happy and confused at his choice of words. "I don't want any medication. I don't want to be knocked out again."

"You're safe. No one can hurt you. Enzo went to get your revenge. Take the drugs, man," Langston says.

Zeke shakes his head, and the nurse stops.

Zeke moans again, biting his lip to keep the curses in as another wave of torment hits him.

"Give him the fucking drugs!" Langston screams at the nurse.

"I can't go against the patient's wishes."

"Dammit, Zeke, if you don't let the nurse give you the drugs I'll do it myself," Langston says.

This is getting us nowhere, so I speak up. "We won't leave you, Zeke. Not for a second. One of us will hold your hand even if the drugs knock you out again. But you need the drugs to heal. Your body is in too much pain; you could go into shock and die from the pain—that's not fair to Enzo or Langston. They both love you, and you need to survive for them. Let the nurse do her job. We promise as soon as it's safe, we will reduce the medication so you can stay awake."

Zeke watches my mouth studying it closely like my mouth holds the key to his decision.

Finally, Zeke nods at the nurse.

"Give him the drugs," Langston says as Zeke's grip on both of our hands tighten as his face scrunches in agony.

The nurse gives him drugs through his IV, and within moments Zeke is calm and quiet again. His eyes slowly flutter closed until he's out again.

Langston looks to me and gives me a nod instead of a thank you. But I didn't do it for him. I did it because Zeke needed it.

Langston's phone buzzes and he looks at it and curses.

"I have to go," he says as he stares at his buddy.

"Go, I'll stay. I promise I won't stop holding his hand or sleep until you return."

"Fuck," Langston says pacing back and forth.

"Go," I say again, holding Zeke's hand tighter. Langston studies my grip on his hand. He knows it causes me pain, but this is my penance. I'll hold his hand all night to comfort him no matter how painful it is for me.

Langston disappears without another word. I don't know what drew him away, but I know it must be serious. Langston wouldn't leave otherwise.

Enzo?

Could Enzo be hurt? It's the only thing I can think of that would cause Langston to leave.

My eyes water again thinking of Enzo hurt like Zeke. I can't imagine it. He's too strong to be injured. Too much of a king to lay lifeless on the ground with blood seeping from his body. But he's human. It could happen.

And I shouldn't care. I should dance on Enzo's grave the second he dies.

But I wouldn't.

I don't understand why, but I care about Enzo. I twirl the ring on my finger.

Don't you dare be hurt Enzo. Don't make me a fake widower.

I continue to hold Zeke's hand through the night and next day. The doctor returns to check on him and smiles when he sees me.

"You love him?" he asks.

I shake my head as I stare at Zeke. "Not like that." I'm not capable of love. And I'm afraid the only man I could possibly even love is the man who also sold me. *How fucked up is that?* He's the only man I can touch without feeling pain. He's the only one capable of stealing my heart.

"How is he doing?" I ask.

"Good. His vitals are strong. He's a fighter. I'll have the nurse lower his meds so he can wake up soon. I can't say with certainty, but I can say confidently he will live."

"Thank you, doctor."

The doctor leaves, and the nurse gives him a new medication to help him start waking up.

Zeke's eyes open and this time the pain has softened.

"Thank you," he says.

"No, don't thank me. I'm the reason you are in this mess. I'm so sorry for letting you get hurt. But you don't need to talk—just rest. Langston and Enzo will be back as soon as they can. They are ensuring you get revenge."

The nurse comes over, helps him drink, and makes sure he's comfortable before leaving us by ourselves.

He stares at my hand. "Have you been holding my hand all night?"

"Yes, as I promised earlier."

He studies me closely. "Even though it brings you great pain to touch me?"

"Yes, I deserve the pain. And I wanted to comfort you."

He grips my hand tighter to see how badly it affects me and a tear rolls down. He softens his grip immediately but doesn't let go.

"Thank you," he says again.

This time I don't argue.

"I'm so sorry, Zeke. I will never let it happen again. Enzo will make all the decisions when it comes to Surrender and the men. And I will do whatever I can to make it up to you."

Zeke shakes his head. "It's not your fault."

"It is."

"No, it's not."

I frown.

"I'm glad Enzo wasn't there. More than likely I wouldn't be lying in this bed if he were, he's strong, fearless, and smarter than any of our enemies, but I don't mind taking a bullet or two for Enzo. God knows, he's taken too many bullets for me."

"But he wouldn't have had to, if he had gone. If I had let him go, all of the men would be alive and well. You wouldn't be here. And Enzo wouldn't be hurt either. He would have protected you."

"Probably, but it still isn't your fault."

"Then whose fault is it?"

"Enzo's."

I shake my head. "No."

"Yes, if anyone is to blame it's him. But I don't blame him. This isn't his fault. He was just protecting those he cares about."

"I don't understand."

"The man who hurt you..."

"Jarod."

"Yes, Jarod. Do you know what happened to him?"

I shrug. "I assume he still sails on his yacht, taking on new women as slaves in every port and fucking them until he kills them."

"No, he doesn't."

I freeze; my body, heart, and soul stop.

"Enzo hunted Jarod down. We snuck onto his yacht. And Enzo tortured and then killed him for what he did to you."

I gasp. *Why? Why would he do that?* He sold me to him. He wanted me ruined, hurt, broken.

Zeke reads my eyes. "Enzo is loyal to the ones who are loyal to him. He protects those he views as innocent. And he gets revenge for those he loves."

"He doesn't love me."

"No, maybe not. But he does care about you."

Enzo cares about me. He got revenge for me. He protected me.

"I may not understand the relationship you two have. I don't understand why he would sell you only to keep you safe here, but don't ever forget he cares about you and will always care about you. That's why he stayed instead of coming to protect us. He won't hurt you."

"Don't make promises I have no intentions of keeping," Enzo says from behind me.

My heart sputters—happy Enzo is alive and afraid of what he will do. Enzo may have cared before, but I betrayed him by not letting him save his friend. He won't forgive me for that. I know because no matter what his intentions were when he sold me, I can't forgive him.

You can only truly forgive those you love, and we will never love each other.

CHAPTER 14
ENZO

She's holding his fucking hand.

Like that is going to absolve her of her sins.

Her eyes smile at me when she first spots me, as if I'm her favorite person and she's happy to see me. But as soon as she sees the pain etched, the lines formed from worry now hardened into rage, her smile drops.

And Kai can't hide the agony streaming through her body as she holds Zeke's hand. Every part of her body is begging her to let go. Her mind is screaming, her heart pumping wildly trying to get her to flee. She holds her hand calm in Zeke's, but the rest of her body is on edge as if Zeke's a lion about to attack her.

Good. She deserves every drop of pain she's feeling. She's responsible for Zeke's condition in the first place.

But when my gaze turns to Zeke, he looks happy, content. Sure, he's in pain from his injuries, but it's like her touch comforts him.

He's fucking forgiven her.

Shit.

How the hell did that happen? Doesn't he realize she's the reason he almost died?

Zeke raises an eyebrow as if to challenge my assumptions about Kai.

I shake my head, not believing he could forgive her. I'll deal with that later. Right now, I need to know he's truly going to make it.

"How are you feeling?" I ask, making sure to stay clear of Kai as I walk to the other side of his bed.

"Like I was shot multiple times," Zeke answers.

"Yea, you look like shit, man," I say, with a grin.

He grins back. "You don't look too good yourself."

I stare down at my blood covered clothes. I didn't want to change until he saw the proof for himself.

"Did you get the bastard?" Zeke asks.

"You know I did."

"Good." Zeke's eyes face forward, and a cloud of gloom glazes over them as if he was back on that yacht reliving the attack all over again.

Kai squeezes his hand, noticing the change. It takes a minute, but Zeke eventually breathes normally again as he gives her a tight smile of thanks.

Jesus, she can't be helping him right now.

"Zeke, you're awake," Langston says from the doorway.

Zeke smiles at Langston, and it finally feels like home having us all here together again.

Langston surveys the room, then he spots Kai, and he fucking smiles at her too.

Does no one see how she betrayed us? How holding Zeke's hand does nothing to earn our forgiveness? She needs to be punished for what she did.

"Did you kill him?" Langston asks.

"Yes, I declared war against Alastar and his men. But after the message I sent in torturing and killing Billy, they would be wise to surrender now instead of fighting."

We all grin and nod. This is when we are our best, when we are together.

But then their smiles begin to include Kai.

No—fucking no!

She isn't one of us. She's the enemy. She will never be one of us. All she'll end up doing is getting one of us killed.

I won't let either of them die because of her.

Kai senses that I'm breaking, losing my cool. And it's time for her to face her punishment for hurting Zeke.

She squeezes Zeke's hand one last time and then looks to Langston who immediately takes her place at Zeke's bedside before she stands up walking toward me with her head high, ready to face her punishment.

Relenting won't make her punishment any easier on her. In fact, it might make it worse.

She walks out of the room first, and I follow. Zeke and Langston both know what I'm about to do, but I won't do it in front of them. Not when they have taken a liking to Kai. But they won't stop this from happening. If either of them had betrayed us, then I would have punished them all the same.

I close the door to Zeke's room behind us calmly, as if I'm not about to explode.

"Enzo, I'm sorr—"

I glare at her.

She stops speaking.

Then, I start walking.

I can't do this here. Not so close to Zeke. He has too big of a heart. If he hears her screaming, he'll tell Langston to stop me.

So I walk upstairs to my bedroom, which I know is soundproof. Kai follows, walking like a prisoner about to go to the gallows.

I expected a fight, but apparently, she agrees she should be punished.

I hold the door open to my bedroom and wait for her to walk through. Then I slam the door shut.

She jumps at the noise.

"Enzo—"

"Don't. There is nothing you can say."

She crosses her arms across her chest looking at me defiantly.

"I should kill you," I say.

"You won't."

I hate how confidently she says I won't kill her. But then I should have killed her when we were teenagers, and I didn't. I won't do it now either. I can't. She knows it, I know it.

"I won't." *That would be too easy.*

She exhales as if she didn't fully believe I wouldn't kill her until this very moment.

"You killed Jarod?" she asks.

"Yes."

"Thank you," she whispers, with tears in her eyes—tears of forgiveness. I could be forgiven so easily if I just told her the truth. She's so close to giving it to me anyway, even if I don't fully deserve it.

But I don't want her forgiveness.

Just like she doesn't deserve mine.

We've both hurt each other too many times for forgiveness to ever be an option.

"I wouldn't do it again. I've saved you too many times."

She narrows her gaze at my cruel words. "Stop pretending you are a monster when you aren't."

"You don't think I'm a monster?"

"Not as often as you are a protector."

I shake my head. "I'm about to remedy that thought. Because I am most definitely a monster. I'm not going to kill you, but I am going to punish you. And when the games start, I'm going to destroy you."

I grab her by the neck and slam her body into the wall.

She doesn't cry out; her body knows how to protect her from pain even though it's screaming out in pain from my touch around her throat. I've barely squeezed yet, and she already can't stand me.

"Punish me, you bastard, but don't think I won't punish you right back."

I laugh. "You have nothing you can punish me with."

She gives me a wicked look. "Yes, I do."

"No, you don't. You're too weak to punish me physically. I know you think you have Zeke and Langston wrapped around your little finger, but it's not enough. They won't hurt me, no matter what you want them to do."

"I know Zeke and Langston wouldn't lay a hand against you."

"Neither would Westcott or Archard or any of the men at the club. Your father won't; he'd lose his job and his life. And you don't have any friends to help you."

She looks hurt at my last statement. But it's the truth. She has no one.

"I don't need anyone to help me extract my punishment."

"Yes, you do." I squeeze tighter around her throat until she can barely breathe.

Stop.

My conscious comes back with a vengeance. *Stop, you aren't a monster.* You have to save her from yourself, or nothing you've done will be worth it. You will become the one thing you've worked your whole life not to be—*your father.*

"I could snuff the life out of you with just my hand."

"But you won't," she croaks barely getting enough oxygen to talk. She should be terrified. But instead, she licks her lips then parts them practically welcoming me to do what I want with her body.

Because I want her.

I have no self-control left. I want her body. I want to dive into the depths of her body and claim every inch of her. I want to be the only one who can touch her. I want to bring her pleasure, not because she deserves it, but because no other man has. And then I want to punish her ass for letting my friend get hurt.

But you did the same thing. You let her get hurt.

And I've gotten revenge for her. I saved her life. And I've kept her alive here. I protected her. I kept her safe. And I've punished myself plenty, but I know it's not enough. I deserve to be punished the same as her.

I'll let her, but first I need to punish her. I need to get the image of Zeke's lifeless body out of my head. I need to heal my bleeding heart.

"Punish me, Enzo. I deserve it. But don't think I won't punish you as soon as you're finished for what you've done to me."

CHAPTER 15
KAI

He thinks he can punish me. *He can't.*

I've suffered every possible torture imaginable.

I've been shot, beaten, stabbed, whipped; the list goes on.

And it wasn't just physical pain; it was psychological. I suffered alone. I suffered without any comforting touch for years. I went without food. I went without light.

I adapted. My body learned to shut down like a bear hibernates to survive the winter. My body learned to lock itself away only leaving the most vital of organs functioning.

No one can truly hurt me.

Yes, I don't like people's touch, but I can handle it. I've held Zeke's hand for the last eight hours. It's not a picnic, but I can endure it.

Yes, I don't like the water or boats, but Enzo threw me into the water, and I survived only suffering through a frantic heartbeat.

Yes, I don't like the light, but I've learned to live in the light as easily as I breathe in the dark.

Yes, I don't like a soft bed, but I've learned to sleep on a blanket of pillows as easily as a hard floor.

Enzo can't hurt me. Whatever punishment he has planned, I can endure. I can survive. I will take the scars in and come out stronger.

And I know how Enzo wants to punish me.

I can see the lust shining in the dark irises of his eyes. It's the same feeling we've both had since six years ago when we first met. And tonight, we will finish what should have started then.

We have a connection—neither of us can deny it.

But it's a connection neither of us understands.

Is the connection because we were both destined to be enemies from the start?

Is it because he was born in the dark and I the light?

Or did it grow as we both realized the other was untouchable?

We are going to find out. We are going to put an end to the tension between us.

He wants to use sex to punish me—and I want him to.

It was inevitable we would eventually fuck. He's the only man in my life. The only person who can touch me without me flinching. The only person I've ever thought of naked.

We've seen each other naked. We are both attracted to each other. We both want each other.

And this is how it has to happen. *As punishment—rough, primal, carnal.*

I don't want it any other way.

If we go slow, trying to ease me into it, I'll back out. It will give me too much time to think about what I'm doing and how wrong it feels. I can't let my brain think about what's happening. It just needs to happen.

This is the way.

Sex will either heal me or break me—maybe both.

We've tried for weeks now, and there is this constant pull back to each other. But once we've finally fucked we will be free. To forgive each other for our past sins. To be the enemies we were always destined to be.

"Punish me, fuck me," I say as he continues to grip my neck. The last time he did this was on a yacht, and we ended up going overboard. His decision then changed my life, as will his decision now. But I have more control now than I ever realized. And I have my own punishment in mind for Enzo.

Once we fuck, we will be even. All will be forgiven, because I can't keep living with the pain. And neither can he. It will consume us. And we both need to be ready for when the games start.

He narrows his gaze as his fingers tighten around my neck until only the tiniest slip of oxygen can make it to my lungs.

"Don't ask for something you can't handle," he growls.

"I. Can. Handle. It."

He bites his lip as if it's taking all of his self-control to hold himself back. His eyes go back and forth as he searches for the answer. Because as much as he wants me, he won't rape me. As much as I've branded him the devil, there is a part of him that isn't.

The world Enzo grew up in was different than mine. He did horrible things in the name of survival. And that hardened him, but there is still a part of the boy inside of him that has hope for something better. Something that isn't so dark and cruel.

And that part of him is the part I will break. Only then will we be even.

"How, when you can barely handle Zeke's touch? How, when you've only just accepted my touch?"

I try to take a deep breath but I can't. My head is dizzy with lack of oxygen. "Because I want it. I want you to fuck me."

"Liar."

This is going to be hard, convincing him to use sex as punishment. I need to piss him off enough so it's the only option in his mind.

"If not then what? You're going to whip me? Beat me?"

"Maybe."

A whipping or beating would be easy for me to tolerate. It's happened countless times. And I know Enzo is mad for getting Zeke hurt, almost killed, but the beating would be nothing compared to Jarod's.

But if he beat me, I couldn't get my revenge.

"So you'll beat me, but you won't rape me?" I spit out.

His eyes darken. "I don't hurt women."

"No, you don't rape them. That's not who you are. You aren't like your father," I say, guessing that his father is a sensitive subject.

He growls. *I guessed right.*

"And beating me, wouldn't be hurting me?"

He glares and tightens then loosens his grip all in the span of a second as if he's arguing with himself about what to do.

Now's my chance.

"Langston did."

"What?" his grip instantly constricts.

"Langston fucked me," I lie, remembering Langston's threat when he was so vengeful and stunned.

He blinks rapidly, not understanding my words.

"I was aching and desperate to feel good after what happened to Zeke. We got lost in the moment, and he fucked me. It was good. Hot, thrilling, passionate. That's how I got him to forgive me, by fucking him like the whore I am."

Pain, anger, rage.

I see it all in his eyes. He's pissed at Langston for touching me, but he's livid at me.

"You aren't the only man who can touch me. If a man earns it, then it doesn't hurt me. Langston did. And his cock—"

"Shut up," his voice booms.

He squeezes until I can't get any oxygen in. My lies work. They prompt him to use sex instead of a whip.

"He wouldn't fuck you."

I raise an eyebrow, still unable to speak. He loosens his grip.

"Langston fucked me. Truth or lie?" I ask.

His face reddens, and the veins on his arms pop.

"Stop distracting me from punishing you. You deserve to be punished for putting Zeke at risk, so you won't do it again."

"I agree. Fuck me, Enzo. Punish me," I taunt.

His eyes darken as he tries to read my body. Attempts to give me one last time to choose a different route. He takes a deep breath trying to control his breathing like he controls everything else in his life. But I just offered him the one thing he's been dying for on a silver platter. And once he starts, he will lose all of his self-control. And the possibility that I willingly fucked another man other than him is driving him mad.

I will hold power. But I will be trading my body to get it.

"Fuck me and find out if I'm telling the truth or if I'm a liar."

"If I fuck you, it will hurt. The only pleasure you will get is when I make you come but only after you've paid your penance," he says, trying one last attempt to stop me from letting him fuck me.

I grin. *This is what I want.* A man practically begging me to fuck him. A man whose desire I can feel taking hold of all the air in the room. There is no doubt in my mind how much Enzo wants me—for me. Not because he thinks of me as a whore. He wants my body, but he also wants all of me. His intentions are clear. He wants to fuck and control me. He just doesn't realize he will be giving me just as much control as he'll be receiving.

And I want him just as much in return. He's not like those monsters who held me captive for years. Enzo is beyond attractive. I've seen him naked. His body is better than any flawless statue of a Greek God. He has thick muscles, a chiseled jaw, and defined abs. *What more could a woman want?*

He's fierce, formidable, and powerful. No one would ever call Enzo weak. And after seeing how he cares about the men he calls family, I've never been so turned on by someone who could be so protective of those he loves. Whoever finally steals his heart and persuades him to marry her will be a lucky woman.

"I'm not looking for pleasure; I'm looking for punishment." I mean every word. Sex will never be pleasurable for me. I'm too fucked up for that. But maybe it can be exciting, thrilling, and dangerous. Maybe with the right man, I can learn to relax enough to enjoy it. And Enzo is the only chance I have of learning to push through it.

My words cut through his dark exterior. And I see a glimpse of the man who is more than a ruthless leader, but the man who is kind, gentle, caring. A man I would love to get to know more, but I never will. After we fuck, we will cement ourselves as enemies with the sexual frustration no longer hanging us down.

"I could make it as pleasurable as you want, Kai. You've never been with a man who wants to make it good for you. A man who knows your body better than you know yourself. If I wanted to, you would enjoy every moment of this."

"But you don't. You want to hurt and punish me—you're the same as Jarod."

His jaw tenses, his hand closes around my throat, and heat pours from his body. "I am nothing like Jarod. I killed that bastard, for you. You should have never been sold to such a heartless man. That was my mistake."

I still, trying to preserve what little oxygen I have while he tightens on my neck. *I will not show fear.*

"Your first time after Jarod should be all euphoria. It should be slow and gentle and kind. It should be healing—this won't be."

"This isn't my first time," I lie.

The promise in his eyes is exactly what I want. This will be rough, and unforgiving.

I try to speak but I can't. He releases me. "I know. Fuck me, how you've always wanted to, Enzo. I need to be punished. I need to be fucked, not made love to with gentle hands in order to forgive myself." *I need this to heal.*

He doesn't give me another chance to change my mind.

He releases me and steps back, while I cough, my throat burning from lack of oxygen and his fingers squeezing my neck.

"Kneel," he says.

I raise an eyebrow. Now that we are doing this, my mind is going a million miles a minute thinking about all the things he could want from me. How he will torture me for almost getting his friend killed.

"Kneel, Kai. If I have to ask you again, you won't come even after I'm finished punishing you. You will hate me and hate sex, forever. I will ruin you."

I kneel immediately. This is what I agreed to. Doing whatever he said. Letting him control how and when we fuck.

Trust him. Trust him not to ruin you.

I look up at him with big eyes as he takes a step toward me in his jeans and dark T-shirt. The man he killed's blood still speckles his clothes.

He undoes his jeans and reaches inside.

Fuck, are we doing this right away? No foreplay? No kisses? Nothing? Just straight to fucking?

He pulls his large, thick cock out. And I stare at his cock eye level to me. I've seen him naked numerous times before. But this is different. This time I'm going to have to touch it. It's going inside my body. And that thought is terrifying. Because his cock is larger than any man's I've seen before. Not just long, but thick and fat.

I know how much stretch it will take to get him inside, and I'm not sure I'll ever be able to fit all of him. Enzo isn't the kind of man to wait for me to adjust to his size.

"Stop thinking; this is your punishment. Don't think except what I tell you to think," he commands.

I don't know how he expects me to shut off my mind, but I try. I moisten my lips as I stare longingly at him. Because a man who has a cock like that surely knows how to work it.

Don't think, just trust. Trust my instincts that even though it will be punishment, it will also heal me. Enzo won't hurt me more than I deserve.

"Suck me, Kai."

Suck him. I sucked too many cocks on that yacht. *I hate sucking cock.*

Images of cocks on that yacht start flooding my brain, but I push them out.

"Suck. My. Cock." Enzo's voice brings me back to reality.

I reach forward to grab his cock with my hand, but Enzo's eyes stop me. Instead, I move forward, my mouth parted as my lips brush against the head of his cock.

The heat from it immediately warms my cold shell that has hardened since Enzo grabbed me by the neck.

I let the heat consume me, and Enzo watches me patiently like he's going to allow me as much time as I need to adjust.

But then he thrusts, and his cock is deep within my throat.

I gag at the intrusion, my eyes immediately water. *Fuck him.*

He grabs my chin as my mouth is filled with him.

"Beautiful tears," he says.

He pulls his cock back out.

"Fuck you!" I shout, already losing my cool. *Why did I think this punishment was a good idea? I will hate him when we are finished.*

He grins. "Taking responsibility for your actions is never easy, Kai."

I wipe the tears from my face. "You like me in pain. You're sick!"

He fists my hair, jerking my head back. "No, I don't enjoy your pain. I enjoy the control. I enjoy knowing you are *mine*. I enjoy watching you pay me back with your tears, but I don't enjoy your pain."

His cock pushes at my mouth again, and this time I let him in easily. I prepare myself for his cock to invade my throat again, but this time he takes his time, pumping into me.

And when his head rolls back, and he moans, I feel the flood of liquid building at my core. I've never seen a man so hot and bothered from the touch of my lips.

So I get bolder with my strokes. I lick over his length, meeting his thrusts and allowing more of his cock into my mouth, until he's hitting the back of my throat again.

The tears still come, but this time I give them willingly. I give them for Zeke—for the pain I caused Enzo. I give them because I want to see Enzo feeling excited. I love the heated desire grow deeper in his eyes with each thrust and knowing I'm the one putting it there.

My panties are soaked as I continue to suck his glorious cock. A cock I already love and want more of. I never knew sucking a man off could bring me pleasure, but it does.

I could spend my life on my knees tasting the tiny beads of his pre-cum. The heat of his blood as his cock grows larger. The thick muscles as it parts my lips.

I want more.

I can't get enough of his cock. The deeper he goes in my throat, the more he moans, the more sensitive my bud grows between my legs, aching to feel more.

Enzo gives me a look, and I know he's about to explode. The look gives me a choice. I can choose where he comes.

I want all of his cum.

So I pull him deeper into my throat, until he's exploding his hot thick cum coating my throat.

He pulls back and stares at me suspiciously.

"You're tougher than I thought."

I smile as I lick my lips, loving the salty taste in my mouth.

"I've had a lot of practice." That was anything but punishment for me.

His body hardens at my comment. I see his hands fist and the thick vein in his neck pops. He hates that any other man has ever touched me. He hates that he sees me as damaged goods.

"Stop looking at me like that," I say.

"Like what?"

"Like I'm damaged. I'm not. Finish your punishment."

"That was the easy part," he warns. And I have no doubt he means it.

I nod, preparing my body for more invasion.

"Strip," he commands.

I've been naked in front of this man before, but it was never leading anywhere. This time it is, and I'm terrified of what he will think of my body.

He raises an eyebrow while he waits for me. He tucks himself back into his jeans but doesn't do them back up. He wants the inequality between us. He'll be clothed, while I'll be naked.

I grab the hem of my shirt and lift it over my head. My nipples instantly point in his direction. I didn't wear a bra, and right now I regret that I don't have another layer of protection between him and me.

He exhales at my naked chest, and I see the appreciation in his eyes instead of the disgust he should feel at my scars. It gives me the courage to remove my jeans and underwear until I'm naked in front of him.

Enzo was angry and mad at what I did when we first entered this room, but now that he remembers what I've been through, I can see his anger dissipate.

"Don't—don't feel sorry for me. Punish me; I deserve it."

He growls.

"You're right. You do."

I walk toward him and grab the waistband of his jeans to strip him, but his hand grabs my wrist and stops me.

"No, down on the floor on all fours."

My eyes widen. *Is he really going to take me the first time while I'm on all fours like an animal?* I won't even be able to look him in the eyes.

I reluctantly get down on my hands and knees, my ass in the air. *What have I gotten myself into?*

I feel his warm hand at my ass as he kneels next to me. *This is it. The moment my life changes again.*

I close my eyes, preparing for the intrusion. I'm wet from sucking him, but I'm not sure it's enough to ease the pain I know is coming.

I jerk forward, but not from his cock entering me, but from his hand meeting the flesh of my ass.

I don't make a sound. I'm used to holding in any signs of pain. I know Jarod used to get hard at any sign of distress he knew he caused me, and I won't let Enzo get the same pleasure.

"You're so used to pain, aren't you? You don't even react to the sting."

He swats my ass again, this time the sting spreads, and I can't help but let my eyes water. I could stop the feeling of the pain. I know how. Just lock myself away. *But do I want to?*

My body starts the process automatically. Stilling, cooling, locking away my mind. My mind goes to the beach, to the sand, to the warm wind.

"Don't you dare," Enzo curses.

His voice breaks through, but it's not enough.

He slaps my ass again, but I can barely feel it.

He flips me over abruptly, until I'm on my back. "You have to feel everything." He spreads my legs open, and his mouth disappears between my legs. At first, I don't know what he is doing. But then, I feel the warmth returning to my body. The heat spreads from his lips to my core. And then I feel the most pleasurable thing I've ever felt —his tongue on my clit.

I've never felt such pleasure before. Never felt such ecstasy. I didn't know how it would feel, but now I never want him to stop.

I arch my back into him, and my toes curl as he licks and sucks over my sensitive bud.

Jesus.

My body comes back to life from his touch. And if sex means I get to experience even a drop of this pleasure, I will never shut down during it again.

"Yes," I moan, grabbing his thick hair holding his head between my legs.

I feel myself building to a place I haven't experienced since he made me come on his bed.

"Yes, fuck yes, Enzo," I curse.

He stops.

He fucking stops.

He grins down on me. "There you are."

"Why did you stop?"

He smirks, wiping my juices from his mouth with his hand. "Because I haven't finished punishing you yet."

I swallow hard, forcing the fear down.

"I will hit you three more times. And you will stay with me for all of them. You will let the tears fall, the cries escape, the moans fill this room. Whatever you feel, you will feel it. You won't lock yourself away—not until you've taken all three."

I nod.

"Do you agree?" he asks needing verbal confirmation.

"Yes."

He grabs my hips and flips my body onto his lap, my ass in the air.

He rubs it gently, and then I still as he presses a finger at my asshole.

I can feel his grin at my body's response. "I should fuck your ass without preparing you, to punish you, but I'm not that cruel. Someday though, this ass will be mine."

Someday? This ends after tonight. This is the only time we get.

"One," Enzo says, slapping my ass harder than before.

I force myself to feel it because it's the only way I might get to the pleasure that comes afterward. And I'm tired of not feeling, even the bad.

My eyes water, but they don't spill.

"Good girl," he says, soothing my ass with his touch.

"Two," he says, striking harder.

I cry out, my tears falling now. My ass is far too sensitive for another. I consider pleading for him to stop, but I don't. I've never felt so alive.

"Three," I brace myself, but it's not enough. This one holds all his rage. All the pain he's feeling inside he takes out in one stroke.

"Fuck," I cry. My tears are full on streams now, my ass burning, my body convulsing.

"It's over, baby."

"Don't, baby me," I cry, pulling my body off his lap. I hate him, but I also want him. I've never been so wet before. I want his cock even though I know it will hurt worse than his slaps. But I am also already tired of feeling—anything, pleasure or pain.

He watches me carefully as he pulls the T-shirt from his head. Then lowers his jeans and kicks them off until he's naked.

"On the bed," he commands.

"No."

I cross my arms over my chest. I don't want him to fuck me on the bed where he's comfortable. If he takes me, he takes me on the floor.

"It wasn't a question. It was a command."

"No."

"Would you rather take the whipping?"

I feel the redness of my ass. I would need to shut down completely to take a whipping. And Enzo wouldn't let me. It would last days, neither of us relenting until I felt everything.

"On. The. Bed. Kai."

I reluctantly lay down on the bed as he walks toward me. But then I remember my own plan for revenge. It's better this way. And as much as he's hurt me so far, I also feel free. I know he's holding back. If he truly wanted to hurt me, he would. His hits were nothing like Jarod's. Enzo's hits were that of a man in pain expressing his emotion to me in the only way he knows how, because words aren't enough to feel his pain.

And I feel pain too. Pain of what I've been through for six years because of this man. Pain at knowing men died because of me. Pain at not being free.

But that ends now. When Enzo's cock enters me, I will give him all of my pain. I will be free. My pain will be his burden to bear.

He takes a rope and a condom out of his nightstand. He tosses the condom aside and then takes the rope.

My eyes widen. I don't want to be tied down. I won't be able to stop him if I can't handle this. I won't be able to feel his body as he enters me. I've noticed I do better when I initiate the touch first. He's noticed that and is taking it away from me.

"Wrists," Enzo says, waiting patiently by the head of the bed.

I close my eyes, letting the fear overtake me.

"Wrists, baby."

Why is it when he says 'baby' it both calms me and petrifies me at the same time? He wants to hurt me, but he also wants to please me. He can't have it both ways. He can't be the monster and the lover. He has to choose.

And I already know which he will choose. Monster. No lover would tie me up knowing my history.

I raise my hands over my head, and he ties them together and then to the bed frame.

I pull, but there is no way I'll ever get free.

Then, he takes a blindfold from the dresser and covers my eyes.

Shit.

I don't even get to see him.

I get to live in the darkness where I've always wanted, but the darkness is no longer my friend. I feel alone.

I hear the crinkle of the condom as he sheaths himself before settling between my spread legs.

He doesn't kiss me.

Doesn't suck or caress me.

He does nothing to prepare me for his cock.

This is punishment. It's meant to hurt and remind me I don't deserve anything better. He's giving me his pain, and in return, I'll give him mine.

"I hope Langston did fuck you and stretched you out first, because this is going to hurt. And I won't let you lock yourself away again. You will feel this. *All of it.* And you will never hurt my family again."

Anger rages inside—sex should never be a punishment. But this is what I wanted. This is how I get free. By showing Enzo he's a monster no more worthy of becoming Black than I am. He's not a saint who just protects his men and those weaker than him. He's a monster. And until he makes amends for what he did to me, and who knows how many other innocent people before me, he doesn't get to think of himself as anything but evil.

I want to tell him I didn't fuck Langston. But it might give him the resolve he needs to stop himself. And I need him to lose control to do this. I need this.

He needs this.

This ends now.

I almost feel the regret oozing off of him into the room. "I'm just warning you. Even the most experienced women I've been with feel pain at my size. This is your last chance. I won't fuck you unless you want me to. But this will not be gentle. I will not give you time to adjust. This will ruin you if you aren't prepared."

His cock rests at my entrance, and I know the pain I'm about to experience.

I will never be ready for this.

But I want to ruin Enzo as badly as he wants to ruin me.

I need this.

I want this.

This first time is going to hurt no matter what. I'd rather feel all of Enzo than slowly face the reality of him. I want to know the worst, so I'm no longer afraid of sex.

I grab his thick thighs with my legs, pulling him to me. "Do it."

My eyes slip below the blindfold, and I watch as he closes his eyes as if to prepare himself. When he opens, I see a look of lust I've never seen before. It's like he released all of his self-control.

He gives me one look of warning knowing I can see beneath the blindfold, and then he plunges inside me.

I cry out, releasing all of my fury and pain as he enters me. His burning heat mixes with my ice cold and causes a hurricane of emotion and feelings inside me.

Tears burn my eyes; my thighs squeeze at his waist, and my voice screams out feeling every bit of him stretching inside me.

I feel myself struggling to breathe. Like him being inside me pushed all my air out.

I can do this; breathe.

I look up at Enzo. His eyes are dark holes as he looks at me. He doesn't give me any words to comfort me—nothing to help my struggle. His lust seems to grow the more I struggle beneath him.

I've never felt so alone.

He inches forward, and that's when I realize my body hasn't accepted all of him. There is still more to go. I struggle against the ropes.

I can't.

But Enzo doesn't give me time to prepare or argue against it. He thinks this is what I experienced on a daily basis on that yacht. That I felt worse than this. That this is nothing in comparison. He thinks the reason I'm in pain is because I'm back there again.

It's not.

The pain is real.

The pain at never thinking a man would ever want to fuck me.

That a man would never find me attractive.

That a man would never see me as anything but broken.

Enzo doesn't see me that way. He sees me as a woman deserving to be punished—a woman he is desperate to fuck.

He thrusts again.

"Fuck you," I scream at the pain.

Although Enzo thinks I'm screaming at him.

Another thrust, hitting me so deeply I can't imagine he can go deeper inside.

His hands are at my hips, sinking inside me deeper and deeper. Stretching me wider than I've ever been stretched.

I feel the blood oozing as he penetrates me. I feel myself being ripped.

I feel the tears dripping down my cheeks. But not from the torture—from the release of the pain and agony.

Enzo is setting me free whether he means to or not. This is what my body needs—not a sweet entry into womanhood. *This.*

I start relaxing, opening myself to the pain as he starts pounding into me in a brutal rhythm meant to torture me with his cock.

But then he changes his angle, and I feel his body rubbing against my clit. The alternating pain and pleasure overwhelm me. Almost forgetting my part I need to release to fully be free. The part he needs to hear.

It takes everything inside me to speak and not in a curse. "I've never been sold."

He stares at me but doesn't slow his thrusts as if he can barely understand what I'm saying.

"I've never been sold. Truth or lie?" I ask.

"You want to play now?"

"Just answer me," I grit out between painful tears.

"Lie."

I nod. But he pounds faster, and the pain turns to quick panting on the verge of coming, but it doesn't make up for the pain he put me through in his journey to get punishment.

"I've never been tortured."

The scars of my torture mark my body, making it an obvious lie.

"Lie."

Faster he pounds into me—rougher, harder. Not relenting, despite my frantic breathing.

It's too much and not enough at the same time.

I hate it and love it.

He hurt me and healed me.

But I will never let him know how much this healed me. He will only ever know of the pain. He will see himself as a monster. When he looks in the mirror, he will only see the boy his father raised him to be—a beast.

I swallow hard, preparing for my next words.

"I've never been raped."

He doesn't hesitate. He thrusts faster, building us both to the edge of everything—pain, joy, forgiveness.

I feel his cock drive into me over and over.

I bite my lip, but it's not enough. I cry out over and over, but I don't know if it's from pain or ecstasy. It all blends together into one mess of emotions.

It is everything.

Everything I've wanted and hated.

I could love this boy, if only he'd let me. Instead, I hate him.

I hate him for selling me.

I hate him for taking me.

I hate him for telling me the truth.

I hate him for punishing me.

I hate him for hurting me.

But I could love him for healing me.

Which is why I'll never think of this moment again. He broke what was left of me, but somehow the final breaking gives me something back. The ability to finally put the pieces back together.

I scream. It's the loudest I've ever screamed. And everything I'm feeling released in one mighty orgasm as I feel Enzo's own release inside as he jerks within my body.

But when he stills, he doesn't relax like a man who just made a woman come. He was so consumed with his own orgasm and revenge, he barely paid attention to me at the end.

We both pant heavily, his cock still rests inside me, and finally, he answers my last truth or lie.

"Lie," he says more cautiously than the rest. "You were raped by Jarod. Langston..." He can't finish his sentence. Still not sure if Langston fucked me or not.

"I've never been raped, and Langston never fucked me. You just took my virginity—ripped it from my body in your seek for revenge. You may not have raped me, but you hurt me instead of loved me. Because you are a monster." And then I say the words I suspect will hurt the worst, "You're just like your father."

I see the crushing pain on his face, and I know I fulfilled my promise. Enzo punished me, but I got my own revenge.

That was her first time.

She's never been fucked before.

Never been raped.

Jarod never touched her in that way.

Langston sure as hell didn't.

That's what she's saying. And I can't think of any reason that she'd lie.

Plus, now that I've regained some of my self-control I can see the evidence for myself.

Blood is stained between her legs from where my cock tore away her innocence, her pussy was far too tight, and the tears that rolled down her face as she cursed and writhed in pain is enough to convince me.

She was a virgin—until I ruined her.

I punished her harder than I ever realized because she never told me the truth of what happened to her on that yacht with Jarod.

I assumed he and the other men aboard raped her, but now I know it's not true. *What the hell happened on that boat?* Whatever it was, it hurt her so badly she may never recover.

And I just made it so much worse.

I feel a torrent of guilt for my actions—instant regret.

This should have been the opposite of her first time. This was far too violent for anyone's first time. Far too brutal for most people's ever times.

I shouldn't have used sex to punish her. But I also knew I would struggle whipping her, beating her, scarring her. Not when I could see the physical scars all over her body the entire time I was doing it.

And then she goaded me. *She wanted this.*

Why?

So I would feel the same pain she does now.

I feel like a monster.

This is something my father would do—ruin a woman's first time.

There is no way Kai will ever let me fuck her again. I doubt she will let any man touch her for years, possibly ever.

And it's my fault.

I hurt her—when I promised her I never would.

At least, not in this way.

I'm a monster.

I brought the torture she must have only dreamed about to life.

Did she even come?

I was so consumed by my own feelings—revenge, punishment, and euphoria, that it all went by in a blur.

From the tears streaming down her rosy red cheeks, I'm not sure any of it was enjoyable for her.

"Baby—" I start, but she immediately cuts me off.

"I don't want to hear your apology any more than you want to hear mine. There is nothing to apologize for anyway. I wanted this. I planned this. I wanted you to ruin me; it was the price I was willing to pay. I was already broken anyway."

"Kai," I try again.

By now she's sniffling hard, trying to suck the tears back into her body.

Did she tell me to stop?

I try to think back; I don't remember her telling me to stop. This wasn't rape, but it wasn't good. Even if she wasn't a virgin, it wasn't good.

I hurt her, and I didn't care.

But I won't apologize for what I did.

She needed to be punished, and this was the punishment she chose.

My cock still rests inside her. And I can feel her muscles tightening gently around me. Her pussy is so tight; I don't know how she's tolerating me still buried between her muscles.

I try a different route. "You win."

She blinks rapidly, trying to expel the tears from her eyes, since she can't use her hands currently tied above her head.

"You win. I surrender. You were right; I feel disgusting. I shouldn't, but I do. This was two consensual adults having sex, but I still feel gross, wrong, sick. It's too easy to compare myself to what my father did."

"What did your father do?"

I hesitate, "Zeke didn't tell you?"

"No, I just guessed. If the myths were true about Black, your father must have been one evil guy. I'm sure he tried to pass that along to you. And I see your daily struggle to manage both sides of yourself. The good and the bad."

"There is no good."

She doesn't respond, but I know that was part of her gaining power here, to make me feel like I'm only evil. Only the bad part of myself controls my actions. It gives her more power if she can predict if she's dealing with the good or bad version of me.

"What happened?" she asks.

I shake my head. She hasn't earned that story. She doesn't get to know why my father was the evilest bastard ever to walk this earth.

She sighs, and her eyes glance down to my cock still inside her. I'm not as hard as I was before, but fucking her once wasn't enough. Her tightness keeps me hard the entire time; I just need to persuade her to try another round. One where I ensure she comes and it feels good.

Because now that I've had her, I don't ever want to stop. She's the most responsive woman I've ever been with. I've never felt a cunt grab hold of me like hers did. And the screams that leave her throat make me possessive and mad. I want her—all of her. The spitfire, the beauty, the fearlessness. Not once was she afraid, no matter the pain I put her through. She took everything.

And as much as she can try to convince me that I've ruined her, other than the tears, she doesn't look hurt. She has a glow about her, which again, might be the tears, but I don't think so. She's radiant, her cheeks have pinked, and her eyes read more confidence and determination in them than I've ever seen.

This changed her.

For worse.

For better.

And I want to know why. Only then will I decide what to do next. Make amends by fucking her, or release her and return to being enemies.

"Tell me what happened on that yacht," I command.

She frowns. "Untie me and get your cock out of me first."

"No."

She glares. "Enzo, untie me. My story is too vulnerable for me to tell when I have no control."

"I think this is the exact position you need to tell me in."

We return stares, neither of us giving in. We are both stubborn, but she forgets that right now, I have all the power. Because she's the one tied to my bed.

"You hurt me; the least you could do is untie me."

"We both hurt each other. I might be the latest person to start the war, but I'm offering an olive branch as soon as I find out the truth."

She takes a deep breath, her back arching and her wrists pulling as if trying one more time to break free. And when it doesn't work, she starts her story.

"When I was first sold, I thought that was all they wanted. I knew the high price they paid for me. I was branded a virgin on that stand when I was sold. It got them a higher price because of it. I knew what my purpose would be when I was taken aboard that yacht.

"But then, the first night, it didn't happen. I was attacked. Men ripped my clothes from my body. They beat me. Whipped me. Forced their cocks down my throat. Did their best to wrench tears from my eyes. But they never came."

She closes her eyes, and I know she's back on that boat.

I rock into her pussy as gently as I can, trying to bring her back to me and away from that horrible place. I watch her nipples peak, and her pussy lips tighten around my cock the tiniest bit, confirming she's still with me. She opens her eyes again.

"That became their game. Their favorite way to torture me. With promises of what tomorrow would bring. Tomorrow they would rape me. That promise came every day for a month, until slowly I stopped believing the threats. I thought I was safe, at least for the moment. I thought they were saving me for another man who had yet to board the yacht. At one point, I thought you had directed them not to touch me."

I shake my head no.

"But then, they started taking other women on board." She winces as she relives it.

"Kai, come back to me."

Her eyes flutter back to mine immediately. "They would rape those women as soon as their feet touched the deck—always in front of me. They would torture me while I watched them violate other women, while I was hopeless to save them.

"The men made me feel like I was disgusting, unworthy, less than. That I wasn't pretty enough for any man to rape or touch."

Her eyes are completely filled with tears, but she doesn't let them fall—not now. She's too strong to let them out.

"But then, my body took over. I had to cope, and in my sick mind, I started wishing they would rape me. I wanted off that boat, and the women who were raped got to leave, usually in body bags, but it didn't matter, it was an end. But it wasn't just that. The thought of being raped seemed easier than the torture I went through.

"Eventually, my brain filled in the dots with other women's rapes. I pretended their rapes were mine until I couldn't even tell I was lying to myself. That was their plan: to torture my brain. Make me believe things were worse than they were. My imagination was worse than anything they could have actually done to me."

"Kai," I say, my heart breaking for her.

"They say there are worse things in life than death. I believe that. What they did to me messed with my head. It's why I can't tolerate anyone's touch. Because the only time they touched me was to beat me. I never got comfort—nothing that could be misperceived as caring. I didn't even get a sexual release. I got nothing. I was nothing but a punching bag that they tormented until my mind broke and I could no longer determine what was real and what was fake."

"I'm sor—"

"Don't. You don't get to be sorry for what I went through. You don't get to be sorry for anything you did. You were the catalyst. You started this. If we went back to that yacht that day with your hands around my throat, I would have chosen death knowing what came next."

"You said no one could touch you, but I touched you."

She stares at me, lips parted, with no explanation as to why.

"You hugged Langston and comforted Zeke even though you were in pain. In time, you will be able to touch anyone you want without the spark of pain. But for now, you have me."

She chuckles. "You just tortured me into submission. You punished me. My body will no longer respond to you the same way."

"That may have been your intention. You may have hoped to make us permanent enemies with this stunt. You may have thought this would ensure we would never forgive each other and squash any connection we had. That from now on, we would be nothing but enemies ready to fight. But that didn't happen, did it?"

She gasps. "What do you mean?"

"I mean, if you really wanted my cock out, you would have pushed me out long ago. That if you were really so hurt, you would be flinching in pain any time I touch you."

I grab her hips and rock forward.

Her eyes glaze over, part from the pain, but also from something else.

"Did you come?" I ask.

She freezes.

"Did. You. Come?"

"That question isn't relevant. Lots of women come from sexual experiences they don't enjoy."

I flare my nostrils and growl low and heavy. "That means yes, you came."

She looks at me like she's going to kill me for telling the honest truth.

I smirk, *damn I'm good.* Even when I punish a woman, I'm still the best she ever had. I guess in Kai's case I'm also the worst. Because I'm the only man she's ever had.

"Don't get cocky. It had nothing to do with you," she says.

"Sure it didn't. But just to prove you wrong, how about I make you come again?"

"Enzo," Kai warns.

I rock my hardening cock, and her juices instantly soak me.

I move slow, letting her decide what she wants.

"You want me—don't deny it. You've had it rough, punishing because deep down that's what Jarod made you think you deserve. It's what your body convinced you was all you could handle. But it's not the truth. The truth is, everything about sex can be magical with the right partner," I say.

Her lips part, and her tongue licks her bottom lip in anticipation.

I have her. Now just close the deal.

"For instance," I jerk my hips forward until I rub against her sensitive clit, and the angle of my cock presses deep within her most likely hitting her G-spot. "When a man knows how to read your body, it can be the most explosive thing you've ever experienced."

I gyrate my hips, making small circles over her clit and within her cunt. Her legs spread wider for me, and a small whimper escapes her lips.

She has to be sore and in pain, but that's not what I want her thinking about when his ends.

I want her to remember the explosive feeling when she comes around my cock. How I was the only man to ever make her feel that way. And how she only wants me to be the one to give it to her again.

She's mine.

And I don't want her to forget that—ever.

Even when we have long finished our time together, I want her to think back to her first and know that no man will ever bring her the same amount of pleasure as me.

"Let me show you how good it can feel."

She throws her head back as I thrust harder and grip her hips, forcing all of my length inside her.

"Is that a yes?"

She moans as I lean down and take a nipple into my mouth, sucking viciously.

"Kai? If I don't get a yes, then I'll stop. What will it be?"

I've teased her, given her every opportunity to know what it will be like now if she lets me fuck her. Now, it's up to her.

"Yes."

Thank God!

Last time was about punishment. This time, it will be nothing but pleasure.

But it doesn't mean I will fuck her gently. Our connection is too passionate for anything gentle. The crash of sparks at a simple touch will ensure anytime we fuck it will be epic.

I lean down and remove the blindfold that had already started falling from her face as I thrust in and out of her slickness.

I lean down and kiss her, like she's the only woman I ever want to kiss. And from the taste of her, it might be true.

Her tongue pushes back, driving into me with a dance showing that even though she wants this, she won't give up power completely to me.

I push her legs back toward her head as I pump into her, allowing a deeper angle to hit all of her depths.

"Fuck..." she moans, and water burns her eyes again.

"Too much?" I ask. *Please don't let it be too much.* I can barely stand to go as carefully as I'm going.

"No, don't you dare stop. It shouldn't feel good, but it does."

I halt, grabbing her chin and looking deep into her sea green eyes. "Don't ever say sex shouldn't feel good. You were turned on when you sucked my cock. You were wet when I spanked your ass. Drenched from being tied up. You wanted this. You enjoyed this, and there is nothing wrong with you. Plenty of women like the unordinary—the dark, the dangerous. You can like this. You can like plain missionary. You can like getting fucked in the ass. Or tied up. Or on top. Or in any position you want with any person you want, male or female. Don't let Jarod take that from you. This—this is right. If it feels good; it's right."

"This feels good," she says with a tiny smile.

"Now, what do you want, baby? Tell me what you want, and it's yours."

She blushes.

"Fuck me hard, fast, and painful—like before. I don't care about the pain; it just made the release all the sweeter when I finally came."

She came. Even though it hurt at first, her first time was still pleasurable. That makes the sinking feeling inside shrink just a little. I'm not completely like my father.

I smile.

"My pleasure."

I push her legs back again as I drive into her with all my force.

She cries out, but this time I listen closely. It hurts her, but it also releases her from the pain of before.

But I want more pleasure than pain for her this time. So I let my thumb find her nub and press against it in tiny circles while I fuck her deeper and deeper.

Her arms pull at the rope, and her body writhes beneath me.

"God, it's all so much. I never knew..."

"You never knew what?"

"It could feel like this." She cries out again as I hit the deeper depths still.

I cradle her head in my hands as I kiss her in rhythm with my thrusts.

I've already come twice, and I'm about to come a third time, far quicker than I want to. But I'm determined not to come until Kai has.

"Come, baby. Let go."

I'm not sure she'll listen to me. She rarely does. But her pretty eyelashes flutter in my direction, her lips part, and her body contracts.

"Damn you, Enzo!" she screams out as her pussy convulses around me, releasing her orgasm in an explosion. Her cry loud enough that I'm sure any visitors outside could hear her.

Her cries are my cue, and I pump one more time, releasing my load into her core before collapsing on top of her body.

For the first time in forever, I feel whole lying on top of her with my cock still buried inside her.

"Enzo?" comes Kai's sweet voice.

"Yes?"

"As much as I enjoy coming, I don't think my pussy can handle any more stretching for today. And my arms would love blood circulation to return to them," she snarks.

I smile.

"Ready?" I ask.

She narrows her eyes, clearly not understanding my meaning. So I go with the ripping the bandaid off method.

I pull out in one stroke, my cock still thick from being inside her.

She winces, blowing out a hiss as I pull myself from her body.

Only then do I see how much she bled and the damage I truly did to her.

She was a virgin—but now she's not.

I remember my first time. I was fifteen, and the woman was a stripper at Surrender. I think eighteen or nineteen. It was expected of me, so I did. It wasn't life-changing.

But this was for Kai.

I pull the condom off that carried two of my loads. I'm not sure how protective using the same condom twice is. Probably not one of my best ideas.

"Let me clean you up," I say, carrying the condom to dispose of.

"No."

For once, I disobey her no. I run to the bathroom, grab a washcloth and then return to between her legs to wipe as much of the blood as I can.

She winces, but I doubt it's from the pain. More from me taking care of her. She feels weak, and she hates feeling weak.

"Thanks," she says when I stop.

I should release her arms, but this is the last moment of complete control I have. So I take advantage of it.

"I'm—"

"Don't you dare say you are sorry."

I cover her mouth with my hand so she can't talk.

"I'm not sorry. Not at all. At least, not for tonight. Because without the excuse of punishment, you would have never let me fuck you. And as painful as it was, it also healed you. I see it in your eyes. When we first met, I was seventeen and you were sixteen, I wanted to be your first. But once you were sold, I knew it would never be possible. You may think you stole something from me, and you did steal power and forced me to face my own evil that lives inside me, but I also got a gift I never thought I'd have. I got the gift of showing you how incredible sex can be."

She tries to speak, but I keep her mouth closed.

"So thank you. Thank you for trusting me with your first time, even if it was meant to hurt me. It did. But it also was the best fucking time I've ever had."

Slowly, I release her mouth, and she stares with her lips parted, her hair a tangled mess on top of her head. I begin to undo the ropes before she speaks.

"You can be a monster, and I did want to hurt you. And I did, if only for a moment. But I did trust you with my first time."

I smile.

"But don't let it get to your head. I trusted you with my first time, because you are the only man who doesn't cause me to flinch every time he touches me."

I laugh. "I'll have plenty more times to show you just how incredible it can be."

She goes silent.

I finally release the ropes from her wrists.

And then an awkward silence falls between us. Neither of us knows what to say.

"I'm going to run you a bath. It will help with the soreness that is coming."

She nods.

I start the bath and then return. She's sitting on the edge of the bed with a blank stare and soft smile on her lips.

"The bath is ready."

I want to scoop her up, but I know her well enough to know that's not what she wants. It's one of the reasons she didn't tell me until it was too late she was a virgin. She didn't want to be treated differently. She wanted to be treated like an equal.

But when she gets to the tub, I can't help but hold my hand out to help her into the tub.

She takes my hand and then sinks down her chin, her eyes close, and she whimpers softly at the warm water.

I smile as I kneel next to the tub.

"You aren't coming in?"

"If I come in, you'll only end up even more sore, which defeats the purpose of the bath."

Her eyes widen, but she doesn't say anything.

What's going on in that head of yours?

A knock startles me.

Kai and I exchange glances, but dread fills me. It could be Langston or the doctor coming to say Zeke took a turn for the worse.

"Be right back," I tell Kai.

I grab a pair of boxers to put on before I answer the bedroom door.

Archard is standing in the doorway, looking concerned.

"Is Zeke okay?" I ask.

"He's fine. Making jokes and hitting on the nurses. I think he'll make a full recovery."

I exhale the breath I was holding and smile. It sounds like Zeke.

"What do you need then, Archard?"

"Is Miss Miller here?"

"Yes, but she's taking a bath."

"I need to speak to both of you."

I frown. I don't like him coming anywhere near her when she's naked. But the bubbles were covering her the last time I saw her, and from Archard's look, this seems important.

I nod for him to follow me. I notice the bloodied sheets on my bed that look like a massacre happened instead of sex.

I smile, I would love to see his face when he noticed the blood. Instead, I hurry into the bathroom first to check that Kai is covered. She is. I give her a look of warning before Archard enters.

Kai tenses when she sees him, but not because she's naked. She has no problem with her nakedness. But because we both know why Archard would want to talk to us together.

"The first event is ready. This is your twenty-four-hour notice. The first task was chosen by Mr. Miller. But that's the only clue I can give you. Meet me at Surrender at nine AM tomorrow."

I glance at the clock realizing it's nine AM in the morning. It's been a long night. And our lives are about to get harder. I may have fucked Kai. She may have served her punishment, and so did I. We may have even started a path toward forgiveness. But whatever our relationship is, it's new. And before we have a chance to explore what sexual connection we could have, we are going to be forced into being enemies. And I doubt after tomorrow we can continue to be both—lovers and enemies. We can only be one. And our only choice is to remain enemies.

CHAPTER 17
KAI

It was supposed to feel like punishment.

The sex was supposed to make him feel regret and pain.

Instead, it brought us closer into a connection I still don't understand.

It was meant to be only one time. Hurt him and heal myself —that's all.

But then I let him fuck me again.

And his words promised another fuck later if I'm willing.

That wasn't supposed to happen.

Enzo wasn't supposed to care for me after he fucked me.

He was supposed to hurt me and make me hate him even more.

Instead, it's hard to look at him as anything but my protector. But tomorrow no matter what he wants, that ends. He can't protect me and beat me.

The games start tomorrow.

Everything up to this point has been playtime.

Now it's serious.

I have twenty-four-hours to prepare for a battle I don't even know.

And right now, I'm sore as fuck.

Enzo's cock was far larger than anything I could ever imagine. He stayed in me for far too long. And stretched me to my limit. But it felt so damn good.

I will never tell him that though. His ego is already too big.

I can't stay in this tub all day, as much as I want to. And when I get out, I can't snuggle with Enzo in his oversized bed like I want to either. I'm not sure he would want to anyway. That's not how we are together.

Archard left us after giving us our warning. Not that his warning is much help. *How do you prepare for a battle where you don't know what weapon will be used? Or how the battle will be fought?*

You can't.

I try to think about what tasks my father might assign to try to give me an advantage. But when he wrote the rules, I was just a baby. He didn't know he'd never have a son. He didn't know that I would be fighting. And he did nothing to prepare me anyway.

I'm destined to lose. And after how I handled the last crisis, getting men killed, and a high-level leader almost killed, it's probably for the best that I don't stand a chance.

"Baby, what are you thinking?"

"That you should stop calling me 'baby' and start thinking of me as the enemy."

Enzo's eyes drop, and he gives me a chilling look.

You don't get to be my friend. You don't get to be my lover. You are my enemy.

Why can't you see that?

This was supposed to cement our hate for each other, not make us want each other more.

"Can you hand me a towel?" I ask.

"Sure."

Enzo grabs a towel and holds it open while I climb out of the tub before wrapping it around my body.

He sold you, don't ever forget that.

Don't fall for the charming grin and seductive eyes.

Forget how good he made your body feel.

Enzo doesn't move out of my way. We stand—both in various

states of nakedness, but it's not just our bodies exposed to each other, but our souls.

"I'm going to get dressed."

"Okay."

"And then I'm going to prepare for tomorrow."

"Okay," his lips tighten.

"Okay."

Neither of us move. When this moment is over, so are we. I'm sure after tomorrow any feelings we have toward each other will be severed.

Finally, I walk past him, our arms touch and then our fingers brush against each other as if we want to hold onto each other's hands.

We could have made a great couple. The sex is out of this world. We are drawn to each other even when we consider the other person an enemy. But it would have never worked out long term. Just like a flame that eventually dies out quickly with a burst of strong wind. We would have been snuffed out just as quickly.

It's a good thing this can never happen between us. We definitely can't have a relationship, and even fucking each other would bring up too many emotions between us. But it would have been fun to ride his cock while we could, before we let the drama come into our lives.

Too bad it took me until the last possible day to decide it was okay to fuck him.

I walk into the closet and pull on some running shorts, sports bra, and tank top. I'm not in the best of shape and decide I should spend today testing my abilities so tomorrow, no matter what I face, I will at least know what my skills are.

When I come back out, Enzo is dressed in jeans and a charcoal T-shirt.

"Going for a run?" he asks.

"I don't want to stay here—not during the games. I should be staying with my father. He could help me prepare."

"I could help you prepare."

I snort. "Yea, you could. And then you would know exactly what my weaknesses and strengths are."

His jaw tenses. "You aren't leaving."

"Let me leave for today. You can send one of your men to monitor me. I just really need to be alone today."

"No."

Enzo turns away, and I know this is a done conversation. He's never going to let me go. He likes controlling me too much.

Damn him.

I don't care if Enzo knows my strengths and weaknesses. He knows mine already, and I already know his. I just need some space after what happened to get my head on straight.

I run downstairs and out onto the sand. The sun is already beating down with plenty of moisture in the air despite a cloudless sky. It's going to be a hot one.

I stretch for a moment, staring at the sea that feels like my enemy.

You will not hurt me.

I take a deep breath, filling my lungs with oxygen, and then I run.

I run as fast as I can for as long as I can on the sand.

I know Enzo's property is vast, much larger than I can imagine. But I intend to run further than the edge of his property line. I know he has dozens of men watching his property. He has cameras and more security than I could imagine.

Enzo can do his best to keep me here, but it doesn't mean I have to stay.

I run, my lungs burning, my legs aching the entire time.

Fuck, I'm weak. Weaker than I've ever been. I've never been much of a runner or exerciser, but working all the time and running from my father's debt collectors kept me fit.

I see Enzo's property line come into view as men patrol the edge with fencing almost all the way to the edge of the beach.

That's my goal.

But five minutes later I lay passed out on the sand, my chest heaving to catch my breath.

Fuck, I'm out of shape.

Hopefully, my father didn't plan anything that involved endurance, because I won't win that fight.

I look at my puny arms. It better not involve strength either.

Fuck, I'm screwed.

It doesn't matter—this all just a formality. Hopefully the tests aren't too dangerous, and I can survive until Enzo wins. Then I can convince him to let me go free.

"What are you doing?" I hear Langston's voice.

"Getting a suntan."

He smiles over me.

I squint as I look up at him, the sun blinding me.

"Decide to go for a run?"

"Yes, although it was more of a crawl. I have no stamina anymore."

He smirks. "That's not what it sounded like last night."

My cheeks redden, and I gasp. "You heard us?"

"I think the entire city heard you."

I laugh. "Sorry."

"Don't worry; I've already scrubbed out my ears."

I nod.

He studies me for a moment, as a thought twists in his head.

"What?" I ask.

"Come with me."

I don't like the swift mood change, but I stand up and follow him. Sweat coats my body, and my legs ache with every step. After the first task I really need to start working out again and at least make an attempt at protecting myself.

We walk back towards the house and around to a private area on the side of the house.

"Zeke!" I say happily. He's sitting in a chair with his feet in the sand.

He smiles back at me.

"You're out of bed. That must mean you're feeling better and out of the woods?" I ask.

He nods. "I'm feeling well enough to help teach you a thing or two."

I cock my head, not understanding. I look from Zeke to

Langston, and then I notice what else is new. Two targets planted in the sand.

"What are you talking about?"

"We decided Zeke and I should teach you some of the basics before tomorrow. We can only do so much with the limited time we have, but knowing how to shoot a gun at least could come in handy tomorrow."

My lips curl up. "Does Enzo know about your plans?"

Langston gives Zeke a worried glance.

Damn, I like these two. Enzo may be their boss, and they would follow him to the ends of the earth, but they also make up their own minds and do what they think is best.

"What Enzo doesn't know won't hurt him," Zeke answers.

I grin.

"Here," Langston says handing me a gun he pulls from the back of his pants.

I take the gun, it feels heavy in my hands, but I don't feel dangerous holding it. I doubt even if I knew how to aim, that I would be able to shoot anyone with it—least of all Enzo.

Langston goes over the basic mechanics of how to load the bullets, how to check the safety, and how to aim, with Zeke jumping in occasionally when he has things to add.

And then I'm standing in front of a target with a gun in my hand, rapidly firing the gun. My first few bullets barely hit the edges of the target, but with a quick adjustment, I hit the bullseye almost every time.

"I think you need to back up and try some more, but you are a natural," Zeke says.

"But don't forget, it's easy when no one is firing back. All dangerous men carry a gun, even when they aren't supposed to. Be prepared for them to turn a gun on you at any second," Langston says.

I nod, taking in Langston's words. Then I exhale deeply as I back up and fire off more shots, hitting the bullseye again and again. It's a thrilling feeling to be holding something so dangerous in my hands and knowing if I aimed it at a person, I could kill them.

Zeke and Langston must really trust me if they feel safe with me holding a gun.

"What are you doing?" Enzo asks, stepping down from the deck as he walks toward us.

We all freeze and stare in Enzo's direction. Even when he's dressed so casually, he holds the power to get a room full of thousands of people to follow his orders with only his voice.

"Teaching her the basics to protect herself," Zeke answers.

Enzo shakes his head as he stops walking a few feet away.

"You aren't protecting her by teaching her how to shoot. You're only giving her false hope that she actually has a chance at winning," Enzo says.

I frown. Any pleasant feelings from earlier disappear with his words. I embody rage, and without thinking I aim the gun in Enzo's direction, but instead of aiming for his heart like Langston taught me, I aim for just off his shoulder.

Enzo looks at me smugly, and I stare back at him.

He doesn't reach for his own gun, even though I know he has one on him. He always does anytime he leaves his bedroom. Langston and Zeke don't try to stop me.

I squeeze the trigger, aiming for a spot on the deck behind him, knowing if I miss and hit him, the worst damage I'll do is to his shoulder. I won't come close to killing him.

As I planned the bullet hits the deck behind Enzo.

The world stops, and I wait for Enzo's retribution.

He smirks. "You missed."

My own smug expression drops from my face. *Enzo wanted me to shoot him.* Maybe I should have, that might make whatever happens tomorrow a more fair fight.

He turns and walks back to the deck, not worried at all I might shoot him in the back.

"Oh, and you might want to teach her how to drive since she can't do that either."

I glare in his direction and consider firing again, but I don't trust myself with a moving target. I could miss and kill him. Which right now wouldn't be such a bad thing. Except then I'd become Black, and I'm not sure I'm ready or willing to take the job.

I don't want to rule an empire. I don't want to spend my days keeping people in line with my gun.

I look out at the ocean. Even if it gives me such beauty and luxury. Giving me a life of ease.

I don't want it. I turn back and see Enzo slip into the house. Especially if it turns me into a grumpy, unfeeling, lonely man like Enzo.

But I can't let his comments go unchecked. I need to feel rage tomorrow; I will need adrenaline pumping through my veins to aid me in my quest. But I don't need all out anger.

Anger will only serve as a distraction.

I start stomping toward the house when Langston calls, "Gun, Kai."

He holds out his hand as if waiting for me to relinquish it to him.

His eyes read serious. He may like me, but he won't let me hurt his boss or closest friend.

I put on the safety, and then toss the gun in his direction. He catches it with ease.

"Thanks for the lessons."

Both men nod.

"But I have other business to attend to." I stomp into the house, intent on giving Enzo a piece of my mind. Because I will not let him win before the games have even started—not anymore.

CHAPTER 18
ENZO

Kai's a good shot.

And it pisses me off. Not that she's amazing at every-thing she does, as I expect her to be, but because no one ever helped her unlock her potential. I don't care that she's a girl, if she had been properly trained she would have been a formidable opponent. But as she is now, I'll destroy her.

For the longest time, I hoped that my opponent would be the stronger one. That it would be clear they were the better man, the one worthy of becoming Black. But then I faced reality. No one would ever be stronger than me; my father ensured that. So I became Black. For three years I've done the job. I lined my pockets with more money. Filled my bed with the sexiest of women. Hired the most dangerous of men.

But I never wanted it. *Any of it.*

And now I don't have a choice. There is no way Kai could win. And even if she could, I can't let her. Only the cruelest of men deserve to be trapped in this life. And I would never wish this life for Kai.

Whether Kai truly wants to become Black or not doesn't matter. It won't stop her from fighting with everything she has tomorrow.

Her father chose the first task. He might have chosen something that plays to her strengths. And I can't let her win—not one round.

I won't let her become Black.

I don't know what I was thinking when I went out there to taunt her. I was angry and pissed that she could stop fucking me so easily. I thought I rocked her world. I know I did, but it wasn't enough.

I should head to Surrender or one of my other bars to pick up a woman for tonight. It would help me blow off steam and be focused for tomorrow. But that thought makes my stomach turn up in disgust.

For the present moment, there is only one woman who would be able to get my cock up. And she almost shot me in the arm.

If she had wanted to, she would have, and I would have deserved it.

I grin.

My fiery woman.

No, not my anything.

She's nothing more than my prisoner and enemy. The only reason I keep her here is to keep track of her. And to protect her—that's it.

The back door opens as I'm standing in the kitchen staring into the fridge, trying to find something light to eat that won't slow me down tomorrow.

"What the hell was that? You've resorted to taunting me now? You really that desperate to win tomorrow?" Kai storms into the kitchen, ready for a fight.

I slam the refrigerator door closed.

Kai crosses her arms, her curvy hips swaying in annoyance.

"Just trying to even the score."

"How so?"

"You ran out this morning like I didn't just fuck your brains out last night. Like that didn't fucking change everything. Like you could live without doing that again."

"I could. I will."

My jaw tenses, my lips thin, and my eyes darken. "No, you couldn't."

She rolls her eyes. "I've lived without sex for twenty-three years.

You think I couldn't go another few weeks until this is finished without fucking my enemy?"

"Stop calling me that."

"That's what you are: my enemy. My captor. The asshole who sold me. I can also call you bastard, jerk, dick, fucktwat, motherfucker, son of a bitch. Which would you prefer?"

I smirk. "That's not what you were calling me last night. If I remember correctly you were calling me 'oh God,' and 'yes,' and 'fuck yes.' I prefer one of those names."

She shakes her head slightly. "Just leave me alone. We should both be preparing for whatever awaits us tomorrow. We both need a clear head so we don't get ourselves killed."

"Exactly," I say taking a step into her personal bubble.

Her eyes heat as my own eyes travel up and down her body letting her know exactly what I think of her skimpy workout outfit.

"Not going to happen," she says.

"Don't act like you don't want me in your bed every fucking night."

"I don't."

"We can be enemies during the day and lovers at night."

"No."

"It would help keep us from being distracted during the game."

"I don't see how."

"Because we still have the same chemistry as before. As much as you tried to put a stop to that by your stunt, it didn't change anything. You want me. I want you. We both know this can't go anywhere. We both hate each other anyway. This would never be anything but sex. And when one of us becomes Black, it ends. We go our separate ways."

"You'll release me."

"Yes."

"Good."

"So do we have an arrangement?"

"About the you letting me go part? Yes."

I shake my head and move closer until I all but touch her with my entire body.

She stills, trying to adjust to me being in her space and knowing I could, and will, touch her. She has to decide how far this will go.

"And the fucking?" I ask.

Kai breathes heavily, her eyes going down to stare at the bulge in my jeans. She closes her eyes as if that will help her change her feelings.

She fucking wants me.

She can't deny it.

I can see the way her perky breasts harden with a look from me.

"Go fuck one of your whores at the club," she says, with devastatingly sad and determined eyes.

She's trying to taunt me into hurting her so she won't want to fuck me. *Not going to happen, sweetie.*

"Not when I could have the sexiest, most fucking gorgeous woman with the tightest pussy I've ever felt; and hear the most beautiful voice screaming my name as I torture her with my cock."

She gasps and then bites her lip to silence her mouth in the adorable way she always does right before I get my way with her.

"You can hate me, and still fuck me," I say.

"I will definitely hate you."

"Is that a yes?"

"That's a—you better fuck me like I'm the only woman you ever want, but I'm going to fuck you like each thrust is a dagger into your heart."

She said yes. I don't care how badly she hates me. The hate only makes everything better. Because there is no better way I can think of to spend the rest of the day.

I grab her curvy hips and jerk her body to me. Her soft body slams to my stone core. And my lips hover over hers, but I don's kiss her yet. She may not hate when I touch her like everyone else, but I've learned if she's begging for my touch, it's better than if I take it.

Her cool breath sends shivers down my spine. She doesn't close the gap though, almost enjoying the anticipation as much as I am.

My eyes heat into burning fires of need.

"Kiss me," she says.

I do better. I devour her.

My mouth takes all of her mouth in mine—kissing all of her. My tongue deepens the kiss instantly needing to taste her. I only just had her a few hours ago, but already that was too long ago.

I need this woman in my bed for nights on end to have a chance of extinguishing my desire for her. But it seems she's going to want to argue every time I want to fuck her, rather than just fuck. And if it makes me this excited to argue with her before I fuck her, it will be worth it.

But what if I can't convince her in the future?

What if this is it? Her hatred for me will most likely intensify if I have to betray her or make her look like a fool during the game.

So I'm going to engrain this moment in my head in case it's the last time. I'm used to living that way. In my life, there is no guarantee I will wake up tomorrow. No guarantee I won't have a bullet in my head and end up six feet under.

But with Kai, it's different. I've never felt anything in my life so intense, yet also pleasurable. There has never been a woman like her, and after I become Black again, there will never be one after. I will return to fucking nameless woman I sleep with once, then never see again.

"Why are you such a good fucking kisser?" she asks between kisses.

I give her an evil, seductive look.

She laughs and then angers. "Oh...that was stupid."

"No question is stupid."

"Mine was. It's because you have countless women in your bed every night."

I should comfort her. I know I should, but I like seeing the jealous side. I haven't been with a woman since Kai came back into my life. But I'm not sure I want her to know the whole truth.

I trail my kisses down her neck. She tilts her head to allow me better access. "But you're the only one in my bed," I say.

I kiss her again, and we both shiver. I love touching her icy skin. It twists with my warm and makes me crazy; seeking the feeling I only get when I touch her.

"Let's go get in that bed now," she says; her voice heavy, her eyelids hooded.

"No."

Her lips drop into a frown. "What? I thought—"

"I need you here first." I need her in every part of my house. I need to mark her and make her realize how much she's mine.

She's only ever been mine.

That thought drives me wild. I know her first wasn't as it should have been. I know her head is fucked up from what Jarod did to her. But I love that she's only ever had me.

I'm the only one who can touch her.

Kiss her.

Fuck her.

I've never cared before, but there is something very caveman about wanting a woman to only be yours.

"But Langston and Zeke could walk in. Westcott could—"

I kiss her, trying to shut her up.

"You insufferable man. We are not fucking here."

"Yes, we are. Westcott's job is to be invisible. He knew the second we started talking to leave. And Zeke and Langston got the message loud and clear to not come into the house."

"Did you text them?"

"No, when I marked you as my territory outside."

"I'm am not an object!"

"Doesn't matter. You're mine."

I see the look change in her eyes. From relaxed to hate. And I'm not mad about it at all. Because the lust is still there.

"I hate you."

"I hate you more."

She dives her teeth into my bottom lip until I'm sure she's drawn blood. *Fucking incredible woman.*

No one stands up to me. *Ever.* And if they do, they usually end up dead. But with Kai, I want more. I both love it and hate it when she defies me. I crave it as much as I crave her pussy.

"Strip," I command.

She laughs. "Not going to happen."

I cock my head and smile. My eyes already imaging her without her clothes on. "Tired of strutting around the place naked?" I ask, even though I know it's not about that. She isn't afraid to show her body. She just doesn't like giving up control to me.

"No."

"Prove it."

"You can't goad me."

I kiss her neck again, and a soft moan escapes her lips.

She claws at my neck, and I know I've won, but she won't go down gently.

I grab the hem of her shirt pushing it upward, needing it off her body.

Her eyes dance, and then she grabs my shirt by the neck and rips until it is in two pieces.

"If you wanted me to strip, you just had to ask, baby."

"Don't call me baby."

I jerk her shirt off her head, before she protests again.

"Shorts off, now, baby."

She glares.

"Fine, I'll do it," I say at her silent protest.

I pull her shorts down, hoist her ass up on the counter, and then kneel in front of her.

"What are you doing?"

"Eating you out."

"But I'm sweaty and—fuck."

I taste her sweet juices as I bury my head in her pussy. I'm used to women waxing and going bare, but after having a taste of Kai's pussy, I don't know if I will ever go back. There is something sexy about the way her hair hides the prize from me.

"Jesus effing Christ," she calls out as she grips my hair.

I grip her ass cheeks in my hands, holding her body tightly to my lips. She wiggles in my grasp, my touch overwhelming all her senses. No other woman responds to my touch as quickly as Kai, and it's sexy as hell.

I want her to come over and over, until any thoughts of her painful first time are all but a distant memory.

She starts wiggling and panting so much I can tell she's close. Her thighs squeeze around my head; her grip on my head death-defying. I can barely breathe, let alone move, she has me so tightly in her grasp, but I've never been so happy to be suffocated by a woman before.

I dip my tongue into her tight cunt. Pushing deeper, preparing her for what will soon be coming—my cock.

I probably shouldn't fuck her again so soon after her first intrusion. I'm sure she's sore, but the way her wetness is already coating my tongue, I have no doubt she wants this.

"Make me come you fucking asshole!" she screams.

I pull my tongue out of her and move back to her clit.

She explodes.

"Enzo!" she cries over and over as she comes on my mouth, her orgasm rippling through her over and over. She throws her head back; it's like nothing exists. Zeke or Langston could walk in right now, and I don't think she'd notice or care.

"Baby, you are going to have to open your legs so I can move my head. My cock wants a turn."

She slowly relaxes, and I spread her legs apart wide enough to unlock my head from her grip.

"That didn't sound like someone who hated me."

Her eyes glisten. "I hate you."

"You may hate me, but you love my tongue. You love my body. But most of all, you love my cock."

I undo my pants, pull a condom from my pocket, and then drop my jeans, letting my cock free.

Her eyes immediately go to its large girth.

I smirk. I've been with women before who couldn't handle my size. They gave up and stopped, unable to handle the pain. Others suffer through but only after several painful moments stretching them out.

It still amazes me how Kai handles me. She's petite, and her pussy is no different than any other part of her.

"I don't love your cock," she whispers, but her eyes tell me differently. She loves it, but she's also scared based on how last time went.

I don't want her thinking about it. It won't help her to dwell on my past mistakes. She does better when she's just living in the moment.

"Tell me how much you fucking hate me, baby."

"I hate how fucking arrogant you are."

"Yea?" I trail kisses up her leg.

"I hate how incredibly bossy you are."

I kiss over her sensitive clit again, and she stops talking, focusing on the touch.

When I kiss her stomach, she starts again. "I hate how controlling you are."

My eyes grow large looking at her breasts again. I take my time tasting each luscious mound—kissing every part and ending, sucking on her hard nipples.

When I bite down, she squeals and tries to swat me away. But I don't stop, loving the fucking sound of her squeals too much.

My cock grows another inch at the sound. I press at her entrance, my dick desperate to feel her tight lips welcoming me in. I consider fucking her bareback, but think better of it. She's not on birth control. And even if she were, I wouldn't risk it. I will never get a woman pregnant. *Ever*. This legacy dies with me.

I rip the condom wrapper open and lean back to slide it on, and then I'm pressing roughly at her entrance.

"And I hate how fucking big you are."

Our eyes gleam at each other, and then I grab her hips, jerk her from the counter, and flip her around so her ass is in the air and she's bent over the counter.

I slip halfway in while she's still adjusting to the new position, instead of giving her time to think about the pain. I kiss her neck and fist her hair giving her enough pain to focus on other than the ripping torment as I stretch her wide.

She winces and her pussy tightens, not used to my size yet.

It takes every drop of self-control inside me to not push in deeper like I need. But I won't hurt her like I did last time.

"How badly do you want to slap me right now?" I goad.

"So fucking badly."

She releases one of her arms from the counter, trying to reach back to do just that. I grab it and force it tightly behind her back.

"I love how feisty you are."

"I hate how cruel you are."

I lean down and kiss her palm as I move another inch inside her. Her slickness swells from my kiss. "It seems you like how sweet I can be to you."

I suck each of her fingers, slipping another millimeter in with each distracting kiss.

"I fucking love your tits, baby."

I grab them roughly, my fingers teasing the points.

"Aw," she moans as I again descend into her tightness.

"How the fuck did you fit the last time?" she pants.

I ignore her question, knowing we need to focus on other things to get her to relax.

I kiss down her back, and I feel her body start to relax allowing more. So close.

"I can't. You're too fucking much," she groans.

"I didn't think you were a quitter, baby."

"I'm not."

"You got this. We are so close."

I'm failing. I don't want her feeling pain. I feel her body tensing and beginning to close up to me. If I were to look into her eyes, I'm sure they would be glossing over, preparing to protect herself as she has done for years before. Then she would never get to feel the pleasure.

Then I get an idea.

I slap her ass.

She yelps.

"And I fucking love this ass."

I rub gently over the redness from when I punished her last night.

"You didn't act like it last night," she pants.

I smile as she soaks my cock from thinking about last night.

I squeeze the reddened cheeks, and she cries out.

"You sadistic ass."

I hear the tiny tears.

Dammit.

"Look at me, baby."

She turns her head, and I see the tears. I kiss her cheeks, removing them from her eyes.

Then I suck two of my fingers. Her mouth parts as she stares at me. "But do you know what I love most of all?"

"My pussy."

"Yes. But I want something else more."

"What?"

"Your ass."

"What? No! I can't."

I press my fingers at the entrance to her ass, putting just enough of my fingers inside to get her to focus on a different sensation. I kiss her lips with everything I have, and then I grind into her body, sinking all of my cock inside.

The moan she cries into my mouth is beautiful. I love the pain, but most of all I love her pleasure.

Tears stain her cheeks, but I can already see the pain easing.

"I can do this. I want to. Jesus, Enzo. Fuck me."

I smile. "You've already taken me. All of me, baby."

Her eyes widen in surprise.

"Hang on," I say motioning to the counter.

She grabs on, and then I fuck her like I've wanted to since I came into the kitchen.

Her pussy welcomes me in more and more with each thrust, as I grip her ass and kiss every part of her bare neck.

"I love hearing you cry, baby."

"Because you are a sadist."

"No, because I love every fucking sound you make. Most of all when you scream my name."

I hit particularly deep inside, and I get exactly the reward I want. "Enzo!"

Her muscles start tightening, her body coming alive.

I reach around, find her clit, and start strumming her. I want her to come so many times that even if she had the highest powered vibrator, she would have nothing left to make herself come.

She arches her back, her ass pushing into my cock more. *Someday, I will have your ass.*

We build ourselves higher and higher in our little bubble. I cling on for dear life as I struggle to hold back my own orgasm until she comes. Fucking her, with how tight she is, brings me back to when I was fifteen and would shoot my load far too fast. Now, I never come before a woman. I may be heartless, but I'm not a bad lover.

I plead with my cock to hold on. *Wait until she comes.*

And then it happens. Her pussy contracts around me, her cries bounce through the house, and her body turns icy from the chill she sends through my body. The look on her face is glorious as she comes on my dick.

I pump one more time, and I lose it with her. I growl at the explosion I wish could last forever.

More, more, more.

The orgasm rolls through us both again. My heat shoots through her, and her ice through me. Only when I return to my usual warm, and she returns to her usual chill, do the orgasms stop.

"That was—Jesus, I never thought it could be like that," she says, repeating her same sentiment from before.

I pull out of her sharply, giving her no warning this time.

She doesn't wince this time though. She's too lost in her orgasm to feel the loss. I turn her to me and kiss her lips.

"No wonder you fuck so many women all the time if it's like that."

"It's not like that every time."

Her eyebrows raise, and she lights up.

Fuck, this woman. One sentence makes her happy.

"Now what?" she asks, innocently.

I stare down between her legs, happy to only see the tiniest drop of blood this time instead of the volcano of blood I caused last time.

She's getting used to my size, and I want to spend most of the night fucking her until we fall asleep completely exhausted. We should spend the night getting the best sleep, but there is no harm if we both get the same amount of sleep.

I'll make sure she gets at least six or seven hours, even though we both function pretty well without sleep.

"I could spend the night fucking you, if you aren't too sore?"

She gives me the slowest smile on the planet, but thank fuck I can read her well enough to answer.

"I'll happily hate-fuck you all night," she says.

CHAPTER 19
KAI

We fucked most of the night.

Maybe that was his plan to have an unfair advantage: fucking me so much I could barely walk. It worked. But I don't care, even if that was his plan. I wouldn't have traded the sex for anything.

I never knew how amazing sex could be—not until Enzo.

I thought it must be horrible—at least that's how my fucked up brain processed how the woman feels during sex. Because of Jarod and his goons. The screams the other women made will live in my head forever.

The torture of countless men pretending to go for my pussy then stop in disgust will live with me forever.

The pain at Enzo's size is a lot—but it's nothing compared to the moments after. The moments he tried to distract me from the pain. The moments he's sweet instead of the devil. The moments when it starts to feel good. *Really good.*

I'm sure sex with a different, smaller man would be less painful, but I doubt any man has the talents of making me wet with solely a syllable like Enzo does.

We slept in the bed all night side by side, but not touching. As usual. I like Enzo's touch, but I'm still not completely calm every time he does it. It can still cause me panic or freak me out if I'm not ready for it. So at night, it's probably best if we don't snuggle.

And Enzo is used to sleeping alone. He has no need for a snuggle buddy.

We don't talk about it. It just happens. We just share his bedroom like an old married couple.

I stare down at Enzo's mother's ring on my hand as the alarm goes off. It's eight-thirty. Only a half hour until we have to be ready.

I don't want to be Enzo's friend today. It will make it harder to hurt him. And it will destroy me if he hurts me. Especially after our night of lovemaking.

He reaches across the bed and tucks my hair behind my ear.

I freeze.

That's too much—too caring. He shouldn't do things like that.

He's just trying to throw you off guard. Make you want him so you won't hurt him when it comes down to it.

Don't fall for his tricks.

I smile. "Morning."

"Morning," he sighs. "Sleep well?" the cocky grin on his face tells me he already knows I did.

I nod, continuing to play with the ring.

"When we get out of this bed, we are enemies again," he says.

"Agreed."

"Until then..." he reaches over and kisses me tenderly. I wonder how it would be to fuck him gently and tenderly. I always thought it would be too mushy and slow to keep my demons away. But after having him hard and rough, I want to find out what sex is like with Enzo in every way possible.

"Here," I say, taking the ring off and holding him out to him.

"Do you want a divorce already? I thought I was doing a good job satisfying you in my bed."

I smile. "No, I just don't want to have any loyalty to you once we get out of this bed. I'm not your fake wife today. I'm your enemy. And I don't want to accidentally lose it or something."

He takes the ring, but instead of putting it somewhere safe, he grabs my hand again and slips the ring back on.

"We can be enemies and fuck buddies. We can hate each other and still want each other. We can be adversaries and still care. I gave it to you to keep no matter what happens. It's yours—not mine. It's your leverage to protect you when the time comes for you to start your life over. I don't want you to forget I want you safe during the game. Because I do. I will do what I can to protect you."

"I don't want your protection."

"But you have it. I won't let anyone hurt you." He kisses the ring on my finger. "This is my promise. I will always keep you safe. No matter how we feel about each other. Our hate won't stop how I protect you."

I look at the clock. Five minutes have passed. We need to shower and eat something before the game starts.

"Good luck," I say.

"Good luck."

We both exit the bed at the same time. We don't talk. We don't acknowledge the other as we get ready for the day. It's like a flip has been switched. Like we didn't just fuck each other's brains out all night. We have no connection anymore.

My stomach is in knots, so I don't eat much. I drink an iced coffee and pick at some eggs. I take as long as I can in the shower, letting the water wash away any remnants of Enzo. I can't think about him.

I get dressed in dark jeans, a tight fitting black shirt, and comfortable running shoes. I don't know what the task is, but I'd rather be ready for a fight than dressed for a ball.

I put my hair up in a high ponytail and decide on a no-makeup look.

I stare down at the ring, deciding to keep it on. Enzo's right, I might need to sell it for money at some point. And if today goes badly and I'm left abandoned in Mexico or something, then I might need to sell it sooner than later.

Then I head downstairs.

We are supposed to meet Archard at Surrender.

I assume Enzo will give me a ride since I don't have a car, money, or any other means of transportation.

"Miss Miller, Enzo is waiting for you in the car out front," Westcott says when I reach the main floor.

"Thanks."

"Good luck to you, Miss Miller," Westcott says as I approach the door.

I nod and step outside. His good luck didn't actually sound like a well-wishing of words. It sounded like a warning.

I step outside expecting to see one of Enzo's shiny race cars. Instead, I see a large blacked out SUV.

I approach the passenger side and see Zeke sitting there. Langston is in the driver's seat.

I smile at them and then walk to the second door and open it. Enzo is already seated on the far side. I climb in and shut the door.

None of the men speak to me, but Langston starts driving.

I can normally tolerate silence, but the silence is suffocating.

I stare at the men, all dressed similarly to my own look: dark jeans, dark T-shirts, and jackets. The only difference is I'm sure they are all caring guns, knives, and any other weapon they can hide beneath their clothing.

I try to forget about what's happening and stare out the window. I let the sun warm my face as I lean it closer to the glass.

Langston stops the car at the back entrance of Surrender. We all climb out one by one and file into the building, walking toward Enzo's office.

No, not his office. Black's office. This could as easily be my office as it is Enzo's.

I notice a large table has been brought in, and Archard is already sitting at one end.

Enzo walks around to one side of the table and takes a seat. Langston and Zeke follow. Zeke looks weak, his steps are careful, and I'm sure he's still feeling a lot of pain.

I take a seat opposite them and watch as the three men stare at me like I'm truly their enemy. I no longer feel welcome here. I knew Enzo would be staring at me with determination in his eyes, but

Zeke and Langston's looks surprise me. I thought I had made headway in making them think better of me. But they are both glaring at me like they want to kill me and they are just waiting for their boss' word.

Archard nods to both of us and pulls out a piece of paper.

"I will read the rules, ask for any questions you may have, and then the game will start. Remember, outside of the rules I read; there are no rules. As long as you don't break the specific rules written here, you are free to win in any way possible."

Any way possible. His words read dark, and I know he means we can kill each other if that is how we'd like to win. I wouldn't be able to kill Enzo. For one, I don't even have a gun. I already know Enzo won't kill me. But could he order one of his men to do it?

"You are free to use any resources, people, etc. you can persuade to your side."

I stare across at Zeke and Langston. Enzo has the loyalty of two great men. They will do whatever they can to help him win. And he has a whole organization of people at his disposal that would help him.

As his fake wife, I might be able to convince a few of them to help me out. But I don't want help. I want to do this on my own.

I stare at the empty chairs next to me. *I'm alone. I'm always alone.*

"Now to the rules. The objective is easy: steal the high school class ring of Mr. Milo Wallace."

He opens the folder in front of him and pulls out two identical images and hands one to Enzo, the other to me.

I stare at the picture of a man's hand with a high school ring on his pinky.

What grown ass man still wears a high school ring?

"The ring has no value other than sentimentality to this man. The rules are simple. You can't take it by force or kill anyone in the process. You have to steal it in a way where he doesn't realize you were the one to steal it. If you get caught taking it, you lose automatically. The winner is the first person to steal it without being caught and without breaking the rules."

Steal, don't get caught, don't kill anyone.

I exhale a long breath. It's like this game was designed for me. I've spent my entire life stealing to survive. I'm a very good pick-pocket. I've never been caught taking an item from someone. I've stolen watches, wallets, purses, jewelry; the list goes on. This will be the easiest task I've ever had.

I stare across at Enzo—my opponent. He's grown up in a life filled with criminals. But as far as I know, Enzo doesn't have any experience with thievery. He's never had to. He has limitless money, and men with fancy weapons to take whatever he wants.

I might actually have an advantage to this game. *Thank you, Dad.* He does love me. He did try to prepare me; he just never told me the truth.

I sigh in relief.

"One more thing," Archard says.

I freeze. I don't like the tone in which he said it.

"Enzo has already broken the rules by parading around as Black for years now, when it's clear he knew Kai was still alive."

Enzo's lips tighten.

"So you will have to face a penalty for that. I've thought long and hard about the appropriate penalty, and I've come up with a solution. Kai will have to agree to the terms, since your fathers never came up with a plan for such a situation.

"Enzo and any men he uses to complete this task will not be allowed to use weapons. No guns, no knives, nothing. You can carry nothing. You can not steal a weapon. If you get caught holding a weapon, you automatically lose this round." Archard looks to me for a response.

But I'm staring at Enzo. I've never known the man not to carry a gun. This would be a lot to ask of him, to not carry a weapon. For no other reason than he wouldn't want to put Zeke or Langston or any of his other men at risk.

But I won't be completing this task with a gun, so they might as well not either. It can't be that dangerous. We are just stealing a high school ring from some guy. It can't be that hard.

"I agree to the penalty," I say.

Enzo's vein in his head pops with frustration, but he just nods at Archard.

"Do you two have any questions about the rules or tasks?"

"Who is Milo Wallace?" I ask.

Archard shakes his head. "I'm sorry, but you will have to find out any information about this man yourselves. It's part of the task."

I stare across at Enzo who is tight-lipped. I'm sure he's heard of this man, if not Zeke or Langston will find out everything about him in a matter of minutes. That is where I will have a disadvantage. I have no access to men, computers, security. I don't have any money, nor a car, a cell phone, nothing.

Enzo will be able to get to Milo in a matter of minutes with ease. Giving him plenty of time to steal the ring before I even find out the man's address.

But once I find this man, I can steal it with ease.

"Any other questions?" Archard asks.

I shake my head. Enzo continues to sit silently.

"Good, then I'll be needing your weapons, Enzo," Archard says.

Enzo stares at me like he's going to kill me for this as he unloads his gun and knife. Langston does the same. Zeke hesitates for a minute. Maybe he's not carrying a gun because he's headed back to his bed after this.

"Zeke?" Archard asks.

Zeke pulls his gun from his pocket, but instead of laying it on the table, he gets up and walks to me.

He hands it to me. I take it hesitantly. He doesn't speak, but I can read his eyes easily. *Take it, stay safe; this is my forgiveness. This is all I'll do to help you.*

Then the men start filing out. Leaving me seated at the table by myself.

I stare at the ring one more time, memorizing it as I try to formulate a plan in my head. I've lived my life with nothing. No money, no car, nothing.

I stare down at the ring I could easily sell to give me all those things now in order to assist me this round and the rounds after.

No, I won't sell it. Only if my life depends on it. It means too much to Enzo. I could never hurt him like that. I still don't understand his compassion when he gave me the ring, but I know I have to keep the ring safe until he accepts it when I return it to him.

I can find a way to make this happen. I've spent my entire life with nothing and I more than survived.

There is a library a couple of blocks from here. I'll research everything I can on him and then form a plan. But I already know what that plan will have to involve. Milo Wallace is a man. I'm sure he's a powerful, rich man. There is only one way to ensure I can get close to him. Use my body to seduce him. It makes me sick to my stomach to think about flirting with a man after I just had a different man in my bed, but what choice do I have?

I don't know if I want to win. I don't know if I want to become Black. But if I lose, I'll end up with nothing. If I win, I'll have an entire empire at my disposal. If I win, I could change things. If I win, I could stop another woman from being sold. If I win, I could end the pain.

CHAPTER 20
ENZO

Kai could win this.

And it scares the crap out of me. I've worked too hard, for too long to give her a chance at winning a single round. Everything would be destroyed if she won. I can't let it happen.

I sit in the passenger seat, while Zeke rides in the back, already on his computer looking things up about Milo Wallace. Langston is usually better at surveillance, but Zeke is too hurt to drive. And I need to be free to focus on formulating a game plan.

Zeke starts rambling everything we know about Milo, "He's wealthy—a one billion dollar fortune. He got all his money selling weapons. He's single, a perpetual bachelor. He lives in France but loves to sail his yacht. He's actually in Miami; he's throwing a big party tomorrow night on his yacht."

I take in all the information Zeke just gave me. In some ways, it would have been better if Milo was in France. Kai has no money to buy a plane ticket, and by the time she came up with the money to buy a ticket, I would have already flown my private jet to steal the stupid ring and be back.

But he's not in France, he's here, on his yacht. That's the second best news. Kai is afraid of yachts and the water. She won't go near him. That gives me an advantage. I'm not sure if he's the kind of man to step foot in Miami, or if he prefers the luxury of his yacht. I can't imagine a man like him ever leaving his yacht. So if she wants to win, she will have to face her fears.

I smirk. I know she's capable, but she might stall. Waiting him out to see if he will come to land first. That will give me a day's advantage.

"Where is he now?" I ask Zeke.

"He's anchored a few miles off the coast. They won't dock until tomorrow evening just before the party. He's a paranoid guy and feels safer on his yacht than on land."

I smile. *Perfect.*

I can easily get an invitation to this party. If I weren't already so focused on this game and Kai, I would have probably already ensured I had an invitation. This is the kind of man I want control and power over. I would have learned everything, found his weakness and exploited it until I was sure I could control him. That's what I do.

My mind spins with ideas of what I should do. But I know there is only one fool-proof way to get Milo alone—a woman.

If I was allowed a gun, I could easily persuade him to talk to me, but I'm not allowed one. Something I'm very pissed about. Kai should have never allowed that stupid penalty. I don't care about my life, but I will not put my men in danger.

"What's the plan, boss?" Langston asks. I share everything with him, and he's usually more involved in the planning and plotting process, instead of being stuck behind the wheel.

"Get an invite to the party tomorrow night," I answer.

"Already done," Zeke says.

I grin. Maybe Zeke is as good at plotting as Langston and I are. I just always think of Zeke as brute force, instead of brains.

"Then make sure I have the hottest date on my arm so Milo will want to talk with me. If for no other reason than to steal my date."

"Good plan, but then what? Do you know how to steal a ring without him noticing you are taking it?"

I shake my head. I don't have a clue. I've never stolen a wallet, let alone a ring. A ring seems impossible to steal.

"Kai might try to steal it from his finger in broad daylight, but that's not my plan. I could never take the ring from his finger without him noticing. No, my choices are to get him to bet it during a poker game. Or have my date take it during sex."

Langston raises an eyebrow. "Do you have a girl in mind that would be up for the task?"

"Yes," I sigh. I just hate asking her, because I know she'll say yes. She would do anything for me. And she's hot enough that Milo will be dying to get his hands on her.

Get him drunk.

Try to get him to play a poker game.

If that doesn't work, send in my date to seduce him.

Fuck, I hate the plan. But right now, it's all I've got.

"The invitation allows for a plus one. I know Milo won't allow you a security detail. But Langston and I will watch guard from the shore," Zeke says.

I don't know how to say this, but I have to. "You aren't coming, Zeke."

"What? You are not going by yourself."

"I won't. Langston will come and watch from as close as he can get, but I'm not putting you at risk."

"I can handle myself."

"You can when you are healthy. But you aren't allowed a weapon, and I don't want to be worried the entire time someone will shoot you again. You stay; I'm not going to discuss it anymore."

Zeke huffs but doesn't argue anymore. Langston gives me a look of thanks.

I turn to Langston. "You will carry a concealed weapon."

"What?"

"No one will know what you choose or where you hide it except you."

"But that's breaking the rules."

"Your life is more important than the rules. I won't carry anything, but I want you safe. Under no circumstances will you use it to save my life. Only yourself. Understand? Otherwise, you can stay back with Zeke."

"Understood, boss," Langston says, only calling me boss when he knows I'm serious.

I pull out my phone knowing I need to get my date figured out as soon as possible. I need to prepare her for the task so we practically share the same brain because I won't be able to change the plan very easily otherwise.

I scroll through the contacts until I find the one. I haven't called her in a few months. I've been too busy dealing with Kai, but there was a time when this girl was my everything. And that's exactly how she's listed in my phone.

My everything.

I hit the contact and wait.

Liesel's voice shines through the phone making it impossible not to smile at her light voice even though I know I'm risking her life by doing this.

"What does my favorite guy want?" she asks immediately, but her voice isn't mad. She's happy I called.

"Why do you assume I want something?"

"Because I know you. You are all business. If I want to see you outside of work, I call you. So what do you need?"

God, this is why I can always count on Liesel.

"I need you to be my date," I say the words I know will make Liesel's year. Because even if the date is fake, it won't feel like that to either of us.

CHAPTER 21
KAI

I've spent an hour in the library learning everything I can about Milo Wallace.

He's rich.

He's single, but always has a hot woman on his arm.

He lives in France.

But he's going to be here in Miami, tomorrow night.

And of course, he's throwing a party on his fancy yacht.

Shit.

Why does it have to be on a yacht?

This will be my only chance to get the ring. Flying to France would be an automatic loss. Enzo will have a private jet fly him before I can even figure out how to buy a ticket myself.

I need an invite to that party. I need a dress. I need the best hair and makeup. And then I need to seduce this man.

I could go to my father for help. But even if he wanted to help me, he has no money. And I don't want his help. He had twenty years to try and help me; he chose not to. He chose to keep me in the dark.

I could go back to Enzo's place, but I hate that idea. I'm sure there is a fancy dress in the closet I could wear, but I don't want his help either.

I want to do this myself.

My wheels turn in my head trying to figure out a plan. *Think, think, think.*

I hate stealing things, but I don't have much of a choice.

I could use the gun tucked into my pants that Zeke gave me to rob someone, but that seems too dangerous. I should just stash the gun somewhere, because I know I'm not going to use it.

I stare down at the ring.

Sell it, pawn it.

No.

I turn the ring, trying to come up with a plan that doesn't make me a thief.

Ring!

I have my mother's ring in my jewelry box at my father's home. He gave it to me when she died. It won't get me as much money as Enzo's ring, but it will be enough to buy a slutty dress, some makeup, and a cab ride to the pier.

Two hours later, I have my mother's ring in my hand. A ring I never thought I would sell, even for food. But here I am standing outside the old pawn shop I've sold things at before, considering doing just that.

Sell Enzo's instead, the devil says in my ear.

No.

I don't need my mother's ring to remember her. And I will not betray Enzo by pawning his mother's ring off the first chance I get.

I take Enzo's ring off and slip it into my pocket. I don't want Jim to see it and try to convince me to pawn it to him.

The door chimes as I step inside, warning my heart of what I'm going to give up for a chance at winning. I'm selling a part of my heart I will never be able to get back. Then I'm going to dress like a slut so I can get let into a party I'm not invited to. All for a chance to seduce a man, so I can get close enough to steal a different ring. Maybe I'll be able to pawn Milo's ring in order to get this one back, but I doubt it.

I have to think of the real reason I'm sacrificing my heart in order to win: to keep other women from getting hurt. Because once I'm Black, I can change everything.

Damn.

That's all that goes through my mind when I pick up Liesel in my Ferrari.

She descends from the doorway of the condo building she lives in in a black dress with a low V-neck down the front and shiny, sparkly shoes. Her hair is down in long curls, and she's wearing the expensive necklace I bought her years ago when we were dating.

"You look good," I say as I lean against my car.

She eyes my tux, practically undressing me with her smoldering eyes. "I know."

I grin.

Liesel always is one of the most confident women I know. She knows what she wants and she goes after it. And she won't settle for less than. Which is why we aren't together. I know she wants me, but I couldn't give her what she needed or deserved, so we broke up.

Looking at Liesel now, most men would say I made an error not giving her everything she wanted, marriage included, but looking at how Liesel is dressed just confirms to me I made the right decision. *She's dangerous.*

Dangerous in a different way from Kai. Kai unnerves me; she

makes me think twice about my decisions and actions; she makes me want things I never knew I wanted. Makes me want to protect her even when she doesn't need my protection.

But Liesel is just pure sex. She doesn't want me to change. She would take me exactly as I am, dangerous job and all. She likes rough sex. She likes my fancy cars. My big beach house. She likes going to expensive parties. She's likes being rich and flaunting everything she has.

Kai couldn't care less about my money. She would trade her living situation for a second to get free. The only money she needs is enough to survive.

"Ready?" I ask.

Her eyes sear into me and her red lips plump. "You know it."

I walk around to the driver's side, not bothering to open Liesel's door. I'm not an asshole to Liesel, but I don't want her getting the wrong idea. She already will when I have to fake being into her.

The truth is, I look at Liesel as more as a sister than a potential wife. Yes, we used to date. Yes, I find her attractive. But she is also the only woman I could ever confide in. The only woman I could ever have real conversations with. And I wouldn't trade that for anything. I will protect her and care for her all of my life.

We both climb in, and I start driving, with Langston trailing behind for protection.

"So I'm here. Dressed to the nines as requested."

"You always dress to the nines, Liesel."

She smiles. "I do, but why did you need me to?"

I sigh. I told her just enough to get her to go with me, nothing more. "Because you are my date."

"Who am I trying to make jealous?"

"No one."

"Then, why am I coming?"

"I need a hot woman on my arm to get a man to want you."

"So I'm a distraction?"

"A hot distraction, yes."

"And, why am I a hot distraction?"

"Because I need to steal a ring."

She raises an eyebrow. "You could just buy a ring."

I stare at her silently, and as usual, she can read my thoughts. "You found her."

"Yes. Well technically, she found me. Kai came back."

She nods. "What do you need me to do?"

"I already told you."

She shakes her head. "I don't want you to lose everything you've worked so hard to gain. Everything your entire life has been about. You were basically born Black. You have never been Rinaldi; I will do anything to help you retain the title. So tell me the truth. What do you need me to do?"

I sigh. There is no bullshitting Liesel; she knows me too well. "I will do everything possible to get the ring. Bet him in a poker game. *Anything*. But if I can't..." I can't say the words.

She smirks. "Say it Black."

"I can't."

She shakes her head. "You always were a pussy. You want me to get him in bed and steal the ring."

I nod.

She smiles. "Who is this man?"

I pull out my phone and pull up the image of him.

"Jesus! He's fucking hot and rich!"

I nod.

"Done," she says. "I'd fuck him for free."

I exhale a deep breath. *Thank God.* If it came down to it, I wouldn't be able to force her to fuck someone she didn't want to. But Liesel likes men and sex. I figured this would be an easy sell. And even though I know she would do anything for me, she wouldn't spread her legs only to help me.

She continues studying the phone on the ride to the pier. Learning everything she can about Milo Wallace.

"We're here. I don't think it will come down to it." I take her hand and squeeze.

"Stop thinking about me as a girl. I like sex. And this man is hot. It wouldn't really be a hardship if I had to. I might do it regardless of if you need me to or not." She winks as the valet opens her door.

I step out and walk to her after talking with the valet. My eyes trail around in the dark looking for Langston, but I can't spot him, which means he's hidden well.

I hold out my arm, and she takes it. She leans in and smiles, making it easily look like we are a real couple. We have that kind of connection.

We board the yacht, and everyone's eyes turn to us. Between my powerful stance and Liesel's sexy dress, we demand attention.

"We still got it," I say leaning into Liesel's ear.

She beams and squeezes my arm. "We do make a good couple."

"Would you like a drink?"

"Do you even have to ask?"

I lead Liesel over to the bar. I get her champagne, not because it's her favorite, but because it looks sexy as hell when she drinks it. And I get a scotch.

"So, this bitch, do you think she will show up tonight?" Liesel asks.

"She has a name and you know it."

She shrugs. "I do, but I prefer to think of her as a bitch."

"She's not a bitch. She is as trapped in this situation as I am."

She stops her drink inches from her lips and studies me. "Do you have a thing for this girl?"

"No, I just don't want anything to happen to her. I protect her like I protect anyone else who is innocent."

"You like her." She shakes her head.

"No, I don't. She's my prisoner."

She raises an eyebrow. "When did that happen?"

"When she lost a bet to me and ended up in my house. I will only let her go free when we finish this stupid game. That way I can control her and keep an eye on her."

"So where is she now?"

I shrug. "Probably trying to figure out how to get her nerve up to get an invite to this party."

She cocks her head, not understanding.

"She's afraid of yachts."

"Interesting."

I shrug, and then I spot Milo.

He has a woman on each arm, a cigar hanging from his lips, and a scotch in hand.

"Game time," I say, nodding in his direction with my eyes.

Liesel's eyes cut over.

"Damn, he's hotter in person."

"And he already has two women you'll have to compete with."

She pushes her boobs up and flips her hair. "Those bitches aren't any competition."

Liesel leans into me, nuzzling my neck, before she lets her tongue circle the rim of my ear.

My body heats, but nothing more. My cock doesn't even flinch. I'm on a mission, and nothing this woman does will affect me.

But it does Milo.

As if he has an alarm out that goes off whenever a hot woman does anything around him, he locks eyes on us.

Well, Liesel to be exact.

I thumb her bare neck, showing him what he could have but doesn't.

Milo shakes off both women, excusing them with just a word.

"Damn, you're good."

Her eyes don't leave mine. "I know."

Milo walks over to us. "Mr. Black, I'm so happy you could attend." He holds his hand, and I shake it, immediately noticing his high school class ring on his pinky as I expected.

I nod, "This yacht is something else."

He smirks. "It would be since you built it."

"I did."

Milo turns his attention to Liesel who is still clinging to me like she wants to fuck me in the bathroom.

"And who is your date, Black?" Milo asks.

I wait; Liesel isn't the type of woman who waits for a man to introduce her.

"I'm Liesel Dunn; it's a pleasure to meet you, Milo Wallace," she says before licking her bottom lip. Her breasts seem to have gotten bigger in the moment since Milo walked over as she presses them up in her dress.

They shake hands, but Milo's hand lingers in Liesel's. His eyes drop to her chest, looking in an obvious way.

"My eyes are up here, Milo," Liesel says, catching him staring.

Milo doesn't apologize, he just peers into her eyes, as lost in them as he was in her breasts. *This will be too easy.*

"The yacht leaves in twenty minutes, as soon as all the guests arrive. There will be drinking, dancing, fireworks. The whole bit. Save me a dance, Liesel."

"I'm not sure I can be torn away from Black here," she twirls her hand into the base of my hair.

But Milo is no longer watching her displays of affection; he's looking at Liesel like she's a piece of meat he wants to devour. Being on my arm makes no difference to him. A man like him is used to getting what he wants. He's rich and good looking enough to usually get his way.

But then he's looking past her and his eyes heat even more.

I turn in the direction of his gaze.

Holy fuck.

Kai.

She's on the yacht.

How the fuck?

I notice her body first. *How could I not?*

She's in a blue-green dress. The same color as the sea and her eyes. Every other woman here is wearing black, silver, or red—not Kai. The color she chose stands out above the rest.

It should make her look childish because the color isn't usually associated with being womanly. But it doesn't.

It makes her look like the ocean itself. It fits her snugly, like it was made to drape over her skin. Accenting her flat stomach, perky breasts, and curvy ass.

A slit rides high up her thigh, and although the dress shows her cleavage, she's not showing as much as Liesel. But it doesn't fucking matter.

Because she looks so goddamn beautiful.

She swept her hair up and wears an innocent amount of makeup in contrast to every other woman here.

It's like she took the perfect woman and did the opposite but somehow came out looking even hotter because she's so different.

I finally catch the look on her face, and it ends me.

She's biting her damn lip and tucks a loose curl behind her ear. Her eyes cut side to side as if danger is all around her. I can feel her heart racing from here.

Her eyes are bulging, allowing the blue from them to pop even more.

She's terrified to be on this yacht, but she's doing it anyway. And that makes her even sexier.

Every man is staring at her, much in the same way they did Liesel when we first arrived. But this is different. She came alone, so the sharks will start circling faster. And her big doe-eyes showing her innocence make men respond in a way they never will to a woman like Liesel.

Men know Liesel is experienced. She'll be fire in bed.

Men know Kai has never been touched. And they want to teach her everything.

They don't know I've already had her. She's as strong as ice but way more inviting. She'd be the best they ever had.

Kai finally spots me. And her timid gaze turns to frigid in a second when she sees Liesel all over me.

I wince. She'll make me pay for that later, I'm sure. Or worse, she will never let me touch her again for bringing a beautiful woman here to do exactly what she's planning on doing—seducing Milo.

She doesn't hold my gaze long. Because she's locked in on her target—Milo.

And he's already smitten.

Fuck.

My only hope now is that Milo thinks stealing a woman from a powerful man like me is more entertaining than the angel that looks like she was born from the sea. Because if not, I'm fucked. If Kai gets so much as a moment alone with him, she will steal his ring with ease. And I'll be down one to nothing.

I see red when I see Enzo with that woman.

Of course, he would bring the hottest fucking woman to this party. And of course, she would be all over him. I would be all over him if I could.

She's not his prisoner.

She has nothing to lose by being with him.

While every time I let him fuck me, I lose more of myself—especially my pride.

I was terrified when I had the Uber drop me off in front of the yacht. For one, I didn't think I would be let aboard. But the security guard didn't even ask for my name to check against his list. He took one look at me and practically escorted me personally aboard. He let me know Mr. Wallace would love to see me in the VIP room as soon as we set sail.

And then I stepped onto the yacht, and everything came back.

The rocking of the boat.

The beatings, whippings, blood.

The pain, agony, and fear.

The women's screaming.

All of it.

I might have pushed it away when Enzo fucked me, but it all came pouring back in at the first opportunity.

But when I spotted Enzo, it all disappeared again, at least for a moment. Because all I felt was fire.

I force my eyes away, needing a moment without the pain of seeing him with another woman.

Enzo isn't mine. I shouldn't care, but I do.

The man my eyes land on are those of my target—Milo Wallace.

My lips part looking at the man who drips sex, much in the same way Enzo does.

This man is older though, by at least five years. But he carries himself with Enzo's same cocky attitude.

And his desire shines when he looks at me.

He wants me.

That was easy.

I let my eyes drop in a bashful way, knowing I look out of place and my only hope of drawing him over is to play innocent.

It works.

I see the shine of his shoes stop in front of me.

"I'm Milo Wallace. And you are fucking gorgeous."

My eyes slowly drift up to meet his.

I blush.

"I'm Kai Miller."

He holds out his hand as I knew he would. I don't let myself hesitate. I put my hand in his, swallowing down the pain at his touch.

I thought maybe a handsome man like Milo might be able to get through my defenses like Enzo does, but it's not Enzo's hotness that gets through. It's his caring, charming way he protects me even when he wants to hurt me.

"It's a pleasure to meet you, Miss Miller," he says holding my hand tightly as he leans down and kisses the top of it. "You are by far the most beautiful woman on my ship."

"Just your yacht? I figured you would call me the most beautiful woman in the world if you are going to feed me a line so cheesy," I say, trying to keep my confidence up as my hand burns with his touch.

I force the smile to stay on my lips and the twinkle in my eyes to remain, despite wanting to get off this boat as quickly as possible.

My words only intensify his desire. I can see it in his eyes, and the bulge in his pants.

Jesus, what am I getting myself into? This man is going to want to fuck me and who knows how many other women. I won't be able to spread my legs if it comes down to it. And as soon as we leave the dock, I'm screwed. I won't have a choice to leave if he wants me. That's why men like him prefer the water to land. On the water, everyone is forced to play by his rules.

"I will have to work on my charm if I'm to be worthy of a woman like you."

I let my eyes smoke trying to show desire instead of fear.

"Excuse me, Mr. Wallace. We need you to approve we are ready to set sail and confirm all guests are on board," a man in a uniform says to Milo.

"Of course," Milo looks at me. "But I can already tell you the only guest that matters has just arrived." He winks at me.

He slowly releases my hand, and I can breathe again.

"I have business to attend to, unfortunately. I'll only be gone a few minutes." He turns to his staff member. "Ensure Miss Miller has a drink and whatever else she wants and that she finds her way to the VIP room."

"Yes, Mr. Wallace."

Milo walks away, and the staff member remains staring at me. "What can I get you to drink, Miss Miller?"

I consider for a second. The woman on Enzo's arm is drinking champagne and looks sexy as hell. If I were smart, I'd drink the same. It's a light drink I will be able to tolerate without getting too drunk. It's a girly drink I would be expected to drink. But it's not what I want. I used to be able to keep up drinking with the best of men. Six years going without a drink have made me unable to tolerate liquor, but tonight I'm afraid I'm going to need the strength of alcohol to get me through this.

"Scotch. Get me your best scotch."

The staff member disappears to get what I demanded.

"I wasn't sure you were going to make it," Enzo says startling me.

How he can sneak up on me so easily drives me mad.

I turn to him with a large smile on my face.

"Doubting my abilities already? Not smart on your part," I answer.

Enzo doesn't hide his desire from me when he stares at me with large eyes even though his date is still hanging all over him.

"I would never doubt you."

"Good."

We both stare. Neither of us backing down.

"Introduce me, Enzo."

Enzo frowns at his date's comment, but I don't know why. I want to be introduced to the bitch.

"Liesel, this is Kai," Enzo says.

I smile when he introduces me as Kai instead of Katherine.

I hold out my hand, wanting to grip this woman's hand.

She takes it, and then her eyes grow big when she spots the ring. I moved the ring from my left hand to the right so Milo wouldn't know I am fake married. And I'm going by Kai Miller instead of Katherine Black, so hopefully, the news of our fake marriage hasn't spread to Milo yet. I don't know how much he knows Enzo. But as far as I know, Enzo hasn't spread news of our marriage to anyone. And I've only told a handful of people at Surrender.

She throws my hand down and stares at Enzo. "You didn't."

Enzo takes a second to see what Liesel was staring at. "We aren't legally married or married in any real way. I thought a fake marriage might be necessary for the men to accept her authority at Surrender, but I'm not sure it's the best idea anymore. We had pictures taken and everything to announce our rushed wedding, but I haven't released them yet. The only person who knows about our fake marriage is dead. So we have time to decide how to handle it."

Liesel shakes her head, not caring about any of his words. "I fucking know you aren't married you asshole. That's not what I'm mad about."

"Then what?"

"You gave her your mother's ring."

My eyes widen. *How does she know that?* This woman isn't just a fling he brought here to make Milo jealous. This woman knows a lot. She didn't seem surprised to see me or ask too many questions. She now knows about our fake marriage Enzo might not even be sharing with the world. And she knows about his mother's ring.

"I did. She needed a security policy in case something happens."

Liesel drops her fascade and crosses her arms glaring at him. "She doesn't deserve your protection. And she sure as hell doesn't deserve your ring."

"Excuse me, sorry to interrupt," the staff member from before says.

He holds out my scotch. "Here is your drink, Miss Miller."

"Thank you," I say taking it and realizing I need it more than I realized.

"Mr. Wallace has requested all of your presence in his VIP room. When you are ready, I can escort you."

I take a deep breath as the yacht starts moving. It's so slow it shouldn't affect me, but it does. My stomach immediately churns, threatening to throw up. I try downing the scotch in my hand, but once the liquid is in my belly I realize it won't help. My stomach keeps churning with the gentle rocking of the ship.

"If you could show me to the restroom first, I would appreciate it; then I'll be ready to go to the VIP room," I answer.

"Of course, right this way Miss Miller."

I hand him my empty glass and follow, forgetting all about Liesel and Enzo.

He leads me to a private section of the boat, then opens the door to the restroom.

"I'll get you another drink," he says with a small smile. "You can head through that door if I haven't returned by the time you are finished." He nods in the direction of a door at the end of the hallway.

I wince, trying to keep myself together.

"Thank you," I mumble and duck inside. I slam the door shut and lean against it just before I fall apart.

The panic attack has me in full swing. My body trembles against the door, my stomach heaves, and I know I'm seconds away from throwing up everything inside, my body twisting in torture.

I feel the ice cold shiver in my spine pulling me to shut down. Shut it all down. It's the only way to save myself.

A tear falls down my cheek. I'm stronger than this. I have to be. If I shut down, there is no guarantee I will be able to leave this bathroom. I'll fail without even really trying.

I can't.

My breathing is fast and uncontrollable, but even so, I can't get enough air in my lungs. My head is pounding. And then my stomach wretches.

I run to the toilet and vomit.

Everything comes up until my stomach has emptied.

I hear a knock on the door.

Shit. The staff member. *Why didn't I get his name?*

"I'm fine," I shout, hoping that's enough to get him to leave.

And then I vomit again. I grip the toilet, hating that even though I'm wearing one of the most beautiful dresses, I'm sick.

Please don't let me get anything on the dress.

The door opens, and my panic rises to a new level.

No one can see me like this.

And then I see the dark eyes of a man who's seen me come numerous times now. A man I'm far too intimate with. A man I'm pissed at.

"Just leave. You win. I won't be able to leave this bathroom until we stop moving," I say.

Enzo shuts the door behind him.

"I'm not winning like this."

I sigh. But then I can't think because I'm dry heaving over the toilet.

When my stomach seems to stop, Enzo holds out his hand, and I take it until I'm standing up.

"Here," he says holding out his own scotch to me.

I take it and swig a few sips back to wash my mouth of the taste of vomit. Then I move to the sink to wash my face.

My stomach is empty, but I still feel like a wreck.

"Go," I try again. "Steal the ring. You win."

"No, that's not why I'm here. I'm not here to gloat."

"Then, why are you here?"

His eyes heat. "To fuck you in that dress."

Everything stops when he says that. And then I finally come to my senses and laugh. "I think your date might get a little jealous."

He shakes his head. "I don't want my date; I want you."

I chuckle quietly. "I just vomited, my face is flushed, I'm ice cold and shivering. In a few minutes, I won't even realize what is happening anymore because I'll have shut everything out. You don't want me."

Enzo grabs my hips and forces me in front of him at the mirror.

"Look at yourself. I don't see a woman who just vomited out of weakness. I see fierce eyes, determined not to shut down. I see warm cheeks and a strong exterior. I seek a kick-ass woman who faced her fears, walked onto this yacht, and captured the attention of every man on the boat, including Milo. And more importantly, me."

I shake my head. "Stop trying to make me feel better."

He presses my ass to his front, and I feel how hard his cock is.

"Does this feel like a man who isn't turned on by you?"

He's hard as steel.

"I'm sure Liesel helped you along."

He growls and pulls me harder against him. "You have no idea how beautiful you are. You are fucking incredible. Liesel was all over me, and I didn't want her. You stood and batted your eyes across the room, and I've been hard and aching ever since."

I breathe out shallow breaths. Wetness pours into my panties. And my heart stops.

"Now, help a man out and fuck me."

I gasp.

"Fuck me, Kai. I need to fuck you. I can't go all night watching you with Milo and not having you first. I want my cum dripping from your pussy every time you smile at him. I want you sore from my cock every time you move a muscle to flirt with him. I want you thinking of me every time you talk to him. Now, fuck me."

I swallow hard. I can't believe he said that to me.

"Fuck me, Enzo."

He growls again. "My pleasure."

His lips go to my bare neck immediately, and every other feeling melts away as his lips ravish me.

I forget about my mission.

I forget about my anxiety.

I forget about Liesel.

It's just me and Enzo.

"God, the second you walked on this yacht I got jealous as hell. I didn't want any man looking at you, let alone touching you."

"No one touched me."

His eyes rage. "Milo touched you."

I smile. "He only touched my hand."

He grabs my hand and brings it to his lips. "This is my hand."

"Oh really?" I smirk.

He runs his hands over the front of my dress, stopping on my breasts. "These are mine."

He kisses my shoulder. "This skin is mine."

His hand trails down the side to my waist and ass. He begins pulling up my dress until he can feel my ass. "This ass is mine."

I hear a zipper and assume he's pulling his large cock out. I'm not scared about it fitting. Not this time. I'm soaked thinking about him. And I'm as desperate for him as he is for me.

He pushes my panties aside, and then I feel him pushing at my entrance.

"Mine," he says as he plunges into me.

I cry out, but not in pain. There is some agony, but mostly it's a territorial and primal need to claim him as much as he's claiming me.

"Fuck," I moan as he sinks in deeper, while his hand reaches around to find my clit.

I feel myself climbing high, and we've only barely gotten started.

I'm panting, wet, and needy and his cock is barely inside me.

"More."

"Baby, you're not ready."

"More, Enzo." I meet his eyes in the mirror, and I know he's losing control. He can't hold back any longer.

I bite my lip, daring him with his eyes. He finally gives me what I want. *All of him.*

"Mine," I cry out, taking all of him.

Our eyes meet again. "You're all mine," I say, again, making it clear if I'm his, then he's mine. He doesn't get to go to that slut tonight after our mission is over.

"I'm fucking yours," he says.

I smile.

And then he fucks me like he's lost all control.

Driving in and out of me with a frenzy I haven't seen before.

I grip the counter and match him thrust for thrust.

It's so much and not enough at the same time.

"Hang on, baby," he says understanding immediately what I need.

He picks up speed, thrusting harder, faster switching the angle until he's hitting that delicious spot inside me.

"Enzo," I cry. *How can it get better each time he fucks me?* I didn't think it could keep feeling better, but it does.

"I could listen to you say my name all fucking night."

"Yes, Enzo," I cry again, barely registering his words or anything else.

"Are you about to come, baby?"

"Yes," I whisper, no longer able to speak, breathe, or move. All I can do is feel intensity as he fucks me into oblivion.

"Then come, baby."

"I'm coming," I cry a second later, loving that his words sent me into my orgasm.

His meets me at the same time, and I feel his orgasm shooting inside me.

Slowly we still, coming down from our high. Enzo pulls out of me, and I straighten my dress out.

"Mine," he says again, winking at me. And then he exits the bathroom. Leaving me to compose myself before I leave.

I stare at myself in the mirror and smile. Realizing I don't feel sick any more thanks to Enzo. I don't know if that was his intention or if he just really needed to fuck me. But either way, I'm grateful.

And then I feel it—his cum staining my panties.

Shit.

He fucked me without a condom.

You can't get pregnant after one time, can you? You can if you fuck a man like Enzo.

I take a deep breath. I can't get pregnant, not on top of everything else. The sex is great, but I'm still his captive. He's still a monster. And we are still competing for everything.

He would make the worst father.

And I don't ever want to be a mother.

I'll take the morning after pill tomorrow. Right now, I have a ring to steal.

CHAPTER 24
ENZO

Fucking Kai was a mistake.

Because when she came to the VIP room, she glowed and hasn't stopped since.

Milo hasn't arrived yet, but his dozen closest guests fill the rear rooms and upper deck, a deck with the best view on the yacht.

And Kai has been munching on a meat and cheese plate in the corner, while drinking her scotch and ignoring me.

Liesel, on the other hand, hasn't stopped asking me questions. "What did Kai say when you went after her?"

"Can I get you another drink?" I ask, ignoring Liesel.

She sighs. "If I'm going to have to keep dealing with you ignoring me, then yes."

Wanting to get Liesel a drink has nothing to do with Liesel and everything with wanting to be near Kai, who is standing at the bar munching on small bites of food to settle her stomach.

She was an absolute wreck when I entered the bathroom. Being on that yacht for all those years truly fucked her up. And it makes me pissed off for my part in it all.

Kai spots me walking toward her and smiles before she realizes what she's doing. She immediately stops. And starts walking away.

Dammit.

I retrieve drinks for Liesel and myself, only just returning to her side when Milo enters.

The room stops, staring at him.

"Thank you all for joining me. We are going to have one incredible night. Enjoy yourselves."

Everyone applauds him, like he's a fucking rock star or something.

Liesel resumes her flirting with me, by wrapping my arm around her waist and leaning into my chest.

Milo notices and starts approaching us, until Kai laughs loudly at something a gentleman next to her said. She hadn't been talking to the man until Milo entered. But I recognize him. He's Abel Frost. Wealthy, powerful, and handsome. Only third behind myself and Milo in wealth and good-looks.

I shake my head. Of course, she found the best looking man here to make Milo and me jealous.

I move to take a step toward her, but Liesel grabs my tie, stopping me. I'm not sure if it was intentional or if she is just continuing her flirting.

Milo abruptly turns in her direction instead of ours when he hears her infectious laugh. Every man in the room turns toward her like she's a siren calling their names.

"Shit, we have to do something," I say to Liesel.

"Just give him a moment to talk to her. He'll get bored soon enough, and then we will have our chance."

I shake my head. "You don't understand. She's a thief."

"Well, I could have guessed that. She's horrible."

"No, I mean she's stolen dozen of times to survive growing up. When we first met, she stole my watch without me noticing. She has a gift for pickpocketing. If she gets even a second with him privately, she'll steal the ring before I have a chance at taking it."

"Shit," Liesel says back.

"That's not helpful. We need to do something, now."

I try to think, but I can't. Not as he nears my woman.

"I have an idea," Liesel says as Kai smiles at Milo.

Fuck.

"Fine, whatever. Just do it now."

"I'll be happy to."

She grabs my face and pulls me into a kiss. I haven't kissed this woman in over a year, but she kisses me like we were making out yesterday. I close my eyes, trying to make the kiss feel real, but all I can focus on is Kai.

And how wrong this feels.

We start moving, stumbling through the crowd. *How the hell will this help?*

And then we crash into someone.

"Oh my gosh! I'm so sorry. Sometimes I just let the passion get the best of me," Liesel says.

That's when I realize who we stumbled into—Milo and Kai.

Kai no longer looks charming. The anger is clear on her face, and there is no hiding it. She's pissed at Liesel for kissing me.

While Liesel on the other hand, looks smug and happy.

"I completely understand," Milo says swimmingly to Liesel, and my anger at Liesel's stunt dissipates.

I pull Liesel to me harder, knowing it will throw Kai off her game while also making Milo crave Liesel more.

"When you find the person you desire, everything else just disappears," Milo says, but his gaze soon turns from Liesel to Kai, indicating Kai is the woman he's chosen for tonight.

Fuck, fuck, fuck.

I need to get him away from Kai now, before he falls any further for her.

"How about a game of poker? I haven't played in years, and I've heard you are the best."

"Nah, I'm good. You are welcome to play. There is a table set up downstairs," Milo says.

In the main rooms, not the VIP area.

Milo continues to stare at Kai like she's the only one in the room.

"I have a cuban, I'd love to smoke. Would you care to join me?" I ask.

Milo looks at me for a second. "After the fireworks, I always enjoy a good cuban after hearing that racket."

The fireworks aren't happening until much later in the night. I've played all of my cards. I don't know what else I can do short of throwing Liesel in between them.

"Will you show me the top deck? I would love to see the view from up there," Kai asks.

Milo grins and holds out his hand, which Kai takes without hesitation or a wince on her face.

Milo starts leading her upstairs.

"We'd love to see the view," Liesel cuts in, grabbing my arm.

We follow them up, and it takes everything in me not to rip Kai from Milo's arms.

Kai leans into his ear and whispers something, her eyes locked in an evil glare with mine.

I thought she got the hint when I fucked her in the bathroom and demanded she was mine, but apparently not.

Apparently, she'd rather cling to Mr. Boring here.

"It's beautiful," Liesel says when we reach the top, trying to barge in on Milo and Kai's romantic moment.

"You're beautiful," Milo says stroking Kai's cheek.

Really? Can the guy be any more cheesy?

We all stand in silence for a minute, watching the stars go by overhead.

"I have a surprise for you," Milo whispers to Kai, holding her in front of his body.

Liesel leans into me, but I don't think the jealousy thing is going to work with Milo. Not when he's so fascinated with Kai.

A firework starts to go off. And we all ooh and ahh.

"I thought the fireworks weren't supposed to go off until later?" Liesel asks.

Milo kisses the top of Kai's head. "I couldn't wait to show Kai."

I bet you couldn't wait.

I rub my neck as I stare up at the sparks in the sky. Other than tackling Milo, I have nothing left. I have no plan.

"Got anything?" I whisper to Liesel.

She shakes her head.

Fuck.

When I look up again, Milo is kissing Kai. His hand is on her ass, and she leans in as her eyes close like she's enjoying the kiss.

I lose it. I growl under my breath.

"Enzo, you can't make a scene," Liesel warns.

She's right. I see two men on the deck who I know are Milo's security. I don't have a weapon to defend myself. And I won't put Liesel nor Kai at risk.

Milo whispers something in Kai's ear, and she smiles brightly, her eyes hooded. And then I watch as they descend back down the stairs without a word or glance in our direction.

I've faced plenty of problems before, but none I couldn't solve or fix.

I'm not pissed because I'm going to lose this round.

I'm pissed because Kai kissed him.

I'm pissed because he's taking her to his private quarters.

And I'm pissed she's going to fuck him with my cum still inside her, all so she can beat me.

"Enzo? It's just a game. There will be other rounds. This is just the first battle. You can still win the war. The next round your father chose, and you know it will be better suited toward your talents."

I don't hear Liesel's words. They don't matter.

All that matters is that Milo is going to fuck Kai, and Kai is going to let him. *Did she play me this whole time? Can she touch other people without feeling pain?* Because I didn't think there was any way she was ready to hold another man's hand, let alone kiss or fuck him.

"Enzo, are you okay?" Liesel asks.

No, I'm not okay. Kai is about to fuck another man, and I can't stop it without getting us all killed. Because if she goes through with this, if she fucks that bastard, I'll kill them both. I'd rather die than let that bastard fuck her.

Come back to me, Kai. You're mine. And I'm not finished fucking you in every way possible. Come back, before he ruins you.

CHAPTER 25
KAI

Kissing Milo is torture.

Every kiss burns my lips, my tongue, my mouth. Pain surges through my body with each slip of his tongue into my mouth. My heart slowly stops, trying to shut him out. My breathing is weak, and my body so cold.

"Are you cold, baby?" Milo asks.

Baby. Milo isn't allowed to call me baby, only Enzo is.

"A little," I say, shivering again.

He grins, his dimples deepening. "Don't worry; I'm about to warm you up."

His lips crash down on me again in a messy, sloppy kiss. He's been drinking, but I don't think he's drunk, just sloppy in comparison to Enzo.

It shouldn't make me feel guilty kissing Milo, not when Enzo kissed Liesel, but I do. I don't want to kiss Milo. I don't care about winning anymore, only surviving. I need to get off this yacht in one piece.

But I also want to punish Enzo and make him suffer for kissing Liesel after he fucked me.

I should be the only woman he kisses.

And he should be the only man I kiss.

Dammit, this stupid game.

Milo presses me hard into a door.

I wince as he fumbles with the door handle.

He doesn't notice my pain. No man other than Enzo ever has.

Finally, he gets the door unlocked, and we stumble inside.

I'm uneasy on my feet. The little amount of alcohol I've had makes me dizzy and lightheaded.

Milo shuts the door and panic rises in my chest. We are in a bedroom, his bedroom by the look of it. The bed is large, filling most of the room. There is a mirror on the ceiling and on the wall. *How many women has he brought here and fucked?* I don't want to be the next woman. *But how do I get out of this now?* First, I need to get the damn ring. Because if I leave now, the kissing him will all be for nothing.

"I could use another drink," I say, hoping more alcohol in both our systems will result in us passing out before he tries to get me to fuck him.

"Of course, anything you want," he grins at me. He locks the door he's standing in front of, his eyes already undressing me as he walks through a door at the back of the room.

I'm exhausted. I want to sit on the bed and get the pressure off my aching feet, but I don't want him to get any ideas that I want to move things to the bed.

He returns a minute later with champagne and a scotch.

I shake my head. He didn't even pay enough attention to me to realize I've been drinking scotch all night, not champagne.

"Here you go," he says holding out the flute glass to me.

I grab the scotch from his other hand and sip it.

He smirks at me. "You are the sexiest goddamn woman I've ever met."

I bat my eyelashes at him, trying to act like I'm turned on by his comment instead of disgusted.

I can do this. Just seduce him. Get the ring. And then get out before he tries to fuck you.

I glance around the room as I continue to sip the scotch. He takes my hand, and we sit down on the edge of the bed. I let my eyes drop to the ring again on his pinky finger. The key that will allow me to leave.

Being sexy will be the easiest way to steal the ring.

He leans down like he's going to kiss me on the lips again, but I grab his hand and instead kiss his palm and set my scotch on the floor. He does the same with the champagne glass.

I kiss him again, and his eyes glue to mine in a heavy terrifying way, because I know what that look means. He's planning all the ways he wants to fuck me.

I continue kissing his palm, stalling.

Do it.

I take his index finger in my mouth, and suck it like I'm sucking his dick instead of his finger.

He bites his lip as he holds in a growl from the sensation.

I force my lips to curl up in a smile as I move to his middle finger.

I get a small moan as my reward. *Disgusting.*

I give the same treatment to his ring finger as I push him hard in the chest making him fall backward on the bed.

I need to give him everything before I move to the last finger, the one with the ring I need to steal on it. Hopefully, the ring is loose and not tightly squeezing his finger, or I'll never get it off.

I keep his finger in my mouth as I force my legs to straddle him until I feel his erection.

I suck in a breath trying to keep my nerve.

I can do this. I'm so close.

But no matter what happens, I can't. *I can't fuck him. Not even to save my own life.*

I move my mouth to his last finger at the same time I ground my pussy over his dick. I take his pinky finger into my mouth.

His eyes roll back in his head, and he presses his erection deep inside me.

I feel sick.

As I pull my mouth off his finger, I bring the ring with me into my mouth.

The boat rocks hard in that moment, as if the sea is finally on my side.

"Oh my god! I think I'm going to be—"

I jump off of him and run to the door I hope leads to the bathroom. There is a small private hallway that leads to a bar and a bathroom. I duck inside, shut the door behind me, and then lock it.

I exhale deeply. My body is still wrecked with panic and anxiety from having to touch and kiss him.

Tears stream down my cheek.

I feel like a whore, and all I did was kiss him. I can't imagine how I would feel if I let things go any further.

I grab the ring from my mouth and stare at it. I smile gently; I got the ring. Now I just need to find a way out of here with my dignity intact.

A rattle at the door makes me jump.

"Kai? Are you okay?" Milo asks.

Shit.

I walk over to the toilet and flush. "Yes, I just get seasick sometimes," I say weakly.

I walk over to the sink and turn it on, pretending to wash my face. "I just need a minute to try and freshen up."

Hopefully the thought of me vomiting will turn Milo off.

I wait a few minutes, then turn the water off. I pinch my cheeks and loosen my hair to try and look more like a mess. Like I'm desperately ill.

Then I look at the ring I'm holding. I need a place to hide it. I can't wear it on my finger. I really only have one choice: my bra. I slip it inside, knowing if he does try and fuck me, he'll find the ring and discover my real intentions.

I slowly walk to the door, like I'm walking to my death. I unlock and open it.

Milo is standing with his arms on either side of the doorframe.

"Feel better?" he asks.

"Um...not really. I'm sorry, I think I just had too much alcohol, and I got seasick. I think some fresh air might help me feel better."

"Or lying down on my bed might help."

I smile weakly. "The fresh air is usually the most helpful."

I try to push past him, but he doesn't move. He glares down at me; his eyes still singular focused on eating my body.

"You don't get to tell me no, baby. No one tells me no."

"I'm sorry. How about a rain check? My breath reeks of vomit. And I don't want that to be the first memory we share together."

"I don't buy it."

"What?"

"I. Don't. Buy. It."

I shake my head.

"Plenty of women have tried it before. Seducing me, but not willing to give it up when the time comes. Hoping that by dangling me along, I will want you more and more. Until I make you my girlfriend in hopes of finally fucking you. It's not going to happen. Not unless your pussy is made of gold or something. I get what I want, and I want you. Now get the fuck on my bed. Naked. Ass up in the air because you're right—I won't be kissing you anymore."

"Fine, I just need air first." I'd rather throw my body overboard into the sea than let this sick fuck have me.

I duck under his arm, walking fast and with purpose toward the bedroom door. I get there before he does. I grab the handle and try to unlock it, but it doesn't unlock.

Fuck.

There is a keypad and screen on the wall.

"It doesn't unlock from the inside or outside without me entering that code first."

"You sick fuck."

He grins.

"Get on the bed."

"No."

He grabs my arm and throws me on the bed. *This can't be happening.*

He removes his tuxedo jacket as I clammer off the bed.

He grabs me again, and I slap him.

"A fighter, huh? I enjoy it more when you fight back."

I scream. "Help! Somebody, help me!" But I know my cries are useless. If his staff heard, they wouldn't come. And everyone else is upstairs listening to loud music. They won't hear me. Enzo might try and save me, but he might just as easily give me space thinking I'm safe and simply trying to steal the ring.

Fuck the ring.

I don't want it.

I'd give it to Enzo if he came and saved me.

Milo grabs my wrists and spins me around before I even have a chance to fight him. He holds my arms behind my back with one hand as he grabs my ass with the other.

"No! Please stop! Let me go," I cry, not caring the tears are falling. Let him see the pain he is causing me.

But my tears only make him harder. I need to stop begging for someone to save me and find a way to save myself.

Think!

A gun.

He has a gun. I'm sure of it. Langston said all dangerous men carry a gun. He showed me the most likely spots. I just need a free arm.

His sloppy mouth moves to my neck, and I let him. Moaning instead of pushing him away in fear.

"I said you would like it, baby. Just give into it. Stop fighting me," he whispers.

It's enough to get him to loosen his grip.

I slip one arm from his grasp and grab the gun from his waistband. I aim it at his heart.

"Get away from me. Now."

Milo grins, backing up. "You're a fiery one."

"I will shoot you if you touch me again. You can ask my husband; I'm a good shot."

He grins and glances down at the ring I'm wearing on the wrong finger. "I knew you were married. Something about you told me you were off limits."

"Then why did you come after me?"

"I like the married ones. The fighters. It's so much more fun this way."

I shake my head, disgusted by this man. I only thought he was a rich douchebag; I didn't realize he was a rapist.

"Unlock the door."

"Not without payment."

I freeze. "I'm not sucking your dick. And I'm not letting you fuck me. You will unlock the door if you still want your cock attached to your body." I aim the gun lower and ensure the safety is off.

"You know how to work a gun; I'll give you that. But are you strong enough to fire it?"

"I am."

He nods. "I have a feeling you are."

"Unlock the door. Now."

"Not without payment."

"I won't—"

He shakes his head. "I want the ring."

"What?" I panic. *Does he realize I stole his ring?*

He nods in the direction of the ring I'm wearing. "It means something to you. It's special. Something your husband gave you. If I can't have your body, then I want the ring."

I tremble. *He can't have the ring.* This ring is Enzo's. It's his mother's. It means too much to him. I can't just let him have it.

"The ring or you don't leave. *Ever.* I don't care if you kill me; you will never get out of this room alive. None of my staff have a way to override the door. You will be trapped in here forever if you kill me."

Fuck.

"The ring for your freedom."

I stare at the ring. *I will get you back. I promise.*

Carefully, I take the ring off. I toss the ring at him. He catches it.

"Good girl."

"Unlock the door."

He moves to the door, and I train the gun on him.

He starts to enter a code, and I hear the door mechanism unlocking. "Move away from the door," I say when he's finished.

I keep the gun on him as he moves away from the door, and I head to it. I try the handle, but it doesn't open. Words flash on the screen.

The door will unlock in twenty-four-hours.

Twenty-four-hours!

"What did you do?"

"I unlocked the door."

"No, you fucking didn't! Do you have a death wish? I will kill you."

"No, you won't." He walks closer to me until the gun is pressing against his chest.

He grabs the gun before I can react. *Why the hell didn't I pull the trigger?*

"You bastard."

He smirks. "I'm not a bastard. I unlocked the door as requested. You were the one who didn't confirm the details first before coming to an agreement. I'm a businessman, Kai. The key to winning is in the details. I unlocked the door; it just won't open for twenty-four-hours."

I tremble. I'm trapped with this bastard for twenty-four-hours.

"You won't fuck me. You promised."

"No, I won't fuck you, not until you beg me—which you will."

I cross my arms. "I think I can go twenty-four-hours without wanting to fuck an asshole."

He grins. "Not if I beat you for every second we are in here, only providing you with relief when you beg for my cock."

The first blow is always the hardest. It's the one that knocks you into reality. I never thought I'd get beaten on a yacht again. Never be trapped in a room while the ship rocks. But when Milo's fist flies into my chest, it all comes back.

The fear.

The agony.

The pain.

All of the memories consume me again. And I hate myself for falling victim again. There was a reason I hated boats. A reason I hated the water. Because you can't run from the monsters when there is nowhere to go.

Kai has been gone for three fucking weeks.

When the yacht docked, she never got off. Langston, Liesel, and I waited in the car all night waiting for her to disembark. To see if she had the ring. If she had won.

But she never got off.

Every day that went by made me crazy.

What happened?

Did she get the ring?

Did she fuck him?

Did she get caught?

What happened?

Milo was photographed a day later giving some grand speech, without the ring.

So I knew she had it.

But where was she?

Then, the rumors started. Milo spread the word he'd fucked Enzo Black's whore and wife.

I hadn't told anyone I was married. I still wasn't sure if it was the right or wrong move entirely.

Milo broke the news to the world—and now he's my enemy.

I've been tracking him for weeks. But it doesn't seem Kai is still on board. Numerous other women have been brought on his yacht, but no sign of Kai.

Did she try to run from me when she had the chance?

"Sir," Langston says stepping into my office at my beach house.

"Have you found anything?"

"No."

"Keep fucking looking and don't come back until you have something." *How could she just disappear?* It's not possible. Not from my team with my resources.

At first, I was worried about Jarod's boss hunting her down. I've been tracking leads for weeks, trying to find out who owned Kai. Who controlled Jarod. And finally, I have my answer. And it's even more fucked up than I could imagine.

"What happens if we don't find her?" I ask Archard, who is sitting on the couch.

He opens his mouth to answer and then stops abruptly staring at my doorway like he's seen a ghost.

I turn in that direction, already knowing what I will see when I glance that way, but unsure of how I'll feel.

Relieved she is alright.

Pissed she has been gone so long.

Angry she fucked that monster.

Just as I knew she would be, Kai is standing in the doorway. Gone is the glamorous look she wore the last time I saw her. Now she wears yoga pants, an oversized sweatshirt, and baseball cap.

She walks into the room without a word or glance my way.

"The ring," she says, holding it out to Archard.

He takes it slowly from her hand and inspects it.

"I'm declaring Kai the winner of this round. I'll notify you both twenty-four-hours before the next round starts," Archard says before leaving the room like he can't get out of here fast enough.

"Tried to run and realized you couldn't, not without my help?" I say.

"No, I wasn't running. I just needed some time to think."

"I'm sure you did after what you did."

"What does that mean?"

"It means you didn't want to face me after you fucked him!"

She glares at me, giving me all of her hatred. But she has no right to be mad, not right now. Now I get to be pissed.

"Do you have any idea the damage you caused?"

Her mouth drops open at my words. "The damage I caused you? Are you serious?"

"Yes! You ruined my reputation. Black's reputation. You told him you were married to me, and then you fucked him. Repeatedly. He told the world he had stolen my whore, my wife. No one will think I can rule when I let my woman get taken from me so easily."

Her face reddens, and for the first time since I've known her, I don't think her skin would feel like ice if I touched her. It would be scalding like fire. Burning and torching my skin from her hatred from me.

"Why the fuck would you tell him we were married?"

"One; you never told me not to. But I didn't tell him."

"Then how did he figure it out?"

"The ring you gave me. He knew it was an engagement ring. He wanted to know whose it was. I couldn't come up with a lie, so I said you."

I stare down at her finger, searching for the ring she claims almost ruined me.

"Where is it?"

Her face goes white.

"Where. Is. The. Ring. Kai?"

"It's gone."

I raise an eyebrow. "You sold it?"

"Milo has it."

What. The. Fuck?

"Spreading your legs for him wasn't enough? You had to hurt me by giving him the only possession I care about?"

I see red. I've never been so angry. So out of control. I knock everything from my desk in one swoop just needing to be destructive. Then I grab the chair and fling it across the room. I want to hurt Kai like she hurt me.

There was no reason to sleep with Milo. No reason she could give that would make me understand how she could fuck me in the bathroom and then five minutes later fuck another man simply to win a game. No reason she could give to explain why she would give him the ring meant to protect her.

"You fucking whore!" I spit out.

"You sold me! You fucking sold me! Did you think I would be loyal to you? That just because you fucked me, I would never fuck another man?"

"Yes, you're mine! I thought I made that perfectly fucking clear."

"I'm nobody's, least of all yours!"

My body shakes from the adrenaline I'm feeling. Without thinking I grab her and push her against the wall. My lips crash down on hers, needing her to fucking know she's mine.

"Mine!" I cry as she fights me off from her lips. She tastes as delicious as I remember, even though she betrayed me, my cock doesn't understand. He still wants her. I still want her.

But I can't have her. Not after she hurt me, again.

"I don't belong to any man. Let me go!"

"No, you're wrong. You belong to me. You had a choice, and you bet your life, all for a chance at getting answers from me. You lost, now live with it. You're mine."

"You fucking bastard. You don't want me; you just don't want anyone else to have me. You won't even let me go free."

"No."

"Who cares that I fucked him? Who cares that I gave him the ring? You don't care about me. You don't love me. Why does it matter?"

"Because you are mine."

I release her. I won't hurt her. Even though I want to. I won't touch her.

She betrayed me. Gutted me. She got in bed and spread her legs for a man I hate. Just to win a game. And then she stabbed me in the heart by giving him the ring. A ring I willingly gave her to protect her.

Unacceptable.

I will make her pay for what she did.

She wants her freedom from me. She will get it. But she will never truly be free. I'll make sure of that.

She hates being here; I'll make her wish she never begged me to let her free.

"Go," I say to her. "Shower, get rid of any remnants of Milo. Then I will let you know what your punishment is."

She doesn't fight me; she just leaves. But I doubt she will shower. She won't do anything to make me happy. Nothing to show I have any power over her.

She thinks I'm the devil. I'll show her how evil I can be. I'll get my reputation back. And I'll retain my name—Black. Because she can't fight for the name if she isn't here to fight for it.

I pick up the phone and dial the number as a plan forms in my head.

I've been beyond nice to her.

I protected her.

I gave her everything she could ever want.

I even helped her in that bathroom by getting over her fear of being on that yacht.

And this is how she repays me—with her betrayal.

No more.

She thinks I'm the devil, so I will be. I'll release the man inside me my father spent years trying to cultivate. But once I release him, I can never go back. I'll grant her reprieve from me, but she won't ever be free. Because she will never stop thinking about me.

CHAPTER 27
KAI

Why does this bedroom comfort me?

It shouldn't.

Enzo is a monster.

He made it even more clear downstairs in his office, when he accused me of fucking Milo. Or willingly giving up his mother's ring.

He thinks so little of me.

That I would betray him like that.

But I wouldn't.

I did everything I could to survive.

Something he will never understand.

It's been over an hour since Enzo dismissed me from his office. And this is where I came—his bedroom. *Our bedroom.*

The room where he held me captive.

The room where he taught me to sleep in a bed.

The room where I learned to love myself.

The room where he made me come with just his voice.

The room where he fucked me the first time.

The room where I healed.

I hug my legs to me, sitting in the middle of the bed, like this room can somehow fix everything.

It can't.

Any feelings I had for Enzo vanished.

I feel nothing.

I'm numb.

I'm broken.

I don't care about the game.

I don't care about winning.

I just want him to let me go. He can be Black; I don't want it. I've suffered enough.

The door opens, and Enzo steps inside with an eery calm to him.

I watch him with big eyes as he walks to the bed and sits down on his side, leaning back against the frame and stretching his long legs out in front of me.

"What are you doing?" I ask.

"I want to play a game."

"I'm tired of games."

"You are never tired of our truth or lies game."

I freeze. I don't want to play that game. I don't want to tell him the truth. I don't want to tell him how wrong he was downstairs. How badly he hurt me. But I can't keep it in. And I want to hurt him as badly as he wants to hurt me.

"Fine, you go first."

"You're a whore," he says.

I growl. "You did not just say that."

"Truth or lie, you're a whore," he repeats as plainly as if he were telling me the weather.

"Truth," I say, because that's what he thinks of me.

He waits for me to say something. Because apparently, this game is more about telling the truth than it is about concealing things from each other.

"I spent the last three weeks hiding," I say.

"Truth," he says almost bored.

Then he looks me dead in the eye. "I never sold you."

"Lies," I answer.

He opens his mouth to speak, but I stop him. I need to get my own truth out before he tries to hurt me with whatever comes next.

"Milo beat me."

"Lies," he says rolling his eyes.

I rip my hat and sweatshirt from my body, revealing the truth. I spent three weeks alone trying to heal so Enzo would never know what I suffered from Milo. So he wouldn't look at me as broken. But the damage Milo did couldn't be healed in three weeks.

My body is as purple and black as it was when I first arrived here after being held captive by Jarod. I'm broken. Milo only had me for twenty-four-hours, but he housed a rage I didn't think any man could.

"Kai," Enzo's voice breaks as he looks at me. And a silent tear drops down his cheek seeing the pain. Seeing what I went through. What I was desperate to stop from happening.

"He beat me because I wouldn't sleep with him. I wouldn't spread my legs and become the whore he wanted me to be."

Enzo winces when I say the word whore, realizing how stupid it was to call me that earlier. I can see the terror on his face at realizing how badly his words hurt me. Almost as badly as what Milo did to my body.

"And your mother's ring—it did save me in the end. It saved me from being raped. It was his payment, because he knew how badly it would hurt you, which in the end was all he wanted."

Sorrow fills his face in a way I've never seen before. Pain, agony, despair all flow through his veins.

"I didn't betray you. I never would. I did everything I could think of to keep him from touching me. To keep him from getting your mother's ring because even though you gave it to me to protect me, I knew how precious it was."

Silence.

There is nothing he can say to fix this. This can't be forgiven. Not easily, by either of us.

"You promised to protect me, and you did, with the ring. The bruises are nothing. I would have died if he had raped me. I couldn't have recovered. But he didn't, because of that ring."

My words hurt him, because whatever he came up here to say he still hasn't said it, and I know his words will be a betrayal of his own.

He needed to get back at me, so he did. And I need to hear the monster he has become. Because despite all of it, I still want Enzo. His ring protected me. And that I can never stop thanking him for.

"Tell me," I say.

His eyes bug open. "I can't."

"Tell me what you came here to say."

"Fuck." He rubs the back of his neck and looks at me with tear stained eyes.

"I didn't sell you."

"You already said that."

He shakes his head. "I. Didn't. Sell. You."

"What?"

He takes my hand, and I pull it away. But he only grabs it again.

"I didn't sell you."

"But that's what the men said. I remember them saying your name when I was sold."

"That's what they wanted you to believe."

I frown. "Why did you hide the truth all this time? Why didn't you tell me you didn't sell me?"

"Because it was easier if you hated me. I wanted you to hate me. It was the only way I could protect you from the truth and keep you safe. Because if I didn't sell you, then someone else did. Someone would be looking for you and try to sell you again."

"Who?"

"I was wrong. No one is looking for you."

"Who. Sold. Me?"

He takes a deep breath and squeezes my hand like the next words are going to hurt.

"Your father."

I gasp; my face goes white.

"What? Why?"

He shakes his head. "Maybe he's crueler than either of us realized. Maybe he thought you were safer being sold rather than staying here and facing me. Maybe he thought he was toughening you up quickly rather than dealing with years of training. I don't know the answer, but he sold you."

I process his words. *My father sold me.*

It hurts beyond anything else, but it's not Enzo's fault. I can forgive him for the worst thing I thought he did to me.

I can forgive him.

And he can forgive me.

And we can move on as what…?

We still have to fight to become Black.

We still can't date.

We shouldn't be lovers.

It doesn't change anything.

We are still enemies.

My father sold me. Of all the things Enzo listed, the only one that makes sense is he did it to toughen me up. To prepare me for what is about to come in these games. That's why I was never raped on that yacht. He couldn't bring himself to order those men to rape me, only break me. Push me to my limit.

It makes sense.

I turn back to Enzo who looks like he's about to be sick. When I'm the one who should be feeling this way.

"What else?" I ask.

He won't look at me. He's told two truths, which meant he was saving the worst truth for the end. *What truth could be worse than my father sold me?*

"Enzo, what was your third truth?"

"I'm so sorry. I thought you had betrayed me, hurt me. I thought you willingly fucked Milo. I thought you gave him the ring to hurt me. It killed me to think you were willing to fuck Milo to win a stupid game. It broke my damn heart."

"I didn't though." And Enzo can't have feelings for me. It's not possible. I'm just a possession to him. Not someone who could hurt him.

"I did."

I frown. "You did what? You fucked Liesel?"

He shakes his head, and I can breathe again. For some reason that would hurt me. Him fucking another woman would kill me as badly as my father's betrayal.

"Then what?"

"I sold you."

"But you just said..."

"I didn't sell you before. But I sold you now, to Milo. He's coming in an hour, and I'm not sure I can stop him."

TRAPPED BY LIES

CHAPTER 1
KAI

My heart healed—wholly and completely. I forgave the man I thought had sold me. I did the impossible. I was wrong about Enzo. He didn't sell me. He's not responsible for all of the hurt I endured for six years.

My father is responsible.

My heart healed, only to break a second later.

Enzo didn't sell me before, but he did now.

He sold me to Milo Wallace.

Milo—a man I only spent twenty-four hours with and already my body became as scared, broken, and bruised as the entire first month I spent with Jarod. Milo has taken women before, that much is clear. He's practiced in breaking people slowly and methodically. I still don't understand how I got out of there without him raping me. Unless, this was his plan the entire time. To let me think I was free, only to buy me back and force me to do whatever he wants.

And I know if Milo gets me back, this time my body won't be off limits to him. This time I won't be able to buy my freedom by enduring beatings or giving him a precious ring. This time, Milo will ruin me.

Milo's coming in an hour, and I'm not sure I can stop him.

Enzo's words cut through the fog.

I blink rapidly, trying to bring myself back to the real world. I'm standing in the bedroom I've shared with Enzo since he took me as his captive. I've spent all this time wishing he would set me free, wishing for a way out, but now I'd do anything to continue to be Enzo's prisoner. I know what Enzo expects of me. And he'd never force me to do anything I didn't want to do. Enzo would never hurt me, not like Milo would.

Sold.

I never thought I would be sold again. Never thought I'd be stupid enough to let it happen. But being sold isn't about being naive. It's completely out of my control.

I could fight.

I could run.

But I won't be able to do either without Enzo agreeing. I can't fight two armies of men.

One hour.

That's how much time I have.

One fucking hour left of freedom, if you can even call my current situation free.

I should be talking to Enzo about what he's going to do to try to keep from letting me go. Or what his plan is to get me back if he does have to give me to Milo.

But I can't.

My heart hurts too much.

Enzo betrayed me, even after I did everything to try and protect him.

It fucking hurts.

I feel a tear well up, but I won't let it fall. Enzo doesn't get to see my pain. And neither does Milo when he arrives.

I'm numb—that's where I'll go. My body has prepared time and time again for this exact situation. I'm not even scared anymore. My body will lockdown for as long as I need to survive.

Enzo says something to me, but I don't hear it. I've already locked him out. He doesn't get to see inside my mind. He lost the right to talk to me, to touch me, to be anything other than my enemy.

His mouth moves again, but my ears have learned to filter out the sound.

The door opens, and Langston and Zeke enter.

My heart starts to open again at the sight of the two men—men I consider friends.

No, close it. Don't open it. They work for Enzo—not me. They will hurt me the same as Enzo. And when the time comes, they will turn me over to Milo with one word from Enzo. They won't try to stop it, no matter how much they want to save me—they won't.

I watch the exchange between the three men, like I'm in a tank at the aquarium filled with water and they are on the other side of the glass. I can see them, I know they are there, but I can't hear them.

Enzo paces frantically in the bedroom. Langston reaches out to touch him, but Enzo swats his arm down.

I think they are yelling, arguing, but I can't imagine what about. Enzo sold me. The deal is done. Enzo Black is a man of his word. He can't back out of the deal now. It would ruin him and Black's reputation. He would never put me above the Black empire. And I wouldn't want him to. Other people shouldn't suffer because of me. I just wish Enzo would have trusted me enough to know I would never willingly betray him. I would never hurt him if I could avoid it.

Never.

Apparently, Enzo didn't feel the same way.

The sound of the doorbell downstairs alerts my senses. It's the first sound I've heard in over an hour.

An hour—has it really been that long?

The bedroom door opens, and Westcott pokes his head in.

Enzo gives Westcott an order, and I'm sure he's going to greet Milo Wallace. My time is almost up.

What will happen to the Black empire with me gone? Will Archard call for the next game, and when I don't show up, will Enzo win by default?

It's better this way. I may have won the first round, but I don't want an evil empire. Not even to try and turn it good. I want nothing to do with this life anymore.

Enzo walks over to me and puts his hands on my shoulders, squeezing tightly. It should burn, the fire in him should light up every nerve in my body like he has countless times before. But I feel nothing. He might as well not be touching me.

He opens his mouth, but again I don't hear him.

I've shut him out. The pain is too much.

"Kai! Listen to me!" Enzo's voice booms, somehow cutting through the brick wall I put up to lock him out.

I blink, the only indication that I heard him.

"I have a plan—trust me. I will never let any man hurt you," Enzo says.

His words mean nothing.

"Kai?" Enzo asks hesitantly, trying to see if I heard him or not.

I snap my head to him; my eyes blacken into slits, shooting all my anger at him. But I don't say anything.

He sighs with a whimper of agony and fear filling the room with his despair.

Good, he deserves to be in as much pain and anguish as I am. I want to hurt him as badly as I can before I leave.

"I will never let another man hurt you. Truth or lie?" he asks.

He waits.

I wait.

The pause stretches.

I want his words to be truth so badly. I want to feel hope.

For him.

For us.

For myself.

But my heart knows the truth—I can't trust Enzo Black.

"Lie," I answer.

His face falls into darkness like I plunged a blade into his heart.

Enzo drops his hands from my shoulders, and then he looks at Zeke and motions for him to stay with me. To watch guard over me and make sure I don't do something stupid like try to leave or kill myself to avoid being sold to Milo.

Enzo wipes the moisture from his eyes and then transforms into the fiercest demon I've ever seen. No one would ever know Enzo's heart was breaking just a moment ago. He's one determined motherfucker. He's just not my black knight, my savior.

He sold me.

The truth rings in my head as I watch Langston and Enzo leave.

Enzo sold me, and he doesn't know if he can stop it.

CHAPTER 2
ENZO

Kai's words wreck me.

I deserve them though. I have to earn her trust again. I have to protect her at all costs.

Even at the cost of the Black empire. I would give it all to Milo today if I thought that would keep her safe.

It won't.

For one, it would only make Milo realize how much I care about Kai. It would make him want her more—hurt her more.

No, sacrificing my men and empire to Milo wouldn't save Kai.

I have to find a way to keep Kai and my men safe. *But how?*

I told Kai I have a plan—I don't.

I could offer myself up in exchange for her. But that would leave Kai vulnerable with no one left to protect her. And Milo has no use for me; he'd just kill me or sell me to my enemies. I'm not a good exchange for Kai. He knows someone else would take my place, and he still wouldn't have what he wants—Kai.

Milo Wallace is a wealthy and dangerous man. He doesn't have as large of an empire as I do, but it's impressive all the same. He won't go down easily. And it's going to be hard for me to back out of the deal I struck with him. That's not who Black is. Black doesn't back down from a deal.

How could I have been so stupid and reckless? Because I was raised by the devil. And no matter how hard I try to fight off that side of myself, it always creeps back in when I lose self-control—when I let the anger in.

Kai deserves so much better. When I find a way to save her, I have to let her go before I hurt her again and again. I have to win to keep her out of this life. I have to protect her always. And getting her as far away from the monster within me is the best way to do that.

Langston and I walk toward my office where I told Westcott to bring Milo. He trades me a nervous glance as we approach. Langston has had faith in my leadership abilities time and time again. He knows I'm capable of leading my men to safety. I will do whatever it takes to keep everyone safe. But Langston, Zeke, and I talked for the entire hour, and I couldn't come up with a plan to save Kai.

The only solution I've come up with is to kill the bastard sitting in my office. But it would ignite a war—one the Black empire couldn't handle fighting at the moment. Not when Kai and I would have to agree before we made any move.

But I'll start the war if that is the only way to keep Kai safe.

I reach the closed door to my office. "Stay here," I say to Langston.

He nods solemnly, and it's the first time I don't feel complete faith from Langston in my abilities.

Zeke already swore he'd take Kai and run off if it came down to it to protect her. Langston feels pretty much the same.

It's the first time I think they would disobey my orders if I told them to turn her over to Milo. And it's the first time I'm thankful for their rebelliousness.

But I can't let them run away with Kai. Milo would hunt them down and kill them all.

There has to be another way.

I let the fire grow, burn, and ignite until the monster within is focused on saving Kai and on protecting my men.

I'm not a superhero.

I'm not a savior.

I'm not a good man.

And right now, no one believes I can or will protect Kai without hurting those who work for me—but I will find a way.

My father may have turned my soul into the devil—the kind to turn on Kai the second I thought she turned on me. But it's also the ruthless kind to destroy anyone in my path. And right now I'm set on saving Kai.

I promised to never let another man hurt her—and that includes me.

I open the door and step into the office like the fucking king I am. Milo Wallace will not know my anger. He will not know my fury or rage. And he most definitely will not see my fear.

Milo will be clueless to my intentions. He will never know offering to sell Kai to him was the worst mistake of my life. When I picked up the phone to call him, I thought this is what she wanted. Maybe not to be sold, but to be with a man she chose. I was idiotic for thinking that. And Kai doesn't deserve to be sold—ever.

"Mr. Wallace, it's a pleasure to see you again," I say, holding out my hand to him.

He grins evilly as he shakes my hand, trying to look into the depths of my eyes to get a glimpse of my feelings. He doesn't have a clue though.

"Please, call me Milo, Mr. Black," Milo says.

I don't offer for him to call me Enzo—not in my office. Not when he's taking what's *mine*. I am Mr. Black here. I am power itself, and by the time this meeting is over, I will have a plan.

"Take a seat," I say, as I take a seat behind my desk. Westcott already has a scotch sitting at my desk, and Milo has one in his left hand.

"How's business going?" I ask.

"Good. You?"

"Good." Neither of us gives anything away. We both know better than to let anything slip out the other could use as leverage.

"Five million is a lot of money for a whore," Milo says.

Do. Not. React.

I force the calm stillness to take over. I kick back in my chair as I nurse my scotch.

"Five million is nothing to men like us."

He gives me a slight nod.

"Still, I usually don't go higher than one million."

"I won't accept anything less than five. One million isn't even worth my time for this meeting." *Is this the way? Can it truly be this easy?* He won't pay more than one million for Kai. I can refuse to sell her because I want more money.

Milo smirks and then reaches into his pocket and pulls out a ring.

A ring I recognize immediately—*my mother's ring.*

The ring Kai gave to Milo so he wouldn't rape her. A ring I owe everything to for saving Kai, yet also want to curse for making me believe Kai betrayed me.

Milo cocks his head. "This looks like an engagement ring to me, Black."

I nod nonchalantly. "It is."

He twirls the ring around his pinky finger. "Why would you sell the whore you married?"

I laugh like it's the most ridiculous thing. "You think I married the bitch?" I hate myself for calling Kai a bitch, but he needs to think she means nothing to me.

"Yes."

I shake my head. "I didn't marry her."

"Then why did you give her this ring?"

"So the world would know she's mine."

He leans back studying me, but I pour all my truth into my words. Those words at least are true. Kai is mine, and I wanted the world to know.

"The scars and bruises weren't enough?" Milo tests me. He doesn't believe I was the one who marked her.

"You know how men are. I beat her black and blue plenty of times, but that wasn't enough to stop other men from touching her. Only that ring did that."

"She didn't look too beat up at my party."

"I've grown bored with her lately. I've had her for six years. She earned a night of freedom, and when I saw your infatuation with her, I realized I had found a buyer willing to pay top price."

"She means nothing to you?"

"Nothing."

He sighs. "Then she isn't worth five million."

I shrug. "Probably not. I broke her easily. You got a taste of her on your yacht, which for that alone I should double the price. You didn't have any right to touch what was mine without paying."

I lean forward, threatening Milo with everything in my body. "I think I will raise the price—ten million. You saw something in her on your yacht. You want her; you pay for her. And you pay for your mistake touching her."

Milo's eyes light up. *Fuck. I fucked up.* He realizes what she means to me. He pockets the ring again.

His phone buzzes. He glances down, and his pupils dilate. He doesn't answer the phone. He silences it only for it to start buzzing again. And that's when I realize *his mistake*. He has enemies here. Someone he's running from.

"When do you leave?" I ask.

"Tonight." He answers, but his thoughts aren't on this conversation. They are on the buzzing in his pocket. "I should be going. Arrangements need to be made for my departure."

"Back to Italy?"

He doesn't answer. He doesn't want me to know where he's going. He wants to hurt me. He wants Kai. But he doesn't feel safe here in Miami. With one phone call I'll find out who his greatest enemy in town is, and then I'll use it to my advantage.

I will keep Kai safe.

"Do we have a deal?" I ask, holding out my hand already knowing he's going to take it. He risked his empire all to claim my woman. He wants to hurt me; I just wish I knew why. At his party he acted like we were great friends. But that's how enemies behave in public, like the best of friends. Only in private do we dare to make moves against each other.

He grips it and then pulls out his phone. He speaks to his right-hand man, and I know the money is in my account. I don't verify it. I don't give a shit about the money. That's not what this is about.

Milo wants power over me, and he's taking it. He set a trap to get me to sell Kai, and I fell for it. He won this round, just as Kai won her first round in our game. But I never lose twice against the same opponent. The next round goes to me, and I will slaughter him.

"The whore?" Milo asks, watching my reaction when he calls Kai a whore again.

"Westcott," I say.

The door opens, and Westcott steps inside. "Have Langston bring me Miss Miller."

"Yes, Mr. Black," Westcott answers.

I want to add—slowly. Take your fucking time so I can make Milo squirm. The second he gets back I know he will depart. I only have minutes to make my plan work, but I don't doubt I can make it happen. I can save Kai while keeping up the ruse that I want to sell her.

I take out my cell phone. "I just need to confirm you made the payment, and then the whore is yours."

I dial Zeke's number.

"Do you have a fucking plan?" Zeke answers.

"Yes, I'd like to confirm Milo Wallace deposited ten million into my account," I say, even though I don't give a shit if the money was deposited, and I know Zeke won't either.

"Shit, Langston said he's here to take her to Milo. You better have a fucking plan Enzo, or I'll kill you myself. We don't sell women. We fight, we kill to protect our empire, but we never sell women like objects." He pauses. "I'm letting her go, but you better have a fucking plan."

"How much longer until you find out if the money is there? Mr. Wallace is in a hurry," I say, trying to let Zeke know he doesn't have much time to do what I want him to do.

Zeke sighs into the phone. "I'll find out everything I can about Milo. But we already know everything. We know his organization. His number two. His allies. And his enemies."

"Yes, can you read that last number again?"

"His enemies? I should focus on his enemies?"

"Yes, thank you for confirming the deposit." I end the call, knowing I gave Zeke all the information to get started searching for Milo's enemy. The one closest to Miami. The biggest threat.

"The money has been confirmed," I say to Milo.

"Good. Now, where's my whore?"

"She's coming. One of my men is bringing her now."

There is a knock, and my heart stops.

I hate this plan.

I would much rather shoot Milo here now, but that could put Kai at bigger risk. Men would know she's my weakness. They would try to take her just to control me.

Langston opens the door and escorts Kai in, holding onto her bicep. Kai doesn't look at me, nor Milo. She's a stone fortress blocking everything out. She doesn't even react to Langston's touch on her arm.

Milo looks her up and down. "Good. Sorry for cutting this short, but I really should be going."

I nod. "Of course, we won't keep you waiting."

I'm heartless. I beg my heart to stop beating because I know this is going to rip it to shreds.

Milo stands up and grabs Kai by the wrist.

She doesn't flinch.

God, she's so fucking strong.

This ends here. This is the last time a man touches her without her permission. I don't care how many times she betrays me; I won't hurt her or let anyone else hurt her again.

I want to tell Kai this with my eyes and soul. I want her to believe me, but she won't—not until I prove it over and over and over.

I nod to Langston, and he releases his grip on her arm. Milo starts leading her out the door, pulling her too forcibly. But I compel my body to stay in my seat until he's gone.

I will get her back. She will not take a step onto that yacht. Even if I have to shoot Milo myself and start an impossible war. I will not let her get hurt.

Kai's eyes fall to mine, surprising the hell out of me.

I promise her with my eyes. "I will save you—trust me," I mouth.

"I know," she mouths back, and then she's gone.

I'm gutted.

How can she put faith in me after everything I did? After I'm letting a man, who has beaten her before, take her? Did something happen up in that bedroom while I was gone? Did Zeke say something? How can she trust me?

Because I'm her only hope. She has no choice but to put her faith in me.

I can still earn her forgiveness, not that I deserve it. I don't want to be redeemed. I only want to keep her safe.

I hear the front door shut from my office where Langston stands looking at me like he's ready to kill me. But I don't have time to explain myself to him. There is work to do. And I will not fail.

I close my eyes letting the pain I deserve in, because watching another man take Kai was the hardest fucking thing I've ever done.

CHAPTER 3
KAI

Each step away from Enzo's office physically hurts.

Each fucking step is another memory of his betrayal. Of the pain he caused me. He fucked up, and somehow I'm the one paying for his mistakes.

Stop.

I can't think about what Enzo did that landed me in this mess. I can't think about what my father did that started this all. I can't think about anything other than finding a way out.

I will never be someone's slave. *Never again.*

I'd rather die.

Have faith in Enzo—trust him. Enzo's done everything he can to protect me, and even though he's the reason Milo is taking me, he's the best hope I have at getting free.

But didn't I learn from last time I can't have hope in anyone coming to rescue me?

Enzo didn't know I was taken, last time though. He didn't make me a promise to keep me safe. To prevent any other man from harming me ever again.

I can't rely on my father or anyone else coming to save me, but maybe I can count on Enzo coming.

Milo leads me to a blacked out SUV. He opens the door and releases my wrist, waiting for me to get into the car, but not controlling me. He wants me to surrender to him—*never going to happen.*

"Get in the car, Mrs. Black," Milo says.

I narrow my eyes and scowl. I know Enzo didn't confirm our marriage. That would look like a weakness if he gave up his wife to a man like Milo.

"It's Miller, Kai Miller," I snap.

"No, it's not. It's Black. I don't buy Enzo's bullshit. You mean something to him. He gave you his mother's ring. But I don't know why he sold you. Oh well, his loss is my gain." Milo sweeps my hair off my neck.

I jump at his touch. Not because his fingers swept over a bruise, but because Milo is the last man on this earth I want touching me.

He grins at my reaction. "You're jumpier than the last time we met. Is there a reason for it?"

I growl. "You're a monster."

"No." He leans down until his breath is at my ear. "I'm your new master."

I shiver.

"And if you don't get in the car right now, I'll beat you until our previous meeting doesn't even register on your pain scale anymore," he says.

I glance behind me to the door of the beach house I've come to feel like home.

It's not my home. It betrayed me.

And even though the only people who give the tiniest of shits if I live or die are all inside its walls, none come for me. None fight for me. I'm on my own.

I take a deep breath, knowing I have to choose my battles if I'm going to survive. And refusing to get into the car won't help me. Not when Enzo will order Langston or Zeke to put me in the car themselves if I try to run.

I climb into the car, all the way to the far side, and then Milo slides into the seat next to me. Two men sit in the front seat. Neither of them speak or turn to look at us; they remain focused on the windshield as if they are statues.

But Milo nods, and the car starts driving forward. As soon as we exit Enzo's property, we are surrounded by half a dozen more cars that feel more like tanks than ordinary vehicles. All driving around us, like Milo is the fucking president or something.

"Is the protection really necessary? Enzo sold me; I don't think he will be rushing to try and get me back," I snap.

"Enzo isn't my enemy—at least he isn't today. I have many enemies in this country. But don't worry, I have the best team; I won't let anyone hurt you but me."

I want to fight—that's my initial reaction. It's been a long time since I truly got to fight.

With Jarod, I learned to lock my mind and heart away. I blocked it all out after the first few months.

But I'm tired of blocking it all out. I won't let my mind shut down and put up walls anymore. I'm still just as fucked up after shutting it all out. It didn't truly protect me. *Maybe if I had continued to fight day after day, I wouldn't be so fucked up now?*

So that's my plan. To never stop fighting. To fight until I have nothing left. To fight until Enzo saves me or I die.

Enzo Black may be a monster. The kind of man who would sell me because of my disloyalty. But that is only half of who Enzo is. The other half protects the innocent and deserving. He will do everything he can to protect me. Even if it takes him years, he will come for me. And I won't lock away what's left of me while I wait. I won't go backward. Enzo helped me heal, and although I have a long way yet to go, I won't let Milo break any of my progress.

When Enzo saves me, I will remain as I am. Not because Enzo deserves to have me whole, but because I do. I deserve to stay healed. I deserve to remain strong. I deserve to remain Kai Miller.

"I can't wait to get you alone," Milo says, reaching over and stroking my arm with his finger.

Fight.

I grab his finger and twist as hard as I can, hoping to break it, and if not, do some amount of damage.

He doesn't make a sound. Not one moan of agony. He removes his hand seamlessly from my grasp.

"You're a fighter, I'll give you that. I wasn't sure after our previous encounter where you just locked that pretty little mind away. This version of you will be so much more enjoyable."

He slaps me across the cheek. I feel the burn of his touch. I feel the sting as our skin collides. My head whips to the side, but I feel nothing beneath the outer layer of my skin.

No fear.

No pain.

Nothing.

I study myself, trying to determine if I locked my soul inside again to protect myself.

I didn't. I'm still here. But my fury is bigger than the pain. My determination at fighting is stronger.

"Tell me about Enzo. Tell me how you two met," Milo says.

I open my mouth to refuse when Milo's phone rings. I hear the buzzing in his pocket, and I look out the window at the passing palm trees.

Milo speaks into the phone, but I don't listen. I try to enjoy the sunlight pouring in. I don't know the next time I'll feel the warmth from the sun on my skin.

He ends the call. "It's time for us to have a chat."

I turn my attention back to him, just as his phone buzzes again. He growls as he looks at the number and decides to answer it. "Yes," he hisses into the phone.

I watch as Milo gets four more phone calls. All from numbers he chooses to answer. Each call lasts five minutes or longer. Each call distracts and irritates Milo further. But he answers them. Each and every one.

Enzo.

Is he arranging these calls? Finding a way to distract Milo to protect me?

Yes, I feel it.

But how long can he keep this up? And once we get to wherever

Milo is taking me, then what? Enzo can't keep having the entire city call Milo.

I need to fight.

I don't know if Enzo is going to be able to get me back for a long time, but I can try now—while Milo is distracted.

I need a weapon.

I can't overpower Milo. The door is locked, and there is no way to unlock it from the back seat so I can't run. The only chance I have is to find a weapon.

I'm sure Milo has a gun on him. Enzo, Langston, and Zeke all carry a weapon near their waist. But I don't see anything visible on Milo from where I'm sitting.

I glance down to his thick boots. Enzo also carries knives in his boots.

I'd rather have a gun. Langston and Zeke taught me how to shoot. If I had a gun, I'd kill Milo. Although, Milo's two goons in the front would probably shoot me before I had a chance to turn the gun on them. It would be worth it to know Milo is dead. His men might finish me off, but not before I destroyed Milo.

But if he's carrying a knife near his ankle, that would be easier for me to get than a gun in a waistband buried beneath his jacket.

Milo's eyes are trained out the window as he barks into the phone. Something about having plenty of fuel by the time we get there, or he'll kill them all.

Fuel?

I look out the front window, and that's when I realize where we are going—his yacht.

Fuck.

I will not get on his yacht. I can't. I'd rather die.

Seeing the dock and his yacht looming in the distance fans my desire to act. I must act—now.

I glance over at Milo one more time, trying to decide where I'm most likely to find a weapon. And one I can easily retrieve. I decide to go for the ankle.

I bend down, pretending to mess with my own shoe. My eyes

focus down, trying not to draw any attention from the three men in the car. When Milo's voice grows loud again, I make my move.

I slip my hand under his pant's leg until I feel metal. Then, I grab it—my body launching over Milo's as the knife lands at his throat.

The car lurches trying to throw me off Milo, but I hold the knife steady to his throat, watching as he swallows carefully.

He laughs and ends the call without a goodbye.

"Easy, guys. I can handle this," Milo says to the two men in the front seat.

I don't let my eyes dart around to see the men behind me, their guns trained on me I'm sure. I keep my focus on slicing the knife into Milo's neck. I should have already done it, instead of waiting to persuade Milo to set me free.

"You are a spirited one. I'm going to have so much fun breaking you."

"You won't touch me."

He tilts his head, allowing me better access to his neck, and I press harder—until one droplet of blood coats the knife.

So close. Just a little harder and blood will be spurting.

Milo chuckles. "You should have slit my throat by now."

I press harder, watching more blood. "And if I slit your throat, your men will kill me a second later."

"Ah, that's your concern." He looks up to his men. "If she slits my throat, you are to do nothing to her. You don't touch her. Understand?"

"Yes, sir," both men say.

I freeze. *What the hell?*

"There, now you are free to slit my throat without any repercussion from my men."

Do it.

"But, you better make sure you kill me when you slice my throat. Because I will make you pay ten times over for any damage you do to me."

His hand comes to my wrist gripping the knife, and he presses it harder to his neck as more blood spills. He doesn't show the slightest sign of agony at the blade's touch. This man understands pain. And this isn't pain to him—I understand the feeling.

"I want you to slice my neck. It will make it so much more fun when I slice your neck right back."

Shit.

What am I doing? I will never get out of here alive. *I don't have to. I just can't get on that yacht.*

He releases his grip on my wrist. "What's it going to be, whore? Slice my neck and see what happens. Because as much as you think you will be able to kill me, you have to slice a lot deeper for me to bleed out before my team of men jumps in to save me."

My eyes cut to the two men driving and the dozens of cars around us. No doubt one of them is a doctor, and no doubt he is carrying a pint of his blood. I've seen what money can do to motivate a doctor to save a dying man's life. Zeke shouldn't be alive except for having the highest paid doctor with the best training to do whatever it takes to save him.

Milo will be no different. One slice won't be enough to kill him. I would need a dozen or more stabs. And Milo will only let me get one before he fights back.

His eyes threaten me, as if they already know my thoughts, and he's a dozen steps ahead of me.

I need to do something he isn't expecting. It's my only chance.

I could stab myself—put an end to this.

I won't.

I want to live.

For no other reason than to kick Enzo's ass for selling me.

There are six additional cars. More than a dozen men ride in the fancy, most likely bulletproof, vehicles all around us. I'm outnumbered by a ridiculous amount.

Milo's phone rings again, but he ignores it—too infatuated by what I'm going to do.

I'm going to crash this motherfucking car.

I pull the knife back and slice across Milo's cheek, needing to cause him some pain for thinking he could buy me like property. And then I fling the knife with everything I can toward the driver.

Hoping to God it hits him hard enough for him to lose control of the vehicle. And then I launch myself at him.

The car lurches as I hoped. The knife lands in his shoulder, and he gasps as my body flings over to him. I grab for the wheel, pulling hard to the right as the car starts spinning.

Yes! This could work!

And then I feel the hands. One pair grabs one arm while another pair grabs the other, pulling me off the man and shoving me into the back seat.

The driver regains control, as the man in the passenger seat pulls the knife out of his back.

The driver curses as the knife is jerked free. Obviously, he isn't as used to dealing with pain as Milo or me.

Milo shoves me down onto the seat, forcing my arms over my head, as his body crushes me down into the black leather.

He's sweating, and a thin line of blood scars his cheek. It may not have caused much damage, but the scar will remain for the rest of his life. A constant reminder on his face of me, at least until I find a way to kill him.

"You okay, Vito?" Milo asks, not taking his heated eyes off of me to check on his driver.

"Yes, it just hurts like a motherfucker," Vito answers.

I don't look away from Milo, but I'm sure Vito is giving me an evil glare.

"Don't worry, Vito; I'll make sure she pays for her crimes."

Milo pulls another knife from his pocket and pushes it against my neck in the same way I did to him earlier.

I hold my breath, trying to remain as still as possible, but I don't let the fear in. I won't. He doesn't deserve my fear.

"How far are we from the yacht?" Milo asks his driver.

"Five minutes."

Five minutes, that's nothing. Once I'm on that yacht, I'll have no hope of getting off. And have no hope of hiding my fear.

"Do it. Slice my pretty neck. I deserve it," I taunt him.

He grins, pushing his weight further into my chest until I can barely breathe. His cock sinks between my legs, and it takes every-thing inside me not to try and pull away in disgust.

"Do it," I say again. My eyes glaze with a fire to have control over this man. Even if it's just to get him to hurt me, he'll hurt me because of what I did, and what I said. If it weren't for me, he'd still be yelling into his phone. I have control.

"With pleasure," Milo says.

The knife presses hard against my throat, and I feel the warmth of my blood trickling down my cool neck.

He won't kill me. I know that much. He needs me alive to torture me later. Even though a part of me wishes he would kill me and put an end to this.

Everything starts to move in slow motion.

The knife slices deeper, until I can't contain the pain. I grit my teeth to try to keep it in, but the pain is unexpected. *Maybe he is trying to kill me?*

The car is spinning the next second. Milo flies from my body, slamming into the back of the driver's seat.

Vito grips the wheel hard, trying to regain control, but we keep whirling.

I grab my neck and feel the blood soaking my hand as my body grows colder.

Glass shatters.

And then everything stops.

The car.

The screams.

The guns.

I'm cold—so fucking cold. It's been a long time since I felt this level of ice hardening my veins.

I don't move. I let the ice consume me, freezing me in place. Soon I'll be a statue again. I'm sinking back into my shell, and I welcome it if it keeps me alive.

My eyes start fluttering closed, until I see men with guns standing over me. Men I don't recognize. Men with evil and wickedness in their eyes.

Fuck, it's just my luck. To get stolen from Milo only to deal with worse men. And Enzo won't have a fucking clue he has to steal me from this new enemy, that I'm no longer with Milo. I've been taken by new men.

I let my eyes drift closed, and hope I'll never open them again. Death has to be better than this.

CHAPTER 4
ENZO

Kai's alive.

And Rowan Evan's men now have her, just as planned. *Thank fuck.*

"They have her," I say, ending the call as I look at Langston and Zeke.

Westcott enters my office a second later. "Is she?"

Even Westcott is worried about Kai.

"She's safe."

Westcott nods. "Do you need anything, sir?"

Langston glares at me, ensuring that I do what I must instead of what I want to do.

"Yes, have my car brought around."

Westcott nods and then leaves. The plan is for me to be seen at Surrender—as publicly as possible for the next hour or so. So that when Milo tries to figure out where Kai is, he won't suspect I took her. He will put all of the blame on Rowan. It's going to kill me and be absolute torture to not be here when Kai returns, but it will be safer for her if Milo doesn't know who has her.

Rowan was more than happy to help us out as soon as I asked for his help. I claimed I too was an enemy of Milo, which is now true.

And I wanted to punish him for crossing me. That the woman he harbored was important to him, so I wanted to steal her back.

I offered Rowan the ten million Milo gave to me for his services. In exchange, he gives me Kai unharmed.

My phone buzzes again. It's Rowan. I still. *Why would he call me back?* Langston and Zeke are supposed to meet his men in half an hour to make the trade.

"Hello," I answer the phone cautiously.

"We don't want to alarm you, but the girl has been hurt."

"What? I told you she wasn't supposed to get hurt. That was the deal."

"It happened before we arrived. The bastard had a knife to her throat."

"Is she?" I can't bring myself to ask if she's alive. If she's dying right now in the back of one of their cars.

"She's alive. She'll survive. Your girl is a fighter. She went into some type of shock, her body shut down, and it seemed to minimize the bleeding. We already have her stitched up. She should have lost a lot more blood than she did. If her body hadn't taken over, that bastard would have killed her."

"Fuck," I breathe.

How could I have been so stupid?

How could I have thought she would be safe for even a second with that monster?

How could I have ever thought it was okay to punish her by selling her? Even if I thought somewhere deep down she wanted him?

How could I?

"We just wanted to let you know so you could have a doctor ready to look her over. Her blood pressure is low, her pulse and breathing are weak, but she's alive. She hasn't woken up yet."

"I'll have a doctor with me to retrieve her."

"Good. Also wanted to let you know we don't want your money."

"Why not?"

"We do some shitty, evil things to make money, same as you. But we don't hurt women; we don't hurt the innocent. It's one rule we never break and never tolerate. It's why we hate Milo so much. He has no respect for women. This I will do for free."

"Thank you. If you need any help putting Milo in his place let me know, I'd be more than happy to help," I say, squeezing the phone hard, knowing how badly I want to hurt Milo myself.

"Of course."

We hang up.

"Change of plan. I'm not going to Surrender. I'm going with you to pick up Kai."

"But—"

"I don't care if Milo finds out I stole her back. He fucking hurt her."

Langston and Zeke's eyes grow big with pain.

"No one touches what's mine. This is my fuck up. And I'm going to fucking fix it."

♡

WE MEET ROWAN AND HIS MEN IN A BACK ALLEY. IT'S STILL daylight, but I doubt anyone will give us much attention.

I step out of the car and race over to the open door of the Escalade.

Kai.

"She's alive," Rowan says. I'm surprised he helped deliver her himself. This thing between him and Milo is personal.

"Thank you," I say, holding back tears and anger.

I lift her limp body out of the car, and then run back to mine. I brought Dr. Patten with us to help take care of her on the way back. Langston and Zeke are driving in the front.

As soon as we are in the car, Langston takes off like we are an ambulance racing to the hospital.

I see the large cut on her neck, now tied together with stitches as I lay her head in my lap.

Dr. Patten starts checking her vitals, takes her blood pressure, and examines the wound.

"Should I head toward a hospital or home?" Langston asks as he drives.

I look to the doctor to determine Kai's condition.

"The cut looks worse than it is. It's stitched up nicely. Her vitals are slower than normal, but I think it's just because her body went into a survival state. Not because she's at risk of dying. The only thing they could do is give her blood, but I don't think she lost much. There isn't much on her clothing or hair. And her cheeks are still pink."

"Rowan said she didn't lose much blood from what he could tell."

"Good, I think all she needs is rest and time."

"Home, Langston."

I stroke her hair. "I'm so sorry. I'm so fucking sorry. Never again. Never."

I repeat over and over as Langston drives us home. And I don't care who hears or knows what I'm thinking. Kai is too important to risk ever again.

She will never forgive me for this.

I will never forgive myself for this.

But I can ensure it will never happen again. I will do everything I can to protect her. Even if it kills me.

As we pull up to the house, Kai opens her eyes. As if she was waiting to feel truly safe before she came back to the world.

She blinks rapidly as she looks at me.

"Enzo?" She croaks. Her voice sounds scratchy, and she winces at the pain.

"Shh, don't talk. You're safe."

Her eyes are immense as she looks at me like she can't believe I'm really here.

The doctor smiles. "I'm glad you are awake Miss Miller. Would you like some pain medication for that neck?" He reaches down to produce a couple of pain pills and a water bottle from his bag.

I take the pills and hold them up to her lips. She takes them, and then I carefully pour water through her parted lips.

"You'll make a full recovery soon. You just need to rest. By tomorrow you should feel a lot better."

"What—" she starts.

I press a finger to her lips.

"Don't use your voice to ask me questions."

I can read her eyes and body well enough to know what she's going to ask anyway.

"We found Milo's closest enemy and hired them to get you out before you got to the yacht. We didn't want Milo knowing we were the ones to get you because we were afraid Milo would attack us and try to get you back. I vowed to protect you, and so I will. Even if I failed you now."

Her pupils dilate before turning small.

"Yes, I had every man I know with a connection to Milo call his phone with various questions—problems with the yacht, questions about partnerships, money transfers, weapons that were supposed to be delivered to him, anything I could to keep him occupied and you safe."

She nods a thanks.

"Don't you dare thank me. Don't thank any of my men or Rowan's men. We should be protecting people that deserve it. And you, beautiful, deserve every inch of our protection. You deserve so much more than I can give you."

"I'm so sorry he hurt you," I stroke her neck where a permanent scar will serve as another reminder of the pain, just like all the other marks on her body.

Her eyes shine, and I realize what she's trying to say. She's not sad about the scar. It's a good reminder. A reminder of something she did to Milo.

I smile. "You hurt him first?"

She nods.

"Good girl. Where?"

She points to her cheek and makes a long line. She's vicious when she needs to be.

I hate that her fighting back almost cost her her life. But I know she's truly healed if she was able to fight instead of locking herself inside.

"You are so incredible." I stroke her forehead and hair. Even though we are stopped outside the house, none of us are in any hurry to go inside. All eyes in the car are on Kai, soaking up everything she tells us with her body.

She looks to Langston in the driver seat and points to his shoulder.

He smiles at her. "You got the driver in the shoulder?"

She nods.

"That's my girl," Langston says.

I shoot him a look when Langston says *my girl*. But he simply raises his eyebrows as if to say Kai's as much his as she is mine. She may be calm and understanding right now, but the second she gets her strength back, she will be fucking ready to kill me for getting her into this mess in the first place. Even though I ensured her safe return, it doesn't matter. I fucked up in the worst possible way.

The absolute worst way. And I deserve every bit of her revenge coming my way later.

She looks around the car smiling at each of us, showing her thanks and gratitude for getting back. When her eyes arrive back on mine, she smiles for a split second before letting it drop. And I know that's the last smile I will be getting.

"I promise you—never again. I will die before I let another man hurt you. I will die before I let another man take you. I will give up everything to you if that will save you. I don't care how you hurt or betray me in the future. You have my allegiance. If you win the empire, I will spend my life serving you and protecting you. I'll even give up the empire to you now, if that's what you want. I'll lose every round until you are Black. And I will spend the rest of my life keeping you safe."

She bites her lip as she studies my distraught face, and I know what she's asking me. She doesn't want to be Black. She wants what she's always wanted. The one thing I'm desperate to give her and not sure I can. She wants her freedom.

"What?" Zeke asks, looking from her to me, not understanding.

"Kai wants me to set her free."

Zeke's face falls heavy. "You can't. It's not safe. Definitely not now that Milo will be doing everything possible, including burning this city down, to get Kai back."

My eyes cut to Zeke, silencing him and the rest of the car. Because his words aren't helpful even though they are the truth.

"You will be free as soon as it's safe. I will take you wherever you want to go. I will give you the ten million Milo paid me in the sale. I will give you everything you want. I just can't let you go yet. I'm sorry. I won't let you get hurt again. But I'll give you as much freedom as I can while you're here. I hope it's enough."

She sucks in a breath and looks around at all of the eyes on her, and I know it will never be enough.

"So I'm trapped here until you can determine it's safe for me?" she asks, her voice weak.

"Yes," I say, my heart breaking.

"Then I'll be trapped here forever because I'll never be safe."

CHAPTER 5
KAI

It hurts to think. The muscles twinge every time I make my neck move, but hopefully, the pain medications will kick in soon, because I have a lot to say to Enzo, and it can't wait.

I'm trapped here. That much I know. Enzo will never let me go until he can ensure my protection, something he will never be able to do. Milo will start hunting me as soon as he tends to his wounds. All of Enzo's enemies have now become mine. Whether the news of our fake marriage spread, or realizing I'm the daughter of a Miller and I have as much right to the empire as Enzo does. The world knows of my existence and will be coming for me.

Enzo continues to stroke my hair, looking down at me like he's terrified of living if I were to die. I've seen something close to this on his face before, but never *this*.

Something changed when Milo took me. Enzo felt pain when I was taken. *Maybe Enzo does have a heart?*

How can I be happy and pissed at someone at the same time? I feel both emotions in equal measures. I'm livid Enzo sold me and got me into this situation in the first place. And I'm elated he saved me. I'm happy he's scared to lose me. I'm thrilled he offered to give everything to me in payment.

He offered everything but my freedom.

Enzo nods and all the men file out of the car.

Langston opens Enzo's door. Slowly Enzo eases out from underneath me, stands, and then his arms are under me scooping me out.

I can walk, I say with my eyes because it's not important enough to speak with my voice and cause myself pain.

"I know you can, brave girl. But you shouldn't have to. I'll be your legs forever if you let me. I'll be your armor. Your fighter. Your protector. Watching you walk out the door took something from me. I don't understand why seeing you go hurt so badly, but it did. Worse than being shot. I won't let it happen again."

I soak in his words. *Truth.* His words are the truth.

He smiles, continuing to read my mind.

I don't ever have to worry about Enzo hurting me again. He won't, even in the game. I'm safe from his wrath.

Enzo carries me up to the bedroom where all the men have gathered. All of their concern is still etched on their faces.

I shake my head with a bashful grin as Enzo lays me down on the bed.

He sighs. "They just need to make sure you are okay. If you weren't, you can count on the fact Langston and Zeke would kill me themselves."

"You okay, stingray?" Zeke asks.

Stingray? I raise an eyebrow.

"Yea, it's your nickname now. We needed a code name for you during the mission. That's what I came up with. Because you pack a punch like stingrays, and you come from the sea."

I reach out, needing to squeeze Zeke's hand. He looks at it in fear.

"It's okay," I whisper. We both need the touch. He finally walks to the bed and takes it, and then I pull him to me so he can hug me. The familiar jolt of energy shoots through me at the touch, but I don't focus on it. I focus on this man who cares about me. Something I don't think I've ever experienced. My own father didn't even care about me.

When Zeke releases me, I look to Langston. I tell him to come here with my eyes. He does and hugs me the same way Zeke did. Two men that care about me. *How did I get so lucky?*

And then I see Enzo. His look is both similar and different from Langston and Zeke's. He cares, but there is something else there I can't place.

Zeke and Langston leave, as Dr. Patten starts examining my wound one more time. He puts a dressing over it and gives me a bottle of painkillers to take. He reminds me to take it easy for a day or two, but I should heal easily. The stitches can come out in two weeks.

And then it's Enzo and me alone in the bedroom we share. And as much as I'm trapped, I don't feel that way—I'm home.

Fuck, it's messed up that the only place I've ever considered home is this house.

Enzo sits on the edge of the bed while I study him. He's lost in thought. His brow has deepened, and the lines near his eyes have creased. I'm sure he's thinking about how to keep me safe from Milo.

Milo will be coming. But it will take some time for him to realize Enzo has me, and not his other enemies. We are safe enough for now.

Right now, I need something different. I know the doctor ordered rest, but I won't be able to rest until I get what I need.

I need to solidify Enzo's promise. I need to heal. And I need to know I will never be hurt by this man again.

Enzo reads my thoughts. He knows what I need. But I think he's going to fight me on it. I think he's going to say I need rest first. I need to sleep.

However, Enzo surprises me as usual.

"Punish me. It will make you feel better. And when it's done, I will spend the rest of my life earning every bit of your trust."

CHAPTER 6
ENZO

Kai needs rest. She needs to heal. She's been through hell today. She's barely recovered from her first encounter with Milo. He only cut her neck this time, but it's enough. Enough to bring back all the painful memories she experienced for years.

And it's all my fault.

I may have thought I was setting her free by selling her to Milo, but it was selfish. I knew even if she wanted to be with Milo that it would hurt her to be sold to another man. I knew by giving her to him, I would win Black. Milo would never let her leave his side long enough to come back and compete for this empire.

I thought it was the best solution. Instead of the nightmare it has become.

Kai needs to rest, but she needs revenge more. She needs to make me pay for the pain I've caused her.

I don't blame her. I know how it feels to feel helpless to the pain —to the anger. She needs me to suffer as she's suffering. When Zeke was hurt because of Kai, all I could do was get his revenge. I couldn't think—the pain clouded my head so deeply. And when I thought Kai had betrayed me by wanting Milo instead of me, all I saw was red.

Kai needs to punish me. She needs to let go of her anger. It's the only way we will ever have a shot at moving past this.

I stand up and meet Kai's gaze. Knowing in my heart we both need this more than we need air right now.

"What do you need?"

Her face scrunches in confusion. "What do you mean?"

"A whip? A knife? Chains? A gun? What?"

Please, anything but a gun. I vowed I would never let anyone shoot me again without fighting back. And I would have to break that promise to myself.

Kai studies me for a moment, as if trying to determine which method of torture she should use.

She shakes her head and pats the empty space on the bed beside her.

"You sure?" I ask.

She nods.

Fuck.

Somehow not using any weapons seems scarier than using one. I think back to the last time she hurt me with her body—forcing me to take something from her so savagely. I won't let that happen again.

I slowly walk around the side of the bed and lie down next to her, my hands folded over my chest, staring up at the ceiling.

I'm not used to following orders. But today, I will do anything she asks, including slitting my own throat if that's what she needs.

I wait.

But she doesn't speak. She doesn't move.

The waiting stretches, driving me mad with what she could be thinking. But I don't dare open my mouth. I don't ask her to move things along faster. This is about her.

Healing her.

Letting go of her pain.

And living through the anger.

I want to close my eyes to shut out the silence, but I don't even allow myself to do that.

I wait.

I suffer.

And then I wait some more.

Finally, I feel her cold fingers brush against mine.

I turn my head to face her. But I don't see the look of wrath I was expecting.

I see fear.

"Kai? Did something happen? Are you okay?" I ask, suddenly worried. I try to roll to her, to understand what's happening.

She puts a hand up, pressing against my chest, stopping me from touching her.

The cold chill shoots through me. I shudder at how cold I feel. Usually, the cold settles my heat, calming me and making me feel whole. But this time, it empties me.

Kai looks at me unblinking. And that's when I realize what's happening. She won't punish me with whips or beatings. She will punish me by showing me everything she's feeling and everything she's ever felt.

I will feel all of her pain. It will be impossible for me not to. The connection we share is too deep not to. I won't be able to shut it out like she does. And I'll never forget the pain.

The torment she has gone through.

Kai releases my hand and then moves her fingers to her neck where the doctor put the dressing. She removes the dressing. And I truly stare at the fresh wound for the first time. I could hardly look at it in the car except to ensure she was still alive.

She takes my hand again and moves it toward her neck.

"No," I say, not wanting to hurt her or disturb the stitches. Like my touch might infect the wound in some way.

She holds my gaze, and her lips tighten. I know she won't let me get away with not doing this. She carefully places my hand over the wound.

It's hot as fire. The only part of her body that isn't cold. And I can't imagine what that feels like to her. Not only does her neck hurt, but it feels like she was branded with sizzling flames.

I close my eyes, and I can feel the sharp blade pressing against her skin. I feel the searing blood warming her much cooler skin. I feel the terror pulsing through her veins as blood spills and knowing the only way to stop it was to shut herself down. Knowing every time she shuts down, it takes a mountain of pain to reenter the world again.

She holds in her tears, but I can't mine. I let a tear fall.

She growls at the sight of my weakness. And I suck the rest in. I pull my hand back, needing relief from the pain and loneliness.

No, she mouths—her face stern.

She grabs my hand again and traces the bruises on her face with my fingertips. The thin lines on her face that will continue to soften with time, but never disappear completely. Most of the scars aren't my fault. They are her father's for selling her the first time. But this is what would have happened again to her if I didn't stop Milo from taking her.

She lets go of my hand for a second and then removes her shirt, lifting it up over her head.

I wince at the discoloration of her skin. Purples, blues, and yellows cover her body, in much the same way her skin was when she first arrived.

I should kill Milo for what he did to her—I will kill him.

She takes my hand and moves my fingers over her broken and beaten skin. And with each touch, it's like a knife is being shoved into my own flesh. I can't imagine the amount of suffering she endured. I've lived with her for months now. But this, knowing I almost sent her to endure this again, it's too much.

Tears fall as I feel everything and realize how much it would break me to see her suffer for even a second.

I feel the cold.

I feel the pain.

I feel the loneliness.

"Here," she moves my hand over her shoulder to a mark I know. A similar mark to several I wear at the hands of my father.

"Here I was shot because I wouldn't willingly suck Jarod's cock. I bled for days. The wound became infected. I became delirious, sick with fever."

I relive my own bullet wound. I know the pain. I remember the blood that never seemed to stop pouring out of me until I was too weak to stand. And she's suffered worse.

"Here." She moves my hand to her ribcage. "Milo beat me until it burned to breathe. He broke ribs that have been broken numerous times before."

Jesus.

She sucks in a breath, and I can see the pain. Not from the wound on her neck. But I see how her lungs move cautiously, never pulling in a full breath of oxygen to avoid expanding her lungs as little as possible.

"The worst was here." She forces my hand down to her lower abdomen. "I was stabbed here so many times. The pain always made me wretch. But worst of all, I faced the fact that I couldn't help but thinking each stab was going into my ovaries, my uterus. I might not be able to ever have kids because of these stabs." A tiny sob escapes. "But at the same time, I begged for them to keep stabbing, because I never wanted the ability to have kids and bring a child into such a cruel world."

She rips my hand from her body.

"You may have fixed your error, but it doesn't mean I can ever forget what happened."

She shoves me back against the bed, and then her body is straddling mine. She's reaching back, and I know instinctively what she is reaching for.

She doesn't need it. I will say and do whatever she wants, but she needs to feel the power of holding the sharp metal in her hand.

Kai grabs the knife from my ankle and then presses it hard against my neck.

Adrenaline drills through my body in spades. Not because I truly fear for my life, I know Kai won't kill me even if I deserve it, but my body reactions to the threat all the same. I grip the sheets to force myself from retaliating. It takes all of my restraint to keep myself planted on the bed instead of disarming her.

Her eyes engulf me, and a sly smile curls on her lips.

"Why?" she asks.

"You already know why," I breathe, careful not to move my throat much to prevent the knife from dragging deeper into my neck.

"I know why, but do you? You say you sold me because I betrayed you, but that's not the truth. Tell me the truth."

"It is the truth."

"No, I don't owe you my loyalty. We are enemies. We are playing a game that generations of our families have played before. You own me. It shouldn't have mattered to you that I slept with another man to win the game. It wouldn't have been a betrayal."

My nostrils flare, and I see red as I think about her with another man.

"You're mine," I curse, rolling us over so I'm on top. The knife is still pressed to my neck, but it doesn't matter. It doesn't matter who is in control anymore. It matters she realizes that even though we are enemies, she is still fucking mine.

She glares like a dragon breathing fire at me. "I'm not yours, not in the way you want."

I lower my mouth, hovering over her tender pink lips. She keeps the knife pressing against my carotid artery, like that is going to keep me from claiming her.

"Admit it," she raises her eyebrows, her confidence never as great as it is in this moment.

"No."

I feel the warm blood draining from my neck, but I know it's nothing more than a nick. She doesn't want me to bleed, at least not from my neck. She wants me to bleed from my heart. But she forgets I don't have a heart. I'm incapable of feeling anything.

Yes, I want to protect her, but in the same way I want to protect my favorite car from getting stolen. She belongs to me, not anyone else. That's all this is.

"You have a heart." Kai trails the blade down my neck, over my shirt, to my chest. She stops it over my heart.

"My heart hardened, years ago. You learned to shut down to survive; I learned to shut off my feelings."

"And you brought me back from my darkest cavern. I was trapped inside the darkness, and you showed me how to live in the light. You may have shut off your heart to protect it, but it's starting to thaw."

"You can't thaw it. You're made of ice."

"And you're fire, but it's going to take more than fire to free your heart."

"I don't want it freed."

She grits her teeth as she pushes the knife harder against my chest until I can feel the metal against my skin. Until I feel the pierce of the blade over my heart. All I have to do to get the pain to stop is lean back, but it would mean removing myself from Kai. I need to feel every inch of her. I want more, not less. I want to shove my tongue so deep into her throat that I taste all of her. I want to nibble and attack her precious neck so the long cut on her neck is nothing in comparison to the marks I leave. I want to spread her legs, throwing them over my head until her thighs are trying to suffocate me as I lick her into oblivion.

"Admit it, you care about me."

"Only as a man cares about his car."

"I'm not an object."

"No, you are the bane of my existence."

"Admit it, Black," Kai says. She never calls me Black. It would be admitting defeat. That I'm the true ruler.

"Not until you admit you like being trapped here. You like my protection."

She pants against my lips. If she wants me to admit I want her, then she has to admit she wants me. That she doesn't feel like a prisoner. That she wants to be here.

We both lock in our determination to not admit defeat. Because that is what it would feel like: *defeat*. We are both too strong to ever develop any sort of feelings toward each other.

"I've already thawed as much of your heart as I'm going to without your help. It's your move Black," Kai says.

I lean down and finally taste the lips of the woman I've claimed, stolen, sold, broke, healed, and cried over. Somehow the tears I shed before is what breaks through all the rest for me. I don't cry. *Ever.*

Not since I was a boy. And then when I'm around Kai, I cry all the time for her. It's just because her life is so tragic.

"You care about me. Truth or lie?" Kai says.

"Truth," I breathe, as I brush our lips together again, my salty fire mixing with her sweet cold.

"You like me. Truth or lie?"

"Truth."

I dip my tongue between her parted lips and both our bodies ease. Her muscles melt against the kiss.

"You like being mine. Truth or lie?" I say.

"Truth," she whispers, pulling my bottom lip into her mouth.

She drops the knife, and I push it off the bed, as I tangle my body with hers. I taste her deeply, our teeth clash, and our temperatures slam together, as we stop fighting with our words and instead fight with our tongues.

Kai grips my shirt, thrusting it up my body over my six pack and then jerks it forcefully from my body. I lay my body on top of her, melting her exterior. But I want more than just the surface. I want all of her. Kai's right, I want as deep as it gets when it comes to her. I just don't think I can give anything in return. But I want her to depend on me, beg for me, live for me.

We shouldn't be making out right now. We are both too angry. In too much pain for this to be the logical next step. Kai should be healing, and I should be finding a way to keep Milo from figuring out I have Kai.

Instead, we devour each other. I'm not careful with her like I should be. She's bruised and physically broken, but fierceness inside her has only grown stronger. It's the main reason why I like her as Kai says I do.

And the way she's biting as much as she's kissing me, I know she doesn't want this easy and gentle. She wants me to push her, show her how desperate I am for her. That was her plan all along, and I fell for it. She may think she tricked me as she did before, but it's not tricking if I'm doing it willingly.

"Does it hurt?" she asks as she kisses my neck where she spilled some of my blood.

"No."

She shakes her head as she bites over my chest and to my heart.

"That's not what I mean."

I cock my head, but I don't want to know what she means. She's dangerous right now.

I grab her neck; she winces as I brush my hand over her wound. I push my hand back, fisting her hair as I claim her mouth. As long as I'm kissing her, she can't speak. She can't do any more damage. And neither can I because when we are together like this—our bodies mixing in a hurricane of temperatures and moans is when we are most right. It's where we are most meant to be.

I like Kai Miller.

I like the fucking.

I like how she makes me fight for her.

I like how nothing is easy, and yet everything is easy at the same time.

I like how it feels to have her in my arms. Her body temperature may be cooler than mine, but it doesn't feel that way to me. It feels like a breath of air when I touch her, grounding me, while also giving me wings to fly.

I hook my thumbs into her pants and pull them down. And then I drop my head between her legs. Her body instantly arches as I find her clit with my tongue. I growl, the vibration in my throat sending shockwaves through her body.

"Jesus, Black."

I tighten my grip on her clit with my teeth, applying just enough pressure to drive her mad. Good thing she doesn't still have the knife, or she'd use it to threaten me to stop teasing her.

"Yes," she moans.

God, I love her voice.

I flick my tongue over and over. I feel her hands grab my hair, but she doesn't get to touch. I grab her wrists and force them apart, glued to the bed.

All I want is for her to feel my tongue on her most sensitive of areas. For her to remember I'm the only man who has touched her here. The only man who gets to hear her cries as she comes.

"Wait...I want your cock," she pulls her hands, trying to loosen them from my grip.

I drive my tongue into her cunt, pulling her juices out and lapping over her clit.

"And you shall have it, but first. *This.* I want to feel your first explosion rattle the entire room."

Kai pants at my words, as if my words are causing the orgasm instead of my tongue. Faster I pull her under my spell. Taunting her, teasing her, until I finally give her the pressure she needs, and she finally gives me what I want—my name in as much of a prayer as a curse falling from her beautiful lips.

"Enzo!"

Her body shakes viciously, her thighs clench as I pull an orgasm from her body. But that was just to prepare her for round two. I might not deserve to sink my cock inside her, but it's not about deserving. It's about need. And we both need it more than we need blood to keep pumping in our veins.

I pull the condom from my pocket and barely get my pants down and the condom on before I explode like a teenage boy.

I grab her and roll her on top, so I don't completely crush her underneath me, and she continues to have some control.

She straddles me with flushed cheeks, and heavy eyes. She claws at my chest as I pull her down on top of my sheathed cock.

Each time we fuck I still can't believe how tight she is. But there is no pain on her face. I slide in easily from her slickness.

She rides me hard, and I'm sure the good doctor would yell at us both for this, but it's worth it. I'd gladly give her all my blood to keep her alive after this and die a happy man.

I thrust into her as she grinds on top of me, her clit angling toward my hard stomach.

I roll my head back for a second before reminding myself to focus on the beautiful woman humping me. Because someday, she won't be mine anymore.

Kai puts her hand over my heart as we pump harder.

"Here, it hurts here," she says.

My eyes are defiant, but there is no use in hiding it. "Just fuck me, beautiful."

She leans down, still riding me but at a slower pace as our foreheads touch.

"You love me. Truth or lies?" this sentence comes out as question more than any of her previous ones. This one she doesn't know the answer to before she asks it. She knows I care about her. I even like her. But love, that's on a whole different level.

"I love it when you scream my name when you come," I wink at her. Thrusting again to try to get us off this topic. But she's determined. She wants a real answer.

"That's not what I mean. Do you love me? Do you have a heart? Are you capable of loving?" she presses against my heart with her palm.

"Do you love me?" I ask.

"Can a slave ever love her master?" she says back.

"Can a predator ever love his prey?" I snap back.

Her face grows determined. She wants me to admit weakness. Admit I love her when she could never love me in return.

"I'm not capable of love, Kai. We are fucking, nothing more. I care about you sure. I want to protect you and keep you alive because I want to protect the broken. But when this is over, when one of us is declared Black, this is over. You want to be free; I'll find a way to make it happen the second this twisted game is through."

"You're too evil for love, and I'm too broken." She smiles sadly. "Just making sure before you start proposing to me for real."

I chuckle and kiss her lips. "You don't have to worry about that. This is the best we will ever have, with anyone. Neither of us can love. Neither wants to get married. Neither wants to start a family. But this connection we have. It's special. And it's real. And it can be the best damn thing we have. Because not being capable of falling in love is the best damn gift either of us has ever received."

She nods. "Fuck me and remind me what I have instead of what I'm giving up."

So I do. I fuck her hard, quickly moving back into our rhythm together. Our blood pumps, and it might as well be flowing through me to her as in sync we both are together.

I drive in harder.

"You like that, baby?"

"Fuck, yes."

"You have nothing to fear. You're safe—always."

I fuck her harder. Deeper. Longer. Until I know we are both going to spend the next few hours passed out in the bed from a sex coma instead of what I need to be doing—finding a way to protect her.

She screams and pants her orgasm out until her screams turn into silent pleas. A single tear rolls down her cheek.

I kiss it away, hoping with its removal so too am I removing her pain and her anger. I know we aren't capable of forgiveness any more than we are capable of love. But we are capable of moving forward no matter what. We are survivors.

We collapse on the bed next to each other. We both pant hard, and I'm too tired to get up to even remove the condom.

We both close our eyes as sleep begins to come for us. But not before I realize what I have to do to keep her safe. And she isn't going to like it.

CHAPTER 7
KAI

I love Enzo Black.

I love him.

I shouldn't. It should be the last feeling I ever feel. But I do. I love him. I thought I was too broken for love. I thought I was undeserving. But nobody told my heart any of those things.

Enzo is cruel. He's dangerous. He's evil.

He sold me, but not out of malice, but because he loves me too, and it hurt him too much to imagine me with another man. It hurt so fucking much he had to get rid of me. He needed me gone in order to survive.

But he's so broken he will never admit he's capable of love.

Love is weak.

Love is fear.

Love is dangerous.

I understand, it's how I feel. I've never felt so vulnerable as I do now—loving him.

I didn't want to admit it to myself. He's evil incarnate. But it doesn't matter. Because he's my evil, and I'm his broken.

And I'm completely fucked. Because as much as I love Enzo, he will never admit his love back. He will never show his love beyond protecting me, beyond claiming me as his.

I thought that could be enough, being his. But my heart is already pierced by his confession. He doesn't love me. He's willing to give me up when this is over.

Enzo deserves to be Black. I already think of him as Black. But I will fight every day to prolong the game as long as possible. Because the longer the game lasts, the longer I get Enzo. And I need him, forever.

I need him to love me like I love him.

I'm only just learning what love means. It's the first time, I've admitted it to myself. I thought I wasn't capable of love. But maybe because I'm not capable of loving someone who isn't broken. And Enzo is as broken as it comes. His life has been just as tortuous as mine.

I should end it. Give him peace. Let him win what he deserves. I spent six years being tortured. He's spent his entire life. But I'm selfish. I want him. I love him. And if I only get a few more months to love him, then so be it. I'll take it. I just won't ever admit it. Because admitting my feelings out loud would hurt worse than keeping them inside.

I've forgiven him for hurting me, which only verifies my feelings for him. Only my love for him could allow me to forgive him for the sins he's committed against me. And these feelings are going to screw me over more than anything else.

I've been tortured, abused, shot, but I've never had a broken heart. Never had love ripped from me. And I know that's where our journey ends. With my heart bleeding for him.

Enzo stirs. His body is draped over me, warming me more than any blanket or heater ever could. I never liked fire, never liked being hot living in the Miami sun, but with Enzo I welcome it.

He smiles at me.

"You're sticky," I say with a smile. The condom fell off sometime while we were sleeping and his cum now sticks to my thigh.

"You complaining?"

I stretch. "I guess not." I smile wider. I'll never complain as long as I keep getting sex like that. It wasn't my intention when we started. I just wanted him to understand how serious this is to me. This isn't a game. This is my life.

But then I made the mistake of touching him, and that lit a flame neither of us knows how to extinguish.

"Shower with me," he commands instead of asking.

He rolls off me, and the bed dips as he stands up.

I nod and slowly follow. Apparently being in love means I don't mind when he gives me orders. Am I doomed to spend the rest of my time with him meek and weak, merely following orders like a lovesick puppy?

Yes, and I'll be all too happy to do it.

I watch Enzo walk; his tight ass is too hard not to watch as we enter his ginormous bathroom. He starts the shower before tossing the condom in the trash bin.

His eyes are fixed on me, and he stops me to examine my neck wound.

"Does it hurt?" he asks.

I shake my head. Of course it hurts, but it's nothing compared to what I know I will feel when we are over.

He frowns. He knows I'm lying. He drops his hand and disappears into the bedroom, reappearing with two pills and a bottle of water. I take the pills without arguing and then take a sip of water to wash them down.

He nods, satisfied.

And then we step into the shower, neither of us keeping our eyes off each other. We stand close together but don't touch. If he moves, I move, like a dance we orchestrated, instead of a stalemate.

"What are you doing?" I ask, as the water beads down on us.

"Watching you."

I shake my head. "No, you are trying to hide your plan. I think you've kept enough secrets from me. Tell me the plan."

"I don't have a plan."

"Liar."

He sighs. "Can't we just enjoy a shower together?"

"No, because it gives you time to figure out how to hide the truth from me."

He rubs his hands through my hair, washing the long strands, stalling even though it feels nice.

"Enzo..."

"I have a plan, but you are going to hate it."

I suck in a breath, already suspecting what his plan is, but he needs to say it.

"Try me."

"Milo doesn't know I have you, and until I figure out how to deal with him, I think it's best if we keep the fact you are here hidden. I know you won't like that. You are half owner of the Black empire. You have every right to show up at Surrender same as me. But that's why I think it's best that neither of us goes near Surrender for a while. We can run the business from elsewhere. I can show you more of the ropes of how to run things."

"You mean you want to leave on one of the yachts," I say flatly, saying what he's been avoiding this entire time.

"Yes."

CHAPTER 8
ENZO

Kai didn't fight me on my plan to board a yacht and sail until Milo is either dead or we have a plan to ensure he will never touch us.

I expected a fight.

I expected a battle.

I expected to have to throw her ass over my shoulder with her kicking and cursing to get her onto a yacht, knowing I can't guarantee when we will touch land again.

I love the sea, so it's no problem to spend years at a time on the ocean. But for Kai, living on the sea is her biggest nightmare.

But she didn't fight me, maybe because she thought it was inevitable. Or maybe because something changed. Being around her feels different. She should be steaming still after what I did. It was unforgivable. I was an idiot. And I know I haven't done enough to make up for it. But she's tolerating me.

More than tolerating me. She beams when I'm around her, and follows my order without argument. I want to ask what's going on, but I don't dare. I need her to do exactly as I say, at least until I get her on that yacht.

I left Kai in the bedroom and sent Westcott to purchase any

items she will need and pack up the rest of what she has because I don't know when we will hit land again.

"What's the plan?" Langston asks, his arms crossed as I enter my office. Both him and Zeke continue to scowl at me, and I don't think they will ever stop after what I did to Kai.

"I'll tell you when you wipe that scowl from your face," I answer, as I collapse into my chair behind my desk.

Langston growls. "Not going to happen. Kai is now a member of this family. You decided that the day you brought her here. And yes, she may have fucked up. But you fucked up worse. She's earned my forgiveness; you haven't yet. So I will keep being pissed as long as I want."

I grin at his loyalty to this family. I truly wish Kai was a part of the family as Langston says. It would be nice to have a girl around. She's not though, and can never be. Because as long as I'm Black, she can never join the family, it's too dangerous. And if she were to ever become Black, she would be in constant danger. Not going to happen.

"Glad to know where your loyalties lie, Langston," I say with a huff. I look at Zeke who is crossing his arms smirking down at me. His muscles are twice the size of mine, which should intimidate me —it doesn't. I know behind the muscles is a big softy who cares about me more than he cares about hurting me.

"The plan is we are all getting on the Savage and getting lost in the middle of fucking nowhere, until Rowan takes out Milo or I find a way to kill him myself. In the meantime, we will run the empire and continue the game at sea. I need you both to make the necessary arrangements to get the Savage prepared and ready to go with a full crew in the next hour. Westcott is helping Kai pack. And I need to make a phone call to Liesel."

"Liesel?" Zeke cocks his head. He's always hated her even though he would never say it to my face.

"Yes, Milo knows about Liesel remember? I took her as my date to Milo's party. It isn't safe for Liesel if she stays here. He could kidnap her and interrogate her to get answers about us. She needs to come with us."

Zeke raises an eyebrow. "That woman isn't going to drop her high paying job and come ride around on a yacht all for an unknown amount of time. Not without payment in return."

I know exactly the kind of payment Zeke in insinuating with his comment.

"Liesel isn't like that," I roll my eyes at him. And even if she is, Liesel means too much to me to just leave behind. Even if it will complicate things a bit.

"Whatever you say." Zeke and Langston exchange knowing glances.

"Just get the yacht ready—one hour," I say sternly as both men walk out of my office.

And then I take out my phone and scroll to the number listed as *"My Everything."*

I really should change that, but she's still my everything. I would never let anyone hurt Liesel. I would fight to the death for her. Kill for her. I have killed for her. Too many times to count.

And she's finally living the life she deserves. She's happy. I don't want to take that away from her. Even if it's to keep her safe. But she doesn't exactly have a choice.

I sigh. I convinced Kai with only a sentence, maybe Liesel will be just as easy.

"Hello, handsome. Didn't get enough at me at the party, huh?" Liesel says seductively into the phone.

I smile. I know she's just teasing. We've dated in the past, but we quickly realized we were better suited as friends than as lovers.

"I need you to do a favor for me," I say, deciding that is the best angle to play with Liesel.

"I already did a favor for you, handsome. I think it's time you do a favor for me. And I know exactly how I want you to repay me. I remember your tongue being especially skilled in the art of licking."

"I have a—" *Wait, was I about to call Kai my girlfriend?* She's anything but. She's my captive for goodness sakes. But it doesn't change how I feel. I don't want to fuck Liesel or any woman other than Kai.

"It's not going to happen, Liesel. You're going to have to figure out a different way for me to repay you, but right now I need to ask another favor."

She practically grins through the phone, but I don't know why. "You like the whore, don't you?"

"She's. Not. A. Whore." If one more person calls Kai a whore, I'm going to turn barbaric. I don't care who it is.

Liesel purrs into the phone. "That's too bad. I would have loved to get into her panties like we used to. Our three-ways were some of my favorite nights with you." She's trying to get me riled up and turned on at the thought of having two women in my bed. Two women that both mean something to me—Liesel and Kai. When Liesel and I were dating, we would try all sorts of crazy things in bed. Threesomes, tying each other up, whips, dildos, every toy imaginable. But I can't imagine needing any of those things with Kai. With Kai, it's different. I don't need all the flashy toys, and I sure as hell am not going to share Kai with Liesel.

I ignore Liesel's last comment.

"I need you to a pack a bag."

"Oh, so this is an overnight booty call."

Ignore her, I tell my temper. I'm trying to save this woman and everyone I care about at the moment, and she is trying to goad me.

"Pack a bag with everything you could possibly need for months. I'll have Langston pick you up within the hour. We are all getting on the Savage, and I don't know when we will make port again."

Silence. For a woman that always has words to say and never shuts up, it's unusual to hear silence.

"Did you hear me, Liesel?"

"Yes," she finally says. "What happened?"

"I don't have time to explain everything, but Milo Wallace happened. I fucked up and betrayed him, and now he will be hunting me and everyone he knows I have a connection with. He'll kill you if he finds you to try and get information on me and to retrieve what he bought from me. So you are going to get your ass on my yacht in the next hour because I don't want to have to worry about your safety. I don't care how many clients are expecting your law skills. You can work from the yacht."

Another pause. *Fucking Liesel, this isn't the time to get silent on me.*

"What did he buy from you?" her voice is soft and quiet as she speaks, and I suspect she already knows the answer.

"Kai, he bought Kai."

More silence, and I know she's judging me. Not for selling Kai to Milo, but for stealing her back. Liesel has always wanted me to be stronger. To stick to my decisions and not look weak. Stealing Kai back, Liesel would see as a weakness.

"Thirty-minutes, Liesel. Langston will be there in thirty minutes." I hang up the phone without waiting for her to confirm she is coming. She will come, if Langston has to drag her ass onto my yacht. I don't care. I'm not leaving her behind for Milo to find.

♡

WESTCOTT DRIVES KAI AND ME TO THE PIER TO GET ON THE Savage, my favorite yacht out of the fleet of yachts I own.

I hold Kai's hand the entire time, but I've been on the phone most of the drive dealing with the logistics of getting everyone that matters onto the yacht as quickly as possible, while also ensuring Surrender and the rest of my businesses are running smoothly. But when we pull up in front of the yacht, I drop the call with Langston. He can figure out what needs to be done; Kai is my entire focus.

"Are you okay, baby?"

Kai doesn't react to me calling her baby. It feels natural falling from my lips. As does every other term of endearment I can think of.

Kai's chest rises and falls slowly, as she forces herself to take a deep breath. The sun reflects off her light olive skin and jet black hair. She tucks her long wavy hair behind her ear and shivers in her pale yellow sundress. She needs a jacket, but I'd rather be the one providing her all her warmth.

I scoot closer and put my arms around her shoulders. She leans back into me, accepting my offer to warm up her body.

"You ready for this? If there were any other way, I would do it," I say.

She shakes her head. "No, you wouldn't. There is another way. We stay and fight instead of running. But it's not about if we should stay and fight or if we should run and hide. You think I need this in order to fully heal. In order to be able to let me go, you need to know that I'm whole. I will never be whole; I can't be. Not anymore. But thank you for trying."

I cup her chin, not accepting she is anything less than whole. Sure, she has more healing she needs to do, but that doesn't change that I think she's pretty amazing as she is.

My lips come down hungrily on hers, determined to wipe away any thoughts that she is less than. I tease her tongue with mine, and suck the oxygen from her lungs, making her feel like enough while also distracting her from what she is going to have to do. Step onto a yacht and not know when it will return to shore—her nightmare.

I want her panties soaked; I want her begging, dying to come before she has to step foot on the yacht. I want her focused on me and my cock—nothing else will be able to distract her.

I hear Westcott step out of the car, giving us at least the illusion of privacy, and then I make my move. I grab her bare thighs, and slide my hand upward, gliding my hand along her shimmering skin.

I move to pull her panties down, when I find none. She's bare.

So. Fucking. Hot.

I want to fuck her right here on the backseat of the Porsche Cayenne. *Thank God, I have great self-control.* Otherwise, I would. And then she'd be spent, but not necessarily distracted.

Focus. You'll have your chance to have her, just wait.

Good thing I believe in delayed gratification.

Kai arches as my fingers dip between her thighs. Her mouth opens wide in a cry, unable to focus on kissing me when I'm teasing her so tortuously.

"Please, yes," Kai moans.

I kiss her neck, careful not to touch the area that has been recovered with a bandage. And I swear I feel every nerve ending in her body switch on like a light switch. I feel the surge of energy swirling and begging to be set free.

Not yet, my beauty. Not yet.

My hand is soaked with her sweet juices as I taunt her clit with my fingers. I slip one inside to feel just how wet. And I know she is seconds away from squeezing my finger as her orgasm pulses around me. When she is one second away, I stop.

Her head whips to me. "Why did you stop?"

I kiss her plump and swollen lips. "Because I want you thinking about me all damn day. Don't you dare touch yourself. I want to know I can make you come whenever I want with just a touch."

I remove my hand from her dress.

"I'm going to be dripping all day," she huffs.

"Yes, and I'll love it." I lick each of my fingers slowly, torturing both her and myself as I do. *You are doing this for her, to keep her from panicking,* I remind myself as my dick hardens painfully in my jeans.

Fuck, why do I have to be such a martyr sometimes?

I open my door, grab her hand again, and jerk her outside of the car.

She takes a deep breath as she stares up at the massive piece of metal looming over every other boat in the harbor. We can't stand out here for very long. I don't want anyone to spot her that isn't a part of the crew. But I know this is a big moment for her. And I'm not going to take that from her like I've taken everything else.

I hold her against me tightly while my men continue to load up the yacht with supplies.

I don't ask her if she's ready again. She never will be, not truly. It's like jumping into the ocean when you know it's still too cold to swim in, you just have to do it and know you'll survive long enough to find the beauty in it.

I start walking, and she walks with me. There is a ramp, but I'm feeling nostalgic, and I'm hoping it will keep her mind fighting me instead of the trepidation of the boat.

I give her a wink as I release her, and then I jump up onto the main deck. It's a big jump, and the consequences of missing mean I'll take a dip into the ocean water below. But I've done it countless times. I never miss.

I turn to Kai still standing on the deck below. "Your turn," I shout.

It's a risky move. She could take the moment to run away; I

already know she doesn't want to do this. But I would chase her down and catch her within seconds.

Her eyes twinkle at the challenge. If we are anything, we are relentless against challenges.

She takes a step back, and I think I was wrong. She's not going to do this. Then she takes a running leap, flying through the air as she sucks all the evil in my life away in a second, before landing firmly on the deck.

She winks back at me. We exchange knowing glances, both remembering the last time we boarded a yacht together all those years ago. And even though it ended in disaster, the moments we stole on that yacht together were something I wouldn't give up for anything.

Our fingers intertwine together as I hear Liesel's voice.

"Am I going to have to pull my luggage up the ramp myself, Black?" Liesel asks.

I smile at her sassiness as I stare down to the deck at her. *She came.* Everyone I care about will be safe. I'll ensure that.

"Zeke and Langston will help you," I say noticing both men hurrying down to collect Liesel's many bags.

I had to practically force Kai to pack an entire bag worth of clothes. She knew we could be gone for months, but she didn't see the need to pack more than a week's worth of clothing. She said she could do laundry. But Liesel, on the other hand, packed her entire life.

It's just another way the two women are so completely different. But they share one thing, I will protect both to the end of my days.

"What is she doing here?" Kai asks.

"Liesel isn't safe from Milo, not after I brought her as my date to his party. I'm making sure everyone on board is safe. Her included," I say.

I feel the tension oozing out of Kai. Her body stiffens, her face pales, and she's no longer thinking about the ache between her legs.

"Are you jealous?" I ask.

"No."

I laugh, because she obviously is.

I lean down and lick around her ear, slowly and seductively. "Don't worry, baby. You are the only one who will be screaming my name later tonight."

I pull away, and her cheeks have flushed as she bites that gorgeous lip I want to taste again.

Mission accomplished.

"Let me introduce you to everyone, and then I'll give you a tour of the boat before we leave." I tighten my grip on her hand as I lead her to where the crew is boarding.

"This is Aidan, the captain. James, Pedro, and Scotty," I say.

"Everyone, this is Kai," I say, not adding her last name. No one needs to know she's a Miller, or pretending to be my spouse, or any other details.

"You will take orders from Kai the same way you would me. She's not just my guest; she's my equal."

Kai smiles at me when I speak. I promised her I'd give her as much freedom as I can while she's still mine, and I plan on keeping my promise.

"And this is my childhood friend, Liesel Dunn. Liesel, this is Kai. I know you two have already met under very different circumstances, but I think you both can become good friends if you want to be."

Liesel holds out her hand to Kai to shake it. Liesel knows exactly what she's doing. She knows Kai doesn't like to be touched.

I frown at Liesel as I pull Kai closer to me, letting Kai know she doesn't need to shake Liesel's hand. She doesn't need to touch anyone while she's here. I will take care of all of Kai's needs.

"Langston can show you which room you'll be staying in, Liesel," I say.

Liesel smiles, cocking her head to the side as she looks to Kai. "We aren't sharing a room? I guess it might get a little crowded if we did."

"Liesel," I threaten with just the one word, and she stops.

Langston scowls at Liesel as well as he grabs her shit and leads her down the where her bedroom is.

I notice Kai out of the corner of my eye giving Liesel a dirty look.

And then suddenly, Kai isn't by my side anymore. She grabs Liesel's hat that has blown off her head and races to her.

I should intervene. This could get ugly. Kai will have no problem punching Liesel, and if Liesel is threatened, she will fight back. These two women have to share the yacht, which is large, but not large enough for these two to never have to interact with each other. But I don't make it in time.

Kai cocks her head at Liesel as she hands the hat to her. "You dropped this. And I wouldn't want you to mistake that I steal things that aren't mine. I don't." Kai's eyes say more. Enzo is mine. And I didn't steal him. He was free for the taking.

That's my girl.

Liesel retaliates by grabbing hold of Kai's hand as she takes the hat back.

Kai just cocks her head and smiles lazily, but I know the touch is killing her. Liesel lets go with a smug smile, but Kai slaps her a little too hard on the back showing she can tolerate touch just fine, especially when she's the one giving it.

"It's good to see you again, Liesel. You look pretty tired though; you should make sure you get some good rest tonight. And make sure Langston doesn't put you in a bedroom near ours. We won't be sleeping much," Kai says, strutting back to me.

Liesel frowns but doesn't say anything as she follows Langston.

"Savage," I say.

Kai shrugs. "Are you ever going to tell me the whole story about Liesel?"

I open my eyes wider. "Do you want me to?"

"Maybe. Not right now."

"Should I give you that tour then?"

She bites her lip again, and I know what she's thinking as her eyelids grow heavy with lust. "Honestly, I just want to explore your body."

I laugh.

"Captain says we are ready to depart," Zeke says interrupting our exchange.

I feel Kai's heartbeat stop next to me. She doesn't breathe; she's a statue next to me.

Don't block this out. Don't block me out.

I pull Kai into me, hoping my arms will warm her enough to bring her back to life.

"Tell him to depart," I say.

Zeke's worried stare moves to Kai. "Is she going to be—"

"She's fine."

Zeke pouts, but does as I say and heads to the bridge to tell the captain it's time for us to leave.

"Kai?"

Nothing.

Fuck.

The tour will have to wait until later. Right now, Kai needs me to bring her back to life. And that's exactly what I plan on doing.

CHAPTER 9

KAI

Dammit, the second Zeke mentions we're leaving I close up. It happens automatically, as it almost always does. And then I'm pushing everyone out, Enzo included.

No, no, no!

I'm stronger than this. I fought to be better than this. I'm not going to let this happen—not again.

I am fucking healed.

I will not give in to the fear.

Jarod doesn't get to win.

Milo doesn't get to win.

The memories don't get to win.

I win.

Enzo scoops up my legs in his arms, and I win the first battle of pushing the cold shield down.

"I'm okay," I say.

Enzo smiles, but it's fake. I know he's worried about me. "I know you are. I know you can take care of yourself. You can heal yourself, but this is all my fault. We wouldn't be running if it wasn't for me."

"It is your fault," I say with a teasing smile.

"I know, so let me fix it," his eyes grow dark, and I know what that means. The tour of the yacht will wait till later.

His lips lean down, and he kisses me softly, barely touching me. But it's enough to spark alive the feelings of torture he provoked before. It warms my core and drenches my thighs, all from the lightest touch of his lips.

He's my anchor—the thing keeping me present instead of drifting away into oblivion.

Even when he fucks up, it still makes me want him. It still keeps me anchored to the moment. He keeps me feeling everything.

"You aren't going to give me a tour?" I ask, even though I already know the answer, I just want him to confirm it as he continues to carry me through a door.

"Nope. The only thing I'm giving you a tour of is my body."

I grab his neck and pull his head back down to my face so I can keep kissing him. I don't care if he can't see where he's going while he carries me, I need the distraction.

We stop outside another door.

"You have to stop kissing me for a second, baby," Enzo purrs.

"Why, when you like it so much?" I ask back, still kissing him.

"Because I'll fuck you right here in the hallway if you don't let me open the door."

"You don't need your lips to open the door."

He chuckles as I push my tongue deeper into his mouth.

"Just my eyes," he says, wiggling his eyebrows.

I stop and watch as the system uses facial recognition, a code, and his fingerprint to get through the door.

I must be gaping because Enzo says, "Don't worry, I'll make sure you know all the codes and the system recognizes you to get to my private bedrooms."

I raise an eyebrow. "Paranoid much?"

"I'm in the security business. Securing yachts is my favorite part. No one will touch you here. Milo will never be able to get to you."

If I was worried before, I'm not now. The way Enzo speaks with such intensity, I know he would take a bullet before he let someone touch me.

"Does every room have this level of security?" I ask.

"No, just yours and mine."

"I like the sound of that."

"The sound of what?"

"You and me."

He grins as he carries me into the room at the end of the hallway. I expected a tiny room with a modest bed; we are after all on a yacht. But this room rivals the one in his beach house mansion.

"Seriously? How is this room so big?"

"The same way everything else about me is big," he wags his eyebrows.

I laugh. I could get used to playful Enzo. I know he's just teasing to keep me distracted from the fact we are now moving. But I could tell the second the engines started. The familiar rock of the yacht starts immediately, and I know it will only get worse the further out to sea we go.

The bed is beautiful, made of light whites and gray linens. I expected it to feel darker in here, but instead, it's heavenly. I remember the cave of a room I stayed in for years; this is the opposite of that. The windows look out into the ocean, but the high ceiling and lights overhead make up for any darkness. I don't feel trapped so much as encased by beauty.

"Put me in the bed and fuck me," I tug on his bottom lip with my teeth.

"No."

I pout. "Why not?"

"Because I want to fuck you against this wall first."

He motions to the almost all glass wall that looks out to the ocean. He flicks a switch, and the wall lights up into beautiful shades of turquoise blue, making the ocean seem illuminated.

"Okay," I bite my lip, liking that idea of being fucked against the wall too much.

He grabs my bare ass under my dress and smirks. "Don't act like you don't like it. You already made it so accessible to reach my favorite parts of you."

His fingers dip between my legs for a split second before retreating back to my ass, leaving me on edge again.

"Enzo, that's not playing fair."

"I never play fair. But then you already know that."

"You're going to kill me tonight."

"And I'm going to love every torturous second of your slow death," he growls.

"Please, I need to come."

He grins. "Do you now?"

"Yes."

He gives me a mischievous grin and then lifts me up until my thighs rest on his shoulders, and my pussy is at his face.

I grab his head. "Oh my god!"

His tongue descends on my already sensitive bud, and I know I'm going to come so fucking hard on his face.

I dig my fingers into his thick hair, holding on tightly as he drives me wild with his tongue, dipping in and out of me before rubbing over my clit.

"Yes, yes, yes!"

He stops.

"Enzo," I growl. I need this. He doesn't get to stop.

I try pressing his head against my pussy, and he chuckles.

"Needy, are we?"

"Yes, please."

He tongue dips in again, swirling, tasting, taunting my lips until I'm going to come and nothing will stop me. He bites down on my clit, and everything stops again.

"No!"

"God, you are so sexy, woman. So goddamn sexy when you are so close and on the edge, but I won't let you come yet. Not until I'm the only thought in your head."

"You are."

He tsks. "I'm not, not yet. You are still thinking about the rocking of the boat. There is still chaos in your eyes. And the second you come, you will start closing the world out again."

"I won't."

"You will."

He licks again, and this time, I let go. I pant. I squirm. I writhe. But I don't shut out the world.

I'm present. I feel the rocking, and instead of shutting it out, I welcome it. I move my hips in rhythm with the boat, putting more pressure on my clit as I ride Enzo's face.

"That's my girl," Enzo moans into my pussy.

"God, I'm so close." And if he prevents me from coming again, it's him I'm going to kill.

"Come, Kai."

I do at the vibration of his words. I explode on his face. My cum is drenching his lips, and my cries are shaking the yacht until I'm sure everyone aboard can hear my screams.

I relax back against the glass wall, unable to catch my breath, and my heart hammering in my chest.

"I'm not done with you yet, beautiful."

"I don't know if I can handle any more. I've never had an orgasm so powerful as that one."

"It's because I denied you so many times. But you are about to have another one."

He slides me down the wall, and I wrap my legs around his waist as he gently tastes my lips.

I taste my cum on his face. I taste too sweet.

"Like how you taste?" he asks.

"Yes."

"Good girl."

He retrieves a condom while holding me up with his other hand. I undo his jeans and push his clothes off as his hard cock springs free, and suddenly I forget about the earth-shattering orgasm I had a moment before. I've never wanted his cock more.

"Hurry," I pant at the sight.

His eyes lust in a deep darkness of want. No man has ever looked at me like Enzo does. Nobody sees me for me. Nobody demands so much from me. Nobody loves me like him.

His sheaths his thick veiny cock with the condom and then thrusts fully into me in one long stroke.

"Fuck!" my nails dig into Enzo's shoulders until I'm sure I'm drawing blood. My mouth devours his as I continue to scream my pleasure into his mouth. My legs squeeze until I'm sure he has trouble breathing.

Enzo doesn't move once he's inside me. He waits for me to adjust to him. Adjust to taking all of him and it never being enough. I want more. I want his cock every damn day. And I want to be the one that claims the invisible ruthless Black's heart.

"You with me, baby?" he asks.

"Yes, I'm with you. Always."

His tongue slowly traces my swollen bottom lip, teasing me before dipping it into my mouth. I realize he's waiting to see if I'm still fully with him or if I've noticed the rocking of the ship has worsened as we've picked up speed.

"I'm here. I don't care about anything but this."

His eyes move back and forth, searching for the truth.

I smile. "I won't shut you out again. I'm here, truth or lies?"

He smiles. "Fucking truth."

And then he thrusts, fucking me like he's wanted to since we got in his car this morning.

His eyes lock on mine as he thrusts, both of us finding a rhythm together as we move in unison. His eyes tell me everything his mouth never will.

How beautiful he finds me.

How much he likes my fighting spirit.

How much he loves me.

Maybe I'm delusional. Maybe he doesn't love me. Maybe I'm so desperate to feel love I'm imagining it. But when I look into his dark eyes, I no longer see the monster who sold me. I see a broken man who needs saving and healing. I see a man who has dealt with too much pain. And I see a man who loves me.

I'VE NEVER SLEPT BETTER.

Never.

It shouldn't be possible for me to sleep so well on a boat, not after everything horrible in my life has always happened on a ship.

But with Enzo wrapped around my body so tightly, after the most incredible fuck of my life, how could I not sleep well?

Enzo rolls onto his back, and I stare at his naked body. I could get used to this forever. I would even take the running and hiding from our enemies.

This can't last.

Enzo said so himself. We have an expiration date. As soon as the five games are over, then we are over. Black will become the king he was always meant to be and I'll...

I don't know what I'll do. I have no education. No career aspirations. No family. I have nothing. Enzo will ensure I have plenty of money to live off of, I have no doubt about that, but money means nothing.

I need a plan. I need to figure out what I want out of life.

Enzo.

I want Enzo.

But I have to want more than just a man.

Yet the pull is there—I love him. Every second I exist, I realize how stupid I was to not see it before. How he treats everyone else like crap, but me like a princess. How he protects me at the cost of everyone else. He loves me even if he doesn't believe it himself.

I love his sexy grin. I love the ruthless fight in his eyes. I love how we fuck. I love how we fight. I love the chaos that is our life.

And I don't know what to do with that love. If I told him, I think he'd drop me off at the next port. He'd think I'm ridiculous. Maybe I have stockholm syndrome or something. But even though I've been his prisoner, I've rarely felt like I am. He's treated me with more respect than my own father ever did.

My stomach growls, and I see the hint of light shining down through the glass windows, submerged underwater. I don't know how early in the morning it is. But maybe after having a full stomach, I will be able to think more clearly. And bringing Enzo breakfast in bed would be a nice surprise.

I climb out of the bed and find his shirt on the floor. I slip it on and watch as it falls to mid-thigh. I slip my panties on underneath.

Good enough.

I go to the door and open it into the hallway.

I see the main, locked door to Enzo's barracks at the other end only Enzo can use to open this section of the yacht. I open several doors but don't find anything that looks like a kitchen.

I sigh. *I guess I'm going exploring.*

I consider putting more clothes on, but I'm never going to get used to wearing clothes. I'm always going to prefer to be naked as often as I can.

I walk through the door that leads to everyone else on the yacht. It was nice to think Enzo and I were the only ones on the ship for a little while.

But as I walk, I realize the yacht is quiet. All of the bedroom doors are shut. It must be early in the morning still.

I smile, realizing I should be good to sneak up and get food and back down without being detected.

I jog up the stairs and find the kitchen on the main level. The sun is only starting to rise over the horizon. I walk to the large fridge and pull the door open.

"You are up early, stingray. Sleep well?" Zeke asks with a wink.

I close the fridge and walk over to the bar Zeke is sitting at. He takes a pot of coffee and pours me a cup.

"Oh, you prefer your coffee iced, don't you?"

I smile. *How are all of these men not taken?* Zeke shouldn't know how I like my coffee, but he does.

"Hot is fine." I take a seat next to him and cup my hands around the coffee to warm up.

Zeke's eyes cut down and then quickly back up. "Enzo isn't going to like you only wearing his shirt in public."

"Good thing I'm not in public."

Zeke shakes his head. "You are good for him; you know that right, stingray?"

I shrug. "I guess. But I'm also very bad for him."

We sit in silence drinking our coffee.

"What are you doing up so early?" I ask.

"I decided to stay awake after you two decided to keep the entire ship up most of the night."

My cheeks redden, and I gasp. "You heard me?"

"Yep, the walls are usually soundproof enough. But apparently not to contain the cries of a Miller."

"Oh my god! I'm so sorry."

Zeke laughs. "I'm teasing. My bedroom is the closest to yours. It shares a wall. I barely heard you. I'm sure no one else heard you."

I bite my lip. I'm not sure if he's telling me the truth or not.

"But seriously, you can't walk around the ship half naked. Enzo would kill me if he saw me sitting here with you."

I roll my eyes. "Let me handle Enzo."

"I would, but it's my ass he's going to hide for this, not yours."

"You're more of a brother than anything else. Enzo has nothing to worry about."

"He won't see it that way."

I chuckle.

"You love him, don't you?" Zeke asks.

I stop breathing. I didn't realize anyone else could see it.

"Yes," I breathe. It makes it more real, admitting it out loud.

He nods solemnly. "I'm sorry."

"Why are you sorry?"

"Because Enzo will never admit he loves you back. I've seen it happen before. I've seen women spend their lives waiting for Enzo to love them back. He never does. He can't."

"Liesel?" I ask.

He nods. "This won't end in happily ever after."

"I know."

"Enzo doesn't know how to love anyone other than Langston and me. And I'm not even sure if he truly considers us as people he loves or just brothers and that makes it a requirement. Liesel came close, but he doesn't love her. He just protects her. You, you might come the closest to gaining his love. But it's a fight that isn't worth fighting. It will only end in heartbreak for you."

I nod.

"I'm sorry. If he could love anyone, it would be you. You need to finish the game and then leave and forget you ever met any of us."

Leave and forget about the most important man in my life.

Zeke's asking me to leave, rip out my own heart, and tear it to shreds. Then pretend I didn't just destroy the only meaningful thing that has ever happened to me.

"What if I can't stop loving him?"

"Then you will live the rest of your life in horrible pain. Worse than anything you've ever experienced before. Trust me—find a way to get your heart back before it's too late."

Someone broke Zeke's heart. And he doesn't want to see me get hurt the same way he's constantly hurting. The same way Liesel hurts.

I sigh.

Get my heart back; it should be easy. But I already know it's too late. My heart belongs to Enzo. I stare at my finger where his mother's ring used to sit with the inscription—*My heart belongs to the devil.* The inscription became truth. Was that always going to be my fate from the moment I wore the ring?

I don't know Enzo's mother's entire story, but I do know it didn't end well. The woman fell in love with the devil. The only problem is the devil has no heart to love back with.

CHAPTER 10
ENZO

"*N*o! Don't take her!" *I yell.*

"Kai doesn't belong to you, Enzo. She never did. She doesn't want you. She doesn't like you. She could never love you," Milo says.

I look at Kai smiling in Milo's arms. She leans over and kisses him on the cheek.

I pull out my gun and aim it at them. "Let her go."

"Does she look like a woman that needs to be rescued? She's happy here, with me," Milo says.

"I'll believe it when Kai tells me to leave. That's she's happy here with you."

Milo cocks his head and runs a finger down Kai's neck—my neck. She's mine, not his.

"Beautiful, would you like to tell Enzo how happy you are here with me?" Milo asks.

Kai kisses him softly on the cheek. "Gladly, hubby."

Hubby? They're married?

She looks at me. "I'm happy with Milo. He's the love of my life. He's strong, handsome, and he isn't a monster."

I'm not a monster.

599

I don't lower the gun, I can't. I don't believe her, or maybe I don't want to believe she could be happy here with him.

Kai is mine.

No, she isn't. She only stayed because you forced her to. You were supposed to set her free. That's how the saying goes. Something like, if you love someone set them free, and if they return they are yours forever.

I could never risk it. I wasn't strong enough to set her free. Because I knew she'd never return to me.

"*You're lying. You'll say whatever Milo tells you so he won't kill you,*" I say.

"*Who has the gun pointed at her? It's not me, it's you she fears,*" Milo says.

I frown. No, she loves me. She wants me.

Milo takes Kai in his arms and forces her to kiss him. He shoves his tongue into her mouth, forcing her to kiss him back. And then she moans, and I lose it.

The gun fires—killing Milo instantly.

And then Kai looks at me, with all of her wrath and I know the truth. She loves him and hates me. I'll never be enough. And I've truly become the monster she thought I was the entire time.

I WAKE UP ABRUPTLY. WHEN I SIT UP, I ALREADY KNOW KAI IS NO longer beside me. I wouldn't have such an evil, cruel dream if she were still near.

I stretch for a second and try to wipe the bad dream from my head.

It was just a dream. It means nothing.

But I know it will stay with me far too long.

I pull on my jeans and a dark T-shirt before I go to find Kai. And I don't even want to know what clothes she put on when she decided to leave my bedroom. Her clothes are still on the floor, and the only thing I notice missing is my shirt from yesterday.

I head to the kitchen first, assuming her stomach decided it needed food and that's exactly where I find her—with Zeke.

I growl when I see him put his hand on her wrist as if to comfort her. But all I see is anger. No one touches Kai without her permission. He knows she doesn't like to be touched, and he did it anyway. It's unacceptable. Especially when she's only half dressed.

I storm toward them and shove Zeke against the wall before either of them hear me.

"What the hell are you doing, touching her?" I scream in his face, huffing out all of my furry into him as I squeeze his neck so tightly he can barely breathe.

"Enzo, let him go! He wasn't doing anything wrong!" Kai yells next to me, trying to pull my hand off of him.

"He touched you for no reason when he knows it hurts you, that's something," I say.

My eyes burn into Zeke's. If he wasn't my brother, I'd throw him overboard for an offense like that. I made a vow to Kai no man would ever hurt her again, and that includes something small like a touch that burns her skin.

"His touch didn't hurt me!" Kai shouts.

"What?"

"His touch doesn't hurt me anymore. At least, it barely registers. And he was just trying to comfort me. Let him go right now," Kai says with her hands on her hips and defiance in her eyes. She will fight me if I don't let him go.

I release my hold. *Damn, that dream fucked with my head and put me on edge more than I thought.*

"Sorry," I say, running my hand through my hair. I walk over to the pot of coffee, pour myself a cup and down it, needing to walk out of the fog I feel trapped in.

"It's okay, man. I'm going to go check on the captain and see if he needs anything," Zeke says, wisely leaving me alone.

I shake my head, trying to brush off the anger flowing through my veins. I can't. The anger is always a part of me. Always ready to explode at a moment's notice. I used to be better at controlling it, but ever since Kai came into my life, my emotions are all over the place. I'm having feelings I didn't even know existed, and the anger is the hardest to keep in check.

"What the hell was that?" Kai says, shoving me backward.

"You don't want to touch me right now."

"I think I do if you are going to act like an asshole for no reason."

"Just leave it alone, Kai."

"No, I can't. I won't."

"Kai," I warn when she steps so close we are all but touching. "Back up."

I cast my eyes down, keeping the darkness in my gaze away from her.

She stops, and somehow she knows. Her voice grows soft, "What happened?"

My eyes flitter and meet her concerned ones. "Nothing, it was just a dream."

She sucks on her bottom lip, obviously concerned but doesn't ask me any other questions.

I close my eyes, taking a deep breath, and trying to drive my demons out. Her arms slip around me, and instantly, I feel calmer. I know it doesn't hurt her to touch me anymore. It's not a sacrifice. But it still feels that way. No one has ever hugged me in order to comfort me. Not since my mother when I was a young kid.

"Thank you," I breathe out.

"I was trying to bring you breakfast in bed."

"I couldn't stay in bed, not without you. From now on, wake me up first."

She nods against my chest.

"Come on, let me give you the tour I never gave you last night. I know Westcott wants to make breakfast for everyone, and he will be up here soon to make it."

"Okay."

I take her hand again, our fingers intertwining far too naturally. Like a real couple. *We are anything but a real couple*, I remind myself.

I walk her out of the kitchen and onto the main deck. There are several seating areas, strings of lights, and tropical plants that decorate this area. But there is also the looming sea all around us. No walls to hide us from the ocean. There is nowhere for her to pretend we aren't on the ocean. She has to face the water and her own demons.

I suck in a breath waiting for her to shut down or panic because she won't let herself hide away anymore. She doesn't. She slowly walks away from me, trying to drop my hand. At first, I hold her tighter, but I know she needs this. She needs to know she can face it on her own. Especially, if she's going to survive.

So I let go.

Even though it kills me.

Kai takes her time walking to the railing. I keep my feet planted firmly on the ground. I put my hands in my jeans pockets. Let her have this moment alone.

She walks right up to the sea and places her hands on the railing. She closes her eyes and takes a deep breath of the salty air I love and she hates. Her hair blows crazily in the wind, and my shirt rides up her body until I can see her perky ass.

I should make her change, but after seeing her like this, I want her to wear only my shirt the entire trip. I'll just force everyone else to stay in their rooms. *She's fucking breathtaking.*

I give her a few minutes alone, and then I walk up behind her and take her in my arms.

"You are so strong—so much stronger than me. Sometimes I think you would make the better Black," I say.

She leans back into my chest. "You're stronger than you realize."

"Only because of you." I kiss her cheek. "Come on, I have more to show you."

I show her the main deck, the captain's room, and where most of the crew is staying below. I give her the password to my rooms and ensure she knows how to get in. And then I show her the one place I know she will love. The place I know will be a step toward freedom for her. And it terrifies me.

Because I like control. I like that I can make her mine and not worry if she is safe. But I know someday, I have to let her go. I'll probably make Zeke or Langston go with her to protect her. Probably Zeke, she seems to have taken a liking toward him the most.

I take her through my rooms to another door with a similar passcode and eye scan.

"What's this?" she asks. "Another secret room?" her eyes go wide.

"Something like that."

I enter the initial passcode, and then I turn around. "You need to enter a new passcode, one only you know."

"Why?" her voice is so soft as the single syllable leaves her lips.

"Because this room is yours. And yours alone. I don't have the passcode. My face won't work to open the door. It's only yours."

"What?"

"Enter a passcode."

She does, and the door opens. I turn around and push her inside. And then she stares in awe at the room I had Westcott decorate for her. It mirrors mine in many ways but has soft shades of grey and more turquoise that gives it a slightly more feminine feel.

She turns back to me, and I can see water in her eyes.

"There's more than just this room."

"More?"

"Yes, you asked for your freedom. I'm giving you all I can give you."

I walk over to the bed where the electronics and wallet are lying.

"Your phone," I say, handing her a brand new cell phone.

She stares at it like it's a foreign object. But then she never did own a cell phone before to my knowledge. She didn't have the money to own something most people take for granted.

"My number is already programmed into it," I say.

She opens the contacts and smiles. "Giant dick, really?"

I shrug. "I figured it would make you smile."

"And how am I programmed into your phone?"

I wink at her. "Stingray." I took the name Zeke gave to her.

She shakes her head. "You're ridiculous."

"I also got you a laptop in case you decide you need to start googling porn or something. That's all laptops are good for."

She giggles, running her hand over the shiny metal that's more expensive than the entire trailer she used to live in.

"And these are your credit cards," I say opening the wallet.

"I don't need credit cards. I don't want to spend your money."

"You won't be spending my money; you will be spending your money."

"I don't have any money."

I suck in a breath. Not wanting to say the next words, but knowing I need to. "Yes, you do. I got ten million dollars from Milo…from selling you."

Her face stiffens, and her eyes turn red.

"I know, you will hate me for the rest of your life for that one. And you should. I'm not asking for your forgiveness. I'm saying I don't want the money. I originally was going to use it to give to Rowan to pay for him helping you to escape, but he didn't want the money. The money is yours."

"I don't want the money either."

"It can get you your freedom. You will never have to work. Or you can use the money to do something good, start a business, anything."

She frowns, staring at the wallet.

I'm not going to let her worry about the money. That will be a battle for another day. For now, I just want her to enjoy the little bit of freedom I can give her.

"Come here," I say.

She moves to me silently. And then I press my lips gently to hers.

She smiles against my lips. "You really do want to give me my freedom, don't you?"

"As much as I can." Which I know isn't enough for her. Giving her her own room and phone is nothing. I want her to be free, but I don't know if I could bear it. Even if Milo is dead, letting her go would kill me.

So I don't think about that. I'm done talking.

I grab her hips, sliding my hands up under my shirt she's wearing to feel the curves of her hips as I pull her body tightly against mine. Kai deepens the kiss, pushing her tongue into my mouth as she moans her desire.

I will never get enough of her, and she will never get enough of me.

I hear the knock, but I don't want to acknowledge it. Whoever it is can wait.

Then the doorbell rings, and the video system sounds at Kai's door, indicating someone needs to speak to her.

"Who is that?" Kai asks.

"Ignore it," I say, taking her mouth back in mine. Kai is the only person who matters right now.

The doorbell rings again, and I moan.

"This better be fucking important," I curse as I walk out of Kai's room still gripping her hand to let her know this is not ending. As soon as I deal with whatever asshole problem is behind the door, I will return to fucking her brains out.

She giggles at me as I storm to the door and open it like she can feel all of the rage inside of me.

When I open the door, three pairs of eyes stare back at me.

I frown. "What the hell do you all want?"

Liesel crosses her arms and sways her hips to one side in her bikini top and cover up skirt. "You were the one that dragged me away from my high paying job to sit on a yacht all day. I don't expect to be fucking ignored all trip."

I growl and then turn to Zeke. I raise an eyebrow waiting, but he just glares at Liesel as does Kai next to me. "I was just escorting Miss Dunn to the pool deck."

I turn my attention to Langston. "I have news from Rowan about Milo Wallace," Langston says.

I crack my knuckles trying to remain calm. I need to get everyone off this fucking boat if for no other reason than for them to stop driving me nuts. If I could just have Kai and myself on this yacht by ourselves I would. For a second I consider moving them all to a second yacht so Kai and I can fuck in complete privacy, but I know it's better for her protection if my best men are here.

"Zeke, continue the task at hand," I say.

"My pleasure," Zeke says, winking at Kai as he lifts Liesel over his shoulder.

"Put me down, you brute," Liesel shouts.

Kai tries to contain a snicker next to me, but it still escapes.

I sigh, running my fingers through my hair. I wish Kai and Liesel could get along. It would be better for everyone, but Liesel doesn't play nice with anyone. She never has. And Kai doesn't understand Liesel and my's past.

Now that I have gotten rid of Liesel and Zeke, I turn my attention to Langston. I want to order him to leave, but I need to hear what news he has about Milo.

"Speak," I order, running out of patience.

"Milo has returned to Italy. He's injured, as are a few of his best men, but they will all make a speedy recovery. He's pissed, obviously, but assumes Rowan stole Kai from him. Rowan is doing some reconnaissance and thinks the best time to attack Milo is when he's on his yacht, not at his home."

I frown, not sure about that. Milo bought one of my yachts; I know its capabilities. But I prefer to attack at sea, and it seems Rowan feels the same.

"I want you to get me the full blueprints of both Milo's home and his yacht. I want to know everything about both locations and have our own plan of attack. Tell Rowan we will be speaking soon; I will not let Milo continue to live and put Kai at risk. I want him dead."

Kai shudders next to me at the mention of Milo's name. I want Milo dead now. I won't let him come near Kai again. I want to protect my men from this dangerous asshole, but with Rowan's team on our side, we have twice the army Milo does. Milo's days are limited. I will kill him. I will set Kai free from any man who tries to claim her, including myself.

CHAPTER 11
KAI

E nzo wants Milo dead.

I'm surprised he's had as much self-control as he's had. I figured now that he has me trapped on a yacht with his best men, he would have gone on a mission by himself to take out Milo. It's only a matter of time until Enzo gets impatient waiting.

Enzo is smart. He's ruthless. He can be patient. But not when it comes to me. He wants me safe, yesterday.

And when he goes to kill Milo, he will go alone. He won't risk his men. He won't start a war with a man as dangerous as Milo over something personal.

Rowan may want revenge, but Enzo needs to heal the hurt he feels for betraying me. Enzo will never forgive himself for what he did. Even after I do. Even after he kills Milo.

And I'm terrified of what will happen when Enzo goes for Milo. Enzo is powerful, dangerous, and strong. I've never seen him fail in hand to hand combat. But Milo won't play fair. I know that from my limited time with Milo. He's cruel in a way that Enzo never will be. Enzo's father may have trained him to be cruel, but deep down that's not who Enzo is. Enzo is fair, ruthless, and he demands loyalty above everything else. But he would never kill or torture just for the sake of killing. He would never kill for his own amusement.

Milo does. He kills because he enjoys killing.

That's why Milo has made so many enemies. That's why Rowan hates Milo as much as Enzo does. I don't know who Rowan lost to Milo, but I know he did. I could see it in Rowan's eyes when he stole me from Milo. He's felt pain I can only imagine. I've felt plenty of physical pain, but nothing like what Rowan has felt.

His pain is different. His pain rocks you to the core and lives inside in a cage that digs deep into his heart, tearing away at it slowly until there is nothing left. He lives with the loss of someone he loved every single day.

While I only live with the scars of what happened to me.

My eyes drift to Enzo still gripping my hand. A second ago, I was prepared to fight Liesel; my jealousy had gotten the better of me. I wanted to rip out her throat for thinking Enzo could ever be hers. But now I realize how stupid I was being. I would gladly let Liesel have Enzo if it meant he was safe.

Because right now, I fear for his safety. I don't know if he will survive a battle with Milo. And that pain would destroy me.

I need more answers. I need a way to protect Enzo while also defeating Milo. Rowan might be that answer, but I don't trust a man I hardly know. I don't trust anyone. Not even my own father.

My father.

He's betrayed me more than any man ever has. Because even though Enzo sold me to Milo, Enzo also saved me.

My father sold me and then never came for me. He didn't rescue me. He didn't save me.

And the only way I can truly heal is by facing him. By figuring out why and maybe learning more about this stupid game that hold Enzo and I captive. We're slaves to such a stupid game, all for a chance at ruling an empire I don't want. And one Enzo suffers too much for. Because I know if one of his men were under attack, if one of his men's wives were stolen by Milo like I was, he would still do everything fucking possible to get them back and make Milo pay.

"I need to talk to my father," I say, seemingly out of nowhere.

Two seconds ago, we were talking about Rowan and Milo; my father didn't even enter the equation. But for all I know, my father was the one who sent Milo. He was the one to set the trap Enzo fell for when he sold me.

Langston takes a step back as if he knows he shouldn't be involved in such a personal conversation, but I don't care. Langston is more family to me than my father will ever be.

Enzo studies me for less than a second, not at all surprised by my change in topic. He's been waiting for me to bring up my father this entire time.

Enzo nods and then turns to Langston. "Arrange for Mr. Miller to meet us at a set location. I don't want him to know he is meeting us. Just give him an order through the usual chain of command."

"Yes, sir," Langston says, disappearing and leaving Enzo and I alone again—at least until Liesel escapes Zeke's grasps and comes begging for attention again. I know I need to talk to Liesel and make things civil between us. I don't know her whole story, but I know her story is important if she was let into Enzo's deepest circle. But I'll face Liesel later.

I should want to jump back into Enzo's arms and fuck him like we were planning to moments before. He gave me everything he could, inching me closer to my freedom, and I've never felt closer to him. But right now we are both too on edge to fuck.

All I want is to cuddle in Enzo's arms while I plan what I'm going to do with my father. I want to hold Enzo close to me for as long as possible, because I don't know how long I have left with him. Whether Milo kills him or Enzo finally sets me free, one way or another—our story ends the same, with my heartbreak.

Enzo squeezes me close to him, and I already feel my heart breaking. *I'm such a goner.*

CHAPTER 12
ENZO

I step foot onto the Raptor, the yacht of mine Mr. Miller captains, with all of my furry flowing through me with a force I haven't felt since I screwed up and sold Kai to Milo. It is going to take everything inside me not to kill this bastard the second I see him. He's the reason Kai was tortured for six years. He is the reason she came back to try and claim the Black empire instead of staying gone. He is the reason I ended up hurting her.

No, I take responsibility for my own actions. I hurt her. I won't let Mr. Miller take any of the blame.

But I am going to make him pay for what he did to Kai. I will pay every day of my life with every breath. I vowed to protect her with more than my life. And I plan on living that way.

Miller will eventually pay with his life, but not before Kai orders me to kill him. She will; she's as ruthless as I am deep down. But I'm not sure she's ready to kill her own father. That's the kind of thing that takes years of abuse to develop. It needs to be personal. It needs to consume your every thought and every nightmare. Only then does someone turn to something as extreme as killing your own father. I should know.

I walk slowly and deliberately to the main office on the yacht in the middle of the night. A few crew members notice me, but they know better than to ask me any questions. I take a seat in the office like I own the place, and I do. I haven't stepped foot on this particular yacht in years—mainly because of fucking Miller. I never trusted him, not when I knew he was Kai's father. Not when I found out he never searched for her when she went missing. Not when I discovered he lived in a trailer for a house instead of a mansion. I pay him well enough to afford much more. And the story he's fed Kai over the years about his wife's hospital bills taking all his money is bullshit.

And all my suspicions were proved correct when I found out he was the one who sold Kai.

I wait for Mr. Miller, but I won't wait for long. I'm giving him five minutes to get his ass into this office before I come after him and shoot him in the leg for making me wait. Kai can't fault me too much for shooting him. Not when she experienced worse for years.

The door opens and Mr. Miller steps inside, his head up and proud, staring down at me like I'm vermin instead of a king. He stares down at me like I am less than, instead of worthy of all his attention. I guess I should thank him for passing the trait onto his daughter, because I love that she is the only woman who has ever truly stood up to me.

"You summoned me," he says, not taking a seat in the chair opposite me.

"Sit," I command.

He hesitates.

"Sit, or I'll make you sit."

He huffs like he knows I won't.

Try me, old man.

When he sits, I notice the wrinkles around his eyes have deepened, the gray in his hair now covers his entire head of hair, even down to his beard. He truly looks like an old man. His muscles have weakened through the years. If he were any other of my men, I would retire him or fire him depending on how loyal he'd been to me over the years. But I can't do either without pissing off Kai and breaking the rules since I'm required to run everything by her as co-Black for now.

I shouldn't even be having this meeting without informing her. But this conversation will stay between us. This conversation will not leave this room.

Mr. Miller folds his hands in his lap while he spreads his legs, taking up the entire chair. He seems relaxed, but I can read people easily. He's not relaxed. He knows I could end him as easily as I snap my fingers. He's afraid of me.

"Why?" My entire body goes into that one word. One question has never been this important.

He laughs like I asked the most ridiculous question. "That's not the question you should be asking. You already know why I sold her."

I growl. He's not even going to apologize for what he did. He made the decision as easily as he decided his breakfast this morning.

"It's the question that matters to me. You hurt her. You answer to me."

He chuckles again. "Why? Because you love her? You don't care about my daughter any more than I do. Rumor is you sold her to our enemies. You don't give a fuck, so stop pretending you do. If you need to take out your vengeance on someone, fine, take it out on me. But don't act like you are any better than me."

I storm toward him and kick him hard to the floor; he falls off balance and slams into the floor beneath him. My boot lands on his chest, pressing hard enough I know it's hard for him to breathe.

"You will tell me everything. Or I will kill you."

He spits at me. "I will tell you nothing more than what you deserve. And you don't deserve the truth. You already know why I sold her, the same reason your father tortured you night after night. To toughen you up in order to win the empire."

My eyes grow wide with anger. "And you know how I felt about my own father."

He snickers using too much of his air as he does. "You fucking slaughtered him."

"What makes you think I won't do the same thing to you?"

"Because as much as you pretend to be cruel, you aren't. You didn't actually sell my daughter, and you are too much of a pussy to hurt her."

I press my foot into his neck, shutting him up, but I'm careful not to leave any visible markings. I don't want Kai to know I roughed up her father before I let her meet him.

I study him and realize he's bluffing. He knows nothing about the game. He didn't trick me into selling Kai to Milo. He's not working with Milo. He knows nothing. He's just pretending to know something in order to stay alive.

Fucking pussy.

"Listen to me. If it were up to me, I'd kill you right here on the floor of this grungy office and never think about you again. But it's not up to me. You're Kai's father. And I know the decision has to be hers."

He tries to speak, but I dig my boot in deeper.

Self-control. Keep it together. Don't give into the anger.

"This is how it's going to go. At dawn, Kai and I are going to board this yacht so she can get her questions answered. You will not let her know you and I spoke. You will answer all of her questions, honestly. You will apologize for everything bad you have ever done to her. You will be a father. You will promise to protect her from now on and never hurt her again. And you will promise to stay out of her fucking life. Do you understand?"

I ease my foot from his throat.

He coughs.

"Or what? You'll kill me? You already told me you wouldn't do that for Kai's sake."

My face reddens as the anger explodes through my body. "I will kill you if you don't do as I command. I've fucked up plenty of times where Kai is concerned. I'll deal with her wrath if I have to. But I vowed to not let any man hurt her ever again. That includes you."

He scowls. "You wouldn't. You are too much of a pansy."

I shrug. "Maybe. Maybe I wouldn't kill you." I press my boot harder into his throat, no longer caring that it will leave a mark. I watch his face turn purple and blue from lack of oxygen. And then I lean down close like I'm telling him a fucking secret.

"But there are worse things than death. Just ask your daughter about that."

I release him and watch as the bastard wiggles on the floor, begging for oxygen. I only gave him a few seconds of what he put his daughter through and he could barely handle it—*the coward.*

I walk to the door, ready to return to Kai who I had to leave sleeping naked in my bed to come talk to this asshole.

"You think you got everything figured out," Mr. Miller says.

I turn as I reach the door. "I do."

He shakes his head. "You don't know nothing. You don't know the fucking truth. You don't know the pain coming both of your ways. There is so much you don't know, boy."

Old feelings stir when he calls me, boy. The only other person that ever called me, boy, was my father. And I hated him for it.

I slam my fist into his face, watching the blood spurt from his nose as I do. So much for not letting Kai know I was here. She'll know the second she takes a look at her father. But I'm done hiding secrets from her, and I don't regret one second of my time with her father.

"Are you ready?" Enzo asks me, as I roll up my sleeves on the buttoned-down shirt I decided to wear.

I wanted something that made me feel powerful, as an equal to my father and Enzo, but I'm not sure it mattered what I wear. I have huge butterflies bouncing around in my stomach.

How can I ever be ready to face a father who sold me?

I nod when I finish rolling my sleeves up, revealing enough of my scars, but not too much.

I want answers.

I want an apology.

I don't want to show him the pain I experienced. He doesn't deserve my pain.

Enzo holds out his hand instead of taking mine like he usually does. He's going to let be the one in control today. If I don't want Enzo with me, all I would have to do is ask him to leave. He'll be right by my side if I want him to, or he'll remain only as a guard protecting me but not interfering.

I want to face my father on my own. But I could use Enzo's help getting to that point.

I take his hand that instantly warms me.

We walk up the decks of the yacht and meet Langston and Zeke on the top deck. Both of them are solemn in their dark jeans and black T-shirts. They look like they are about to do battle. And I have no doubt they know as much as I do about my father, possibly more.

I notice the other yacht anchored next to us and the ramp that leads from ours to theirs that Langston and Zeke have been guarding.

Enzo gives them a nod, and they silently traipse across the ramp. Enzo and I follow with my hand still gripped in his. When we reach the yacht my father captains, all the men stop as if we are royalty. They practically bow at us as we walk.

I don't feel like a scared little girl anymore. I feel like a woman about to deliver her vengeance.

We reach a door, and our group stops. Langston and Zeke face away like they are ready to jump in front of a bullet to protect me. All the men on this yacht work for Enzo, so I don't know what we have to fear here. I think they are more likely here to intimidate my father.

"Your father will meet you here," Enzo says hesitating outside the door waiting for me to invite him in. But he already knows I won't. I need to face my father on my own. Enzo doesn't protest or ask to enter with me.

He leans down and kisses me on the cheek. "You got this." He doesn't say he'll be here if I need him. The confidence in his voice tells me he doesn't think I will need him.

I open the door and leave the only men who care about me outside while I enter the room where I'll face my father.

The lock of the door behind me sounds like a closing to my soul. I'm trapped in this room that smells like blood and musk and men. A room my father and the rest of his crew enter to handle business and probably beat the shit out of each other when one of them fucks up.

I take a deep breath in and out, filling my lungs to prepare to speak to my father. My neck still throbs, but my voice is easier to use now. I don't even have to wear the gauze covering anymore, but the stitches are starting to itch like a motherfucker.

There is a large oak desk with an executive chair I know I'm supposed to sit behind. It would give me control over the situation.

Sitting behind that desk would make it clear I'm the boss and my father is nothing but a peon who needs to follow my orders.

But he's still my father, and I don't want to face him with a desk between us. So I pull the two chairs on the opposite side of the desk apart until they are facing each other and take a seat in one and wait.

My stomach does flips while I wait, which isn't long. The door opens, and my father is standing in the doorway only minutes later. His face is bruised, and there is dried blood on his nose and the collar of his shirt. His hair looks disheveled, and his neck is heavily bruised.

He looks like he got in a fight mere hours ago. I notice Enzo standing behind him, staring at him with intense disgust. Like he wants to put a bullet between his eyes, instead of letting him into this office.

My eyes return to my father. Enzo did this. It has his mark all over him. He met with my father before he let me speak with him.

I should be angry at Enzo for controlling my life, but I'm not. I'm grateful. My father deserves every bit of pain he's in and more, and I'm not strong enough to deliver the same level of punches Enzo can.

"Take a seat," I command, not getting up from my own chair.

My father stiffens before the door is closed behind him. Then he takes a seat opposite me, crossing his legs like we are meeting for a casual lunch instead of meeting to discuss why he sold me.

He folds his hands in his lap, and for the first time, I realize how old he looks. He's in his late sixties and still working, but I doubt he can handle the physical nature of this job much longer.

Questions fill my head—so many questions. But I don't ask them. I let the silence fill the room, letting the silence stretch and unnerve him.

"What are you doing?" he asks.

I cut my eyes to him. "Thinking of all the ways I could kill you."

"You wouldn't kill your own father."

"Maybe not, but I'm not sure I consider you a father anymore. Fathers don't sell their daughters. Fathers don't lie to their daughters their entire lives."

"That's what you are pissed at? That I didn't tell you about the stupid game? The empire you could inherit if only you were strong enough?"

"No, I'm pissed I thought I grew up with a father mourning the loss of my mother, doing everything he could to survive, and instead, I was raised by an evil sack of shit who didn't prepare me for my own future."

"Ask your fucking questions, I have work I need to get back to."

I lean forward, putting all my anger into my stare. I consider sitting in silence so I can piss him off further, but I can't stand to be in this room with him any longer than I have to.

"My mother's hospital bills, are you really in such debt that you can't afford a house bigger than that trailer?"

"No."

Fuck, this is going to gut me.

"Then, why did we live in a trailer?"

"Because I wanted to toughen you up. I didn't want you to become a princess like how Enzo was raised. You learned how to handle yourself in that trailer."

I close my eyes, willing myself to ask the next question.

"Did mom really die from cancer?"

"No, your mother was an alcoholic. She drank too much and killed herself."

My mouth falls open as my heart breaks. I don't remember my mother. All I know is the story. She fought so hard to stay alive for me that we incurred an incredible debt we could never repay. It was a lie. All of it. *A fucking lie!*

But then every word out of my father's mouth is a lie.

And it doesn't shock me that my mother didn't care about living for me either.

I want to get out of here. I want to get back to the Savage with Enzo and pretend I'm an orphan, that my father died along with my mother back then. But I have one more question I need to ask. A question I already know the answer to, but I have to ask it. I need to hear it from his lips.

"Why did you sell me?"

His eyes look into my soul, and I know it's not out of love or compassion or sorrow for what he did to me. He doesn't tear up thinking about it. He doesn't regret putting me through the pain.

He hurt me because he wanted me to be stronger. He hurt me because he thought I was too weak to win without experiencing pain.

"I sold you so you would have a chance to win. I did it for you."

"No!"

My single word vibrates through the room until it consumes both of us.

"No, you didn't sell me so I had a chance to win. You sold me because you are evil and cruel. You sold me so if I were to win, I could give you a better life. Promote you in the ranks, and the Miller line would continue on ruling for another generation. You didn't do this for me. You did this to me. You hurt me. Broke me. Caused me more pain than my body could physically handle, until I learned to shut it out."

I think back to Enzo's father. I don't know what he did to prepare Enzo to become Black, but I know it wasn't kind. It was personal and dark and cruel. But at least he was a father. At least he didn't pretend to be something he wasn't and hide behind a lie. He spoke the truth to his son and showed him his darkest side, while my father pretended all this time.

"You are nothing but a coward. There were other ways to prepare me that didn't involve selling me. Teaching me how to wield a gun and weapons. Teaching me how to fight. Educating me on how this business runs. Preparing me for every scenario. You didn't have to sell me!"

A sob escapes my throat, and I curse myself for showing weakness to this man.

"Are you finished?" he asks.

I grit my teeth together to keep from launching myself at him. "No. You haven't even apologized for what you did."

"And I'm not going to. You had to be sold."

"Why? Why was that the only way your twisted little brain could think to prepare me?"

He leans forward, glaring right back at me. His nostrils flare, and his anger spreads from his face to his bones.

"I've been in this world a lot longer than you, Katherine. You don't understand the dangers you will face. You don't understand how strong you have to be to become Black."

"One, don't call me Katherine. My name is Kai."

He shakes his head.

"And two, you don't understand the strength required to be Black. You failed, remember? Enzo's father won, not you. You have no right to think you know better than me the strength it takes."

My father sighs, falling back in his chair in defeat.

I win.

But it doesn't feel like a win. It feels like pain.

"I don't want to ever see you again," I say.

"Fine, then stop summoning me and I'll never see you again."

It's not enough. I want him out of my life forever. I consider going outside and retrieving Enzo's gun, but then I think better. That's not who I am. I'm not cruel. I will not kill my father.

"I want you to leave Miami. I want you to move to California or Canada or Belize or Ireland. Anywhere that's hundreds of miles from me. Anywhere not connected to the sea or Miami."

He cocks his head. "I can't exactly leave Miami or the sea when I'm a captain."

"You aren't a captain anymore. You're fired."

That gets his attention. His face goes pale. "You can't fire me."

I cock my head to the side. "Did you forget the rules you helped to create? While the games are being played, Enzo and I have equal control of the company. And I'm currently in the lead one to nothing. So I have plenty of power. And I'm firing your ass, effective immediately. This ship's next mission will be to get your ass to the farthest away land, away from me."

"You can't fire me," he whispers like I just ripped out his heart.

"I just did."

I stand, effectively dismissing him. I never plan on seeing my father ever again. It's not the same as killing or punishing him for what he did to me, but it's enough.

He stands too, facing me. And I can tell he has more to say, but it's too late for an apology. I won't change my mind about firing him.

I walk to the door and open it. Enzo's eyes meet mine, searching to see how much pain I'm in, but the pain is gone. My father no longer exists to me.

Enzo smirks when he reads my face.

"My father is fired. Tell the men they are to drop him off at port as far away from here as possible and to promote the second in command."

Enzo raises an eyebrow.

I step closer to him and whisper so only he can hear. "And if you have a problem with me ordering that without discussing with you first, we can have a discussion about you meeting with my father first and beating the shit out of him."

"I don't have a problem with you making the decision. It's yours to make."

I nod. "And thank you for beating the shit out of my father. He deserved every punch."

He grins.

My father walks to the door where I'm standing. He glares at Enzo like he's the devil. He is, but he's my devil. The kind I can trust to protect me. The kind who fucks up and then makes up for it. Not the kind that sells me and pretends that is somehow saving me.

My father leans over to me, alcohol heavy on his breath as he says, "There is so much more you don't know, Kather—Kai. So much more. Find the truth before Enzo does. It's the only way to win."

I straighten and look my father dead in the face and speak loud enough so everyone can hear my declaration. "I don't want to win."

CHAPTER 14

ENZO

We return across the plank to our ship in silence. I hold out my hand to her as I did before. Walking onto the ship, she held my hand like we were a team. Walking off, she didn't take my hand.

I don't know what her father said to her, but it wasn't an apology. It wasn't what I told him to say.

She fired him. That was her vengeance. She's hoping by sending him away she will be able to heal and get over this. She doesn't realize a child never gets over the betrayal of their own father.

Never.

It's something I will live with the rest of my life.

And so will she.

Kai walks straight for our private rooms once aboard our yacht. She is in no mood to talk or be around other people. I unlock the doors for her because it will be faster than waiting for her to do it herself. I hold the door open, and she steps inside. She heads directly toward her room.

She hasn't slept in that room since she boarded the yacht. She's stayed in my room, but right now, it looks like she wants to be alone.

And I can't handle that. I want to help her. I want to heal her. And I can't do that if she locks me out.

I put my hand on the door to her room, stopping her from opening it.

"Want to get a drink with me before bed?"

She looks at me, and I see the pain etched on her face. I want to make her smile. I want her to be happy. But she can never be happy here with me. She will never be happy until she is free of this life.

She takes a deep breath, probably to tell me off.

"We can play a game while we get a drink," I say, hoping that getting to play a game of truth or lies with me will sweeten the deal.

She smiles softly. "Okay."

It's the most beautiful word I've heard. It warms me to know I get to spend a few more hours with her. Even if she doesn't share my bed tonight, I will still have this.

I don't hold out my hand to her again; I already know she won't take it. I think she thinks that by not touching me she will break our connection, that I won't be able to read her mind as easily if I can't feel her.

But I don't need to touch her to understand her. I feel her heart fluttering too quickly in her chest. I feel the throbbing ache in her chest. I feel the coolness of her breath. She wants to shut down so she doesn't feel. That's why she wanted to go back to her room alone. So she could go back to her icy cage and not feel anything.

I open the door to the lounge, decorated with beautiful, elegant white couches and soft lights to make it feel light and airy. There is an all-glass bar in the corner, and the room could easily fit fifty people for a party. Instead, it usually only holds me, and now Kai. I don't need more than that.

"What do you want to drink?" I ask as I walk behind the bar.

She stares at all of the high priced liquors floating on a glass shelf overhead.

The yacht rocks hard, and we both grip onto the cool glass of the bar to keep from falling over. My eyes lock with hers trying to calm her, but I don't see as much fear as I would expect. Her father hurt her too much to care about a rocking ship at the moment.

It rocks again, and I know we are heading into treacherous waters. Storms are coming, both natural and man-made. Milo will be coming soon if we don't attack first. And we still have to face the second round of games.

Kai steadies herself and grins as she stares up at a bottle of liquor. A cheap bottle. I don't even know how it got onto this yacht.

"No," I say.

"Yes," she says.

"No way. We are not drinking that poison."

She nods hungrily. "Yes, we are. If you don't want me to head to my room right now and shut everything out, then you are drinking with me, and I get to choose the drinks. And I choose shots of Jager-meister."

"Ugh," I moan. "I don't think my stomach can handle it."

"Come on, Black. I thought you were made of stronger stuff."

She's back to calling me Black again. And I didn't miss her declaration to her father. She doesn't want to be Black. She just wants this to be over. She wants to pretend this life never existed. *That I never existed.*

It hurts, but not as much as drinking this liquor is going to.

"Fine."

She smiles triumphantly and climbs up on the counter to reach the bottle herself.

I reach for a couple of high ball glasses so I can at least mix coke or something into it to disguise the taste.

She wags her finger at me. And then reaches behind me for the shot glasses.

Oh, hell no.

"Seriously? Shots?"

She nods. "We are about to get wasted."

I sigh. I would do anything for this girl. She has somehow snuck onto my very limited list of people I would lay down my life to protect. That list includes Langston and Zeke. Both brothers who would protect me as readily as I protect them. Then there is Liesel and Kai. Only four people I truly care about.

Kai carries the bottle and shot glasses over to the biggest couch, sits, and pours two shots.

I sit next to her and reluctantly take one of the glasses. She holds hers out with a huge smile on her face, and suddenly this is all worth it. I'd drink myself to death with the shitty liquor just to see her smile.

We both slam the drink down, and I try not to vomit from the taste.

"Why do you like this so much?"

"I grew up on this shit. You think my father could afford better?"

Yes, I think your father could afford a lot more on the quarter of a million dollar salary we paid him each year.

She frowns, realizing her mistake, and pours another shot for each of us.

"So what do you think the next round in the game will be?" she asks, trying to move on from her father.

I sigh. "I don't know. But if I know my father, it will be cruel and twisted. Something neither of us wants to do."

Her eyes grow bigger at that thought. Stealing from Milo was easy. He was a rich asshole who stole and beat women. He deserved everything and more than we did to him. But my dad could order us to kill an innocent. And at least one of us would have to do it if we want the games to stop.

She raises the new shot. "To shitty fathers."

"To shitty fathers."

We both down another shot of poison. This time it goes down a little easier.

"You start," she says, referring to the game of truth or lies I promised. She pours more liquor into both of our glasses while I lean back, getting comfortable on the couch.

I say the first thing I'm thinking, "I healed after what my father did to me, and so will you. Truth or lie?"

"Lie, drink," she says. She downs her shot, and so do I. She refills our glasses before she speaks.

"I forgave my father for selling me."

"Lie," I say as we both slam another drink down.

Kai wasn't kidding about getting drunk. With the number of shots we are drinking, we are going to be completely hammered.

The ship heaves again—and maybe that's a good thing. She will pass out and be able to sleep through the storm.

"I forgave myself for selling you."

She frowns like my lie is painful to her. It shouldn't be. She will never forgive me, and I will never be able to either.

"Lie," she says quietly. We both drink, but it's more somber this time.

She bites her lip, considering her next truth or lie.

"I could never forgive you," she says.

"Truth," I sigh, knowing it's true.

She shakes her head. "I already forgave you."

My pupils dilate, and my heart races as if she admitted her deepest secret. She didn't, but the emotions that spill from her words consume me. *How can she forgive me?* She's lying—to me or to herself.

What I did was unforgivable. But we are both too drunk for me to argue with her about it now. So I keep playing the game instead.

If she wants to get deep, then so will I.

"I killed my father," I say, admitting something I've never said to anyone.

Kai looks at the scars she can see on my hands. She looks at the pain in my eyes and the fire in my soul. She's seen how black my heart can get. I've never told her any stories about how my father trained me. I've never told her stories about how cruel my father could be. But she knows. She sees the evidence on my skin and heart.

She didn't kill her father for what he did to her. But I did mine. And she will probably hate me for stooping to his level.

"Good, he deserved to die. Did you make him suffer?"

"Yes, when I became stronger than him, I snuck into his office. I made him bleed on every surface of the office he loved and then painted the walls with his blood. Only when he showed how weak he could be, did I kill him."

She licks her lips like what I just said turned her on.

I shake my head. *We are two messed up motherfuckers.*

The boat rocks and I wince, preparing for the fear and pain on her face. She downs her last shot.

"I'm not afraid of the water anymore. The rocking doesn't scare me. Not when there is something so much more treacherous I fear."

Milo?

Does Milo now consume all her thoughts that she no longer has more than one fear?

I don't get to tell her I think it's a truth. I don't get to ask her what she's terrified of. Because she launches herself on top of me, her lips meeting mine as her hips grind onto my crotch.

We've both drank so much our bodies literally shouldn't be able to fuck at our level of intoxication. But with one kiss I sober up quickly, and my cock hardens into stone.

Her tongue dips into my mouth as if she's been doing it for years, and I'm the liquid she yearns to taste, not the liquor. She tastes like cheap alcohol. It should turn me off; instead, it makes me crave more.

Shit, now I'm going to want to drink Jager all the time because it reminds me of her.

I slip my hand under her shirt, letting her cool skin ease my senses. The self-control it takes to keep the devil inside instantly takes over when I touch her. Her skin makes me feel human in a way I haven't felt since I was a young kid.

She makes me think I'm not a monster. But I'm just fooling myself. She only pushes the monster away for a few minutes while I focus on her.

I reach for her pants, and she swats my hand away.

"Just kiss me and hump me like two teenagers making out on their parents' couch. Only when you can't help but not have me do I want you to fuck me."

Jesus.

I'm already there, but I don't tell her that. I flip us over and do exactly what she asks. She wants to get a teenage experience she never had, fine. But after that, she is going to get all man.

I drive my hips into her spread legs, letting her feel as much as she can through our clothes as I dip my tongue in and out of her mouth, kissing her like she's never been kissed before.

My kisses should be messy and drunk, but they've never been so focused on my mission of getting Kai to beg for me to strip her naked and fuck her with my fingers, tongue, and cock.

I want it all tonight.

She didn't tell me what she fears yet, but I want to take it all away. I will drive it away with sex—at least for tonight. And tomorrow, I'll figure out what looms over her.

I grind my cock again into her core as her body grips my waist with her legs, begging for so much more than she will ever admit to me.

What are you hiding, pretty girl?

I want to fuck it out of her, but that's not fair. She told me her truth during the game. Now I just have to figure out my own truth.

I don't know how teenagers make out on the couch anymore. That was something I was never privileged enough to experience. Not because I didn't have women lining up for me at that age, but because my youth was stolen too soon. At that age, I was treated like a man. My fucks were with women, not teenaged girls.

"Are you okay?" Kai asks, stopping our kisses and looking into my eyes like she can see what haunts me.

I smirk. "Yes, I'm about to fuck the most beautiful woman in the world."

She cocks her head. "You already decided you are going to get lucky, huh? You still have to win me over, convince me to fuck you."

I nuzzle her neck and kiss the tender spot there. "I already have."

I want to torture her slowly, but I have no patience or self control when it comes to her. She controls my body and soul. I've never been in a more dangerous position than when I'm with her.

"Fuck me, Black."

One command and I yield to her.

I could never deny her.

Before this is all over I'm going to sacrifice everything for this woman, I can feel it deep down to my bones.

I pull her pants down before sliding my own down. I barely have time to sheath myself with a condom before my cock grows a mind of its own and slides into her slick pussy.

She groans, and I lose my shit.

Why does making her feel good drive my every action?

Why does she have this hold over me?

I thrust, feeling her tightness and enjoying the beautiful glaze of her eyes as she releases whatever fear she's dreading.

What is it about Kai that makes everything different?

She has a pussy and a tight body like every other woman I've been with. She's beautiful and smart and fearless, but there are plenty of women in the world with similar attributes.

Is it because we share similar life experiences? Both raised by fathers more concerned with winning an empire than raising children? Both spending our entire adult lives fighting for something we don't really want?

That's part of it, but there is something deeper I don't understand. And when my cock is inside her, like it is now, I have no hope of figuring it out.

I watch her mouth change into a beautiful O shape as she cries out her orgasm. With every other woman, I make her come because it stokes my ego. It makes me feel godlike to know I can control something so intimate. With Kai, simply seeing her orgasm brings me as much pleasure as my own.

Her body settles down, her orgasm finishing its course, and I'm frozen. I just awe in the beauty on her face.

"Enzo? What are you doing?" Kai asks bashfully.

"Watching you."

She bites her gorgeous lip.

"Aren't you going to come?"

"Yes, but I didn't want to ruin this moment. I wanted to be able to watch every second of your orgasm."

"I'm done now."

I laugh. "You aren't anywhere close to done."

I pound into her body and watch as her body responds. And I know I'll pull another orgasm out of her soon.

This woman.

This beautiful, broken woman is going to be the end of me.

She is going to take everything.

My house.

My money.

My men.

My family.

My empire.

It will all be hers by the end. I don't want the empire any more. It means nothing if I can't keep her safe. I don't care about winning; I only care about protecting her.

Tomorrow I'll do more surveillance of Milo Wallace. He's her biggest threat at the moment. He's my new mission. Killing him, and then sending a message to the world that Kai Miller is never to be touched.

Kai may never belong to me, but she doesn't belong to them either.

She's like the wild ocean waves, uncontrollable and with the power to take over the world with one crash if she wanted to. Her wrath will eventually decimate me in one mighty hurricane. Because that is who she is. She can pretend she forgives me, but deep down, she will never let that pain go until she destroys me.

Body, heart, and soul.

It will all be claimed by the sea. Kai doesn't fear the sea anymore because she's taken on its power.

And I'm fire—even with all its mighty power, I can be easily extinguished with one crash of her waves.

What do you fear now, Kai? How do I protect you? Because I no longer care if I survive, only that you do.

It's not because I love her; I'm too fucked up for love. But because I believe Kai is truly better than me. She has the power to change everything in our world. She has the power to stop the cycle of Rinaldis and Millers battling each other for a dark world that shouldn't even exist.

And because the only way to keep my empire and who I am is to give her up now, not wait until the end of the game. The fucking would have to stop. The kissing. The touching. The connecting. All of it needs to end in order to keep myself whole.

But I can't.

I want her too much.

I'm about to lose everything to this woman.

And the sacrifice will be worth it.

CHAPTER 15
KAI

Enzo Black is broken.

How did I not realize it before?

Yes, I thought he was a little fucked up like all of us are. His father did a number on him. I understand the feeling now that I know my father did the same or worse.

But how did I not realize he's as broken, if not more so than I am? He doesn't even think he is capable of love.

Of being loved.

Of loving others.

Of falling in love.

I know Enzo can never love me. We are enemies. We've both betrayed each other and will continue to betray each other in different ways, but he needs to heal enough to love again. He helped me heal so I could love him. The only way I will be able to truly walk away from him is if I know he can love another—even if that person isn't me.

I lie in Enzo's arms on the couch in his bar area. My head pounds from the amount of alcohol we drank last night, but not once did I truly feel drunk. I always feel sober around Enzo. *I feel alive.*

He snores gently beneath me, naked and adorable. *Why don't you think you are capable of being loved? Why, why, why won't you let me love you?*

I run my hand through his hair, outgrown and in need of a trim. But I like it a little too long, a little too messy. It fits him better. Enzo isn't perfect. He's far from it. When he fucks up, he does it in a huge fashion. But that's what attracts me to him. He may fuck up, but he makes up for it just as effortlessly. Life with Enzo is never boring.

I reluctantly climb off him, knowing I need a gallon of coffee to have a chance of ridding myself of this headache.

Enzo grabs my hand before I fully leave him. "Where are you going?"

"To get coffee to try to stop this pounding in my head."

He frowns and pulls me to him, touching my head as if he can feel the pain there.

"I'm sorry, baby. I knew we shouldn't have drunk that disgusting liquor."

I raise an eyebrow. "You seemed to drink it just fine after you got a couple of tastes of it."

He sits up, grabbing his own pounding head. "Ugh, I haven't had a hangover since I was fifteen and just getting used to the stuff."

"You really shouldn't drink that much. It's not good for you."

He smirks. "You aren't good for me. Should I stop you too?"

Oh, God, please no.

"No," I kiss him hungrily on the lips. "I think we both just need a taste of our poison."

He kisses me back, his tongue sweeping into my mouth and tasting every last drop of the alcohol in my mouth.

A buzzing sound stops both of us.

We look over at Enzo's cell phone lying on the floor next to us.

I moan.

The buzzing continues, and we know he needs to answer it. My cell phone still lies in the bedroom I have yet to use. I like having it there in case I need it, but I also prefer sleeping in Enzo's arms.

Enzo pulls me to his stomach as he reaches down and grabs the cell phone from the floor.

"This better be important," Enzo snaps into the phone.

I watch as he listens carefully and then ends the call without speaking.

"Who was that?"

"The real world calling. I need to start going to work on a plan to take out Milo and every man who would step into his place. His empire is similar to ours. Ending Milo won't end the war. There is always another heir ready to take his place. I have to destroy the entire clan."

I nod. I know he needs to work. It's the only way we will ever get off of this yacht. Although, after last night, I don't plan on ever leaving this yacht again.

He hesitates as he opens his mouth.

"What?" I ask.

"I really don't want to include you in the Milo stuff, but I will if it's what you want. I know you are strong and very capable with a gun. But this fight is going to be between men that have been firing guns their entire lives. Used to hand to hand combat. Know how to wield a gun and a hundred different ways to kill. These men watch others die on a regular basis, and I don't want you anywhere near it when the time comes.

"I promise to share the important details of the plan once we have one, but I don't want you spending any more of your time thinking about Milo than you have to." He strokes my cheek. He thinks Milo is who I dread more than the sea. He doesn't realize the only thing I fear is losing him and having my heart ripped out because I fell in love with the wrong man.

"Go, involve me in what you want to include me in."

"This isn't a tactic to get another penalty against me in the games, is it?"

I laugh and kiss him quickly on the lips. "Maybe." I waggle my eyebrows.

"I'll win, even if I have to take a penalty."

"Who is ahead again?"

"You are, baby." He kisses me again and then throws my clothes at me. "Get dressed if you want to leave this room."

I sigh but put the clothes on. Someday we are going to have a place where I can go naked everywhere.

I shake my head. *There I go again, planning for a future that will never exist.*

Enzo dresses too, and we head toward the door that leads to the rest of the yacht and the world. We open the door, and as always, it seems like the entire yacht's passengers have decided to greet us.

Enzo frowns when he sees Liesel, but I need to stop putting off the inevitable. I need to talk to her. She's Enzo's friend. He obviously cares about her, and I need to know how much. I need the two of us to at least get along, and maybe she can help me understand Enzo better if I befriend her.

"Hello, Liesel, would you like to join me for coffee while the boys work?"

She grins. "I'd love to."

Enzo, Zeke, and Langston all frown at my idea.

"I don't think that's the best idea. Why don't you join us, stingray?" Zeke asks, always protecting me.

I smile at him and wish Liesel would find Zeke or Langston attractive and within her reach, instead of looking at Enzo like he's already hers.

"No, Liesel and I need some female bonding time. We are tired of the boys running the show all the time. You guys go play with your fancy computers and guns and leave us before a while," I say.

Zeke tells Enzo with his eyes that he hates it and he can stay back to keep an eye on us.

Langston shrugs, as if to say he's not getting in the middle of it. *Smart man.*

And Enzo turns to me, seeing there is nothing he can say to make me change my mind.

"Behave," he says, kissing Liesel on the forehead like she's his.

Chills of jealousy course through my veins. It was just a friendly kiss on the forehead, probably to try and persuade Liesel to be nice to me more than anything else.

Enzo looks to me, and I know he wants to kiss me on the lips to show Liesel just how much he's taken by me, but he thinks better of it. Instead, he kisses me identically to Liesel. On the forehead, but he doesn't tell me to behave. In fact, his eyes tell me to give her hell.

I smile. I know he wants the two of us to get along, but I can't, not until I understand what Liesel means to him.

The men reluctantly disappear, leaving Liesel and me alone.

"Change into your swimsuit and meet me upstairs in five minutes. I'll make sure Westcott has plenty of coffee to help you deal with the bags under your eyes. You want to hear my story. You'll get everything you want. And you are in desperate need of a tan. Your skin is far too pale," Liesel says.

I freeze, looking at Liesel truly for the first time. She's already wearing a gold and black bikini with a see-through white sarong around her hips. She has a full face of makeup, and her hair is curled in thick blonde ringlets. Her hair was darker the last time I saw her, but now she's dyed it a lighter shade of blonde. And to top off her look, she's wearing heels. *Fucking heels! Why?* We are on a yacht in the middle of nowhere, not going to the Met Gala.

But reluctantly, I agree. I haven't swum in the pool or laid out at all since we got in the yacht. If I'm going to understand this woman, then I need to do it on her terms.

And the only way I can truly understand Enzo is to know more about his past. Enzo will never face the fact that he needs to heal as much as I do, but maybe Liesel will be able to tell me how to repair him before it's too late.

I sit down on the lounger looking up at the sun. There isn't a cloud in the sky. This should be my heaven. Sunning myself on one of the most expensive yachts in the world. Instead, it's my hell.

Because the only man I've ever loved is here with another woman. A woman he could love if he ever let himself love again.

I hate her. She's competition. And she could destroy Enzo.

But I also love her for loving him. I can't fault her for falling for him. *I did.* Enzo isn't easy to love. He fucks up as much as he does right. But when he lets you into his inner circle, nothing can feel better than being protected by him.

Kai obviously loves Enzo. It's easy to see. I understand the feeling. I've been in love with him since we were fifteen. And the one month I got to date him was the best month of my life.

My heart broke when I realized I loved him and he could never love me back—that's Kai's fate. Loving a man incapable of love.

I'm not much of a saint. In fact, I'm the opposite of a saint. I have a law degree, and instead of helping the innocent, I work for big banks ensuring they, and I, get richer. I like money. Enzo has given me plenty to live off of, but when the love of your life has been taken from you, you find other things to pretend you love to occupy your time. And I love the thrill of chasing money, pretending that fancy cars, high-end clothes, and big condos are what get me up in the morning. That somehow those things will love me back.

"What can I get for you, Miss Dunn?" Westcott asks as he stands over me.

I shade my eyes to see him. "Coffee for Miss Miller and a pitcher of mimosas."

He nods. I'm surprised he hasn't already brought me a mimosa. It's what I've had every morning here so far as I sit by the pool by myself, with Zeke or Langston stopping by every once in a while to give me an evil look like I'm the bad guy.

They may have decided Kai has the best chance at getting to Enzo's heart, but they forget, I used to be her. I used to be the best and worst thing for Enzo. And all it did was rip out my heart and make Enzo put up more walls, ensuring no one ever gets through.

"Is this seat taken?" Kai asks.

I shield my eyes again as I look up at the scrawny woman standing in front of me. She's wearing a simple black bikini that looks like it came from Target, it's definitely not designer. She doesn't have any shoes on, and she's wearing a baseball hat to shade her eyes.

She has jet black hair. I have blonde.

She's a bit of tomboy; I'm a princess.

Her body is covered in scars; my body shines from all the plastic surgery I've gotten to hide mine.

We are so different, yet exactly the same. Both broken and hopelessly in love with a man who is more broken than either us. Because his emotions run deeper than either of us have ever felt.

I force a smile on my lips and nod to the lounger next to me.

Kai sits just as Westcott returns with our drinks.

"Iced coffee, for you, Miss Miller," Westcott says, handing her a glass. "And mimosas to share." He places the pitcher on the end table between us and then pours each of us a glass.

"If you need anything else, I'll just be in the kitchen, and I'll check on you soon," Westcott says.

I nod and sip my drink, waiting for him to leave before I speak.

"You look like shit," I say, not sugarcoating anything. That's not my style; I'm blunt and honest to a fault.

"Oh, um, I thought this was going to be a civil conversation where we try to get along for Enzo's sake. I'm sorry if I was mistaken, I'll just go," Kai says.

"Sit down," I say, jerking on her arm to keep her in the chair as she tries to get up. "I'm not trying to be a jerk; I'm just honest and have no filter."

Kai glares but doesn't say anything.

"I'm not going to apologize for anything I say either, so don't expect that. All I was trying to say is that you've been through hell, and it shows."

Kai narrows her eyes. "That doesn't sound any better than what you said before."

I sigh and lift my hair from my neck where a scar similar to the one she will wear forever on her neck lies.

Kai's eyes grow big, and her hand automatically goes up to trace the thin line.

"I used to look similar to you—not as bad. I only suffered for a few months before my own savior came for me, but I have the scars. With time, I've hidden them. Most with plastic surgery. Some with tattoos." I hold out my wrist where the word *beautifully* is written in script over a scar on my wrist where I tried to kill myself rather than keep dealing with the pain.

"All I'm trying to tell you is that you and I are more alike than you may think. And I'm trying to prevent you the same heartache I once suffered."

"You look pretty happy to me," Kai says as her eyes travel over my healed body.

"You of all people should know you can't judge a book by its cover. I look happy, but I will never be happy again."

Kai bites her lip as she finally understands what I'm saying. "Tell me. Tell me everything. Enzo saved you. He took care of you. You loved him, and then he ripped out your heart."

I nod. *And the same thing will happen to you.*

"Tell me, I need to hear the truth. I need to hear it so I can let him go."

I shake my head. "You will never be able to let Enzo Black go. Trust me, I've tried. But hopefully, you haven't fallen as deeply in love with him as I did."

"Tell me," she whispers again.

I close my eyes, letting myself travel back to the worst moments of my life.

♡

"THIS IS OUR NEW HOME, LADYBUG," MOM SAYS, SQUEEZING ME HARD to her chest as I stare up at the big dark mansion.

It's ugly and big and horrible. It looks more like a medieval castle than a home, and not the good kind. The kind with evil ghosts, and monsters, and dank rooms.

"What do you think?" Mom asks.

I can't tell her any of that. Mom has a job as a maid here. It won't pay much, but we get a free room in the guesthouse, and the money will be enough to feed us so I can't complain. And hopefully, the guest house won't give me the same creepy vibe the house does.

"I think we will have fun here."

She grins and squeezes my scrawny ten-year-old body tighter. "We will."

She lifts one of the two boxes from our car and carries it to the guest house. I follow, carrying the other box that contains all of our belongings.

This will be a better life. It has to be. *At least here we won't starve.*

We take the next hour to settle in before Mom announces she needs to get to work. She tells me I'm allowed to explore the main house, and the owners, a Mr. And Mrs. Black, have a son around my age I should go introduce myself to.

No, thank you.

I'll stay here and lock myself in my new room and decorate it. I've never had my own room before, and although I don't have any paint or decorations to style the room with, I have paper and crayons that will have to be enough for now.

Mom leaves, and I get to work coloring pages various pinks to line my walls. I can't paint them pink, but at least the pages will allow me to pretend the walls are pink.

I've colored twenty pages when I hear the noise. It's a sound I know all too well when we were living on the streets of Miami.

Gunshots.

No!

I saw the walls surrounding this property. I saw the men who guarded it. I saw the security cameras watching us as we pulled up. This house was supposed to be safe.

We were supposed to be safe here.

I don't think; I run out of the room and out of the small guest house.

I know better. My best bet at surviving is to hide under the bed or closet until Mom returns. But she is all I have. I have to make sure she is okay.

I hear more gunfire, and instead of running away from it like I should, I turn toward it.

I find the door and enter the creepy house. It's too big, too dark, and too old.

More shots.

I run up the stairs.

"Mom!" I shout, hoping she will pop out at any second and then we can run away from here. I'd rather starve every night than deal with the threat of guns in our own home.

I don't see her anywhere. "Mom!"

And then I hear a different voice, that of a boy's and he too is crying for his mom. His cry is different. It's louder and more panicked than my cry. He doesn't long for her to be found; he longs for her to be taken. Because he too feels the pain that looms in the darkness of this house.

I creep quietly toward the door, needing to comfort this boy more than I need to find my own mother. I've never heard or felt such pain. And it draws me in even though I know how dangerous and stupid it is.

When I reach the door, the sight I see terrifies me. The door is mostly closed, only open a crack, but it's enough for me to wish I'd stayed in my bedroom and never left.

I see a man with demons in his eyes, standing over a boy who can't be much older than I am. The only difference is where I have scrawny arms; he already has muscles. But those muscles are marked with bruises and scars. Scars I have no doubt the man standing over him caused.

But that's not all I see.

I see a woman lying on the floor gasping for air as blood oozes from her body.

"Are you really going to make your mother suffer?" the evil man says.

The boy's hand trembles, and I see the shiny black metal gripped in his hand.

No! His father can't be serious? He wants the boy to shoot his mother. He can't.

But I look to the woman who is already so broken and bleeding so profusely. Even if the boy doesn't shoot her, she's going to die. He might as well put her out of her misery. The pain in her eyes is unbearable.

"You failed her. You were supposed to protect her. To save her. And you couldn't. You weren't strong enough to protect those you love," the vile man says.

I need to do something. Either go inside and try to stop it or run and get help. This is wrong. But I do neither. I'm frozen watching the catastrophe in front of me.

A shot fires. And I squeeze my eyes shut, not wanting to see what happened.

Slowly, I open them and see the boy now lying on the ground, blood oozing from his leg. He doesn't scream or cry like I would from being shot. He welcomes the pain, like the pain is helping him avoid the torment his mother is feeling as she dies on the ground next to him.

"Now, be a man and put your mother out of her misery. She's in pain, much worse pain than you are. Show her mercy."

The boy's eyes are filled with tears as he looks at his mother.

She looks back and tells him she loves him. Then she looks at the man and tells him she loves him too.

How messed up is that? *She still loves this man who is most likely responsible for her death and for her son's pain. But I realize then that you don't get to choose who or how you love. You can't prevent it or stop it, no matter how much a person fails you, you still love them.*

That's when I vowed I would never fall in love—never.

Finally, the boy lifts the gun with too many tears in his eyes, and he fires.

I finish the story and look at Kai, who is crying buckets. I would be too if I hadn't already cried too many tears for that broken boy. That boy who was hurt more than any person ever should.

"Enzo killed his mother?"

"No, his father did. Enzo simply pulled the trigger. But that was the day Enzo learned he could never love. He'd be punished for loving, alongside the person he loved. And that he wasn't strong enough to save those he loved. But it didn't stop him from trying."

I've stayed away from the boy since that night. He scares me, but his father scares me more. I hide in the guest room, doing my school work there so I never have to leave. I'm not even sure they know I exist. I don't let them see me. The house has too many ghosts and demons, and I've learned to stay as far away as possible. I won't even swim in the pool out back, even when I know the boy and his father have gone.

I've become my own ghost. I lock myself in my room and pretend I'm Rapunzel locked away in a tower until her prince comes. But unlike Rapunzel, I will never be rescued.

Mother went into town to buy us groceries. And the water calls to me. The longing to swim in the beautiful pool pulls me out of the safety of my bedroom.

I think they were gone. They often are. The father takes his son out on missions for weeks at a time. I don't know where they go, just that they are gone. The sun seems to shine a little brighter over the house when they are gone.

Mom bought me a swimsuit only last week. A simple bikini for my newly starting to bloom body. I am a teenager now. And I deserve to get to leave my room. My mother has tried everything to get me out of the room, not realizing the danger lurking so close to our home. She doesn't realize the evil man she works for, or if she does, she pretends he would never turn his evil gaze our way.

So I take a chance. I put on the bikini, and I creep out to the empty pool.

The pool is rarely used. The boy occasionally sneaks out to swim, but he never throws any parties. And the father never swims.

The blue of the pool practically sparkles, inviting me in. And so I jump in, not bothering to hide my splash. Mom said we were allowed to use the amenities. And I have occasionally seen staff use the pool when the father was gone so I know it is allowed.

But it still feels wrong to enjoy something so grand.

But once I start swimming back and forth, I realize how right it feels. The water feels fantastic, and my muscles ache to get some exercise.

I swim hard, imagining I am a dolphin swimming free in the ocean. I would gladly turn into a dolphin and trade my sad life to become an animal. It has to be better than my pathetic life where I am destined to become a maid like my mother.

I hear another splash, and I stop, hoping it's one of the staff members. When I surface though, panic shoots through me.

It's the boy.

Although, I'm not sure I can call him that anymore. He looks like a man now, even though he's not older than fifteen. His muscles are large and defined. He has a six pack, or is it an eight pack? I can't tell as half his abs are submerged under the water.

"I'm sorry," I say, swimming toward the ladder to climb out.

"Don't go, Liesel."

He knows my name. He knows I exist.

I stop and stare at him. "How long have you known who I am?"

"Since the first day when you saw my mother die."

"How?"

He shrugs. "It's my job to know about everyone who lives and works in this house. And my room looks down into your room. I watch you sleep most nights."

"Don't you sleep?" I ask, feeling like he's a vampire from Twilight or something.

"No, never."

I frown. No one can never sleep. You need sleep to survive.

"I like what you did to the room. The pink suits you, and I like all the glitter you added."

I blush.

And then our world changes. His father yells in the distance, and the boy's ears immediately perk, sensing the danger.

"I have to go, you should go inside," he says.

I nod. I need to avoid the man at all costs.

We both climb out of the pool. I didn't even remember to bring a towel, so I drip the entire way back to the guest house my mom and I are staying in.

The boy starts running toward the house. The boy that knows everything about me, but I don't know anything about him.

"Wait...what's your name?" I ask.

He hesitates, looking at me like I'm a lost cat.

"Black. My name is Enzo Black."

And then the boy is gone.

Black. *It's such a dark name. A name meant to send chills to anyone who thinks of crossing him.*

I smile, watching the boy disappear. Maybe living here will be more tolerable than I thought. The boy didn't say it, but I know he's been watching over me, protecting me from the darkness. He will keep me safe here. He will become a friend, and then my life won't be so miserable anymore.

The smile remains as I walk back to the guest house. I am so lost in my own little piece of happiness, I don't notice the shadow covering the door. I don't notice the man creating the shadow. I don't notice the evil finally come for me.

"Black!" I scream as the man's hands grab me. But I know it's too late. The boy won't be able to save me. Not this time. This time evil won.

CHAPTER 17

KAI

I try to hold in my tears, listening to Liesel's story, but she makes it impossible not to embrace everything she felt.

Enzo's life was a nightmare. His father trained him to become evil like him. He forced him to shoot his own mother to end her suffering, and then his father hurt the only friend Enzo had: Liesel.

I know Liesel didn't tell me the story so I would feel sorry for her. She told me to better understand her and Enzo's relationship. She told me their history to teach me a lesson.

"Enzo's father raped or beat me several times over the next few months. It was the worst time of my life," Liesel says.

I swallow down my tears, doing everything I can to listen and understand her pain.

"Enzo's father did unthinkable things to Enzo. Tortured him in the worst possible ways to try and make him strong enough to become Black. But Enzo would rather have the pain himself than watch someone he loves getting hurt."

"He loved you," I say, agreeing.

She shakes her head. "He wouldn't let himself after what happened to his mother. The only people he ever let himself love are

Langston and Zeke, and he only allows himself that love because they chose this life. And he knows whether he loves them or not, they are going to put themselves at risk right next to him."

I shake my head. "He loves you, Liesel."

"No, I tried for years to get him to love me like I loved him. When we were teenagers, he learned to piss his father off enough so he would torture him instead of me. He took the punishment meant for me. And of course, I fell in love with him for protecting me. But he wouldn't let himself fall for me.

"When we got older, I persuaded him to date. It didn't last long. And even though we were both screwed up, I fell hard. He was the one for me. He protected me. He saved me. He worshipped me. And he vowed to never let another man hurt me again. The fucking was incredible, and his lifestyle was intoxicating. But he never let himself love me. Eventually, he realized he was hurting me more than helping me by dating me, so he broke it off."

For the first time since Liesel started talking, I see tears in her eyes.

"I loved him, and he broke me. And I can't ever heal from that."

I want to tell her how sorry I am. I want to tell her how I understand. But I can't. It won't make her feel any better.

"Enzo can't save those that he loves, so he doesn't allow himself to fall in the first place."

"But he protected you," I say.

"Only after months of abuse."

I suck in a breath, realizing what Liesel is saying.

"Enzo can't protect those he loves.

"He couldn't save his mother.

"He couldn't protect me.

"He'd rather face the pain himself."

"What do you want me to do, Liesel? I know that's the point of the story. Some lesson."

She cocks her head, shielding her eyes from the sun so she can look at me. "Not a lesson, but a warning. Enzo will never love you. I know you've already fallen for him. But you have to let him go."

"And what if I can't?" I whisper, clutching my coffee in my hands like it's a lifeline.

"Then protect him like he would protect any of us."

"How?"

"You already know the answer to that."

I nod. I do. Enzo can't handle those he cares about in pain. He can't handle not being able to save them. He can't handle not being enough.

"Promise me you will protect him, put his needs above your own desire to play superhero," Liesel says.

"I promise," I say, knowing exactly what I'm promising. That I have to keep myself safe at all costs, even if Enzo gets physically hurt. Because that hurts him less than seeing me suffer.

Liesel and I don't speak again. We just drink and soak up the sun, waiting for Enzo to finish his surveillance of Milo's residence.

I thought this whole time I was the broken one. That I was the one who needed healing. Enzo may refuse to love, but he couldn't stop the feeling from happening. His love saved me. And maybe my love can heal him back.

But what happens if I were to succeed? If I healed him and showed him he is capable of loving? And that love is what makes life worth living. That he can't fear it. *Then what?*

Would he choose me, a broken girl who he has to fight for an empire? Or would he pick his childhood friend, who has never betrayed him?

I know everything there is to know about Milo Wallace.

I know he's as evil and cruel as my father was.

I know he already bought a new whore to replace Kai.

I know his mansion in Italy is impossible to tackle without risking suicide.

I know he owns several of my yachts and prefers the sea, like I do.

I know he's a monster I will soon kill.

And I know I need to go interrupt whatever is happening between Kai and Liesel, because both of them are strong-willed and not afraid of a fight. And if I leave them alone for too long, one of them is going to end up going overboard.

I walk to the pool deck and find them both tanning themselves in their bikinis while sipping on mimosas.

They aren't speaking, which might be a good thing. It means they aren't planning anything against me.

"It looks like you two have spent your time productively," I say as I lie down on one of the loungers next to Kai. I'm wearing jeans and a black T-shirt, and there is no way I will last out here in the beating sun dressed like this. But I don't plan on staying long.

"We had a very productive time," Liesel says.

I put my hands behind my head, trying to seem relaxed, but I'm anything but. Not when two of the people I care most about have spent the morning together most likely threatening each other. "So does that mean you are friends now?"

"No, just not enemies," Kai answers.

I look at her, searching her eyes for more truth, but she's not going to give it to me. I look over at Liesel, and she's as much as a closed book as Kai is.

These women are my everything. They are both smart, beautiful, and fearless. They have both faced more evil than any person should.

I should have fallen for one of them by now, but I can't. *I can't love.*

And both of these women deserve more than I can give them.

I look at Liesel, my childhood friend I've tried to protect with my life countless times. Sometimes I was able to save her, sometimes I wasn't. But when we became adults, I vowed no one would hurt her. No one has. I've at least kept that promise.

And then I look at Kai, a woman I've let down so many times. And in many ways, I have failed more than Liesel.

Liesel learned a long time ago I'm not worth loving.

But I'm not sure Kai has learned the same lesson yet. I need to remind her we are enemies at the end of the day. That we are two people drawn together by the need to fuck, nothing more.

I want to go remind Kai of that lesson right now. Take her to my bedroom and fuck her hard instead of gentle, remind her I'm rotten to my core. But I don't want to hurt Liesel.

Liesel may know there is no chance at us having anything more, but I don't want her to think there is any chance I'll be with Kai either. I just want to fuck her.

"Go," Liesel says, dropping her sunglasses over her eyes, looking bored.

"Go where? We are in the middle of the fucking ocean, Liesel."

She raises her sunglasses so I can see her roll her eyes. "Go fuck her."

Kai freezes at Liesel's words.

Liesel starts shooing us away, and I'm not going to miss out on a chance to fuck Kai. If Liesel is okay with it, then I'm not going to miss this opportunity.

I grab Kai's hand and pull her to me.

She blinks rapidly, and I can already feel her pulse speeding just being in my arms.

"We should stay. It's not fair to leave Liesel all alone," Kai says.

Liesel laughs. "I've been alone my entire life. I think I can handle a few hours alone on this big fancy expensive yacht. Although, if we do ever decide to make port, I will be bringing some boy toys on for me to play with. It's only fair."

"Come on," I tug on Kai's hand. Liesel is a big girl. She knows I want Kai. And whatever these two talked about while I was gone didn't change anything. They still hate each other and with good cause. I used to fuck Liesel. She used to be everything to me. And that makes Kai jealous. But now I'm with Kai, and that pisses Liesel off.

I can't win. I'm an asshole. I deserve any grief I get from either of these women.

I hold onto Kai's hand as I pull her down to our cabins. She doesn't resist, but she doesn't walk willingly either.

I unlock the main door to our cabins and slam her body into the door as it shuts, caging her in with my body and raging emotions.

I didn't realize how badly I wanted her until Liesel pointed it out. Something about hunting an evil man who wants to take Kai from me turns me into a caveman who wants to show the world Kai is mine by fucking her over and over again.

Kai crosses her arms though, seemingly pissed at me. That isn't going to save her.

"That wasn't very nice."

"I would think by now you would realize I'm not a very nice man. In fact, I'm very bad. And I want to be bad with you right now."

I move in to kiss her neck.

She slaps me.

Which only turns me on more.

"What did Liesel tell you?"

"Everything."

I nod.

Liesel knows my past better than anyone. She could tell all my secrets. And it appears she did. And now Kai is going to look at me with pity. I don't want her sympathy. I want her fire.

"It doesn't change anything," I say.

"It changes everything."

I narrow my gaze, and then grab her wrists, forcing them up over her head so I can kiss her without her stopping me.

I don't want to talk about feelings and emotions. I don't want to talk about how I'm as broken as she is. I just want to fuck until we both forget about everything.

My tongue dances over her bottom lip, teasing her and letting her know I have all the power, and there is nothing she can do to stop this. I know all her buttons to press. I know what turns her on, and that pressing those buttons will send us into an endless spiral neither can control. Once we start, her mind will be shut out, and she won't want to stop us.

But her eyes turn into dangerous blue orbs as she bites at my tongue before I can retreat.

I growl as she holds her grip on my tongue.

When she releases, my tongue darts back into my own mouth. Afraid of the vixen taunting me with her perfect body in her skimpy bikini.

"Really? You don't want me to fuck you?"

"You have to beg first," she says, batting her long eyelashes.

Not going to happen, baby, I don't beg.

"Fine, you aren't the only woman on this boat. I'm sure Liesel will have no problem playing. She was, after all, looking for a boy toy to play with. And she knows how good I am in the sack," I say, releasing her and going for the door handle.

Kai slides in front of the door with a scowl I've never seen on her face. Not even when I betrayed her by selling her to Milo.

"You are the biggest ass on the planet."

"And you are the most stubborn. You want to fuck me, so why are you denying yourself?"

"Because we need to do more than just fuck. I have things I want to talk to you about."

"I'm not in the mood for a game of truth or lies, sweetheart," I say.

She hisses. "I don't want to play a game. I want to talk."

I shake my head. "Not going to happen. Now, do you want to fuck, or should I go find Liesel?" I wouldn't really fuck Liesel. I would just find a bottle of bourbon and drink with her until the sun fades. But Kai needs to know she isn't my boss. *I am.* Liesel may have shared my past, but that doesn't mean I'm willing to talk.

I stare at Kai who is just as stubborn as I am, and I know I'm not getting laid.

I reach again for the handle, but Kai shoves me back. I barely move, her body is about a tenth of the size my body is, but I step back giving her room.

"Fine, have it your way, asshole," she says.

She stalks toward me, and I back up like I'm fucking prey. The look of intensity on her face tells me to not stand in her way.

"You think that's all we are to each other—fuck buddies?" she asks.

"Well, we are also enemies fighting each other for a game."

She narrows her gaze and stops as my body collides with a wall.

"We are so much more," she hisses.

"I'm your protector. I'm your enemy. I'm your fucker. Nothing more."

"You're also my fucking drug. I want nothing more than to storm out and show you that you can't just demand I fuck you whenever you want. But one hit, and I'm yours. I can't quit. I want hit after hit."

My eyes darken with heat. "And you're my addiction. One I need to give up for my own survival."

She reaches her hand behind her body and undoes the ties of her bikini top. I watch as it falls to the floor, giving me the perfect view of her gorgeous tits.

"Then what are we going to do?" she asks.

"Fuck each other until one of us overdoses."

Her eyelids grow heavy as I remove my shirt and she takes in my sculpted abs. Her gaze drifts to the v that dips into my pants. And her breath hitches.

I love that I make her body respond like that. She can't control how her body reacts to me.

"I'm the only man who makes you feel this way," I say, caging her in again.

"Yes."

I hover close but don't fucking touch her. When I touch her, an explosion will go off.

I know it.

She knows it.

And I'm prolonging the feeling as long as I possibly can.

"I'm the only man who can touch you and give you pleasure and not pain." My lips almost make contact with hers, but I stop them.

"Yes." She pushes her bikini bottoms down, completely vulnerable to me.

I undo my jeans and push them down, retrieve a condom, and put it on. My cock is already hard, and I haven't even touched her yet.

I look between her legs and see the moisture. She's dripping, already demanding for me, and I haven't even kissed her.

My cock will be the first thing that touches her.

I stare at the condom I hate. I want to feel her skin to skin. But I don't dare get her pregnant.

She spoke once about not being sure if she could conceive. But in order to fuck her without a condom, I would need to have a serious conversation with her. Possibly call a doctor to look at her, and I don't want to share anything more serious with her. I've already led her on too much.

I will protect her, nothing more.

And fucking her without a condom would be more.

"Turn around," I command.

She does, sticking her ass out, pushing it so close it almost brushes against me.

She turns her head in my direction, her big eyes anticipating the collision of our bodies in a fierce battle neither of us will be able to quit.

I lick my lip instead of hers like I want—the anticipation taunting both of us.

For a woman who doesn't like being touched, her body is begging for me to grope her all the fucking time. We are magnets pulling toward each other, but also ripping each other away from everything else in our lives.

I stare at her ass.

"Don't you dare," she says.

I chuckle. "Your ass will be mine someday soon, little virgin. I will take all of your firsts.

"I took your first kiss.

"I took your first touch.

"I took your first fuck.

"I will take your ass."

She stiffens.

"But not today. Today, my cock is begging for your dripping pussy."

Her shoulders relax, and that's when I take my cue.

I plunge inside her and ignite the spark that only exists between the two of us as I find her tight walls with my cock.

"Jesus, fucking Christ," Kai cries, not from me pushing her pussy too hard, but from the fucking sweet electricity pulsing between us.

Everything ignites.

The pleasure.

The shock.

And emotions that shouldn't exist.

I don't know what this feeling is when I'm in her; the only thing I can describe it as is home. I feel at home when I'm in her. But not the kind of home that comforts and protects you, the kind that pushes your boundaries and creates a chaos of emotions.

I grab her hips, needing more connection as I push into her deeper.

Her legs spread for me, and her ass pushes higher as her face pushes into the wall.

"God, why do we ever stop fucking?"

"I don't know. We should never stop," she purrs.

I move my lips over hers. Tasting her purity and desire pouring from her lips. I get drunk on her lips as I thrust into her.

And the cries leaving her throat tell me she's lost in me.

I slap her ass, watching the pinkness spread and intensify our connection. My heat pushes through her cold, and I can practically see the spark of energy from the firm touch.

"God, it's too much."

"Never."

I slap her ass again as I thrust.

Her body trembles, and I know she's trying to hold onto her orgasm so this feeling can last longer. But it's impossible to hold onto. Just like us, the feeling is fleeting. Every day is a gift, and tomorrow it could all be taken away from us.

"I can't hold on," she cries.

"Then let go."

She bites down on her lip, trying to wait, but it's impossible to hold onto. She lets go. Her orgasm ripples from her head to her toes. Her body trembles. Her body flames. Her pussy tightens, coming hard on my cock.

And as much as I want to hold on, I let go too. Spilling everything I have into the condom still deep within her core.

I need a bed to collapse into, I'm so spent from fucking her against the wall. She is too. I wrap my arms around her, holding her up, knowing I'll need to carry her to a bed.

She has her own bed she might want to sleep in. I gave her the choice of freedom, but tonight I'm not giving her that choice. And she's never once chosen her bed over mine anyway.

So I lift her body and cradle her as I carry her to my bed. As soon as I regain my strength, I will fuck her again, and that's easier to do if she's here in my bed instead of hers. I would have to break her door down to get to her otherwise.

I climb into bed next to her as the buzzer on my door goes off. I really need to have that removed.

I dig my phone out of my jeans I threw on the floor next to the bed to see who is at the door.

Archard.

Fuck.

"What's wrong?" Kai asks, so in tune with my emotions right now I couldn't hide anything from her.

"It's Archard."

She frowns.

I press a button on a panel that connects me to the outside.

"What do you want, Archard?" I ask.

"I need to speak to both you and Miss Miller."

I'm not about to let him into my personal cabins or anywhere near a naked Kai again.

"You are speaking to both of us," Kai says, reading my thoughts.

I see Archard's reluctant face. He wants to talk to us in person—too fucking bad.

"Tomorrow. The next game will happen tomorrow. You won't have to leave the ship. But you will face your greatest weaknesses. Those you care about and love will be at risk. And you won't be able to save them, even from yourselves," Archard says.

Kai and I exchange glances at the warning for the game. The clue proves a problem because Kai no longer has anyone she loves. Her father was the only person she loved, and after his betrayal, she hates him.

And I am not capable of true love. Sure I love Zeke and Langston. I care about Liesel and Kai, but my father, who created this game, wouldn't know about my feelings for any of them. And the clue specifically said love; my father made sure I never loved anyone.

Love equalled weakness to my father. And my father made sure I never showed weakness by doing something as stupid as falling in love.

CHAPTER 19
KAI

Archard's words haunt me all night.

Someone I love is going to be hurt, and there is nothing I can do to prevent it.

It scares the crap out of me.

And I don't sleep one second all night.

Enzo doesn't either.

But neither of us talk about what the game could be. He just holds me in his arms all night.

After our first fuck, we both intended to spend the rest of the night fucking each other's brains out. But after Archard spoke, we couldn't. They only way we could have had sex would have been slowly, intimately, and vulnerably. And neither of us wanted that moments before we were going to have to compete.

So we didn't.

We didn't speak.

We didn't fuck.

We simply held each other all night, both of us dreaming about what tomorrow was going to hold.

Hurt someone I love.

The only person I love is Enzo.

But I doubt I will be the one hurting him.

And Enzo loves no one.

I thought he did, and he just didn't show me. But after hearing Liesel speak, after fucking him so hard last night, I know he truly doesn't love me. He can't love. His heart is too broken to love. Whatever his father did fucked him up in a way I'm not sure I can fix him. And that breaks my heart.

We've been living in the shadow of Milo hunting us. So consumed by running from him and trying to figure out how best to kill him that we both forgot about the game. And that we were going to have to compete against each other.

I'm the first to leave the bed.

I'm the first to shower and get ready.

The first to declare us nothing but enemies.

This round is going to be harder than the first. The first round, my father chose the game. This round, Enzo's father designed it. And somehow, despite my father being the man who sold me, I think Enzo's father may have been worse.

The game Enzo's father chose for us is going to be much harder than the first. And even after one of us wins, who knows what the consequences of that win be.

After the first game, Enzo sold me because he thought I betrayed him. It led to a war we will eventually have to wage against Milo.

That was before I realized I had fallen for him. Now that my heart is involved, I don't know how I'm going to handle any pain Enzo exerts against me during the game.

It's just a game. We don't have a choice. I can't let anything Enzo does get to me.

That's what I continually tell myself as I walk to the main deck where Archard is waiting for us—alone.

I walk over to Archard without a word, dressed in dark jeans and a gray T-shirt. My hair is pulled back in a low ponytail. I might as well have painted war paint on my face, because that is what I'm preparing for—war.

Enzo approaches Archard as well. Dressed similarly, jeans, boots, and a dark T-shirt. The only difference is the bulge in his waistband where he carries his gun as always.

Unlike last time, Langston and Zeke aren't by his side. He comes alone. Most likely because he is no longer sure if Langston or Zeke would be on his side or mine. Or maybe he's trying to make the fight fair this time.

Enzo's eyes hold the weight of the world—like he is walking to his own funeral. He knows his father better than anyone. And he knows that whatever his father planned for us is going to kill, or at least ruin, us.

Archard looks to each of us, then down at a piece of paper in his hands. The paper has the rules of this game on it. The paper will destroy whatever relationship Enzo and I have built.

"Get on with it," Enzo growls, no longer having any patience for this game or process.

This is only the second game. And already it's too much for either of us.

Archard doesn't react, completely unfazed by Enzo's outburst.

My eyes snap to Enzo's, and I see the worry and pain in the frown lines of his face, and my stomach flips again, knowing whatever we will face will be personal in a way the last game wasn't.

"If you will follow me, Mr. Rinaldi," Archard says to Enzo.

Enzo frowns as Archard begins to walk away.

"What about me? What about the rules?" I ask, not liking being left out.

"I will share the rules when I get back. The game is to be told to each of you individually," Archard says.

I hate it. If we are told together, then maybe I will get some clue from Enzo about how to handle the game. But now, we will both be in the dark.

Enzo doesn't look back as he follows Archard into the depths of the yacht. I'm left standing on the main deck alone, with nothing but the warm salty breeze to keep me company.

Why couldn't the game be something easy, like chess? Some sort of strategy game that determines how well our brains work. But I know that isn't what this is. Whatever awaits me in the rooms below deck is dark, and most likely, the cruelest thing I have faced yet.

Alone I stand.

Alone I wait.

Alone I tremble.

The wait stretches, and the fear creeps into every nerve in my body. I'm shaking, I'm cold, and I'm worried.

But I can't let the fear win. This is part of Enzo's father's plan. I will not let him destroy me, not like this.

I close my eyes, already feeling my body shut down. Maybe, just maybe, I can use that to my advantage for once. I don't want to shut everything down; I won't be able to do any task that way. I need to feel, just not the fear.

Let it go.

Let it out.

I feel the fear as I push it out of my core. And I focus on Enzo.

The love I hold in the depths of my heart is everything. I didn't let myself feel that love before—not fully. But I do now. Because his love is the only thing that might save me.

I force myself to feel instead of shutting the world out. Feel the torture I felt when I watched Enzo walk away from me and not knowing what he was about to face. Feel the love I felt when he held me in his arms all night, the man who shot and killed a man for wanting me. Enzo Black may be most people's hell, but he's my heaven.

Archard returns silently, my eyes are still closed, but I can feel him near me. Because he brings Enzo's pain. I feel it as clearly as I feel my own heartbeat.

Enzo is in pain. The kind that will stay with him for the rest of his life.

Fuck.

"Is there any way to stop this? Can I just withdraw?" I ask, my eyes still closed.

"You can withdraw, but Enzo would still have to complete the rest of the games himself in order to keep the empire. Once the games have started, there is no stopping it," Archard says.

Fuck Enzo's father. Fuck my own father. Fuck generations of our families before us, wanting us to play this twisted, vicious game all so the strongest would rule the empire. *Fuck it all.*

"Are you ready, Miss Miller?" Archard asks.

I laugh. Such a ridiculous question. I'm not ready—never.

I open my eyes until I'm sure the blue in my irises has turned to red. That's all the answer Archard is going to get. But it seems to be enough.

He starts walking.

I follow, the fear gone, replaced by rage. Enzo is hurting, and there is nothing I can do except end this game as quickly as fucking possible. But if I win, then that puts me up two to nothing. I don't want the empire. I can't handle ruling. Enzo deserves it all.

It's a no-win situation.

I push those thoughts out of my head for now. I don't even know what the game is yet; I need to focus on that first.

Archard goes to one of the cabins I've never been in before. I know this is where most of the crew sleeps, in cabins near here.

He opens the door silently and holds it open for me to step inside.

Zeke.

He's standing inside looking as clueless as to why he's standing there as I am entering the room.

He's wearing the usual uniform of jeans, boots, and a dark T-shirt. His hands are in his pockets, making the muscles in his arms bulge. The man is huge. Like Jason Momoa huge. And Zeke has the long locks to match tied up in a man bun.

Is Zeke here to help me complete this game?

That should comfort me. Instead, the butterflies in my stomach return in the form of wasps, stinging, and raging in my belly.

"This game is simple and is all about testing the belief that you are able to put the Black empire first, above everything that you hold dear," Archard starts.

Zeke looks at me with a nervous expression. We both know where this is going.

"If you were to become Black, you need the ability to extract important information out of any man you capture. No matter if they are your enemy or friend."

Please, no.

"Zeke has a past, a secret he has never told anyone, even you, Miss Miller."

No, no, no.

"Your job is to extract this secret via any means possible," Archard continues.

FUCK!

"You can use any tools or weapons you deem necessary to extract this information." Archard points to a table in the corner with various weapons.

Shit.

I can't use any of that on Zeke. And even if I wanted to, he's stronger, more powerful than I am.

"You can bring in any person you need to help subdue him, but you are the one who has to do all the torturing. And you can torture him, even to death, so as long as you get the information."

I can't bring myself to look at Zeke as I feel the tears in my eyes. There is no way I will be able to hurt him.

"Who does Enzo have to torture?" I ask, my voice stronger than I feel.

"I'm sorry, but I'm not allowed to tell you that information. That is part of the game. Enzo doesn't know who you are torturing, and you don't know who he is torturing."

But I already know who he's torturing, the only person he would give his life for—Liesel. *His everything.* I saw how her contact was written on his phone when he was scrolling absentmindedly through his phone last night, trying to distract himself from what is to come. It broke my heart at the time, now it destroys me.

"Any other questions?"

"So the winner is whoever extracts the information first?"

"Yes."

I can't let Enzo hurt Liesel.

But I can't hurt Zeke.

There has to be another way.

"I have monitors in both rooms I will be watching. I know the information each prisoner contains, and I'll know when that information is extracted. Otherwise, there are no rules."

"I don't get to know what information I'm looking for?"

"No."

Archard walks to the door, "When the fog horn sounds, you may begin."

And then he's gone, locking the door behind him.

And I'm left alone with Zeke. But I still can't bring myself to look at him. I need a second to breathe, to think, to find a way out of this mess before I lose my soul by torturing a man who doesn't deserve it.

The fog horn sounds, giving me no time. Not enough time to figure out how to save us all.

And then I hear a scream so loud it sends vibrations through the entire boat. A cry that will live inside me forever. A cry of a heart breaking.

Enzo's cry, scream, growl all rolled into one. It's a cry of a warrior about to face a battle. The cry of a man so destroyed by what he has to do. And I know I have limited time to save Enzo. Because there is no way he's going to back down from this challenge, even if it destroys him in the process.

♡

THE FIRST THING I DO IS WALK TO THE DOOR, TESTING TO SEE IF I'm locked in.

I am.

I'm trapped in this nightmare.

And the only way to get out is to torture one of the few people in the world who loves me.

Slowly, I turn to face Zeke, who is still standing there with his hands in his pockets. He's still weak from getting attacked before because of me. And scars etch into his tan skin. I can't cause more.

I bite my lip as I try to figure a way out of this. It's just a puzzle I need to solve, that's all. I don't have to torture anyone.

"What is your secret, Zeke?" I ask, maybe it will be that simple.

Zeke cares about me, loves me even, not in a romantic way, but in an —I'm your big protective brother who will beat the shit out of anyone who touches you, sort of way.

"I can't," he says.

I frown. "Why not? You care about me. You definitely care about Enzo. He's in the other room right now, torturing Liesel. She's suffering. He's suffering. You can end it all if you just tell me."

"I can't," he repeats.

"Why not?" Maybe the secret is truly so big he can't spill it. Even to save himself. To save me. To save Liesel. To save Enzo.

We don't speak, just peer into each other's souls. *What are you hiding, Zeke? What is so important you can't tell me to stop the pain?*

"Because you can't win," he finally says.

"What?"

"I can't let you win."

I frown. "But I thought..."

Zeke walks over to me and puts his arms on my shoulders, like I'm the one who needs comforting instead of him. He's the one about to be tortured.

"I can't let you win because I love you, Kai. And I love Enzo too."

I nod. "I know that."

"And I can't let you win, because you deserve better than this life. Enzo doesn't know anything different. He doesn't know how to handle his problems without using his fists or a gun. You haven't killed anyone. You are still innocent and pure. You can be free when these stupid games are over. You can find a life with true happiness. And if I tell you my secret, then you will be one step closer to being trapped in this life forever. I would never forgive myself if I did that. Enzo would never forgive me. And if you are being honest with yourself, you would never forgive me."

"Will Liesel give away her secret to help Enzo win?" I ask, my voice filled with hope.

"No."

"Why not? She'd rather him win than me."

"Probably, but I know what her secret is. She'd rather die than share it with Enzo."

"Enzo won't torture her. He loves her," I say.

He doesn't blink as he says his next words, "Not as much as he loves you."

My eyes water. I've wanted Enzo to show me he loves me this whole time. I want him to tell me he loves me. But not like this. Not by keeping me from torturing a man. Not by keeping me innocent. Not by hurting the only woman he ever loved before me. Not by breaking his own promise to her to keep her safe.

"Don't hurt her," I send out a plea to Enzo. If neither of us tortures our prisoner, then neither of us can win. But then I'm pretty sure we'd all die in these cabins, because I'm sure the rules that Archard is following states to not let us out of these rooms until one of us has extracted the secret.

"What do I do?" I ask Zeke.

He opens his mouth to speak but is interrupted by another horrendous scream. Liesel's scream.

Fuck, I'm out of time to decide. Enzo has chosen. And he chose to torture Liesel.

I feel the tears drop down my cheek as a tiny crack in my heart forms. Enzo isn't perfect. Far from it. But I love him. I love how fiercely he protected me, even from himself, *but can I forgive him for hurting a woman as broken as I am?*

Zeke's eyes are filled with moisture too, and I know his heart is breaking just as mine is, but he won't relent. He won't tell me his secret, because he needs Enzo to win, at all costs. And the cost this time, might be too great.

"What do I do?" I repeat my question.

"Whatever you need to," Zeke answers.

Whatever I need to.

What I need to be able to live with myself.

What I need to do to save Enzo.

Because he is the man I love above all else.

I love him. And I won't let him torture Liesel, and in turn, destroy himself.

I love Enzo—I would eventually forgive him for this. That's what love is.

But Enzo doesn't love anyone, including himself. He won't be able to forgive himself for this. And I know that pain is something he will never be able to stop living with.

I walk over to the table and examine every weapon. I run my hands over each of them, feeling the pain they will enact with only a touch because I've felt every one of these weapons myself. I've felt the pain.

I close my eyes, sucking the tears back inside as I pick up my weapon. Already knowing my soul is about to turn black. My heart and soul are about to be given to the devil, freely. I'm about to curse my soul to hell, all to save a man I love. And I'm going to deserve every moment of fire and torture I'll get.

CHAPTER 20

ENZO

My scream is primal and evil and love and sacrifice and fucking everything. The scream sucks my life from me, while also energizing me.

And I curse my father who is burning in hell for creating this disgusting, cruel game.

But then what did I expect?

My father prepared me my entire life for this exact game. Which is why I learned to never truly love another person, so if I was forced to hurt them, it wouldn't truly matter because I wouldn't love them. My heart is guarded from the world because I don't love. And the world is safe from me because I can do what is necessary to prevent truly evil things from hurting the innocent, even at the cost of my friends.

But there is just one problem with my plan. Somehow along the way, my heart opened, maybe not enough to love, but enough to make vows of loyalty. Vows that tiptoe on the edges of loving another person.

I've only ever made two vows in my life. One to protect Liesel. The other to save Kai. And I'm about to break one of those vows today, because I can only save and protect one of them.

This shouldn't hurt me; my soul is already stained black. I already surrendered my heart to the devil years ago, when my mother died because of my gun. Because I couldn't save her.

And if I don't decide quickly, I won't be able to save either woman.

"What is your secret?" I ask Liesel. Hoping she will spare us all a lot of pain by just fucking telling me. But then Liesel was never one to save me back. I've protected her countless times, but she's never protected me. Not that I deserve anyone's protection.

"I can't tell you," she says, crossing her legs as she takes a seat on the chair I'm meant to interrogate and torture her in.

"Why?" I growl.

"Because I want to protect you."

I scoff. "You've never wanted to protect me before."

Our eyes burn into each other, sharing our pain, the love we could have had if we weren't both raised in this fucked up world.

"Fine, I want to protect myself. I want to protect what little love you have for me, because if I tell you my secret, it will break you. You will hate me, and I can't live with your hate," she says.

Finally, the truth.

Hearing Liesel's truth is so different from when Kai spills a secret to me. When Kai tells me a truth, it's because she wants me to know her better. When Liesel tells a truth, it's to hide more of herself from me.

"Tell me, Liesel. Make this simple, easy. Get back at my father. You hate him as much as I do. It would be like killing him all over again if we defied his game, and I learned your secret without hurting you."

She smirks, looking bored. "It would be great revenge."

Yes, please, just tell me. I don't even care what it is. Just tell me.

"Tell me your secret. Whatever it is won't change things between us."

"It will break your heart."

"You forget, I don't have a heart to break."

"That's a lie, and we both know it."

I frown. *Come on, Liesel. Just tell me.*

I reach into my back pocket and pull out my phone and scroll until I find her number. Then I hand it to her. Hoping to pull on her heartstrings.

She stares at the phone, at the name I've given her number in my phone.

My everything.

Liesel tears up at the contact entry. She never cries. Never. But she does now.

I kneel down in front of her. Knowing this could be it—the moment where I win a game before it even starts.

"You see, there is nothing you could tell me that I wouldn't forgive you for. You wouldn't even have to ask for my forgiveness; I would just give it—freely. I give it now, before you even tell me, because there is nothing you could say that would make me feel differently about you. You are my everything. You have been since your big brown eyes showed up on my doorstep when we were ten. You mean the world to me. I've vowed to protect you, to never let anyone hurt you, including me. Don't make me break my promise to you."

Liesel reaches out and touches my heart, feeling the unrelenting pounding in my chest. I wish I could say it was beating so wildly because of her. Maybe then she'd tell me her secret, but it's beating for Kai. Longing to go rescue her from her own torture in the other room.

Because I know who's she's trapped with—*Zeke.* A man she's formed a bond with I can't understand. It could be Langston, she's formed a relationship with him as well, but Langston is still mine, while Zeke has become hers.

I send out a silent plea to Kai. *Don't you dare touch him. Just wait. Let me win this one. I'm so close.*

I don't send the plea because I'm worried about Zeke. He's withstood plenty of torture before, and I know Kai can't physically hurt him too badly. But because I don't want Kai to relinquish the part of herself that is pure and innocent. The part of herself that makes her her. The part that is holy and sacred and hers. If she sacrifices her soul, it will only be for one reason. To save me. And I don't deserve her saving.

I look down at where Liesel still rests her hand against my chest. I take her hand calmly and bring her palm to my lips. I kiss her palm sensually.

"Please," I beg. "Please tell me. I already forgive you for whatever it is."

"You're a liar, Enzo Black."

I frown. "I'm not."

She shakes her head, hands me back my phone, and then pulls her palm from my grasp.

"I'm not your everything, not anymore. And you will never forgive me."

"Liesel, please," I beg again. I've never begged a woman so much in my life. But there is only one woman I would beg like this for: Kai, the woman who means sea itself. A woman that has conquered the sea, along with her fears and my heart.

"Please," I whisper one last time.

"I can't."

I stand, closing my eyes and turning away from Liesel. And then I let the darkness in. It doesn't take much, it's always in my heart, locked in the deepest part. It takes everything I have to keep the evil in and not let it out without me telling it to be free. But it's always there. Always ready when I need it, even when I don't.

It's the part of me that escaped its cage when I thought Kai had betrayed me. And I almost burned us all down in the process.

It's why even when I have to do evil things, I rarely let the monster out. I prefer to handle all the cruel things myself. I let myself feel every drop of pain, but that only feeds the monster more.

But this time, the only way I'm going to be able to hurt Liesel and save Kai is by letting the monster out.

So I do.

I stare at the table filled with weapons, and the monster laughs. I don't need a weapon to torture Liesel. Even the cruelest part of me isn't that cruel to hurt a woman in that way. And even if I did, Liesel is too strong to be broken with knives, whips, or guns.

She's faced it all at my father's hand and never broke.

But I know what Liesel is truly afraid of because I know her better than any other man. And I know I won't have to lay a finger on her to force the truth from her. Because the threat of pain is worse than the actual pain for her. And I know how to play with her head to get to the truth.

"Stand up," I say not turning to look at her, keeping my voice calm and cool.

The monster is out and ready; my body is flaming with the fire always burning inside me. What I wouldn't give to touch Kai right now and steal some of her cold, cool calmness.

I pick up the rope, the only weapon I will touch.

And then I turn to face Liesel, sliding the two strands of rope into my back pocket so she can't see which weapon I chose.

She's standing almost eye to eye with me in her ten-inch heels. I used to admire her for looking so fierce in shoes and outfits like the one she's wearing. A dark red dress and shiny silver shoes that make her look like sex and nothing else. But now, I see nothing but the scared little girl I saw in the hallway all those years ago when she watched me shoot my mother to end her pain—the moment I let the monster in.

Liesel stands not because she chooses to follow my orders, but so I can see the defiance in her eyes, and I know how much I'm going to have to break her to end this. And have a chance at saving Kai from creating her own monster.

"Back up," I say, taking a step forward.

"No," she says defiantly.

And then I use a voice I've never used with Liesel before. A voice I hate.

"Back up," my voice booms, bringing with it the fire of hell.

She stumbles back, the fear creeping over her now pale skin.

My eyes blaze with the fury my father put inside me all those years ago. I stand taller as the monster grows inside me.

I take another step, pushing Liesel back with my body without touching her because she fears what I might do to her. She stops when her back hits the wall behind her.

"Strip," I growl, my voice low.

She grips her dress and pulls it over her head quickly. And I can see what she thinks, that seeing her naked will somehow turn me on and make me stop this. I won't hurt her when I remember she's a woman, and I don't hurt women.

But I don't lust after Liesel, not anymore. My cock only points toward one woman these days—Kai.

Liesel smirks, but it doesn't reach her eyes as she stands naked in front of me except for her shoes. Her long flowing hair and large tits make her look all woman, and sexy as a goddess. But it does nothing to my body. My cock doesn't even stir.

"Turn around," I say low and breathy.

She smiles and does as she spots the rope I bring out from my pocket.

"Kinky," she says.

"No, Liesel. I am anything but kinky right now."

I don't want to do this, but I must. I won't lay a finger on Liesel. Not one finger. I'll only make her think that I could. That I will. That I'll hurt her.

"Give me your hands."

She extends her hands behind her back, and I tie them, careful not to touch her skin as I force her wrists together. And then I bend down and tie her legs.

"You're my prisoner, Liesel, nothing more."

She scowls at me as I look at her.

And I know the way to break her. Not with threats of fucking her, but with threats of never touching her. Of her never being enough. Of her meaning nothing to me.

I take a step back as she turns around, balancing precariously on her heels, now that her feet are tied together.

"You're nothing but a sick bastard. You're just like your father," she spits out.

I grin. "I'm nothing like my father. My father wanted you. He raped you. He took your innocence. I want nothing from you."

Her face drops.

"I want nothing but your pain."

She narrows her eyes, trying to understand what I'm doing, but I see her fear. I see her pain. She's exposed to me, and I see all of her.

I take out my phone, pulling her number out again, I type in the change to her contact.

"You are nothing," I say, showing her my phone.

"Take it back," she sobs.

"No, you are nothing. Nothing but the daughter of a maid—*my maid*. You should be cleaning this yacht, not living the life of luxury in your penthouse condo."

"Stop."

"The only reason you have anything is because of me. Because I let you. I let you leave my house. I paid for your college. I got you into Harvard. Me—not you."

Her eyes darken, and I see the fierce fire. Let it out *Liesel, let it go, stop making me hurt you.*

"I ensured your grades were straight A's by bribing your teachers. Every friend you ever met was me. I paid people to befriend you."

"Liar."

"Am I?" I walk toward her, and she tries to hop away, but it only gives me room to circle her like she's prey.

"Then how come you know I speak the truth? Everything good in your life was because of me, and I didn't even care about you. I still don't. You were just a puppet for me to play with."

"Stop," she says again, this time her voice is weak, not fierce. *We are getting closer.*

"You were my father's greatest fascination, and my biggest pain in the neck. It was fun watching my father play with you though. And you enjoyed it, didn't you?" I seethe against her neck.

"I didn't," she cries out loudly, so loud I'm sure everyone heard her.

Fuck, I hate myself. I hate myself so much for this.

End this. Now.

"Admit it, you've hated me this entire time that I've hated you. Since the moment you met me and saw me kill my mother, you hated me. All of your supposed feelings for me were just a trap. Just a way to gain knowledge about me to use later. So you could hurt me later."

"No," she whispers, her voice weak as her head drops.

"How does it feel?" I purr over her shoulder.

"What?" she looks up.

"To know that you are nothing."

I hook my foot under the rope tying her legs together and pull. She collapses to the floor, dropping to her knees before me. If I was my father, I'd make her suck my cock. She is at the right height for it, after all. But I'm not my father. I never will be.

But then why do I feel like I am?

I walk behind her and squeeze my tears down because I feel every drop of Liesel's pain. And I hate it. I hate myself. I hate my father. I hate all of it.

End this.

Stop the pain.

"How does it feel to know I chose Kai over you?" I circle back to the front so she can see me. See the pain and thinking all of my pain is for Kai, and none of it is for her.

I stand tall over her, looking like the complete demon that I am.

"How does it feel to know I broke my promise to you because of her? I will always choose her over you."

And then I choose the words that will break her. The words will be a lie, spoken full of truth.

"How does it feel to know I love Kai when I could never love you?"

She sobs. All she has ever wanted was to be loved by me. And I could never give it. She thought it was because I could never give it to anyone. And she was right. I can't. But she thinks I love Kai in a way I could never love her.

"I hate you," she finally says from the floor, naked, exposed, and vulnerable.

"I know; as I hate you."

Then the fire returns, and I prepare myself for the storm she's about to blast me with.

"I could have saved your mother," she shouts.

Her truth.

Her secret.

It guts me, just as she said it would.

"How?" I growl.

She couldn't have, could she? I killed her with my bullet. She was dying, and I ended her suffering.

"Your father and you left your mother to die on her own, but I stayed. I watched. I snuck into the room, and she was still alive—very much alive."

No, that's not possible.

She sits up straighter, watching how her truth hurts me. "Your mother begged me to save her. To get help. I could see that although you shot her, it wasn't fatal. She would die a slow death, bleeding out. She collapsed to the floor when you shot her so you could think you were saving her from the pain by putting an end to her suffering. But she didn't die."

"Why didn't you save her? Why didn't you call for help? My father and I left the premises that day. You could have saved her. Called an ambulance. Nothing was stopping you."

And then I see the monster in her eyes. I wasn't the only one who gained a monster that day. "Because I saw the pain in her eyes. I saw the evil. She still loved your father despite everything he did to her. She loved him—the monster, the devil himself. And because she loved him, I couldn't let her live. So I left. I let her die on that floor alone."

I close my eyes holding in my pain. It's not fair to hate Liesel. We were young.

My father was the one who started it all.

He shot her.

I finished her.

Liesel left her.

We all betrayed my mother. We all played our own little part. And nothing we do now will bring her back. The only woman who could ever love me. She may have had her faults when it came to loving my father, but she loved me and that's all that matters.

I reach into my boots and pull out my knife.

Liesel's eyes go big, thinking I'm going to hurt her with it to get my revenge, but I will never seek vengeance when it comes to her.

I slice through the ropes, freeing her, and then I remove my shirt and pull it down over her arms, dressing her like a broken doll. Because she's as broken as Kai and me.

The pain of her words hurts me, but I deserve them. Because I hurt Liesel. And she will never forgive me for it, just like I can't forgive myself for hurting her to win a stupid game.

So I turn and walk to the door that unlocks now that I've succeeded in my mission.

I won the second game, but somehow, I also lost. I let the monster out, and now that he's free, it's going to take everything to cage him again.

I let the monster win, and I lost everything in the process.

Fuck you, father.

CHAPTER 21
KAI

I pick up the gun.

I know it's the deadliest weapon. The only one I know how to yield because Zeke taught me.

How ironic that one of the men responsible for teaching me how to use a gun will be the first I use my skills on.

Ironic and sad. Because I don't want to hurt him. But the only way to save Enzo from himself is by ending this—fast.

As quickly as possible.

The other weapons would only draw it out. I don't know how to use a whip. I've thrown a knife, but that was mostly luck, and I can't get that close and hurt Zeke. He's not tied up. He would never let me hurt him. The only weapon where I can keep my distance and still hurt him is a gun.

I hold the metal in my hand, hoping that me holding it will be enough for Zeke to change his mind. Enough for him to stop this.

"Don't make me hurt you, Zeke. End this. I will have only won two rounds. I won't win more than two rounds. I don't want to be Black any more than you want me to."

"I can't. We don't know what the next round will be. We don't know if Enzo will be able to beat you. I can't let you win this round," Zeke says, still keeping his hands in his pockets. He doesn't look afraid. Not one bit. He doesn't think I'll shoot him, but he forgets how much I love Enzo. I will do whatever I can to save him.

"Enzo is strong enough. He can win at anything."

Zeke shakes his head. "He's strong, but so are you. You are more equal in this fight than either of your fathers ever imagined you would be. Enzo may have grown up in this world. He may be better prepared, but your father prepared you more in the single day he sold you than Enzo's father prepared Enzo over the course of a lifetime. You developed more strength in a single day facing that kind of pain and loss of control than Enzo ever has."

I hate Zeke for speaking the truth.

He stares down at the gun I'm loosely gripping. "You'll shoot me; I don't doubt it. You might even kill me in order to save Enzo. You love him. You want to protect him. But you forget you aren't the only one who loves him. I love him too. And I love you. And I will do what I can to protect you both—including die. My life means nothing compared to yours."

Who hurt you, Zeke?

"The love between you two is epic. It's the kind of love that only happens once in a million times. A love that will bring about change. Maybe it will end the world, or maybe it will save it. But it's that big of a love. You have already figured that out, and as soon as Enzo stops fighting it, he will realize he loves you too. And once you declare your love to each other, you will be unstoppable."

Tears, dammit.

So many tears pour down my face. Zeke is as hurt and broken as Enzo and I am. *Why didn't I realize it before? Why did I let him get hurt the first time?* This would be so much easier if I didn't already care about Zeke. If I hadn't already betrayed and hurt him.

"Dammit, Zeke," I say, dabbing at my eyes with my shirt.

He smiles gently, like the gentle giant he is. Any woman would be lucky to love a man like Zeke. He shouldn't give up his chance to save Enzo and me.

I hold up my hand; the gun pointed at Zeke as I feel my time running out. Already, Enzo could have hurt Liesel. He could have whipped her. Beat her. Hurt her. And I can't let him.

"Please, Zeke, just tell me," I whisper through my tears.

"It's okay," he says, knowing what I have to do, but it doesn't change what he does.

"If you say you want to save the love Enzo and I have, then you won't make me do this, you will end this. You will stop Enzo from hurting me, because if he hurts Liesel, I will never forgive him."

Zeke cocks his head. "Yes, you will. You love him. Love can forgive anything."

My hand shakes. "I can't forgive this. I've already forgiven too much."

"It's okay, Kai. I'll forgive you. Enzo will forgive you. And you will eventually forgive yourself."

My heart breaks so far open I'm not sure I can put it back together. A giant hole forms, endangering everything I care about.

Not time.

Not love.

Nothing will fix it.

I'm permanently broken. Because I have to choose between two men I love, and I already know who I'm going to choose—Enzo.

And that breaks me more than anything. Most love isn't tested like this. Most love isn't this big. Most love doesn't require you to give up everything and everyone you love in order to keep that love. But my love for Enzo does.

Our love is toxic. It's wrong. As Zeke said, our love is destined to destroy the world.

All the more reason to let go of it. *Save Zeke. Choose Zeke. Let Enzo go.*

But saving Zeke means I'll end up alone—never to fall in love again. Because Zeke is right, the love I feel for Enzo is a once in a million kind of love, and once I've felt that I will never settle for anything less.

But I'm selfish to keep Enzo's love even though it will end up destroying me and everyone else who enters our lives.

"Zeke," I warn, as I blink away the tears.

Zeke takes a deep breath as he ties his hair back, and then he closes his eyes, putting his hands in his pockets, letting me hurt him.

I swallow.

I can do this.

I can do this.

I can do this.

But when I fire, more of me breaks. I only graze the outside of his shoulder, but it's enough to cause pain and for me to know I've sacrificed everything because there is no coming back from shooting someone you love.

"Ready to talk?" I ask. *Please.*

"No, never, stingray. You're not strong enough. You can't hurt me," Zeke taunts—trying to make me shoot him again. Trying to take away some of my pain. But then he shouldn't have used his adorable nickname for me if he wanted me to shoot him.

Fucking, dammit.

It only makes me love him more.

I aim again, this time for his other shoulder.

And then the door opens.

I turn with wide eyes as I see Archard standing at the door.

"The game is over," he says.

I drop the gun so fast I'm afraid it will go off from the impact when I realize I didn't put the safety back on. But thank God, it doesn't.

It's over, all over.

The relief that washes through me is everything.

But then, I realize what it means. *Enzo hurt Liesel. He got her secret.*

And it crushes me.

First, I walk over to Zeke and examine the flesh wound I caused on his shoulder.

He laughs, shaking me off. "I'm fine. You barely hit me. If that's your aim, we need to practice some more. If you are torturing someone, the goal is to shoot them where it hurts."

His words are meant to make me laugh, to make me feel better, but they don't.

"Hey, stingray." He lifts my chin with his finger. "I forgive you, but honestly there is nothing to forgive. You were protecting Enzo, and I love you even more for that."

He pulls me into a hug before I can argue.

We are okay.

This won't come between our friendship.

Even though it should.

Even though it hurt me to hurt him.

Even though the cut is only skin deep, it's enough to know what I would have done.

"Go," he whispers, knowing I need to see Enzo. I need to find out the truth. I need to know what he did to win.

Archard has already left. So I run out searching.

Nothing.

There is nowhere to go down here except our rooms. And I don't think Enzo went there. At least not until he has officially been declared the winner.

So I go up. Up to the top deck and I find them—Archard and Enzo.

I walk slowly over. Enzo won't meet my gaze. In fact, I'm not sure he recognizes I am here at all. And I can't feel him like I usually can.

I can't feel his cold.

I can't feel his love.

I can't feel his pain.

"Good job, everyone. Round two is officially over," Archard says.

I hiss when Archard says 'good job' like we are competing in a track event.

Fuck him.

"Enzo is the winner. That means you are tied—one to one. I will schedule the next round soon, determined by Kai's father. Until then, I guess it's back to sailing the ocean," Archard says trying to lighten the mood. But the mood will not be lightened.

Archard realizes he is no longer welcome and leaves us alone on the small top deck. The deck has the best views, but the smallest surface area. It is empty except for the two of us.

Enzo still doesn't look at me. He hides—like a coward.

"What did you do?" I ask.

Finally, he looks at me. And the anger etched there is not what I was expecting.

I was expecting pain, agony, regret, and the need for forgiveness. Instead, I got rage.

So I push more. "What the hell did you do?" I step into his space, filling it with my own anger.

"I won. What the hell does it look like I did?"

I see the sweat on his brow. The bulging of his veins. The grip of his hands. Whatever he did to Liesel was physical. It was painful and required all of him.

I take a step back. "I can't believe you hurt her."

He growls at my words. "Does it shock you, that I'm a monster? I thought you had already learned that lesson, baby."

"Don't call me baby," I say, and I feel the hole in my heart expanding. *Bigger, bigger, bigger.* If it gets much bigger, it will rip completely in half. As it is, I'm not sure I can forgive him, and I don't even know how he hurt Liesel, just that he did.

"What. Did. You. Do?" I ask again. I need answers. I need to see the monster. I need to know how big of a monster I am when I forgive him.

His eyes dig into my soul and pull out my truth. "The same as you. The only difference is I was faster. I found my monster sooner."

"I hate you."

"Good, at least we agree on something."

"Stop!" Liesel's voice booms over everything. We both turn in her direction as she stands at the top of the ladder that leads up here, looking more like a girl than the sexy woman I know her to be.

She looks at Enzo. "You don't get to hate yourself. You did what you had to do. What you did wasn't that bad. I'll heal, I always do. Just give me a few days."

Then she glares at me. "And you, you don't get to be pissed. You don't get to determine if you forgive him or not. There is nothing you need to forgive. She lifts the T-shirt I realize is Enzo's to reveal her untouched body. I hadn't even realized Enzo wasn't wearing a shirt; I was so consumed with my own pain.

"He didn't hurt me, at least not physically. He found another way to get my secret. And my secret hurt him more than it hurt me." Liesel stares up at the man we both love. "And he chose *you*. He saved *you*. His father forced him to choose, even from his grave. He saved you. He kept his promise. Don't hate him for it."

And then, she's gone.

And I know her words are the truth. I shouldn't hate him because he did save me from completely ruining myself. From physically harming Zeke. He found a way to save us all with the least damage done.

"You hate me, truth or lie?" Enzo says.

I think for a second, but I already know my answer. "Truth."

He nods.

"You hate me, truth or lie?" I ask.

"Truth."

I swallow hard. We both hate each other, but only because of how much we love each other. You can only truly hate those you love, and I know now that Enzo saying he hates me might be the closest I ever come to hearing him say he loves me.

Taking away the hate isn't about forgiveness. We don't need to forgive each other. Our love just lives on a spectrum between love and hate. Right now, our feelings are at one end of that spectrum, and someday they will end up on the other end. It's when one of us stops loving each other and removes themselves from the spectrum that my world will end.

"Show me your hate. Show me your pain. Take it out on me. Use me," I say.

He shakes his head. "No, I'm going to my room. I'll see you when I see you."

I move in front of him, preventing him from going anywhere. "Did I ask you? No, I told you. Use me, and I'll use you right back."

I push hard against his bare chest, and my hands instantly burn. His skin has never felt as hot as it does right now. And I realize it's because the devil inside him is out right now, and he doesn't know how to cage it again. That's why he burns. And if he's not careful, he'll burn himself down, along with everyone on this ship.

"You're hot."

"You're wet," his eyes dip down to between my legs.

I roll my eyes. "I meant temperature hot."

"I meant soaked like you just got caught in a rainstorm."

I bite my lip. I was always taught never to play with fire, but I have a feeling playing today is going to do more than get me burned. Playing today will mean giving up everything to the fire and letting it consume me.

But maybe my ice is enough to save myself, at least this time.

"I'm warning you I will destroy you if you don't let me pass. I will take everything and never give it back. I will burn you to the ground. I will feed on your fears and show no mercy."

"Good, because I have no fears left to feed on. And I've always wanted to tame a beast."

I move in to kiss him hungrily, planning on nipping and biting my way over his body. But he catches my chin in his hand. *Fuck.*

"I'm not here for your kisses," he says.

"Then what do you want?"

His eyes heat. "I want you to pay for what I had to do to Liesel."

I grab his jeans, jerking our bodies together. "Oh, I'll gladly pay, and take everything I deserve from you."

I grab his cock through his jeans. "Because your cock will be my payment."

He gives me an evil smile, and my body tingles, trying to figure out what is going to happen next.

His hands go to my T-shirt, ripping it expertly down the middle. *T-shirt.*

That's when I remember Liesel was naked except for his shirt. *Naked!*

And now I'm pissed off.

I grab his balls and twist.

He jerks and winces at my grip.

"You fucking bastard. Did you fuck her? Is that how you got her to surrender her secret?" Although, I don't think fucking Liesel would have convinced her to talk. She wants to fuck Enzo.

"I didn't touch her."

I don't stop twisting.

"Lies."

He shakes his head and spins me around, pushing my stomach into the railing and my ass into his throbbing cock. "Oh, baby, when will you learn to tell the difference between when I'm telling the truth and lying?"

He grinds into my backside. "My cock only gets hard for you." He rubs it into me until I can feel just how hard.

"I made her strip so she would feel vulnerable."

He jerks my pants and panties down until I'm naked.

"I tied her up so she would feel at my mercy."

He pulls my hands behind my back as if I'm tied up.

"And then I pulled the truth from her with lies," he whispers into my ear.

I hear his pants going down.

"But I tell you when I'm lying, and when I'm telling the truth. And I don't plan on speaking much longer. I plan on fucking you until you fear me again. Until you want nothing to do with me. Until you run away, because now that I've let the monster free, he won't go away. Not without a fight. And you will get hurt in the meantime."

And then, we are falling. Down into the fucking ocean. To the place Enzo still thinks I fear. But I don't. I don't fear the ocean, especially not with Enzo wrapped around me.

The water is the same temperature as my skin, which means it must feel cold to Enzo. The surface of the water consumes me in one gulp. The impact of the water separates us for a second as we become submerged under the water.

I open my eyes, knowing the salt water will sting, but I don't care. I want to see him.

And when I do, it feels like magic. Like we are the only two people left in the world swimming in the depths of the ocean. Enzo's eyes meet mine, open just as wide despite the pain, and I see every-thing—the pain, the fear, the love.

He's as scared to love me as I am to love him.

But we don't live our lives letting fear win.

It's more than the dread controlling his love. At least it's not his fear, but his fear for me. All those he loves end up hurt by him or his enemies.

Liesel is the latest casualty. He didn't physically hurt her, but he still caused her pain her even after promising he never would.

I know. I know you can't love me.

And then we both break the surface, breathing in air we both desperately need.

We don't connect immediately, the connection we had under the water was enough to overwhelm both our senses.

And suddenly just as fast as we took the dive into the water, Enzo is upon me, running his hands over my naked wet body.

"You really aren't afraid?" he asks. His question has a double meaning. *Am I afraid of the water? Am I afraid of loving him?*

"No, I'm not afraid of the water," I say, because the other question I'm terrified of.

He nods, understanding.

My legs go around his waist as his cock presses between my legs begging to be let in.

I want nothing more than to let him in, but fucking in the ocean, as romantic as it sounds, is very difficult to actually do. I want to press my lips to his, but I realize from his expression he still won't let me. He doesn't want to let me all the way in. So I'm left clinging to him with my body, hoping it's enough for him to feel the emotions I reaching out for him.

"We have to swim," he says suddenly.

"What?"

He laughs, realizing I haven't noticed our predicament. He nods in the direction behind me. I turn and realize the yacht has continued moving away from us.

Shit.

But why, despite my brain fearing the yacht stranding us in the middle of the ocean, does my heart not care? *Because I'm with Enzo.*

Enzo reads my mind.

"Swim, we will figure the rest out later," he says.

He waits, and I start doing the breaststroke, not sure if it will be enough to catch up to the yacht, but surely someone will notice us both missing soon and stop the yacht or turn it around to search for us.

I swim hard with Enzo by my side. And I swear the only thing missing from my perfect piece of heaven would be if some dolphins came up next to us and started swimming, leading us back.

Instead, it's just the two of us. And it's the first time in years I don't fear the ocean. Even if we died here in the water, this moment would be worth it. This moment of connection with a man I love. That's what I want out of life—love. I realize how empty my life was before without it.

And I'd rather have love and die young from heartbreak than spend a long, lonely life without love.

We both stop automatically as we near the yacht. As I suspected, someone noticed our absence and stopped the yacht. We climb up on the back, soaked, exhausted, and naked.

But it's not time for rest.

Enzo pushes me down onto my back as his body engulfs me. We don't have a condom, but neither of us cares. The chances that I am capable of getting pregnant are slim. What's more important is this connection.

Enzo enters me, and my entire body feels home again. This is what has been missing from my life, and I'm never letting it go.

Milo will have to pull Enzo from me with all the force of the world to keep me away from him. And I know that Milo doesn't have that kind of power. The kind is bigger than anything of this world. That's the kind of power needed to separate me from Enzo.

He thrusts so deep inside me I can't distinguish from where he ends and I start. I've never felt so connected to him.

"The games can't hurt us," I start as he thrusts silently.

"The truth can't hurt us," I continue.

"The lies can't hurt us," he finishes.

"Because we have something greater—"

Enzo doesn't let me finish my sentence. His lips crash down on mine. Taking my breath away with a kiss I've been desperate for. A kiss I needed more than I needed air. And the kiss is everything. It is love itself even if Enzo would never admit it out loud.

Nothing can hurt us, not anymore, because we have something greater...

"Sir, Rowan Evans is here," Vito says, stepping into the office.

I sit in my chair behind my desk—pissed and angry.

I don't know why the man who stole Kai from me wanted an audience. But I allow him to come, if for no other reason than I can shoot him in person.

The door opens again, and Rowan steps inside.

"Well, isn't this a surprise. I didn't think you would ever be willing to face me, not after what you did," I say.

"Did I hurt you?" Rowan asks, his eyes searing.

"Not physically, but you took from me."

"And it earned me Enzo Black's trust."

I study him. "Why do you hate Enzo Black?"

"Because his father took someone I loved from me—my wife. And I swore on her life I would get retribution. He's already dead, but I'll settle for killing his son."

My eyes darken. I was ready to kill this man for taking from me, but I might be willing to forgive the sin if he helps me take down Enzo Black.

"I assume you gave him the whore back?" I ask.

"Yes, but she's not just a whore. She is so much more."

I huff. "I don't care if she's a fucking princess. I want to steal her back and make her my whore. Then I want Enzo Black to die slowly, and watch him suffer."

He smirks like he thinks I'm a fool. *How dare he!*

"Kai is Katherine Miller, Kai Miller. We all thought Enzo had already fought to claim the title of Black. But we were wrong. She's the woman he has to fight for power of his empire."

How did I not make the connection myself? She really is a princess, and what she could inherit is more powerful than inheriting any throne. The Black empire makes more money than most small countries. It has men and spies in almost every country. But that is not where the Black empire shines. The technology that has been developed for security purposes is greater than anything else. That's why I buy all my security systems and yachts from him. But I know Enzo keeps the best technology for himself, that way he is always protected.

What I could do with that kind of power! If my empire were melded with his, I would be unstoppable.

"But the girl can't have a chance at winning, not against Enzo," I say sadly, realizing the girl really has no use beyond my initial plan.

"I heard you are missing a ring," the man says, staring at my empty pinky finger. "That was the first task. She won. She stole it."

An evil grin forms on my face.

"They are tied—one to one. The first to three wins. Enzo is strong, but so is Kai. And with your help, the girl could win."

I nod, a new plan forming. I can now see why Enzo was so fascinated with her. She's his enemy. And she equals him in every way.

I need to steal her. *Or I need to steal him.*

I need to threaten something she cares about to ensure she is on my side. *Or threaten someone he cares about.*

I need to train her to win. *I need to force him to fight for me.*

I need to weaken Enzo. *I need to weaken Kai.*

I need to take the Black empire. It doesn't matter which of them I choose. I have leverage on both Enzo and Kai. And I won't need either for long, just long enough to win the empire.

That's the endgame—getting Black's empire. And Rowan will help me accomplish that.

"I have a plan, and you are going to help me enact it."

Black is about to lose everything he cares about. His friends, his family, his woman, and his empire. And only when he's lost everything will I rest. Only when Enzo Black is nothing but a name people whisper in memory will I stop.

It's been weeks since I won the game.

I thought the game would destroy us, but instead it healed us. And something happened inside me in the ocean with Kai I can't explain.

It's like the ocean healed me along with Kai.

I've never felt so calm as I do now. I didn't think the monster would ever go back in its cage. And I don't think it did. Instead, I've learned to live with the monster free. And in turn, I've never felt so free myself.

I'm not the only one who has healed.

Kai leans over the railing on the top deck where we dove into the ocean together weeks ago. She smiles as she stares out at the blue abyss she has so much in common with.

Kai and I have healed—together.

I don't know what you would call our relationship. There is no label to accurately define our relationship. We aren't dating, we aren't boyfriend and girlfriend, we aren't married. We aren't in love. But our relationship is different than anything I've ever felt before.

I'm no longer in constant pain every day. I'm no longer guarding my heart or holding back any part of me. I'm free.

Our relationship isn't the only one that has healed.

Kai and Zeke have grown closer, until they seem closer than my relationship is with Zeke. They share secrets like they are best friends.

Langston on the other hand has grown closer to me as he sees his best friend grow a relationship with Kai, leaving him in the dust. Langston has grown more and more unsettled as the days pass, and I know he's missing the comfort of a woman in his bed. He used to enjoy countless dates and women in his bed every night. But here he can't have that. His playboy lifestyle can't exist here.

Zeke, on the other hand, is used to being alone. And having Kai welcome him so openly has brought him to life.

I don't know exactly what happened during the game. I don't know how Kai tried to hurt Zeke or why Zeke didn't just spill his secrets to Kai immediately to ensure she won. But Zeke doesn't look physically hurt. And whatever happened is nothing but a distant memory between them.

And even Liesel and I's relationship has mended. At least enough where we can tolerate being in the same room with each other. Liesel is no longer my everything, but she is still worth protecting. She's still a woman worthy of protection, even if she has secrets and pain like all the rest of us. That only makes her fit into my life more.

I walk over to Kai and lean against the railing next to her.

"Rowan wants to meet. I agreed. We need to end this fight with Milo," I say.

Kai nods. "I agree."

"You will stay here," I say, knowing it's a shitty move, but I don't want to risk her. I trust Rowan, but I don't trust the sea. This yacht is the safest place she can be. Nothing tops the security built into it.

She takes a deep breath. "I knew that's how you'd feel."

"So you aren't going to argue with me about it?"

"No, as long as you make one promise to me. You won't hide anything from me. You will tell me your plan when it comes to attacking Milo. And you will let me participate in the planning. You will let me judge if the fight is too risky. I won't go with unless it's safe for me, but I won't let men fight on my behalf if it's too risky," she says.

"My life means nothing compared to yours."

Her eyes burn. "My life means nothing without you."

Love has never been spoken between us. The word doesn't exist in either of our vocabularies, but sometimes when she says things like this, I wonder if she feels it—love. But then just as easily, I dismiss the thought. We don't love each other. We can't love each other. This is still going to end with one winner and one loser.

"I need to go. I'm taking Langston and Zeke with me. They both need to know the plan and earn Rowan's trust."

"I'll be safe," she says.

"I know you will. Westcott has as many skills with a gun as I do. No one knows where the yacht is or that you are on it. And if you feel unsafe, go to your room. Take Liesel and everyone else with you. No one can hurt you there. The walls are impenetrable."

She kisses me softly on the lips. "Go, make a plan. The sooner you talk to Rowan the sooner we can all head home. Everyone is getting far too antsy as it is. If we don't go home soon, there might be a mutiny."

I smile and then disappear before I change my mind and decide to spend my day fucking her again, like I have every day since the game.

I find Langston on the deck watching Zeke pull the small tinder boat around for us to meet Rowan away from this yacht. I trust Rowan, but I don't want him to know where Kai is. If one of his team members aren't as trust worthy as he is, they could tell Milo. And then we'd be fucked.

"Let's roll," I say to Langston as Zeke inches forward with the boat.

But Langston stops me. "I don't trust him."

"Rowan? I don't trust anyone fully, but he is our best chance at taking down Milo. He is the reason we have Kai right now."

"No, I meant Zeke."

"Zeke?" *What the fuck?* "He's like a brother to us. He's sacrificed his life for us."

"I know. But he's hiding something. When he did a surveillance run last week, he was gone longer than he should have been. He said he was checking out another yacht nearby, but our radar showed no other boats. There is something he's not telling us," Langston says staring at Zeke who has pulled the boat to us.

"Are you fuckers coming or not?" Zeke hollers.

I frown at Langston. "He is your brother. Trust him. We will be lost if we start fighting between ourselves. The three of us are family. Don't forget that."

I hop onto the boat and Langston follows.

I don't need Langston doubting right now.

I don't need Zeke losing focus.

I need everyone ready to take down Milo.

I need to protect Kai, and then I need to set her free as promised.

I thought I should wait until the end of the game, but the longer we are together, the more damage I'm going to do to her.

She needs to be free. And the only way to set her free is to destroy Milo.

CHAPTER 24
KAI

I feel uneasy with Enzo gone.

Like a piece of me was taken. I feel unsteady and unable to live. It's like living under a dark cloud. Everything is in shades of grey and white. Color no longer exists in my world.

A storm has started to roll in in the distance, and I wrap my arms around my bare shoulders as I stand on the top deck looking out at the horizon where I watched Enzo leave with Langston and Zeke. They've only been gone an hour, but it feels like a lifetime.

"Here," Liesel says from behind me. She's holding out a shawl to me.

I take it and put it over my shoulders as I'm only wearing a bikini top, and short shorts cover my ass.

Liesel is dressed more conservatively in sweatpants and a long-sleeved T-shirt. I've never seen her dressed so down before. She's usually glamorous and sex on heels.

"You okay?" I ask. We haven't talked since the games. Enzo and her seem to come to some sort of agreement between them, but I know it's not the same as it was before.

Liesel doesn't answer me. "You know he's coming for you."

I frown. "Enzo? He's coming back."

She shakes her head. "Milo."

"How do you know that?"

"The same as you, we can feel it. People like us who have been hurt before. Who have experienced true danger. We can feel it in our soul when danger is approaching. It doesn't always help us escape it, but we can feel it coming."

"It's just the storm you feel."

She closes her eyes as the wind picks up.

And then I see it. The light of a large vessel in the distance headed our way. And I feel it in my bones. I feel what I've felt this whole time, but pushed out because there was nothing I could do anyway.

"Get everyone and head to Enzo's cabin," I say.

"We can't enter, not without you," she says.

Shit.

"I'll go unlock the door. Get everyone. Now!"

I run downstairs as I text Enzo on my phone. The first text message I've made since getting the phone.

ME: MILO IS COMING.

I RACE TO THE THICK CABIN DOOR THAT IS AS SECURE AS ANY bunker built for a president.

I unlock the door ,and then I wait. Westcott is the first to arrive. "Get everyone inside. Stay here and hold the door for everyone. I'm going to make sure everyone gets inside."

"You need to get inside. Let me and Liesel handle getting everyone," Westcott argues. And I know Enzo has given him an order to lock me inside.

But if Milo comes I know he is coming for me. And I won't let anyone else die because of me.

I wiggle free of Westcott's hold easily and start running, Westcott tries to follow.

"Hold the door open, or none of us will survive," I order.

Westcott stops, staying by the door.

And then I run up pushing as many people as I pass down into the cabins as I can.

A buzz alerts me to my phone. I stare at it as Enzo's name pops up on my screen. I changed it from Giant Dick...

MY LOVE: FIFTEEN MINUTES.

I TAKE A DEEP BREATH FEELING LIKE A PIRATE ABOUT TO HAVE HER ship invaded. I need to hold Milo off for fifteen minutes. I need to keep everyone safe for fifteen minutes.

It could take that long for Milo's vessel to get here.

But when I get back to the main deck, I know my time is up.

Milo Wallace is standing on the end of the pool deck with a cheshire grin on his face.

But no other men accompany him. He knows Enzo is on his way here. He knows if I wanted to, I could hide away in the cabins below, and I would be safe from him. But that wouldn't keep Enzo safe.

"I think you and I should talk," Milo says.

"I agree." And then I step forward, surrendering myself to someone worse than the devil, in hopes of saving my love.

CHAPTER 25
ENZO

Milo is coming.

The text message both startled me and pissed me off.

We have a traitor. Someone on my ship, or Rowan's, betrayed us to Milo. It's the only way Milo would have known to attack while we were most vulnerable.

Fuck.

"We attack tomorrow," I say, ending the argument about when is the best day to attack.

"Agreed," Rowan says with a growl.

If Milo took Kai, I need to get her back as soon as possible. "And if he already has her, we attack tonight."

Rowan nods solemnly as I jump off his yacht and back onto my small boat.

We take off racing back to my yacht, and I hope to God Kai listened to me and went to our cabins. If she's there, she's safe.

I text Westcott, who I tasked with making sure Kai went to the cabins where it is safe.

. . .

ME: IS SHE THERE?

I WAIT.

One second.

Two.

My heart beats a million times in between each second.

WESTCOTT: I FAILED, SIR.

FUCK.

"Faster," I yell to Langston.

And then I take my anger out on Zeke, the only remaining man. I pull out my gun and shove it in his face. I need answers—now.

Zeke puts his hands up, his body movements are slow and cautious, filled with uncertainty as he watches me wield a gun.

"Did you betray us? Did you betray Kai?" I ask.

Zeke frowns looking from me to Langston.

"I would never hurt Kai. I would protect her with my life. I would protect her even from you," Zeke says.

"Then what the fuck happened? How did Milo know to attack?"

"Rowan," Zeke says.

Fuck. And I know he's right. Rowan betrayed me to Milo.

"Why? Why would he?"

"Your father made many enemies, Enzo," Langston adds. "When we return, I'll do more research to see why Rowan would hate the Black name."

"Fuck!" I put the gun back in my pocket. Happy that Zeke didn't betray us, but pissed that Rowan did and that I was stupid enough to trust him. Because it would be so much easier to take down Milo with his help. Now I have to face two enemies. Two enemies that are playing me.

And I will make them both pay.

We reach the yacht faster than fifteen minutes. I jump onto the yacht with my gun drawn, ready to face Milo here and now, but I find the yacht empty.

No other yacht is near. *He's gone.*

If he took Kai, I'm going to do more than just kill him. I'll kill everyone he's ever met.

And then I see her, standing out at the front of the boat, like a goddess protecting all on her ship.

"You're here," I breathe out relief and run to her to throw my arms around her body.

"Yes, Milo left as soon as he saw your boat approaching. He was just trying to scare us and let us know that he knows you have me," she says.

My hands run over her body, looking for any evidence of injury. I run my hands through her hair, touching her scalp, her face, her neck, her arms. Then over her stomach, hips, and legs.

"I'm okay. He didn't touch me. He was just threatening us, letting us know our time is up," she says.

"His time is up."

"You have a plan?" she asks.

"I have a plan. But it doesn't involve Rowan. I think he's a traitor. I think he's on Milo's side."

"Then how are we going to defeat Milo without Rowan's help?"

"I have a plan," I lie.

"Tell me."

I promised to tell her, but I can't. I don't want to worry her. I don't want to make promises to her I can't keep. And the only promise I've made so far is that I won't let another man hurt her. And I won't. *I fucking won't.*

Instead of answering her with words, I answer her with my lips.

I kiss her so hungrily I don't know how her lips don't detach from her body.

She throws her arms around my neck, clearly okay with me distracting us with sex instead of answering her questions.

But I don't want to fuck her here. I want to fuck her in her bed where she belongs. And where she will stay until Milo is dead. And I've dealt with Rowan.

I grab her ass, and she throws her legs around me easily without a fight. She wants me as badly as I want her.

Our lips dance with each other, vicious and reckless as I carry her from the upper decks down to ours. We pass plenty of my crew on board, but they quickly move out of the way.

When I unlock the door to my cabin, I shout for everyone to get the fuck out. Westcott is all who is left. And I give him a disappointed glare. He had one job, to keep Kai safe, and he couldn't do it.

Fuck him.

He's lucky if he has a job after I handle Milo.

I slam the door shut behind us, effectively locking out the entire world. And then I carry her to the door only she can unlock.

"Unlock it," I say.

She looks at me hesitantly, and I'm sure she can guess why I want to fuck her in her room. This is where I told her to go, and she defied me.

If she defies me now, she will regret it.

Slowly, she enters the password and shows her face, the key to unlocking her door.

I carry her inside the room that has never been slept in.

I throw her onto the bed.

"You promised me you would come here. You promised me you would be safe. Do you usually break your promises, Miss Miller?"

She breathes, heavily panting as her legs fall open on her bed. "I was safe."

I growl. "No, you weren't. The only place in the world you are safe is here."

She gives me a defiant look back. "You can't keep me trapped here forever."

"Oh, baby, you have no idea the lengths I will go to keep you safe."

"You promised you would set me free."

"And I will, when it's safe too."

"The world will never be safe."

I sigh. "It will be safer than it is right now."

"Promise me. Swear to me, you will let me go."

"When it's safe."

"No, when Milo is gone. When he is no longer a threat, you let me go free. Vow to me."

"I vow, when Milo is gone, you will be free."

We stare back at each other, neither of us relenting. Neither of us backing down from our threats and promises.

"And you promise me you will stay in this room until it's safe."

She doesn't answer me with words. She just shrugs off the shawl and unties her bikini top, knowing it will distract me from my goal.

"You'll stay here where you are safe from everybody, but me," I say as I remove my shirt over my head.

Her eyes soak me in, giving my body an appreciative stare. Most women appreciate my body, until they see the scars. The marks scare them. But not Kai, not when she understands the scars make me stronger, as they do her.

I slowly undo my belt and toss it on the bed next to her. She stares at it with wide seductive eyes. I don't usually bring toys into the bedroom, but tonight I need them. We both need to be punished for our actions.

Then I remove a condom from my pocket and toss it next to the belt. Only then do I remove my jeans and boxer briefs.

Kai looks at me with appreciation, like she's safe with me. She is anything but safe.

I attack. My body flying forward as I remove her shorts and bikini bottoms before my face plunges into her pussy. I'm relentless with my tongue. Building her too far, too fast, not caring enough to be merciful.

That's who we are. We are defiant and strong and push every button the other has.

And as much as I want her to follow my orders for once, it's why I care about her. It's why I'm so attracted to her. Because this is everything.

"God, Black! You're going to make me come in record time," she cries, her legs tightening around my ears.

I stop. She doesn't get to come. *Not yet.*

She moans at the loss of an orgasm.

I grab the belt in my hand. "Turn over."

She huffs, and her eyes gleam defiant. "You aren't using that on me."

I flip her over. "You deserve it after you broke your promise to me to stay safe." I pull her ass in the air and run the leather of my belt over her ass. The monster wants to beat her until her ass is so red she will never defy me again. But the other part of me, the part I've only just discovered wants to whip her until her pussy is dripping in pleasure.

I don't know which part of me will win, and neither does she—that's what makes me so dangerous.

My cock hardens at the sight of her warm ass in the air. If my cock gets his way, I will pound into her ass and forget all about the whipping part.

"Enzo," Kai warns, as I run the belt over her perfect ass again. I know what her threat means. If I hurt her, she will do something to retaliate.

"You need to be punished," I say.

"No more than you. I'm not the only one who broke a promise."

"My vow to protect you overpowers any other promise. Every. Fucking. Time. I won't apologize for that."

Finally, she pushes her ass into the belt I have yet to use. "Then what are you waiting for?"

She knows exactly what I'm waiting for, the battle inside me to finish and winner to be crowned—either the monster or the protector. I don't know which will win.

But then her ass is pressing against my cock, and I don't have time to wait for the battle to finish.

I drop the belt, and my cock pushes against her ass.

"I guess my cock won," I say, hissing into her ear as I rub my cock against her sweet slickness between her legs.

"Enzo," she warns again, both concerned and thrilled by where my new thoughts are leading me.

"It's time I take another first. That seems like the proper punishment." And then I push my cock against her asshole. She clenches, not liking the intrusion.

"Relax, baby. Trust me."

My words are magic to her. Because even though I broke one promise, I kept the most important one. I kept her safe. And I'm going to do better than that. I'm going to keep her safe forever.

I push harder as I kiss down her spine.

"Wow," she says, as I spread her open.

"I never imagined something could feel this tight," I groan as her ass cheeks clench around me.

I reach between her legs and find her most sensitive spot.

She relaxes immediately as I push all the way in.

"How does that feel so good?" she asks through a heavy breath.

"Because it's you and me, babe. We make everything better."

I pump into her as my fingers tease her clit, making her wetter and wetter. Her almost earlier orgasm is holding on, ready for a release.

"Why are you fucking me in the ass instead of my pussy? And why not before? This feels so incredible!" she cries.

"Because I wanted this to feel like a new beginning instead of a goodbye," I answer honestly.

We are both silent after that. Just feeling each other. Racing to make this moment last longer instead of shorter.

Hold out, don't come.

But of course, the moment ends as all the best moments do. With an explosion, new feelings stirring, and an empty feeling when it's all over.

I get dressed quickly, but she doesn't. She knows I won't let her out of this room again until Milo is dead.

When I'm finished dressing, I look at her almost reluctantly. I don't know what to do. *Tell her goodbye.* That I'm going to fight Milo. That I don't care if she hates me for holding her here. *She's safe.*

"Don't worry, I'm not going anywhere. You kept your promise; I'll be safe," Kai says.

But there is something haunting behind her words. Some truth she isn't speaking. She has her own secret. But then we always keep secrets from each other. It's one reason we would never work in a real relationship.

And I feel it. The moment our time is up. I'm losing her. And I can't keep holding onto her in this cage. She needs to be free. It's time for me to slay the dragon to save the princess. But this isn't a fairytale. Once, I defeat the dragon, I won't be walking away with the princess.

And so I walk out without a goodbye or a promise. I walk away, hoping I can free her. And hoping her secret won't destroy her. I walk away without a goodbye, even though I know it is one.

CHAPTER 26
KAI

Enzo leaves me naked and alone.

He leaves without a proper goodbye. Although, after what he did to my body, it felt like a goodbye.

It felt like death.

Enzo left me to keep his promise to me—the promise that no man will ever hurt me.

But he doesn't know I made my own secret promise. I would never let him risk his life to save mine.

I couldn't let him die saving me.

Enzo won't understand. He thinks after how royally he fucked up that it's his responsibility to protect me.

But I'm the one who is in love with him. He doesn't love me. He will get over my absence. He will be able to move on with his life —eventually.

But if Enzo were to die, I wouldn't live. My love is too much. And his death would end us both.

So I did the only thing I could to ensure one of us survived. To ensure Enzo survives long enough to keep the Black empire thriving. To bear an heir. To continue the legacy.

I didn't betray Enzo before, and I didn't now. But to Enzo, what I did will feel like the biggest betrayal of all.

But waiting now is the worst part. Now I have to put my trust in other people to keep Enzo safe. I know they will because they want what I have to offer. And I will do anything to keep Enzo safe.

Slowly, I get up and get dressed, putting my bikini and shorts back on as time moves too slowly.

I pace around the room, not really taking any of it in.

This isn't my room, it never was, and never will be. It's just a cage Enzo created to keep me locked in.

I try to focus on anything else, the gentle rocking of the boat, the humming of the air conditioning, or the warmth of the sun through the window. But it's useless.

All I can feel is him.

He's everywhere.

Inside me.

Around me.

Engulfing me in everything he is. And I want to revel in every drop of him. Because the beauty encompassing Enzo squashes all of the darkness.

But that beautiful floating feeling changes quickly.

I can't describe the feeling.

But my gut clenches.

My heart stops.

My world ends.

Something happened.

Something is wrong.

No!

I run to the door and to my surprise, the door opens. I assumed Enzo had locked it from the outside, but there is no need for him to lock it when he left a guard to watch over me—Zeke.

"What's wrong?" he asks.

I hold my stomach, feeling something in the depths of my core. I've never felt this way before. It's like a stirring of danger.

I glance at Liesel, who is leaning against the door in the hallway behind Zeke. Everyone Enzo left must have been ordered into the cabins behind the safety of the security system. I was to stay behind one more level of security in my bedroom.

The feeling is what Liesel described earlier—knowing that danger is coming.

"Danger. Enzo is in danger," I say feeling it so intensely that I can practically feel the pain myself.

Zeke looks into me trying to understand how I could be feeling this. "You're sure?"

"Yes."

"Fuck!" he curses, letting me go, obviously torn between going to Enzo's rescue and staying here and protecting me.

"We need to go," I say.

"No, Enzo's orders were clear. I keep you here where it's safe."

I smile softly, "Since when do we follow Enzo's orders?"

Liesel frowns from behind Zeke. "You promised to protect Enzo. You swore to me."

"This is me keeping that promise," I say.

I look up at Zeke. "What do you say? Are we going to save the world or what? At least our little piece of it?"

"Not until you put something a little more protective on you," he says.

I hide my smile as I run back into my room, throw on some jeans and a sweatshirt and return.

Zeke hands me a gun, which I take and tuck into my jeans like I've seen all the men do. My hair falls into my face as I do.

He pulls the scrunchie tying his own hair back and hands it to me. "Tie your hair back. I don't want the reason you miss shooting Milo is because your hair was in your face."

I raise an eyebrow as I smile and tie my hair back out of my face. "What about you?"

"I have perfect aim whether my hair is in my face or not. Let's go," he says.

Liesel stands in my way as we try to leave. "Don't hurt him."

"I won't. I love him."

"Then live long enough for him to learn to love you back," Liesel says before walking away, letting Zeke and I go.

The pit in my stomach doesn't leave; in fact, it intensifies as we get on the smaller boat and speed off into the night. I don't know if I'm making the right move or just putting Enzo into greater danger. But I can't just stay behind. I have to try, even if I die.

CHAPTER 27
ENZO

I stand on the stern of my boat, watching Milo's yacht face my fleet. Rowan's yacht is to my left. But this isn't going to be a battle of yachts; this is a battle of men.

Rowan may pretend to be on my side, but I know he's not. Langston confirmed the truth. Rowan has a vendetta against my father. He may not truly be on Milo's side either, but the two enemies may form together to take down a worse enemy. And I'm that worse enemy. I'm the worst it gets.

Because I have nothing to lose. And I fight like death means nothing to me. And I'll face my father's crimes, even though I didn't commit them.

They think I have something to lose—Kai.

But I can't lose her, not when she's locked away in the safest place possible.

And dying isn't a curse; it's a blessing. So I will fight as fearless as I always do.

"You ready to surrender?" I shout to Milo.

He laughs. "Are you? I think we have you outnumbered."

"We? It looks like just you," I say, putting my foot up on the railing like I'm going to a cruise instead of about to launch myself over the railing onto his yacht. I pretend I don't already know the truth, that Rowan is on his side.

Milo's eyes cut, and I know that's his cue.

But I'm faster.

I shoot Rowan before he has a chance to make a move on me. I watch his lifeless body drop to the floor.

Seconds later, my men have Rowan's entire crew surrendering.

"Now, as I was saying. Would you like to surrender?" I ask. "It seems you are a bit outnumbered."

Milo frowns. "I don't surrender to men who can't keep their word."

"I kept my word. Your quarrel was with Rowan. He's dead now. Now you deal with me."

Bullets fire, and we attack.

The rest goes by in a blur.

The orders I give.

The gunfire.

The screams of pain.

The bloodshed.

All of it moves so slowly and so quickly. Until all that I'm left with is me and Milo. Everything disappears into the background.

"You hurt her," I say.

"I did. And I will again," Milo answers.

"Over my dead body."

"That's the plan."

Our guns are pointed in each other's direction, but I feel her before I see her—Kai. *What the hell is she doing here?*

And then I hear the crack of the gun, and I know I've lost her.

"Kai!" I yell, begging for the bullet to miss. To not hit her. To go anywhere but her.

Zeke is standing next to her, I spot Langston holding is own wound on his side, but he will never make it to her in time. But Zeke can and does.

He dives in front of her and pushes her to the ground. The bullet hits him square in the heart.

I knew I loved Zeke, but not until this moment of watching him die, saving my woman did I realize how much. I thought my heart was a cage of metal and stone, only there to hold my monster inside, but it's a heart all the same. A heart capable of breaking, shattering, and ripping in half. And that's what I feel. *All of it.*

No amount of pain my body could experience is greater than losing someone I love. I learned that with my mother, but I thought it was because I was a kid. I was young, but now I know it wasn't because I was a kid. It's because this is what love does; it is everything when you have it and then takes everything away when it's gone and leaves nothing but the dull pain behind.

I don't have time to go through all the stages of grief in a single moment, but that's what my body tries to do. I feel denial, reality, bargaining, pain, all of it. *And I hate it.*

Kai sobs over Zeke's lifeless body.

She's alive, and I made a vow to protect her—no matter what. No matter how she fucked up. It's time to make good on that promise.

All of my anger, rage, and pain take over, and I charge at Milo. This won't be won with guns. He made this personal, and I'm going to kill him with my bare hands.

My fist connects with his face, bloodying his nose, and making contact with his eyes.

He stumbles backward, but I don't relent. I attack ruthlessly over and over. My fists flying, my legs kicking. He tries to fight back, but it's clear he's not used to fighting hand to hand with someone his own size. So instead, he moves to a defensive stance. His body blocking blow after blow. It will take longer for me to kill him this way, but I don't care. *I have time.*

But the world is never on my side.

A storm is coming, and I don't mean just my fists. The ship begins rocking at an unsafe level as rains pour down upon us.

This needs to end—now.

"This is for Zeke," I scream, putting everything into my attack, my entire body drives into Milo's. I don't care about the consequences of my attack on myself; I just want this motherfucker dead.

My force is too much for either of us, as our bodies collide, we hit the railing that breaks, and then we fall down to the ocean depths.

Our bodies stay connected as we hit the water, and now we both rely on the other for survival. The only way we live is if we both live. If we both surface. But I'd rather us both die, than Milo live.

So I force our bodies lower under the water. Milo fights against my hold on his neck and body, keeping him down. But my hold is tighter. Our oxygen levels deplete more and more with every second that passes. It will happen soon. Death is coming, and it will be sweet.

I look up and see light. *This is it—the end.*

A light descends further upon us.

Wait, it doesn't make sense. In death, I shouldn't be headed for a light. I should be headed to the darkness of hell.

But that doesn't stop the light from grabbing me. I let go of Milo and watch his body float down, away from me as the light takes me up.

I hit the surface of the water and take a deep breath, my lungs heaving for oxygen but not getting enough. I vomit up the salt water before I can finally take a breath.

"Thank fuck, you're alive," Kai cries, holding me to her.

She saved me.

I look behind me, but I don't see Milo surface.

She kisses me hard as the rain pours down on us, and I know as much as I want to spend my life making out with her here, I can't. *It's not safe.*

"We have to go," I say.

She nods, and we swim for the ladder on the yacht. When we reach the deck, Langston finds us, gripping his side where a bullet grazed him.

"The men have the yacht ready to go. We need to leave," Langston says.

I nod. "Where is Zeke?" I ask. *I need his body. I need to bury him properly.*

"He's gone. Went overboard in the storm," Langston adds.

"Let's go," I say, even though I want to dive back into the ocean and pull Zeke's body from the depths myself.

We all board the boat that will take us back to our yacht and stand on the edge, looking out into the dark ocean. The moon and stars twinkle overhead as we mourn a man we all loved.

Langston loved Zeke as a brother.

I loved Zeke as a friend.

And Kai loved Zeke as her protector.

"He deserved better than to be shot by a man like Milo," I say, refusing to cry as I lean over the railing looking down into the water.

"He would have been honored to die protecting someone he loves," Langston says, and a tear drips from each of our eyes.

"And he'll rest in the sea he loved," Kai finishes. She removes the scrunchie from her hair and places it on her wrist. A scrunchie I recognize as Zeke's.

His hair wasn't always long. He'd go through periods of it being long and short. But when it was long, he always carried a scrunchie for when his hair got in the way. We used to make fun of him, calling him a girl. Now I want him back just so I can tease his giant ass. I want him back so he can tease me back. So he can tell me how stupid I'm being. I want him by my side when we fight, when we drink, when we sail. But he won't be, ever again.

Kai kisses the scrunchie. "We will miss you big guy. You have no idea how much you were loved."

I meet her eyes; you have no idea how much you are loved, stingray.

CHAPTER 28

ENZO

We sailed back to Miami.

There is no reason to keep running on the ocean now that Milo is gone. All that is left is to keep my promise to Kai to set her free.

Kai has used her own room since we got back on the yacht. She hasn't been in my bed since before I went after Milo. At first, I thought it was because we were all mourning Zeke's death and needed our space, but then I realized the truth, she's distancing herself from me to make the next step easier.

We made port in Miami yesterday. There is nothing keeping her here anymore, except the truth.

The truth could keep her here, trapped forever. But I realized something the second that Zeke died. I realized just how capable of love I am. *And I love Kai Miller.*

I love her more than I could ever love Zeke or Langston. The love is different. It's all consuming, unhealthy in some ways, and like breathing air in other ways. My love for Kai is greater than anything I've ever felt before. It's greater than the pain my father made me endure.

It's greater than losing my mother.

729

It's greater than losing Zeke.

Losing Kai would top everything I've ever felt. But I can't keep her trapped here any longer. If I love her, she deserves to be free. She deserves the chance to choose her own life and future. I won't take that from her any longer. Even to keep her safe. There are other ways to protect her.

I take out my phone and scroll to Kai's contact. I change it until it reads, My Love. And then I text her.

ME: Meet me in the lounge.

MY LOVE: FIVE MINUTES.

THOSE FIVE MINUTES ARE THE LONGEST OF MY LIFE. BECAUSE I know what I'm about to do, and I don't know what the outcome will be. But I have to do it; if I truly love Kai, I have to set her free.

She looks like a goddess in an all white bikini cover-up, her jet black hair cascading down her back in thick strands, and Zeke's scrunchie on her wrist—I doubt she will ever take the scrunchie off.

"One last game of truth or lies?" I ask, pouring a couple of shots of the disgusting alcohol she poured us before.

"Last?" she asks, stepping into the room.

I nod.

"Okay," she says, looking concerned as she takes the shot glass from me. This time we don't make ourselves comfortable on the couch, there will be nothing comfortable about this. This will be the most uncomfortable, painful thing I've done.

"I promised to protect you forever, truth or lie?" I ask.

"Truth," she says, not taking the shot, just holding it in her hands.

"And have I kept that promise?"

"Yes."

"I promised to set you free when Milo is gone, truth or lie?"

"Truth."

"Milo is dead, truth or lie?"

"Truth," Kai says, swallowing hard.

I hold my shot up, as does she, and then we both drink it, because we both know what is coming next. The drink burns going down, but it doesn't hurt as much as what will come next.

I won't tell her I love her. It's not fair to her if I do. If I tell her I love her, that might make her decision for her. And that's not what freedom is about. Freedom is about giving a person a chance to choose, and that's what I'm doing.

"You are free, truth or lie?" I ask, my voice breathy.

"Truth," she breathes back.

I nod.

"Thank you," she whispers.

Stay. I love you. Stay. We will figure out everything else. I will keep you safe. Just stay.

"I should go," she says.

I nod. *I can't form words.*

She opens her mouth like she wants to speak but then closes it.

"You aren't going to try to protect me anymore, right? That's what being free is," Kai says.

I clear my throat. "I won't protect you anymore," I lie.

"Thank you."

"And you won't protect me," I say.

"I won't protect you," she lies.

And then she's gone.

I follow up to the top deck to watch her leave. Langston joins me.

"Why are you letting her go when you know Milo is still out there? You know he survived," Langston says.

"Because it's the only way to save her."

"What? That makes no sense."

"It doesn't, but it's the truth." Unlike everything we just said to each other. Everything we said before was lies. I will always try to protect her. And she will always try to protect me.

We both knew Milo is still alive.

We both knew the other tried to make a deal with the devil himself.

But Milo will only take one of our deals—mine. He will not take Kai. Kai will be free. And when the deal is done, Kai will disappear into the crowd. She will no longer be in danger. She will get a fresh start.

She will be safe; I'll make Langston swear to that.

She will always be protected; even if she never learns of the love I have for her, she will be safe. That's the promise I vowed to keep no matter what. No matter if I have to sacrifice my own life to keep it.

CHAPTER 29
KAI

Kai's Lie

Enzo gave me my freedom.

Or at least the illusion of freedom.

He set me free. He gave me the one thing I've been asking for since he took me.

I should be happy, grateful, elated.

Instead, I'm focused on saving Enzo from the danger.

I'm tired of fighting.

I'm tired of losing people. Zeke is enough. I can't bear to lose Enzo too.

So I lied to Enzo.

Repeatedly.

I lied when I said Milo was dead, when I overheard Enzo and Langston talking about Milo being alive.

I lied when I said I wouldn't protect Enzo, because the only thing I care about is keeping him safe.

And I lied to myself when I pretended I can survive being separated from Enzo—I can't.

I made a deal with the devil to keep Enzo safe.

When Milo came to the yacht searching for me before the war started, we had a moment to talk—alone.

And I gave him what he wanted—me.

I would give myself to Milo freely and willingly for the rest of my life, if he sparred Enzo. If he let Enzo live, then I would be his. If he let the Black empire remain Enzo's, I would be his.

Milo said he would consider my offer and left. I yelled into the darkness if he killed Enzo, even if Enzo provoked him first, the deal was off. I would never be his.

And I could see in Milo's eyes as he drove off into the night how badly he wanted me. He wanted me more than he wanted the empire. That's who Milo is. Women he keeps as slaves are his ultimate goal. Not money, and not power over men. Power over women —that's what he wants. *And I'm his ultimate prize.*

I know Enzo tried to make his own deal with Milo. But I know Milo will take my deal, because he loves controlling women more than he loves money and power.

I will save you Enzo. I will save you from any more pain or loss. You've already lost too much. I will keep you from losing more.

I find the number Milo gave me to contact him when I'm ready to make the deal. And then I dial.

CHAPTER 30
ENZO

Enzo's Lie

"**W**here are you going?" Langston asks.

"To make a phone call," I say, walking back into my private cabins. I don't need Langston following me and trying to stop me.

The guilt eats at me as I walk. *Is it okay to lie to those you love, even to protect them?*

I'm sure it's a sin, but one I'm willing to commit again and again to keep Kai safe.

Because the lies I told her were limitless.

I claimed Milo was dead when we both knew he wasn't.

I lied when I said I wouldn't protect her—I always will.

And I lied when I didn't tell her I loved her.

I should have told her. Maybe that would have changed everything. Or maybe it would have risked everything. Because the only way to keep her safe is to make this deal. She deserves a life free of all of this.

Away from Milo.

Away from Black.

735

Away from me.

I made a deal that ensures she will be free and protected forever.

As soon as I realized Milo was alive, I lost it. I wanted him dead. But we watched him. After news of Rowan's death spread, my enemies all converged and sided with Milo. They will all attack together because they see the Black empire as too big, too powerful. I'm too big of a threat. And it would be suicide to fight them all at the same time.

The only way to end Milo and keep Kai safe is to give everything to Milo.

So when I realized Milo was alive, I made a phone call. I offered up everything he has ever wanted. I named him my heir. Found some deep buried blood connection and said if I were to die, he could fight in my place to become Black.

When the games start, Langston will make sure Kai never shows up to fight. Milo will win by default. He will become Black. He will get my entire life's work. He will get what my father and generations of Millers and Rinaldis before fought so hard to build.

He will get to kill me and claim the Black empire. He will get everything he's ever wanted.

I know Kai made her own deal with Milo. But he won't take it. She offered him her body, while I'm offering him a chance to kill me and take an entire empire.

Milo will choose my deal. Kai will be safe.

I find Milo's contact and dial the number. I will sacrifice everything to save her.

CHAPTER 31
MILO

I sit on my throne in my home in Italy, triumphant.

I won.

Enzo Black thought he did when we hit the water. He had no idea days later he would surrender everything to me.

He had no idea the woman he loves had already surrendered herself to me before the war even started.

I had won before the battle begun.

Enzo needed his woman to save him in the water that day, but I grew up in the sea. I know how to fight, hold my breath, and swim for the surface.

I know how to survive. And that's what I did until my men found me.

And now, I have all the power.

Because I get to choose which life I take. I get to choose between the two fools.

Both Enzo and Kai are willing to give up everything to save the other—for true love.

Ugh, it makes me sick.

I can't believe either was foolish enough to fall in love.

Love is a weakness. It makes you vulnerable. Case in point, both of them are willing to give up their lives in order to save the other.

And it makes getting to choose who I take all the sweeter.

Both are strong.

Both are fighters.

Both are stupid enough to fall in love.

Both hold the key to me taking over the Black empire.

But I have to make a choice.

I can't pick both, as tempting as it is. If I kill both, then I won't get to watch as the other crumbles into a pile of dust—self-destructing from the loss of the other.

Both think they are doing the right thing by saving the other. But neither realize by sacrificing themselves they are killing the one they leave behind. *That is how love works.*

So I must choose. And I know exactly who I will pick. I will pick the strongest. The one most likely to become Black. The one who will fight until they become Black and earn me an empire. And then I will make them sacrifice their life, love, and empire to me.

♡

Thank you so much for reading Taken: A Truth or Lies World Collection! Kai and Enzo's story continues in STOLEN: A Truth or Lies World Collection.

I never thought that with him, I would find my home. Until I was stolen...

One-click STOLEN now >

"I. Am. Dead. Seriously. This tale just gets more twisted with every turn of the page...and I love it!"

JOIN ELLA'S NEWSLETTER & NEVER MISS A SALE OR
NEW RELEASE → ellamiles.com/freebooks

Love swag boxes & signed books?
SHOP MY STORE → store.ellamiles.com

Definitely Yes

Definitely No

Definitely Forever

STANDALONES:

Pretend I'm Yours

Finding Perfect

Savage Love

Too Much

Not Sorry

ABOUT THE AUTHOR

Ella Miles writes steamy romance, including everything from dark suspense romance that will leave you on the edge of your seat to contemporary romance that will leave you laughing out loud or crying. Most importantly, she wants you to feel everything her characters feel as you read.

Ella is currently living her own happily ever after near the Rocky Mountains with her high school sweetheart husband. Her heart is also taken by her goofy five year old black lab who is scared of everything, including her own shadow.

Ella is a USA Today Bestselling Author & Top 50 Bestselling Author.

Stalk Ella at:
www.ellamiles.com
ella@ellamiles.com